COURT OF
SHADOWS

COURT OF SHADOWS

CYNTHIA MORGAN

BALLANTINE BOOKS NEW YORK

Library of Congress Catalog Card Number: 90-93218
ISBN: 0-345-36651-4

Text design by Holly Johnson
Cover design by William Geller
Cover painting by Jeff Barson

Manufactured in the United States of America

First Edition: March 1992
10 9 8 7 6 5 4 3 2 1

For my mother

This project took years to complete, and many people have helped along the way, but I especially want to thank:

My family, for their love and support.

My friends—particularly Mark Dahmke, Gary Carey, and David Allen—for their encouragement and advice.

Joan Buhlmann, for her help in translating some lines of dialogue into French.

My editors—Lesley Malin Helm, Elizabeth Rapoport, and Joëlle Delbourgo—for their patience and insights.

And, finally, my agent and friend Russell Galen of the Scott Meredith Literary Agency, for believing in this book even before it was done . . . and for nagging me to finish it.

COURT OF
SHADOWS

PROLOGUE

May 1, 1570

He followed his quarry through the darkness, shivering in his threadbare frieze jerkin. The night's breezes reminded him more of late winter than of the month of May that had begun an hour ago. Now and then his boots slid across damp cobblestones or splashed into stinking puddles where the residents of Knightriders Street had emptied their jordans, but he had no time to pick his way carefully. Lord Harwood was already well ahead of him, far enough to be out of sight were it not for the white ruff he wore, glimmering faintly as it caught the light from the linkboy's torch. What mattered now was keeping the nobleman within sight. Tomorrow Sparrow could buy him a new pair of boots to replace these . . . and he would do so gladly, the man thought with a fleeting smile, when he learned what his spy had overheard.

Suddenly the torch bobbed and swerved to the left, then vanished from sight, the pale shimmer of the nobleman's ruff disappearing a moment later.

He swore to himself, quickening his pace despite the treacherous footing. He had been glad when Lord Harwood hired the linkboy at that last Cheapside tavern he visited, but he had not expected then to be led on this meandering walk toward the Thames, as though by some will-o'-the-wisp, some errant fool's fire that had left its marshes for London's streets. Were that torch to vanish completely down some unfamiliar lane, he might wander, lost, till morning. And worse fortune would face him if Lord Harwood disappeared before he discovered the baron's destination. He sucked in his breath at the thought of how angry Sparrow might be.

The stench of rotting fish reached his nostrils then, but it was too late a warning. His feet skidded across a slick, fetid pile of refuse thrown out by one of the many fishmongers whose shops lined Knightriders Street. He fell to his knees, fish carcasses squishing beneath his hose. 'Sblood! He would never be able to get the stink from the wool. He would need a new pair of hose, which meant he needed Sparrow's good will even more. Scrambling to his feet, he ran to the entrance of the lane Lord Harwood had turned down.

He thanked God the torch was still visible, but the linkboy was far down the lane and had turned yet again, onto Thames Street, this time right, to the west. The spy ran as softly as he could down the street, praying for dry footing. He was less than halfway to Thames Street when a man stepped from a doorway into his path, the blade of his upraised sword catching the light from a nearby lantern.

"Hold, sirrah." After a day of listening to that voice, it was instantly recognizable to the spy. "I would know why you follow me."

Staring at the nobleman's sword, he wished, of a sudden, that he had never heard of Sparrow, let alone met the man. He wished he were still back in Lancashire, happy with the two pence a day he earned as a thatcher. Tonight, as was the custom before May Day, he should have been out in the wood with some willing maid or widow, dallying there till morning, when they would rush to gather dew for her to bathe her face in . . . not here, on some street whose name he did not know, facing a steel rapier that soon might part his soul from his too-mortal flesh.

"My l-lord," he stammered, and fell silent for a few desperate seconds. Then the linkboy came back around the corner, bringing inspiration as well as light with him. "My lord, I followed your light, not you. I could not afford to hire a linkboy, and thought to follow you for as long as possible, so as not to be entirely lost, and so I could call for aid if some rogue set upon me."

"I'faith, 'twould take a desperate rogue. You stink of fish."

"Pray your pardon, my lord." He stepped back, hoping that the nobleman would not follow him, but to his dismay, Lord Harwood did.

The linkboy approached them, a curious look on his young face.

"Let me see this varlet," Lord Harwood directed.

The spy wanted to flinch from the light as the linkboy held it near his face, but he knew that his life depended on his standing here as though fearless of the nobleman's scrutiny. Would Lord Harwood recognize him as the man who had loitered but ten paces from him in St. Paul's that morning, then followed him on his course among the booksellers in the churchyard, and thence to Southwark? He shivered slightly, and prayed the nobleman would assume it was from the cool breeze.

Lord Harwood was frowning, but there was no look of recognition on his face. "Where were you bound?" he asked abruptly.

"To Southwark, sir. I saw that you made your way toward the river, and thought to follow, and hire a boat."

"Southwark?" The nobleman laughed. "No doubt to the stews. But not even the most diseased whore would bear your stench without complaint. 'Twould be best if you swam the Thames first." He frowned again, his eyes narrowing as he stared at the spy, then shook his head slightly.

Taking a coin from his purse, Lord Harwood handed it to the link-boy. "Here. There's a shilling for you to lead this wretch safely down the hill to Paul's Wharf, where he may hire that boat—if any wherryman will accept a cargo that stinks of dead fish. See him there. I would know, the next time we meet, that he was put safely on his way to Southwark, lest some more suspicious soul run him through for following his link-boy."

The boy wrinkled his nose, but obediently set off down the street, stopping after a few paces to look back. "Will you follow?"

He knew he had no choice. Lord Harwood stepped aside, gesturing with his sword for him to follow the linkboy. The nobleman was smiling. *A pox on you*, the spy thought. What pleasure Sparrow would otherwise take from the news he would bring him would be abated when he learned that Lord Harwood had suspected he was being dogged and now knew the spy's face well enough that he would henceforth be useless as an intelligencer in the baron's vicinity.

At the corner of Thames Street, he stopped and looked back up the hill. Lord Harwood was gone, vanished in the darkness. The spy knew that Sparrow would berate him tomorrow for not having glanced over his shoulder tonight to see which way the nobleman had gone, whether west or east on Knightriders Street, or north, up the lane he now realized was the one known as Paul's Wharf Hill, toward the great looming bulk of St. Paul's Cathedral, pitch black against the starry heavens.

He hoped Lord Harwood's choice had been Knightriders Street. He hoped the nobleman had retraced his steps toward the east.

Let him slip on those fish, the spy thought bitterly, then turned and trudged down the lane toward Paul's Wharf and the water stairs.

CHAPTER 1

"I would know more of this danger, Master Sparrow."

Nicholas Langdon's face was alight with curiosity. Seeing it, Walter Cadmon, whom some knew as Sparrow, bit back an oath. His master, Francis Walsingham, had sent him down to Sussex to recruit Langdon, not antagonize him. But God's bones! How could Master Walsingham—that usually reasonable servant of Sir William Cecil, the queen's principal secretary of state—believe that matters important to the safety of England and Queen Elizabeth could be entrusted to a popinjay such as this?

Grating his teeth, he looked away from the youth in an attempt to keep his temper.

All around them in the orchard, the apple trees were in bloom, and the warm breeze was heavy with their scent. Looking back the way they had come, Sparrow could see, beyond the tree tops at the far side of the orchard, the red tile roofs of Beechwood Manor. Smoke curled up from the kitchen chimney. He could hear the sound, faint with distance, of a maid singing. They had walked most of the way across the orchard to ensure their privacy, following meandering strawberry-bordered paths of colored sand before stopping at last beneath an old walnut tree. The only sounds nearby were rustlings in the branches high overhead, followed by a flurry of wings as a bird took flight, and the songs of other birds in neighboring trees.

It was a peaceful scene, and Sparrow should have been able to enjoy it. He should have enjoyed the ride south from London, too, with Sussex's downs fresh and green in early May, and the weather fair and dry enough that even the notoriously bad roads were tolerable. But he had been unable to shake free of his doubts about Langdon, doubts that had been confirmed the moment he set eyes on the boy.

He glanced sideways at Walsingham's newest agent, his mouth twisting a little in distaste.

Dressed in doublet and hose of straw-colored satin, his cloak of gilded Spanish leather, perfumed gloves in his hand, Nick Langdon looked every inch the London gallant. When Sparrow was first told he would be meeting the new man in Sussex, he had hoped for a stolid, reliable country squire—a hope that had faded as Walsingham mentioned that Master Langdon had attended Cambridge and then studied law at Gray's Inn. Sparrow knew that both Cecil and Walsingham were Cambridge graduates, and both had also been at Gray's Inn. But they were mature men, well seasoned by earlier, troubled times. The younger graduates whom Sparrow knew were too often little more than idle fashionmongers. And though Sparrow's dashed hopes for recruiting a sturdy squire had been revived somewhat when he heard that Nicholas Langdon had not been to London or the court for a year, staying at Beechwood since his father's death last summer, Sparrow suspected that whatever had kept him at home was not common sense.

"So quiet, Master Sparrow? Are these dangers so great that they tie your tongue? Or do you perchance fear me unequal to them?" Smiling, Langdon rested his hand for an instant on the hilt of his rapier.

If he thought to inspire confidence with that little gesture, he erred. Sparrow looked at the long, slim, foreign weapon with contempt. 'Twould be just his luck that the youth would not even fight in honest English fashion, with sword and buckler. Nick Langdon had obviously been wasting some of his time around masters of fence, learning the Italian style of fighting with rapier and dagger and chattering of *stoccatas* and *pararlas*. There was entirely too much Italianate about the youth, Sparrow thought, remembering that Langdon had twice referred to Machiavelli already. And Walsingham had said that Langdon had a friend studying at a university in Italy and had once wished to study there himself. Even Italians had a proverb for such a man as this: *Englese Italianato, è un diabolo incarnato—An Englishman Italianate is a devil incarnate.*

Unable to curb his dislike of the youth, Sparrow said coldly, "You will be in danger only if you are fool enough to let Lord Harwood suspect your reasons for being at the Jerusalem Tree."

Langdon's face flushed with anger, and for a moment Sparrow hoped that he would refuse the mission. Then another intelligencer would have to be chosen, and with no time to return to London for further instructions, Sparrow would be free to choose one of the dependable men he knew.

"Sirrah—" the youth began sharply, then checked, shaking a little from suppressed fury. He drew a deep breath. "You must needs tell me more, then, to protect me from my own folly."

With another, older man, Sparrow might have wondered if this new humility promised later caution, but he would not give Langdon that much credit. If the boy were restraining his pride, accepting rudeness from an inferior, it proved merely that he was that eager for what he saw as adventure. Tell him that Lord Harwood was both the most dangerous swordsman in the land and the possessor of a diabolical ability to recognize his enemies no matter how carefully disguised, Sparrow thought sourly, and odds were good that the youngling would be off to the Jerusalem Tree Inn faster than ever.

Sparrow sniffed at the thought, looked the young gallant over, and sniffed again. 'Twas poor stuff, but all he had to work with for now.

"I must be on my way soon," he said, starting back toward the manor house. "So mark me. 'Twould be best if you did not use your own name . . ."

"I would know more of this danger, Master Sparrow."

Wakened from a light sleep by her brother's voice, Katherine Langdon stirred, about to turn over, then froze just in time. Her eyes flew open. Overhead was a latticework of branches and fresh green leaves, dark against the bright blue of the sky. She rested twenty feet above the ground, her perch a natural arrangement of branches that had been her favorite hiding place when she was a child, a sanctuary she could retreat to whenever she needed to think about something. She had all but forgotten its existence until a few hours ago.

She tilted her head to one side, listening. The only sounds were the rustling of leaves and bird cries. She must have dreamed she had heard Nick. *Master Sparrow,* he had said. When they were children, it had been his wont to amuse her at times by addressing the creatures about them with mock formality: *Master Falcon,* he would say, or *Mistress Bee.* A dozen years had passed since he had played that game. Odd that she would dream of it now, when her last thoughts before falling asleep had been so far from the concerns of a child.

She shifted uneasily in her perch, startling a lark into taking wing.

How long had she been asleep? She looked toward the sun, surprised to see that it was well down the vault of the sky from the place it had occupied when she had climbed up here. Had anyone missed her yet? She knew she should return to the manor house, yet she was reluctant to do so. She frowned as she remembered why she had come here.

"God's death!" Her hands shaking, Kat set the glove aside. It had been a mistake for her to offer to help her aunt, Anne Norland, embroider the gloves Anne had bought for her husband in London. Kat had become bored and less careful of her work, and the last several stitches were uneven. She feared she might have ruined the glove, an expensive one of fine perfumed chevril.

Anne's maid, Madge Dunstable, had been reading aloud from Foxe's *Book of Martyrs,* one of Anne's favorite books. She had just reached the passage where Foxe told of how John Rogers, Bloody Mary's first victim, had gone valiantly to his death and had washed in the fire "as though it had been cold water." Now she stopped reading and looked up at Kat. Anne was also staring at her niece, an expression of sympathetic concern on her face.

"Is aught amiss?" Anne leaned over from the pillow on which she sat and picked up the glove. While she studied it, she groped for the platter of comfits on the low Italian table beside her, rolled the rose-flavored sweetmeat in a bowl of musk sugar, and then popped it into her mouth. She wiped her sugary fingers carefully on a napkin, then began to pick at the stitches. " 'Tis simple enough to fix," she said, glancing up at Kat.

"Not for me," Kat said, and her aunt vainly fought a smile. Anne had struggled for years, during her frequent visits to Beechwood, to turn Kat into an accomplished needlewoman, but finally had admitted that Kat would always handle reins better than needles.

"Would you have me finish this for you?" Anne asked.

"Yea, and I thank you. I must see to the work in the kitchen. I would know how the cooks are progressing with the—with supper," she finished lamely. She had almost spoken of the elaborate sugarwork she had ordered prepared for her aunt, a miniature garden with statues and topiary work. Anne loved sweets more than anyone else Kat knew.

She stood up, stretching limbs that had become cramped. They had been here since dinner, more than two hours ago. 'Twas a poor way to spend an afternoon, she thought as she walked down the gallery toward the great stairs. She passed the fireplace, where a branch covered with fragrant apple blossoms had been added to the evergreen boughs that perfumed the air. Perchance she would take a walk in the orchard after checking on the work in the kitchen, or else have one of her horses saddled and go riding. She had not been out riding since May Day, when she and Nick and their guests had visited the neighboring villages to see the Maypoles, gorgeously decorated with flowers and ribbons and paint, and to watch the dancing by villagers and morris dancers alike under the gaze of the May queen and her consort.

She was downstairs, only a few paces from the kitchen door, when she stopped suddenly, hearing the voices of her two cousins. The girls were begging the cooks for pieces of the sugarwork garden. Alack, there would be nothing left by suppertime.

Kat was about to intervene when the begging gave way to a conspiratorial whisper, so low that no words were distinguishable.

Then Eleanor, at twelve the younger of the two, said more loudly, "But Kat's not old!"

"Seventeen," her sister Frances replied.

Kat knew she should leave, but eavesdropping was an old habit. She had often eavesdropped on her brother and Edward Neale, their neighbor's son and her betrothed since their childhoods, so she would know of their escapades and join them whenever possible. Now that old habit kept her standing near the kitchen door, listening intently, though she was not at all sure she wanted to know what Frances said about her behind her back. *Old!* God's light, seventeen was not old!

"She lets her opportunities to marry slip past," Frances continued, and Kat smiled thinly. Frances was fourteen, and engaged to the son of a neighbor of theirs in Suffolk, a baron. Belike she thought that made her an expert on marriage. "Soon no one will wish to marry her."

"Ned Neale wished to marry her."

"Neale is dead these three years," Frances said bluntly, unfeelingly, and Kat flinched a little, her smile vanishing. She still grieved for Ned, who had been killed, thrown from his horse while hunting, less than a month before they were to have wed. "She has turned away all suitors since then. If she does not change her ways soon, she'll lead apes in Hell, as do all women who fail to marry."

Eleanor was silent for a long time, then said, so quietly that Kat could barely hear her, "She may not wish to marry yet. She lives the life she wishes here."

"She's selfish," Frances replied coldly. "She thinks of herself, and never of Nick."

"She loves Nick well!"

"Not so well that she'll marry so he'll be free to bring home a wife. Were he to marry now, while Kat is still mistress here, would she be content to let Nick's bride order the servants in her stead? He must fear that. Why else would he not have married yet?"

There was no immediate reply, and Kat did not wait to hear if her younger cousin would eventually speak in her defense. Though what defense could there be? She had never considered that she might be the reason Nick had not married, but now it seemed the simplest explanation. She retreated to her bedchamber, using the back stairs to avoid going through the gallery again. She did not want to talk to Anne now.

Kat's maid, Louise Pickard, was in the bedchamber, sewing pearls back onto a straw-colored satin sleeve. "Faith, y'are pale," Louise said. "Are you ill?"

"Yea, from needlework," Kat replied, drawing a laugh from Louise, who had served her for twelve years now. The maid shook her head slightly and went back to work, while Kat paced up and down the chamber.

Why had she not given more thought to Nick remaining a bachelor? Although he would not have been able to meet many suitable women since returning to Beechwood from London's Inns of Court a year ago, after their father's death, he must have met scores of eligible, attractive maids during his time in the city. And yet, while he often jested about his loves, he had let Kat know that they were no more than dalliances. Why had she never asked him his reasons for not seriously looking for a wife?

He had never urged her to marry any of the men who had courted her since Ned's death, and she was sure she knew why: he had loved Edward Neale as much as she had, and, grieving as much, had understood when she had decided, with each of her suitors, that she could never love him as she had loved Ned. But had Nick sacrificed his own happiness out of concern for her?

"Y'are restless of a sudden," Louise said. "What's the matter?"

" 'Twas something that Frances said . . ." She hesitated to say more.

"*Frances.* I will not be sorry to see *her* leave tomorrow, though I would fain have your aunt and Eleanor stay longer. I wonder that you have spent so much time with the girl. D'you remember how you would sometimes disappear to avoid her company, and she never could find you?"

"Yea, I do," Kat said, smiling.

"I could tell anyone who wished to see you," Louise said calmly, not looking up from her work, "that you had a headache and went to bed, and are asleep."

"I trow you could," Kat agreed with a laugh.

She went to the chest at the foot of her bed and began rummaging through the clothes stored there. What she sought was near the bottom of the chest, neatly folded, untouched for the last three years: an old doublet and hose, castaway garments of Nick's. She had worn these clothes often during the year before Ned's death, when she would go fishing or hunting or hawking with him and Nick, or simply ride with them through the neighboring countryside. She had not taken them out since Ned died. She had newer doublets and hose of her own, garments made for her to wear while riding or hunting or hawking, but these old clothes would be better for what Kat had in mind . . . if they still fit.

They did. Kat was no longer as thin as she had been at the age of fourteen, but the doublet and hose were large enough to conceal her slender curves. As she gazed at her reflection in the looking glass, she realized that if she were to tuck her hair into the old cap she had worn then—it was somewhere in the chest still—she would again be able to pass as a boy. How strange, that she had changed so little outwardly, when those carefree days seemed so long ago.

She twisted her long blond hair into a knot on top of her head and pinned it securely, then picked up the black satin mask lying on the top shelf of her press and put it on. She could not risk a sunburn: she had spent too many hours washing her face with rosewater and buttermilk, in an effort to keep her complexion fair, to ruin it now.

Then she scrambled up onto the windowsill and climbed down the brick wall. She still remembered all the hand- and footholds. In less than a minute she reached the ground and set off at a run for the orchard, and the ancient walnut tree that was her old hiding place . . .

"So quiet, Master Sparrow? Are these dangers so great that they tie your tongue? Or do you perchance fear me unequal to them?"

Hearing Nick's voice startled her. So she had not merely dreamed that she had heard him earlier! But that surprise was nothing compared to the astonishment she felt when a stranger replied, in an insolent manner that she was certain Nick would never tolerate. She could scarcely believe it when Nick made a soft reply.

Who *was* this Master Sparrow?

She started to turn her head, as though moving her ear an inch closer to the ground would make it easier to hear them, then froze as leaves rustled with her movement. She prayed that neither her brother nor the mysterious Master Sparrow would look up and see her.

Then they were walking away. Kat could have screamed with frustration as Master Sparrow's voice faded in the distance. She knew she had to follow them, but waited a bit longer, not wanting them to hear the noise of her descent. She puzzled over what they had said. She had heard of Lord Harwood, a baron residing in Hampshire. And she had once visited the Jerusalem Tree, an inn a day's ride southwest of London, with her father and Nick. That had been several years ago. To the best of her knowledge, Nick had not been to the inn since, as it was not along his usual route to London.

When she could no longer hear them, she climbed down the tree as quickly as possible, then removed her boots and set off after them, toward the orchard gate, her stockinged feet soundless on the path.

The gate was closed when she reached it. She hesitated a moment before opening it and peering through. Nick and his visitor were nowhere in sight. Her first thought was to hurry to the courtyard, where the stranger's horse must needs be, and ask one of the grooms who Master Sparrow was, but there was too much chance that she might encounter this Sparrow himself, and she dared not do that until she had changed to more presentable garb. She pulled her boots on again, then set off at a run toward the wing of the manor house where her bedchamber was located.

———

Louise was still sewing pearls back on the sleeve, but as soon as Kat peered over the sill, she dropped her needlework and ran to the window.

"Your aunt was here," she said as Kat climbed back inside. "When I told her of your headache she went away, but she came back with conserve of violet—"

Kat chuckled. Conserve of violet was Anne's sovereign remedy for all ills.

"—and she told me that Master Danvers is here, and will wait to see you when you feel better."

Kat shook her head, not at all happy with that news. It was as well that Nick was busy with Master Sparrow. Her brother could not abide Christopher Danvers.

"Your aunt said she would return soon," Louise warned.

"And she must not find me like this. I know."

She changed clothes as swiftly as she could, fretting at the long minutes it took to don smock and French farthingale and petticoats, then her kirtle. She waited impatiently while Louise fastened the row of hooks down the left side of the bodice, then pinned the bodice's front hem to the half-kirtle's waist while Louise pinned the back. Thank God her sleeves were still securely pinned to the bodice, or that would have taken minutes longer.

She wanted to talk to Nick. She could make some excuse to her aunt later. Looking around the chamber, she spotted her slippers, placed neatly beside a chest. She was sliding her feet into them when she heard a knock on the door.

Kat sighed. "Let her in." She had taken the pins from her hair and was combing it when her aunt entered the chamber.

"Do you feel better, Kat?" Anne asked. "You look well."

"Yea, I do feel much better. Thank you for the conserve of violet."

"I thought it would help. Do you feel well enough to see Master Danvers?"

"Indeed, madam."

She went over to a shelf along one wall where she kept her paints and perfumes in an assortment of gallipots. Sitting down on a cushioned stool, she studied her face in the small mirror propped against the wall, then opened a pot of red fucus and applied the paint lightly to her lips and cheeks.

"What think you of Christopher?" she asked Anne as she was replacing the lid on the gallipot.

"I like him well. He is very handsome."

Kat nodded. She could not deny that. "Think you that I should marry him?" she asked.

"If you wish to marry him."

Kat looked intently at her aunt, at those familiar features, very much a softer version of her father's. Anne's open, benign expression was also familiar: like Henry Langdon, his sister wished only the best for Kat, as she had shown so often during the ten years since Kat's mother had died. Anne had spent weeks at a time at Beechwood, helping her brother order the household and teaching Kat the womanly skills that Mary Langdon had not insisted that her daughter learn, since Henry was content to have his daughter follow her older brother about, riding, fishing, hunting, hawking, and sharing lessons with Nick and his tutors. Anne had taught Kat how to govern the maidservants, how to oversee the work in the dairy and brewery and stillroom, so that Kat had been able, by the age of thirteen, to manage the household without Anne's help or advice. Kat owed her aunt much for that, and also for the sympathy and comfort she had given after the deaths of Kat's parents and Edward Neale. Anne had come to Beechwood to nurse Henry back to health after he fell ill of an inflammation of the lungs last spring, but she had found her brother on his deathbed, and had stayed to help Kat and Nick through the first black days of grief.

Anne would never advise her to marry Christopher Danvers if she knew Kat did not love him . . . no matter how important it might be for Kat to marry so Nick would be free to bring home a bride.

"I have not yet decided." Until a few hours ago, she had planned to discourage Christopher, but now she must needs look at him with new eyes, and see if she could not abide him as a husband. No longer could she afford the luxury of waiting to meet someone who pleased her as much as Ned had.

She smoothed a cream perfumed with musk and roses on her wrists and neck, then checked her appearance in the tall looking glass. She did not feel like a woman ready to see her suitor, but she looked like one.

"Where is he?"

"In the gallery," Anne replied. "Frances and Eleanor are keeping him company."

Christopher Danvers usually disliked being kept waiting while in the country—he had enough of that at court—but he was content for at least a little while longer to stroll up and down the gallery. Sunlight from the tall windows gilded the rush matting covering the floor, the warm air was sweetly scented with pine and the perfume of flowers, and the gallery's furnishings reminded him pleasantly of the prosperity of the woman he hoped to wed. Tall sideboards displayed gleaming silver plate and Venetian glasses; fine Turkey carpets covered two chests and a long table. Three smaller, marble-topped tables from Italy were set at intervals along the inner wall. Two of the tables supported vases of flowers, but the third—where Christopher's companion paused almost every time they reached it—bore a platter of sweetmeats.

Frances Norland had a weakness for sweets, and would someday, much sooner than she expected, be fat.

Amused by the thought, Christopher smiled down at the girl and was rewarded with a coy, dimpling smile and a fluttering of the eyelashes. He found her attempts to dally with him enchantingly clumsy. Her open admiration of him was balm to his injured pride—especially since Kat Langdon, though friendly enough, seemed indisposed to succumb to his wooing. Were he not certain that Kat was as innocent as a protective family and a life spent in the country could make her, he would wonder if she were not akin in spirit to Mistress Lettice Fielding, his leman for the last year. Mistress Fielding had been happy enough to share a bed with him while her feeble old husband was alive, but after the old man died two months ago and Christopher had asked her to marry him, she had laughed at his proposal and told him that she would as lief marry the pet squirrel she kept on a chain. Undeceived by the gifts he had presented her with, she had made inquiries about his fortune, and she had no intention of sharing her late husband's wealth with him. He had retreated to Sussex to lick his wounds away from the court . . . and to think more carefully about an offer from someone who was wooing him.

Christopher twisted the massive ruby ring he wore on his right index finger. He had no quarrel with the gift from his suitor, only with the intent behind it: it was not an offer he wanted to accept. And yet it had seemed inevitable until he once again met Kat Langdon.

He had seen her occasionally when she was a child, during the times he was down from Oxford. His family's home lay only ten miles from Beechwood, and he had first noticed Kat, clad in doublet and hose, when she was out riding with her brother and Edward Neale. He had thought then that she was a younger brother to one of the youths, but his father, who was hunting with him, quickly set him straight. Christopher had then thought her a poor, strange creature indeed. His father had told him four years ago that Kat had become a lovely young gentlewoman, but Christopher had neither believed that nor cared, since he knew her to be betrothed to Edward Neale. His trips home during the years when he had been at the Inns of Court had been brief, since he preferred Clement's Inn and the court to life in the country; he knew that Edward Neale had died, but Christopher had not realized how important that was for him until he encountered Kat in Southampton a month ago.

He would not have suspected who she was if she had not been with her brother. He knew Nicholas Langdon from the Inns of Court. They had not been friends, but Christopher had not let that stop him from riding over to greet Nick warmly so that he could get a closer look at the woman beside him. Her hair was the color of honey, as was Nick's, and her eyes, like his, were seawater green. When she removed her mask it became impossible not to notice the resemblance: they had the same high cheekbones, the same short, straight nose, the same sweetly shaped mouth. She had been wearing a cloak of azure camlet lined with white silk over a matching kirtle, and he had thought her more than the equal of any beauty at the court, with her lovely oval face and delicate features. When he remembered that the Langdons were said to be wealthy, he was completely captivated . . .

"Pray tell me more of the court, Master Danvers," Frances said. "Would that George knew as much of the court as you do."

Her mother's maidservant coughed to remind them of her presence. Christopher looked to where Madge sat, embroidering a glove. She had her eyes fixed on her work, but he knew he should heed the warning. 'Twas not the first time Frances had said something comparing Christopher to her betrothed, to George's disadvantage. He did not want anyone, but most especially Kat, to think that he had been trying to woo Frances or make her discontented with the match arranged for her.

"I trow I have said too much of the court already," he said truthfully enough, and smiled. "I fear I'll weary you with my stories."

Before she could respond, he strolled over to the window seat to which her shy little sister Eleanor had retreated after stammering out a greeting to him.

"How now, Eleanor! What's this, that you read so diligently?"

" 'Tis the *Book of Martyrs*, sir." She surrendered the book to him when he held out his hands. "My mother's favorite."

He could have guessed what book it was from its sheer size. This copy had been bound in fine Cordovan leather, with an ivory plate bearing the carved figure of an angel over the spine. The Norlands must needs love the book, to have bound it so carefully. He knew others who would as lief have burned it.

He opened the book to the title page and read the familiar words.

ACTES
and Monuments

of these latter and perillous dayes
touching matters of the Church, wherein
ar comprehended and described the great persecu-

tions & horrible troubles, that have bene wrought
and practised by the Romishe Prelates, special-
lye in this Realme of England and Scot-
lande, from the yeare of our Lorde a
thousande, unto the tyme
nowe present.

The page was illustrated: at the top, angels sounded trumpets to the glory of the Lord. On the left side of the page were the Protestants, meeting for prayer, being burned at the stake as martyrs, glorifying God in Heaven. On the right side were devils and the earthly followers of Rome.

He leafed through the book, stopping at another illustration, this one of Protestants roped together as they were led to London for trial. There was a verse from Matthew: Ye shall be led before Princes and Rulers for my names sake.

" 'Tis a brave ring, Master Danvers," Eleanor said shyly.

He glanced down at the ruby ring, suddenly aware that he had been toying with it. "Thank you, Eleanor." It was indeed a fine ring, with the stone as large as the nail on his little finger. He had been given it, he was told, to remind him how highly he was valued, but it seemed at times like the first payment on his soul. He would be glad to give it back, when Kat and her dowry were his to command.

"I'faith, Christopher, you look melancholy!" said a light, mocking voice. He started, then looked up to see Kat entering the gallery with her aunt and maid. "I am sorry to have kept you waiting."

To Kat's surprise, her words brought a guilty look to Christopher's face. Then that expression was gone, replaced by a practiced smile as he came to greet her and made a leg as elegantly as if he were at court.

"I was melancholy," he said teasingly, "but seeing you dispels that humor."

"Pray do not tell anyone, Christopher. I should find myself more in demand than any physician who has only wormwood and tamarisk and bugloss wine to help him cure melancholy."

"Then I'll tell no one, for I would be your only patient."

She felt her cheeks growing warm. It still embarrassed her that he was so open in his wooing. Her other suitors had been more discreet. Was this the practice at the court? She distrusted his flattery. Her father had often warned her, and Nick too, of court incense and court holy water, the insincere compliments of courtiers.

"You must have healed yourself, Kat, for you look well, and your aunt said you were plagued by a headache."

"I have my aunt to thank for that cure. She brought me conserve of violet."

"The best remedy, I have heard." He smiled and bowed slightly to Anne, who looked pleased.

Damnable jackanapes. Kat could hear Nick's contemptuous term for Christopher as clearly as if he were here and had just spoken aloud. Her brother had no patience with the courtier, and said he rued the day they had met Christopher in Southampton. He had told her, too, that it was rumored that George Danvers had been forced to sell some land recently to pay his son's debts and had sworn that he would no longer support Christopher's expensive habits. *'Twill be Christopher's undoing if he cannot soon find a rich wife,* Nick had said. *He has nothing to commend him at the court except his fine clothes, and he will not be able to afford them much longer. He may be desperate—*

Desperate enough to marry me? she had asked.

Mayhap even more desperate than that. A friend of mine saw him in an apothecary in Bucklersbury, making some purchase that he did not want witnessed. My friend thought it might have been some poison, to hasten his father to his grave.

Nick!

'Twas said more in jest than in earnest.

Such jests do not bear repeating, she had told him angrily, and he had looked abashed.

Likely we have wronged him, he had said, unusually somber. *Mayhap he sought only a purgative, after so many rich meals at court, and was buying cassia or epithyme.*

Likely that was it, she had agreed with mock seriousness . . . but that day, for the first time, she had invited Christopher to supper, as if in some confused way that would make up for the gossip of her brother and his friends.

Now she studied Christopher, as she had that evening, wondering once again about Nick's dislike of the man. Certainly there was nothing to object to in Christopher's appearance: he was the handsomest of her suitors, with his pale blond hair and bright blue eyes, his wide shoulders and well-muscled legs. He wore fine clothes—today a suit of watchet taffeta. Two years older than Nick, he had spent more time at court and could claim to be the more accomplished courtier. Perchance that was it? Jealousy? She knew that her brother was attracted to the courtier's life, despite their father's warnings about the insincerity and ruinous expense of the court. Nick's copy of Thomas Hoby's *Book of the Courtier*, the translation of Baldassare Castiglione's *Il Libro del Cortegiano*, had been read so often that it was nearly falling apart. Of certain he was as well-suited for court as friends of his from Cambridge who now spent much of their time there, for they were of no more gentle birth than he, their lineage no older or more honorable, their wealth no greater. She wondered now if it so chafed him to stay here in Sussex, after having spent more time at court before their father's death, that he resented Christopher all the more for being free to go where he could catch the queen's eye and perhaps secure her favor . . .

"Shall we go for a walk?" Christopher suggested. " 'Tis too lovely a day to spend inside."

"Indeed," Kat murmured.

Christopher turned to Anne. "Will you join us, madam?"

"Thank you, sir, but I have much to attend to here." Anne glanced at Frances as she spoke, and Kat had to suppress a smile, knowing that her aunt must also have seen how the girl had been gazing at Christopher a few minutes ago. "Will you sup with us this evening? I would enjoy talking with you again, before we leave for home in the morning."

"Gladly."

"We will see you at supper," Kat told her aunt. Christopher offered her his arm, and they left the gallery, Louise following at a distance.

Their talk was light and inconsequential as they made their way through the house and outside to the flower garden. While Christopher told her of a hunt on his father's land yesterday, Kat looked around for Nick, but he was nowhere in sight. When they reached the garden, Kat suggested that they walk down the vine-roofed alleyway bordering the stone walls. The yew hedge forming the alley's inner wall was high enough to conceal Nick and his visitor, but they were not there. Leaving the alleyway, she and Christopher strolled to the center of the garden, where a honeysuckle-covered banquet house stood. Kat seated herself on a bench facing one of the open sides of the banquet house, far enough away that the scent of the honeysuckle was sweet but not overpowering. She plucked a rose, and looked around at the garden. It was deserted, save for Christopher and Louise and herself. She could not hold back a sigh.

"Cry you mercy, Kat, if I bore you with this talk of the hunt."

"Never, Christopher. I sigh only because I wish I could have hunted with you." She and Nick had been invited, but had declined because of their guests.

"You shall be able to hunt at Colmeade as often as you like, if you marry me."

In the past she had always turned away and changed the subject when he spoke of his plans for their future, but now she continued to gaze at him directly. "How so? Would we not be with the court much of the year?"

He looked surprised. "Would you wish that? You have said that your father warned you against the court, and that you love the country. Would you not be content to live at Colmeade?"

Would you? She but thought the question; his obvious disquiet had already answered it. It had never occurred to him that she would wish to accompany him to court. She wondered if he were now calculating just how quickly her dowry would be spent if she, too, would have to be outfitted for court, rather than staying quietly at home while he preened himself in one of the queen's palaces. For she was certain that he had no intention of living the life of a country squire.

Never having considered him seriously as a suitor until now, she had given no thought to what their marriage would be like. Now she was stung by the discovery that he had planned to keep her at home in Sussex, like some caged bird, while he flew free. It was not an uncommon pattern for marriage, she knew, but neither was it one she would accept for herself.

She rose and started walking again, past a sundial that reminded her how much time she would have to spend with Christopher before supper—soon after which, pray God, he would leave to ride back to his own home. She was near despairing of how she would endure his company when it occurred to her that the time could be well spent.

She returned to Christopher, who seemed to be waiting anxiously for her answer to his question.

"I would fain see London," she said. "You have made it sound so marvelous."

"In good sooth, you would weary of it soon."

"How so? You have not wearied of the court."

"I have not spoken of my weariness, but I tell you, Kat, you would sicken of the court and its schemes and rivalries. After a few days there, you would be happy to return to the country."

"Then why do you not stay at Colmeade?" she asked, feigning innocence.

He flushed slightly. "I must needs keep close to the queen, lest my enemies take advantage of my absence. Were someone more favored by the queen to lay claim to what is rightly mine to inherit . . ." He shrugged. "Who knows? Colmeade might be lost."

Had she known less of him, she might have believed him. Her father had once admitted that he was free to avoid the court only because he had no enemies against whom he needed to cultivate powerful allies. But Nick had told her enough that she knew that the greatest danger to Colmeade was Christopher himself.

"Then you truly do not enjoy the court?"

He hesitated before speaking. "I would be lying if I told you that, sweeting. There are aspects of the court that are pleasant . . . but you would not find them so. Country life suits you, Kat."

"And court would not?" she asked tartly. "Do you fear that a country wife would be out of place at Whitehall?"

"Nay, sweetheart, for you would dazzle the court."

Kat nodded, smiling, then looked down at herself. "I would dress more finely than this. Were I at court, I would wear only the finest silks, the most gorgeous velvet-on-velvet from Italy . . ." Christopher looked so dismayed that she was hard put not to laugh. "You would not be ashamed of me, Christopher."

"No, Kat. Never."

"And," she said mischievously, remembering that he rented his London lodgings, "were we to be at court often, we would buy a house in London."

"First let us see if you like London, sweeting."

"I warrant you, I will love it, for both you and Nick have told me so much of London—aye, and London's shops—that I trow I could spend all my time there. Yea, and all my money, too," she added with a little laugh, and went on to tell him all the things she might wish to buy, the better to adorn herself and the house she must needs have, were she to live in London.

Half an hour before supper, Kat, saying that she had to talk to the cooks, left Christopher in the garden to admire the late-blooming jonquils and peonies that Louise wanted to show him. He was in a quiet, contemplative humor by then—one well suited, mayhap, to appreciating the garden . . . though she suspected that his thoughts were less of flowers than of how ruinously expensive a wife she would be. She congratulated herself on discouraging him as she hurried back to the house, then up the stairs to the gallery.

Anne and her daughters and maidservant were not in sight. They must have gone to prepare for supper, leaving their needlework behind. Kat was glad not to have to answer any questions as she hurried toward Nick's bedchamber.

He was not there.

She stopped in the doorway, stunned at the disarray. Clothes had been pulled from chests and the press and flung across the room. Most lay on the bed, but a buff jerkin and a fine linen shirt lay on the floor, a doublet had been tossed on one chair, and hose were draped sloppily over the side of an open chest.

"Nick?" she asked weakly, gesturing around the room.

Nick's bodyservant, Walter Eakin, nodded grimly but did not pause as he carefully folded a silk shirt before replacing it in a chest.

"Where is he?" she asked, fearing to hear the answer she was given a moment later.

"He's gone, my lady. He did not say where, nor for how long he would be gone."

"And he did not ask you to go with him?"

"He said he would have no need of my services." The servant's voice was taut with anger and pain that Kat understood. Since Nick had returned to Beechwood from the Inns of Court, he had never left the manor for more than a day without Walter accompanying him, as Walter's father had accompanied their father on his journeys.

She looked around the room, which was almost as familiar as her own. There was the leather case for Nick's lute; he played it so often that she had given him three sets of lute strings last Christmas. Had he expected to be away for any length of time, he would have taken the lute—she was sure of it. Several of his books lay on a table near the fireplace. She crossed to it and looked curiously at the volume that lay open. It was Thomas Tusser's *Hundred Points of Good Husbandry*. Of certain that book would tell her nothing of his reason for leaving so hastily. Nor would the others, she realized, smiling crookedly as she looked at them: all were books on heraldry.

She let her fingertips trail over the books, then touched her lips as she looked around the chamber again. There was nothing here to explain Nick's mad errand for Master Sparrow.

"Did he say anything to you, madam, about where he might be going?" Walter asked.

He was looking at her shrewdly: all the servants knew how close she and her brother were. She shook her head, feeling vaguely guilty for not telling Walter that Nick had left for the Jerusalem Tree.

"He's never kept secrets from you before now," Walter said, and she wondered if he had guessed that she knew Nick's destination.

"I am not my brother's keeper, Walter," she said lightly, then left the room quickly, before he could question her further.

The *Book of Martyrs* was still lying open where Christopher had left it. Kat closed it, but not before noticing the illustration of Protestant captives. Though she had read the book often, it made her uneasy now. This evening the perilous times Foxe described seemed too close, the danger too likely to return.

The greatest threat now came from Mary Stuart, the Catholic Queen of Scots. Mary had been Queen Elizabeth's guest and prisoner since leaving Scotland for sanctuary in England two years ago, fleeing her own rebellious subjects. But the far-from-royal behavior that had driven the Scottish lords to rebel against Mary and imprison her—crowning her infant son King of Scotland and making the Earl of Moray, Mary's half brother James Stuart, the regent—did not seem to disturb Mary's sympathizers, mostly Catholic, in both Scotland and England. There had been the botched plot of the Duke of Norfolk to wed Mary last year. And only a few months had passed since the end of the rising in the north of England. The rebellion had begun last November, led by Thomas Percy, the Earl of Northumberland—*Simple Tom*, they called the earl, who was said to be governed by his wife—and the equally thoughtless young Earl of Westmorland. The English rebels had planned to free Mary and place her on England's throne, overthrowing Elizabeth, but they had never reached the Scottish queen and the rising had been crushed within a few months, with the traitorous earls escaping across the border to sympathizers in Scotland. Then, too, in January the Earl of Moray had been assassinated, shot from ambush by one of the Hamiltons of Bothwellhaugh; Mary was said to have rejoiced in the murder of her half brother. Kat could not doubt that the Queen of Scots was still plotting to overthrow her cousin Elizabeth, and that she would continue to seek aid from the Catholic monarchs of Spain and of France, where her Guise relations wielded great power. Kat had often wished heartily that the inquiry into Mary's role in the murder of her second husband, Lord Darnley, had led to a clear decision about the Scottish queen's guilt; that might finally have tarnished her in the eyes of the English Catholics who had rallied to her cause these last two years.

And now Kat wished that she knew whether Lord Harwood had played a role in those conspiracies. Had she not heard something once—some scrap of gossip, idly mentioned and at that time scarcely heeded—that linked Lord Harwood to Spain and the Catholic cause? But she could not remember the details now: the recollection was as elusive as any *ignis fatuus*.

She looked out the window, hoping against hope that she would see Nick returning.

I, too, would know more of this danger, Master Sparrow, she thought with sudden anger. *Much, much more.*

Then she went back downstairs to join her guests for supper.

CHAPTER 2

"Madam . . ."

Kat groaned and pushed her face into the pillow, trying to ignore her maid's attempt to wake her. "Madam!" Louise's hand was on her shoulder now. "There is someone here to see you!"

"Nick?" Kat sat up suddenly, brushing her tangled hair back from her face.

Louise, looking puzzled, shook her head. " 'Tis Master Danvers."

"I'faith, at *this* hour?" Kat could scarce believe he would return at all; she had thought herself well rid of him. Marry, had he not heard what she said yesterday? Was it possible he had already forgotten? "What does he want?"

"He is waiting in the gallery, madam. He has brought you breakfast."

"Jesu." Kat rubbed her eyes. She would have to set Christopher straight, make it clear to him that she would never marry him . . . but 'twould be more difficult than ever now that he had come like this, humbling himself to bring her her breakfast as though he were her servant . . .

"Madam?" Louise said. "Did you expect to see your brother this morning? He has not returned yet."

Kat glanced quickly at the maid, then away. How many of the servants would know by now not only that Nick had left, but that he had left in great haste? She doubted Walter Eakin could keep such news to himself. But she would not add to this gossip.

"Thank God he has not, since Christopher is here," she said with a laugh. "Nick would tell him we already have servants enough to serve our meals."

"Aye."

Louise had sounded skeptical, and Kat glanced at her again. She looked skeptical. *Would that I had not mentioned Nick,* she thought.

But was it any wonder that she awoke with his name on her lips, when she had dreamed of him half the night? She had twice awakened from bad dreams in which she had seen him dragged to London to be burned as a heretic by a Catholic monarch. *'Twas merely that picture I looked at last night,* she told herself as the dream images came back to her, but she could not push her fears for him from her mind, and it was a relief to have Louise interrupt her thoughts to ask her which nightgown she would wear over her smock.

The patience that had served Christopher Danvers so well as he waited for Kat in the gallery yesterday was gone today. He strode restlessly back and forth beside the table on which he had set the wicker basket.

He had slept very little last night. At home he had found a letter brought by a messenger: his suitor, made uneasy by Christopher's retreat from the court, wanted an answer. Yet Christopher was unwilling to give that answer without trying Kat once more.

He wished now that he had not let her talk of London cow him yesterday. He could deal later with her foolish, expensive dreams of life at court. For now, he had to make sure of her . . .

"Master Danvers?" Louise was standing in the doorway. "Pray come with me."

Kat was sitting up in bed, pillows propped behind her back, when he entered the chamber. He was pleased that she had not dressed for the day, but instead wore a nightgown of murrey velvet.

"Good morrow, Christopher. You woke early this morning."

"I could not stay away." He set the basket down on the writing desk. "I could not sleep."

"And so you thought to share your sleeplessness with me." She smiled. Her unpainted face seemed unusually pale to him, but she was still very beautiful . . . even when, as now, he suspected that she was laughing at him.

"I would share all my sleepless nights with you," he said, and she blushed. Her maid, who had taken up a post beside the bed, frowned at him. "I have brought you breakfast."

"So Louise said."

He took two finely wrought Venetian glasses from the basket. "Do you like these?"

"They are lovely, Christopher," she responded, looking slightly confused.

"They are yours, then. My first gift to you today."

Her reaction stunned him. He had hoped to see delight on her face, but after her remarks yesterday, he had steeled himself to accept even the sort of complacent greed with which Lettice Fielding had taken his gifts. What he had not been prepared for was Kat's look of dismay.

"Marry, I hope you'll like the wine better than the glasses," he jested. " 'Tis charnico, which you told me was one of your favorites. And I have brought some tarts my cook baked this morning from apple-johns."

"Also my favorite," she said quietly, her expression softening as she smiled faintly. "Why did I think you paid too little attention to things that I said?"

He shook his head, not sure what she meant, but she had nothing more to say for the moment.

Turning so that his back would block their view of the writing table, he reached into a pocket of his doublet and withdrew a small glass vial containing a fine powder. He dumped the powder into Kat's goblet as he filled it with wine, returned the vial to his pocket, then filled the other glass. The powder dissolved quickly, as promised; if any had not dissolved, it had settled to the bottom of the glass, where it mixed with the lees.

He took both glasses over to the bed and watched anxiously while she tasted the wine.

She made a slight face, then smiled. " 'Tis very sweet."

"D'you not like sugar in your charnico?" he asked innocently, then took a sip from his own glass. It was much too sweet for his taste. The old Frenchwoman who had sold him the powder had advised him to mask its bitterness by mixing it with a sweet drink.

"Sometimes."

He went to get the apple tarts then, glancing around the room as he did so. The bedchamber was as richly furnished as the gallery, with velvet upholstery on the chair by the writing table, lavishly embroidered satin hangings on the huge four-poster bed, and a fine Turkey carpet draped over one of two large chests. Here, instead of the matting he had seen in the gallery, the floor was strewn with fresh rushes mixed with meadowsweet and rosemary. The fireplace had been scrubbed clean and filled with fragrant pine branches. It was a pleasant room, one more assurance that Kat would be a competent wife . . . once he convinced her 'twould be folly to squander her dowry on clothes to wear at court.

He was glad to see that she washed down each bite of the pastry with a swallow of wine. Her face gradually became flushed. Was that a sign that the love philter was working? he wondered. He wished he had asked the old woman in the apothecary in Bucklersbury more about this potion, but while she had been in the back of the shop, crushing herbs with a mortar and pestle, an acquaintance of his had come in to buy some tobacco. Christopher had feigned interest in the conserves and perfumes until the old woman had returned, then had paid her and left quickly, before his acquaintance could ask questions about the powder—

and he might well have, had he heard the same rumors about the apothecary that had led Christopher there.

That had been two months ago, after Lettice Fielding's husband had died, a day before he had proposed to her and been mocked and humiliated in response. He had not even been allowed to stay long enough to drink with her, so that he could have added the philter to the sack-and-sugar that was her habitual drink. He had been shown out of her house within a few minutes after proposing. Out of all of his memories of that day, only the fact that he had not presented her with the expensive clock he had bought for her was consolation for his injured pride.

Now he wondered whether the philter might have lost its potency after two months. He prayed that it had not. But the Frenchwoman had said that the powder should be used soon . . .

Kat's face was very red by the time she finished a second apple tart and followed that last morsel with the dregs of wine from her glass. He took the glass from her hand.

"And what is your usual breakfast?" he asked as he went to refill the goblet.

"Cold beef and ale, or, mayhap, eggs and butter with a glass of wine."

"*Watered* wine," Louise added sharply. Kat gave her a scathing look, and after a few moments the maid lowered her gaze.

Watching out of the corner of his eye, Christopher felt cheered. "I would have my next gift brought up from the hall now," he said as he brought the glass back to Kat. "I left my man waiting there. If your maid could bring him to us . . ." He let his voice trail off, hardly daring to hope that Kat would send her maid away—though this seemed as opportune a moment as any.

"Of certain. Louise?"

"Madam! You should not—"

"And," Christopher interrupted, "I would have your aunt here to see this gift. If your woman could bring her as well . . ."

Kat nodded, then looked at the maid. "Anne should be awake by now. Ask her if she'll join us." Then, when Louise hesitated: "Now."

Looking grimly unhappy, the maid hurried away.

As soon as the door had closed behind her, Christopher turned to Kat. "Sweeting, we must talk, for— Is something wrong?"

She had been touching her forehead; now she lowered her hand and shook her head, smiling wanly. "Nothing, nothing of import. You speak truly, Christopher, for we must talk, now that we have some privacy." She paused, a pained look on her face, and this time her hand touched her belly lightly. "In sooth, that was too sweet a breakfast . . . and I do not think I can drink this," she said, handing him the glass of wine, which he set on the floor.

"I would have brought the sort of breakfast you favored, love, had I known it." He moved closer to her, becoming aware of a gentle perfume of roses, so faint that it was barely noticeable against the lavender-scented bedclothes. Putting his arm around her shoulders, he tried to kiss her, but she averted her face at the last moment, and his lips brushed her cheek.

"Christopher," she whispered, pushing against him. "Please you, let us talk of what you said yesterday, of your offer."

"If you wish, sweeting." He released her, and she slumped back against the pillows. She looked ill. She stared at him for what seemed a long time, then closed her eyes. He noticed there was a sheen of sweat on her face.

"Is this gown too hot, Kat?" he asked. He reached for the top fastenings, rejoicing when she did not move to stop him, even when he brushed the heavy velvet away, revealing the almost sheer smock underneath. Her eyes were open now, but she stared at him as though entranced. The philter was working! And just in time, too, for he heard women's voices outside in the hall; the maid was returning with Anne Norland. Feeling triumphant, he slid his arms around Kat and waited for the door to open.

He was stunned when she shoved him away with enough strength to break free of his grasp. "Oh, Christopher, I am sick!" She flung herself out of the bed and ran to the basin and leaned over it, retching. Christopher rose, uncertain what to do, terrified that he might have poisoned the girl.

The door opened. Anne Norland seemed frozen to stone for an instant, then she ran to her niece. Louise shot Christopher a look of pure hatred that quelled any explanation he could have given, then went to assist Anne.

Christopher's servant stood in the doorway for a few moments, looking baffled, then walked heavily into the room and set a massive gold clock down on the writing table. "There." He grinned with simple pleasure until he saw the look on his master's face.

Kat was sipping from a cup of water Anne had given her. She set it down, wiped her face with the towel, and smoothed her hair back from her forehead. "Thank you, madam." She looked at her guest then, her cheeks reddening with what he suspected was shame this time. "Cry you mercy, Christopher. I must have a weak stomach this morning. Else I had too much wine."

"Only one glass," Louise reminded her, looking at the goblet filled with wine that still sat on the floor beside the bed.

"But unwatered," Kat reminded her. The maid did not respond, and Christopher thought he saw a look of suspicion in her eyes.

How much of the philter would have been left in the glass when he refilled it? Was it possible that someone could detect its taste even when it was diluted with a second glassful of charnico?

He hurried to help Kat back to the bed, directing Louise to stand on the other side of the weakened girl. As they reached the head of the bed, he swung his foot into the goblet, shattering it, spilling wine across his boot and into the rushes, where bright shards of glass glittered dangerously.

"Oh, Christopher!" Kat cried in dismay.

"A plague on my clumsiness! Kat, I am sorry to break your glass. I'll buy you another."

He helped her settle back against the pillows while Louise, after giving him another suspicious look, hurried to clean up the spilled wine and broken glass. *Prove your suspicions now*, he thought, feeling a bit giddy with relief. Kat did not seem terribly ill, and any evidence that he had drugged her had vanished among the soaked rushes that Louise was clearing away.

The clock chimed then. At the unexpected noise, Anne and the maid jumped, and Kat cried out in surprise.

"Do you like this gift, sweeting?" he asked, gesturing toward the clock. "Nay, do not tell me you have no stomach for this."

Kat opened her mouth to speak, then shut it again and looked helplessly at her aunt.

"Sir, she should rest now," Anne told him.

He nodded, though reluctant to leave. What might the maid say about him once he was gone? What suspicions might she voice? But he was unable to think of a reason to stay here. "I would fain stay at Beechwood until she is well enough to see me again."

"As you will," Anne said absently, turning toward the bed.

"Beshrew this sickness!" Kat said suddenly. "I promised Eleanor that I would take her hawking this morning before you leave."

" 'Tis of no matter," Anne assured her.

"But she will be disappointed!"

"Let me take her hawking instead," Christopher offered, and to his relief was rewarded with a smile from Kat. Mayhap all was not lost . . .

An hour later, as he rode back to Colmeade, Christopher was bitterly regretting that offer.

The outing had seemed promising at first. It was a lovely, warm morning, and the tercel-gentle that Kat and Nick had given Eleanor was a fine hawk. But Frances had insisted on coming along, and then had begged Eleanor to let her fly the hawk. And he had agreed—worse, had persuaded Eleanor to accede to her sister's request.

And now the hawk was lost, for Frances had so mishandled it that it had raked away almost at once. He had perforce offered to replace it. 'Twould have been ungracious to do otherwise. Foolish, too, for Kat might have blamed him, when in truth she was to blame for not warning him against Frances. And that was one more expense the day had brought him.

Yet even that had not been enough to crown the morning's mischances. As he had crossed the shallow stream bordering Beechwood, his horse had slipped on the muddy bank, throwing him into the water and ruining his fine new suit . . . and in full sight of Kat's cousins and servants. He would be a laughingstock at Beechwood now.

He was still in a dull fury when he reached Colmeade, and it did not help his humor that a carrier had brought another letter from London. *I would know your heart,* it said, and no more. He burned the letter and set about bathing and dressing himself to visit Beechwood again, where this time, without question, he would know Kat's heart.

Late in the morning, Kat wandered restlessly about her room. She had offered to help Anne with the final preparations for their journey back to Suffolk, but had been relieved when her offer was refused, for the truth was that she still felt slightly weak and ill. In no way would she show it, though, while her aunt was here, lest Anne decide she should stay and nurse her back to health. Kat very badly wanted her aunt and cousins out of the way.

Nick . . .

She had sorted through all her books, but there was no comfort there, not a moment's distraction, not in Cato's *Distichs,* or in Plutarch, Homer, or Dante—not even in *Celestina* or *Pyramus and Thisbe* or *Guy of Warwick,* which her aunt, an advocate of Vives's advice, disapproved of her reading. Nor could she find any amusement in reading her copy of the *Hundred Merry Tales.* She fretted too much about Nick. That, and her illness, had left her so peevish that she had snapped at Louise a few hours earlier.

I trust him not, madam. I believe he may have drugged your wine.

What? Kat had stared at Louise, stunned by the possibility. She could not help but recall what Nick had told her, of his friend who had seen Christopher in an apothecary in Bucklersbury, buying something that might have been a poison to hasten his father to his grave . . .

'Twas no poison, she had thought. No purge, either. It must have been some potion to make a woman more amenable to his suit. Nick had told her of the rumors that Christopher had courted a widow. She would have to tell Nick—nay, she dared not. Nick would likely challenge Christopher to a duel, and she could not have that. Nor could she have Louise gossiping about her fears to the other servants, for such gossip would soon reach Nick's ears.

A plague on your suspicions! she had said quickly. *But an hour ago you were telling me that I was drinking too much wine, and then you had no thought of drugs and potions. You were right to tell me then that I was not used to such strong drink so early. Do not now seek to blame Christopher for my carelessness. 'Tis an idle, mischievous thought.*

Louise had begged her pardon, and promised to say nothing to anyone else of her suspicions, but Kat found little satisfaction in that. She had rarely spoken so harshly to the maid, and though she had apologized soon after, Louise had said very little since then.

Devil take Christopher, Kat thought. Devil take his gift, too. She glared balefully at the clock as it struck again, as it had every quarter hour, loudly enough that there had been no chance of her drifting off to sleep. It was a handsome clock, more than twelve inches tall, gilded and ornately wrought with choppy waves at its base and fountains of water supporting the artfully sculpted figures of a mermaid and a dolphin. Like Christopher, the clock was fair to look upon, but its company could be borne only when it was silent.

"A pox on him," she muttered, finally sitting down on the bed again. She hoped Christopher would return to Beechwood soon, but not before Anne had left. What Kat had to say to him was best said without an audience.

It was with relief that she finally heard a knock on the door and Anne's voice announcing that they were ready to leave.

Down in the courtyard, whither Kat had insisted on accompanying them, she bade them all farewell—even Frances, whose eyes were red-rimmed from crying after the verbal lashing she had received from Anne.

Kat glanced toward the gate from time to time, and Anne, noticing, asked, "D'you suppose any mischief has befallen Master Danvers?" Her voice was distinctly cool. Her fondness for Christopher had vanished once she heard of his insistence on seeing Kat in her bedchamber.

"He takes great pains with his appearance. Perchance he is having a new suit sewn for his next visit."

Anne chuckled, but sobered quickly. " 'Tis my hope that his new suit will suit you even less than his old one."

" 'Twill never suit me," Kat said, hugging her. Were it not for her worries about Nick, she would be sorry to see her aunt go, especially now that Anne no longer was Christopher's advocate.

One of the grooms helped Anne into her saddle, and she gazed down at Kat, smiling a bit crookedly. "Pray tell Nick that he need not leave home just because he finds farewells so awkward."

"I shall tell him," Kat said, forcing herself to smile in response, though her throat ached suddenly.

She stood in the courtyard, surrounded by her servants, waving until Anne and her retinue were out of sight. Then, as the servants began to disperse, she called to one of the grooms.

"Go bid Hal saddle the Blackamoor for me. I will be leaving for Stamworth in an hour."

He nodded and ran toward the stables. Kat went back into the house, ignoring Louise, who stood astonished in the middle of the courtyard for several moments before hurrying after her mistress.

Upstairs Kat changed to her newest riding garb, a linen shirt and a doublet and hose of murrey silk, and donned her boots, while Louise, complaining but obedient, packed her cloakbag as ordered. Kat was taking the old doublet and hose she had worn yesterday, and also a kirtle and gown. She doubted she would be wearing the women's garb, but she did not tell Louise that.

Finished dressing, she went to Nick's room. All was in order again; there was no trace of Nick's hasty packing yesterday afternoon. Kat easily found what she sought, and, wrapping it in one of Nick's cloaks, left the room to find Louise already waiting for her in the gallery, the cloakbag in her hand. The maid looked suspiciously at the long, bulkily wrapped bundle her mistress was carrying, but a glance at Kat's face forestalled questions.

Downstairs in the great hall, Kat sent Louise away, calling for her steward to bring writing gear. She had to leave Christopher a message, and it was wiser to entrust it to the steward than to Louise, who might see fit to add a few choice words of her own.

They were short of supplies for making ink, the steward told her. She nodded absent approval to his requests for new supplies while she wrote swiftly in her neat secretary hand. She folded the letter deftly, softened a lump of scented wax between her fingers, and pressed it onto the paper with her seal ring.

"This is for Master Danvers, the next time he comes to Beechwood," she told him. "I want his gifts returned, too—all of them. Tell Louise to gather them for you."

The groom was waiting for her in the courtyard, holding the Black-amoor's reins. The horse stamped restlessly. It had been days since she had ridden him, and she knew he would be eager to run, which suited her today. While a stableboy fastened her cloakbag and the awkward cloth-wrapped bundle to the saddle, she stroked the Blackamoor's neck, careful to avoid the scars that still testified to a previous owner's brutality. The wounds had been fresh when her father bought the stallion at Smithfield, in London, nearly four years ago, and he had stayed in town an extra week while his groom tended the wounds and soothed the horse until he could be led home. The Blackamoor—so they had named him, for his coal-black color—could not be ridden then, nor for a year after that by anyone. No one could ride him yet but Kat, who, during the bleak days after Ned's death, had spent hours at the stable, gentling the stallion until finally the Blackamoor accepted saddle and bridle again and allowed her to ride him. A cross between a Barbary stallion and an English mare, the Blackamoor was by far the swiftest horse at Beechwood, which was why Kat had chosen to ride him, despite his tricksy spirit. Her ultimate destination this day was not Stamworth but the Jerusalem Tree, and she wished to reach it before dark.

Riding out of the courtyard, the groom following on a gray jennet, she looked anxiously toward the west, toward Colmeade, and was relieved to see no rider there, no one who might be Christopher, returning before she could get away. She turned east, toward Stamworth, and let the Blackamoor run at the fastest pace that her groom's mount could match.

It was but ten minutes later that Christopher Danvers was met by the steward in the great hall at Beechwood. He knew even before reading the letter what he would find in it: it had been clear the moment he saw his gifts to Kat, gathered together for him to take back to Colmeade.

His hands were shaking slightly as he broke the seal and read the brief sentences Kat had written, from her apology for having been called away and hence prevented from delivering the message in person, to her cool explanation that she had realized they would not suit and so should not marry.

He folded the letter and pocketed it. Were it not for the servants who were watching, he would have torn the paper in two or crushed it and discarded it on the rush-strewn floor. The servants, with their studiously blank faces and carefully deferential manner, must, he felt, be laughing at him inwardly, knowing that he had just been spurned by their mistress.

For a moment he was tempted to sweep all the gifts onto the floor and leave them there, so much glittering rubbish. The thought of the servants' reaction stopped him—that, and the more important thought of how much those gifts had cost him and might still be worth.

So he took the gifts with him when he left, in bulky packs strapped to his manservant's saddle. Once they were out of sight of Beechwood, he spurred his horse to a gallop, leaving his servant and the heavily laden horse far behind. The clock and other gifts would reach Colmeade, he was sure, by the time he was packed and ready to leave for London.

CHAPTER 3

Jane Spencer leaned over the pot in which the year's first batch of rosewater was being prepared. Two days ago she had watched her maids set the roses to steep in their own juice, with yeast added. Now the heady, vinegarlike smell of the mixture assured her that it was time for the first distillation. She nodded and stepped back out of the way as the maids set to work. She would be glad when the new rosewater was ready. Last year's was gone already, and she had been forced to go to an apothecary for the rosewater she had used last week for flavoring syrup to candy flowers. Her late husband would have disapproved of such lack of thrift.

She hurried out of the stillroom. Other household tasks demanded her attention—many more now than during her brief marriage, when her husband, thinking his child-bride incapable of running the manor, had managed it himself with his steward's help. But she had found, after his death, that she was capable of managing Stamworth, and that she enjoyed it.

Early this morning she had gone with the dairywoman to a neighboring manor to buy two milk cows, then had settled a dispute between the butler and his assistant. She had greeted the candlemaker, who had not visited Stamworth for a few months, and he was now at work making rush candles for the servants with the tallow saved from cooking. She had seen that the broken meats left from breakfast were sent to the porter's gate to be given to beggars, and had searched through her volumes of Ruscelli's *Secrets of Alexis*, which Nick Langdon had purchased for her in London, for a salve one of her maids required. With luck, now, she would have some quiet time to sit with those of her maidservants who were spinning flax, while Meg Allen, her youngest maid, read the Scriptures to them in her clear, sweet voice—and, Jane remembered, she would have to talk to Meg about her dowry: the girl was twelve, old enough to marry . . . and already a month older than she herself had been on the day of her wedding five years ago.

As she passed through the great hall, her steward came toward her.

"Mistress Ophelia bade me thank you for the jumbolds and dainty butter."

"I am glad they pleased her." Her great-aunt was seventy, ailing and querulous, but Jane still preferred her company to that of any of the other relatives who might have insisted on keeping her company—or, worse, insisted that she live with them—after her husband's death, to protect her reputation. Jane had been relieved when Ophelia had agreed to move to Stamworth. She would have risked being known as a lewd, lecherous widow before she would have returned to her home and the parents who had married her off to a sickly man in his fifties.

Both she and her steward looked around as a groom ran into the hall.

"Madam, Mistress Langdon is here!"

"Is anyone with her?" she asked, then flushed a little, wondering how much that question gave away. "I know her aunt is visiting Beechwood."

"Nay, she's alone, but for her groom."

Jane tried not to let her disappointment show. Perhaps this was for the best, anyway. She had not painted her face that morning, or given much care to her dress. During her fourteen months of marriage to Andrew Spencer, she had, at her husband's bidding, dyed her dark brown hair yellow, and painted her face with white and red fucus. It had been a relief, after his death, to do without paint and dye. Only during the last year had she begun to paint her face again, when she expected Nick Langdon to visit, or when she herself visited Beechwood . . . and even then she had almost laughed at herself. She could not make herself taller, nor—no matter how little she ate—much slimmer. Her hair would perforce stay brown, since dye turned it to straw, and though paint could make her skin look fairer, it could not make her round face one whit thinner. And what magician could sell her a paint to change her eyes from brown to blue? She had been told that she was lovely, but she feared Nick would never find her so. The few times she had heard him speak of some beauty he admired, he had mentioned fair hair and blue eyes. She would have lost all hope, had she not reminded herself that perchance he found other sorts of women fair to look upon. Would that she could find out for certain, but she dared not ask him—or Kat, for that matter.

Kat was coming up the steps, followed by one of her grooms carrying a cloakbag and a long cloth-wrapped bundle, by the time Jane reached the door.

"Well met, in sooth." She smiled warmly at Kat, for she was glad to have her here, even without her brother. "We have missed you."

"And I you. I would have visited sooner, and Anne and her daughters with me, had not Eleanor suffered from a cough."

"Has she recovered?"

"Aye, Mistress Physician," Kat said with a laugh. "You need not delve through Master Alexis's secrets. They left this morning." She hugged Jane. "You look well."

"So do you. Their company must have agreed with you. Or, haply, Christopher Danvers . . . ?"

Kat flushed, started to speak, then closed her mouth and merely shook her head. Jane was suddenly aware again that her steward and the two grooms stood nearby.

"Have you dined yet?" she asked, and, when Kat shook her head, "Then pray have dinner with me. Will you be staying overnight? Would you like the bedchamber overlooking the orchard? Mitchell can show your man where to put your cloakbag."

Soon they were seated at the table in the parlor, the meal spread before them, all the servants withdrawn and the doors shut. Jane had decided to serve her guest herself, that they might talk privately.

"What will you have?" she asked, gesturing at the dishes before her. "There's salad, and chicken pie, and cold beef. And I should tell the cook now to prepare soused pig for supper, as you like it, with white wine and ginger and nutmeg and bay leaves."

"Jane," Kat said, and something in her guest's voice stopped Jane as she rose from the table, "I thank you, and I am sure the soused pig would be wonderful, but I cannot stay for supper. I must leave soon."

"But you sent your groom back to—" She broke off as Kat nodded. "I see. You do not want it known at Beechwood that you are not staying here."

"I may be back tonight, very late, but 'tis not certain."

"Whither are you going?"

"I cannot tell you that, nor why. Pray forgive me."

Jane stared at her friend for a time, then nodded. "Very well." She busied herself with serving the food, then said grace, and they began to eat.

"Does this concern Master Danvers?" Jane asked after a few minutes of silence. "It seemed that my mentioning him earlier troubled you."

To her surprise, Kat laughed. "He's no longer a troublesome matter. I have rejected his suit." And she told Jane of her conversations with Christopher during the past few days.

"Do you think it was wise to reject him with that letter, rather than telling him yourself? He's a proud man, and will not take it well."

Kat shrugged. "I could not wait to talk to him. Then, too, I was not sure whether—" She stopped talking, her face pale of a sudden.

"What?" Jane prompted.

"Swear that you will tell no one else of this?"

Jane so swore, then listened in growing anger as Kat related her suspicions that she had been drugged that morning, rather than—as she had earlier said—just sickened by the wine.

" 'Tis only gossip," Kat said, shrugging again as if that could dismiss the story Nick had heard from his friend who had seen Danvers at the apothecary.

"Gossip that suits the facts too well. What does Nick say? Does he not wonder at your sudden illness, knowing of Christopher's fondness for apothecaries?"

Kat shook her head slightly. "He knows nothing of this. He's away."

Jane nodded. "And does his absence have aught to do with this business y'are about? I would ask if you were on your way to tell Nick of Master Danvers's perfidy, had you not already told me that this does not concern Christopher. Something of greater import, then?"

"I beg of you, Jane, no more questions."

"What will you? That I go along with your pretense of staying here, while you ride off someplace alone—you were planning on traveling alone, were you not?—into dangers I cannot even guess at?"

" 'Sdeath, thirty miles by well-traveled road is scarce a voyage to Cathay. What's this about dangers you cannot even guess at?" Kat looked down at the table suddenly. A few moments later she sighed, wiped her mouth with one of Ophelia's lavishly embroidered linen napkins, and pushed her chair back from the table. "No more questions?" she asked softly, a plea in her eyes as she looked up again. "I know I ask much of you, but I will leave you a sealed letter, telling you where I have gone, if you will agree not to open it unless I fail to return by noon tomorrow."

"What shall I then? Raise the hue and cry?"

"Mayhap the carrier would serve you better," Kat said, smiling crookedly. "I shall write the names of those you should alert."

So you do think danger at least possible, Jane thought, staring intently at her friend. *Thirty miles by well-traveled road* . . . Toward London? Perchance, but there were other possibilities. Southampton? Winchester? Portsmouth? Uncertainty fretted her. Yet she dared not insist that Kat reveal her destination now: Kat was capable of going off without leaving her so much as the letter she had promised.

"Well enough," Jane said at last. "Now. Is there any other way I can help you, any other aid I can give?"

Kat relaxed visibly. "Yea, and thanks. I would have some soil from your garden, a scant handful, not too wet, and," she added with a mischievous smile, "without any compost in it."

"Will it serve, d'you think?" Kat asked an hour later.

Jane stared critically at the bizarre figure that now stood in front of her, holding her looking glass and tilting it from side to side. "I warrant you, no one will suspect that you are a gentlewoman," she said at last, "and 'twill be fortunate if they take you for a gentleman, rather than some rogue."

Kat laughed and set the glass down. The face she turned toward Jane was far from clean. Jane had winced as she watched her friend rub her face and hands with dirt, then carefully brush the excess away, leaving only enough to make her beautiful fair skin seem coarser and darker. Jane had helped Kat wind her hair tightly around her head and pin it securely into place, then cover it with a large and ancient cap that was battered into shapelessness. And Jane had brought her a length of cambric so Kat could bind her breasts flat before donning an old doublet and hose that had once belonged to Nick.

Now Kat went over to the awkward bundle her groom had carried up here and left on a chest. She untied the strings that bound it, then unrolled the cloth—a cloak, Jane saw—to disclose a sword in its scabbard, and a sword belt.

"Welladay, what's this?" Jane had spoken sharply, and Kat jumped slightly but did not look around.

" 'Tis Nick's Toledo blade. He took the better of his two new swords. I would have taken the other, were the scabbard not too fine for this garb." She struggled to fasten the belt about her waist.

"And have you studied fence?"

"I have watched Nick."

"You have watched birds, too. Think you that you can fly?"

"Have I made that boast? Look you, Jane, I shall not use this sword, but I must needs wear it. What youth of our age would be without a sword?"

There was no gainsaying that. Jane shook her head helplessly, her hands clenched as she watched Kat walk up and down the bedchamber, accustoming herself to the weight of the sword on its belt, reaching behind her to touch the hilt of the dagger that hung in its own scabbard at the back of the sword belt. *And why do you do that,* Jane asked silently, *if you think you will not use a weapon?*

Kat drew the sword partway from its scabbard, then sheathed it again. She had begun to swagger in a way that reminded Jane of how Nick had walked a few years ago. Jane suspected it was an imitation, but was it a conscious one? Of one thing she was sure: this was unwise.

"Katherine," she said dryly, "should you play the swashbuckler too well, you might find yourself challenged."

That stopped Kat, and the look she gave Jane was abashed. " 'Twas Nick's manner, when he was first at Cambridge with—with Ned."

"Yea, and they were often foolish then, were they not?"

Kat nodded after a moment. Her walk, as she went to pick up her cloakbag, was less ostentatious, though still closer to Nick's usual gait than her own.

" 'Twill serve you well," Jane said more generously. "None will suspect you in that guise. Pray God, it will keep you safe."

"Amen," Kat added under her breath, shouldering the cloakbag. Her eyes met Jane's for an instant, and Jane thought she saw fear in them. Then Kat turned away, moving resolutely toward the door.

Jane led the way down to the orchard, avoiding curious eyes.

"Were anyone to see us," Kat asked as they slipped out of the house, "would they think this some tryst?"

Jane laughed. " 'Twould confirm their worst fears."

"Then all Ophelia's efforts are for naught."

The Blackamoor was waiting at the orchard gate, his reins held by Jane's head groom, an elderly man who could be trusted. Even he appeared disturbed, though, by the appearance of the youth at her side.

"George, do you remember Mistress Langdon?"

"I saw you but last September," Kat reminded him, "when you helped us eat the Michaelmas geese."

His mouth fell open. A moment later it snapped shut. He bowed, apologized, and would have helped Kat into the saddle, but she waved him away, easily mounting without help. While she held the reins, steadying the horse, he fastened her cloakbag to the saddle. Finished, he retreated to give them privacy.

"Thirty miles of well-traveled roads," Jane said in a low voice. "Will you reach your destination before nightfall?"

"Easily," Kat answered, but averted her eyes.

There were risks in any travel, Jane knew. There would be more should Kat still be on the road after dark. Nor had she given any assurance that she would find safety at her destination . . .

"Is this about Nick?" she blurted out. "Is he in danger?"

Kat stared at her, and Jane felt as though her face were on fire.

"Jane, are you—" Kat began wonderingly, then broke off. "Nay," she said a few moments later. "Nay, he is in no danger—or so a sparrow said. Bid me God-speed."

"God speed you," Jane said obediently, and Kat wheeled her horse and rode away before Jane could ask what she had meant about the sparrow.

CHAPTER 4

Kat rode to the Jerusalem Tree at an easy false gallop—what Nick called a Canterbury pace—which, riding the Blackamoor, was nearly as fast as a full gallop on other horses. She kept to the verge of the rutted roads, her boots sometimes brushing against hedges of yew and hawthorn.

She passed a tinker, who was walking and leading a packhorse; the pots and pans clanged against each other, but both horse and tinker seemed deaf to the noise. Scarcely had she left the clatter behind when she heard the sound of bells far ahead. A minute later she caught up with a carrier's train bound for London. A middle-aged couple in out-dated finery, belike too poor to hire post horses, rode with the train. Glad that she did not have to travel so slowly, Kat soon left them far behind.

Nick, she thought, remembering Jane's crimson face when she had asked about him. *What would you say if you knew of this?* For it was certain that Jane loved Nick, and Kat doubted that Nick had thought of Jane much at all, other than as a pleasant neighbor. Neither when Jane was Andrew Spencer's painted toy of a wife, nor at any time during her widowhood, had Kat heard Nick say aught of Jane, unless she first mentioned the woman, or unless he had happened to meet her. Small wonder, though: Jane could not be further from the *buonarobas* Kat had once overheard Nick discussing with a friend of his from the Inns of Court. As near as Kat could tell, those glorious wenches were nothing but more costly sisters of the Southwark punks Nick and his friend had disparaged.

She reined in the Blackamoor as she approached a ford by which a boy in ragged clothes and oversized riding boots was watering his horse. It was a postboy she knew—a rather idle postboy at the moment, as he lounged on the bank of the stream, chewing on a blade of grass. His leather satchel lay on the ground beside him. She knew the satchel must needs contain a packet of letters to and from officials of the court, but whatever was there must not have seemed too urgent. None of those letters would have *Haste, post, haste for life* written on the outside, with a drawing of a man hanging from a gallows sketched beside the words

41

to let even illiterate postboys know that they were to ride as though carrying a pardon that would save a man facing execution.

The boy glanced around then, and scrambled to his feet. There was a look of guilt on his face. He quickly mounted his horse and set off south again at a gallop, blowing on a hunting horn to warn anyone along the road to give way to the post.

The sun was already setting when Kat first caught sight of the crown of the enormous, ancient oak tree that gave the Jerusalem Tree its name. A moment later, as she crested a gentle hill, the inn itself came into view, smoke wafting upward from its chimneys. It was a welcome sight, for the exhilaration she had felt during the first hours of the ride had given way to weariness.

Two riders coming from the south reached the inn just before her. She followed them into the courtyard, reining in several yards away.

A gentleman and his servant, Kat thought, for a moment envying the gentleman. She wished she could have brought Louise with her, then chuckled as she pictured the way she would appear, garbed as she was now, with a maid in attendance.

The gentleman looked around then, and Kat could not help but stare at him. He was the handsomest man she had ever seen, tall and slender but well muscled, with a face that might have been carved by a sculptor, thick reddish-brown hair that seemed ablaze in the sunset, and carefully barbered beard and mustache. His clothes were fine, too: a doublet and hose of russet velvet, and a cape of russet-and-black-striped silk. But she felt her admiration for him fade as he stared back at her, too clearly surprised by her odd appearance. He looked over the Blackamoor then, and shook his head in wonder, and Kat began to regret having worn such old clothes when she was riding such a magnificent horse. His tawny-haired manservant—also a handsome fellow, Kat noticed—said something in a low voice to the gentleman, who laughed shortly. Kat felt oddly ashamed and angry at the man who was laughing at her, and she looked down.

As the two men dismounted, the innkeeper hurried out to greet them.

"Lord Harwood!" he called, and Kat looked up. The innkeeper bowed, then clasped pudgy hands together as he smiled up at the gentleman, who was a head taller than his stocky host. "My lord, you are most welcome here!" He called to the ostlers.

While two grown men came running to take their horses, Kat found herself attended by a boy no more than ten. "Shall I see to your horse, sir?"

She slid to the ground, wincing as she took a few tentative steps. The boy was staring at the horse's neck.

"Those scars are whipmarks," Kat said quietly. "Do not touch them. He'll shy away."

"Someone whipped *this* horse?"

Kat smiled despite herself, reminded of the youngest groom at Beechwood, who had the same love of horses she saw in this lad. "He was no judge of horseflesh, and the Blackamoor is well rid of him."

"Aye, that he is! What breed of horse is he? He looks like a Barb, but he's much too big."

"My father was told that he's a cross between a Barbary stallion and an English mare." She handed the boy the reins. "Feed him well."

"Yea, I will," the young ostler promised, "after I have walked him and rubbed him down."

She gave the child a coin, then started toward the inn's door, but before she reached it she heard the Blackamoor snort.

Whirling, she saw the young ostler, clutching the Blackamoor's reins in one hand, run his free hand curiously across the horse's scarred hide.

"No!" she shouted, but it was too late.

The Blackamoor screamed and threw his head back.

The boy clung to the reins and was yanked off the ground as the horse reared. A hoof struck his shoulder and he fell, landing below the Blackamoor's hooves.

Kat began to run toward them, but Lord Harwood and his manservant got there first. The servant scooped the child up and carried him to safety as the baron seized the flying reins. For a moment Kat thought he would be the horse's second victim, but then, miraculously, the Blackamoor was standing still, trembling, as Lord Harwood stroked his neck and spoke gently to him.

"Thank you, my lord. I'll take him now." She held out her hand, but the nobleman kept the reins as he looked down at her coldly.

"My lord, are you all right?" the innkeeper asked. "I apologize for this young ruffian." He turned a glowering face on the boy, who was on his feet again but holding his arm, wincing but not crying out as the manservant probed for broken bones. "He's a poor excuse for an ostler."

" 'Twas not his fault, I trow," Harwood replied. "How badly is he hurt, Tandy?"

"A bruise," the servant said. "Nothing more. He'll be mended in a day or two."

"He'll need longer to recover from the whipping he's earned," the innkeeper said, and the youth blanched.

"Hold, Master Bruning. I said 'twas not his fault." Lord Harwood pointed at the scars crisscrossing the Blackamoor's lathered hide. "This horse was badly abused once, and still shies easily." He looked at Kat. "Why did you not warn the boy?"

An angry retort was on the tip of her tongue, but she held it back after glancing at the boy again. A thrashing might not be the worst he would suffer. He might lose his place here, too, if the innkeeper knew he had disobeyed Kat's orders.

"I forgot."

Her answer had sounded sullen, and Lord Harwood's lip curled derisively. "You forgot." He gave the reins to another ostler, an adult, who had come up; then, after a final, contemptuous glance at Kat, he set off toward the inn's entrance, the innkeeper close on his heels. A few moments later the servant, Tandy, walked past. He glanced at her, and she was steeling herself to face his contempt, too, when to her surprise he winked and gave her a friendly smile.

"Sir?"

She turned, almost colliding with the young ostler, who had approached her silently.

"I thank you for your lie," he said solemnly.

"Y'are welcome to it," she replied, with equal seriousness. "Will you do me a favor now?"

"Anything."

"Follow that man"—she nodded toward the ostler leading her horse into the stable—"and see that no one touches the Blackamoor's scars. The next one might not be so lucky."

"No, sir. I mean—yes, sir. I'll tell him." And he was off, running toward the stable.

She sighed and turned back toward the inn. It was an inauspicious start, she thought, recalling Sparrow's advice to Nick to watch without being observed. She did not even know yet if Nick were here, but she had already made certain Lord Harwood would not overlook her.

She stepped into the firelit dimness of the inn's common room, then moved out of the way of a blue-clad drawer carrying pots of ale on a tray. The room was crowded. Men called for food and drink while a trio of musicians in one corner tried vainly to compete with the noise. Kat saw the innkeeper talking to a corpulent middle-aged woman clad in a kirtle and gown of fine wool: his wife, as like as not.

She scanned the crowd, looking for Nick, praying he was not also disguised. Not seeing him, she felt despair begin to erode the confidence with which she had set out to find him. How was she to ask for him? It was not likely that he would use his own name here.

The heavy woman came toward her, heading toward the door.

"Mistress Bruning?" Kat ventured, and was rewarded by a smile that gave way to a look of puzzlement as the innkeeper's wife looked her over carefully. "I seek a young gentleman, of this height"—she held her hand a few inches above her head—"and favoring myself." *And pray do not ask me his name,* she added silently.

"Oh, him!" Mistress Bruning was smiling again. "His brother, are you? Or his cousin? Go out again and up to the gallery. You'll find him in the third room, the one with the swan carved on the door."

Kat thanked her and went back out to the courtyard. Up the stairs, and a short walk down the gallery, was a door with a carving that looked more like a goose than the swan Mistress Bruning had described. She raised her fist, hesitated a moment, then rapped on the door.

"Meg?" Nick called. "Is that you? Come in. I left the door un—"

His voice cut off as Kat opened the door and slipped inside.

"Who the devil—"

"A relative, sweet coz," Kat said quickly. Fortunately, Nick was alone in the room. He was lying on the bed, wearing a nightgown that was much too large for him. "Do you not know me?"

His jaw fell. "Kat?"

"Not at the moment. You tell me your name, and I shall tell you mine."

He looked confused.

"Your name, coz. The one you are using now."

"Oh. Matthew. Matthew Ramsey."

"I am Edward Dyer."

"You are an idiot. My God, Kat—"

"Ned."

"—what are you doing here? How did you know I was here?"

Kat winced. "Softly, Nick. Else they'll hear you even in the common room." She bolted the door, then crossed the room to the bed. "Still abed at this hour? So lazy now? Or are you just returning to bed? And who, pray tell, is Meg?"

"My questions first . . . coz. How did you know where to find me?"

"I heard you talking to someone in the orchard—"

"Sparrow?"

"It sounded much like a man. And you mentioned this inn."

"But where were you? We were well away from the gate and the walls. There was no one—" He paused, then groaned. "In the tree?"

Kat made a leg in mocking salute. "Discovered, i'faith."

There was no answering smile from Nick. He brushed his untidy hair back from his forehead and closed his eyes wearily. Kat watched him for a moment, puzzled, then looked around.

It was a small room, but neat and airy, with windows in two walls.

One looked out toward the inn's namesake, the enormous, gnarled oak that according to legend was centuries old, having been planted by a knight before he rode off on a crusade to the Holy Land. The knight had promised his lady wife that he would return from Jerusalem before the tree was his height. There was disagreement as to whether he had kept his promise, but his descendants, and the innkeeper's predecessors who had bought the land from them, had thought enough of the tree to leave it untouched.

"How much did you hear?" Nick said suddenly. His eyes were open again, and he was looking at her with an expression of pain on his face.

"Enough that I wish to know more. Tell me of this talking sparrow."

"I cannot, Kat."

"*Ned.*"

"A plague on your masquerade! This is too dangerous a matter for such games."

"Not unless y'are foolish, quoth sparrow. Tell me more of Lord Harwood."

"You heard us mention him, too?"

"Aye." She hesitated, weighing whether she should tell Nick of her encounter with the nobleman, and decided against it. 'Twould wait till later. Crossing to the table beside the bed, she began to toy with a small, stoppered glass bottle. "Have you seen him yet?" she asked lightly.

"No. I might almost believe that Sparrow had his information wrong, but . . ."

"But Sparrow is not likely to have incorrect information?" she guessed, and knew from Nick's expression that she had guessed rightly. She set the bottle down. "Tell me more of Sparrow."

"Kat . . ."

"I'll stay here, Nick, until you do. You'll not be rid of me."

"Jesu, Kat, you sound like a child again! And look like one, too."

"Frances would not agree with you there. Howsomever, we were discussing Sparrow."

Nick sighed. "Will you promise me that you'll tell no one else of this?"

"I swear it," Kat said with a smile, "on my honor as a gentlewoman . . . and a gentleman, too, if you will."

A shadowy smile crossed Nick's face, then was gone as he sat quietly looking at his hands. "Sparrow is Francis Walsingham's man," he said at last, very softly. "And Walsingham is Cecil's."

"The queen's secretary?"

He nodded.

"Walsingham . . ." Kat bit her lip. "You mentioned him once . . ."

"He's the queen's spy-master, Kat."

"And he wanted you to work for him? To spy on Lord Harwood? But why?"

"Walsingham heard of me from Anthony Holmeden."

Kat nodded; Nick had shared a room with Holmeden at Gray's Inn.

"Anthony may have worked for Walsingham himself. I do not know. But Walsingham wanted someone trustworthy who was not already known to Justin Lisle—that's Lord Harwood's name. So Walsingham sent Sparrow to talk to me. I knew who Lisle was—he had been pointed out to me once at court—but we had never met. On that condition, at least, Sparrow was satisfied. He seemed displeased otherwise."

"He did speak to you most strangely," Kat agreed.

"I trow he would rather have chosen another, had Walsingham given him leave."

"So he sent you to watch Lisle," Kat prompted, not allowing Nick to change the subject. "Why?"

" 'Tis believed he's a Church papist, and a friend of Spain."

"God's death! Are all papists to be suspect now? Even Church papists?" Kat shook her head. Horrified as she had been by the rising in the North, she could not bear the thought of all adherents of the Roman faith—even the Church papists, who attended Protestant services to avoid the fines and penalties but practiced their own faith when they could—becoming suspect. Especially a peer of the realm, for the nobility were usually free of scrutiny into their religious practices unless they made trouble. Had the revolt of Northumberland and Westmorland ended that privilege even for those who had not shared their cause? Or had Lord Harwood—

"Lisle's grandfather harbored several Catholic priests until Mary's accession," Nick said, interrupting her thoughts. " 'Tis said that it is well he died during her reign, since Elizabeth's accession would have killed him."

"And his son? Lisle's father?"

"He worshiped the bottle. The old lord saw more to admire in his grandson than his son. 'Tis believed, though it has not been proven, that Justin Lisle is secretly Catholic."

"There must be more, Nick. Walsingham would be busy until the last trump if he investigated every Catholic in England."

"Aye, there's more. There is Lisle's cousin Margaret. She was a maid of honor at Queen Mary's court. She married a Spanish nobleman and now lives in Spain."

"Oh."

"And Lisle was in love with her when he was younger. 'Tis said he still is."

"And he would betray the queen for his cousin? Another man's wife?"

"Greater malice has sprung from less cause. And there is more—that is, Sparrow hinted that they had evidence linking him with Spanish plotting. But he would not tell me what it was. I know only that I am to wait here for Lisle, and observe him and any man he meets, as well as I can."

Kat shifted uncomfortably, remembering her encounter with Lord Harwood. What chance now that Nick could observe him closely, should Lisle learn she had come here to see him?

"Does this trouble you, Kat?" Nick asked. "I confess that this does not seem a matter for gentlemen, but you know—do you not?—that the queen cannot depend on soldiers alone to protect her."

"Not while the Queen of Scots is in England."

"Nor even before. Two years ago there was a plot—Sparrow told me of it—by the Cardinal of Lorraine—"

"Mary Stuart's uncle?" Kat said bitterly. The cardinal and his late brother, François, Duc de Guise, had used their niece the Queen of Scots to increase their power in France; now she was a chess piece that the cardinal and his nephew Henri, now the duke, could play in England and Scotland.

Nick nodded. "That great cleric"—his voice was very dry—"had Italian agents in England. Walsingham was kept informed of them by another Italian, one Thomas Franchiotto, a Protestant, who advised that those about the queen be very careful of her food and furnishings."

"So the cardinal would have Italians do his poisoning for him?"

"Why not? Who knows more of poisons?"

Kat sighed. "I am glad that there are people to handle such business for the queen, but I am not sure it suits you, Nick."

"Sparrow, I fear, would agree. As will Walsingham, if I have missed Lisle. I cannot spend all day wandering about the inn—"

Kat raised an eyebrow in query, but he ignored her.

"—and though I have my own intelligencer"—he smiled wryly—"I cannot be certain I'll know when Lisle is here."

"Oh, he's here," Kat said lightly. "I saw him arrive. We had an argument over a stableboy."

Nick stared at her, disbelieving. "Upon my life, Kat! You let me sit here, knowing I should be watching him?"

" 'Twould be difficult to spy on him in his chamber, and he was not in the common room when I came in."

"But I must be ready when he comes out again. And I must know if anyone arrives looking for him." He swung his legs off the bed, then grimaced and clutched at his right thigh.

"What's this, Nick? Are you hurt?"

"Merely a flesh wound," he said, but an instant later, as he got to his feet, she heard him catch his breath sharply.

"Merely? How did this come about?"

Surprisingly, Nick reddened. "There was a fight in the common room last night. Several rogues had come in, claiming to be strolling players. No one here had ever seen them. Their leader said that they had played at inns in London."

"A likely story last year," Kat said, remembering the bands of players they had seen who had left London when plays were banned for a few months because of the plague, "but not now."

"They seemed too dull-witted to have thought of that. I took them for common vagabonds, and though they had coin to pay for their drink, Master Bruning was considering sending them away even before one of them took an interest in a servingmaid and began to fondle her despite her protests."

"And you sprang to her defense?"

"Nay, I sat, and bade him leave her be. Then he drew his knife and threw it. He was drunken, and his aim was poor."

"Jesu," Kat said under her breath. "And what became of this whoreson rogue in players' feathers?"

"He's now playing jailbird, and should have time enough to perfect that role, at least. He had enough coins in his purse, according to the bluecoats who took him, to pay for his keep for many weeks . . . God's bones, you look as if you wish him in his grave!"

"Better him than you."

Nick shrugged. "He was drunken. The innkeeper was so grateful he refused to take money for my room. Though no doubt he wishes that the maid would spend less time here."

"Meg?" Kat asked, remembering the name he had spoken when she knocked on the door. "Grateful, is she?" She chuckled. "And well she might be! 'Twas a noble act, saving the honor of a serving wench. A plague upon Lisle and this spying! You must tell Walsingham of the maid."

Nick sighed.

"No doubt he'll tell the queen. 'Twas a brave deed, Nick. She'll knight you for it!"

He swung a fist at her. She dodged, laughing, and brought him his doublet and hose and shirt.

The bandage on his thigh was thin enough that he had little trouble drawing the silk hose over it. Still, he grumbled about the way it ruined the appearance of his leg.

"You would liefer bleed to death, I suppose," she chided, "and the women would sigh and say what fine legs the corpse had. Tush, Nick."

He looked abashed but smiled, then lost the smile as he hobbled away from the bed. Alarmed at the lines of strain on his face, Kat sprang forward and took his arm. He stopped, leaning on her a bit.

"Merely a flesh wound, is it? Is it infected?"

"It was. The infection's nearly gone now. But I have had little sleep . . . and no, not because of the maid," he added with a sigh. "The leg seems to hurt more at night. It has kept me awake."

"And could not this innkeeper, with all his gratitude, have given you something to help you sleep?"

"Laudanum." He gestured toward the small bottle Kat had noticed earlier. "I'll have none of it, not when I must be alert to watch for Lisle."

"You would suffer this much for Sparrow?" Kat asked indignantly.

"For the queen," he answered softly, and Kat's gaze fell.

Someone knocked at the door.

"Who's there?" Nick called.

"Meg."

He looked at Kat uncertainly.

"Ned Dyer, remember?" she murmured. "I am your cousin."

"Alack, must I confess to it?"

She laughed and went to open the door.

"Marry, Matthew," the maid complained good-naturedly, "why did you lock—" She stopped and gaped at Kat.

"Meg, this is my cousin, Edward Dyer."

The maid was a year or two younger than Kat, almost as tall, and even thinner. Though Meg was attractive enough, with glossy blond hair and a pretty, pouting mouth, Kat felt the few fears she had harbored that Nick might be interested in the maid slip away. The girl was heavily painted, and her kirtle was less than clean. There was something coarse, too, in the way she stared at Kat, a bright gaze that shifted from sudden interest to puzzlement—as she took in Kat's outlandish headgear, old clothes, and grimy face—and then to disdain, visible for an instant before she turned to Nick.

"More guests have arrived," Meg said as she set down a tray bearing a jug of ale and two cups, after first pushing aside two other cups on the table. She told him briefly of the arrival of Lord Harwood and his man, as well as three others.

"Thank you, Meg."

"Why are you dressed, Matthew? Surely y'are not leaving yet?"

"Ned and I have decided to eat in the common room. You need not bring me my supper."

Meg looked disappointed. She cast a resentful look at Kat, but voiced no other protests.

They went slowly along the gallery and down the stairs, Nick supported by Meg on one side and his sister on the other, and Kat could not help but notice the way Meg clung possessively to Nick's arm. The maid left them at the foot of the stairs, and returned to the kitchen. Kat helped Nick to a table in a corner opposite the door, from which they could see whoever entered the inn or came down the stairs. It was likely that Lisle would choose to eat in his room, but in that case Meg would be able to tell them whether anyone arrived to see him.

Justin Lisle only half listened to his host as he climbed wearily up to the gallery. Master Bruning was describing the feast his cooks could offer that night, but the baron had little appetite now. It had been a long ride, and had seemed longer yet because he felt uneasy about this rendezvous. Nor had it helped to be confronted with that foolish young rogue when he arrived here. 'Slid! What was such a rampallion—a hedgeborn rogue, from the look of him—doing with such a fine horse?

He was relieved when Master Bruning soon excused himself to greet another arriving guest, a local justice, rather than staying to attend Justin himself. The nobleman was in no mood for company now. He had thought the muddy, willow-shrouded bank of the Thames a poor place for that last meeting, but at least there he had been able to think more clearly than he could here, with Master Bruning's clacking tongue never ceasing.

"My lord?" Tandy, who had gone ahead to make sure that the chambers were satisfactory, had finished inspecting the bedlinens for lice. Now, after Justin seated himself on a chair beside the fireplace, he helped his master remove his heavy riding boots, replacing them with velvet slippers. "What will you for supper?"

" 'Tis your choice, Tandy. I'll trust your judgment." He looked out the window at the thickening twilight. The man he was waiting for should arrive soon. Even with servants for protection, he disliked being out in the English night. "Master Bruning has already recommended the roast swan."

He took the glass of wine Tandy brought him—a good Madeira, which Master Bruning knew he favored—and settled back into the chair. Some moments passed before he became aware that Tandy had made no move to leave the chamber.

"What's the matter?"

"My lord, about the boy in the courtyard . . ."

"Are you concerned for him too? Give him a few shillings from me. He was lucky to escape death today."

"The stableboy, my lord?" Tandy asked, puzzled.

"Who else? Did you think that I would reward that ill-clad young rogue who brought on that trouble?"

"I'faith, my lord, he did not," Tandy answered quietly.

None of Justin's other servants would have contradicted him so boldly, but then, Tandy was nothing like the other servants, for all that he had been born and raised at Harwood Hall.

William Lofts—as Tandy had been christened—was the oldest son of Justin's grandfather's steward, and would have become the steward in time. Justin's grandfather, George Lisle, had given Tandy his nickname, calling Will Lofts *that tandy boy*, using the old word for *tawny*. The old baron had been fond of Tandy, showing him almost as much affection as he showed Justin—and more than he showed his own son, Robert, who had disappointed him with his drunkenness and black rages. Less than a month after the old man's death, Justin's father had given Tandy, then only fifteen, a choice between marrying a pregnant scullery maid who claimed falsely that Tandy had fathered her child, or else leaving Harwood Hall. Tandy was gone the next morning.

Eight years passed before Justin saw him again. Tandy had not been forgotten by his friends and family, but they, not knowing his whereabouts, had given up hoping that he would return, and Tandy's younger brother was trained to fill the steward's post. Robert Lisle had died after five years as baron, and Justin, who had used his studies as an excuse to stay away during those years, had returned to live at Harwood Hall. He was in London visiting friends one day when, riding near Aldgate, he spotted Tandy, who was just then leaving the city, vanishing into the crowd beyond the gate.

Justin had spent a miserable evening and night on the north bank of the Thames to the east of London, stalking up and down Wapping's filthy alleys, searching through tenements inhabited by sailors' victuallers and taverns where the drunken mariners were outnumbered by cozeners and whores, until he finally came across Tandy playing a seemingly honest game of mumchance-at-cards. It had been a hardened, cynical Tandy, sporting a fresh crescent-shaped scar on his left cheekbone; a Tandy who had been wary of Justin at first and more doubtful yet when told he could return to Harwood Hall. The rest of the night had fled before Justin had succeeded in talking his old friend into returning. It had helped that Justin, after joining the card game, had been lucky enough to win every coin Tandy carried. They had returned to Harwood Hall a few days later.

Justin never learned exactly what Tandy had been doing during those eight years, but it was clear that he knew much of ships and sailing. He was wise to cozeners' tricks and all the ways of cony-catching, too, and could warn Justin against men who would cheat him, or speak to the rogues in their own canting tongue, which Tandy called pedlar's French. And he was quicker with a sword and dagger than he had been in the days when he practiced fence with Justin at Harwood Hall. Unwilling to assert his right to the steward's post again, he now served as Justin's chamberlain instead, both at home and away. The arrangement suited them both, and Justin had long ago returned to treating Tandy as he had during their youth, more as a friend than as a servant.

So now he merely looked curiously at Tandy and asked, "Why do you say that? The rampallion admitted he was to blame."

"I overheard him warn the ostler to be careful with the horse."

"Then why did he not say as much?"

Tandy shrugged. "Belike he was as concerned for the stableboy as you are. He could not defend himself against your accusations without himself accusing the boy, and with Master Bruning there . . ." He shrugged again, already moving toward the door. "The roast swan?" he asked, and at Justin's nod, went out, closing the door quietly behind him.

There had been no reproach in Tandy's words, only a simple statement of fact. Nevertheless, Justin sat motionless for a time, brooding over the mistake he had made. Finally he shook his head. He needed to think of other things now, and he forced himself to consider what he had heard the day before May Day, and what he had learned from the slyly worded letter he had received later.

He was still musing when Tandy returned with two servingmen bringing their supper. The roast swan was as good as Master Bruning had promised, and the innkeeper had sent along more of his finest Madeira. The servants waited to make sure all was satisfactory, then took the coins Tandy offered them and left.

"He's in the common room," Tandy said as soon as they were alone.

"Already?" Justin's appetite deserted him again at the thought of this meeting.

"The lad, I mean. The one you spoke to in the courtyard. He's there with another youth, perhaps a few years older. His brother, mayhap. They look much alike."

Justin's eyes met Tandy's, and after a moment the nobleman laughed. "Very well, Tandy. I'll apologize to him."

He rose and, picking up his glass of Madeira, started away, only to pause when Tandy asked, "Now?"

"D'you think there will be time later?" Justin asked, glancing back over his shoulder.

"No, my lord." Tandy's reply was muffled, the expression on his face unhappy. Justin knew that his servant was not looking forward to this meeting either. *At least*, Justin thought, *I can divert myself for a time, if only by admitting that I spoke too hastily an hour ago.*

The common room was crowded, and Justin caught a few unpleasant whiffs of tobacco smoke as he walked through the door. He looked around quickly, scowling as he noticed the man who was to blame. The rogue looked so pleased with himself that one would think drinking tobacco was natural—even proper—rather than the latest odd fashion. Damn him, Justin thought angrily, and damn Sir John Hawkins for bringing that filthy herb back from the New World. That had been only a few years ago, but it was already difficult to avoid tobacco smoke in most public gathering places.

He moved away from the man who was drinking tobacco and scanned the room until he spotted a large, shapeless cap, worn by a slender man seated with his back to the nobleman. Needs must that it was the same youth, Justin thought wryly; there could not be two such caps in England. A young gentleman was seated across the table from the boy, and Justin studied his face but could not decide if there was a resemblance. In truth, what Justin remembered most about the boy's appearance was the grime on his face and the eccentric clothing. The two young men were talking to a pretty servingmaid. As the baron watched, she reached flirtatiously toward the youth in the cap. The boy shrank away from her touch, to Justin's surprise: the other lad clearly enjoyed the wench's company.

"Lord Harwood!" Master Bruning called, and the oddly dressed youth turned around, a look of alarm on his face as he stared at Justin. The light from a nearby fire set off the boy's delicate features—features so much like his companion's that Justin was certain then that he had completely misjudged the lad. This was no rogue, but a close relative of the gentleman seated opposite him: perhaps a poorer cousin, perhaps even a younger brother, who for some reason—shyness, belike—preferred a slovenly appearance to the beauty he could have displayed.

He looked away to answer Master Bruning's concerned inquiries about the supper and to tell the innkeeper what Tandy had explained. After receiving Master Bruning's assurance that the young ostler would not be punished, and his promise of a stoup of wine, Justin excused himself. The lad now had his back to the nobleman again, and his companion watched Justin approach with some wariness. *No welcome there*, Justin thought, but accepting that he was to blame, he forced himself to smile as he reached their table.

CHAPTER 5

You told me that you quarreled with Lord Harwood about a stableboy, Nick had said as soon as they were seated at the table. *What manner of quarrel was this?*

Kat had told him of the encounter with reluctance.

The Blackamoor! he had exclaimed when he learned which horse she had ridden. *Shall I let you tell me which of my horses I may ride, coz?* she had replied, and Nick, reminded of her disguise and aware of curious gazes, had said no more about her choice of steed, only grimacing from time to time as she told him the rest.

Perhaps I should not have come down to the common room with you, Nick had said after she had finished her story. *I cannot watch him unobserved, if he notices you.*

Think again, coz. Seeing you with me, he'll assume that I have told you of my meeting with him. And so he'll find it less odd if he notices you watching him.

Those had been brave words, Kat thought as Nick told her Lisle was approaching their table. They would have been less brave if she had guessed then that Lord Harwood might come over to talk to her now. Finally she forced herself to look around at him.

He was only a few feet away, towering over them. In the firelight, with his reddish-brown hair and russet velvet clothing gleaming, he appeared burnished, and Kat felt more uncomfortable than ever with her own attire. She noticed again how handsome he was. He was not much more than thirty, if that, and with only fine laugh lines radiating outward from his blue-gray eyes to show his age. She was aware of only a faint smell of perfume as he came closer, and approved: more than one of the courtier friends Nick had brought home had been drenched with perfume, as if the scent of flowers and musk could cover the odor of unwashed clothes and bodies. He had changed from his riding boots to velvet slippers, and Kat could not help noticing how shapely and well-muscled his legs were. He was a fine-looking man, i'faith. Under any other circumstances . . .

Suddenly he smiled—a dazzling smile; unlike most men his age, he still had good teeth—and Kat began to smile in response, then quickly looked down, shivering. How could she have forgotten, even for a second, that this man might be a threat to the queen? And a threat to them, too, should their masquerade be discovered.

"Good even, gentlemen." Kat looked up again, reluctantly, to find him gazing directly at her. "My manservant has told me that you had given a warning to that ostler. I owe you an apology."

"Perhaps my warning was not loud enough."

"Tandy had no trouble hearing you," Lisle replied, looking amused. "It was praiseworthy of you to save the boy from being punished."

"Thank you, my lord," Kat said after a moment, unable to think of anything else to say. Nick saved her the trouble.

"Ned feels sympathy for younger lads," her brother said. "But, my lord, we must thank you for restraining the Blackamoor before the boy was hurt worse. Will you join us, sir? Drink with us?"

Disbelieving what she had heard, Kat could only stare mutely at Nick as the nobleman accepted and dragged a stool over to their table, then sat down. His eyes met hers and she drew back a little and looked away. At any moment, she feared, Lisle would see through her disguise.

Heedless of her fear, Nick gave Lisle their assumed names. He paused then, and Kat realized with horror that Nick must not have given any thought to continuing the conversation. The silence dragged on, an island of silence in the sea of noise around them: theirs must have been the only table at the inn where no one was talking.

Lisle looked from Nick to Kat and back again, apparently made a bit uncertain by their silence. He toyed with the glass he had set on the table. It was fine Venetian glass, Kat noted, better than anything in the common room; no doubt the wine it held was also better than anything served to guests of lower rank.

"Are you students?" the nobleman asked, finally breaking the silence.

"Ned is a student at Cambridge," Nick replied with relief. *Too obvious relief,* Kat thought, but Lisle did not seem to notice. "As was I, until a few years ago. I studied at the Inns of Court, Gray's Inn, until last year."

Lisle nodded, then turned back to Kat. "Which college?"

"St. John's," she said, naming Nick's college.

"That was my college," he responded cheerfully. "Do you enjoy Cambridge?"

She could have groaned aloud, so dismayed was she that he would seek to prolong this conversation. Thank God Nick had told her much about the university, for now she must needs play parrot, and hope that Lord Harwood would not see through her role.

So she complained about Cambridge's cold and rainy weather, and then told of fishing in the River Cam, and of keeping a ferret in her room. Both were forbidden to students, but she had erred in hoping that confessing to such transgressions might encourage the nobleman to seek other company, for he merely smiled and admitted to keeping a hawk as well as a ferret.

She looked helplessly at Nick then, not sure what to speak of next, and he came to her rescue, reminiscing about Stourbridge Fair, which was held each September near Cambridge. It was the most famous fair in England, and the largest. "And the finest fair of all," Lisle said, and agreed a moment later with Nick's statement that 'twas a pity that the townspeople had to dispute with the university over income from the fair.

"Have you ever been to the fair?" Lisle asked Kat, and she shook her head. "You would love it," he told her. "If you went for so much as an idle look, you would want to spend all day there. And you would swear that the ale you drank at Stourbridge Fair was the best you had tasted all year."

Nick laughed and agreed.

"But if you like Madeira, you will find no better than what is served here," Lisle said, and called for more wine. Three silver stoups of the fine Madeira he was already drinking were brought to them.

The nobleman continued to trade reminiscences with Nick, recalling tennis and fencing and dancing lessons . . . all of which had busied them so much that both Nick and Lord Harwood had been forced at times to hire bellringers to wake them early so they could spend an extra hour or two at their books. Only once did the topic of conversation change, when Lord Harwood noticed that Nick's leg was bandaged. He was amused by the explanation Nick gave him. Kat found herself laughing with him, and enjoying his laughter. She had to remind herself constantly that if Sparrow were right about this man, he was her enemy, a very real threat to the queen.

She spoke only rarely, her brother being quick to come to her aid whenever Lisle turned to her, making some remark that quickly drew the nobleman's attention back to him. But she would nod and smile often, as if agreeing with much of what the two men said. She smiled now as Nick recalled how much he had enjoyed drinking with his friends at the White Horse Tavern.

"Flapdragons," he said. "We drank flapdragons."

Kat nodded again, remembering how shocked she had been the first time she saw Nick add raisins to a drink, set the liquor aflame, then catch the raisins in his mouth and eat them.

Lord Harwood nodded, too. "And we would drink dozens of toasts, to everyone we could think of, from the queen—"

Which queen? Kat wondered. Justin Lisle must have started at Cambridge during Queen Mary's reign . . . though, if she guessed his age aright, Mary would have died while he was still at the university. Had he toasted the bloody Catholic queen, with her Spanish husband? Had he found it harder to toast Elizabeth, that end to Catholic hopes?

"—to the host of the White Horse and all his able servants."

"Shall we drink a toast?" Nick said then.

Kat stared at him in amazement. 'Sdeath, he must needs be drunken, to have forgotten her disguise. Were they to drink a toast, she would be expected to remove her hat.

"I remember returning from a football match at Chesterton one day," Kat said quickly, as though she had not heard what Nick said a moment earlier. "We were late, my bedfellow and myself, so we were forced to gallop, and with the other riders often in our way, I took out a hunting horn I usually carried in my cloakbag and blew that as we rode, as though I were the postboy, warning anyone ahead to clear the road." She chuckled slightly, recalling when she had heard the story from Nick, who had laughed himself as he told her of the afternoon when he had made that ride from Chesterton back to Cambridge. "There was a yeoman taking a wagonload of corn to market. He had whipped his team off the road and was mired to the hubs in soft mud by the time we sped past. I tried to hide the horn, but 'twas too late. He saw us and realized he had been tricked, and he cursed us, and was still cursing when we rode out of earshot."

Nick laughed, but Lord Harwood merely shook his head, an expression of distaste on his face. Kat went on with her story, but less confidently than before.

"It was hours later before the yeoman reached Cambridge, and he made the rounds of the carriers, and stopped at the university too, trying to find the horses he had seen and discover who the two boys were. As if our horses looked like common carriers' jades! He wasted his time, but he had all the carriers in town sweating for fear that two of their horses might have been ridden faster than at a journey's pace." She shook her head. "We met the yeoman ourselves late that night. We had changed our garb since our ride back from Chesterton, and he did not know us. We bought him a round of drinks at a tavern and toasted him and wished him all luck in finding the rogues who had driven him from the road. 'Twas the finest jest." Kat's voice faltered, and she was looking down at the table as she finished the tale. 'Twas no jest at all, but a poor, shabby trick, she realized. And now Lord Harwood was again regarding her with contempt. Why had the story seemed so amusing when Nick had told it? Had she been so caught up by her brother's infectious laughter that she had been unable to see the churlishness of the behavior he had described?

There was a scraping noise: Lisle had pushed his stool back from the table. In a moment, Kat was certain, he would take his leave of them. She felt shamed and relieved at the same time.

Then Nick spoke.

"Were you at Cambridge during the queen's visit?"

She raised her head. Lord Harwood was still seated, but he looked impatient. "Would that I truly looked so young as you must think me. No, I was not."

"I was," Nick continued, undaunted. " 'Twas in 1564, during my second year at Cambridge. All was in readiness for the queen—even the townspeople finished paving the streets."

"All was readied but an ample supply of beer, as I heard."

"True enough," Nick said, laughing. "The queen and her courtiers would have stayed longer, had the beer and ale lasted longer. You should have been there. Cecil arrived first, and lodged at St. John's. Then Leicester came to stay at Trinity, before the queen arrived at her lodgings at King's College. The road itself was strewn with rushes and flags. The queen's own tapestry had been hung in King's College Church. The queen praised our disputations and orations, and responded herself in fine Latin and Greek. Would you not say," he demanded suddenly of Lisle, "that she is the most learned queen ever to reign? Far superior to the Queen of Scots, who studied naught but the French court's licentiousness . . . and murder?"

Kat held her breath as she glanced at Lord Harwood, then quickly away. Would he challenge Nick's brutal comments on the Queen of Scots? Half the papists they knew would be tempted to reply to that by telling Nick that he lied in his throat, a deadly insult that could be answered only with a challenge to a duel.

"I would praise Elizabeth Tudor's learning," Lisle replied calmly, and Kat had to steel herself not to slump with relief.

"There was only one presentation that did not please the queen," Nick went on, and Kat felt her muscles tensing again: she knew what direction he was taking—an even more reckless one than before. "Not counting, of course, the performance that was planned of a play of Sophocles's—"

"*Ajax Flagellifer*," Kat put in. "The Latin translation."

"—which was not given, the queen being too weary to see it, her last night at the university. Some friends of mine were so disappointed by this that they followed the court from Cambridge to Sir Henry Cromwell's home at Hinchinbrook—"

"I heard of this," Lisle said coldly.

"—to perform a masque that was to have followed the presentation of *Ajax*. A most clever piece. 'Twas a wonder that this displeased the queen so."

"How so?" Lord Harwood asked. "Why would they have thought to entertain the queen with a burlesque of the mass? 'Twas thoughtlessly planned."

"I'faith, the masque was much kinder to papists than some of the plays my father told me he saw, that first Christmas after Elizabeth was crowned. He said he saw a masque at court in which a cardinal—or was it an abbot?—was shown in his true guise, as a wolf."

"Such foolery was ended by royal proclamation just a few months later."

"Only because the Spanish ambassador complained that his master, King Philip, was being mocked as well. Besides, 'tis common knowledge that it was Cecil himself who directed the argument of those masques."

"Is it?" Lisle said. "Then your knowledge must be much more common than mine."

Nick seemed stunned by the insult. Before he could answer, a strange voice interrupted, speaking in a broad Devonshire accent.

"God's bones, Justin! What's this?" The speaker, Kat saw, was a man nearly as tall as Lord Harwood, with sunburned skin and thick beard and mustachios. "Do you waste your time quarreling with striplings now?" the man continued, turning his gaze to Nick, whose face burned with anger. "And one in his cups, by the look of him."

"No quarrel, Henry. In sooth, a most pleasant conversation, until a moment ago. I fear my young friend has drunk too deeply, and I must take some of the blame, having paid for the drink."

Nick seemed about to speak, but Kat glared at him in warning and he kept silent.

"Gentlemen," Lord Harwood said, "you are now in the presence of Henry Malcomb, a sea captain from Devonshire, and the finest source of wares from Turkey that you will ever meet."

"Honesty forbids that I deny that," the man said. "I am but recently home from a voyage, and my cargo—most specially the carpets—betters any that I have ever seen."

"Good carpets, you said?" Lisle asked.

"In truth, my lord, the finest in England."

"And the dearest?"

The sea captain shrugged. "Priced fairly."

"We must discuss this." He bid Kat and Nick farewell, speaking in a manner more gracious than Kat felt Nick deserved, then left with the sea captain.

Kat watched them till they were out of earshot, then turned back to Nick. "Marry, have you drunk enough, and said enough, for one night?" she said in a furious whisper. "Or would you follow him now and declare him a papist traitor and challenge him to a duel? Do you think this is what Sparrow meant when he asked you to observe Lord Harwood—and to be *careful?*"

"God's life, Kat, I do not need to hear this." Nick's face, inflamed but a few moments ago, now looked ashen. "I had too much wine. D'you think he may have guessed my purpose here, and bought more wine to loosen my tongue?"

"You confuse munificence with subtlety."

"And you defend him far too much, Kat. What womanish—"

"Hush!"

He shut his mouth then. He had one hand on the table. As she watched, he clenched the hand into a fist, then relaxed. "We can do no more here," he said a moment later. "Will you help me back to my chamber?"

He leaned heavily on her as they made their way across the common room and up the stairs, and she realized he was not only drunk but tired. All of a sudden her irritation with him gave way to remorse. Why had she not insisted that he stay in his chamber, rather than eating in the common room? Would it not have been better if she had come downstairs alone to watch for Lisle?

And then talked to him alone?

She shivered violently at the thought, bringing a muffled curse from Nick as his arm slipped a little from her shoulders. She started to murmur an apology, then stopped, in midword and midstride, bracing herself against the weight of Nick's arm as it struck the back of her neck. She raised a finger to her lips to silence him.

"What the devil!" he blurted, not turning toward her until it was too late. The voice she had heard had stopped, and now there was only silence from the chamber they had just passed, the first along the gallery.

Fearing that the door might be flung open at any moment, Kat hurried Nick back to his own chamber. She shut the door behind them and latched it before helping Nick cross to the bed.

"What the deuce, Kat!"

"He was speaking in Spanish, Nick. I heard him."

"Who?"

"Captain Malcomb. Did you not hear him? Nay, you are too deep in your cups."

"I warrant you are the one in your cups, if you thought Henry Malcomb able to master Spanish, when he so tortures English with that

damnable accent. You imagined it, Kat. I have said too much to you of
this plotting, and now your brain is fevered.''

She shook her head. She had paid no attention to the quiet, indistinct conversation behind the door of that other chamber when she had
first heard it, but for just a few moments a man's voice had been raised
in anger. *Madre de Dios*, he had said, *esto no lo sufro! La reina*—

Then Nick had complained of her sudden stopping, and the voice
had been cut off, either because the man who had spoken had overheard
them outside the door . . . or because his companion had, and had
warned him to be silent.

And that companion must have been Lord Harwood. For the speaker
had been Captain Malcomb: she was sure of it. The Devonshire accent
had been gone; he had spoken Spanish as perfect as that she had heard
from a tutor their father had hired because of his experience of Spain.
Yet even without the Devonshire accent, the voice—that light, musical
tenor—had been Malcomb's.

"He was saying he could not suffer something, and then he started
to say something about *la reina*—the queen. I am going back to listen
again,'' she told Nick, but before she could get away, he seized her arm.

"No! Jesu, Kat, this is not me and Edward you wish to spy on. What
do you think would happen, should someone discover you eavesdropping? This childish masquerade of yours would not survive any interrogation. You would bring suspicion on both of us. I have seen enough of
that vagabond player—I have no wish to join him in jail.''

Kat dropped heavily onto the bed. Nick was right: she dared not
attract too much attention. But it rankled her to be so close to Lord
Harwood and Captain Malcomb, yet not be able to overhear their conversation.

Someone knocked at the door, and she jumped in alarm, fearing
the worst. Nick also looked uneasy. He wet his lips but kept silent.

"Matthew, 'tis I, Meg. How fare you?''

Nick sighed with relief, and gestured for Kat to open the door. Meg
stood there, holding a tray on which stood a flagon and two silver
goblets.

"Were you in pain, Matthew?'' The girl stepped into the room at
once, ignoring Kat. "I did not think you would return to your chamber
until I could help you.'' There was an undertone of resentment in her
voice.

"He's sore wounded by our good host's Madeira, but feeling no
pain,'' Kat said quickly, before Nick could respond. She wished the
maid would leave, so that she could again talk freely to Nick. "Is that
tray for us?'' Only two goblets. No doubt Meg had hoped to be alone
with Nick, but Kat would not allow that to happen.

"Nay, though I wish it were. 'Tis Master Bruning's best Madeira. I am to take it to the baron."

"Well enough," Nick said. " 'Twould not suit me. I have drunk too much already."

Meg eyed him doubtfully. "Then you'll want no company—"

"In sooth, we do want company, good Meg," Kat said suddenly. Nick gaped at her, but there was no way to tell him of the thought that had just occurred to her . . . and no chance that he would have approved. "Matthew missed your company at supper."

Meg looked pleased. Kat moved to take the tray from her, and when she would have resisted, said, "Come, you must have a drink with us. Some of that fine ale you brought earlier. And pray sit on the bed and talk with my cousin, who is, I fear, sorely tried by my company this evening."

"None could argue that," Nick muttered. Meg looked baffled, but obediently settled herself on the side of the bed. Her back was to Kat now. Kat opened the bottle of laudanum—the stopper was mercifully quiet—and poured some into a cup before filling it with ale. She handed this to Meg, then poured a second cup for Nick, then one for herself. Nick had watched her, wide-eyed, but had dared say nothing.

She sipped her ale, and was glad to see that Meg drank thirstily, in between chatter about the guests. *Nick has a useful intelligencer here,* Kat thought, *but now she can best serve us by sleeping.* And the maid was yawning already, thank God.

"I should take that tray to Lord Harwood . . ." Meg said at last, but her voice was blurred.

"Tarry with us but awhile longer," Kat told her. "Matthew is tired, and may be asleep before you return."

"Marry, I am also tired," Meg said, illustrating her comment with an indelicate yawn.

"Were you to lie down for a few moments, and close your eyes, you would rest enough to see you through your work tonight."

Meg nodded sleepily, handed her cup to Nick, then slumped sideways onto the bed. Her eyes closed at once. Kat waited but a minute, then tried to shake the girl awake, but without success.

"Done," she said, but any satisfaction she might otherwise have felt had been stolen from her by memories of Christopher Danvers's trick that morning. That had been for an ignoble cause, and this one was worthy, yet it still troubled her to have to use such means. Had she been able to think of aught else . . .

"This is mad," Nick whispered. "You are mad."

"Am I?" Kat raised an eyebrow. "I think not. But Meg will be mad, if I am not back and her clothes back on her before she wakes. Will you take her clothes off, Nick? I must wash."

"Take her clothes off?"

"As you have done before, good brother." He flushed angrily, but before he could object, she added, "Pray hurry. I do not know how long she will sleep."

"Aye, and that's another argument against this foolish plan of yours."

"Is it? Then perforce I must go dressed as I am, and stand listening outside Lord Harwood's door, and pray that no one discovers me and marks me for a spy. You cannot stay me from this course by not helping me," she insisted. "You can only assure that I am more likely to fail." He shook his head, but he was looking more doubtful now. "And would you have me fail? 'Twould be to fail Sparrow as well. Would you not know what is being said in that chamber now? I know you, Nick, and I warrant you, that if you thought you could play the maid yourself, then you would already be borrowing Meg's clothes that you might spy on Lord Harwood in that guise."

His laugh sounded unwilling, but she knew she had won.

"Pray hurry," she said again. "I would fain be back there before this Spanish sea captain leaves."

As soon as she saw him begin to undo the laces of Meg's bodice, she turned away. There was much to do, in very little time. She scrubbed her face and hands until her skin was clean and glowing, then went over to her cloakbag and rummaged through it. Her own half-kirtle and bodice were of no use to her now—none of the servingmaids wore such fine apparel—but she had packed two gallipots, closed tightly and wrapped securely in fabric. She daubed her cheeks and lips with red fucus, deliberately applying the paint with a heavy hand, and was equally careless as she applied her perfume, which she hoped would cover any odor of sweat or horse that might still cling to her after her long ride. She grimaced as she looked at her reflection in the tiny mirror she had brought along: a Southwark punk might paint herself so.

Nick thought so too, and complained, especially when Kat changed from her boys' garb to Meg's clothing and discovered that the bodice was indecently tight. "Would you have me play the bawd, Kat, to let you go to Lord Harwood's chamber in this guise? Will you at least scrub off that paint?"

"And shall I let out this bodice, too? A plague on your fears, Nick. What better guise than this, to prevent Lord Harwood and Captain Malcomb from seeing in me the youth they met downstairs? How better to conceal myself? Even Anne would not know me."

"Nor would she wish to. 'Slid, I do not like this. But if you must go, then go quickly, and leave faster yet."

"What, to return before I have left?" Shaking her head, she went over to Nick and put her hand on his shoulder. "Look you. I must needs have time to listen at the door, and then I will have to deliver up the wine, lest Meg come to more harm, by this shift, than the cold she will suffer if you do not cover her better than that." She nodded toward the sleeping girl, whom Nick had draped but partially with a sheet. "Do not fret yourself. Lord Harwood is an honest man, no rogue playing a player who would trifle with his host's servants."

"Unless he thought such trifling invited."

"He'll have no invitations from me."

"Kat, you wear it!"

"Enough! We have argued this already. Now wait, and while you wait, think how much we might learn."

"Marry, I have learned a great deal already. I'll never again discuss secrets within earshot of a tree."

Kat laughed and picked up the tray. After a final glance at Meg, peacefully slumbering under the coverlet, she went to the door and stepped out onto the gallery.

It was quite dark, for the lantern nearest their chamber's door had been allowed to go out, and the lanterns at either end of the gallery cast but a feeble light. She stood just outside the door for a few moments, suddenly uncertain.

Nick was right: this was mad. How had she come to this? But a few hours ago, she had left Beechwood with every intention of assuring that Nick would come to no harm on behalf of Master Sparrow, and now she herself stood poised, ready to risk her own safety to observe this man that Sparrow had sent Nick to watch. It seemed impossible . . . and yet each step that had led her to this had seemed logical, even inevitable, at the time. *As no doubt it seemed to any cat that ever walked out onto a limb . . .*

Still, she could see no way to go back now. Her eyes had adapted to the darkness, and she walked carefully and almost silently toward Lord Harwood's chamber, wishing that the lantern at the head of the stairs had also been allowed to go out. She would have welcomed a cloak of darkness. The light that had seemed so feeble moments before seemed much too bright now. Yet there was no one below in the courtyard, no one climbing the stairs. She stopped in front of the door and leaned lightly against it, her ear to the wood.

Silence. It dragged on so long that she became certain that Henry Malcomb had left and Lord Harwood was asleep. She had wasted her time, and put poor Meg to sleep for naught. She was about to turn away when she heard Henry Malcomb's voice again, as he spoke very softly.

"*Preferiria que* . . ."

His voice trailed off into an indistinct murmur, and Kat pressed closer against the door. *I would prefer that* . . . He would prefer what? In her frustration, she had forgotten the tray, and now she swore under her breath as the flagon slid an inch to one side, the scrape of metal on metal seeming as loud as a scream to her imagination. She swiftly moved away from the door, toward the gallery railing: she dared not be leaning against the door, if either of the two men had heard that sound and came to investigate.

"Ho, Meg!"

She jumped. Wine splattered her face. Below, in the courtyard, a face was upturned toward her: she recognized the balding head and full beard of one of the drawers she had seen in the common room. She waved and stepped back from the railing, praying that the darkness that had allowed him to mistake her for his fellow servant had sufficed to keep him free of suspicion. God forbid he should come up to speak to her.

Then the door opened behind her and she whirled around, blinking at the brightness of the candlelit room.

"What's this?" Justin Lisle asked. "Yet more wine?"

"Aye, my lord." She had little choice but to enter the chamber. "Compliments of Master Bruning."

"I'faith, my lord, I had thought this a rare wine," Henry Malcomb said, in the same broad West Country accent Kat had heard when she first met him. "Yet it must not be so rare, if the very servants here wash themselves in it." He grinned at Kat.

She looked away quickly, ashamed of her clumsiness and also frightened that his intense gaze might see through her disguise. The baron had scarcely glanced at her so far, and she felt grateful that servants were overlooked as she placed the tray on a table by the fireplace.

"Are we agreed, then?" Lisle asked.

"Perforce we must agree," Malcomb said in a complacent tone.

Kat rearranged the goblets and the flagon of wine. Dared she hope that they would discuss their business now, even in veiled terms? Would they feel so little concern about a servant? She picked up a napkin that was lying neatly folded beside a platter of untouched food and used it to mop up the spilled wine, moving as slowly as possible to prolong the time she could stay here.

They were no longer talking. Were they looking at her, waiting for her to leave?

"Shall I pour the wine, my lord?" she asked coolly, looking around for Lisle's response.

He had not been looking at her after all, but had been gazing at the fire, seemingly lost in thought. Now, as his eyes met hers, she saw a look of surprise cross his face. *Alack! He recognizes me!* She would have bolted for the door, had it not been too obvious that both men could block her way easily. She continued to stare at him, trying to seem tranquil, while her heart hammered wildly.

After what seemed an eternity, he nodded and looked away. Her hands were shaking as she poured the wine, but she managed not to spill it. She kept her gaze lowered as she took one goblet to Lord Harwood, then offered the other to the sea captain.

"Not for me, lass. My business here is finished, and I have miles to ride yet tonight."

"Very well, sir." Kat turned back toward the table, but before she could set the goblet down, Lisle said, "You drink it, sweeting."

"My lord?" She looked uncertainly at the nobleman.

"What, is not Master Bruning's best wine good enough for you?"

Any maidservant, Kat guessed, would have been flattered by the offer of the wine . . . and also by the baron's smile. But she could only think of how far away the safety of Nick's chamber seemed at this moment.

The sea captain laughed suddenly. "God's bones, my lord, I warrant she'll refuse you. How now, sweet maid? Is there more work awaiting you this night?" He rose and picked up his cloak and hat. "I must away, my lord." To Kat: "Will you walk downstairs with me, lass? I would thank Master Bruning for his hospitality."

He offered her an escape from this chamber—but how could she go downstairs with him, where Master Bruning or any of his servants would spot her deception in an instant? Nor was she certain that she could slip away from him on some pretext and escape to Nick's chamber. If he insisted on following her and saw them together, would he then see through this masquerade?

"She'll stay, Henry," Lisle said, and after only a brief hesitation, Kat nodded.

The sea captain shrugged gracefully. "I lose again. Were it to anyone but yourself, my lord, I would resent it."

"Think of your profits, Henry."

"Will profits keep me warm?"

"If you buy enough down."

"You would have me take my comfort from a goose?"

"Aye, a Winchester goose! Now get you gone, you rogue!" Lisle replied, laughing, and the sea captain bowed, bade his lordship farewell, and turned away. As he reached the door he turned back again.

"My head's muddled from too much wine. What was that date you mentioned? The evening you wish me to bring those carpets to Harwood Hall?"

"The nineteenth," Lisle said. "Of *next* month, not this month."

"That much I remembered. I will be there . . . but 'twill be late."

"God speed, Henry."

"The same to you, my lord . . . and a pleasant ride tonight."

Kat grated her teeth. Her feelings must have shown, for as soon as the door closed, Lord Harwood said quietly, "You must forgive Henry's manners. He's but a yeoman's son and sometimes acts the rudesby . . . though never, I trow, as much as that player who was here. Yea, I was told of that, and met the young gentleman who defended you, and now I see why he leapt to your defense. Will you not drink, sweeting? I fear there is too much wine for me alone, and you already hold the goblet."

Kat took a sip of the wine. "I can tarry here but a short while, my lord."

"We'll see." He came closer, and Kat had to fight the impulse to retreat. "I see, Meg, that you have had too much wine already." He touched her sleeve, and Kat saw to her dismay that the pale fabric was dotted with wine stains.

"Oh, no! My lord, I must leave, that I may wash this at once, lest—"

" 'Twill stain, girl. Naught can be done now. I will pay for another pair of sleeves and a kirtle."

Kat glanced down at the stained kirtle, then turned away. Her plans had gone awry. Not only had she failed to hear more than a few words spoken in Spanish, but her clumsiness had ruined Meg's clothing.

She jumped when Lisle took her hand and placed a coin in it.

"Nay, my lord," she said, and sought to give the coin back, but he stepped backward.

" 'Tis payment for your clothing, Meg, not for you. You had not planned to dally here, had you?"

Kat stared at him, amazed, then, looking down, shook her head.

"You should not paint yourself thus," he said quietly, "lest your intentions be misunderstood. I have seen Winchester geese in London who use less paint in a week than you wear now, and yet none would mistake them."

"Winchester geese?"

"Have you not heard of them? 'Tis but a name for the strumpets of Southwark, who live on land owned by the Bishop of Winchester."

She flushed, but kept staring at the floor and said nothing. She would be free soon: she could ignore an insult.

"Come here." As she looked up, she saw him pour water into a basin. "Wash yourself now, before you lead anyone else astray."

She stared at him dumbly. Wash off this paint? She would as lief remove her clothes . . .

" 'Sfoot, can it be that you take pride in how you look? Who taught you to paint yourself so? Do you wish all who see you to think you a common whore?"

"I am *not* a whore."

"You paint yourself as one. Would you be treated as one?"

He moved toward her swiftly, catching her hands. She dropped the coin. It rolled away unheeded as he pulled her against him. His head bent toward hers, then he swore and pushed her back, holding her at arm's length. Holding both her wrists in one hand, he dunked a towel in the basin and began to scrub her face.

For some moments she was too stunned to react. Then old memories flooded her, of times when Nick and Ned had treated her roughly, attempting to discourage her from following them. She had felt humiliated then, and she felt doubly humiliated now. Perchance a maidservant would tolerate this, but she would not.

"Devil take you!" she sputtered, twisting and kicking at him. He yanked her against his side, put one arm around her and caught her wrists with that hand, and continued to rub the paint-smeared towel across her face. Suddenly he began to laugh, which infuriated her even more. She landed a kick on his shin, and was gratified to hear him gasp with pain.

"You shrew." He dropped the towel and grabbed her hair, forcing her head back. "Would you have me get half your paint on myself when I kiss you?"

His mouth came down hard on hers, but an instant later the kiss became gentler. Kat had been kissed before, but the kisses she and Ned had exchanged had been those of children, sincere but clumsy. Lisle's mouth moved expertly on hers, coaxing her lips apart, and when she finally drew away from him, she was breathless. Shaken, she buried her face in the fine material of his doublet.

He laughed raggedly. "Run, Meg," he whispered. "Run while you can." And, unbelievably, he released her.

She continued to lean against him for a few moments. She wanted to flee, yet she wished, absurdly, that he was not letting her go.

Then the door flew open, and Nick was standing there. With his face flushed, his hair wildly awry, he would have looked a comic figure—save for the unsheathed sword in his hand.

"Unhand her!"

"What's this? Another rescue? By God's blood, will you make a career of rescuing this wench? Best tell her, then, to leave off painting. She plays the whore—"

"You lie in your throat!"

Kat shook her head, gesturing for Nick to leave, but he was too drunk to mind her.

"Boy," Lisle said, and Nick bridled at the insult, "I had thought you gently born, but your manners betray you. I will not fight with a common stripling. Take your wench and be gone."

"You kissed her," Nick said furiously, and Kat saw to her dismay that there were a few streaks of paint on the nobleman's mouth.

"She was not unwilling," Lord Harwood said, glancing at Kat, who flushed and looked away.

"Again, you lie in your throat," Nick said, advancing into the chamber.

Lisle lunged to one side, catching his sword and unsheathing it as he turned to face Nick.

"Now, popinjay," he said softly, taking a step toward Nick. "Out! Be quick about it, and I'll forget your bad manners."

Nick stood his ground. Kat knew it was useless to beg him to retreat now, though she doubted he could win any fight with the baron, who was taller and more heavily muscled—and more sober—than her brother. Worse, Nick was handicapped by his wound. It was madness for him to fight, and she would have screamed to bring others in to stop this duel, were it not that her masquerade would be discovered then.

As Nick and the baron edged toward each other, she looked wildly around the room. There was his dagger, still in its sheath on his sword belt. She moved to seize it, then hesitated. She did not know how to use a dagger. Nor did she wish to kill the baron. Nor could she merely wound him, for then he would call for help . . .

Nearly sobbing with frustration, she grabbed the half-empty flagon instead, ran up behind Lord Harwood and brought it down on his head. He toppled forward, and Nick caught him clumsily, staggering a bit beneath the larger man's weight.

"There. Get his sword before it falls!" He lowered the baron gently to the floor, then felt the back of Lisle's head. "No blood. I doubt you have killed him." He straightened. "By the mass, he should be more wary of wine."

Kat sobbed aloud. She still held the flagon, which was dented now. Disgusted, she hurled it onto the bed, where the last dregs of wine spilled.

"Fear not, sweet sister, he'll have nothing more than a headache to remember this by. Now set that sword down and help me. We must bind him, and quickly."

They used the points of Lord Harwood's hose, and were careful not to tie the leather thongs too tight. "Men have lost their hands after being bound too tightly," Nick explained as he gagged the nobleman with a strip of cloth torn from his shirt. "Though it would be no more than he deserved, for how he handled you."

Kat looked away.

"I am sorry that I did not come more quickly, Kat. Had I heeded my fears—"

"You came soon enough, and I am in your debt, good Nick. Now, shall we leave him here?"

"Would that we could deliver him to Sparrow, trussed like this."

"And untrussed like this," Kat remarked, bringing a smile from Nick. "Dare we attempt it?"

He shook his head.

"Nick, I heard them—"

"Later, sweet sister. We must away. But first let's put him to bed."

They left the baron lying on his side, his face away from the door and the coverlet drawn up so that it would seem, to anyone looking in, that he was simply asleep. Before they slipped away, Nick checked once more to make sure that Lisle was still breathing. Watching him, Kat swallowed hard. Could she have killed Lord Harwood so easily, with such a clumsy weapon?

Back in Nick's chamber, Kat made short work of shedding Meg's clothes and donning her own. She rubbed the soil she had brought along in a paper onto her face and hands while Nick struggled to dress the maid, then joined him in fastening the numerous hooks and eyes.

"Marry, she'll sleep till Doomsday," Kat said guiltily.

"Till morning, belike. And wake wondering how she spent the night."

"In dalliance with you, of course." Nick blushed, to Kat's surprise. "What, was that not how she spent last night?"

"Last night, Kat, my only bedfellow was pain."

"Then Meg will think her dream fulfilled." Nick moved to the door and looked out. She started to follow, then hurried back to the bed and added a few coins to Meg's purse. 'Twas less than Lord Harwood had tried to give her, but it would suffice to buy the maid new clothes.

Nick looked at her curiously, but before she could explain, he put a finger to his lips, warning her to be silent, and led the way out onto the gallery.

CHAPTER 6

Downstairs, whatever questions the innkeeper might have had about his guest's decision not to stay the night were answered when Nick began to chide Kat for not telling him sooner of his sister's illness. He kept up the complaint as the grumbling ostler, whom they had roused from his sleep, saddled and bridled their horses. Nick was still berating Kat as they rode out of the innyard and turned north, toward London.

"Enough, Nick! Have mercy!" she pleaded as soon as she was certain that all at the inn were out of earshot.

He grinned and set spurs to his horse's sides.

They rode north for half a mile, though the first rise had lost the inn to their sight. Then, leaving the road, they struck off across country in a wide half circle that eventually brought them out onto the road leading south from the inn, toward home. They kept their pace to a Canterbury gallop, with Kat holding the Blackamoor back from time to time so Nick's horse could keep up. She was anxious, and would as lief have given the Blackamoor his head and raced toward the haven of Beechwood, but Nick was not up to riding at a full gallop. He agreed readily when she suggested stopping to rest after they had put several miles between themselves and the Jerusalem Tree.

They halted by a brook. She helped him dismount and walk down the bank—he was limping badly now—and watched anxiously as he drank from cupped hands, then splashed water across his face. He shuddered. She dug her fingernails into her palms. Until now, she had thought only of putting as much distance as possible between themselves and Lord Harwood. It had been foolish of her to think Nick could manage this ride.

"Mayhap you should rest here, Nick, and wait for me to return with servants and a litter."

He stared disbelievingly at her. "With my Lord Harwood and God knows how many others looking for me? No, thank you. I wish to be safely and inconspicuously home by daylight, not traveling along in some great slow litter, drawing all eyes to myself."

"Yea, but wishes will not mend your leg. You cannot deny that it is worse. You can scarce walk."

"Then I must thank God that I can ride. Look you, Kat, my wound has not reopened. The dressing is still dry. Come, now, bring me that flagon in my cloakbag."

She had thought he wanted to fill the flagon with water, but instead he unstoppered it and drank from it.

"What's this?" she asked sharply. "Have you not drunk enough?"

"Not near enough," he said regretfully. "Do not upbraid me, sweet sister, at least not until I am too drunk to ride."

"Much good it will do me to upbraid you after."

"Nay, for then you need not fear that your audience will flee. Now, Kat. Tell me what you heard, that you would have told me at the inn . . ."

After she repeated what she had overheard, Nick was silent for a time. " 'Tis very little," he said at last.

"Will you not tell Sparrow? Would he not wish to know that Lord Harwood met with a man who spoke like one from the West Country while in the common room, yet in private speaks Spanish like a man born in Castile?"

"Of that you are certain, that his accent was that of Castile?"

"Did we not share the same tutor? And did he not say that I did better than you in our lessons?"

"He said so merely to encourage you, lest you lose interest in your studies."

Kat waved a hand, dismissing the comment. "Do you doubt that I can recognize the accent of Castile?"

Nick hesitated, then shook his head.

"So you'll tell Sparrow?"

"Marry, I will."

Kat opened her mouth, planning to ask Nick if he thought that Sparrow would give the information to Walsingham at once, then shut her mouth again. 'Twas obvious that Sparrow would give the information to his master if he felt it significant. And then? Imprisonment for Lord Harwood? Torture? Execution? She closed her eyes as if that would shut out the unwelcome images. Yet why should it trouble her if Lord Harwood met with a traitor's death, if he were a traitor? And why else would he be meeting with a man who spoke perfect Spanish when he thought no one else overheard?

"Kat?" Nick sounded concerned.

" 'Sdeath, but I am weary. Would that we could rest here longer, but we must away . . . if you are ready to ride again."

As she helped him back up the bankside, she thought of taking the flagon away from him but decided against it. Most of their journey still lay ahead of them, and belike he would need to drink more before they reached home. She felt tempted to drink herself . . .

They rode at the fastest pace Nick could bear, a pace that became slower as the night wore on. Whenever they stopped, which was often, Nick would take a drink from the flagon. He said nothing except when he asked that they stop to rest. Kat was also silent, and so weary that only fear kept her in the saddle. Partly it was fear of pursuit, but more and more she feared meeting vagabonds who preyed on travelers. Nick, she knew, would be unable to defend them now.

Finally they reached a bridge she knew well, as she knew the yeoman's house beyond that. They were not far from home now. She looked at the sky. Judging by the stars, they had an hour yet till sunrise. More than enough time to reach Beechwood, if they could ride but a little faster.

She turned to Nick, and cried out as she saw him sag forward onto his horse's neck. Before he could fall off, she was at his side, steadying him as he straightened up again. His voice sounded very blurred as he thanked her. Perchance it was the drink, yet . . .

She touched the dressing that covered his wound, and very nearly sobbed as she felt the stickiness of blood-soaked cloth.

"Why—" she began, then bit back the words. This was no time to rate him.

"Have we much further to ride?" Nick asked, not bothering to look around.

Kat made a decision. "Nay," she said, and taking his reins and looking back frequently to make sure that he was not about to fall, she led him across a field and onto the lane leading to Stamworth.

Dressed in her warmest nightgown, shod only in light slippers, Jane hurried across the courtyard to where her visitors still sat on their horses. Nick, she saw, could barely sit up. As she approached, the reek of wine struck her. *Drunken. Too drunken to ride all the way home.*

"Good morrow, Jane," Kat said softly. "May we speak to you alone?"

Jane waved her servants—the maid who had followed her downstairs, the grooms who had come out to tend the horses—away from them.

"We need shelter," Kat said wearily, "and Nick has need of your skills in healing."

Jane looked at him, contempt for his drunkenness warring with her affection for him. "There's no remedy for too much wine. What would—" She broke off then, seeing for the first time the dressing beneath his hose. "Wounded?" she asked in a whisper.

"Aye, and we would not have your servants gossip about it. If you trust your maid, pray bid her walk with us, helping Nick. Let all think him merely drunken."

Jane nodded and went to speak to the maid.

Together they helped Nick across the courtyard and upstairs to the chamber that Jane had prepared earlier that day for Kat's visit. There was already a small fire, to warm the room. The maid added more wood to the flames as Jane and Kat helped Nick onto the bed, placing a towel beneath the seeping bandages.

"How did this happen?" Jane asked, and saw Kat glance warily at the maid.

"He encountered a rogue," she replied. "The less said about this, the better."

"Are you in so much trouble, then?" Jane asked, and without waiting for an answer, went to her maid and asked her to bring the medicines she needed: distilled water of mayflowers, and comfrey for a poultice.

Then, after Kat had helped Nick remove his hose and don an old nightgown that had belonged to Andrew Spencer, Jane began the slow work of removing the blood-soaked dressing. Nick bore the pain until she had to rip the last bit of cloth away from the wound. Then he gasped and mumbled something about torture.

"Would torturing you make you answer my questions?" Jane asked lightly. "Will you tell me how this happened?" She frowned as she saw Kat and Nick exchange glances and Nick shake his head. "Come now, speak. My maid is gone. You may speak freely."

"I beg of you, no more questions," Kat said.

"Right. What's this, Jane? You serve us with questions when we would have wine." He gestured toward a flagon on the table. "Will you pour—" He gasped then, as the edge of the nightgown slid across the open wound. Closing his eyes, he swallowed hard.

Jane took pity on him and brought him a cup of wine, which he drank straight down. "Would that I had syrup of poppy," she told Kat, "but the last of the opium was given to a carpenter whose leg was crushed by a beam that fell on him."

"I forgot to bring the laudanum Nick was given."

"Given by whom?" she asked, and to her annoyance Kat shook her head again.

Jane had had little sleep. She had sat up till midnight, hoping for Kat to return, and had slept fitfully during those few hours before her maid woke her to tell her that Kat and Nick were in the courtyard. Now, in her exhaustion, her patience was worn out. Had she not known these two long enough to deserve their confidence?

"Why have you come to me?" she demanded of Nick. "Since you wish to be physicked by one who will ask you no questions, why did you not seek another? Shall I call some wisewoman to attend you? Shall I send for Alice Cowley?"

Kat made a choking sound, and Nick looked at her curiously. "Do you know aught of Mistress Cowley?"

"Aye," Kat responded after a moment. "I have heard of her. She's known for her cures with mice."

"Mice?"

"Mice?" the maid echoed. She had just come into the room, and now she looked inquiringly at Jane.

"Nay, not for me," her mistress said hastily. "I was telling Master Langdon that he might wish to ask advice of Goodwife Cowley."

The maid looked puzzled as she handed the medicines to Jane. "I thought you did not believe in her cures," she said after a moment, "but my own sister swore that her husband's cousin was cured of warts, after the old woman tied a mouse cut in twain to his hand."

"Mark you," Jane said soberly to Nick. "A cure, i'faith. And merely by the laying on of a mouse. Mistress Cowley also prescribes the eating of a mouse, a flayed mouse—"

" 'Tis most important that it be flayed," Kat added, her voice unsteady.

"—as most efficacious for all manner of ills."

"Does she use that for aught but toothache?" the maid asked, and Jane nodded firmly, not daring to look at Kat.

She thought Nick looked a bit paler than he had a minute before, but he raised his cup in a mock toast to her.

"Then bring on your mice! I am proof against mice!"

"Aye, but are you proof against this?" she asked, and poured the distillation the maid had brought onto his wound. His gasp was a satisfying answer, and he had nothing more to say as she prepared the poultice and then bound the wound again with clean strips of linen.

While she dressed the wound, Nick had sagged back against the pillows. He lay motionless now, his eyes half closed, locks of hair plastered against his sweaty forehead, and again she felt pity for him.

"Would you have more wine?" she asked softly, and when he shook his head, "Can you sleep? I have no laudanum, but I could make a posset with wine and valerian."

He shook his head again, and closed his eyes. He seemed to fall asleep at once. Jane whispered his name, but he did not respond.

She turned then and took Kat by the arm. "Come. I will have another chamber prepared."

"Nay, good Jane. I shall sleep here, in the trundle bed. You need wake no manservant to tend Nick. Pray wake no more of your people."

"Lest they ask more questions?" Jane signaled her maid to leave them. After glancing toward Nick to make certain their conversation had not disturbed his sleep, she drew Kat towards the fire and sank down on a cushion there. After a moment's hesitation, Kat also sat down, her movements stiff and awkward.

"Is there naught you can tell me?" Jane asked again. "You bring Nick back with a knife wound in his leg. And you seem fearful, Kat. Is there danger to you still? Shall I set guards at the gate? Shall I send for the bluecoats?"

"No, and no, and again no. We have left all danger behind us."

"Yet you will not name this danger. Do you fear that naming it will summon it again, like some hell-spawned fiend?"

"Sweet Jane—"

"Nay, not sweet Jane, not when I am galled by your silence. Can you not trust me?"

"Nick would not have trusted *me*, had he been free to choose!" Kat seemed abashed by her own outburst. "Pray question us no further. There are reasons that I can tell you no more, and the reasons themselves must remain secret."

Jane turned to look into the fire. After a few moments she sighed. "Can you recall telling me how your father was fond of commonplace books, and bade you and Nick read them and take their advice to heart? That he most valued William Baldwin's treatise?" Kat nodded. Jane glanced down at her hands, remembering how she had then read a copy of Master Baldwin's *Treatise of Morall Philosophie*, hoping to understand more of her neighbors. What she had read had shaken her. " 'There is so little difference between our enemy and our friend, and so hard to know the one from the other,' " she quoted now, " 'that there is great jeopardy lest we defend our enemy instead of our friend or hurt our friend instead of our enemy.' " Her hands were trembling slightly; she pressed them firmly together, almost as though praying. She had convinced herself that neither Nick nor Kat had heeded the advice their father had bidden them read: they had seemed to trust her. But now, in such a weighty matter, they would not confide in her even when they required her help. " 'Doubt them whom thou knoweth . . . They that trust much to their friends know not how shortly rivers be dried up . . .' "

Kat was shaking her head. "I have never believed that."

"Have done! You will not trust me. As you will." She got to her feet. "What shall I tell my servants? You must have *some* explanation . . ."

"Tell them that Nick met with a rogue . . . and that said rogue swore revenge, so naught is to be noised about of this, lest the rogue's friends search Nick out."

The answer had been given too easily. Jane nodded, and could not resist saying, "Now at least I know what did not happen." Then she turned and left the chamber.

For a long time after Jane had left, Kat remained sitting by the fire. She drew her legs up and wrapped her arms around them, then rested her chin on her knees and stared into the flames. Despite her exhaustion and the fire's lulling warmth, she was no longer sleepy. Jane's words had cut deeply, and Kat could find no balm in the thought that Nick had warned her against confiding in Jane, for Nick had thought only of Sparrow's concerns.

Sparrow.

" 'Beware of spies and tale-bearers,' " she murmured, quoting William Baldwin, whose words she remembered well. In that, at least, he had been right . . . "You have done us a disservice, Master Sparrow." She turned her head to the side and closed her eyes, remembering times they had spent with Jane, pleasant occasions uncomplicated by thoughts of traitors . . . uncomplicated, too, by the knowledge that Jane loved Nick. Kat wished she could force time to run backward a scant two days: how much she would change since then!

She jumped at an especially loud snore from Nick. Had she been sleeping? The fire had begun to burn down before she closed her eyes, but now it was little more than embers. She added wood, then got up stiffly and shuffled over to the bed she must sleep on this night. A trundle bed, a servant's bed. A harder bed than she was used to. *You have wronged us, Master Sparrow,* she thought, and fell asleep.

She woke as the door opened. Jane tiptoed into the chamber and crossed to the trundle bed. Her face was wet with tears.

"I could not sleep," she whispered to Kat, "so I again began to read Master Baldwin's *Morall Philosophie.* And it came to me that he was right as well as wrong in his philosophy. 'Doubt them whom thou knoweth.' In that he was wrong, and yet I followed his advice and doubted you. —No, let me finish," she said hastily when Kat would have interrupted her. "Master Baldwin was wrong in that, but when he wrote that there is great jeopardy lest we hurt our friend instead of our enemy, then he was right. I hurt you by doubting you. Had my questions and doubts forced you from sanctuary here—which they would have, had not Nick been wounded—"

Kat said nothing. She could not honestly deny what Jane had said, much as she would have liked to comfort her friend, whose eyes were again shiny with tears.

"—I would have helped your enemy. I would have you know, now, that your enemy is mine, and I will aid you in any way I can, with no more questions asked."

"Generous Jane," Nick said quietly. Kat started; she had not realized he was awake and listening. "We are in your debt already. Your offer will make us your debtors forever. How could we repay you?"

Jane had whirled around to face Nick the moment he spoke. Now she lowered her head, and Kat could see that she was blushing.

"You should sleep," she said, and Kat could not tell whether she was making a jest in response to Nick's question, or merely speaking the first words that came to mind. "Both of you should be sleeping. Cry you mercy, I should not have awakened you." And she fled the room.

Nick stared after her, bemused. "In sooth, I did not think it would disturb her so much to know that I was listening. Did she wish to speak to you privately?"

"Alas, to think that the queen's safety might rest on your skill as an intelligencer," Kat muttered. A moment later, as he looked at her wonderingly, she wished she had not spoken so hastily. Jane would not want Nick to suspect how she felt toward him. "Did you not hear her ask me if I was certain you slept?"

Nick shook his head.

"Well," she said, and turned away from him, hoping to fall asleep again at once.

But this time sleep eluded her. In her mind she saw Justin Lisle again, reviewed every instant she had spent with him. She imagined his lips touching hers again, and she writhed and then nearly cried out in pain as she dug her fingernails into her palms, punishing her traitorous flesh. For as much as she had tried to deny her feelings until now, here at Stamworth, where it was safe to think and she could be alone with her thoughts, she could not deny that she had found him more attractive than any man she had met since Edward Neale . . . more attractive, perhaps, than Ned. She bit her lip. *You goose, Kat. Not even Frances would approve of this match.* She chuckled at the thought, but it was much later, and the sun was already above the horizon, before she fell into a mercifully dreamless sleep.

CHAPTER 7

Justin woke to the sound of a cock crowing outside his window.

His head ached as though someone were hammering on it. His mouth tasted foul, and his legs and arms were cramped. His first groggy thought was a curse at his own stupidity for having had so much to drink, but as he tried to turn over, thinking to recapture oblivion, he realized he was bound.

He opened his eyes on a dark room.

For a few moments he panicked, struggling against the bonds and twisting his head from side to side as if that would free him of the gag, until memories seeped back. He lay still then, his anger congealing into an icy calm. He had no doubt that he could wriggle to the edge of the bed; if he toppled off, the sound of his fall might bring someone to his aid. But did he really want to draw anyone's attention to his humiliation?

He began to work at the thongs binding his wrist. Whoever had tied him—the boy, he guessed—had been hasty, and it was a simple though time-consuming matter to free his hands. He tore the gag from his mouth, then sat up so he could untie his ankles. Dizziness felled him. For a few moments he lay still, staring at the gray dawn light seeping through the window. When his head had stopped whirling, he drew his legs up and undid the points binding his ankles together. Then, carefully, he sat up and trussed his points. When he was sure that his hose were fastened securely to his shirt and would not fall down about his ankles when he stood, he grasped the bedpost and pulled himself up onto his feet.

The room reeled about him. He sat down, hard, then dropped back against the pillow.

Meg would pay for this. And so would that boy. He would see to that.

Smiling a little at the thought, he fell asleep.

He woke again when the sun was already well above the horizon. Someone was knocking on the door.

"Come in," he called, thinking it was Tandy.

Instead of his manservant, a plump girl with dark hair entered the chamber, bearing a tray with his breakfast. She bade him a cheerful good-morrow as she set the tray on the table. Then her gaze fell on the dented flagon, and her smile faltered.

She looked around at him, her eyes widening as she noticed the wine stains on his clothes. He sat up as she came toward him; his head throbbed, and he reached up to clutch it. His eyes closed for a few moments. When he opened them again he saw that the maid was about to pour him some wine.

"Hair of the dog that bit you, my lord?"

" 'Twas more like a shrew," he said, half to himself. The maid looked at him quizzically. "Yea, I'll drink." As he took the glass from her, he asked, as casually as possible, "Have you seen Meg this morning?"

"Aye, my lord."

It was not the answer Justin had expected. He had thought that Meg and her young swain would be well away from the inn by now, and that he would have to search for them. Could it be that the encounter with that player—and the innkeeper's generous treatment of the youth— had led them to believe that last night's quarrel would be seen in the same light? If so, they had sorely misjudged Master Bruning.

The maidservant cleared her throat. "Sir? Would you have Meg sent to you?"

"No, not now. I would speak to her, though, before I leave. Pray tell Master Bruning that."

A few minutes after she had left, Tandy came in. "Good morrow, my lord! I trust that your meeting—" He fell silent, staring in bewilderment at Justin's stained and rumpled clothing. He shook his head as he noticed the wine-stained floor and bedlinens.

"No, we did not carouse it," Justin said irritably. " 'Twas after he left that this happened."

Tandy raised an eyebrow. *Conclude what you will from that,* Justin thought sourly. His head was still throbbing, and he was in no mood to explain.

He waited in the common room, standing near the door to the courtyard, while Tandy settled their account. He had been there only a few minutes when Master Bruning came bustling toward him, a young blond woman at his side.

"Good morrow, my lord! I hope that you slept well. Joan said that you would speak with Meg."

"Aye," Justin said.

"What did you wish with me, my lord?" the girl asked, a bit nervously.

"Meg?" He gazed at her wonderingly.

"Yea, my lord." Her voice was shaking now. "What did you wish with me?"

She was somewhat fair, and yellow-haired, but there her resemblance to the maid he had seen last night ended. Never, no matter how drunk, could he mistake this girl for the other.

If this was some jest, then it seemed that the innkeeper was not in on it—Master Bruning was no experienced player, to so portray the innocent. But it was clear that the maid was nervous. What troubled Justin was that she also seemed uncertain, as though she did not know in truth why he wished to speak to her.

"Cry you mercy, my lord," the innkeeper said, "if she has done aught to offend you." His face was reddening, but whether it was from embarrassment or from anger at the wench, Justin could not tell. "I have never heard any complaints against Meg, which is why I sent her to bring you the wine, but I should have known that something was amiss when she was not found in her own bed this morning, but instead was discovered fast asleep, like some Jill-a-dreams, in another bed . . . and all bespattered with wine." By now the maid's face was as red as Master Bruning's. "If she spilled wine on you as well as herself . . ."

So Joan had told him of the disarray in which she had found Justin, and the innkeeper was choosing to believe the story most favorable to the nobleman . . . For a moment Justin was tempted to let the misunderstanding continue: he had no wish to have Master Bruning think he had drunkenly spilled wine over himself. Then, too, he felt the maid was somehow involved in what had happened last night. She had at least lent her clothing to the other girl. Yet she seemed to be unaware of just how that maid had dealt with him—else she would have run away by now.

Making a sudden decision, he told the innkeeper, "In sooth, she behaved most courteously in bringing me the wine. A most seemly maid, and a graceful one. 'Twas my clumsiness that caused the wine to spill, and I asked to see her only to apologize, and to offer to pay for her ruined garments."

Master Bruning sputtered in confusion.

"Nay, do not call her a Jill-of-dreams," Justin said. The maid looked surprised by his defense of her. "Was she not in Master Ramsey's chamber? I was told that she had looked after him, after he was wounded defending her. Mayhap she but meant to watch over him while he slept, then fell asleep."

"Ramsey left last night," the innkeeper said.

"Marry, did he?" Justin asked, feigning surprise. "Then he must have left quietly, so that he did not wake Meg from her sleep."

Bruning shook his head. "Nay, he was far from quiet, for he so rated the youth he was with—"

"His cousin?" Justin asked

"Was he?" Master Bruning shrugged. "A milk-livered boy, I warrant you, to accept such a rating from the other. Yet a careless one, too—and haply deserving of the scolding—for having forgotten to tell young Matthew that his sister was sick."

Justin smiled thinly. What a fatbrain the innkeeper was, to believe that a youth who had come to the inn seeking his cousin would have forgotten the reason for his journey until hours later. It was a mad, bastard story, born no doubt of fear and recklessness—yet it had worked. He wondered which of the youths had thought of it.

He took a coin from his purse and handed it to the maid, who thanked him and then, at a gesture from Master Bruning, left them.

Tandy had concluded his business, paying the innkeeper's wife, who kept the accounts. He and Justin walked out into the courtyard, where their horses were waiting, held by two ostlers. Master Bruning would have accompanied them, but his wife had asked his help with a dispute among the scullery maids: even outside, Justin could hear shrill voices raised in anger, then a bellow that was far from the innkeeper's usual dulcet, obsequious tone.

"Good my lord . . ."

Justin turned to see the yellow-haired maid.

"I must thank you, my lord. I was scolded this morning, after I was found, and when I saw how my clothing was stained, I feared the worst. In truth, I should not have drunk the ale that Matthew offered me."

"You feared the worst . . . ? You cannot remember?" The maid blushed and looked down. "You truly do not remember bringing me the wine."

"Nay, my lord," she responded, her voice barely audible. "I am ashamed. 'Tis the first time that ale affected me so."

Drugged, in truth. Justin was about to tell her so, but then decided to hold his tongue. It would do no good to tell her that he believed Matthew Ramsey had drugged her: she clearly knew nothing of what had happened while she slept, and could not help him there. More, he had no wish to make her curious about who had served him the wine. That he intended to find out from Ramsey, when he located the boy.

"Did Master Ramsey tell you where he lives?" he asked hopefully.

"No, my lord."

She bade him farewell, then thanked him again before leaving. Watching her, he thought how ironic it was that he should have felt compelled to lie to save a servant's reputation. *Just as Ned Dyer did.* And how deeply was that boy involved in his cousin's mischief-making? After hearing that account of the trick played on the yeoman, Justin would never again be misled by the boy's angelic features—

He caught his breath then, his mind superimposing one heavily painted profile on another that was curiously begrimed.

" 'Slid, what a fool—" he said under his breath. Tandy looked at him questioningly, but Justin ignored him.

'Twas a girl. He might have been less sure of that, had Meg's dress had a high-collared bodice, but the neckline had been low and revealing. Perchance that was why he had not noticed the wench's resemblance to the young gentleman he had met earlier. That, and the paint that she had been loath to part with . . .

He swore again, and when he went to mount his horse, the ostler looked at him fearfully. Tandy, too, was regarding him warily. At any other time, Justin would have told Tandy what had happened, but he had been galled too much by the way Ramsey and Mistress Ned had treated him. He had no desire to let others know yet how he had been the butt of their jest. So he was silent as he rode away from the inn, spurring his horse to a gallop as soon as they were past the gate of the courtyard. Tandy followed, also silent, belike not daring to interrupt his master's thoughts. Justin was already composing a letter in his mind, thinking of all those at Cambridge to whom he could write, asking about a youth who fit Ramsey's description. For that Ramsey—under one name or another—had once been at Cambridge, Justin had no doubts at all.

CHAPTER 8

"Teach me to fence."

Nick looked up in surprise at his sister's question. He had been half reclining on his bed, playing his lute. "What did you say?"

She repeated the question, and to her annoyance Nick shook his head. "Nay, Kat, why would you learn the art of fence? 'Tis no art for a woman. Do I ask you to instruct me in needlework?"

"No, and you would learn little if you did," she said, putting aside the velvet purse, a gift for Louise, which she had been embroidering while she listened to him play.

Though she would never have thought it possible, in the last few days she had found herself picking up her needlework projects just to keep busy, in the vain hope that she might be able to occupy her thoughts with something other than the events of three days ago. She would have spent more time outdoors, but Nick still limped from his wound and kept to his bedchamber much of the time. She spent much of her time there too, hoping that he would want to talk about what had happened, but he discouraged her attempts to draw him out on that subject. Though she could scarcely believe it, Nick had acted as though nothing out of the ordinary had occurred. Some of this was pretense, she knew, a show of carelessness about the cause of his wound that was intended to reassure the servants and lull any suspicions they might have. But she was beginning to wonder whether, except for that wound, he was truly untouched by the events at the Jerusalem Tree.

Kat's own thoughts had never been more unsettled. She slept so poorly that there were circles under her eyes. No remedy she knew had helped, not even placing a sack of rose petals under her pillow. Her mind remained too restless, for she could not deal directly with the matters that troubled her most—her failure to overhear more of the conversation between Justin Lisle and Henry Malcomb, and, more disturbing yet, Lisle's effect on her.

But there was one fear that she could take action to end—if Nick would help her . . .

"While we rode back from the Jerusalem Tree," she began, and paused when she saw Nick glance toward the door to be certain it was closed. Lowering her voice to little more than a whisper, she continued, "I feared that we would be set upon by rogues, at a time when you were unable to defend yourself, let alone me. I could not have defended us then against any rogue armed with more than a club. Nor could I have defended myself, had anyone attacked me on the way to the inn."

"An argument for your staying at home, I trow."

Kat refused to let him divert her into a quarrel about whether she should have followed him. "And how would I defend myself here, should that prove necessary? It has been but half a year since the rising in the North—"

"And nearly as long since it was put down."

"Yea, but for how long? You cannot tell me of plots against the queen at one time, Nick, and then try to lull me into security at another. Were there no threat, you need not play the intelligencer; if there is a threat, then I must be ready to defend myself."

" 'Tis but sophistry, good Kat. You have men to defend you."

"And how many women in France these past ten years were told that by their menfolk? And how many of them have been killed, or raped, or both?" Suddenly Nick looked uncertain; she had been wise to remind him of the fighting between the Catholics and the Huguenots that had torn France asunder for much of the past decade. Had the rising in the North not been put down so quickly, England might have been similarly rent by civil war. "I do not ask this from any vain ambition to master the art of fence, Nick. 'Tis not my aim. But I must needs be able to use a sword with some skill, should I ever be forced to do so."

He was silent for some moments, then abruptly lurched to his feet. He limped across the room to a small chest, opened it and pulled out a book. "How well do you remember your Spanish?" he asked.

"Will you turn language tutor now, when I require a master of fence?"

He tossed the book to her, and she looked at it curiously. It was the *Filosofia de las Armas*, written by Don Jeronimo Sanchez de Carranza. She remembered Nick's delight at receiving a copy of the book a few months ago.

"I hope you remember your Italian, too," Nick said as he went to his writing cabinet and unlocked the drawer where he kept his private papers. He withdrew a letter of several pages. "This is from George Calvert."

"Your friend who went to study at Padua?" she asked, remembering how envious her brother had been when George had been sent to the university of Padua rather than the Inns of Court. Nick had asked their father to let him go study abroad, once he was through with his studies at Gray's Inn.

"The same. He has made the acquaintance of an Italian master of fence, one Giacomo di Grassi, who is preparing a manual on the art. George has promised to send me a copy of *Ragione di adoprar sicuramente l'Arme* as soon as it is printed. In the meantime, he has sent me notes of what Giacomo has taught him. I would have you read this." He held out the letter to Kat, but just as she reached for it he drew it back out of her grasp. "Nay, wait. You need study only part of this. The rest will be of no interest to you." He looked over the papers, finally separating out four pages of tiny writing that he handed to Kat.

"Could I not learn from the rest?" she teased. "What news is there for you? Does he write of the courtesans of Venice?" Nick reddened. "Ha! Pray God, that George brings back nothing from Italy but learning . . . or at least nothing that requires a physician's cure." She glanced at the papers, then shuffled through them in mock horror. "God's light! May his Italian be better than his writing. Else I will need a year to decipher this."

"We can start as soon as you have finished reading it."

"Tomorrow, then." She turned to leave, already poring over George Calvert's crabbed writing.

"Kat?"

She stopped and looked back over her shoulder at Nick.

"Is this in truth what you want? To learn fence? I have noticed that time crawls for you these past few days, and that idleness has even driven you to needlework." A fleeting smile. "Are you unhappy? Perchance lonely? I was told that you no longer welcome Christopher Danvers as a suitor."

"Do you object?"

"Nay. You know my opinion of him . . . but I hope it was not my opinion that guided yours. Was that why you bade him look elsewhere? Pray tell me it was not, for I could have learned to like him, if you loved him."

She shook her head. She dared not tell Nick of her suspicions that Danvers had drugged her wine.

"Well, then, even if Danvers did not please you, would you not be happier if you had a suitor? 'Tis an offense against all order that a gentlewoman so lovely should go unwooed."

She swallowed hard. So Nick did wish her to wed, so much so that he would tolerate Christopher Danvers as a brother-in-law if Danvers were her choice. She bowed her head, not wanting him to see that her eyes held unshed tears.

"Perhaps," she said, as lightly as possible, "but it can be but a slight

offense when there are no suitors in the neighborhood." And she hurried from the room, the book and sheets of paper still clutched in one
hand, yet all but forgotten for the moment.

"Hold, Nick," Kat gasped. "I must rest."

The sword felt as though it would drag her arm from its socket as
she crossed the rush-strewn floor of the gallery to the table where she
had set her cup of ale. Her arms and shoulders ached, and beneath the
heavily padded leather jerkin she wore, her shirt was clammy with sweat.

It was the fourth day of their practice, a practice that had, in the
first grueling hour, destroyed any illusions she might have had of easily
mastering this art. 'Twas one thing to read the advice of de Carranza
and di Grassi, another to attempt to employ it. She had not guessed
that one of Nick's splendid rapiers, so fine and delicate in comparison
to the heavy longsword their father had used, could feel so heavy after
only an hour in her hand. That first day it had been a struggle for her
even to learn the various wards—the high ward, the low ward, and the
broad ward—that she must master if she would defend herself against an
enemy's strikes. Nick had shaken his head, avowing that she had not
the strength to use a sword, but she had persevered. She had finished
the scant two hours of their first practice with her muscles protesting
more than they ever had before, and had barely been able to move her
right arm when she awoke the next morning, but she had insisted that
the practices continue every day, for as long as Nick himself could
tolerate the exercise.

She knew now that as soon as she drew her sword she could keep
the point downward to use the high ward for protection. Then, with a
step forward, she could make a thrust—a *stoccata*—abovehand at her
enemy . . . but she would need much more practice before that stroke
would be accurate and powerful. The first time she had tried it, Nick
had not even needed to protect himself with a parry—a *pararla*—since
her blade had come nowhere near him, and it was still easy for him to
defend himself when she tried a *stoccata* from the high ward. She was
equally skilled—and unskilled—in the other wards, and in blows made
both with the edge and the point of her sword. Faced with her own
incompetence, she had finally begun to appreciate the many hours that
Nick had spent in fencing lessons, lessons that she had often disparaged
as mere play for gallants and fashionmongers.

Nick had taught her that the fourth part of the sword's blade—that
part nearest the point, all but the last four fingers' breadth, which was
too weak—delivered the strongest blow when the sword was swung. She
learned to use the first and second parts of the blade, the half nearest
her hand, to ward blows from Nick's sword. He spoke incessantly of

lines and circles and times, reminding her always that a straight line for a thrust was the shortest, that the outer part of a circle described by her blade carried the most force, that all her movements took time and so the best blow was that which took the least time. He warned her that while a thrust was usually the swiftest blow and the most dangerous, a side blow was best—because it was quickest—when her point was out of line so she could not thrust at him without first realigning her sword. And when she made a mistake and he criticized her and she pleaded with him to give her time to think, he reminded her that time to think was something she would not have in an actual fight. That put an end to her pleas for easier lessons.

So that she would be accustomed to different swords, he insisted that she practice with all three that he owned: the Toledo blade she had carried to the Jerusalem Tree Inn; the Isebrook, a fine sword made in Spain, but of steel forged in Isebrook, which the Germans called Innsbruck; and the bilbo, from the city of Bilbao in Spain. Proudly showing off the bilbo, he bent its blade until the point touched the hilt—then warned her never to try to do so. She was not even tempted; her fingers already bore numerous small scratches from careless handling of the swords.

Today Nick had begun to teach her to use both dagger and rapier.

"Come, Kat," he said now, scant moments after she had sheathed her weapons; she had taken no more than a few sips of ale. "You will rarely get so much as a second's respite in a swordfight. Draw your sword and dagger."

She sighed, but did as he asked, and waited lying in the low ward, with the sword hilt held a few inches outside her right thigh, the point raised slightly, in line for a direct thrust at Nick. This was the best of the three wards, Nick had told her. The high ward was the quickest to use if forced to draw a sword and fight at once, with no warning. The broad ward, with the sword held out well to one's side, might tempt an enemy to strike, to his own perdition—unless one forgot and allowed the sword point to be out of line, as Kat had, most of the times she had tried it. *Never use it*, Nick had told her at last. This low ward she would use, though. She felt comfortable in it, even with the unfamiliar weight of the dagger in her left hand. As she waited, her right shoulder was turned toward Nick: she no longer had to remind herself not to face him directly and so present him with a larger target.

"Now," he said, and drew his sword, paused when she made no move toward him, then twisted his hand to raise his rapier's blade and struck at her from the high ward with an edge blow.

She took a slope pace forward, moving out of the line of his sword, which was well, for when she caught the descending blade with her dagger's hilt, her arm was forced down. Nick yanked the sword back an instant before it would have touched her.

"No, Kat! Did I not tell you to use both sword and dagger to parry?"

"Yea, but then I must disengage my sword for a thrust, while now 'tis ready—"

"For what? You would have been struck down by an enemy. Look you, you have not the strength to ward a blow with just one arm. Use both sword and dagger to catch my blade and stop it, then you may continue to hold my blade with dagger alone. Again."

This time she was more successful, but she knew she was too slow at drawing her sword back again.

"Fear not," Nick assured her. "Your speed will improve with practice. And you learn quickly."

"Take care not to praise me too highly, brother. You'll have me believe myself invincible."

"Not yet," he said with a laugh, and threw his arm wide so that he lay in the broad ward. "Strike me now."

She had been lying in the low ward. Her thrust was the fastest she could make, but it seemed she had scarcely moved her arm before his sword blade slid along hers, and with a flick of his wrist he wrenched her sword from her grasp and sent it spinning across the chamber to bury itself among the rushes.

She gasped and rubbed her wrist.

"You still have much to learn," he said, grinning at her affectionately.

"I'faith, I do. 'Twas a neat trick, and one I would fain learn. And when, pray, will you begin to teach me the Spanish art of fence? I have already practiced the *pasada*." She took a step of approximately twenty-four inches; she had measured out the length of the Spanish fencing paces on the floor of her bedchamber, marking them with spools of thread, and practiced them there. "And the *pasada simple*"—another step, this time of thirty inches—"and the *pasada doble*." She took two steps forward, combining the other two paces, then bowed with mock formality to Nick. "Do I not perform them precisely?"

"Indeed," Nick said, clapping his hands. "Yet such niceties serve you well only when your opponent also practices them. 'Twas thoughtless of me to ask you to read the *Filosofia*, when it is the Italian style of fence that will serve you best."

Kat nodded. Nick was right: in the type of attack she feared, she would not be able to ask her attacker to pause while they measured out a circle's diameter, as Carranza taught, by extending their swords toward each other until the points touched. Nor could she insist that her attacker keep within the circle, in the best Spanish fashion. She chuckled at the thought.

"Do you take this so lightly?" Nick asked unexpectedly. " 'Tis no game, Kat. I hope that you will never have to use the lessons I teach you, for I would not have you forced to kill a man. Should you ever again go dressed as a man and carrying a sword, you must needs take care what you say, lest you lead someone to challenge you to a duel."

"I should not, then, while talking to a papist, declare that the Queen of Scots is a wanton and a murderer?"

He flushed. " 'Twas folly," he admitted, "and I would not have you speak so foolishly. Needs must that you be courteous at all times, and avoid quarrelsome men. And above all, never give anyone the lie nor let anyone find cause to give it to you."

Kat nodded gravely, remembering how at the Jerusalem Tree she had feared that Lord Harwood would call Nick a liar, forcing a duel.

"Good morrow, sir! Mistress Katherine!"

They turned to see their steward coming toward them, a small packet in his hand. "A carrier passed by and brought this letter from Master Gardiner in London."

He gave Nick the letter and then took his leave, only a startled glance at a new gash in Kat's jerkin showing that he found anything unusual about their practice at fence. The servants had quickly adapted to Kat's latest fondness.

Kat waited impatiently while Nick broke the seal, revealing a letter of perhaps a dozen pages. He had scarcely begun to read when he laughed with delight. "Blanche is with child. William writes of this most soberly, as though 'twere no great matter, but I can see him crowing as he wrote this."

"Yea, and every time he thinks of it." Their cousin William Gardiner had been married now for more than five years, and he and Blanche had almost despaired of having children.

"Do you think Blanche will now stay at home more," Nick asked, "and not attend so many prophesyings?"

After a moment's thought, Kat shook her head. Blanche was too much a Puritan, too involved in the activities of the godly.

"Listen," Nick said, with a chuckle. "He writes, 'We have not yet decided what to name the child. For my part, I had hoped, if the child is a boy, to name it after my father, and if 'tis a girl, after my mother. Yet though Blanche had once concurred, she now believes that our child should have a more godly name.' "

Kat groaned. "By my life, I pity the child. What think you she will call the poor young Puritan? Praise-God Gardiner?"

"Nay, Repent. No, not you, unless needs must. I meant the child. Mistress Repent Gardiner. Or young Master Deliverance."

"Deliver us!" Kat said vehemently. "No, she'll call the babe Reformation, and together they shall sing psalms all the day long."

"Poor Will."

"Poor child," she said, then, after thinking over the matter for a time, while Nick continued to read the letter silently, amended, "Nay, 'tis wrong to say so. Blanche will be a good mother. And haply Will may curb her desires to fashion her child as a Puritan as soon as it is born."

"Peradventure with our help," Nick said quietly. "We are invited to visit them in London." He read aloud: " 'For though we will be leaving the city by the end of June, to stay until late autumn in the country, where we will by God's grace avoid the pestilence that has afflicted London these past summers, we would welcome your company at any time—and for any length of time—until then. I would have you see the city at last, Katherine, and as for you, cousin Nick, I remember well how you enjoyed being in London on midsummer eve for the vigil of St. John the Baptist.' "

Nick broke off reading to look up at Kat, his face radiant with excitement. "You should see it, Kat! The fires in the streets, and the tables set out with all the food they can bear! The streets are thronged, with dancing and feasting everywhere, and all is safe, for the Midsummer Watch protects the citizens from any rogues that are about. Yea, you should see London then, with the houses decked with birch branches above the door, and St. John's wort and white lilies and garlands of flowers, and all the houses lit by glass lamps, with the oil kept burning till dawn. You can walk about the city all night, and stop at friends' houses for sweetmeats and drink. And mayhap our good cousin Blanche, for all that she is a Puritan and belike frowns upon such things, will not mind if you set up fern fronds in a dish, should you be in love by then and anxious to learn if the man is true to you."

Kat shook her head. She knew the custom well, and the havoc it sometimes wreaked. Last year on St. John's Eve, one of their maidservants had found the two fronds, which she had left leaning together in the dish, lying apart at sunrise of midsummer day. It had taken much pleading by the mason who was wooing her to convince her that, despite the ferns' evidence to the contrary, his love was true, and Kat had been told that even now, several months after the wedding, the woman had doubts about her husband's faithfulness.

"Were you in London, Nick, half the fair gentlewomen in the city would find that their fronds had spurned one another, warning of their future disappointment."

"No, good sister, I am not that fickle. But think: you may have enough time in London to find another suitor before St. John's Eve. Would you not like that? And would you not wish to learn if he would be true to you?''

She was silent. It had not occurred to her that London might be the best place for her to find a husband. But it obviously had occurred to Nick. "Yea, of certain," she muttered to herself.

"Then we'll to London," Nick said cheerfully, "where you shall find a new suitor."

She was confused by his words until she realized he had taken the bitter thought she had spoken aloud for her answer to his questions. So they would go. 'Twould seem odd if she argued against it now, and in truth she was looking forward to the trip—though not, she would warrant, for the same reasons as Nick.

"It would be good to see Blanche and Will again," she told him. " 'Tis more than three years now since they last visited Beechwood. And perchance she would listen if I suggested a name or two for her child. When shall we leave? Tomorrow? Or the next day?"

Nick shook his head. "They must have time to prepare for our visit. I shall send them a letter to tell them that we're coming. John Baker's son can take it."

"Will you have him leave today, then? Or tomorrow morning?"

"Jesu! Why such a great hurry?" he said testily, then was instantly repentant. "Cry you mercy, Kat. This wound pains me." He turned his attention to the letter again, scanning the remainder of it quickly. "Most of this seems to be about the law—"

"As always." Will Gardiner was a barrister, and had hoped at one time that Nick, too, would complete his study of law at the Inns of Court.

"—yet I am sure you will wish to read it." He refolded the letter and handed it to her. "Shall we practice more tomorrow? I know we have been here but an hour today, but I must rest."

She offered to help him back to his room, but he refused.

She looked after him wonderingly as he limped away. 'Twas the first time he had complained of his wound during their practice. Nor had she seen him limp so badly before. He might truly be in pain, and yet . . . She felt guilty for doubting him, but it did seem to her that he had wished to escape her presence as soon as she pressed him to make plans for their journey to London.

Halfway to the door, he stopped and looked back over his shoulder at her. "Will you go to Winchester to buy some syrup of poppy tomorrow morning?" he asked, his voice unusually plaintive. "There is an apothecary there, a man whom I trust to prepare medicines most carefully, from whom I would have you buy the syrup."

"You cannot send Walter or another servant to buy the laudanum?"

" 'Tis an important matter to me, and I trust you more. If you leave early enough in the morning—"

"Then I shall be well away from here by the time Sparrow arrives."

He whirled around, and she noted with a mix of satisfaction and disappointment that he had put his weight on his wounded leg and seemed not to notice.

"How did you know?" he demanded.

"I know that you have not met with Sparrow since our return, for Walter has dogged your steps since then, whenever I was not with you. Nor have you sent any letters. Sparrow will not wait forever to hear what you have learned. Therefore, you expect to meet him soon . . . and you would have me away from here at that time.

"Howsomever," she added softly, undeterred by the look on his face, "I shall stay, and stay near you, for I would fain meet this Master Sparrow . . ."

Her muscles aching, Kat picked up the longsword once again. It was late, nearly ten, and she had been practicing alone for more than an hour. The sword she held was her father's. It was so much heavier than the Spanish rapiers Nick used that Kat had at first wondered how Henry Langdon had ever been able to wield it with such skill. But it was the extra weight she had wanted, so much so that two days ago she had asked the steward to bring the longsword to her chamber. Years ago, she had heard their father insist to Nick that he practice also with the longsword, if only to add strength to his arm. Nick had not suggested the same to her—no doubt he thought her totally incapable of managing the heavier sword—but she had not forgotten their father's advice, nor the fact that Nick had followed it and profited from it.

She sheathed the sword, then drew it swiftly, held it for a few seconds in the high ward—ignoring the pain in her side and shoulder—then drove the blade forward and down toward the invisible enemy who stood before her. In her imagination she missed as he stepped to one side, and as she drew her sword back again she raised her dagger instinctively to stop his strike at her from the low ward. She thrust at him—"The *stoccata*, the *punta dritta*!" she whispered—and then pretended that he had parried her sword's blade with his dagger, an instant before he aimed a *stoccata* at her face. "The *pararla*!" she cried, using her dagger to beat his sword away, to her left side. "The *punta riversa*!" She turned her sword hand, gasping a little at the unexpected strain on her wrist as she delivered the backhand thrust. In her mind she saw her sword's point pierce his shoulder: 'twas merely an imaginary flesh wound, but inflicted in very little time. Nick would approve. Satisfied, she relaxed for a few moments, lying in the low ward.

Louise cried out, and Kat looked to where her maid sat doing needlework. Louise had her finger in her mouth.

"Wounded?" Kat asked. "By my life, I have suffered often myself from that point. Would you care to wield this instead?"

Louise shook her head, not taking her finger from her mouth.

The low ward, then . . . Her opponent had retreated, so she took a slope pace forward and thrust at him, finally impaling him neatly . . . and just in time, for as she made that *stoccata*, it felt as though the muscles in her right arm and shoulder would tear asunder. She sheathed the sword, unbuckled the sword belt and set it on the chest at the foot of her bed, then dropped heavily onto a cushion on the floor. She was exhausted. Her eyes closed, she began to knead her right arm. How had Nick tolerated this? She had never heard him complain.

Unaware of Louise's movements, Kat jumped when the maid touched her shoulder.

Louise held out a small gallipot. "Liniment?" she asked.

A scattering of wilted petals lay on the ground, victims of a heavy rain the night before, but otherwise the orchard looked just the same as it had nine days ago. And so did Nicholas Langdon, Sparrow thought dourly. He had hoped that the mission he had sent the youth on might sober him, but Langdon had seemed as exuberant as ever as he greeted Sparrow in the courtyard and led the way to the orchard.

Sparrow could feel no such exuberance himself, but rather only impatience to be done here and on his way back to London. A few days ago he had been shown a copy of a letter about three Spanish spies in England. One of them, John Delgado, lived in the Spanish ambassador's house, and another, Peter Benavides, went there occasionally. The third, Diego Ridiera, was said to travel about England. 'Twas he who most interested Sparrow. According to the letter, Ridiera was "a tall man of person eyed like a cat." Sparrow had already passed on this news to his most reliable intelligencers. Now he was curious to learn what Langdon had discovered. The spy sent to dog Lord Harwood in London had reported that the baron met with a tall fellow, but had noticed nothing unusual about the man's eyes. Still, it could be the same fellow. And however poor a spy Langdon might be, surely he could at least describe any men Lord Harwood had met with at the Jerusalem Tree.

But Nick Langdon was still prattling about a horse he wished to buy. Finally Sparrow could take no more.

"Tell me of your stay at the Jerusalem Tree. Was it without mishap?"

"Yea, except for a flesh wound suffered in a fight."

"A fight?" He did not bother to keep his voice lowered. They were well into the orchard now—not far, Sparrow estimated, from where they had stopped during his last visit here. No servants were likely to overhear them. "You fool, you were not to fight with Harwood, you were—"

"To observe him, sirrah. As I did." The boy looked furious, and Sparrow, reminding himself that Walsingham wanted this lad's cooperation, bit back the vicious comment that had been on the tip of his tongue. Langdon continued, "The fight was with a drunken player, the evening I arrived. Lisle did not arrive until the following evening."

"Then he did stay at the inn." He would have to commend the rustic who had brought him that information. Perhaps he would even ask Walsingham to agree to pay the swain for the hose he had ruined in Knightriders Street. "Had you opportunity to observe him?"

"At close hand. We sat talking over wine that evening."

"You spoke with him?"

"He came to my table in the common room."

Sparrow had not anticipated that possibility. He had planned on Nick observing Lord Harwood without being noticed in particular by the baron, had recommended that Nick avoid speaking to the man. "Did he know who you were? Did he remember you from court?"

Nick shook his head.

"And you were using an assumed name."

"As you advised."

" 'Twas well done," Sparrow said, a bit grudgingly. "He should not know you when he meets you again, for the walnut stain I bade you use would have so transformed—" He broke off, seeing that the young gallant looked uneasy. "You did stain your hair and skin?"

Nick shook his head. " 'Twould have been difficult to remove, and more difficult to explain. My sister would have noticed and—"

" 'Sdeath! And what if you meet him again at court?"

" 'Tis unlikely, when Lord Harwood is so seldom at court. And should we meet, I need but concoct some story. Perchance I shall tell him that I wished to travel through the district without encountering a sworn enemy who has informants at every inn."

" 'Twould have been better to use the stain."

"How so? Did you not hear me say that I was wounded? The innkeeper summoned a barber-surgeon, and he and the maid who changed the dressing would have seen that my leg was unstained. You bade me stain only my hair and my hands and face. Had I done so, I would have been instantly under suspicion. I would likely have had no choice but to leave, and would never have seen Lord Harwood.''

Sparrow let the subject go. It had been pure luck that the boy's decision to go undisguised had been the right one, but 'twould be a waste of time to argue that. Nor was there any point in telling Langdon that the explanation he proposed to offer Lord Harwood, should they meet at court and the baron wonder why this young gentleman had used another name at the Jerusalem Tree, would certainly not be believed. He would offer his opinion to Master Walsingham, though . . .

''What did you learn of Lord Harwood?'' he asked.

''Other than that he's fond of Madeira, and of reminiscing about his days at Cambridge?'' The youth paused, smiling a little, his defensiveness gone. No doubt he enjoyed making Sparrow wait for his information. 'Twas an attitude Sparrow had seen before. ''He met with a sea captain, a Henry Malcomb,'' Langdon said at last, an irritatingly smug look on his face.

''You had met Malcomb previously? No? Then you mean that he met with a man who was introduced to you as a sea captain.'' The name *Henry Malcomb* was unfamiliar to Sparrow, but he would remember it and make inquiries later, after returning to London. ''Was this man perhaps tall—yea?—and was he also eyed like a cat?''

''Nay, he had rather melancholy eyes. Spaniel eyes. He was swarthy, with dark hair, thick and curling. And thick mustachios and beard. And he spoke with the broad accent of Devon.''

Sparrow shook his head. The description meant no more to him than the name, but it was clear the man was not Ridiera. The letter Sparrow had been privileged to read had mentioned a fourth spy, a Burgundian who spoke both English and Irish, and who was wont to write his letters with alum water, but that man was said to have been sent into Ireland. As like as not, the sea captain was no more than what he appeared to be.

''Do you know why he met with Lord Harwood?''

'' 'Twas apparently an accidental meeting, for he arrived while Lord Harwood was in the common room, my second night at the inn,'' Nick said, a bit defensive again. ''Malcomb told Lisle of a cargo of Turkey carpets, and they withdrew to his lordship's chamber to discuss it.'' He looked as though he would say more, but did not.

It was just possible that Lord Harwood could have met a sea captain of his acquaintance at the Jerusalem Tree. Still . . . ''Would that you could have heard all their conversation.''

''Some of it was in Spanish.''

Sparrow blinked in surprise. ''You heard them converse in Spanish? In the common room?''

"Nay, not there."

"You eavesdropped on them while they spoke in Lord Harwood's chamber?" 'Twas the first indication he had been given that the youth might be a useful intelligencer after all.

"Not I—another." Nick turned away, then looked up into the branches of a nearby walnut tree: the same tree, Sparrow realized, that they had stood beneath nine days ago. "Kat!"

The youth was addled, Sparrow thought. He felt like grabbing Nick by the shoulders and shaking him until he explained this riddle. But then he heard something scrape against bark, high up in the tree.

He took a few steps closer to the tree's trunk and looked up, then stepped back, swearing, as a fragment of bark nearly fell into his eye. Shielding his eyes, he glanced up again, seeing boots, dark hose, a dark doublet . . . and, gleaming against the dark fabric of the doublet, long honey-colored hair. His mouth, which had sagged open, shut with a click. He was grinding his teeth together by the time the woman reached the ground.

"My sister, Katherine," Nick said. "And this, sweet sister, is the Sparrow I told you of."

The introduction had been unnecessary for Sparrow: he had seen the resemblance at once. He glared at the girl, so angry he could not speak.

"A very quiet Sparrow," she said. "Will it not sing while I am here?"

"You told her of this?" Sparrow asked Nick, so provoked by her levity that he was nearly shouting. "You took her to the Jerusalem Tree with you?"

Kat stepped back, wincing. "More softly, sir. We would keep this private. Nick did not tell me of his conversation with you. I was here, hidden in the tree, unbeknownst to you, when you spoke to him that day. You see how easily one may miss a person hidden among the branches? And for my going to the inn—that was my own decision. Nick was unaware that I knew his whereabouts; he had left before I could speak to him. Then, when he did not return that day, I followed."

"Foolishness."

"You are mistaken, sirrah."

The insulting way she addressed him stung him. It rankled him, too, that she was taller than he, so that he was forced to look up to meet her gaze.

Not trusting himself to speak to her, he asked Nick, "Think you that I am mistaken? Did you approve her decision?"

Nick shrugged. " 'Twas too late for me to approve or disapprove by the time she reached the inn that afternoon."

Sparrow shook his head, then froze as he realized that the girl must have reached the Jerusalem Tree before Lord Harwood. She had been there while Nick spoke to the nobleman.

"Pray God, you did not also share a table with Lord Harwood." Seeing the expression on their faces, he nearly groaned aloud. 'Twas bad enough that Nick had conversed at length with the nobleman, when he had no practice at such dissimulation. What chance was there that both these nestlings could have spoken for any time with the baron without arousing his suspicions? "Did you not think, madam, of the danger you put yourself in? A maid traveling alone, and meeting with a man such as Lord Harwood."

She blushed then—as well she should, Sparrow thought.

"I wore these garments," she said, and explained the rest of her disguise. "And so I traveled safely enough"—she hesitated, exchanging a look with Nick that Sparrow could not interpret—"and Lisle did not know I was a woman. Nor would he recognize me again, should we meet."

"In sooth, he would not," Nick said. "Kat has often traveled garbed as a boy, as a jest."

"Did you think this a jest?" Sparrow asked, and the younger man looked away. He turned back to Kat. "You—you in your old doublet and ancient cap, with your face begrimed—why would Justin Lisle have shared a table with you?" His hands clenched into fists. This foolish maid might have spoiled all his plans. "He must have seen through your clumsy disguise, and sought to learn more of you."

Kat shook her head. "We had quarreled when we first met, and he came to our table to apologize."

Sparrow listened, appalled, while Kat described her first encounter with the baron. He could think of nothing further from the discreet, unnoticed observation he had wanted from her brother . . . who would now also be suspected by Lord Harwood, simply because he had been with this Amazon.

" 'Tis beyond hope that you could have learned aught of use to us about Lord Harwood after this," he said bitterly to Nick. "Think you that anyone conspiring against the queen, if faced with such a spectacle as this"—he pointed to Kat—"would risk a meeting with another plotter? Nay, he would have sent him off, with a few words, or a signal. Your sea captain was no more than that."

"But he spoke Spanish!" Kat said. She came toward Sparrow, then stopped when he took a step back. "I heard him. Once, when we walked past the door of Lord Harwood's chamber, returning to Nick's room. And again—"

"And you know Spanish well enough to be certain when you hear it?"

"She and I studied with the same tutor," Nick said, "a man who had traveled in Castile and knew the language well. He praised Kat often for her command of Spanish."

"Did he?" asked Sparrow sarcastically. To Kat: "And what, pray tell, did you think you heard this Spaniard from Devonshire say?"

She hesitated, wetting her lips nervously, before responding. " 'Madre de Dios'—that is, 'Mother of God,' he said, 'esto no lo sufro' . . . which means 'I cannot suffer this.' "

"Nor can I," Sparrow muttered.

"Then he said 'la reina,' which means 'the queen' . . ."

"And?"

"I heard no more then."

"So that was all? Even if you heard that correctly, 'tis nothing. No more, belike, than a parroting of something that was said to him, or, perchance, part of some story about a Spaniard that he—"

" 'Twas a lengthy story, then," she said, interrupting, "for he was still speaking in Spanish when I returned to listen outside the chamber later. And he spoke no more in Spanish after my presence was discovered."

"You were found there?" He shook his head again. "This is much too much. You had as lief carried a placard announcing your business, and rung a bell to draw attention to it."

The girl's face grew red with anger. "He knew me not."

"His memory was wondrously poor."

"Nay, sirrah, for if you would hold your tongue for the space of a minute, you would learn that I had returned to the gallery outside his chamber after disguising myself as a servingmaid—"

"I might hear it, but why would I believe it? I have heard of bands of strolling players who traveled with fewer costumes."

" 'Twas the garb of a servingmaid at the inn, who"—she glanced at Nick—"who was sleeping then. With my face heavily painted, I looked in no wise like the youth Lisle had seen before. And mark me: I heard Henry Malcomb speak in Spanish again."

"And what said your Spaniard from the West Country this time?"

"He said, 'I would prefer that . . .' And then I heard no more, for he spoke too softly. 'Tis but little, I confess, but it was in Spanish."

Sparrow snorted. "Women. 'Twas all too accurately written that those of your sex are 'weak, frail, impatient, feeble, foolish, inconstant, variable, cruel and lacking the spirit of counsel and regiment.' Most especially lacking the spirit of counsel, in your case. Aye, and impatient and foolish, too."

He turned to go, but Kat, to his amazement, moved forward swiftly to seize his arm. "I, too, have read the *First Blast of the Trumpet Against* the *Monstrous Regiment of Women*," she said furiously. "Do not forget that the queen disliked it so much that she forbade John Knox to come into England from Scotland. Would she welcome hearing that her servants refer to Knox to disparage her own sex?"

Gazing at her livid face, Sparrow felt afraid of these children for the first time. As gentry, they had access to the court; any stories they told might reach the queen's ear. He had once, while in Walsingham's company, met the queen, and she had greeted him courteously before he took his leave a few moments later. But he was of humble birth, and though he served Walsingham—and might, in some dispute, be able to count on his support—Sparrow could not forget that not even Sir William Cecil himself had been able to help John Knox. It mattered not that the Scottish Protestant divine's vitriolic pamphlet had been directed against Elizabeth's Catholic sister Mary and the other female Catholic monarchs of Europe, and that Knox had aided the cause of the Protestant Elizabeth and had later told Cecil in a letter that he excepted Elizabeth from the failings of others of her sex: Knox remained *persona non grata* in England.

He thought quickly.

"Would the queen welcome learning how you have interfered with her intelligencers, lady? I think not." He yanked his arm free of her grasp, then swung around to face her brother. "I shall be in touch with you later . . . should your help be required." And he stalked away, oblivious of his pleasant surroundings, conscious of nothing for the moment but his contempt for Katherine Langdon.

Kat watched silently until Sparrow was gone from sight, then turned to Nick, who wore an expression of dismay. She shrugged and tried—unsuccessfully—to smile. "A choleric humor, in sooth. He would do well to avoid hot spices and wine, and purge himself with wild hops and rhubarb."

Nick continued to look dismayed. Finally he said, "We should have told him that Lisle planned to meet with Henry Malcomb again."

"Why? So that he would know that Lord Harwood plans to buy more Turkey carpets? God's blood, Nick, you heard what he thought of our intelligence." Sparrow's remarks had stung her. She knew that there were men who held women in complete contempt, but her father and brother had shielded her from them.

"Y'are right. He would not have heeded us." He looked in the direction Sparrow had gone, his expression so forlorn that Kat regretted her decision to follow him to the Jerusalem Tree. She did not believe that Lisle had seen through her disguises and so had become wary of them and of other possible spies, but it was clear that Sparrow believed

it and now thought even less of Nick. *Not that he showed much respect
to Nick before*, she thought, remembering the conversation she had overheard.

Somewhat cheered by the thought that she was not solely responsible for any problems Nick had with Sparrow, she took her brother's
hand. "Come. You promised me a fencing lesson this afternoon, and
another after supper."

"Hold, Kat!"

Poised to deliver a *punta riversa*, she froze, fully aware of her brother
for the first time since they had begun to practice that evening. She
had concentrated only on his movements as they fenced. Now she noticed that he was sweating freely, and that he limped slightly as he
walked over to the table where the servants had left a flagon of ale for
them. He had been able to walk without a limp earlier, when he first
met Sparrow and was undecided whether to tell the little spy of his fight
with the player.

"Cry you mercy, Nick. I had not meant to press you so."

He laughed, but the sound was not a happy one. "I had never
thought you must needs make such an apology. Nor would you have,
Kat, were I fully recovered—or were you not fighting as one faced with
a demon. Did you take me for Sparrow just now?"

Kat smiled ruefully. She had, indeed, been thinking of the offensive
little man.

"Is there any ale left?" she asked, sheathing her sword.

She had hoped the exercise would help distract her from thoughts
of their meeting with Sparrow that afternoon, but it had not worked for
her. Neither, she now realized, had the practice distracted Nick.

"Shall we go to London?" she asked. "We could send a letter to
Will tomorrow, and leave in a few days, for I would send the carts off
a day or two early rather than travel at their pace. 'Twould be long
enough, would it not, for your leg to heal so you could bear the ride? I
would not have you make the journey in a litter." Her remark brought
a laugh from him, and this time it was genuinely merry, which pleased
her. "We could postpone all fencing practices, if that would help you
heal more quickly."

He nodded, and she thought she saw a look of relief in his eyes.
"But will you continue to fence with the empty air, alone in your chamber?"

"You were told of that?"

"By the steward."

"And you did not mind?"

"At first I doubted the wisdom of your solitary practice . . . but then your strength, and your skill, have improved so quickly . . ."

Kat could not help but smile with pleasure at his compliment. "I would like to continue our practice in London, but what would Blanche say?"

"Nothing, if she believes that I am practicing fencing with Walter, and you are merely watching. But you may find you have no time for such practice, with all of London to entertain you, and, mayhap, a new suitor."

"Mayhap . . ." She leaned back against the table, looking out the windows on the opposite side of the gallery. Sunlight still burnished the tops of the garden walls, but the garden itself was in shadow except for the few tall trees that were crowned with the reddish light. Although her trip to London might bring an end to her life at Beechwood, she felt content for the moment. Only one small matter—very small, i'faith; a few inches shorter than herself—still troubled her. "But what of Sparrow?" she asked. "What if he comes here to speak to you?"

"Then he can fly back to London again," Nick said lightly, and she knew he was beginning to put their problems with the little man behind him.

CHAPTER 9

Three days later, with Walter and Louise following them, Kat and Nick rode away from Beechwood, north across the downs toward London. They traveled swiftly. It had not rained for several days, and though the roads were often tangled skeins of dried ruts, the ground to either side usually provided safe and solid footing for their horses. Kat had not taken the Blackamoor: that temperamental steed had been judged an unwise choice for London's crowded streets. *Nor,* Nick had said, *would you want to trust the beast to the ostlers at the inn where Will keeps his horses.* Instead Kat rode her father's reliable dapple-gray Neapolitan, while Nick rode his favorite, a roan Barbary gelding.

Kat had not been out riding for several days, and she exulted in this ride. The day was bright and warm, and all around them were the signs of spring ripening into summer. The forests of oak and beech were lush with new leaves. They passed gardens bright with French marigolds and honeysuckle, blush pinks and roses, and stopped once to admire a late-blooming lilac. By midday, when they stopped to dine on the cold mutton and bread and ale that they had brought with them from Beechwood, they were more than halfway to the inn that was their destination that day.

There had been no sign of the carts they had sent ahead with their baggage. Nick, who had traveled much more than Kat and had more than once overtaken carts he had sent ahead that had become mired in the road, could scarcely believe their good fortune.

"They may yet reach London before us," he said, then laughed. "Not that it would matter, good Kat, if our clothes failed to reach London at all. You must have a new wardrobe for the city and the court . . . and so must I."

"Last year's suits will not do?"

"Nay, for fashions change too swiftly."

Kat shook her head. Nick's addiction to the most fashionable clothing had caused many an argument with their father. "Do what you will, Nick. I shall not turn fashionmonger. You cannot force me to do so."

"Perchance not I, but London will. Mark me. You must needs have new suits to attract new suitors."

It was not the first time in the last few days that Nick had casually spoken of Kat finding a husband while in London. She had learned to act as though he had said nothing upsetting to her, but she still had some difficulty responding lightly, and she had less to say that afternoon than she had that morning, and pleaded weariness when he finally noticed and asked what was the matter.

" 'Tis but a few miles further to the Three Swans," he assured her.

She did not know the inn, but Nick had stopped there often on his journeys to and from London. It lay some fifteen miles east of the Jerusalem Tree: that had been distance enough to ensure that Nick was not known there two weeks ago, and she prayed that tales of his stay there—and descriptions of him—had not reached the Three Swans.

They had ridden less than a mile further when they heard a horn sounded in the distance.

"Some postboy, belike," Nick said, "making a show of speed when he leaves the inn. I warrant he'll be going at a slow amble before we meet him."

But the postboy was riding at a hard gallop when he came into sight soon after that. He swept past them without slowing, and Kat saw that he was spurring his mount constantly. Nick turned around to shout cheerfully after him, "Haste, post, haste! Haste for life!" He turned back to Kat. "He'll kill his horse before he reaches the next post stage," he said, and though he still sounded amused, she thought he looked somewhat worried.

She, too, felt uneasy. What could have caused such haste? What news?

That was the first question Nick asked of the host of the Three Swans when he came to greet them, and the answer Master Wiley gave stunned them.

"The queen has been excommunicated," the innkeeper said. " 'Tis in a bull from the pope. 'Twas found posted on the Bishop of London's gate in Paul's Yard yesterday morning."

Kat's eyes met Nick's over Master Wiley's head, and she could have sworn that he shared her thought. Did Lisle have knowledge of this?

"And the queen's good Catholic subjects?" Nick asked in a taut voice. Kat was sure she understood the reason for his tension. Were a rebellion to begin now, there would be danger for them in staying at an inn hosted by a Catholic . . . and they did not know Master Wiley's religion.

The innkeeper snorted. "They're good subjects only if they disobey the pope, for Brother Woodenshoe has absolved them of their oaths of loyalty. He has declared Elizabeth no longer a queen and has commanded English Catholics not to obey her laws. All those who stay faithful to the queen are themselves excommunicate."

Brother Woodenshoe. Kat had often heard the derisive nickname for the former Dominican friar, but no Catholic would speak thus of Pope Pius V. They were safe here.

"Pray God, they will not heed him," she said, dismounting easily without the help of an ostler. Turning to their servants, she saw an expression of anguish on Louise's face. "They should not, after the failure of the rising in the—" she began, meaning to reassure the maid, but she was interrupted by Master Wiley.

"Pray God as well, that Spain and France will not send their armies now," he said, and was answered by a wail from Louise.

Kat looked imploringly at Nick, who took the innkeeper aside to arrange for their rooms, then led the entire party upstairs. Louise was crying all the while about "Jack Spaniard." Kat knew that her maid's family, staunch Protestants even during Mary's reign, had bred in Louise this fear of the Spanish, but still she was annoyed and rather snappish as she set the maid about the task of unpacking their cloakbags and neatening the already tidy chamber.

She wished she could have gone downstairs with Nick, to hear the talk in the common room, but the din they had heard from there even outside the door had persuaded Nick that it was no place for his sister. "And Louise needs you," he had said, and had ordered food brought to their chamber. So she sat watching her maid while disordered thoughts churned through her mind, whirling like dancers around a Maypole, bound together by only one central figure: Justin Lisle.

Had Lisle known? Her hands shook as she thought of what part he might have played in the plots surrounding the queen. Was he even now rousing his papist neighbors in Hampshire to a rebellion that might succeed where their northern countrymen had failed? Now she rued her inability to do him harm, when she could have seized his dagger and used it against him. Far better to have killed him then, if he were involved in this. She began to understand Sparrow's anger when he thought they might have been clumsy enough to alert Lord Harwood to the spies about him. She prayed that they had not, that there was still time for the queen's intelligencers to locate her enemies and eliminate them.

She could still hear the low babble of voices from downstairs when the door opened and Nick came in.

"How now, Nick? What news?"

"No more news of substance than our host told us, but a hundred airy rebellions and invasions. At least there seems no danger of immediate rebellion in London. Or so said a merchant who left the city this morning. As for what news the post carries . . ." He shrugged. Not even the innkeeper, the postman at this stage, dared open the packet containing the official letters from the court.

"So we are not returning home?"

Nick shook his head. "I would be in London, and know all the news, and quickly." He looked at Kat's untouched plate. "You should eat. I would leave early tomorrow, and we will not stop until we reach London. You'll need your strength." He smiled of a sudden. "Do not look so frightened, Kat. I doubt there is much to fear in this"—his gaze slid to Louise, and Kat knew the reassurance was meant for her maid—"but I would reach London as soon as possible, and learn more."

It was early in the afternoon when they rode up Long Southwark, the high street running north through the borough of Southwark toward London Bridge. Kat was still anxious, though she kept her feelings to herself. She was tired from the long ride, and hungry, too, for they had not eaten since breaking their fast with cold meats and ale before leaving the inn at dawn. But now she forgot all other concerns in the wonder of the sights around her.

They rode past Long Lane, which ran east from the high street across the fields of Bermondsey Abbey. Just past Long Lane was St. George's, a once beautiful church that was falling into disrepair. Nick pointed out the many small cottages across the high street from the church.

"There stood the house of the Duke of Suffolk, which he built during King Henry's reign. 'Twas taken over by the Crown, and Queen Mary gave it to the Archbishop of York, who sold it to a merchant. That is what he made of it. Those who rent the cottages are charged dearly, but then they are thieves and rogues who are wont to resort here."

Kat shook her head. Nick had told her that London was as patched as a fool's motley, with thieves living next door to priests, but she had scarcely believed it, till now.

The buildings directly north of St. George's reinforced what he had told her.

"That is the White Lion," Nick said. " 'Twas once an inn, but now 'tis a prison. The next is the prison of the King's Bench, and then Marshalsea prison." Kat could see arms outstretched from some of the windows, and hear pleas for alms and food from the prisoners within. She was glad to put the prisons behind them as they rode past a line of inns.

There were too many to remember: the Spur, the Bull, the Christopher, the Queen's Head, the King's Head, and others whose names she quickly forgot. They stopped for a few moments at the Tabard, the most ancient of the inns, with its famous sign depicting a sleeveless herald's coat.

The middle of the wide street—where Nick told her a fair was held in September—was now a marketplace, clogged with sellers and their carts and baskets. "Oatcakes! Fine oatcakes!" cried a woman in gray serge, and Kat would fain have stopped, were it not that Nick continued onward. "What d'ye lack?" was the common chorus, but the individual cries shot through it:

"Matting! Good matting for your floors!"

"Soused eels! Caught just this morning!"

"Lettuce for your salad! Tender lettuce!"

Kat spurred her horse forward to catch up with Nick. They passed a pillory and a cage, empty now of caitiffs—"But not often," Nick assured her—in the middle of the street. To their right was the aptly named Thieves' Lane, running past St. Thomas's Hospital to the meadows of east Southwark. To their left, as they rode down the market hill, was a district of churches and churchmen's palaces, and Nick pointed out what he could from the high street. There was the parish church of St. Savior's, which had once been part of the monastery of St. Mary Overy. North of that, across Pepper Alley, was Montague Close, once a prior's house but now occupied by the Catholic Lord Montague; west lay the palace of the Bishop of Winchester, with its several courts and the great hall with its famous east window, said to be the finest in England. South of the palace lay the Bishop of Rochester's house, which was in ruins. West of that was again the Southwark of infamy: a stream with a ducking stool, the prison of the Clink, and then the brothel houses that the Crown had once licensed, and Bankside with its bear- and bull-baiting, and Paris Garden. Kat knew that Nick spent much more time there than in the churches of Southwark, or even its inns— and he always kept a hand on his purse, so he said, and an eye on any stranger who approached him.

They were near the bridge foot now, and the noise of the water rushing beneath the bridge drowned out most other sounds. Nick rode close beside her while he pointed out the parish church of St. Olave's, within a stone's throw of the bridge on the east side of Long Southwark. "There are many Flemings in the parish now," he shouted. "They have settled here in Southwark, many of those who fled the Spanish armies."

Kat nodded. She had already met a number of Flemings who had escaped the Netherlands during the past few years, fleeing the Spanish reign of terror there, the Duke of Alva's Council of Blood.

They stopped for a drink at the Bear Tavern, the last house on the west side of the high street before they reached the foot of London Bridge. Inside, away from the roar of the Thames and the din of the street cries, it was possible to talk more quietly. Kat was impressed with all she had seen so far of London, but the image that stuck in her mind was that of the prisons, with their alms-begging inhabitants. Clearly those prisons were already as full as the inns they had ridden past. What would happen if they suddenly had to jail hundreds—even thousands— of religious prisoners, Catholics pushed to rebellion by the pope? Would they then turn out all the other prisoners?

Nick roared with laughter when she asked the question aloud. "Heaven help us if they do," he said, then, noticing that Louise was again becoming alarmed, added quickly, "But I see no sign of rebellion here. Think of all the carts and sellers we saw. See yon merchant, with the fat purse that he would do well to conceal before some cutpurse separates him from the profits he made in the city? I have rarely seen Long Southwark busier, except during a fair. All's well, in truth."

Indeed, as they crossed the bridge half an hour later, they saw no freshly chopped pates among the traitors' heads displayed above the tower on the gate north of the drawbridge dividing Southwark from the City of London. Nick looked disappointed, and called to her that he hoped to see at least one new head there soon, following the execution of who- ever had brought that papal bull into London and posted it on the bishop's gate.

Gazing up at the heads stuck on pikes, Kat wondered if Lisle's head would soon be among them. Or would he, as a nobleman, be given a more seemly punishment? She could ask Nick—but would her voice betray her? For all that she would wish Justin Lisle punished, if he proved to be a traitor, she shuddered at the thought of that head—that carefully barbered head, with that handsome face—stuck up there on a pike with the other grisly reminders of treason, its fair flesh a banquet for the scavenging red kites.

She shook her head, tearing her gaze away from the skulls.

Ahead of them the way narrowed again. Tall houses lined both sides of London Bridge, sometimes meeting overhead and plunging the road into darkness. People thronged the narrow way, their cries and the bel- lows of animals melded into an echoing din. She preferred the open drawbridge, though the roar of the water below reached them more clearly here.

She dismounted and walked to the east edge of the drawbridge. Looking back the way they had come, she admired the fair houses, built there over several of the great arches that were, Nick had told her, some sixty feet high and thirty feet across. Counting the drawbridge, he had said, there were twenty arches, twenty feet apart. She tried to calculate the length of the bridge, but gave it up: the din was too great to think clearly. Instead she gazed out across the Thames, across the Pool of London, with the spires of the boats moored there rising like some grove of strange branchless trees; and beyond the masts, past much of the city on the north bank, the domed turrets of the Tower of London.

Would Lisle be imprisoned there?

Annoyed that she could not expel him from her thoughts, she turned and led her horse back across the drawbridge to stand on its western edge. For a time she gazed northwest at London, admiring in silence the fair buildings with their red tile roofs . . . and there on its hill, dominating all about it, the enormous, spireless structure that was St. Paul's Cathedral. It was imposing enough without the spire, for the blunt stone steeple soared to a height of two hundred sixty feet, high above all the other roofs of London. But until nine years ago the church had been crowned by a spire ascending another two hundred sixty feet, topped by a huge weathercock, a copper-sheathed cross surmounted by a four-foot-long eagle of gilded copper. Lightning had struck the spire, destroying it and doing great damage to the steeple and the body of the cathedral. All that damage had since been repaired, but the spire had never been rebuilt, and Kat thought wistfully that she would have liked to have visited London at least once with their father, to have seen the spire then. Henry Langdon had told them of it, and had sent ten pounds to London to aid in the repair of the cathedral, one of the few things about London that he had admired.

"Look, Kat!" Nick cried, his mouth close to her ear so she could hear him over the roar of the Thames.

He was pointing downward, to where a waterman guided his boat toward one of the arches. At the best of times, the waters were dangerous enough where they swirled treacherously about the wooden starlings that had been built around the stone piers to protect them from the force of the current and any objects it swept along. But this was ebb tide, and the starlings so blocked the flow of the Thames that the water, backed up, formed a waterfall of a few feet at the bridge. Kat half expected to see the waterman's boat smash against one of the starlings, but somehow he kept it guided directly beneath the arch as it vanished from sight. *Shooting the Bridge*, this was called, and she had noticed without surprise that the waterman had no passengers. Were he taking anyone down the Thames, they would likely have disembarked at the water stairs west of London Bridge and walked to another water stairs east of the bridge before boarding again.

Unable to restrain her curiosity, she pushed through the throng to the east side of the drawbridge again, in time to see the waterman, who had somehow kept from capsizing, guide his craft toward the bank. So he did have passengers waiting . . .

"Kat, you must try that!" Nick said excitedly, and she recalled how he had once shot the bridge with some friends who were, like himself, drunken after a day in Southwark.

She looked at him cynically. "Have you not told me, sweet brother, that 'tis said that London Bridge is made for wise men to go over and fools to go under?"

"Yes, but who enjoys the trip more?"

She shook her head but could not help but smile. In truth, it had looked like an exciting ride, for all the danger.

They resumed their crossing of the bridge then, and were again closed in by the impressive houses on either side.

"Who lives here?" she called to Nick.

"Haberdashers and mercers," he replied. "And all London comes here to buy pins—as will you, sister, if you lose as many in London as you lost in Sussex."

She groaned. He had often teased her about how the pins she used to fasten bodice to half-kirtle, and sleeves to doublet or bodice or gown, tended to vanish, so that it was rare when Louise did not discover at least one pin missing after a day's wear of some garment. The maid complained that her mistress was too active, and suggested that Kat use hooks to fasten her garments instead, but Kat had demurred: pins were faster, and hooks, too, came undone.

"By my faith, Nick, 'tis a sore point with me," she called to him.

"Aye, and a sharp one made by me," he said, and she groaned again.

Leaving the bridge, they rode up Fish Street Hill, with its fishmarket, then at the top of the hill turned west into Great Eastcheap, with its butchers' and cooks' shops lining the street. Smelling roast beef, Kat realized again that she was famished, and when an urchin came toward her with a basket of meat pies, she would have stopped, had not Nick wanted to press on to the Gardiners' home by Fleet Street.

From Eastcheap they rode along Watling Street toward St. Paul's. Nick debated aloud whether to enter the churchyard by the Augustine gate in its eastern wall, so called for the church of St. Augustine at the end of Watling Street, but finally decided to avoid the bustle of Paul's Yard. They rode south again, around the churchyard, and then north up Creed Lane to Bowyer Row. There, by the west gate of St. Paul's, an acquaintance of Nick's hailed him.

"Nick! Have you heard what Brother Woodenshoe has done?"

"Aye, we heard when we reached the Three Swans. The news had traveled that far by yesterday."

" 'Tis said the queen is greatly perturbed and has kept to her chambers since hearing of the bull."

Nick glanced warily at Louise. "Indeed. Tomorrow we shall speak of this, but now I must needs bring my sister to my cousin's house by Fleet Street."

The man stared with interest at Kat, who met his gaze calmly. She knew that she looked well enough, dressed in white hose and an artfully fitted doublet of carnation silk. Finally he smiled. "Bring her with you tomorrow, too," he said to Nick, then turned back to a group of brilliantly clad gentlemen who had been trying to get his attention.

Nick rode on, though Kat wished with all her heart that they could have stopped. She had heard so much of Paul's, and nowhere but at the court could one learn more of the news of the realm. But she knew that Nick was being sensible. They were all tired, and her trusty old Neapolitan gelding, which had behaved quite well until they reached Watling Street, had finally become overwhelmed by the tumult about them. It shied at a cart that lumbered past, its metal-rimmed wheels clangorous on the cobblestones. It shied again when a youth clad in the blue garb of an apprentice ran past, and then again when a water carrier spilled water into their path from the huge tankard he bore on his shoulder. It tried to rear when the bells began to ring in a nearby church, and when two beggars surged toward them, holding their clack-dishes out and crying "Alms, good people, alms!" the gelding bucked, almost tossing Kat from the saddle. They were near Ludgate then, just within the west wall of the city, but though the street was yet more busy there, Kat stopped and tried to calm her horse while the traffic parted to flow around her, like the waters of the Thames around a starling under London Bridge.

Nick made his way over to her with some difficulty.

"Shall I lead you the rest of the way?" he asked.

She shook her head. It would not help. If the gelding reared or bucked again, she wanted more control than she would have if Nick held her reins. She patted the horse's neck, noticing how its flesh quivered beneath her touch.

"Perhaps I could walk," she said, but Nick shook his head, pointing down at the street. The cobblestones were slimy with refuse. Whoever chose to walk in London, she thought, would do well to stand on the thick cork soles of pantofles. She had no desire to ruin her good leather boots by walking through that muck.

Finally she decided that the gelding was calm enough to move forward again, and they rode through the gate and down Ludgate Hill, across the bridge over stinking Fleet Ditch, and down Fleet Street. They had crossed Fleet Ditch as fast as possible to avoid the reek of the stream that flowed along the westernmost wall of the city, but Nick still slowed, after they crossed the bridge, to point out to her, to their left, near the Thames, the beautiful palace of Bridewell, which King Henry had built half a century earlier to house the nobles who had accompanied the Emperor Charles V on his visit to England, and which his son King Edward had given to the mayor of London to be used as a workhouse for the poor and idle of London, who might be less offended by the stench of Fleet Ditch.

They passed the water conduit built where Shoe Lane intersected Fleet Street from the north, and paused so Kat could admire the tower over the cistern, with its images of angels and St. Christopher. Then they rode on, toward the Gardiners' house on Fewter Lane by Fleet Street.

Nick had told her that Will Gardiner had bought a house here chiefly because of its location between Westminster and the City of London: had the location not been so desirable, he would have chosen a quieter neighborhood. Kat could well believe it, as they rode past busy taverns and printers' shops. Here there were jugglers and puppeteers, and one could find freak shows, too: Nick had once paid a penny to see a two-headed calf, but his money had been returned after he had complained that the stitches where the second head was sewn to the calf's body were visible from several feet away.

What Kat found difficult to believe was that Blanche Gardiner—quiet, pious Blanche—could be happy in this street that seemed even today like a boisterous fair. But then, Nick had said that she did not want to be far from the city and the prophesyings where she could meet with other Puritans. Perhaps she would change her mind, now that she was with child . . .

Kat nearly rode past Nick before she noticed that he had stopped. He was looking up at a fair stone house, four stories tall, with many tall, mullioned windows.

"This is it?" she asked, and as he nodded, she felt the weariness after the long journey, which had felt like a cloak of lead on her shoulders, drop away in an instant.

Inside, they found welcome and comfort.

Though the Gardiners' house lay a good distance from Fleet Ditch, Blanche took care to keep the air sweet by burning perfumes in censers. The tables and chests were covered with fine Turkey carpets, and all chairs were padded with cushions of embroidered velvet or gilded leather. Venetian glass, Majolica ware and gold plate were displayed on the sideboards, and one cabinet held Will's collection of old Roman coins. He had inherited many of the coins from his grandfather, who had begun to collect them after seeing Sir Thomas More's collection of ancient coins, and though Will was still wont to tell visitors of the collection's origins, Blanche tactfully overlooked his references to the papist.

Will and Blanche showed them through the house while their servants laid out a late dinner in the parlor. For Nick and Kat they had prepared the two larger bedchambers on the top floor, rooms they often leased to courtiers who needed lodgings near the court. From what Nick had told her, Kat knew that they used the rents from the two bedchambers to help offset the expense of maintaining a household in London— Will had extensive holdings in Suffolk that brought him a good income, but he also maintained a fine new house there. Kat was feeling troubled by the thought of the expense their visit meant for the Gardiners, until Will, answering an artless question from Nick, told them that the courtier who had been leasing the bedchambers for himself and his servants had become ill and had gone home to Kent to recover. "Not the plague, or any such pestilence," Blanche quickly assured them, "but terrible gout from a surfeit of rich food and drink."

The cart they had sent ahead had arrived that morning, and the chests of their belongings had been carried upstairs. Louise and Walter were already unpacking, putting their clothes in the ambries and presses and large cypress chests. Kat noticed that Blanche was looking at her wardrobe carefully, but before she could ask what was the matter, one of the Gardiners' servants came to tell them all was ready in the parlor.

The dinner was an excellent one: chickens and veal with well-seasoned dressings and sauces, a salad, early strawberries with cream, oranges, cheese, and bread and butter. The bread, a fine white manchet, was not baked in the house, Kat learned, but purchased—"Too dearly," Will complained cheerfully—from a baker in the city. There were also Naples biscuits that Blanche had bought from a confectioner, and the musk and violet comfits she had made herself. Sated, they watched the servants clear the dishes from the table while they sipped at their drinks: beer for Nick, and Will's favorite, Rhenish wine, for Kat.

For some time after the servants had left, there was silence in the parlor. Will, a stocky, ruddy-faced man dressed in doublet and hose of purple velvet faced with gray satin, had monopolized the conversation until now, welcoming them, showing them around the house, then hosting their dinner. He had said nothing yet of the papal bull, and Kat, for her part, had been reluctant to spoil the warmth of their welcome by bringing up such an unpleasant subject. Nick, she was certain, felt the same. But now Will stared at them for a time, and then said, his eyes twinkling:

"Would you rather go to your rooms and rest, or speak of what Brother Woodenshoe has done? I'll warrant you have learned discretion at last, Nick, for I know you must be eager to hear the latest gossip."

"Will, you may assume too much, if you assume that they have heard the news already," Blanche said gently. Kat looked at her curiously. Unless Blanche drew her loose gown of tawny silk more tightly about her, it was impossible to tell that her body was already swollen with the child she carried. Yet there were lines of strain on Blanche's thin, pretty face: from this pregnancy, Kat wondered, or from this terrible news?

"We heard talk of nothing else when we stopped at the Three Swans yesterday," Nick said.

"*You* heard the talk, good brother," Kat corrected, "while I perforce stayed upstairs in the bedchamber to keep Louise calm, when I would liefer have been in the common room with you."

Will turned to Kat and raised an eyebrow. "I had thought you more like your father. Does politics interest you, in sooth?"

"More than you will ever know," she said fiercely, and Nick gave her a warning glance before adding smoothly:

"This news concerns all."

"That it does," Will said, nodding. "How much have you heard?"

He listened soberly while Nick recounted what they had learned at the inn and from the man who had hailed them near Paul's, then nodded again.

"You have the pith and marrow of it," he told them. "A friend of mine will be bringing me a copy of the bull this evening. 'Tis said it was promulgated in Rome in February." He smiled fleetingly. " 'Twas intended to help the rebel earls."

"Late help," Nick commented, "as good as none. Then this is not tied to any current plot?"

"None that is noised abroad," Will responded, and Kat suppressed an urge to glance at Nick. She was sure he would not want Will and Blanche to know of the mission Sparrow had sent him on. "But no one knows what may spring from this. There is nothing but speculation."

" 'A hundred airy rebellions and invasions,' " Kat murmured, looking at Nick then.

"A thousand," Will agreed. "But so far the bull has produced nothing but an outcry against the pope."

"Who posted the bull?"

"One John Felton. With the citizens in a fury yesterday, there was a general search, and a copy of the bull was found in the room of a student at Lincoln's Inn, who said—"

"Which proves again," Blanche interjected, "that something must be done about the influence of papists in the Inns of Court."

Kat glanced at Nick, who had winced at Blanche's remark. She hoped he would not get into an argument with their cousin, yet she knew he was vexed by such comments about the Inns, "which have produced," he often said sarcastically, "such notable papists as Sir William Cecil and Francis Walsingham."

After a long look at his wife, Will continued, "This student said he had obtained the copy of the bull from Felton, whose wife was a maid of honor to Queen Mary."

Kat closed her eyes for a moment. Had not Nick said that Lisle's cousin, too, had been a maid of honor to Queen Elizabeth's sister?

"And have they arrested him?" Nick asked.

Will nodded. "He lives at Bermondsey Abbey. The lord mayor and two sheriffs went there, and with their men surrounded his house. He gave himself up."

"And no doubt pleads innocent," Nick said bitterly.

Will shook his head. "He has confessed already."

"He'll die for this," Kat said.

"And be a martyr for his cause," Will said in a dour tone. "And the Spanish ambassador, who many believe gave the bull to Felton, will be left to make more mischief, unless Felton names him . . ." He sighed.

A heavy silence enveloped the room.

"A plague on this gloom!" Blanche said suddenly. " 'Twill do none of us—nor the queen—one whit of good to fret over this. Will, produce your smile again! These are our guests." She took Kat's hand; the smile she turned on the younger woman was dazzling but also seemed strained, brittle. " 'Tis too long since we have seen you. You were a lovely child then, and you have become a lovely woman. But, coz," and she frowned in mock dismay, "you need new clothes!"

CHAPTER 10

"Which prefer you, Kat? The white velvet, or the ivory satin?"

Blanche's question brought Kat out of her reverie. She had been looking out the window of the Gardiners' bedchamber at the walled garden behind the house. Small but pleasant, the garden contained fir and apricot and walnut trees, with roses planted among them. There were flower beds for the marigolds and gilliflowers and matted pinks and violets that Blanche loved; an alley planted with wild thyme and water mint, whose sweet scents filled the air as they were crushed underfoot, followed the vine-covered walls. Kat had spent many hours there already—much more time there, she had been thinking ruefully, than she had spent seeing London. Brooding over what had begun to seem like a captivity, she had shut out of her awareness the room behind her, with the lengths of fine cloth and the voices of the sempsters who had been hired to work on Kat's new wardrobe, forgetting them completely until Blanche spoke loudly enough to get her attention.

Kat felt her face redden as she turned toward her cousin. Behind Blanche, the sempsters—three women and a man, the latest four of the eleven they had engaged during the past week and a half—had fallen silent and were watching her.

"The ivory satin, I trow," she said uncertainly. What garment had Blanche meant? A bodice? A kirtle? A pair of sleeves, or a gown, or a cloak? She was too ashamed to ask, humiliated that she could have so rudely ignored her cousin when Blanche had so tirelessly set about helping Kat acquire the clothes she would need in London and at court.

Blanche stared at her intently for a few moments, and then smiled: a slow, sympathetic smile. "I would agree that ivory satin would be best for these sleeves," she said, obviously aware of Kat's confusion. "Now, if you have them cut so . . ."

With an effort, Kat brought her attention back to the trivial details of fashion. She might have had more interest in this, she thought ironically, if she had herself seen more of the elegantly dressed courtiers who could be found at St. Paul's, but she had been there only twice in the twelve days since their arrival, each time to hear the Sunday

117

morning sermon preached from Paul's Cross, the lead-roofed stone pulpit in the churchyard north of the cathedral. Many of London's citizens came to these sermons, including the lord mayor, but with Blanche standing beside her, Kat had not felt free to look around and study the newest fashions of London. She had left the house with Blanche a few other times, to buy fabrics from drapers in Watling Street and haberdashers on London Bridge, but on those trips Kat had been unable to enjoy the sights of the city, for Blanche insisted on traveling in a coach which so jolted and swayed that Kat had to concentrate on staying in her seat. Deprived of personal knowledge of fashion, she was forced to rely on advice from Blanche and the sempsters they had hired. 'Twas fortunate, she thought, that Blanche was still interested in fashion, unlike other Puritans.

Blanche had turned out to be unlike other Puritans in many ways, as Kat and Nick had discovered to their relief.

The differences were not in Blanche's feelings about the English Church, its teachings and practices. She was as zealous as any other Puritan in her desire to reform the church, so she went as often as possible to prophesyings, meetings where clergy and laymen prayed and heard sermons and discussed the Scripture before the clergy met in private to discuss doctrine and advise and correct each other—meetings that were increasingly dominated by Puritans. Then, too, Blanche would read only from the Geneva Bible, published two years after Elizabeth's accession. Its principal author, William Whittingham, had become an exile in Geneva during Mary Tudor's reign and had stayed there, even after her death, until he had finished his translation of the Bible and the commentaries that were strongly influenced by Calvin's teachings. The English bishops, not approving of the Geneva Bible's Calvinist tone, had brought out their own Bible two years ago, but Blanche refused to buy a copy.

Within her own house, however, Blanche felt free to ignore many of the strictures the more zealous Puritans placed on their private lives. She did insist that all under her roof speak with respect of those of her faith: Kat and Nick had quickly learned that they could not use the word "Puritans," but only "Precisians," or better—to Blanche's ears— "the godly." Beyond that, however, the Gardiner household was much like any other. Though Blanche, to Will's regret, no longer attended plays herself, she never showed disapproval when Nick spoke of them. Nor did she say anything about Nick's more licentious activities when he alluded to them . . . and Kat was not sure she was glad of this, for she would fain have lectured Nick herself, but knew he would simply tease her for being more pure than a Puritan. Will's fear that his wife's religious zeal might mean that only psalms would be welcome in his house, and that there would be no more madrigals, had proven to be unfounded. The Gardiners still played music and sang, and sometimes hired musicians to play while they taught Kat the dances she had had little opportunity to practice in the country but would need at court: the pavane, the galliard, the lavolta, the coranto and the brawl. And late in the evening they would play at cards: gleek and primero, noddy and God-make-them-rich. Blanche appeared to see nothing wrong with such innocent pleasures, and Kat suspected that her cousin would even have attended plays, were she not fearful of being observed there by some other Puritan who would denounce her at one of the prophesyings.

While Blanche and the sempsters discussed the best pattern for pinking the ivory satin sleeves to reveal the black taffeta lining, Kat wandered over to a shelf of books. There was Blanche's copy of the *Book of Martyrs*, bound even more elegantly than Anne's. Blanche was eagerly awaiting the new edition of the book, of which she had regular news from the printer, John Day; the new *Book of Martyrs* would be two volumes totaling twenty-three hundred pages, and Blanche had excitedly told them last night at supper that John Foxe was writing another new preface, the third, addressed to papists and warning them that the pope's actions against the queen were contrary to Scripture. Next to the *Book of Martyrs* was a copy of Foxe's *Sermon of Christ crucified*, which he had preached at Paul's Cross on Good Friday. Blanche had heard him there. He had preached without text or notes of any kind, and when friends had urged him to publish the sermon, he had had to reconstruct it from memory. " 'Tis somewhat longer now," Blanche had said, but Kat had heard a note of pleasure in her voice and realized it was not a complaint.

And there, next to Foxe's sermon, were the books that Kat had been borrowing, the books that concerned the threat from Spain.

The first of these had been a gift to Blanche from a friend of hers in Southwark, an exile from the Low Countries. *A Declaration & Publication of the Prince of Orange. Contayning the cause of his necessary defense against the Duke of Alva.* Kat had read it and discussed it with Blanche, who was very concerned about the suffering of Protestants in the Low Countries; she had twice given money to her Flemish friend to send to those opposing Alva and his Council of Troubles, which had rightly become known as the Council of Blood. Below that pamphlet lay one by Reginald Gonsalvius Montanus: *A Discovery and playne Declaration of sundry subtill practises of the Holy Inquisition of Spain.* Reading that one had left Kat shivering with fear at the thought of what would happen to England if Spain should successfully invade. Blanche had told her that she would feel the same way after reading the next two books.

Kat picked them up now. Sir John Hawkins's *A true declaration of the troublesome voyage of M. J. Hawkins to the parties of Guynea and the west-Indies.* And *A True and perfect description of the last voyage or Navigation, attempted by Capitaine John Rybaut,* by Nicholas LeChalleaux. Kat had already heard some stories of Hawkins, but not until she had come to stay with the Gardiners had she heard of John Rybaut—or Jean Ribaut—the Huguenot captain whose Florida colony of French Protestants had been slaughtered by the Spanish.

She would read these next . . . and, as with the other two, she would keep them from Louise. The maid had still not ceased fretting aloud about the threat from Jack Spaniard, and needed no further encouragement. It had been all Kat and her brother could do to stop Louise from packing again a few days ago, when they first heard the rumors that William Cecil himself had packed some of his belongings to prepare for flight.

The books tucked under her arm, she went over to where Blanche was examining the intricately cut swatches of cloth the sempsters had brought with them. They finally settled on a pattern, then began to consider the new ruffs Kat would need. Blanche recommended a three-inch width of fine lawn edged with lace, but Kat was dubious that the flimsy material could be starched properly.

"My maid excels at this," Blanche assured her. "Years ago I sent her for instruction to Mistress Dinghen Vanderplasse, one of the Dutch women the queen brought over for this sort of work. None know this art better than the Dutch."

"Very well," Kat said, and would have asked if Louise, too, could study with Mistress Vanderplasse, but then an exuberant voice interrupted them.

"Holloa! What's this? I'faith, a mercer's shop!" Nick stepped into the bedchamber and looked around, his eyes wide in mock surprise. " 'Tis not only the wrong house, but the wrong street! This must be Watling, or else London Bridge! I cry you mercy"—he made a leg to the prettiest of the sempsters, who giggled behind the hand she had raised to her mouth—"but I sought my sister, and shall never find her here. No fashionmonger she, or so she claimed."

"Then it is all the more tragic that you have driven me to this, good brother, and made a liar of me," Kat said sternly.

"Nay, Kat, would I give you the lie? 'Sblood, you would run me through." The sempster giggled again. "By the mass, she would," Nick assured the girl solemnly. "You have not seen her with a good Toledo blade."

Blanche had frowned briefly at Nick's last oath; of all his oaths, she least approved of his swearing by that papist ceremony, and when he had reminded her that it was a favorite oath of the queen, too, she had simply replied, "To the jeopardy of her soul, alas." But even she could look disapproving for only a moment. Nick was merrily drunk, after no doubt spending the morning in some tavern, but not yet drunk enough to be less than enchanting; one could no more resist his exuberant good humor than one could resist a mirthful child. Kat was smiling fondly as he came up to her and took the books from her arm.

He shook his head as he read the title pages. "There's scant amusement here. You would do better, sister, to spend the rest of the day with me. Would you go to Paris Garden, and then to a bear-baiting?"

"Yea, I—" Kat had taken a step toward her brother, whom she would have hugged, but now she hesitated as she remembered Blanche. She looked warily at her cousin.

"Go," Blanche said, smiling. "You have spent long enough in this chamber today. But will you stay for dinner?"

Nick shook his head. "Thank you, but we will dine at a tavern."

Kat surveyed the cloth-strewn room, the waiting sempsters. "Coz, if you would have me stay, to finish this now . . ."

"Get you gone," her cousin said with a laugh. "I had wished myself to have the afternoon free, for there is to be a prophesying at St. Dunstan's."

"Pray come with us instead," Nick teased.

"No, good coz," Blanche said, appearing shocked, then added with a mischievous smile, "Would you not rather come with me to St. Dunstan's? 'Tis closer, just across the lane."

"Nay, sweet Blanche," he replied. "We're to Paris Garden instead, but we would have you remember us in your prayers this afternoon, for we venture into the wilds of Southwark."

Blanche shook her head, but still looked amused as they took their leave. Nick stopped to pay some silly compliment to the pretty sempster, and Kat's last glimpse of the room as they left was of the girl's blushing face.

Kat could have skipped for joy as they left the house, and would have had it not been for the thick-soled pantofles she had donned to protect her velvet slippers. " 'Tis a joy to be outside," she murmured to Nick.

"Has your stay thus far truly been so bad?" he asked, looking concerned for the first time, and she realized that his decision to take her with him to the South Bank must have been a whim and not some well-thought-out plan to rescue her from the tedium she was enduring.

"I would prefer to see more of London than what can be seen from a window overlooking Fleet Street."

"More than this?" He made a sweeping gesture with his arm. "Why, all of London can be seen here, at one time or another."

Kat could not deny the truth of that. Indeed, were she not so eager to see all of London, she might have been content to stay in the house for weeks at a time and simply watch the people who thronged Fleet Street. There was a juggler, dressed in yellow; a weary water carrier shifting his tankard on the soaked towels on his shoulder; a well-dressed middle-aged woman—belike some merchant's wife—with her little page in attendance. Yesterday she had watched a thief pulled down the street tied to the tail of a cart, as he would be carted down other streets in London to be heckled and abused by the crowd. Standing in a tavern door watching—as if daring such punishment herself—had been a woman in the flame-colored taffeta of a whore. Courtiers rode past now and then, the rich fabrics of their clothing like vivid blooms among the duller hues of the garments of the poorer folk, and at those times Kat had leaned far out the window to better observe their costumes. She had seen much in the past twelve days, but it only made her long more to see the entire city and walk among its people and sample its pleasures.

"Do you not enjoy meeting with the sempsters?" Nick asked. He sounded as though he felt somewhat guilty for having insisted that she have new clothes made.

" 'Tis necessary, so 'tis well enough," she replied, "but were it within my power, I would do thus"—she raised her hand and snapped her fingers—"and have my wardrobe appear, without all these meetings and fittings."

"By God's head, you would not! You would be tried as a witch."

"Yea, but the most elegantly garbed witch in Christendom," she replied, laughing.

Her laughter died as one of the men who had been walking just a few paces in front of them stopped and turned to stare at her. He had a thin, sour face, and his somber-hued plain garments and long, unkempt hair proclaimed him a Puritan.

She and Nick slowed and then moved to walk around the man when they realized he would not budge. Kat saw the Puritan's gaze shift to Nick and take in at once the rich clothing of a gallant; then those dark eyes again fixed on her. He opened his mouth and she was certain he would speak to them—*Pray God, he does not provoke Nick to an argument,* she thought—when his companion, who had just noticed that he had walked on alone, turned back and called, "Master Ludham?"

The Puritan glanced back at his companion—also a Puritan, Kat saw—and in that instant she felt Nick take her arm and pull her further out into the street, so others now walked between her and Ludham.

Ludham. Could that have been Thomas Ludham, then? Blanche had spoken of him, for his was one of the loudest—and harshest—voices at the prophesyings in London, as he railed against such popish practices of the English Church as the clergy's wearing of copes and surplices, the use of rings for betrothings, the use of the sign of the cross at baptisms. He had said, too, that the queen, with her attachment to the old Catholic ceremonies, was the greatest obstacle in the reformers' path, and he came close to asserting that she had no true authority over church ministers. Such zealousness made Blanche and others uncomfortable, but so far they had tolerated Ludham, who had such influential friends as Thomas Sampson, the former dean of Christchurch, who had helped Whittingham with the Geneva Bible.

Kat looked back, curious for another glimpse of the dour Puritan, but an ox-drawn wagon had come between herself and the place where she had last seen Ludham, and by the time it had passed, he was no longer in sight.

"What the deuce, Kat," Nick complained as they left Fleet Street to walk down Crocker's Lane, which ended in a water stairs on the Thames, "if you wish to see Puritans, mayhap you should go with Blanche to St. Dunstan's."

Kat shook her head. "I have seen enough. Tell me, Nick, were you at Paul's this morning? Is there more news of the bull?"

"No, and no. No news at all of substance, though there is much gossip from men with idle brains and busy tongues. They read a storm into this lull."

"Perchance with reason." Kat still felt chilled when she thought about the bull. She had read the copy that had been brought to Will their first evening in London, and had since looked at it often enough that the words were engraved on her mind.

Flagitiorum serva Elizabetha, pretensa Angliae regina, Pius V had written, branding Elizabeth a servant of crime and the pretended Queen of England. He had listed at length what he saw as her crimes against the Catholic Church, had declared her and her adherents heretics and had excommunicated them. He had declared her deprived of her title and had absolved from their oaths all who had sworn fealty to her, and had followed the absolution with a threat. *Praecipimusque et interdicimus universis at singulis proceribus, subditis, et aliis praedictis ne illi eiusve monitis, mandatis et legibus audeant obidere. Qui secus egerint, eos simili anathematis sententia innodamus*, he had written: *We charge and command all and singular the nobles, subjects, peoples and others aforesaid that they do not dare obey her orders, mandates and laws. Those who shall act to the contrary we include in the like sentence of excommunication.*

It was a declaration of war. But whose armies would act on it?

The pope lacked soldiers of his own in sufficient numbers to attack England. The rebellion in the North that he had hoped to aid had been so thoroughly quashed—the people there so cowed after hundreds of poorer rebels were executed and wealthier rebels impoverished by fines and confiscations—that there seemed to be little danger now of another uprising in that region. If armies threatened England, they would be the armies of Spain or of France . . . and either or both might be in league with the Queen of Scots, that treacherous chess piece who could move herself as well as be moved by others.

Yet even more dangerous than rebelling or invading armies were the secret traitors in the kingdom, the papists who might now feel it their duty to act individually to harm the queen. Was Lisle—

"I pray you, Kat, do not frown. They'll not let us in Paris Garden if you wear a face meet only for a funeral."

She smiled despite herself and shook off the dark mood. She had walked past Whitefriars as if in a dream, seeing nothing, but they were already at the top of the water stairs and too much lay before her now for her to look back.

The Thames was London's true highway, Nick had told her, and certainly it seemed so now, with dozens of boats plying the gleaming expanse of water. Here and there she saw a small ship with sails, but most of the boats were powered by oarsmen. Far away most plentiful were the small wherries that were for hire, but she saw one brightly painted barge hung with gleaming cloth.

"The queen's barge?" she asked Nick, pointing.

He shook his head. " 'Tis some noble, as like as not, returning to Hampton Court from the city. The queen's barge is much larger, with two cabins most richly furnished, and twenty-one watermen in all."

Hampton Court . . . The queen would be in residence there until she left on her summer progress through her kingdom. Nick had vowed to take Kat there, when her wardrobe was ready. She was excited by the thought but also a bit frightened.

Nick walked down the water stairs. "Oars!" he shouted. "Southward ho!" A few moments later a wherry that had been drifting nearby, seemingly aimlessly, glided toward the bank, past swans that seemed unperturbed by the nearness of the boat.

"No one hunts the swans here?" Kat asked her brother.

"None dare. They belong to the Crown."

While Nick opened his purse to give the waterman a penny for their fare, Kat looked curiously at the man. Sunburned and wrinkled, with his light brown hair streaked with gold, he was dressed in clothing similar to that of the other watermen she had seen: doublet and breeches of canvas. She had heard that watermen were known for their wit— often a coarse wit—and she had hoped for a sample, but this one was silent as he guided his craft to the South Bank, landing at Paris Garden Stairs.

She was still unused to the pantofles, having worn them only a few times, and as they climbed the stairs she stumbled and would have fallen had Nick not caught and steadied her.

"Thank you! A plague on these things! How do you ever learn to walk in them?"

"You must travel to Venice, Kat. 'Tis said the courtesans there wear chopines with soles twelve inches high."

"They may not care if they break their necks, when otherwise they may only look forward to dying of the pox. But what would you know of the courtesans in Venice? Did George Calvert in truth write to you of them? Was that what you did not wish me to read?"

He smiled but did not respond to her questions. Instead he asked, "Is that a new perfume?"

"Yea, a gift from Blanche. And she showed me how to make it. 'Tis a concoction of rosewater, sugar, Damask water and musk. She says it is much like a perfume favored by the queen. Do you like it?"

"You would like my approval when you already have the queen's? Yea, I like it. And I like your new gown and kirtle."

She had been wondering if he had even noticed that she was wearing the only outfit the sempsters had already completed for her: a gown of cream-colored water camlet lined with white silk, which she wore over a kirtle of peach-colored silk. She had chosen the peach silk after first being shown peach-colored cloth-of-silver. Blanche had wanted her to buy the cloth-of-silver and use white cloth-of-silver to line the gown, and Kat did in truth prefer the rich stuff to plain silk, but she had changed her mind about the purchase after learning the price was almost two pounds a yard. 'Twas said that it was easy for a courtier to turn a hundred acres of land into a trunkful of clothes; entire estates had vanished that way, divided up among haberdashers and sempsters and jewelers. She was determined that she would not be so foolish.

She wished she could feel confident that Nick would also avoid such folly.

His behavior since their arrival in London had not been encouraging. Though she knew that he had spent many hours during the first days in the city at Paul's, learning all the news he could—and though he still walked in Paul's at least some time each day—he spent less and less time there, more and more time at more costly pursuits. He had four new suits, including the doublet and hose of tawny satin that he wore today with a cloak of gorgeous tuft-taffeta, the tawny tufts on a background of silver. Kat had seen similar cloth at the mercers' shops she and Blanche had visited, and had been stunned to learn that the price was fifteen shillings a yard. She suspected that she would also be stunned if Nick ever disclosed the fees charged by the Neapolitan riding master with whom he now studied, but she had not even asked for she knew she could never sway his decision. " 'Tis all the fashion," he had told her at dinner, "to study horsemanship with an Italian riding master." He had purchased a copy of *The Fowre Chiefyst Offices belongyng to Horsemanshippe*, Thomas Blundeville's interpretation of the Italian master Federico Grisone's *Gli Ordini de Cavalcare*, and he prattled constantly of the turn *terra terra* and the *incavalare* and the *chambetta*.

It was the fashion, too, for gallants to bet on cockfights, and Nick had spent the last two Sunday afternoons at a cockpit near St. Giles in the Fields. He had admitted losing five pounds betting on a cock owned by a friend of his, and had even talked of buying a cock of the game, a black-breasted red cock owned by a trainer whose gamecocks, another friend had told him, won nearly all their battles. To Kat's dismay, Nick allowed that the cock had never yet fought a battle, having just reached its maturity at two years of age, but both Nick and the trainer had high hopes for the bird, which had the small head, strong back, thick legs and long spurs prized by followers of the sport. "Were I to wait until the cock wins a battle," Nick had said, "the price would be twice as high" . . . but he would not tell her what the price was now.

Kat fingered her purse strings uneasily, scarce aware what she was doing. She had only a few coins with her, a very small portion of the money they had brought to London, but she vowed to herself to be careful with it. Her thriftiness would do only a little to offset Nick's wanton spending, but it would be foolish to turn spendthrift herself for that reason.

"Ware this crowd," Nick said as they stopped to watch two bowlers at one of Paris Garden's bowling alleys. "There are all manner of rogues and shifters here, more cheaters and cozeners and simple thieves than you would dream. Look! There's young Jack Cutpurse, awaiting his chance . . ." He gestured toward a boy of ten or eleven wearing a faded purple jerkin much too big for him. The youth stood a few feet from a corpulent middle-aged man dressed in dark brown velvet, a merchant, perhaps, or even a prosperous yeoman, who was so intent on a bowling match that he seemed oblivious to everyone around him. The boy was trying not to look as though he was watching the man, but Kat noticed his gaze flick now and then to the purse hanging from the man's broad belt.

"Let's warn him," Nick said, and went up to the older man and began to speak quietly to him. Suddenly the fat man's head shot around and he stared hard at the boy, who stepped back into the crowd and quickly vanished from sight.

A few moments later Nick returned to her side. "Young Jack may go hungry tonight, unless he finds another purse to cut and makes himself less obvious about it," he said, and chuckled.

Kat could not share his amusement. In the instant when the boy realized that he was no longer unobserved, she had seen a look of disappointment that was nearly despair cross his face, and she had then noticed that he was painfully thin, with a pinched, hungry look to his face. As he retreated she had seen, too, that his jerkin was threadbare and would provide little warmth on a chill evening. She prayed he would not end up in Bridewell, where the prisoners were regularly flogged under the gaze of people who paid admission to watch the flogging. But what else could there be for him, other than the stocks or a hangman's noose? He was not likely to put aside the knife and the horn thumb-sheath of a cutpurse and become an honest apprentice.

They had a late dinner at a tavern, which was much like other taverns Kat had seen, save for the heavily painted women who she guessed—and Nick confirmed—were Winchester geese. She felt less sympathy for the punks of Southwark than she had for the cutpurse at the bowling alley, since she remembered too well the torments suffered by one of their servants several years ago, when the man contracted the French pox during a visit to London and its stews. The whores had assured him that washing with vinegar and hard pissing into the jordans they kept for their customers would prevent him from catching the pox. Nick had told her that the strumpets, too, believed that, and were not merely lying to their customers, but Kat had scoffed at that. Why, then, were any of the whores poxed? Or any of the men who frequented the brothels? She still felt bitter about the fate of the man's wife, a chaste girl of fifteen who had deserved better than to die of the pox because of her husband's lechery. And she had worried incessantly about Nick after he went to the Inns of Court, until he assured her that the *buonarobas* he visited were no common whores and were free of pox.

Now she watched him closely, and though he seemed to have no interest in the punks, she felt relieved when he finished the last of his ale and set the cup down.

"Come," he said. "You must see Ned Grimes."

Half an hour later they sat on the highest tier of seats in the bear garden.

It was a large building, its circular walls ending some distance beneath the roof, which was supported by massive timbers and open in the middle so that it covered the tiers of seats but left the arena floor open to the sky. It was already so crowded that her first thought had been that everyone in London who could afford the admission was here this afternoon. Nick had paid their admission, a penny apiece, and had paid more pennies before they were allowed onto the scaffolding and finally onto the highest tier. Kat had clung to his arm as he pushed through the jostling throng, past the vendors selling nuts and apples, the workingmen reeking of sweat and ale, and the wealthy whose rich clothes stank of sweat as well as perfume after a warm afternoon on the Bankside. Holding her pomander near her nose, she had savored its sweet perfumes and prayed they would also protect her from any contagion in the foul air, which was ripe with animal smells as well as human. Finally reaching the uppermost tier of seats, she had been able to return the pomander to its chain on her girdle and enjoy the fresh breeze sweeping into the building under the roof.

Ned Grimes, she had learned, was the name of a bear, so named for his trainer, and she had been unable to stop Nick from wagering on the bear, though he had restricted his bet to ten shillings, when two other men were wagering several pounds each. Perchance he had taken her remarks about his gaming to heart, she thought, and she smiled as she looked around the bear garden, surveying the crowd.

Suddenly she caught her breath, seeing an elegantly dressed man with thick reddish-brown hair who sat across the arena from them. His face was turned three-quarters away from them as he spoke to the gentlewoman at his side—a lovely woman, Kat noticed, aware of a painful tightness in her throat. She remembered that his beard was cut just so—

"Nay, 'tis not him," Nick murmured in her ear. "Fear not, Kat. He rarely comes to court, for all that the queen would have him there. You will not see him in London this summer."

At that moment the reddish-haired gentleman turned toward the arena, facing fully toward them, and Kat saw for herself that it was not Lisle. *Not so handsome.* She shook her head, irritated at the thought. Her heart was still hammering, and her throat still hurt, though not so much as when she had thought the gentlewoman was Lisle's love.

There was an appreciative roar from the crowd as a bearward led the first bear into the ring.

" 'Tis Ned Grimes," Nick whispered. "Look at the size of him!"

Kat was impressed. The bear was half again as large as the bears she had seen as a child in Sussex, and she thought a bearward would have to be extremely brave or else mad to work with an animal that large. Yet Ned Grimes seemed docile enough as he followed the bearward to the center of the arena, where he was fastened to a stake with a thick rope about fifteen feet long. The bear stood there quietly, seemingly immune to the crowd's excitement, until the mastiffs were set on him.

They were Lyme mastiffs, huge beasts, pale yellow save for black ears and muzzles. While the audience cheered each dog by name, Nick sat in silence beside her, his expression unusually somber. Kat did not ask if he was familiar with any of the dogs they had heard mentioned by other spectators. No doubt Nick had had his favorites, but in the months he had been gone from London they would either have been killed or maimed, or removed from participation in the baiting by owners who had wanted them used here only a short while, to aid their training as watchdogs.

She leaned forward as the dogs, barking furiously, moved closer to the bear. Suddenly one mastiff darted forward to seize the bear's muzzle. Ned Grimes roared and reared back, his front legs closing around the mastiff in a bruising grip. Then the other dogs shot in. The bear fell to one side, rolling, and the dog that had seized his muzzle was shaken free. As the bear lurched to his feet again, a dog he had fallen on lay still for a few moments, then climbed to its feet and shook itself. It bounded away an instant before a blow from the bear's front paw would have crushed its skull.

The baiting went on for nearly half an hour, and more than a dozen fresh mastiffs were brought in to replace the dogs that were killed or wounded. One mastiff—Harry O'Dare—lasted till the end, but more through its agility in dodging the bear's swipes than because it was sturdier than the other mastiffs. The bravest dog, which had flown at the bear and immediately seized its muzzle when it was released halfway through the baiting, had been killed a moment after the bear shook it loose. 'Twas a sad waste of what would have been a good watchdog, Kat felt, beginning to think this was poorer sport than the bear-baitings she had seen in the country. She agreed readily when Nick asked her if she wanted to leave; he was restless again after collecting his winnings, no more in the mood than she to sit through the next baiting, this time with bandogs, or to see the ape riding the pony: such amusements could be had at any fair. London awaited them outside the bear garden, and she was free for the rest of the afternoon.

They strolled east along the bank of the Thames, past the whitewashed stews, past Winchester House, and onto London Bridge, where they stopped again on the drawbridge to look out over the Pool of London. A ship was being unloaded, barges hugging its sides like suckling pigs. Now and then Kat could hear the shriek of a whistle that was loud enough and shrill enough to cut through the roar of the waters beneath the bridge. Gilt figureheads gleamed in the late afternoon light. She would have willingly stood there an hour, watching the ships, had not Nick suggested that they go to St. Paul's, rather than hiring a wherry to take them west up the Thames to the water stairs at the end of Crocker's Lane.

The walk to the cathedral was a long one, and Kat's feet felt bruised by the time they reached Paul's Wharf Hill, but she forgot her discomfort as they went through Paul's Chain, as the southern gate was called, into the hurly-burly of the churchyard.

There were booksellers everywhere, it seemed to Kat; their stalls and houses clung like barnacles to the outside of the cathedral and to the churchyard walls. Nick was searching for an Italian romance that a friend of his had told him of, but to Kat the most interesting items were the pamphlets and ballads attacking the pope. London's printers and booksellers had wasted no time in responding to the papal bull. Kat was looking over several, unable to make up her mind, when Nick, laughing, thrust another pamphlet into her hands: *A disclosing of the great Bull and certain calves that he hath gotten and specially the Monster Bull that roared at my Lord Bishop's Gate.* She chuckled too, and bought it. "This will please Blanche, if I know her at all," she told Nick.

Then they went into the cathedral itself, entering through the south door.

Kat was but a few steps past the door, her eyes not yet adjusted to the dimness of the cathedral's interior, when Nick pulled her to one side, out of the path of a pannier-laden mule being led by a florid-faced man in black russet who seemed impervious to the furious denunciations of a curate in a threadbare cassock.

"He takes a shortcut through the transepts," Nick said, answering the question Kat had been too astonished to ask.

Kat had been to fairs that were less busy than the main aisle of the nave. As her eyes adjusted from sunlight to the fainter light entering the cathedral through the clerestory windows, she looked around in amazement. The space between the tall columns that soared to the groin vaults of the ceiling was thronged with people and buzzing with mingled conversations that only occasionally resolved into individual words. Paul's Walk, it was called: it was here that Nick came to learn the latest gossip, or simply to meet his friends in the morning or afternoon and walk to get a stomach for dinner or supper.

They strolled past coyly masked ladies making assignations with finely dressed gallants, past scriveners waiting to be hired to write letters, past mercers who had spread their cloth in rich display on the tombs. "What need had I to go to any mercer's shop," Kat teasingly asked her brother, "when I could have come here?" A few moments later, after Nick was stopped by a man who wanted to study the cut of his doublet—and who, despite Nick's suspicions, proved to be the tailor he claimed to be and not a pickpurse or cutpurse—Kat added, "Why, you even have your tailors here, and belike your sempsters, too."

" 'Tis not uncommon to find tailors here. I'faith, they know where to hunt fashionmongers."

"Marry, the prey declares itself. Not that you could do otherwise, brother, in such brave new feathers."

Pointing past a costermonger hawking his apples, Nick showed her the lawyers, there seeking new clients, who stood clustered near one pillar. Another class of men stood at the *Si quis* pillar, so called for the first words—*If anyone*—of the bills posted on it, advertising the skills of the masterless men who were seeking employment. One youth sat at the base of the pillar, idly swatting his boots with a holly wand like those used by grooms. They walked past Duke Humphrey's tomb, and Nick told her that the men who came here in the hope of meeting someone who would buy their dinner, and failed, were said to have dined with Duke Humphrey. " 'Tis unwise, I was told, to spend too much time in the cathedral, lest I be classed with them," he said, and Kat shook her head, marveling that Paul's Walk should have its own society and its own rules.

They met a group of young gentlemen known to Nick, though Kat recognized none of their names when he introduced them: no doubt these were more of his fellows from Cambridge or the Inns of Court. They had spent the early hours of the afternoon at an ordinary, and two of them had clearly had too much to drink. One of them, a lanky youth in a suit of fine carnation damask that was now grease-stained, railed against Cecil, blaming the queen's secretary of state for the pope's decision to excommunicate the queen. "I warned Leicester," he said in a slurred voice, "that something must be done about Cecil. I told him that the queen's Spirit had failed her." He chortled at the poor joke he had made on Cecil's nickname. "Now she will soon be Spirit-less, if the rumors are true and Cecil plans to flee."

"He would not leave the queen, nor would she let him leave," said another, more sober member of the company.

Kat nodded, though she said nothing. She, too, believed that the queen would not be alienated from the man she referred to as her Spirit . . . even though Cecil was often at odds with Robert Dudley, Earl of Leicester, the queen's favorite.

"Nay, I have heard that she blames Cecil for this. I shall know more when I speak with Dudley next—" He left them abruptly, staggering a little as he made his way toward the west door.

"God's death!" Nick said when the drunkard was out of earshot. "If he has ever said more to Dudley than 'Cry you mercy, my lord, pray let me step out of your way,' then call me liar."

"None of us will give you the lie, Nick," said the gentleman who had spoken in Cecil's defense, a pleasant-faced man in a suit of murrey velvet. Nick had introduced him as Thomas Heyford, Kat remembered now. "But pray do not give John the lie, for his fancies that he has Leicester's ear suffice to content him somewhat. He frets like gummed velvet at times like this, when enemies may be anywhere but there is naught that we can do."

Kat watched her brother and was not surprised when, after a few moments, he nodded slowly. The sober gentleman had voiced a frustration she too had felt, and was sure Nick shared. With Elizabeth Tudor's enemies now urged to act with the pope's sanction, danger *was* anywhere, and Kat often felt derelict in her duty to the queen because she could do nothing. Even worse, she and Nick had once been in a spot where they could have aided the queen, but—if Sparrow's judgment were true—they had failed. She chafed at the thought, and suspected that Nick felt worse yet.

After a few moments all Nick's acquaintances but the fellow in murrey velvet took their leave. It was late in the afternoon: the sunlight passing through the clerestory windows to pierce the cathedral's gloom gilded the vaults high above them. In common but silent agreement, she and Nick and Thomas Heyford began to walk toward the west door. It would be time for supper soon, and they were still a long walk from the house in Fewter Lane.

"Well met in London, Kat."

She whirled around, stunned to find Christopher Danvers here.

"How now, Kit," Thomas said, smiling. "So you know Nick's lovely sister?"

Christopher glanced at him briefly, then nodded, his gaze returning to Kat. She was unable to speak. What could she say now, after the letter she had left him that doubtless had shamed him in front of her servants?

"And did the goldsmith I recommended pay you well for that clock?" Thomas asked Christopher.

"A fair price," Christopher said grudgingly.

"I hope he does not melt it down," Thomas continued. " 'Twas a most wondrous clock, with a mermaid and a dolphin, marvelously worked. Kit bought it as a gift for a widow he had courted this past spring, but she rejected him too soon, and never saw it."

Kat looked at Thomas: that pleasant face was guileless. This was no jest of Christopher's, no studied attempt to make her believe that she had been wooed by him only after he was spurned by another. This was the truth, as a look at Christopher's reddening face confirmed.

" 'Twas her loss, then, to have rejected Christopher before she saw the clock." She emphasized the word *before* just enough to make her meaning plain to Christopher, but Thomas seemed not to notice the insult.

Nick had noticed and raised an eyebrow in inquiry, but she shook her head slightly. The blood had drained from Christopher's face. He stared coldly at Kat, then, after a venomous look at Thomas, turned and walked rapidly away.

"Cry you mercy, Kit, if I offended you," Thomas called after him, then turned back in confusion. "Perhaps I should not have mentioned the widow, but I thought little of it. 'Twas not the first widow Kit had wooed."

"Indeed," Kat murmured coolly, but she was shaken.

They resumed walking toward the west door, Nick close at Kat's side. "You know of this clock?" he asked, just loud enough that she could hear him.

"I once owned one just like it," she replied. " 'Twas a gift." Despite her attempt to keep her voice light, she feared she sounded somewhat bitter. It had stung her to learn that Christopher had turned to her only after being rejected by another . . . and though she knew it was foolish, it had stung even more to know that the clock had been bought as a gift for another . . .

"You no longer have this clock?"

She shook her head.

" 'Tis best," he said, and smiled and squeezed her arm.

Thomas left the cathedral with them. He was to meet a friend at the Inner Temple, where he had studied until last year. Kat had been right in guessing that he knew Nick from the Inns of Court. He was a pleasant companion as they walked along Bowyer Lane to Ludgate and then down Fleet Street, telling Nick of the building going on at the Inner Temple and the Middle Temple.

When they reached the Gardiners' house, Thomas asked Nick if he would come see the construction and sup with them tonight. Nick declined.

"Well, then, would you see a play tomorrow? 'Tis to be at the Bel Savage," Thomas said, pointing back toward an inn they had passed, "and 'twould please you, I warrant. As it would please me, Mistress Kat, if you would join us."

"Well, good sister?" Nick asked.

"Yea, I would love to go," she said, delighted.

"Then I shall meet you here at two in the afternoon. The play begins at three, but we would do well to be early."

After Thomas had bidden them farewell, Nick turned to Kat, a mischievous look on his face. "I warrant you have met both an old suitor and a new suitor today."

"How now, Nick? Thomas, a suitor?" She would have laughed, but was stopped by the realization that this was what Nick wished: a new suitor for her. Her lips pursed, she looked thoughtfully back over her shoulder, seeing the murrey velvet of Thomas's cape. She would not have recognized him by the color or cut of his hair: she had not even noticed what color his hair was. Nor had she paid much attention to his face, other than to note the pleasant expression. She had never, she reflected, had a suitor who had made so little impression on her when she met him.

Unlike Justin Lisle.

She banished the unwelcome thought at once, and as Nick looked at her curiously, she managed a smile.

Blanche was unusually quiet at supper that evening. Was it because of the play? Kat wondered. Nick had told Will and Blanche of their plans as soon as the meal began, and Blanche had said no more than a few words since then . . . and nothing, oddly, of the prophesying that afternoon. Perchance it had been unwise to mention the play to her, so soon after her return from St. Dunstan's. Belike some other Puritan at the prophesying had spoken out against the performance of plays. Kat knew that Puritans often denounced plays as abominations—*the food of iniquity and riot*, one Puritan had told Nick. Yet it was unlike her cousin to keep such opinions to herself.

Kat glanced again at Blanche, only to discover her cousin staring fixedly at the dishes before her. Her eyes met Will's, and he shrugged slightly: he, too, was perplexed by his wife's behavior.

"Will," Blanche began, startling them, "I have come to a decision about the name I would wish our child to be given. You know that I shall honor your decision, whatever it may be, but you have told me that you wish to hear my opinion."

"Yea, so I have," Will said. To Kat's ears, he sounded wary.

"I spoke with Master Ludham at the prophesying today," Blanche said, and Will's eyes closed for a moment. Not seeming to notice, she continued, "He told me that he believed that our child should bear a godly name. Should our child be a girl, he would have us name her Bethankful. And, should this child be the son that we have prayed for, he would have us give him the name he gave his own son, Fight-the-good-fight-of-faith.''

Will looked stricken. Kat shot a glance at her brother, who appeared stunned: too stunned, she judged, for it to be necessary for her to signal him to keep silent.

"I told him . . ." Blanche's voice trailed off. Her gaze swept over them, then returned to the dishes. "I told him," she said again, her voice firmer, "that while I, too, would raise my children to be godly and willing to proclaim their faith, I would not have them forced to do so each time they are asked their names." She faced Will then, her expression oddly shy. "I would have them named as you wish, husband, for your parents."

"A brave choice," Nick said, applauding. He was silenced abruptly by a sharp look from Will.

"This is your choice, in sooth?" Will asked his wife, and when she nodded, said more softly, "But Ludham . . . ?"

He did not finish the sentence, nor did he need to. Even Nick's expression was grave now. Blanche could not have chosen any more vociferous opponent at the prophesyings.

"He bade me rethink my decision, of course," Blanche replied. "He said 'twas deplorable . . . sad proof that I was too much swayed by the wantons he had seen leaving our house this noon. He told me he had already troubled to ask about them and had learned they were my cousins."

Kat felt sickened. She had never dreamed that a few careless words, spoken where they could be overheard on a London street, could lead to this.

"And so I told him," her cousin continued, "that 'twas a pity he had not troubled to learn more, for my cousins were no wantons. And I bade him look to his own life, rather than others'."

"You told him *that?*" Will asked in disbelief. "Was he not sorely angered?"

"In sooth, he betrayed a choleric humor," Blanche said, and Kat could have sworn that her cousin was fighting a smile.

"He'll never forgive you," Nick said.

"Mayhap he will not, though the Scriptures counsel forgiveness. Yet had I said nothing, I should never have forgiven myself." She reached out and took Will's hand. "Fear not, husband, that I may come to any harm. Peradventure I may never see Master Ludham again."

He looked at her wonderingly. Kat, too, was confused: not see Ludham, when he was at nearly every prophesying?

Blanche looked at each of them in turn, then smiled. "I have been too often away from the company of those I love. I shall spend no more time at prophesyings." She turned to Nick. "I would fain go with you to the play tomorrow. Husband, will you go?"

"Yea, if it is what you wish."

"With all my heart," she replied, and Will left his chair and went to kiss her.

CHAPTER 11

At half past three the next day, Kat, her brother, their cousins and Thomas Heyford sat in a stall on the gallery of the Bel Savage Inn. Here they were well above the jostle and tumult of the groundlings and screened by cloth hangings from the eyes of the gentlefolk seated to either side. Both Kat and Blanche were discreetly masked: Blanche had suggested it, and though Kat chafed at the need to wear the mask when she had recklessly gone without one yesterday, she had acceded at once to Blanche's wishes. She wanted this afternoon to be perfect for her cousin, who now sat leaning against her husband. Since last night Blanche and Will had been acting as if it were still honeymoon with them. Kat smiled as she looked at them now. *Would that you could see what you have wrought, Master Ludham.* Nick, seated next to the Gardiners on the bench, appeared alternately pleased and abashed; Tom Heyford, too, had been unable to overlook the couple's obvious delight in each other's company, but had accepted without question Kat's explanation that her cousins had just ended a long quarrel. To her relief, he did not take the Gardiners' display of affection as a license to treat her too familiarly; while he sat close to her, he was as far away as the bench allowed.

During their walk along Fleet Street and up Ludgate Hill to the inn, he had entertained her with gossip about the court, but once at the inn he had spoken only occasionally, sensitive to her interest in the scene below them. She had attended plays before, but only a few—not nearly enough to lessen her excitement.

A rough platform had been erected in the courtyard below. The back of the platform was hidden from view by painted cloths that were often shaken by the movements of the players who were back there preparing for their performance, and from time to time the cloth would be drawn aside as one or another player peeped out to look at the crowd. On either end of the rush-strewn platform, in lines leading out from the drapery, were stools occupied by young gallants. "They would be players themselves," Nick had told her, his tone derisive, but Kat guessed that under other circumstances Nick himself would have chosen to sit on that stage, himself the cynosure of the crowd's eyes. A few of the young gallants, two of whom were dicing on a cloak they had spread on the rushes, were known to him, and they had bidden Nick and Tom come down to join their game, then grinned appreciatively at Kat when her brother and suitor refused to leave her company.

Suitor. Somehow the word seemed more apt today. 'Twas partly Tom's attentions, but some of her own change in attitude, she felt sure, had begun yesterday, just before supper, when Nick had mentioned Tom's name and discovered that his friend was well known to Will Gardiner. The Heyfords' house in Suffolk was near Will's own, and Will had spoken very favorably of their estate, which Tom, their only child, would inherit. " 'Tis said he already manages the estate, since his father is in his dotage. A most prudent manager, in sooth." Kat had been watching Nick's reaction to this news and noted his expression of satisfaction: Tom was no Christopher Danvers, likely to spend all his wife's dowry and be looking for more funds in a year or two. Her brother would approve of this match.

But would she?

Tom nudged her then, and she started, wondering for an instant if he had read her thoughts. For once she was glad that the mask concealed her face, which felt as though it were on fire. To her relief, she discovered that Tom merely wanted to draw her attention to the youths selling nuts and apples and bottled ale who had stopped at their stall.

Though she said she was neither hungry nor thirsty, he still bought an apple and a bottle of ale for her, and the same for himself. The bottles of ale hissed loudly as he opened them.

"Pray God, the playwright did not hear that," Tom remarked cheerfully. "He'll fear himself hissed before the play's begun."

He ate the apple he had bought for himself, but demurred when she would have given him hers. "Nay, keep it. 'Twill do to hurl at the players if they deserve it. No, I jest. I know this band of players. You will have seen none so splendid in Sussex."

"Not even last year, when no plays could be performed in London?"

He smiled ruefully, and his hand enveloped Kat's for a moment. "Cry you mercy, lady. 'Twas thoughtless of me to assume you have not seen the like of this play, merely because you have not lived in London."

Yet he was right, she realized soon after the trumpets had sounded and the prologue had appeared and been followed by the actors' appearance on the stage. The play was an Italianate tangle of deception and revenge, the players so skilled and so well suited to their roles that she almost forgot she sat in the courtyard of the Bel Savage. Only once was she forcibly recalled to her surroundings, and that was when Tom nudged her and pointed out to her a heavyset, bald-pated man who stood on the highest gallery on the other side of the courtyard, gazing anxiously down at the platform below. "The innkeeper," he murmured. "He fears fire." She had nodded then, and when she looked back at the stage, where two players held burning tapers as they pretended to make their way through the dark halls of a castle, she was suddenly very aware that the surface on which they stood was rush-strewn wood, not bare stone: 'twould blaze like a tinderbox. "Then why does he—" she began, then answered herself: "No, 'tis plain enough. He loves profit more than he fears fire." She shook her head, turning her attention again to the play.

After the performance had ended—to applause, not hissing or the hurling of crude missiles—Kat waited in the stall with the Gardiners. Will, solicitous for his wife, had said 'twould be best to stay until the groundlings had departed, so as to avoid the jostling crowd. In the meantime Nick and Tom had descended to the courtyard, to talk with their friends who still lingered on the stage. Bored and wishing she could join them, Kat toyed with the apple in her hands. The crowd below was thinning rapidly, but Will, deep in conversation with Blanche, seemed not to notice. She was debating whether to wait for them below when she heard a distinctive voice from the other side of the drapery separating them from the stall to her right.

She was instantly as still as a statue, straining to hear more, scarce believing what she had heard. Then, following a woman's soft laughter, she heard the voice again. Despite the warmth, she shivered violently. How had she missed that voice before? Unless—and that must be the case—the man had kept his voice so soft during the performance that she could not hear him . . .

Unable to restrain herself, she leaned over and seized the drapery, pulling it aside just enough to peer into the stall.

Dark skin . . . Seen by firelight, it would look deeply tanned, but she now saw it was olive in hue. Dark hair: that was the same. No beard or mustache—but those were easily acquired, as any of the players below could testify. And dark eyes, fastened on her in smiling curiosity now—so unlike the flashing blue eyes of the fair-haired woman seated between him and Kat.

Kat let the cloth fall back into place, praying that she had not roused their curiosity—and likely the woman's ire—so much that they would now approach her. She had meant to glance into the stall for only an instant, but now realized she must have stared at the man for several seconds, at least. Thank God she was masked, for she had given no thought to the possibility that he might recognize her.

'Twas Henry Malcomb—she was sure of it. Not only did he look much like the sea captain, but the voice was the same, though now it lacked any accent that she recognized. No one hearing Henry Malcomb now would suspect he was anyone but an Englishman, and one from the area around London. There was no trace of the West Country in his speech now, but then, there had been none when he spoke to Justin Lisle in that perfect Spanish . . . nor, for that matter, had his Spanish accent crept into his English when he spoke at the Jerusalem Tree weeks ago, or here, just now. He was adept at changing accents as well as languages, as adept as he was at subtly changing his appearance—too adept for him to be an honest man with no need of such skills.

She folded her hands in her lap, hoping that would stop their trembling. Her cousins were still intent on their conversation: they either had not noticed her actions just now or saw nothing unusual about them. She gazed down at the gallants on the stage. Tom turned to look up at the stall, and she forced herself to wave at him. To her relief, Nick did not look around. *Pray God, Malcomb has not seen him,* she thought, *for if Lisle has told him of what happened that night . . .*

Then she heard the sounds of the couple in the next stall rising, their silk clothes rustling. A moment later the cloth was drawn back and Henry Malcomb and his companion walked behind Kat on their way to the stairs. Kat turned her head to look at them for just a second— to avoid doing so would appear unnatural—and Malcomb gave her a dazzling smile . . . as he had at the Jerusalem Tree. Then they were gone, hidden from sight by the other drapery. Some moments later Kat heard the woman begin to descend the stairs.

She closed her eyes. Her heart was hammering wildly. Then, just as she finally felt herself safe, relief was overthrown by shame. She had behaved as though she were the prey and had counted herself fortunate to escape detection, when in truth she was a hunter and had failed by not being bold enough. She should have spoken to Malcomb and his companion: belike he would not have known her, since she was masked and dressed as a gentlewoman. Now he had slipped away once again, and there was little she could tell Nick . . . and naught that he could tell Sparrow.

She rose suddenly and hurried after them, ignoring the Gardiners' looks of surprise. By the time she reached the top of the stairs, Malcomb was already on the ground. She would have run down the stairs if she could have, but she wore pantofles and could only take slow, heavy, careful steps downward. It seemed an eternity before she reached the bottom of the stairs.

She walked toward the entrance of the courtyard, no longer able to see Malcomb among the people before her, but knowing he could not be far ahead unless he had left his companion. She had taken less than a dozen steps away from the stairs when a hand closed on her arm.

She cried out in alarm and whirled around, but it was only Nick.

"Soft, good sister. Did you take me for some rogue?"

She shook her head. To her exasperation, she saw that Tom stood behind Nick: she could not speak too openly of Malcomb now.

"Did you see him?" she asked artlessly, looking back in the direction Malcomb had gone.

"Who?" Nick's confusion appeared genuine.

"He wore black damask," she prompted. Peradventure Nick had noticed Malcomb but had not recognized him; he had not, after all, had the chance she had had to observe Malcomb in Lisle's chamber at the Jerusalem Tree. Then, too, Nick had been drunk.

Nick looked even more baffled now.

"Who did you see?" Tom asked.

Kat sighed. 'Twas too late now to attempt to follow Malcomb. At least she could hope that if Nick had not noticed the man, then perhaps he had not been facing in Malcomb's direction long enough for Malcomb to recognize him. The man who called himself Henry Malcomb would, she suspected, be quick to ask questions about her brother . . .

Both Tom and Nick were regarding her with puzzlement. What could she tell them to explain her behavior? She looked away, frowning, then almost laughed aloud at the idea that came to her.

" 'Twas Master Ludham, I thought," she told them. "I would have sworn it was he, and that he had of a sudden turned fashionmonger, for he had been to a barber and he wore a new suit worth showing in Paul's Walk. Yet it could not have been him, could it?"

"Alas, no," Nick agreed.

" 'Alas'?" Tom asked.

"Alas, for nothing would have pleased Blanche more," Nick said, and began to tell him of the Puritan while they waited for Blanche and Will to join them.

It was evening, after supper—to which Tom had been invited—before Kat found a chance to talk to Nick alone. He was in his bedchamber, playing his lute, trying to remember the exact notes and words of a song from the play.

" 'Tis no good," he said as soon as he noticed Kat standing in the doorway. "I must needs see the songbook. Well, Kat. How like you the new suitor?"

"He's pleasant company," she said. "But Nick, I would speak to you of Henry Malcomb. I saw him at the Bel Savage."

He gazed at her without speaking for what seemed a long time. "God's blood, was that what those questions were about? So 'twas not Master Ludham you thought you saw?" She shook her head. " 'Tis a pity. Blanche much liked the idea of Ludham turning gallant. Where did you see Malcomb?"

"In the stall next to us, on the other side of Tom. I heard him speaking, after the play had ended and you and Tom had gone." She took a step toward him, her hands clenched into fists. "Nick, 'twas him! He spoke without the West Country accent, and his beard and mustache were gone, but 'twas the same man! Can you reach Sparrow? Or his master, Walsingham?"

"Soft, good sister." Nick set the lute aside, rose, and then, taking her hands, drew her over to sit on the bed. "Think, Kat. What would you have me tell Sparrow? That you saw a man—a man you cannot name, nor locate again—who sounded somewhat like the man at the Jerusalem Tree—save for a different accent—and who looked much like him, too—save for the loss of a beard and mustache?" He shook his head. "No, Kat. Sparrow would only tell me that I wasted his time. Imprimis—he would say—you have only the word of a woman, your sister, that this Henry Malcomb spoke Spanish and is thus suspect. Nay, look not so spiteful. I only play Sparrow here . . . Then he will remind me that this man in London neither looked nor sounded the same."

"Jesu! Can you not believe that I can recognize a voice, or a face, even if it is changed somewhat?"

"I can believe you, Kat, but would Sparrow?" He shook his head again. "And then too, Master Sparrow would say, there are so many men in London, that odds are you would meet one who reminded you greatly of another you knew. 'Tis more likely here than in Sussex, in the country."

She pulled her hands free of his. "You believe that, too."

"As one possibility. Pray do not fret too much over this, sister. It may not have been the man, and there is naught that we can do, knowing so little. Think on other things."

She sighed. *Nick may be right*, she admitted to herself. She had been certain that the man was Henry Malcomb . . . but she had given no thought to how many men—tens of thousands of men—were in London, and in sooth, of all that number, some would belike favor the man she had seen at the Jerusalem Tree. She had been a fool, she thought, and sighed again.

"Nay, not so melancholy," Nick said. "Please you, sit here with me and help me remember this song. Perchance no printer at Paul's will have the play yet, and I would fain recall it exactly."

"Why? So you may play the faithful lover?" Kat teased.

" 'Tis the only kind I would play, the only kind a maid should have," he responded, taking up the lute again. "Such as Tom. I am glad you will see him again this Sunday . . ."

She recalled his words two weeks later, as she sat with Tom and Nick in a tavern on Fleet Street. They had decided to stop there for ale before returning to the house after watching a puppet show.

She had seen Tom almost every day during the past two weeks. The last two Sundays they had walked in Moorfields with the Gardiners: 'twas a custom for the citizens of London to walk there after church services, showing off their finery and enjoying the fresh air. She and Tom had seen three more plays together: one that first Sunday at the Red Lion Inn in Stepney, a parish east of London, the next at the Bull in Bishopsgate Street, and the third at the Cross Keys in Gracious Street. Tom had hired a waterman to take them downriver past Richmond and Greenwich and back. He had taken her to Finsbury Field to watch Nick and other gallants practice at the archery butts there. Tom escorted her as well on visits to the Inner and Middle Temples, where she admired the halls being built, and to Westminster Abbey, which awed her. And some days he chose to leave off his role as her guide about London, and simply came to the house on Fewter Lane to spend a few hours in her company. Twice he brought gifts: a fan of white plumes with a handle of inlaid mother-of-pearl; a pair of gloves of fine chevril perfumed with musk and orange blossom and lavishly embroidered. Remembering Christopher Danvers, Kat was loath to accept the gifts, but she could think of no polite way to refuse them: was Tom not after all her suitor?

Of certain, Nick believed so. At least he seemed content with Tom's interest in her, when in the past he had often mocked her suitors or teased her about them. He found nothing to object to in Tom, it seemed.

Nor, she feared, did she. Tom was unfailingly considerate of her, and of all others around him: a true gentleman. If he sometimes played the court gallant, then he did so without excesses: she need never fear scandal, nor being bankrupt, if she married him. Though not a serious scholar, he was well-read and could on occasion be witty, if not profound. Not quite handsome, he was at least undeniably pleasant-looking. He was, she realized, a suitor to please any but the most fickle or ambitious woman, and she knew she could do far worse. Poor Jane's marriage had proven that.

And yet . . . she did not love him—at least not as more than a friend. She had always hoped to meet someone whom she could love with all her heart, someone she could love as an adult the way she had loved Ned when they had been children. *And that, you goose, is why you have waited so long to marry and made Nick wait, too,* she chided herself as she listened to Tom and Nick talk.

She smiled fondly at both of them. They were reminiscing about their days at Cambridge—Tom had not known Nick then, not meeting him until they were both in London—and Nick was recounting the story of the wild ride back to Cambridge. *The story I told at the Jerusalem Tree,* Kat recalled, suddenly uneasy. She found herself watching Tom's face as he listened to her brother, and her heart sank as she saw that his enjoyment of the tale was a simple thing, untouched, it seemed, by any awareness of the cruelty of Nick's jest. It pained her to see him less sensitive than Justin Lisle . . .

She drew her breath in sharply, dismayed at the thought. Why must she judge Tom so harshly? She herself had seen nothing wrong with Nick's story until she had noticed Lord Harwood's reaction. Tom was even younger than Nick, and as easily swayed by Nick's ebullience as she was. Would she have him be as cynical, at his age, as a nobleman ten years older? Would she have him be identical to Justin Lisle, save for the treason she feared Lisle plotted?

Yea, she would.

'Twas folly, she knew, but knowing that was no help. She did not even love Justin, so her heart was her own to bestow as she willed. If anything, she told herself, she hated the nobleman for concealing such a traitorous, black heart—if he were a traitor, as it seemed he was—behind such a beautiful appearance, such pleasing ways. But, love him or hate him, she could not forget him long enough to cease comparing all other men to him. And that was not fair to Tom. For if she had been wounded to learn that Christopher Danvers, whom she had not loved, had wooed her only after being rejected by another, then how much more would Tom—who seemed to love her—be hurt if he ever learned that he came second in her thoughts after a man with whom she had spent no more than an hour or two one evening? He deserved better than that. She would have to discourage him somehow . . .

"Marry, Kat, y'are no longer with us," Tom said, gently touching her arm.

She tried to smile but failed. How long had she been lost in thought? No more than a minute or two, she hoped: Nick at least seemed unconcerned. How like Tom to notice her feelings, even when he gave no thought to the poor man whom Nick and his friend had run off the road near Cambridge . . .

"Cry you mercy," she told him. "I was thinking of the visit to Hampton Court."

"Are you still fretting about that?" Nick asked. "I have told you that you have naught to fear there. You will do well."

"Haply too well to suit me," Tom said. "I fear you will find yourself wooed by some great lord, and forget me entirely."

She managed a smile at last, but it felt awkward. "So say you. *I* fear I shall be overlooked completely."

"No chance of that, alas. But I shall be there, to beg at least one dance with you."

Tom paid their bill and they walked down Fleet Street toward the Gardiners' house in a companionable silence.

Suddenly Tom spoke. "What will you do next month, when Will and Blanche leave the city? Do you plan to stay in London?"

Nick shook his head. "We'll return to Sussex."

"Would you not come to Suffolk instead? I would like to show you my home and have you meet my family."

Nick gave Kat a sly look, and to her alarm she saw that he was pleased by the invitation. 'Twas obvious—much too obvious—that Tom wished her to meet his parents.

" 'Tis kind of you," she said quickly, answering Tom before Nick could, "but we must discuss this. I have never been absent so long from Beechwood, and I am loath to be away much longer than we had planned."

"Yet our plans are not immutable," Nick said, the moment she had stopped speaking. He looked at her sharply. She, too, saw the dejection on Tom's face and felt miserable.

"No, they are not yet fixed," she said, agreeing with Nick even though she was not certain it was right to give Tom more hope now.

"Then we will discuss this again," he said, and took his leave of them a few moments later.

Nick's hand closed on her arm. His fingers dug into her flesh a little as he led her into the house and immediately out the back, into the garden.

" 'Sdeath! What possessed you to speak so to Tom? Would you discourage him?"

"Yea, I would," she said unhappily.

Her reply seemed to stun him. "How now, Kat? Have you turned trifler? 'Twas a poor trick on the man."

She shook her head. Turning away from him, she seated herself on a bench bordered by roses. Nick sat down beside her. She felt like crying, and it was all she could do to keep her voice steady as she told him of overhearing Frances and Eleanor talking, of her fears that he had wanted her married and away from Beechwood.

"That minx should have her tongue cut out. And you, Kat, should have more sense than to believe such silly talk."

"So you have not wished me to marry?"

"Not unless you wish it . . . and, I trow, you do not wish to marry Tom, should he ask—which he will soon, if I am any judge."

"What shall I do?"

"Let me explain this to him. 'Twill spare his pride somewhat. I warrant I know where he will be now, seeking to drown his sorrows in wine." He stood. "Will you tell our cousins I may not be back for supper?"

But he was. Kat had no chance to talk to Nick alone before the meal, anxious though she was to learn what he had heard from Tom. While they ate, they spoke of Hampton Court. 'Twas but a few days now till Nick would take her there . . .

"You must practice dancing some more," Nick told her late in the meal, as he helped himself to a sweetmeat. "The lavolta especially."

"Must I dance the lavolta?" It was new to her, and she still felt uncomfortable with the leaping that was part of the dance.

"Fear not, Kat, we shall yet teach you to leap as gracefully as you must," Blanche reassured her.

" 'Twould be a pity if you refused any dance," Nick said. "Especially if Tom should ask you. He bade me remind you that you promised him at least one dance."

He was smiling. She felt relief wash over her. Tom did not hate her, then.

"I doubt there would be another with whom I would rather dance," she replied, smiling herself. Out of the corner of her eye, she saw Will glance at Blanche knowingly. They still thought Tom was her suitor, and she regretted that, but could think of no way to explain the true situation to them. And in sooth it might not be necessary, since she and Nick would be returning to Beechwood within two weeks.

After she had been to court . . . The prospect still filled her with as much fear as elation. Suddenly her throat seemed too dry for her to swallow the sweetmeat she had just taken a bite of, and she reached hastily for her wine glass. Four days now. Only four days . . .

CHAPTER 12

Nearly ready to leave for Hampton Court, Kat stood staring at herself in the tall looking glass that Blanche had asked servants to bring up to her chamber.

Her newest gown, of peach-color cloth-of-silver lined with white double sarcenet, still dazzled her eyes. She had seen it for the first time only this morning, when Will and Blanche presented her with the costly gift, which they had ordered made secretly by the sempsters who had sewn the first gowns she had had fashioned here in London. Kat had planned to wear a gown of white silk over her finest kirtle, which was of peach-color wrought velvet with the embroidery done in silver thread, but her cousins had ordered the gown expressly for her to wear to court. They had even brought two of the sempsters with them in case the new gown did not fit as perfectly as the others, but no alterations had been necessary.

"Blanche, I cannot thank you—" she began, but her cousin interrupted her.

"Yea, you can, for you have thanked me already at least a hundred times since this morning. How well the gown suits you. 'Tis likely immodest to say so, but I knew it would when I first saw the draper hold the cloth up against you. 'Tis your color. You must have more clothes of peach-color."

"Yea, and of seawater green—though not, please you, to wear with the peach."

Kat turned to see Nick standing in the doorway. "What a splendid new suit, Nick!" she cried, clapping her hands with delight. His doublet and breeches were of purled satin dyed that brave new shade of reddish bronze called horseflesh, and the tiny loops of gold thread interwoven with the silk glittered in the sunlight as he passed a window to come stand beside Kat. With the new suit he wore his best cape, of black damask lined with gold tissue.

"You look beautiful, sweet sister . . . as do I," he said, with an approving glance at his reflection.

"And you must say so, for modesty would ill become you," Blanche

147

said, but she had spoken lightly and was smiling; there was no rebuke
in her words. Kat looked fondly on her cousin, who wore a plain gown
and kirtle today. Blanche had been easily wearied this past week, and
her doctor had warned her against going to court. The next time she
left the house to travel any distance, it would be to journey to their
home in the country.

"But pray do not advise Kat to wear seawater green," Blanche went
on, more serious now. It was advice she had given Kat often during the
past few weeks. " 'Tis a changeable color—"

"Like her eyes," Nick interrupted.

"—and betokens a fickle heart."

"Again, like her eyes."

"And yours," Kat retorted. Her brother's eyes were the exact same
shade of greenish-blue as her own, and just as changeable, looking blue
in one light and green in another.

Nick chuckled, then took from his purse—a new one, of horseflesh-
color satin worked with gold thread—a small pouch of black velvet,
closed tightly with drawstrings. "This is for you," he told Kat.

" 'Tis a very small purse," Kat said softly, very aware that her heart
was beating fast in anticipation and fear, "and will not match this
gown."

" 'Tis fortunate then, you mocker, that you are to wear not the
purse but what is within it," he said, opening the pouch and pouring
into his palm a gleaming chain of small pearls interspersed with gold
and silver beads.

Kat gasped. *This is too dear,* she thought, but could not tell him so
now. "It is beautiful," she whispered as he fastened the chain around
her neck so carefully that he never disturbed her neck ruff of white lawn
worked with gold and silver thread. *Both* gold and silver: Blanche had
insisted on it. She glanced at her cousin.

"Yea, I knew," Blanche admitted with a smile. She looked at the
clock on the mantel. "You should leave soon."

Kat thanked her brother, hugging him, but carefully so as not to
muss their finery. She fastened the fan Tom had given her to her girdle,
next to her purse, which like Nick's was a new one; hers was of white
damask embroidered with flowers of peach silk, small replicas of the
embroidered flowers on her white silk petticoats and satin sleeves. Finally she slipped her silk pumps into the pantofles that would protect
them, picked up the gloves Tom had given her, then followed Blanche
downstairs, Nick taking her arm to steady her. She prayed that few of
the court would wear pantofles while they danced, though Nick had
said 'twas becoming the fashion.

Louise was already waiting in the coach. Kat had at first rebelled

against the foolish notion of riding the distance to Hampton Court in
this great lumbering vehicle. "I would as lief walk the distance," she
had told Nick, "or be drawn there in a cart," but he and their cousins
had insisted. As she settled herself back against the cushions, which
she knew would provide little protection from the constant jolting, she
watched enviously as Nick mounted his horse. *He* would not ride in the
coach, oh no: 'twas thought womanish for a man to do so. Nay, only
frail women or invalid men were fit to ride in coaches. 'Twas past folly,
Kat thought: it was outright lunacy. Riding about London with Blanche,
she had feared that her cousin might miscarry from the jouncing, but
Blanche had seemed not to mind. She had even laughed when Kat,
prompted by the sight of strings of teeth in a barber-surgeon's window,
had said that barbers should all have coaches: 'twould loosen their patients' teeth and save them some work.

Suddenly the coach lurched forward, throwing Kat back against the
cushions and nearly unseating her maid, who sat opposite her. "Sit here,
Louise," Kat said, patting the cushions beside her. She gathered her
half-kirtle and petticoats more closely about her to make room for Louise. *I hope these clothes will not wrinkle*, she thought, but even if they did,
it would be no worse damage than would be done if Louise were to land
in her lap . . .

It had been early afternoon when they left London. It was late afternoon
before they reached Hampton Court, a magnificent, sprawling palace of
red brick with a profusion of towers capped by spiny cupolas. As they
approached the palace, Nick rode beside the coach and pointed out, far
to their left, at the end of the wall running south from the east end of
the palace, a large domed building. "The water gate," he said. "For the
queen's barge."

They rode past the north side of Hampton Court, past the tiltyard,
and entered through the imposing gatehouse in the west wall of the
palace. Beyond the gatehouse was a vast courtyard, and there, in the
confusion of people afoot and on horseback and in coaches, Tom was
waiting for them.

She felt a moment's trepidation when she saw him, but he greeted
Nick affably, then, when she alighted from the coach, made a leg and
paid her a pretty compliment.

"Court incense," Nick scoffed. "Ware this man, Kat. He has been
too long at court."

"But a few hours today," Tom protested.

" 'Sblood, but you shall be unbearable in another few hours," Nick
complained, to Tom's amusement.

He led them to a corridor overlooking the courtyard from the south, then up a flight of stairs and into a bedchamber whose window opened onto a view of the garden between the palace and the Thames. " 'Tis a friend's chamber," he explained, pouring wine for them from a silver flagon. Kat stood by the window, sipping her wine and looking out over the garden. There were ponds, and neat squares of lawn; red and white square patches that Tom told her were filled with brick dust and sand; roses and violets and sweet williams; pillars surmounted by brilliantly painted dragons and lions and unicorns that each bore a shield with the royal coat of arms; and cherry and apple and pear trees. A fence painted the green and white of the Tudors surrounded it all. She had never dreamed that such a garden could exist, and would have been content to stand there looking at it until the last light had left the sky, but at last Nick's manservant was through brushing the dust from her brother's clothes. She finished her wine and, with Nick at her side, followed Tom to the great hall.

Here was grandeur of man's artifice to match the grandeur that nature, guided by man, had created in the garden. The walls were hung with gorgeous tapestries, but their jewel-bright colors were no more brilliant than the garb of the courtiers who wandered about like a flock of peacocks. The supper had just ended—the coach had traveled too slowly for them to arrive in time for the meal—but Kat, too excited to feel hungry, did not care. She watched as the long tables were cleared of damask and gold plate and then moved aside to prepare for the dancing. Sometimes, through the clamor of voices, she could hear the sounds of instruments being tuned, but the musicians were hidden behind the wooden screen of the gallery.

"Nick! Well met!" A gallant clad in velvet of popinjay blue, his beard streaked with dye to match his suit, came toward them. Nick introduced him to Kat as George Rosseter, a friend from Cambridge.

Kat had but a few moments to talk to George before a group of young courtiers descended upon them. "Like flies to honey," Tom murmured to Kat, his mouth twisted in a wry smile at odds with the sadness she saw in his eyes. She reached for his hand, but he was already moving away and stood apart from them while she was introduced to these other acquaintances of Nick's.

Richard Meade . . . did she not remember him from St. Paul's? He had been there when she first met Tom . . . Robert Harrison . . . Nicholas Thayer . . . William Dutton . . . . They were of Cambridge and Oxford and the Inns of Court: gentry who had perhaps mortgaged their estates to pay for the cloths of gold and silver, the tissue and tinsel, the velvets and taffetas, that they wore. God knew they reminded her more of Christopher Danvers than of sober Tom Heyford. She looked towards him, but he was studying the nearest tapestry: she would find no rescue there. And she was suddenly aware that she wished for a rescue, for a friend, someone she knew—and knew to be steadier than Nick—who would stand beside her while she dealt with these flatterers, these would-be suitors. God's light! Will Dutton was already trying to compose verses in her honor, but was stuck on the problem of finding a word to rhyme with "Katherine." She thought she heard Tom snicker, but when she glanced at him she saw he was still looking away, apparently uninterested in their conversation. And now Robin Harrison was insulting Will . . . She prayed they would not quarrel. How in God's name did the queen deal with these strutting young gamecocks?

"The queen," Nick said quietly, and for a moment Kat wondered if she had thoughtlessly spoken aloud. Then, hearing silks rustle, she turned to see the courtiers a half-dozen yards from them sink to their knees. She heard a woman's voice, cool and authoritative, but could not see who spoke. "Remember to kneel if she should stop to speak to us," Nick reminded her.

'Twas unnecessary: he had reminded her a score of times already, for there was very little chance that the queen would pass them by if she saw Nick at all. They had met before and she would be aware that he had not been to the court for some months. 'Twould be a great snub if Elizabeth looked at him but passed him by, as though she had forgotten him or he had fallen somehow into disfavor. Kat prayed that would not happen.

She felt the now-familiar mix of fear and elation again. To meet the queen! She well remembered Nick's jubilation when he first told her of Elizabeth's visit to Cambridge, how dazzled he had been by the pageantry, how impressed he had been by the scholarship the queen had displayed. *Let no one tell you that a woman cannot rule*, he had told Kat—to her bemusement, for she had never agreed with John Knox's views. *She is a most splendid and subtle prince, and seems scarce mortal.*

Then Nick was on his knees, pulling her down beside him. She knelt as gracefully as she could, envious of the skill shown by the gallants around her. For some moments she wondered if Nick had erred, if perchance the queen's gaze had not fallen on them, and then the courtiers around them parted to allow the passage of a tall, slender woman in blush-colored velvet-on-velvet who stopped in front of Nick.

"Nick."

"Your Majesty."

"We welcome your return to our court. You have been away too long."

"It could not be helped, madam."

"I was sorry to hear of your father's death. He was a good man, and loyal." She looked then at Kat, who returned the gaze curiously.

Kat saw a woman no longer young but not yet truly middle-aged. *Mortal, all too mortal,* she thought a trifle sadly, seeing that the queen's face had the sheen of egg-white glaze applied to help hide wrinkles. Elizabeth was not beautiful but nonetheless commanded attention with her regal bearing and confidence, and would have done so even if she were not a queen. Her face was pale, heavily painted to hide the faint scars that were said to be left from her bout with smallpox years ago. The red hair was, mayhap, a wig. The mouth was small and thin-lipped, the nose long and somewhat hooked, the eyes so dark—the pupils enormous—that Kat could not judge their true color. Realizing that she was staring, Kat lowered her gaze, only to find her attention caught again, this time by the queen's hands, which were indeed beautiful, the fingers exquisitely long.

"Is this your sister?" the queen asked. "You look much alike."

"Yea, Your Majesty. My sister Katherine."

"You are welcome to our court, Mistress Langdon."

"Thank you, Your Majesty," Kat responded, raising her eyes again to meet that gaze that was both dark and brilliant.

"Is it Mistress Langdon? Or peradventure you are married . . . ?"

"Not yet, Your Majesty."

"Not yet? Then you are certain you shall marry?" A brittle laugh. "God's death, you would be, for these would give you reason enough." Her gaze swept the gallants kneeling beside them. "How now, gentlemen? Think you that she can dance with all of you at once?" Kat heard cloth rustle as at least one of the courtiers shifted nervously. The queen preferred bachelors to married men at her court.

One of those bachelors stood beside her now, smiling as he looked down on the young men who might dare to rival him. Tall and swarthily handsome, Robert Dudley, the Earl of Leicester, was the queen's favorite. Kat well remembered her father's fears that Elizabeth Tudor would marry Dudley, then only her Master of Horse and no proud earl, after his young wife, Amy Robsart, died . . . or was murdered, as many said. But the young queen had been too prudent, had heeded those who warned her against the match, and Dudley was still dancing attendance . . . though now he was forced to share Elizabeth's attentions with others, especially Christopher Hatton. That lawyer-turned-courtier, seven years the queen's junior, had quite literally danced his way into her favor, first catching her attention at a masque in the Inner Temple; a year ago he had become a Gentleman of the Privy Chamber. Hatton's preferment rankled Dudley, and the earl would of certain not welcome another rival, should Nick or any of his friends become one. Leicester was not himself faithful to the queen—he was known to be the lover of the recently widowed Douglass Sheffield, and it was said by some that he had hastened Lord Sheffield's death—but he reacted to Elizabeth's dalliances as if he were a cuckolded husband.

A dangerous rival for Nick . . . The queen, who loved Leicester, called him her "Eyes," but others at the court, Nick had told her, remembered all too well that he was a Dudley, one of a tribe of traitors, whose grandfather and father, and whose brother Guildford, husband to the ill-fated Lady Jane Grey, had all been executed for their ambitions. His nickname to most of the court was "the Gypsy," for he was as dark as any of those Egyptians, and no more honest. Others, stung by his arrogance, called him *Dominus Factotum*, the Great Lord.

. . . and the Great Lord was studying her.

As though from a great distance, she heard the queen ask Nick if he still remembered how to dance, heard her brother make some light reply. Her gaze locked with Dudley's for a long moment, then his eyes lowered as he stared at the upper curves of her breasts revealed by her bodice's low neckline, which she had filled in with a partlet of white cypress edged with silver lace. Now she regretted the transparency of the material, and wished she had taken Blanche's advice and ordered a partlet of satin to match the sleeves. She had never before suffered any man to stare at her so lewdly. Pray God, the queen would notice and admonish her Eyes for looking where they should not. Or would she rebuke Kat instead? 'Twas a fearful thought.

Then, abruptly, they were gone, moving on to speak to another group of courtiers. Feeling dazed, Kat remained on her knees while the others around her stood, and finally had to be half lifted to her feet by her brother.

"You have caught Dudley's eye," he said softly. "Shall we flee the court now?"

She laughed shakily.

One by one, the young gallants who had come to speak to Nick and to meet her drifted away, on one pretext or another, seeking food or drink or conversation with a friend. By the time the musicians began to play, she was left alone with Nick and Tom . . . and then, a few moments later, with Tom only, after a young gentlewoman clad in straw-colored taffeta came to ask Nick to dance.

"It seems your admirers were but shadow men, in no way substantial," Tom remarked.

Kat nodded somberly. They had vanished, and while she knew them to be cowards, she could not deny that they were prudent cowards, well aware of the cost of angering either the queen or the Earl of Leicester.

"Will you dance?" Tom asked her. " 'Tis but a simple galliard. You'll do well."

"Will I? Well, then, chide me not if you find your faith was misplaced," she warned, but allowed him to lead her out toward the center of the hall.

She had meant to leave her pantofles in the bedchamber Tom had escorted them to earlier, but had forgotten. Now she realized that it was not as awkward to dance wearing pantofles as she had feared: these fitted snugly enough that she could manage the five quick steps quite easily, and even the caper, that spring into the air with the heels clicked together, was not much more difficult than in slippers or pumps alone. The fear she had felt for weeks—that she might be so clumsy that she would appear fit only for country dances, disgracing herself and embarrassing Nick—began to leave her, carried away by the music of the viols and rebecs and lutes.

The musicians played another galliard, then a coranto, whose quick, gliding steps she enjoyed still more. By the time the coranto was done, she could see small beads of sweat on Tom's forehead. She was feeling warm herself: the layers of silks she wore were too heavy for such exercise.

"Shall we rest awhile?" she asked Tom, and he nodded. They began to walk toward the side of the hall, but had taken only a few steps before their path was blocked by the Earl of Leicester.

"Pray dance with me, Mistress Langdon," he said, taking her hand. He smiled, and of a sudden his dark eyes seemed alight with mischief and he looked much younger than a man nearing forty.

Should she refuse? She looked at Tom, but saw only weariness and resignation on his face, and she let herself be drawn again out into the center of the hall. She hoped the next dance would not be a lavolta . . .

It was a coranto again. She gave thanks for that, but the thanksgiving was premature. Dudley's nearness robbed her of all enjoyment of the dance, rendered her movements as awkward—or at least so they seemed to her—as they had been when she was first learning the coranto. She would have done better, she knew, if she could have all but forgotten his presence, but she was constantly aware of him, of the warmth of his hand, of the musky perfume he used. She had scarce noticed Tom's perfume. And she could not stop herself from stealing glances at the earl. With his thin face and wispy beard, he was not as pretty as Nick, nor so handsome as Lord Harwood, but he was one of the best-looking men here—tall, broad-shouldered and athletic, dressed superbly in a suit of branched velvet. Like the queen, he appeared supremely assured, confident of his power. He smiled whenever their eyes met, and he was no longer staring at her breasts. It would be easy to be attracted to this man, she realized, if one did not know so much about him . . . and if he were not the queen's favorite.

Then she looked around for the queen, and saw that Elizabeth was dancing now with a gentleman younger than the earl and even more handsome. Christopher Hatton? If so, Kat was but a pawn, to be used to remind the queen that her favorite would not stand idly by while she danced with another. *At least*, Kat thought wryly, *he has no further interest in me . . .*

But when the music ended, and she would fain have left the floor, Dudley held tightly to her hand, keeping her there.

"You dance prettily, madam."

"Thank you, my lord."

"I am glad you have come to join the court. Do you stay here in the palace?"

She shook her head. "I am but visiting my cousins in London, and will return home soon." She turned slightly away from him. Where was Tom? Would he not come ask her to dance again?

"Please you, madam, reconsider. 'Twould be a great mistake to leave the court."

He had spoken lightly, but her head snapped around and she stared at him in alarm. Did he mean then to keep her with the court? Could he do so?

"Would you not rather go with the queen on her progress this summer?" he asked.

"I had not planned to be away from my home for so long," she said warily.

"You trust your steward so little?" That smile again, crinkling the outer corners of his eyes.

Nay, I trust you so little, she thought, but dared not say the words. Oh, where was Nick, to help her now?

"The queen would speak with you, my lord," said a quiet voice.

Kat turned to see the man who had been dancing with Elizabeth.

"Thank you, Master Hatton." He took his leave of Kat at once. Hatton remained at her side, though his gaze never left Dudley as the earl approached Elizabeth. The musicians began to play again.

"Will you dance with me, madam?" he asked politely.

Kat looked around at the dancers. 'Twas a lavolta. Would it be so rude to refuse him? He was not even looking at her, but stood staring at the queen again.

"In sooth, sir . . ." She paused, abashed. "I dare not attempt this while wearing pantofles."

He turned back to her, a look of surprise on his face. Then he laughed, an open, merry sound. "Yea, 'tis easier without them," he said, and slid his feet free of his pantofles, so he stood in his slippers on the clean-swept floor.

His gesture was so generous that she could give no more thought to refusing. She worked one slippered foot free, but the other pantofle was too snug to remove without using her hands. She reached down and began to pry her slipper loose from the confining velvet. She had stood bent over for several seconds, and had finally freed her slipper, before recalling the transparency of her partlet. She straightened immediately, flushing, but Hatton was again intent on the queen, completely unaware of Kat. Looking at him, she was struck by how much he reminded her of Nick, who had worn that same worshipful look when he spoke of the woman at whom Hatton was now gazing. For there was a look of worship on Hatton's face, aye, and of longing, too. *He truly loves her,* she thought, stunned to see a courtier so vulnerable. Not all at court, then, were dissemblers, treacherously dispensing court holy water and incense. She was not sure whether Hatton should be pitied or admired . . .

Then, as if he had just recalled her presence, he turned to her, took her hand and led her a few steps further into the hall.

They began to dance.

She had feared that she would seem more clumsy and unpracticed than ever as Hatton's partner, that the dance would be a prolonged torture for her, but the opposite was true. Hatton, attuned to her every movement, moved so gracefully beside her that she felt more graceful herself, even when his hands closed around her waist to help lift her into the air during the leaps. She was dismayed when the music stopped, certain that the musicians had quit playing too soon, but when she looked around she saw that no one else appeared surprised that the lavolta had ended. 'Twas but her imagination, then.

She turned to Hatton, wanting to thank him for having made her feel so at ease, but he was again ignoring her as he watched the queen. Kat's enjoyment began to dissipate. She had been looking forward to dancing with Hatton again—would have gladly danced with him the entire evening—but now she realized she would have to set him free somehow, perchance by telling him that she must needs rest for a while. Then, to her relief, she saw Tom approaching.

"Will it please you to dance with me again, Kat?" he said when he had reached her.

Hatton, to his credit, feigned disappointment well, then took his leave as gracefully as he had danced.

"There goes a man who loves the queen well," Kat murmured as soon as the courtier was out of earshot.

"Yea, i'faith. Would that she preferred him to Dudley." He smiled at her. "Will you dance, Kat? Or would you rather cool your heels? I have discovered your pantofles, and put them where they will trip no one up."

He led her to where he had left the pantofles and helped her fit her slippers into them again, then went to get glasses of wine for them. Kat stood contentedly watching the dancers. Hatton had again persuaded the queen to dance with him, and he was a pleasure to watch. As was Elizabeth. The queen's energy amazed Kat. Elizabeth had danced every dance so far this evening, but showed no signs of tiring. Nick had told Kat that the queen frequently danced till midnight, then rose the next morning at dawn for a brisk walk with her ladies before attending to state business. Few of her councillors could keep up with her.

But where was Nick? Aware that she had not seen him for at least a quarter of an hour, she took a few steps along the wall, scanning the dancers. She saw another gallant in bronze satin, but his hair was dark, not fair like Nick's. She would have liked to look for him further, but dared not wander too far from where Tom had left her. Disappointed, she turned back, nearly colliding with a gentleman dressed in black and white silk.

"Cry you merc—" The word caught in her throat as she looked up at a familiar olive-skinned face.

"Pray your pardon, lady," he said in that too-familiar voice. "I see I have startled you, when I meant only to ask you to dance."

With a supreme effort of will, she tore her gaze from his face. She looked away from him, her head lowered. Would he recognize her? At the Bel Savage she had felt no such fear, as she had been masked. Now her only mask was the paint she wore. She could only hope that the light, flattering paint she had applied this afternoon was different enough from the heavy, strumpetlike paint she had worn at the Jerusalem Tree that she would appear a different woman now, especially with her finery.

"Nay, you have not startled me." She spoke quietly, wishing she had not begun to apologize to him a few moments ago. She would have tried to alter her voice somewhat, but could not do that now. " 'Tis I who must pray your pardon, for, good sir, I cannot dance with you, as I have promised to dance with another." She all but turned her back to him, looking around for Tom, who was nowhere in sight.

"*Dios*, I envy him! Please you, tell me how I may win such a promise."

She spun around to face him. Stunned by his use of the Spanish oath, and by the faint Spanish accent she had heard in his speech, she could only stare at him mutely.

Gradually his face took on a puzzled expression. "Have we met, lady?" he asked. "You look familiar . . . and yet I will not believe that I could have ever seen you and then forgotten you."

"Fie, sir, such court holy water! I warrant we have never met. Like enough, you have seen other women who favor me. 'Tis not such an uncommon face."

"You wrong yourself, madam. 'Tis a face to inspire heroes—"

"And think you, sirrah, that you are one?" Tom asked. She had not noticed his approach. His face was red with anger; she had never seen him angry before. "Belike you think it bravery to come to court now, but others would call it foolhardy."

Kat stiffened. Should this Spaniard, who had once been introduced to her as Henry Malcomb, call Tom a liar, then a challenge to a *duello* would follow—to the queen's great displeasure and, haply, Tom's greater harm. But she could think of nothing to stop this now.

The Spaniard's eyes had narrowed. He stared at Tom for what seemed a long time before saying at last, " 'Twould be foolhardy to respond in kind." He turned to Kat. "Good even, madam," he said quietly, and then walked away.

"An arrant knave and coward," Tom said—but not, Kat noticed, loudly enough for the Spaniard to hear him. He handed her a glass of wine. His hands were shaking, but she guessed that was from rage rather than fear. Tom might be discreet enough to avoid pressing an argument to the point of a *duello* while at court, but he did not seem to be afraid of the man she knew as Henry Malcomb.

"A Spaniard at court?" she asked, trying to keep her voice light. "Now? Who is he?"

"He is Francisco Muñoz de Herrera, a secretary to Don Guerau de Spes, the Spanish ambassador. 'Sblood, that he should be welcome here! I trow there are too many at court who mistake the knave's ability to speak good English for a sympathy with our country, and he does all he can to encourage their foolishness."

Kat nodded. There would still be people at court who remembered that Queen Mary's husband, Philip, had not considered it necessary to master English, for all that he would have mastered England's treasury, had his wife allowed it. Muñoz de Herrera's easy command of the language would be a pleasant contrast to their memories of Spanish arrogance and scorn for the English—especially pleasant in comparison to the current ambassador from Spain, who, Nick had told her, was a contentious malefactor who seemed to rejoice in his ability to infuriate the officials he had to deal with, even the normally calm and reasoned Cecil. Were Muñoz as agreeable at court as he had appeared to be at the Jerusalem Tree and at the Bel Savage, then he would be attractive indeed to those who felt it necessary to conciliate Spain. Here, they would feel, was a man they could talk to . . . and in their own language.

Which, when at court, Muñoz spoke with just enough of an accent to remind his listeners that he was Spanish.

. . . but not all the time. Though she could not be sure, it seemed to her that his English had been free of any foreign accent when he first spoke to her, that he had spoken English as one from Spain only later. Perhaps he had himself been so startled that he had forgotten to pretend that his command of English was less than it was? Yea, certainly, for she knew she would not have failed to notice that accent. She must tell Nick.

Dear God. *Nick!* She looked around for him wildly. She must find him before he encountered Muñoz, try to get him away from here. It was all too likely that the Spaniard, though failing to recognize her, would remember Nick from the Jerusalem Tree . . .

Yet he was still nowhere in sight.

She turned to Tom, gripping his arm in her excitement. "Have you seen Nick? I must speak with him."

"I saw him when I went to get the wine. There." He gestured toward the far end of the hall. "He was talking to Francis Walsingham."

Kat suppressed a cry of dismay. Should Muñoz see Nick with Walsingham—and if he knew Walsingham's work for Cecil, which was likely—then he would suspect that he and Lisle had been spied upon, and Nick might be in yet more danger. She handed Tom her wine glass and started toward the place he had indicated, walking as fast as her pantofles allowed.

Nick had danced with three gentlewomen already, and was still basking in the warmth of their sweet welcomes and compliments as he stood quietly watching the glittering courtiers. So he had been missed. By God, he should have returned to court sooner, bringing Kat with him. He glanced toward where he had seen her a few moments before, dancing with no less a favorite than Christopher Hatton, who had, thank God, separated her from Leicester—though that may well have been the queen's doing, for Leicester now danced with Elizabeth. Nick turned toward the slim figure in blush velvet just in time to see the queen leap into the air, Leicester's hands on her waist. He had heard gossip that Elizabeth was suffering from a sore leg, a painful ulcer like the one that had plagued her father, but no one seeing her now would give credence to such stories . . .

"Good even, sir. I am glad to see you at court again."

Nick started slightly, then turned around, amazed to find Francis Walsingham standing just a few feet away.

A somber crow among the peacocks of the court, Walsingham, in the plain black that suited his Puritan inclinations, should have been instantly noticeable. Nick could scarce believe that he had failed to mark his presence here tonight, and as he responded to Walsingham's greeting, he wondered if mayhap there were truly such magics as cloaks to make a man invisible. Of certain Walsingham had been all but invisible, as befitted the queen's spy-master.

They spoke of personal matters for some minutes. Walsingham offered Nick his condolences on Henry Langdon's death, then asked about Beechwood and the Gardiners. He was so agreeable that anyone listening would have thought them old friends, but Nick had spoken to Walsingham only a few times previously, and then no more than a few polite words each time. At first it troubled him that the man knew so much about him, but then he dismissed that worry from his mind: eliciting information was, after all, Walsingham's business. And he was content to talk idly, for he dreaded the questions that he was sure would be asked eventually about his encounter with Lisle. It was one thing to be at odds with Sparrow, quite another to displease his master.

Then Walsingham said, very pleasantly, "I feel I must apologize for my Sparrowhawk. He takes too much upon himself sometimes."

"Sparrowhawk?"

Walsingham smiled. "So the queen nicknamed him, after the one time she saw him with me. You may know him as Sparrow, for so most men call him, and 'tis said he accepts it himself. He's a good man, though limited, like his namesake. A hawk to be sent after small prey, and close to home. I erred in setting a sparrowhawk over a gerfalcon."

Nick could think of nothing to say: the last thing he had expected to hear was such a compliment. Baffled, he studied Walsingham's dark, austerely handsome face, but could read nothing of the man's thoughts there. Dark hair, dark eyes, dark skin: Elizabeth, with her penchant for nicknaming those about her, had dubbed Walsingham her "Moor."

"I would have you know that your work at the Jerusalem Tree was appreciated," Walsingham said.

"Thank you, sir. I was glad to be of service."

"My Sparrowhawk tells me you are fond of things Italian." He chuckled. " 'Tis something he is wont to notice. Tell me, have you ever traveled to Italy?"

"No, Master Walsingham," Nick replied, a bit warily. Surely Walsingham already knew the answer to that question?

"Italy can be a marvelous place to study. I studied there myself, years ago."

"So I have heard." Walsingham had lived abroad during most of Queen Mary's reign, leaving England soon after Sir Thomas Wyatt's abortive rebellion in 1554: a wise move, as some of his family had been involved in the rebellion. But he had made more of his exile than the enjoyment of a time of safety away from England's Catholic queen. He had studied Roman civil law at the university of Padua on Venice's *terra firma*, and had even been elected Consolarius of the English nation at the university, a post that had given him a role in choosing the rector of the university and had made him responsible for both upholding the rights and overseeing the behavior and finances of the English students. *And he was then scarce older than I am now*, Nick thought, of a sudden ashamed of his idleness since leaving Gray's Inn.

Walsingham had learned more than law in Italy, Nick knew. Others, like George Calvert, might while away their time with Italian masters of fence and horsemanship, or the famed courtesans of Venice, but Walsingham had apparently studied the turbulence of Italian politics, learning most of all from the Venetians and the wily Jesuits, both masters of open statecraft and hidden machinations. Nick remembered Anthony Holmeden saying that Walsingham had once told him that books were but dead letters; true knowledge could be had only when those books were given life through conversations with other men. Where better than Italy, then, to study the statecraft expounded by such philosophers as Machiavelli? The knowledge gained there now benefited the queen.

"Should you wish to study there," Walsingham said, "I have friends who can make all necessary arrangements."

"A kind offer, sir. I have family duties keeping me here for the nonce, but I will consider it."

"Very well," said Walsingham with a smile, seeming not the least disappointed that Nick had not expressed interest in leaving for Italy immediately. *But then*, Nick thought, *he would not have expected me to do so, as he knows so much of my affairs.* Walsingham was content to wait for a time, for all that it was obvious that he wanted another intelligencer in Italy.

What had Walsingham called him? A gerfalcon—a hawk suitable for capturing larger, swifter prey than could be brought down by the reliable but limited sparrowhawk. Nick knew it was flattery, but still his spirits soared, no longer burdened by Sparrow's criticism. He knew he would go to Italy: there was no question of refusing this opportunity presented by Walsingham. But he could not make plans to leave without arranging first for someone to protect Kat. Perchance she could stay with the Gardiners . . .

"How now, sirs! What's the matter? My Moor and my squire stand here in idle talk while my maids want for partners! Are you not dancing this evening?"

Nick turned to see the queen approaching, Leicester still with her.

He sank to his knees, hardly aware of Walsingham also kneeling beside him. Her squire. She had called him her squire. The queen tended to bestow nicknames on those for whom she felt affection or contempt, and he could not believe that it was the latter. He glanced at Dudley, only to see the earl glowering at him. Nay, Dudley did not think it was contempt, either.

"Our talk had just ended, Your Majesty," Walsingham replied after the queen bade him and Nick rise again.

" 'Twas of important matters, I hope," Elizabeth said. "The proper width of a ruff, or the best perfume for gloves?" Her eyes seemed to dance with amusement as she regarded her plainly dressed official. The queen was said to respect Walsingham's abilities, but she had little sympathy for his staunch Protestant beliefs and austere tastes. For his part, Walsingham was said to consider the queen's tolerance of Catholics—that is, those Catholics who outwardly complied with her laws—deplorable.

"Less important, Your Majesty. We spoke of Italy."

"Nay, Master Walsingham, say not that Italy is less important. Do you not know that I am half Italian?"

"I have heard that you have said so, madam," Walsingham replied slowly, and Nick smiled. He, too, had heard that Elizabeth was known to make that odd boast when she spoke of her love of things Italian.

"You smile, my squire," Elizabeth said, turning her attention to Nick. "Think you Italy is unimportant?"

"Nay, madam. Truth to tell, I would study there."

"Study what? Velvet patterns? I would fain have someone in England who would see that we have velvets as fine as those from Genoa."

"I would gladly turn weaver, madam, if that is your wish."

"And would you sing psalms then, as our Flemish weavers do?"

"Not unless you wish it."

"A most agreeable weaver," Dudley interposed. "I warrant you, madam, he weaves a net for your heart."

"Nay, Robin," the queen said, shaking her head, "for I bade him make velvets, not nets." Her gaze returned to Nick. "Pray tell me, what would you study, in sooth?"

"Politics, Your Majesty."

Her laughter was a crow of delight. "Politics? Then I must call you not my squire, but my politico! What say you, my lord?" She looked mischievously at the earl, whose face had turned masklike as he tried in vain to hide his displeasure.

"Truly," Dudley said at last, "the time cries out for politicos. Her Majesty and I were discussing the Queen of Scots, Master Langdon. What think you of her?"

Elizabeth raised her brows but made no comment on Dudley's challenge, though Nick prayed that she would say something, anything, that would give him a clue as to how he should respond. He remembered now that her favorite motto was said to be *Video et taceo—I see and I am silent.* That silence had served her well in the past, when she chose to use it to avoid committing herself at times when delays and indecision could be to her advantage. But he felt like cursing her for remaining silent now. Did she peradventure enjoy Leicester's attempt to draw him into a treacherous quicksand?

For the subject of the Queen of Scots was a quicksand, and Nick would as lief have juggled lighted matches amidst fireworks as voiced his opinion on that subject, especially before Elizabeth. There had been no more vexing question for the queen than what to do with her Scottish cousin, and the issue was more pressing than ever now that there was the possibility that France or Spain, or both together, would heed the pope's wishes and invade England. But what answer would Elizabeth want to hear from him, when she had already heard so many conflicting opinions from her councillors?

Nick thought he knew what answer Walsingham would have him give. Walsingham had written a pamphlet about the Queen of Scots a year ago, when the Duke of Norfolk was considering marrying her, a marriage that had the approval of others on the council. Holmeden had given Nick a copy of the pamphlet, and Nick had been struck by Walsingham's arguments. He could recall every word of the section of the pamphlet dealing specifically with Mary's character, Walsingham's *Consideration of the Q. of Scotts person.*

> *In religion she is either a Papist wch is evill, or ells an Atheist wch is worse, and in league joyned wth the confederate enemies of the Gospell by the name of the holy league, to roote out all such Princes and magistrates as are Professors of the same. A thing well knowne, though not generallie.*
>
> *Of nation, she is a Scott, of wch nation I forbeare to say what may be said, in a reverend respect of a few godly of that nation.*
>
> *Of Inclination, how she is given, let her own horrible acts publicly knowen to the whole world witnes, though now of late certen seduced by practise seeke to cloke and hide the same.*
>
> *Of Allyance on the Mothers side how she is descended of a race that is both enemy to God and the common quiet of Europe, every man knoweth, but alas too manie have felt.*
>
> *In goodwill towards our soveraigne she hath shewed herself sundry waies very evill affected, whose ambition hath drawen her by bearing the Armes of England to decipher herself to be a Competitair to this Crowne, a thing publiquely knowen . . .*

Nick could perhaps please Walsingham by voicing opinions like those in the pamphlets, but would not that brand him, in the queen's eyes, as merely Walsingham's creature? Nor was he entirely sure that Walsingham would welcome such slavish agreement . . .

The Earl of Leicester, pleased that Nick had not responded immediately, began to smile. Nick knew, too, what answer would suit Dudley. 'Twas said that Dudley and those of his party favored releasing the Queen of Scots from her long captivity as a way of appeasing the Catholic powers of Europe. But Nick was in no mood to agree with the earl, especially if he might by doing so merely be adding weight to any arguments that Dudley had just made to the queen.

Nor, he realized with a feeling of exultation, would it be necessary either to agree or disagree with Dudley. There was a safe path across this quicksand, for the earl had asked only what Nick thought of the Queen of Scots, not what he thought should be done about her.

"I have never met the Queen of Scots," he said softly, "but I have talked with those who have, and they have described her to me. 'Tis said . . ." He paused. Elizabeth's smile had become a forced and brittle thing, and her eyes had narrowed to slits as she regarded him. Did she fear that he would praise Mary Stuart's beauty, as so many did, to Elizabeth's great displeasure? Yet those who had met Mary also marveled at her height: at six feet, the Scottish queen was taller than most men. " 'Tis said," he murmured, "that she looks too high."

There was a moment of silence, and then another delighted crow of laughter from the queen. "By God's precious blood! I must agree! Too high indeed! She looks too near my throne!"

"Truly, madam, I believe he meant only that she is too long a woman," Dudley said coolly.

Elizabeth shook her head. "Nay, Robin, he meant that and more. 'Twas a most subtle and politic answer, Master Politico."

"A most careful answer," Dudley agreed ill-humoredly. "Are you always so careful, Master Langdon? For, as they say, care killed the cat, though it had nine lives."

"Careful, but not too careful, my lord," Nick replied, meeting Dudley's gaze calmly.

"Indeed, this cat is not too careful," Elizabeth remarked. "Nor is that other cat, his sister."

Nick looked at her wonderingly. Did she know that Kat had followed him to the Jerusalem Tree? Did her officials tell the queen so much? "You do not, I pray, think we should have been more careful?"

"No, Master Politico. You were careful enough, and no more."

So she did know. And she approved—or at least did not disapprove.

Smiling a little with satisfaction, Nick glanced at Dudley, who seemed confused.

"Now, gentlemen," the queen said, "will you forget all your cares and dance?"

"All our cares?" It was Walsingham who spoke.

"Yea, for I have this evening," the queen told him. "I have forgotten my cares and feel secure."

Indeed, Nick thought, she looked as though she had not a care in the world. Whatever she and Leicester had said of the Queen of Scots, it seemed to have left her good humor untouched. Gazing at her admiringly, Nick began to doubt the stories that the queen's reaction to the papal bull had been to retreat tearfully to her private chambers. Other rumors had said that she had instead laughed and made up verses about the pope. That seemed much more likely now.

"While I would have you feel secure, madam," Walsingham said, "I would not have you forget that there can be great danger in security."

"Not for me, Sir Moor," the queen responded. "Not while I have you to be careful for me. Pray God, you will always serve me."

"With all my heart, madam." Walsingham bowed, clearly pleased by the compliment.

"Now dance, gentlemen! Find partners and caper! 'Tis my command, and you will obey it if you would not lose your heads." Laughing, she was gone, sweeping away with Dudley to join those dancing a galliard.

Dazzled, Nick could only stare after her. Not until Walsingham cleared his throat did he remember that the official was still standing beside him.

"Most subtle and politic indeed," Walsingham said with a smile. "Yea, you are meet for Italy, and will do well there. But that is for the future, and for now we must dance. Good night."

Nick watched him walk away, then jumped slightly as he felt a hand on his arm, smelled a familiar rose-scented perfume. Had the queen returned? But no, 'twas only Kat. He tried to mask his disappointment, and smiled as he took her hand.

"Come, sweet sister, we must dance." Jesu, but she looked troubled. Perchance the court did not agree with her? Then mayhap she would not object to staying with the Gardiners while he traveled to Italy.

"No, sweet brother, we must leave," she told him in a whisper. "Henry Malcomb is here, and he is no sea captain, but a Spaniard serving de Spes. Quick. We must go, lest he see you and know you. I pray he has not seen you already . . ."

————

Half an hour later their coach rattled away from Hampton Court. Nick rode inside with Kat and Louise, as she had requested. He was so curious to hear her news that she had not had to ask him twice.

Louise, fast asleep and reeking of wine, lay across the seat at the back of the coach. Kat and Nick sat facing her, their backs to the driver, their feet braced on the floor.

"Think you she truly sleeps?" Nick asked quietly when they were a mile or two from the palace.

"She sleeps, by my faith. I know that snore."

"Good. So tell me where you saw Malcomb."

She recounted her conversation with the Spaniard.

"Are you sure this was the man?" Nick asked when she had finished.

"By God's holy body! Do you take me for a fool or a blindwoman, that my own senses cannot be trusted?"

"Cry you mercy, Kat, but I must be certain of this before I say a word to Walsingham," he said edgily. " 'Twould not do to look foolish now," he added, so softly that Kat wondered if he were talking to himself.

"Tom said you spoke with Walsingham."

Nick nodded.

"Of what did you speak?"

She listened carefully as he described his conversation with Walsingham. As more became clear, she was torn between happiness and sorrow. God knew she wanted Nick to be able to study in Italy, since that was what he wanted. But she would miss him.

"You should go," she said at last. " 'Tis best for you."

"Would you stay with the Gardiners?"

"With the Gardiners? Why? Can I not stay at Beechwood?"

Nick shook his head. " 'Twould not be proper for a maid to live alone."

She looked away, her heart sinking. She knew that. 'Twas the reason Nick had stayed so long at Beechwood after their father's funeral, rather than returning to the Inns of Court.

After a time, she asked, "What of Muñoz? What shall we do about him? Will you not tell Walsingham?"

They had pulled the curtains aside to let in the fresh night air, but even with some moonlight entering the coach, it was still too dark for her to see Nick's expression. He was silent for a long time.

"If I were wrong again . . ." His voice trailed off.

You mean, if I were wrong again, Kat thought, but kept the thought to herself. "There is one way to be sure. If you will not tell him what I have discovered, so that he may have someone endeavor to spy upon Lisle and Muñoz when they meet again, then we must be there. 'Tis but three days hence," she added, recalling the date the two men had discussed at the Jerusalem Tree. "We must needs leave tomorrow."

"We? Nay, Kat, you will stay here."

"If I do, I shall tell Walsingham where you have gone."

"You would not."

"Yea, I would. I swear it."

"You tomboy! You would seek out danger, when I would protect you from it?"

"How protect me, when Lisle and Muñoz wander freely abroad? And how cage them securely, unless we learn more of their treason?"

"I can learn of that treason alone."

"Nay, good brother, for they spoke in Spanish at the Jerusalem Tree, and my Spanish is better than yours."

"Unkind, good sister."

"Yet true. And you must acknowledge it, as you are an honest gentleman—when you are not a rogue. But come, Nick, no arguments now. You may well need me there, for if they contrive their plots in Spanish, 'twill be a quick business. They will not wait for you to check each word in a dictionary, nor would you dare ask them how some word is spelled, that you may find it more readily."

She drew a chuckle from Nick, but he said nothing for quite a while. When he spoke at last, his remark startled her.

"The queen knows that you were at the Jerusalem Tree."

"So Sparrow told her!" She felt almost sick with fear. "Then I shall tell her that he would have John Knox order our opinions of women."

"No need for that, for I trow it was Walsingham who told her, and he thanked me for what we did at the Jerusalem Tree. Nor did the queen speak ill of you, Kat. She said you were just careful enough, and no more."

"Well, then. So shall we be when we go to visit Lisle. Just careful enough. For," she added musingly, "any more would be a waste."

To her annoyance, Nick thought that some jest.

CHAPTER 13

" 'Travel not by the way with him that is brainless lest he do thee evil,' " Kat whispered, quoting the well-remembered words from Ecclesiasticus, " 'For he followeth his own wilfulness, and so shalt thou perish through his folly.' "

"What?" Nick asked, also in a whisper.

" 'Twas nothing," Kat muttered, not daring to repeat the warning from the book that had been one of their father's favorite parts of the Bible. Nick would think she meant him, and in truth she had when she first recalled the words, but now she had to admit that the warning given by Jesus the Son of Sirach applied as much to her. Perhaps even more. But at least one thing was certain: their father would have called both of them brainless, if not lunatic, had he seen them now.

They crept in deepest shadow beside a wall. To Kat's right, topiary beasts shaped from yew raised their leafy heads toward a starry sky. To her left, sometimes catching the shabby cloth of her old doublet with grasping thorns, was a mass of roses trained against the stone, their scent heavy as any perfume. Ahead of her loomed the brick and stone and glass of Harwood Hall, light showing only through the open window of a chamber on the second floor.

It had been late afternoon before they first came in sight of the fine new manor house set on a wooded slope a mile from the village of Harwood. By that time they had been riding since dawn, except for a brief stop at Stamworth and a short break for dinner at an inn. Kat, dressed in Nick's shabby castoff garments and pretending to be his manservant, had ridden the Blackamoor, and Nick his swift roan Barbary gelding. They had gone past the manor, then left the horses in a nearby wildwood. Knowing it might be hours before they returned, they had unbridled their horses and hobbled them, leaving them tethered, contentedly cropping the grass, in a small clearing surrounded by thickets.

'Twill be late, Muñoz had told Lord Harwood at the Jerusalem Tree, after inquiring again about the date they were to meet next. Kat and Nick had gambled that his plans had not changed. They had hidden themselves in a clump of bushes near the road, within sight of the gatehouse, and waited. It was well past sunset, with the twilight fast thickening into night, when two riders came galloping toward Harwood Hall. Even in the gathering dusk, Kat was close enough to feel certain that the rider in the lead was Muñoz.

"Malcomb?" Nick had whispered, a look of confusion on his face. "But the beard . . ."

"Yea, a neat, small beard, like to the one he wore at the Bel Savage. Either Henry Malcomb—if there is such a man—has turned barbermonger since last we saw him, or this is Muñoz, and he changes his beards as often as other men change their shirts." She shifted uncomfortably, was stuck in the arm by a branch, shifted again. " 'Sdeath! Would it were full dark . . ."

Twenty minutes later, cloaked by darkness, they had left their shelter and scaled the wall of the garden, leaving a rope hanging from the stone knob on one corner of the wall, ready for when they needed it.

Thinking of that rope now, Kat wondered if leaving it there had been a mistake. Should anyone be wandering late in the garden—lovers, perchance, or someone suffering from melancholy and seeking out darkness and solitude to match his humor—the rope might be discovered, and a search begun for them. Mayhap they should leave now? Was it not enough to be able to tell Walsingham that Muñoz had ridden so far to meet secretly with Lord Harwood?

Yet she knew it was not enough, not nearly enough, to repay them for the lengths to which they had gone to be here.

First, there was the explanation they had given to Blanche and Will—who had, thank God, been willing enough to accept their story that Kat had reason to fear the Earl of Leicester's intentions. Indeed, she had been so quick to agree that Kat would be safer from the earl in Sussex that the younger woman had half feared that Blanche would send all her menservants along to serve as guards.

And then, after deceiving the Gardiners about their reason for leaving London, they had again taken advantage of Jane's good will. After leaving their steward with orders to contact Jane for advice about the estate, should they not return within four days, they had ridden to Stamworth early this morning to ask Jane's cooperation.

It was an uncomfortable memory for Kat now, and had been a painful scene then. Jane, already awake for an hour and busy with the day's tasks, looked particularly lovely in a kirtle of watchet calico, yet Nick, impatient to be on his way to Hampshire, had paid her no more heed than if she had been one of their maidservants. Kat could not doubt that her brother's indifference had hurt Jane. And then they had perforce asked her to help them without knowing what they were about.

"Yea, I will be glad to help your steward, should he need my advice," Jane had told them. "But where, please it you to tell me, may I reach you in Hampshire, should I need to send a message? Pray your pardon if you have told me before of these cousins you will visit, but I do not remember hearing of them before." Her voice had been so sweet, surely that had not been an accusation. But Nick had responded as though it had been . . .

"Must you know?" he asked sharply. " 'Twill be but a few days, and we might well pass any messenger you send on our return to Beechwood."

Now Jane did look suspicious.

"No messages will be necessary, I trow," Kat said quickly. "But should we not return within four days, pray write to the court—"

"Kat!" Nick took a step toward her.

"—to Master Francis Walsingham."

"Jesu, Kat!" His face was flushed with anger.

"By my faith, Nick! Someone must know, if aught goes awry."

"Walsingham," Jane murmured. Her face was as white as Nick's was red. "So this is the queen's business y'are about? As you were at the Jerusalem Tree?" She looked at first Kat and then Nick; both were as still as statues. After a moment, she nodded.

"You may not need to write him," Kat said in a small voice.

"You will not," Nick asserted. "We'll be back in a few days."

"So say you," Jane said, her voice unsteady.

Kat went to her and took her hand. "You may hear from a man of Walsingham's, a man named Sparrow." She described Sparrow briefly. "He is of small stature, as drab as his namesake and just as noisy. But you may trust him to fly straight to his master with any message you give him."

"And what message would you have me give him?"

Kat was silent for a few moments, having given no thought to the matter before. "You may tell him that we have been away longer than expected, on a visit to a friend in Hampshire."

"A friend? Not cousins?" Jane laughed. "You lose cousins so easily, and with no sign of mourning . . . Nay, I shall not jest. Would you have me keep those cousins alive for the sake of your steward?"

"Marry, we would," Kat replied. "All our household believe we have gone to visit our cousins."

"Then I shall suffer their ignorance." Suddenly she looked anguished. "But must I suffer my own? Can you not tell me of this friend . . . ? Nay," she answered herself after a glance at Nick, "I see you cannot."

" 'Twould be a danger to you, to know any more," Nick said.

"And you would fain protect me," Jane said bitterly, her tone seeming to shock Nick. "Very well, then. I will pray for your quick return, but if that is not to be, then I shall keep watch for your Sparrow. God speed."

There had seemed to be nothing more to say, so they had taken their leave. Nick's relief at escaping Jane's presence had been obvious enough to rankle Kat, and she had not spoken to him during the first few miles of their ride . . .

Was Jane still angry? Pray God, she would come to understand that they truly could have told her no more.

Nick had stopped where the stone wall of the garden met the fine new bricks of the manor house. He put his fingers to his lips, warning her to keep silent. Perhaps he had thought he heard a footstep, but she could hear nothing more than the bright gurgle of a nearby fountain and the music of a breeze sifting through myriad leaves. At last he moved, stepping free of the shadow by the wall. Moonlight gilded his hair and skin, and Kat wished of a sudden that they had thought to bring dark hoods.

He gestured for her to follow him, and she did, walking silently on the grass beside the path. Past a darkened window, with other windows, equally dark, above it . . . Past a doorway . . . Past another window . . . And at last they stood below the single window that showed a light.

A man was speaking. Lisle. She shivered as she recognized his voice, which she had thought never to hear again after leaving the Jerusalem Tree. Then Muñoz spoke. She dug her fingernails into her palms. God, would neither of them speak any louder? She could recognize no words, though the cadences were those of English, not Spanish. But wait—had that been Spanish? She felt like screaming. To be so near, and yet unable to hear them!

She jumped when Nick touched her arm. Leaning so close that his lips nearly touched her ear, he whispered, so softly she could scarce hear him, "Can you hear them well enough to tell what they are saying?"

She shook her head.

"Then"—a pause—"can you climb?"

She stared at him in disbelief for a few moments, then looked at the wall. There was just enough light for her to see shadows marking possible hand- and footholds beside the window at which they stood, and the ornamental stonework above the window might allow her to pull herself up another few feet. She could manage the climb, as Nick had realized. And she knew he could not: he had never been able to climb as well as she could.

"Yea, I can climb this," she breathed.

She gazed up at the stone cornice. Reaching that would put her ten feet closer to Lisle and Muñoz, haply close enough to hear a few more quietly spoken words. But was it worth the risk?

"Kat, if you fear to do this—" Nick began.

She shook her head. "Nay, I am merely reluctant, like the cat that would eat fish but not wet its feet."

"Would that wet feet were the only danger here."

She raised a finger to her lips. Muñoz was speaking again, in English, his voice raised.

"But, God! if he could see the queen . . ."

She swore under her breath as he lowered his voice and she again lost the sense of his words, but she had heard enough to make a decision. If they were even now plotting for some traitor—some assassin, maybe—to be brought into the queen's presence, then she must take the risk.

She reached up to probe the first shadowed niche in the brickwork, tightened her fingers around the edge of the brick, and tugged. Then she let herself drop, most of her weight hanging from that brick. It held firm. Good enough.

She turned to Nick. "Help me to the window ledge?"

He lifted her until she could set her foot on the ledge, then held her steady while she sought new handholds and finally stood there balanced, pressed against the mullioned window. Above her, Lisle and Muñoz continued their conversation, but she no longer concentrated on that. All that mattered to her at the moment was that they not hear her begin her ascent.

Setting her hands and feet in niches beside the window, she climbed toward the stone carving overhead.

Muñoz was an ass.

Tandy had recognized that the first time he saw the man last summer. Muñoz had been walking with de Spes in the garden of the petty canons at St. Paul's, and both of them had been loudly lamenting the garden's existence and the loss of Pardon Churchyard, with its cloister walls painted with the Dance of Death, which had stood there until late in the reign of Henry VIII. Tandy had followed them unobtrusively as de Spes took his new secretary on a tour of London's churches and former church sites, with the ambassador pointing out what had been lost or defaced as a result of Henry's break with Rome. The church of the Gray Friars, where the marble tombs and gravestones had been torn down and sold. The old site of the parish church of St. Alphage near Cripplesgate, now replaced by the saw pits of a carpenter's yard. The taverns and tenements built in place of St. Martin's le Grand. The ruins of the priory of St. Bartholomew. The defaced monuments in the churches of St. Pancrates and St. Mary Bow and St. Mary Aldenbury and all the others they visited . . . And at each church or site, the Spaniards had sighed so heavily, and wrung their hands so, that any unknowing observer would have thought the two about to expire of melancholy. Tandy had never seen a clumsier miming of grief.

But it was in the garden that had replaced Pardon Churchyard that Muñoz had carried this public display too far. After hearing from de Spes that the Dance of Paul's, as the mural painting on the vanished cloister had been known, had been copied from the Danse Macabre of St. Innocent's in Paris, Muñoz had loudly bewailed the desecration. He had visited St. Innocent's, he declared; he had seen those fabulous painted walls, and so knew that what had been lost here was an invaluable reminder of mortality, of the fleeting nature of man's life on earth compared to the immortality of the soul. Was that what was the matter with these English, he asked aloud, that they gave no thought to their own deaths? Was it such blindness that led them to accept their filthy church, that abomination born of Henry VIII's adultery with Anne Boleyn, that abomination that was the first of the two surviving bastards born of Henry's lust for the Boleyn witch?

Muñoz had spat out the name of the queen's mother, as though he felt even speaking it defiled him, and he crossed himself when he called her a witch. That was too much for a young gallant who had also been listening. The youth began to draw his sword, and Tandy had to move with lightning swiftness to stay that motion, wrestling the youth away from the two Spaniards before Muñoz even noticed how close he had come to making an end of his own fleeting life.

It was a rescue Tandy almost regretted. Had his master not been interested in Muñoz, he might have let the gallant strike to avenge the insult to the queen. But Justin had been unwilling to approach de Spes, who was far too clumsy and obvious in his plottings and would have brought suspicion on them almost at once. Fool though Muñoz was to make this show of grief—even if it was done, as Tandy suspected, to impress de Spes, who enjoyed anything that enraged the English—at least he offered them the chance to avoid the elaborate snares the ambassador unwittingly set for himself with his conspiracies. Lord Harwood's Spanish brother-in-law had warned them against de Spes, so Muñoz it must be, and would be, if he would let Justin counsel him so their meetings might escape detection. Thus, some hours after saving Muñoz's life, and despite his personal dislike of the man, Tandy had arranged for a letter to be delivered to the Spaniard that led him to meet with Lord Harwood that night. And so it had begun.

Tandy thanked God now that he rarely had to deal with Muñoz himself.

He gazed at his master, who was seated on a leather-upholstered chair across from Muñoz. Good Cordovan leather, that: a gift from the Spaniard, a token of friendship. No one observing the baron casually would guess that he felt anything but friendship for Muñoz, but Tandy knew Justin well and could interpret the complete stillness of his hands as they rested on the chair's arms. His perfect outward quiet meant inward trouble. Muñoz, as always, tried what little patience Lord Harwood had.

And now there was this matter of George Wilford . . .

"If he is willing to take the risk," Muñoz asked, almost pleading, "should he not? There are none who suspect him—"

"So say you."

Muñoz's face darkened with anger. "You need my help, my lord. Never insult me thus."

"Pray do not insult me, either, with such harebrained schemes. Trust me to know the court, and what will succeed."

Muñoz was silent for some moments. Tandy heard leaves rustle outside, then, faintly, a scrabbling noise. Perchance some rat seeking admittance at one of the lower windows . . .

"Better than he does?" the Spaniard asked at last.

Justin laughed. "Much better."

Muñoz sighed. "He may not stay this action . . ."

"Pray God, he does. There is too much risk in this."

"Then I shall tell him so." Muñoz rose gracefully, and let Tandy help him with his cloak. "You need not see me out," he said when he was ready to leave, "since your foot still pains you." There was a flash of white teeth.

Justin thumped his bandaged-wrapped heel on the floor. "I'faith, it does. Yet I predict a sudden healing by tomorrow."

"Then I must bid you God-speed. Please you, remember the friends of whom we spoke—"

"And the messages you would have me give them. Marry, I shall. Fare you well."

As soon as the door had closed behind Muñoz, Justin sagged back in the chair and shook his head. "What fools we must traffic with," he said, so quietly that Tandy could barely hear him.

"More wine?"

"Yea. Thank you. And pour some for yourself, if you will."

He would. It was Lord Harwood's best canary, and Tandy was thirsty. He had not drunk with the baron and Don Francisco; the Spaniard was too conscious of his rank.

They sat in companionable silence. There were not even any noises from the garden: the faint breeze had died down, and the rat must have gone off to try another passageway into the house. We must get some more cats, Tandy thought; he would mention it to his brother. Half the manor's cats had been killed last week, savaged by a mastiff that had turned out to be unexpectedly vicious and had since been killed. The other watchdogs were penned up, until the kennel master recovered from the ague and could discover if they, too, had become dangerous. Tandy hoped they would be able to free the mastiffs again soon, for they would be able to kill any rats too big for the cats.

Then, suddenly, he heard nails scratching across stone. For an instant he thought again it was a large rat; then he realized it was too near the window: no rat could have climbed so high. He leapt up and ran toward the window, Justin right behind him.

There was a muffled shriek, then a grunt, then a thud.

Tandy leaned out the window, staring down at two people lying on the ground, one half on top of the other. The one looked familiar, but it was a few seconds before he recognized the youth they had met at the Jerusalem Tree, the cousin of the boy Justin had quarreled with. The youth struggled to his feet, then began to tug at his companion, who seemed dazed. Slowly the other boy lifted his head, tilting it back so he gazed straight up at Tandy and Justin. Yea, it was the same boy from the Jerusalem Tree. 'Sblood, what were they . . . ?

"Get them, Tandy!" Justin ordered, and he whirled and ran toward the door.

"Run, cat!" one of the boys called to the other.

Tandy stopped abruptly, turning back to Lord Harwood.

"Shall I use the dogs?"

Justin shook his head. "I want to question them, not piece them together for burial. Now get you gone!"

Tandy ran, down the gallery and then downstairs, calling loudly for two men he knew he could trust.

"Run, Kat!"

Nick grabbed his sister's arm, almost dragging her off her feet as he pulled her along after him, toward the corner of the garden where they had left the rope. She seemed dazed but otherwise unharmed by her fall—and why not, when she had landed on him? She stumbled once as he drew her after him now, but his grip on her arm held her up, and then they were running across the garden, both sure-footed, able to see well enough in the moonlight to avoid any obstacles in their path. The men inside would need time for their eyes to adjust to the darkness, so he and Kat had an advantage there . . . and one they badly needed, Nick thought. He had heard that tawny-haired servant calling to others for help . . .

He let Kat go over the wall first, even giving her such a shove that she nearly sailed over. Then he was pulling himself up the rope, quick and careless, the rough stone tearing his hose and rubbing the skin from his knee as he slipped over the top of the wall and let himself drop to the long, soft grass on the other side. Kat, the fool, still stood there waiting for him. He pushed her toward the wood where they had left the horses.

"Run!"

She ran.

He sprinted after her. From behind them—not far enough behind them, alas—he could hear men's voices, but, mercifully, not the baying of hounds. Not yet. They had a chance to reach the horses before their pursuers caught up with them. If only Kat were not so slow! He was even with her already.

And he knew he could not afford to wait, not when they had left the horses tethered and hobbled.

He seized Kat's shoulder, stopping her. She cried out as he yanked her around.

"I must needs run ahead," he gasped, "so the horses will be ready to ride by the time you get there. Can you follow me? Can you at least remember where we left them?"

He could see her face well enough to tell that she was frightened, but she nodded without speaking, and he squeezed her arm before releasing it and running ahead, into the wood. He could hear Kat following him, and, well behind her still, the sounds of their pursuers.

Branches snagged his clothes and whipped at his face as he neared the section of the wood where they had left their horses. He wasted precious time searching through the bushes for the narrow pathway they had taken into the thicket, then, finding it at last, hurried along it, his arms raised to shield his face. He was gasping for breath, his chest aching, when he burst into the clearing.

The horses were gone.

Disbelieving, he turned around and around, scanning the shadowy undergrowth as if somehow their horses could have hidden there. Then he stopped, his head whirling.

The hobbles were gone, and the tethers. In the moonlight there was no sign that any horses had ever been here. He would have thought that he had mistaken the place where they had left the jades, had he not recognized the pathway, and the bare branches of a dead tree beside its opening into the clearing. This *was* the place. But the horses were gone, and with nothing else left behind—no broken hobbles or tethers—he could only think that they had been stolen.

Then Kat screamed.

He hurled himself back into the single opening in the thicket, running too fast for the curving pathway. A branch snagged his foot. He stumbled, recovered, and was tripped again, recovered again. He fought his way along the narrow path, flinging himself forward until he could finally see the outer opening. Then his foot skidded on a fallen branch.

He fell, branches that might have tripped him while he ran now snapping under his full weight. Then his head struck the unyielding bole of a small tree, and he knew nothing more.

The wood had not seemed half so dark only a few seconds before.

Now, as Kat swung around to face the man whose fleeting grip on her doublet sleeve had nearly yanked her off her feet before she surged free, she was painfully aware that shadows cloaked him too well. His tawny hair gleamed like a faint halo around his head, but his features were so shadowed that she could not read his expression, and shadows thrown by a nearby tree draped his arms, half concealing their movements. She might as well be half blind, she realized, as forced to fight in this darkness.

Nevertheless, she drew her sword. At the sibilance of blade sliding from scabbard, Lord Harwood's servant—for it was the tawny-haired man she had seen at the inn; she was sure of it—took a step back.

Two other men came running up, then stopped when they saw her. The tawny-haired man glanced over his shoulder at them, then gestured impatiently for them to go around him. "Find the other," he told them. "I can deal with this one."

"So say you," Kat muttered, glancing uneasily from the two other servants to the man in front of her.

"Yea, youngling, so say I," he responded imperturbably. "Now put up your sword, lest you hurt yourself."

She laughed and struck at him from the low ward.

He took two light, almost dancing, steps backward.

"Skip now! Nimbly, nimbly!" Elated, she closed on him, then retreated just in time as he drew his own sword and struck a side blow at her from the high ward, accomplishing the movements in half the time it would have taken her. She scarce managed the parry, and stopping his blade left her sword hand numbed for a moment. Belatedly, she drew her dagger. He followed suit.

"So y'are a rapier-and-dagger man?" the servant asked, almost cheerfully. "By God's body, boy, I would have thought you too young for such games. Would you not do better at ninepins? Mind your left hand, now, and ware my dagger."

He struck at her, a *punta dritta* from the low ward. As she parried with her dagger, he tried to strike a dagger blow at her shoulder. She parried it with her sword, but just in time. Retreating, already breathing raggedly, she knew that only his own warning had spared her from injury, and only his pausing now instead of pressing his advantage kept her safe.

"Put up, lad," he said again. "You must needs practice more, to hold your own in—" He broke off as she aimed a *stoccata* at his face. Lunging toward him, she slipped on the leafy mold underfoot and fell to one knee as he easily parried her awkward thrust. She turned her hand, about to attempt a *punta riversa*, then cried out in pain as his sword grappled with hers and broke her weapon free of her grip, sending it flying. Unthinkingly she flung herself toward him, dagger extended, but before the small blade could touch him he had swung his sword back and with the flat of the blade knocked her sprawling to the earth, where she lay face down, sobbing for breath, the dagger loose in her fingers. A moment later he plucked it from her hand, then spanked her lightly with his sword.

"Up, youngling," he said softly. "My master would speak with you."

CHAPTER 14

'Twas fortunate, Justin thought, that Muñoz had left before they discovered the trespassers. Like enough, the Spaniard would have wanted to stay and speak to both of them, and only mischief would have come of that. Justin wanted no interference from Muñoz if it did prove true that the girl and her friend were spying on him. And if they were not—if this were merely some prank—he wanted even more to keep Muñoz innocent of it. The man was more discreet than his master, de Spes, but that was saying very little. Justin shook his head as he remembered how Muñoz had seemed eager for dalliance with the maid when she came to his room at the Jerusalem Tree. God's light, what folly that had been! There was risk enough in the disguise the Spaniard had chosen, without trying it further by spending more time than necessary with strangers; Muñoz had too much confidence in his own acting. And he had taken a greater risk before that, at Hampton Court in March.

It was a sunny day, and the queen was walking in the garden by the Thames, several courtiers beside her. Justin had paused to admire a statue of a greyhound when Muñoz came toward him, a distraught look on his face.

Justin nodded to the Spaniard, then looked away. They had agreed never to seem too friendly at court, lest Walsingham and his agents become suspicious. But de Spes's secretary must needs have forgotten that, for he stopped beside Justin, not more than three feet away.

"George Wilford wants more money—fifty pounds more!" he blurted.

Justin glanced around, praying that Wilford was not in the garden. He had warned Muñoz never to mention his name to other conspirators, but even if Muñoz heeded him, 'twould be for naught if Wilford saw the Spaniard come up to him like this.

"He's not here," Muñoz whispered. "He's in his bedchamber still, half drunken. He lost a wager at cards early this morning."

"And bade you make it good?"

Muñoz flushed. "Would you have him turn against me and tell all to Walsingham?"

Think you that George Wilford would risk hanging at Tyburn rather than a few months' imprisonment in the Fleet? Justin thought, but kept

179

his skepticism to himself. Muñoz was proud and touchy. It would not do to tell him that he had been made Wilford's fool.

"You have promised the money already?"

Muñoz nodded. "I have some, but I lack twenty pounds, and dare not ask Don Guerau."

"Nay, do not bring de Spes into this," Justin said. He began to unfasten his purse from his belt. It contained more than twenty pounds, but he would attract even more attention if he stood here counting out money. "Take this," he said, handing the purse to Muñoz and hoping that no eyes had spied them.

But one pair of eyes, not half as nearsighted as some people believed, had noticed.

"What's this, Lord Harwood?" the queen called, turning toward them. "I see you have awarded a purse to Don Francisco. Pray tell me how he has won it, for if you are awarding purses, then I would fain have a chance to win one myself."

" 'Twas no award, madam," Justin said. "I was but paying a debt, for I lost at cards to the don."

"Did you?" the queen asked, looking curiously at Muñoz. "I thought you a better player than that. May I have the purse? Thank you." She hefted the purse, frowning as she gazed at it, then looked up at Muñoz and laughed. "I'faith, Don Francisco, you look fearful! D'you fear that I will not let you take your money back to Spain? Has your master warned you that I will keep all Spanish money that falls into my hands, whether I have a rightful claim to it or not?"

Muñoz looked more fretful than ever: no doubt he had no wish to be drawn into the dispute between England and Spain that had begun fifteen months earlier, a dispute that his master, de Spes, had done much to cause.

The winter before last, Queen Elizabeth had claimed the cargo of five Spanish treasure ships bound for Antwerp. The ships had been carrying some eighty-five thousand pounds in specie, a loan from Genoese bankers to the King of Spain, money intended to pay Spain's army under the Duke of Alva in the Netherlands. The ships had taken refuge in English ports, fleeing bad weather and French pirates, and the English had only discovered what the chests taken off the ships contained when the Spanish ambassador, de Spes, asked for some of the coin to pay his expenses.

Then the queen had learned that the coin was not truly Spanish property until it reached Antwerp. She was advised by the Antwerp branch of the Genoese bank that the loan could be transferred to her instead of Philip. 'Twas a tempting offer. With Alva's army in the Low Countries, there was little certainty that England could continue to obtain loans from the bankers in Antwerp. And Elizabeth had just learned from William Hawkins that his brother, the trader John Hawkins, having anchored his fleet for repairs in the Mexican port of San Juan de Ulloa under a truce, had been deceived by the

Spanish and attacked, losing one hundred twenty men and all but two of his ships, including one owned by the queen. Hawkins had requested of Cecil that the Spanish treasure be held in England till damages could be paid.

Yet even before Elizabeth made a final decision to take the loan for herself, de Spes had written to the Duke of Alva, urging a trade embargo against England and the seizure of all English ships and property in Spanish and Low Country ports. Alva complied, and the queen responded in kind. There the matter rested, with English cloth merchants now trading in Hamburg instead of Antwerp and officials at English ports happily seizing the Spanish ships that were still sometimes driven to seek shelter from storms and pirates.

"I have never heard such a statement from Don Guerau," Muñoz said at last. 'Twas possible that he spoke the truth, for he had not come to England until some months after the trade embargoes began, but Justin doubted it. Still, it was a politic answer.

"Would that I could say the same," the queen said dryly, and one of her maids laughed. The queen glanced around, the laughter stopped, and then Elizabeth's gaze returned to Muñoz.

" 'Tis said that the Spanish love a wager," she said. "Will you play against me, for this purse?"

Muñoz dared not refuse. A table was brought, and chairs, and they sat down to play a game of primero. Whether Elizabeth might have won in any event, Justin could not say, for she was a fine and intelligent player. But Muñoz dared win no more than he dared refuse the game. He wasted good hands like someone who had never held cards before, and was so obvious about it that Justin wished he could have warned him to play differently, but before he could think of a way to do so, the game was over and the queen was holding up Justin's purse as if it were a great trophy.

"So I have kept English money in English hands," she said. "Will anyone argue that 'twas not done honestly?"

"Not I, Your Majesty," Muñoz said, then looked anxiously at Justin, and the baron realized that Muñoz had not forgotten the money promised to Wilford. He swore inwardly: needs must that he borrow money himself from one of his friends at court, if he were to give the money to Muñoz. Unless . . .

"Madam," he said as the queen started away, "please it you, will you play against me?" The queen was in a good humor; perchance she would merely make some jest if he succeeded in winning his purse back.

Now she smiled sweetly at him. "By the mass, my lord," she said, a mischievous look to her face, "did you not see how easily I beat the man who beat you? I would count myself a very poor prince indeed, if I let you lose such a sum twice over. Let me hear no more of your betting at cards, till you have learned to play more wisely."

*And she laughed and walked away, leaving him to arrange a later meeting
with Muñoz before he set off to find someone to lend him money.*

He sighed now, remembering how the incident had made him a
laughingstock for the remaining few days he had spent at court. But it
could have ended worse—much worse.

However often Kat had imagined meeting Lord Harwood again—and
she had done so more often than she would admit even to herself—she
had never pictured him thus: seated in a chair like an invalid, clad in
a nightgown of ash-color silk even though it was still early in the evening, his foot swathed in bandages. He was leaning forward and toying
with those bandages when she entered the room. She stopped when she
saw him, too stunned to move even when the tawny-haired servant
prodded her. After a moment the baron looked up.

"Hal and Roger have not yet returned with this lad's companion,"
the servant said, "but I warrant they'll bring him back soon." His words
had no apparent effect on Justin, who continued to stare at Kat, such a
look of contempt on his face that anger flared in her.

"Gout, my lord?" she asked, speaking as sweetly as possible but
remembering to keep her voice low-pitched. "Alack, the torments of
age . . . You must forgo Madeira and all other rich food and drink, and
instead have your maids boil a mixture of oil of roses and egg yolk and
milk and saffron for a poultice. Or perhaps you would do better with
leeks and oatmeal seethed with sheep's tallow—" She cried out as the
servant cuffed her.

"Nay, Tandy," the baron said. "Let our visitor be. Can you not see
that this is but a fool, here to entertain us?" His gaze challenged Kat
to respond, but she held her tongue.

"For a truth, my lord, that would explain these," Tandy replied,
and tossed Kat's weapons onto the floor. " 'Tis clear now that he did
not truly mean me to take him for a rapier-and-dagger man."

Justin's expression changed to one of honest surprise as he looked
at the weapons, then up at Kat. "You fought with these, in sooth?"

"He sought to kill me," Tandy asserted.

"Nay, I meant but to wound—" Kat broke off as Justin laughed.

"How fared you, Tandy? You were not wounded by this nestling?"

The servant shook his head. "Not so much as scratched. He has
more knowledge than skill, has studied the method but not practiced it
sufficiently."

"No doubt there have been few opportunities," Justin said reflec-
tively.

"My lord?" Tandy asked, clearly puzzled, but the nobleman did not
respond.

Lord Harwood began to tug at the bandages around his foot yet again, and now Kat realized that he was unwinding them. She watched as he uncovered his foot, which was stockinged and seemed neither inflamed nor wounded, then put on a leather slipper matching the one he already wore. He stood up then, took a step away from the chair—with no sign of pain or weakness when he stepped on that foot, she noticed—and then unfastened his nightgown and removed it. Underneath he was wearing a white silk shirt and dark hose, also of silk.

She shivered. There was nothing of the invalid about him now, and she was forcibly reminded of the power and strength she had sensed when she first met him at the Jerusalem Tree.

" 'Twas a quick recovery, my lord," she said lightly, knowing that she risked being cuffed again, but feeling a need to speak, to mock him if possible, to keep her own emotions at bay.

"Would that I could say your presence healed me," he replied, his tone equally light, and she reddened as she remembered Christopher Danvers saying something similar as he wooed her, "but I doubt that is why you are here. Why were you lurking beneath my window?"

The chamber was suddenly completely silent. Why, indeed? Kat thought wildly. She and Nick had given no thought to stories that would explain their trespassing here, should they be discovered. That they might be caught had been unthinkable.

"Come, now, answer," Justin said after a few moments. "If you wished to speak to me, you need only have gone to the gatehouse and announced yourself."

Relief washed over Kat as she saw an opening through this maze.

"Yea, my lord, but we wished to speak to you alone."

"Why?"

The simple question left her facing another wall of the maze, until Lord Harwood spoke again.

"Perchance you had some unfinished business with me . . . ? I know that at the Jerusalem Tree I would fain have spoken with you again in the morning, and was sorely disappointed to learn that you had left the inn during the night."

"Haply you wished to speak to—" She hesitated. 'Sdeath, what *had* Nick called himself at the inn? "—to my cousin Matthew about—"

"And not to you?" he interrupted, with an odd smile. Flustered, she hesitated, and in the silence heard footsteps in the hall, then a knock at the door. Tandy went to open it.

"We cannot find him," said a man's voice that Kat had never heard before. " 'Tis too dark, and he had too great a lead. He's escaped, of cer—"

Justin swore, and the servant broke off. "Then get you gone, sirrah.

Think you that you can find your way back to your bed in this darkness?"

The man peered around the edge of the door, not even noticing Kat, obviously too frightened to care about anyone in the room except the baron. "I pray your pardon, my lord, but we have searched—"

"Yea, a full five minutes longer than Tandy. Now go!"

The servant vanished.

Justin returned his attention to Kat. "Now, what was it you thought I wished to speak to Matthew about?"

Rejoicing in the news that Nick had escaped, Kat had almost forgotten her own predicament. It was a few moments before she remembered what she had planned to tell him.

"Maybe you wished to speak to him about the servingmaid who—"

"Meg was her name, was it not?" Justin asked carelessly.

"Yea, my lord, as you well know. 'Twas unfortunate that your treatment of her so angered Matthew"—she hesitated, confused: why was Lord Harwood smiling again?—"that he acted as he did, and he sought only to explain that he had not rescued the maid from one man's lusts to see her become the victim of another." To her fury, the nobleman laughed. "And moreover, my lord, he wished to know why an honorable gentleman such as yourself would have treated the maid so shamefully, seeking to keep her with you when she came to your chamber on an honest errand, to bring you wine from the innkeeper."

"Perhaps Matthew should have asked Meg if she felt she had been treated shamefully," Justin replied, still smiling. "The wench was willing."

"She was not!" In her anger, Kat started toward the baron, only to be yanked back by Tandy.

"Oh, she made a show of rejecting me at first," Justin said good-humoredly, "but she was willing enough when she was in my arms, and made no move to leave even when I bade her go."

"You lie in your throat!"

"What, will you challenge me?' Justin asked, taunting her now. "Was not one sword fight enough for you tonight? And why, in faith? The maid not only would have stayed with me then, had I wished it, but she now seeks me out at home. Take off her cap, Tandy." After a moment, he gestured impatiently at the servant, who, like Kat, stood stock still. "Are you deaf, sirrah? *Her cap.*"

Tandy looked at Kat, and for a moment she read confusion in his gaze. Then, before she could move out of reach, he snatched the cap from her head. She yelped as he inadvertently pulled on tresses still fastened to the cap by pins, and he dropped the cap, which fell against her back, still pinned to a few long strands of hair. She glared at him.

"Now, Kat," the baron said, and she swung around to face him.

"Yea, so it is Kat, and not Meg," he said triumphantly, and she flushed, feeling more vulnerable than ever now that he knew her name. "I thought I heard Matthew—if that is his name—call you Kat. I met Meg at the inn, the morning after you left. I warrant she was shamefully treated, but not by me. You and your cousin have much to answer for."

"We did her no harm."

"Mayhap none that she remembers," he said sharply, and she flushed, unable to respond. He looked at his servant. "Some wine, Tandy, for all of us."

Kat was thirsty, so she drank, after first watching carefully to be sure that her wine was poured from the same flagon as theirs and that nothing was added to it. Tandy had moved away from her, though he was still looking at her with an expression of bemusement. Lord Harwood was studying her coolly. Uncomfortable under their scrutiny, she looked around the room, which seemed to be a withdrawing chamber, elegantly furnished and pleasant. *No place for such a scene as this,* she thought, noting her weapons, which still lay on the floor. Two steps would take her to them, but she had no illusions about being able to pick them up and wield them before either of the two men reached her. Nor could she have fought either man successfully, she knew. Tandy had already bested her, and she suspected that Lord Harwood was equally skilled in the use of the rapier whose expensive hilt, gleaming with gilt and semiprecious stones, protruded from the gilded leather scabbard hanging from the back of his chair. She would have to depend on her wits to get free again.

Yea, the same wits that brought me here, she thought, torn between laughing and crying.

Nick, then. Nick would rescue her. Surely he must have heard her scream and would know she had been captured. He must be somewhere outside the house even now. He would have brought their horses closer to the house, and would be watching, trying to learn which room she was being held in. Pretending casualness, she began to walk toward the window, skirting the place on the floor where her weapons still lay: she did not want either Tandy or Lord Harwood to suspect her of trying to escape. She wanted only to stand at the window for at least a few minutes . . .

She was still several steps from the window when Lord Harwood moved to stand in front of her. She flinched as he touched her cheek, but he made no further attempt to touch her, instead staring down at a rusty-looking smudge on his fingers.

"Jesu, Tandy, did you have to drag her back to the house? Was there any need to deal so roughly with her?"

Kat raised her hand to her cheek, aware for the first time that what she had thought was only a slight scratch, barely deep enough to break the skin, had left dried rivulets of blood down the side of her face.

"I did not drag her, my lord," Tandy said. "She fell when she lunged at me during our fight."

For a few seconds Kat thought the baron was going to laugh. The corners of his mouth twitched as he no doubt fought a smile, and she seethed with anger and shame. Then, to her surprise, she saw a look of sympathy on his face.

"Like enough, she was not used to such footing," he said mildly, then shook his head. "Howsomever, she's not only scratched, but has brought enough dirt for a garden into the house."

"Not willingly, sirrah," Kat said under her breath, and at that Justin did laugh.

"Indeed not," he agreed, "but you must needs bathe just the same. Tandy, have a bath prepared in my bedchamber. And summon Mistress Colwich, and have her bring some ointment for this scratch."

Well satisfied that Mistress Colwich could guard their prisoner, Tandy went looking for the baron.

He found Justin in a bedchamber strewn with women's clothes: gowns of watchet cloth-of-silver and maiden's-blush taffeta and white velvet-on-velvet; kirtles of primrose damask and pearl satin and white cloth-of-gold; sleeves of watchet and blush-color damask and primrose and white satin; a cloak of black silk grosgrain; nightgowns of carnation satin and white velvet. They were Margaret's favorite fabrics, in Margaret's favorite colors, and Tandy—whose opinion of Justin's cousin was no higher than her opinion of him—could not help but feel some disgust that all these garments, with their rich linings and fine embroiderings set with pearls and gems, were meant for her. She would be pleased with the thoroughness of the English-made wardrobe Justin would bring her: there were also four petticoats of silk and sarcenet; several pairs of silk hose; three smocks of the finest cambric with the sleeves and collars wrought with exquisite blackwork; two pairs of perfumed gloves; and two hats, one a copintank of black velvet trimmed with a white plume, the other of lavishly embroidered white taffeta.

He had not expected to find Justin here—would, in fact, have walked past the room had he not seen the door ajar. Now he looked on wonderingly as the baron picked up the white velvet nightgown. The gold embroidery on its wide collar shimmered in the candlelight.

Justin sighed, then looked around at Tandy, apparently not at all surprised to see him there.

"Think you that the lady Margaret will feel herself scanted if she's given but one nightgown?" he asked with a wry smile.

"No, my lord. But why—For the *wench*?" He stared at the Justin in disbelief. That nightgown had cost more than ten pounds.

"Yea, for the wench . . . unless her own garments are to be returned to her, filthy as they are . . . or unless, after her bath, I am to converse with her while she is unclothed . . ."

"Belike she would feel uneasy," Tandy ventured, and Justin laughed. "But is it necessary that you give her one of these? One of the maids might have a nightgown she could spare . . ."

"So I should send you through the house to wake each maidservant in turn and ask to borrow her clothes?" Justin shook his head. "Nay, Tandy, 'tis sufficient that Mistress Colwich knows—and I warrant none of her garments would fit our visitor."

"Joan Bostocke, the brewer's daughter, is near to Kat's size."

"No, I said. This will serve my purpose better. I would woo the girl and have her trust me, so that she tells me in sooth why she came here."

Tandy bit his lip. 'Twould do no good to object. But to give the nightgown to the wench, even for a single night, seemed more a waste than to give it to Margaret . . .

Lisle glanced at a clock on the mantel. "Think you," he said, "that she would be done bathing by now?"

Warm water lapping round her shoulders, Kat gazed over the rim of the bathing tub at Mistress Colwich. She had hoped that the warmth of the room, with a small fire lit and the steaming tub placed before it, might have lulled the woman back to the sleep from which she had been wakened, but there seemed little chance of that. Mistress Colwich— some thirty years older than Kat, a few inches taller, and perhaps half again as heavy—still sat calmly watching her from the chair against the opposite wall. Both her hands rested on the long candlestick of gleaming brass that lay across her lap. It would make a most effective club, should Kat give her cause to use it.

Sighing, Kat closed her eyes against the sight. With the image of her guard and the unfamiliar chamber shut out, she could almost pretend that she was enjoying a bath at home. Sweet herbs had been added to the water, and their scent now mixed pleasantly with that of the soap, which was perfumed with oil of almonds. Large sponges had been placed on the bottom of the tub and against one side, so she need not touch the wood at all. Were it not that the water was slightly too warm for her taste—and she had been able to do nothing about that, for the tub had been filled while she was held in the other chamber—she would have pronounced it a perfect bath . . . that is, if she had been at home.

Tomorrow evening, she thought. Tomorrow evening she would have Louise prepare such a bath. Nick would rescue her tonight, and by tomorrow afternoon they would be back at Beechwood. A long bath then would help soothe her muscles after the ride, as this was soothing her now. 'Twas kind of Lord Harwood, she mused—and her mouth curved in a faint smile at the thought—to provide her with this chance to relax and recover from the long journey here before she returned home . . .

Then the door was flung open and a rush of cool air swept her reverie away.

She opened her eyes to see Lord Harwood standing in the doorway, folds of white velvet piled atop one hand. She gasped and ducked lower into the water, then grabbed sponges to hold over her body.

He shook his head, then strolled into the room, stopping when he was several feet away from her. Turning toward Mistress Colwich, he said pleasantly, "Still in the tub? Has she not washed yet? Does she know how to wash?"

"Yea, my lord, I have washed. When you have returned my clothes, and left this chamber again, I'll leave this tub."

He looked back at her and raised his eyebrows. "Marry, 'twould seem you are wearing sponges, which become you better than the garb you wore when you arrived here. Will you not continue to wear them?"

"I lack pins to hold them together."

"I can provide pins."

"And they are somewhat wet."

"No doubt we can provide dry sponges. Look for them, Mistress Colwich. I warrant this will set a new fashion."

"And why, my lord, would you want to start a fashion that would drive all the mercers in London to jump off London Bridge? Now, please it you, have done with these games. *Bring me my clothes.*"

"Alas, they have been washed, and are no drier than those sponges. Will you have this instead?" he asked, and shook out the folds of velvet.

This time it was Mistress Colwich who gasped. Kat stared in silent wonder at the nightgown, impressed despite herself with the richness of the material and the embroidery and the profusion of gold buttons. 'Twas equal to the best nightgown she had ever owned, and she could not believe he meant her to have it.

"Enough of this jesting, sir," she said when she could speak. "Pray bring me my own clothes. I will wear them wet, and if you fear damage to your fine velvet-upholstered chairs, I will stand."

"I fear rather for your health—"

"Yea, so your servants have showed me."

"—and would have you wear dry clothes. Now dry yourself and put this on." He sounded impatient. Mistress Colwich set the candlestick down, picked up a towel in each hand, and moved toward Kat.

"Not. While. You. Are. Here," Kat said, her gaze locked with Lord Harwood's. She lifted her chin in a defiant gesture that she hoped was not ruined by the water streaming down her neck. 'Twas difficult to defy someone while looking up at him from a tub.

Justin opened his mouth, then shut it again. He looked with exasperation at Mistress Colwich, then flung the nightgown toward her. She caught it between the towels.

"I shall wait outside," he told Kat, "while I count to one hundred."

"Higher, my lord," Kat said. "There must be nearly one hundred buttons on that gown."

He pretended not to hear her as he turned and strode back out the door, slamming it behind him.

Since counting to one hundred did little to cool his choleric humor, he counted to two hundred, then three hundred, before again opening the door and returning to his bedchamber. Kat was dressed in the nightgown, which was closed from collar to hem. It amused him to see that she had buttoned only every other button in her haste.

His amusement vanished when he noticed the expression on Mistress Colwich's face. The woman seemed caught between anger and tears.

Kat, intent on refastening the top button, which had begun to work its way loose, glanced up at him for a moment. "I fear your maidservant was little help, my lord. She's too clumsy to serve as a maid for a lady."

"That might concern me, had I asked her to attend a lady," he replied in an icy voice, and Kat looked up again, color draining from her face. He took Mistress Colwich by the shoulder and escorted her to the door. "I must needs thank you," he told her, his tone as soft and kind as he could make it, "for your work tonight, and will see that it is well rewarded. Pray remember to say nothing of this to the other servants."

"I will, my lord," she replied, a smile pressing creases into her heavy face. "If your lordship requires more help . . . ?"

"I shall summon you," he promised, and shut the door behind her. Turning again to Kat, he saw that she had given up buttoning the nightgown and now stood quietly before the fire, her head bowed in an attitude of meekness that he did not believe for an instant.

"Cry you mercy, my lord," she said after a time. "I should not have complained, and indeed must thank you for waiting outside and so allowing me to maintain my dignity."

"I would not think," he said, dryly, "that dignity would be much concern to someone who would climb the wall of my house to perch beneath a window and eavesdrop on my conversations. I must, however, applaud your agility."

"It comes with much practice."

"Yea? I would have expected climbing to come naturally to a Kat. Or should I call you Katherine?"

Her gaze flicked across him and then away, her expression unreadable. "Call me what you will."

"Nay, Madam *Feles*, for there are words I will not use in front of women . . . even if they are not ladies."

She was still for some moments, and then shrugged. Reaching up, she unpinned her hair, which had been secured in a coil atop her head during her bath, and shook it free to settle in a gleaming but slightly frizzled tangle about her shoulders. She began to comb through it with her fingers, all the while gazing at the fire, her expression dreamy. It seemed to him that she was far away in spirit, unconcerned with the fact that she was his prisoner, alone with him in his bedchamber. He felt like shaking her, but restrained himself, knowing that in his fury he would be tempted to throttle her.

"Will you have some wine?" he said at last, not knowing what else to say, though he felt foolish beyond measure for speaking to her as if she were a welcome guest.

She shrugged again. "If you are drinking, too," she replied, and he remembered then how carefully she had watched Tandy pour the wine for them an hour ago.

"You fear the wine will be drugged?" he asked, and she looked down. "So that is how you dealt with the maid at the inn. What was it you gave Meg?" he asked easily as he picked up the flagon and poured some wine. "Some medicine, peradventure, that she had been kind enough to bring to your cousin Matthew? Syrup of poppy, mayhap?" Turning, he could tell from the rising color in her face that he had guessed correctly. "Fear not," he assured her as he gave one goblet to her. "I would not trust myself to have your skill in drugging unsuspecting young maids. But tell me—did you give any thought to what might have happened to Meg, had some shameless man discovered her, too soundly asleep to be wakened, alone and defenseless in Matthew's bed?"

"Truth to tell, we did," she replied, her face still flushed yet her voice surprisingly calm, "but we believed you securely trussed."

He stared at her without speaking for some moments, then: "Maybe you think your agility exceeded only by your wit. But mark me, wench. This is my home, and I will not be bearded here.''

"Then you must needs shave,'' she responded at once, then looked away, biting her lip.

There was silence again, which he broke at last by saying, "I would not wish such an ungovernable tongue on my worst enemy. Even fools deserve to have enough wit to know that they should keep silent at times.''

"Is that what you think me? Your worst enemy, and a fool?''

"I have already said, girl, that I will not say what I think you.''

Her mouth opened, then shut again, and she pursed her lips. For once she seemed capable of holding her tongue.

He sat down in the chair Mistress Colwich had occupied, then unfastened the top hooks of his shirt collar. It was warm in the room, the air close and heavily scented with the herbs used in the bath.

"Open the window,'' he told the girl. She raised an eyebrow in apparent surprise at the order, then went to obey it. A cool breeze swept past her as she stood there, unmoving, a statue of white and gold against the darkness outside.

Minutes passed, and she stayed at the window, drinking her wine. Watching her, he realized that she was deliberately showing herself to anyone outside, no doubt hoping that her companion—her cousin, or perchance her lover: and why did he feel a twinge of jealousy at that thought?—would see her and come to her rescue. Justin, too, hoped the boy would try. He would be glad to have both these trespassers in his hands.

"Who is your master, Kat?'' he asked suddenly. "Who sent you here?''

"My master?'' She appeared genuinely surprised. "I have no master.''

"And no one sent you here? You mean to hold to this story that you came here of your own accord?''

" 'Tis a true story.''

He shook his head angrily. "You bade me leave off jesting, Kat. Now I would have you do the same. Who is your master, that I may send a message to him and discuss your release?''

"If you will not discuss my release with me, sir, then I fear I shall remain a guest of yours, for I tell you again: *I have no master.*'' She regarded him with impatience.

"Then tell me where your family lives, that I may write to them and they may come get you. Assuming—and perhaps this assumes too much—that they would want you back.''

She shook her head. "There is no one you need contact about me.''

"Not even the sheriff?'' he asked, and for perhaps half a minute it seemed that she had in truth become a statue, she was so still. Then she shook her head again, and, turning her back to him, knelt and then sat in the window seat, facing the garden.

" 'Tis a lovely garden," she said after a while, her voice so muted that he almost missed noticing that it was trembling, too.

"Yea, much lovelier than the inside of a jail. Think you that a Kat could turn jailbird?"

There was a longer silence this time. Gazing at her back, he wondered again who had sent her. He could not believe that she would prefer jail to punishment by her family if they learned of this prank—so this was no prank. But which of his enemies might have sent her to spy on him?

"I see that your garden has many roses." She made the observation in an idle tone, almost as though she were forced to make polite conversation with someone who bored her. "Roses are lovely, but stingy with their fragrance. You should plant musk roses and lavender and white double violets as well."

"I have," he told her, somewhat amused.

"And you should have alleys planted with thyme and water mint, which will scent the air when you walk on them."

"I'll speak to my gardener tomorrow. Have you more advice that I should give him?"

To his amusement, she did. She recommended lime trees for their blossoms' scent in midsummer, and topiary work of juniper for its color in midwinter; for his garden to bloom early in the year, she told him, he must have crocuses and tulips and primroses. She had much to say about fountains, and then, for a longer time, about orchards. She particularly recommended walnut trees—"Though not secret discourse under them," she added with a laugh, and then was silent.

He shook his head. The last, idle remark had been completely foolish, and he might have thought her mad, had she not seemed quite sensible until then. Who—and what—was she? He could imagine now that she was some gardener's daughter, to have so much knowledge. With her father part of a gentleman's household, she would have seen and heard enough of the gentry to be able to ape them, as she had at the Jerusalem Tree. He could readily picture her coaxing some young gentleman to tell her of his studies at Cambridge—had she not done just the same with him? So give her, at least, an honest if poor birth. Then what had brought her here? No honest prank, of certain, or by now his threats of jail would have brought her to a tearful confession. So who was her master now?

Walsingham? Justin could not believe he had been careless enough to draw Walsingham's attention, nor could he believe Walsingham would employ this madcap wench as an intelligencer. De Spes? No doubt the Spanish ambassador would be jealous of his secretary if he knew of Muñoz's plottings: de Spes would be, if not the only Spanish Machiavel in England, then at least the master. But Justin already knew of most of de Spes's agents—more, even, than the ambassador dreamed he was aware of—and not only was this maid not among them, she was also nothing like them. No, de Spes would not have sent her.

One of his rivals at court, then. Justin sighed. 'Twould be difficult to guess which one, for though he spent most of his time away from court, the moment he returned he found himself entangled in disputes, both political and personal. There was never an end to it.

He shook his head.

The girl was still silent, slumped now against the cushions of the window seat. Even huddled there, she seemed to glow, white and gold against the darkness. She was lovely, especially now that her face was scrubbed clean of both the grime she had worn when he first saw her in boys' garb and the heavy paints she had worn when disguised as a maidservant. He wondered what she would look like in a fine kirtle and gown, attired as a lady. He remembered how she had looked while in the bath, the long white legs, the curve of hip visible past the sponge she had clutched against herself, the pale, flawless skin. Too pale? For an instant his image of her as a gardener's daughter threatened to shatter, but then he reasoned that even a servant's daughter could learn to protect her skin, were her parents lenient enough. And 'twas certain Kat had been spoiled, or her mocking impudence would have been beaten out of her long ago.

But was she still being spoiled, by whoever was her master?

He crossed the room to his writing cabinet, opened a door and removed a worn leather purse. Tandy had taken it from the wench before he brought her inside, in case she had hidden some small knife in the purse. The tiny knife carried by cutpurses—a weapon Tandy seemed familiar with—could be just as easily hidden in a purse as in the palm of the hand. There had been no knife, however, nor any letters or seals that would identify Kat's master. The purse had held only coins, to which Justin had paid scant attention. Now, though, he opened the purse and poured its contents into his hand.

A shilling, two half-groats, a sixpence, and a few pennies. A trivial amount. Enough, perchance, for the initial payment to a rogue who would expect the remainder after completing his assigned task, but hardly the amount of money that would be possessed by a trusted and valued servant sent on a mission of some danger.

He looked thoughtfully at Kat, remembering that she had seemed impressed by the gift of the nightgown. Impressed, but also skeptical.

What, he wondered, would she make of greater largesse from him? It would be well worth a few pounds, and more of the fine clothes intended for Margaret, to win Kat's allegiance and mayhap even set her to spying on her former master . . .

Her head slumped forward a little. He moved quickly but silently to her side. Belike she merely slept . . . but there were poisons that would kill swiftly, and he had heard of captured spies using them. He was aware of his heart hammering as he took her hand and felt for her pulse. There, strong and regular. So she slept. 'Twas a deep sleep already, compounded no doubt of exhaustion and wine, for she did not stir when he placed her hand back on her lap.

For some moments he stood gazing down at her. She looked very vulnerable and very young. The breeze blew a strand of hair across her face. It was chilly here by the window. He could not leave her to sleep here.

He picked her up, as gently as if she were a child, and carried her to the bed. She stirred in his arms and murmured something but did not wake as he set her down and drew the covers over her, then moved away to sit at the foot of the bed, watching her.

After a time, aware of his own weariness, he went to the other side of the bed and lay down, but it was a long time before sleep claimed him, and he woke soon after that to find that she had cast the covers aside while she slept. A few of the nightgown's buttons had already come undone: the sempsters must have made the buttonholes too large. The collar of the gown was open now, fallen aside to reveal the upper curve of one breast. His breath quickened as he looked at her, but he forced himself to turn away. He wanted her as a spy, not as a leman. He closed his eyes and eventually slept again.

Only to wake, disbelieving, to the sound of her sweetly whispering his name.

CHAPTER 15

She was dancing in the great hall of Hampton Court, dancing with Justin Lisle . . .

"Your admirers were but shadow men," he told her, and she agreed. Not just that flock of brightly feathered young courtiers, but Tom Heyford and Christopher Danvers and even Dudley and Hatton had all seemed to be in the hall a moment ago and now all had vanished, exorcised with all the other shadows by the dazzling light that surrounded them, light that played over Justin's doublet of cloth-of-gold and struck fire from his russet hair.

'Twas the coranto they danced, and Justin was all grace, even more graceful than Christopher Hatton, and she looked around for Nick, wishing he could see her, but her brother was nowhere in sight.

Disappointed, she turned back to Justin, who had stopped dancing and was now holding two fine Venetian glasses filled with wine. He gave one to her.

"Let's drink a toast," he said, "to us."

The wine was sweet and slaked her thirst like the coolest water. They danced again, then rested on a bench in the middle of the hall. There was a scent of honeysuckle in the air. She leaned against Justin, her head on his shoulder. He put his arm around her, and she looked up at him. "Justin?" she asked, half afraid, half elated. He bent his head to kiss her, his mouth gentle on hers. His hand came up to her neck, and a moment later she felt her ruff fall away. He began to kiss her neck, and she whispered his name, over and over. His hand trailed down her shoulder, brushing the partlet aside, and the touch reminded her of Christopher Danvers.

"Christopher!"

She came awake with a start. There was a taste of wine in her mouth, and she remembered a sickeningly sweet aftertaste. But the man leaning over her was not Christopher.

She screamed and raised her hands to claw at Lord Harwood's face.

He caught her wrists, but she managed to scratch his neck deeply before he rolled away from her, swearing. She tried to kick him, but there were still covers across her legs, hindering her.

"Whoreson!"

He held her hands against the bed now, forcing her to lie on her side, and swung one long leg over hers before she could kick free of the covers. " 'Sdeath, what madness is this? Or were you ordered to lure me and then attack me?"

"Lure you?"

"You whispered my name just now, Kat, as softly as any lover. You welcomed my kisses."

"I—" She broke off, shamed as she remembered the dream, which she had forgotten after the first unpleasant reminder of Christopher Danvers. Her cheeks felt as though they were on fire. She turned her face toward the sheet, closing her eyes and wishing she could hide from his gaze.

"Was it but a dream, then?" he asked after a moment. She made no response. "At least," he said with a laugh, "I know how you would have me treat you in your dreams. Alas, that I am not the only lover you welcome. Who, pray tell, is Christopher?"

Had there been a note of jealousy in his voice? She opened her eyes and peered up at him. He did not look jealous.

"Is he your master?"

She could not help but laugh at the thought of Christopher Danvers as her master. He shook his head, a wary expression on his face, then released her wrists and turned away. He touched his neck where she had scratched him, and a few drops of blood fell from his fingers to the sheets.

"By God's wounds, Mistress *Feles*, you scratch like the cat you are. I pity any man who shares your bed."

"Were you not eager enough to share my bed?" she asked recklessly.

He stood up, then turned, all cool serenity despite the wrinkled clothing and bleeding scratch, to look down at her. " 'Tis my bed, Kat. And you did call out to me."

She could not meet his gaze. "Think you that no other men are named Justin?" Her head bent, she began refastening the buttons of the nightgown.

He laughed cynically and shook his head, but said nothing more to her as he left the room, closing the door behind him. A moment later she heard a key turn in the lock.

She ran to the window, flung it open and leaned out, gazing downward at the wall, then caught at the window frame as the floor seemed to rock beneath her feet. For some time after the dizziness passed she stayed there, motionless, then made her way slowly back to the bed and sat down. Even if she were not so weak and dizzy from lack of food, she could not have made that climb down—especially not dressed as she was in the confining velvet folds of the nightgown. Nor could she have scaled the garden wall without a rope. She was trapped here.

Only until Nick rescues me, she thought, and lifted her head and looked around the chamber. Was there haply some evidence here of Lord Harwood's plotting against the queen? She must needs search, for Nick would be curious about how she had spent her time in Harwood Hall. Then her cheeks burned as she remembered her dream and its aftermath. *He need not be told all*, she decided, and set about her investigation.

Lord Harwood, thought Tandy, looked as though he had spent a sleepless, troubled night.

The baron still wore the shirt and hose he had worn the night before, but the fabric was badly wrinkled, as if he had lain down to sleep for at least a short while. And he had not bothered to comb his hair, though he had been raking his fingers through it to tidy it somewhat as he stumbled groggily into the parlor where he and Tandy had met for breakfast these past several days to discuss the progress of their plans.

Experience counseled silence on mornings like this. After bidding his lord the necessary "Good morrow" and getting a cynical stare in reply, Tandy mimed his way through the serving of breakfast, letting minute changes in Justin's expression tell him which of the dishes set on the table the baron wanted. Finally Lord Harwood leaned back in his chair and looked across the table at Tandy.

"Remind me," he said, the tone of his voice the usual pleasant one, "to let all trespassers leave freely in the future. And if needs must, have them seen with all courtesy to the gate, and there bidden God-speed."

"You would be rid of this one?" Tandy asked, a bit warily.

"With all my heart," Justin replied, "if only the wench would tell me where to send her—other than Hell, of course, where, I trow, she will eventually find herself."

"So she still has not told you who she is, or who sent her?"

"She is a cat, of parentage unknown. A base cat, like enough. A garden cat." He chuckled, then shook his head. "Yet proud and disdainful for all that. I threatened to hand her over to the sheriff, but to no avail."

"You truly wish to turn her over to the sheriff?" Tandy asked dubiously. Surely Justin could see the dangers there . . .

The baron shook his head again. "Nay, I would turn this cat in the pan, and set her to spying for me, on her own master if that is possible. I would have you take some breakfast to her, and see what you can learn. Play not the inquisitor, but instead assume a mantle of friendship and talk to her."

"In pedlar's French?"

"If you will."

Tandy nodded. He piled slices of meat and bread onto a platter and poured some ale into a cup. Justin still sat leaning back in his chair, his eyes closed now, the skin beneath them looking bruised. Not a word had been said about their plans, and although that might be in part because little more could be done until they heard from Southampton, Tandy felt that the wench was mostly to blame. He was not looking forward to talking to her. They had enough complications to deal with now; they did not need another.

The writing cabinet was locked.

'Twas almost proof in itself, Kat had thought when she made that discovery, that Justin Lisle was a traitor and involved in vicious plots against the queen. No honest man would feel a need to hide his correspondence so.

She searched two other chests, the press, then the shelves of books, opening and shaking each book so any letters hidden between the pages would fall out. By the time she had finished, she had acquired a certain amount of grudging respect for the baron's taste in clothes and books, but she had yet to find a single letter written to him . . . or a key to the wretched cabinet. She stared at it balefully, then looked around the room again.

Two tables: she checked to see if they had concealed drawers or shelves, but there were none. The chairs she checked as well, and with no more luck. Then she turned to the fireplace, with its mantel of gleaming, ornately carved marble. Her hands were dusty from searching the furniture, and she would have wiped them on her nightgown but caught herself just in time. Smudges on the white velvet would have been difficult to explain, but then, so would fingerprints on the fine marble mantelpiece. She rubbed her hands. The dust made her sneeze. Wiping at her watering eyes with the back of her hand, she was beginning her examination of the mantelpiece when someone knocked on the door, then opened it.

She took a quick step away from the fireplace and turned toward the door as Tandy entered the chamber. Her cheeks burned. *You blush too easily*, Nick had once told her. *Your very blood gives you away.* She swallowed hard and averted her face from Tandy's gaze, praying that he had not already read her guilt there.

"In truth, girl, you need not cry," he said, and she felt she could collapse with relief at his mistake. "There is nothing to fear from us," he continued in the same concerned tone. "No one will harm—" He broke off, and she heard a sudden sharp intake of breath.

Glancing back over her shoulder at him, she saw he was staring at the bed. Curious, she followed his gaze, and saw the bloodstains Lisle had left there, dark reddish-brown now on the white linen sheet.

"A virgin?" Tandy whispered, turning to her again, and this time she felt as though her face had been set afire by her shame. It was on the tip of her tongue to tell him the truth, that Lisle had not taken her virginity and it was his blood and not hers, but at the last instant she hesitated. Could there not be some advantage in this? If Tandy were sympathetic to her plight when he thought he had found her shedding a few tears, how much more sympathetic would he be if he believed that his master had deflowered her after taking her captive?

She turned away, stumbled to a chair and dropped into it, then lowered her head and covered her face with her hands before he could see that she was smiling. She prayed that he would take the hiccuping noise she made after a few moments, trying to stifle a giggle, for a stifled sob.

She heard him set the platter down.

"I have brought your breakfast," he said awkwardly, and she waited, unmoving, for him to leave. Minutes passed. The residue of dust left on her hands made her eyes water again and tickled her nose. She dared not sneeze now: it might make him wonder if he had misinterpreted the tears on her face earlier. Sniffling, she rubbed her itching nose and then slowly raised her head, to find Tandy watching her with a concern that she would have found touching, were he not also her captor, and were she not still too aware of bruises from their fight in the wood last night.

"I warrant you, I could not eat a bite," she said.

"You must," he told her gently. "Come, have at least a slice of bread. 'Tis freshly baked, still warm from the oven."

He brought the food to her, setting it on the table beside her chair, and stood over her while she ate. She did not glance up at him, but his hands were in view, and judging from the way they tightened into fists from time to time, he was holding back a great anger. Toward his master, she prayed.

She finished all but the last slices of meat and bread, and would have eaten those, had she not belatedly remembered her assertion that she could not eat. She pushed the platter away, then looked up at him, her eyes wide.

"Pray help me, sir," she said in a plaintive voice.

"Kat . . ." He sounded helpless. Dropping to one knee, he took her hands in his. "Where are you from, Kat?" He stared at her, a puzzled expression on his face. "From Romeville, perhaps?"

"Romeville?" she echoed, puzzled now herself.

"I trow I have seen you somewhere, somewhere other than the Jerusalem Tree. In Romeville, as like as not. Mayhap we have been in the same bousing ken or stalling ken at some time. Mayhap we have couched a hogshead at the same house in Southwark."

She shook her head in bewilderment.

"Nay?" he said, with the ghost of a smile. He let go of her left hand and began to touch her sleeve, his fingers tracing the embroidery, toying with the lace. "Bene duds."

It sounded somewhat like a compliment. "I thank you."

He chuckled. "Nay, thank Lord Har—" He broke off, seeming to flinch, and averted his gaze for a few moments. His face became mask-like in its lack of expression.

A neat trick, that, Kat thought enviously. *'Twould be useful in a card game.*

"Do you play oft at cards, Tandy?" she asked impulsively.

He looked startled, and she wished she had not spoken. The question must have made her seem a clotpoll. Then, to her surprise, he smiled warmly at her and squeezed the hand he still held.

"Y'are a cony-catcher, dearling? Are you a verser or a barnard?"

She snatched her hand free. "Do you mock me, sirrah, with such talk? I understand you not."

"No?" His smile had become slightly crooked. "Cut bene whids, mort."

Astonished by the unfamiliar words and the too-familiar tone—a tone that was almost contemptuous in its familiarity—Kat could not speak for a few moments, could only stare at him, her mouth open a little. Finally she said, harshly, "Get you gone, sirrah. I will not talk to you. Tell your master that."

For an instant he wore a look of mingled confusion and disappointment, then the mask was back in place. He rose to his feet gracefully, then made a leg—the courtesy full of mockery—and left her. She did not look around until she heard the door close behind him. He had taken the dishes. A careful servant, that, even when dismissed angrily.

Aware of a sudden that she was trembling, she took a deep breath and tried to calm herself. God's body! She wished she had not ended their conversation thus. It had seemed so hopeful at first. Something had gone awry, but she did not know what—any more than she knew what senseless language he had been speaking. And why, i'faith, had he expected her to know it?

Finally she got up and walked to the window, where she stood looking past the garden, past the walls, to the fields and woods beyond. Where was Nick?

———

Tandy found Justin in the great hall, talking to a youth garbed in dust-covered clothes and heavy riding boots. The baron sent the boy on his way as Tandy came down the last few steps of the great stairs.

"News from Southampton," Justin said cheerfully. "The ship will be ready to sail by tomorrow."

His lordship's fatigue had vanished. Now he seemed restless, impatient with energy that Tandy guessed had come from the news.

" 'Tis good news," he said, though his own reply was a bit muted. He now felt for himself some of the fatigue Justin had experienced after dealing with Kat.

"D'you have more good news?" the baron asked. "Pray God, you do, though I have seen more cheer on mourners' faces. Nay, do not tell me here." He led Tandy back to the parlor.

"Now," he said when the door was shut and they were alone. "What did she say? Did she complain of how she has been treated here?"

Well she might complain, Tandy thought, wondering if he had truly heard a guilty tone in his lord's voice or if he had only imagined it. He shook his head, for a few moments not trusting his own voice to conceal his feelings, which had swiftly changed from anger at Kat to resentment of his master's churlish behavior toward the girl.

"No, my lord," he said when he dared speak again. "I served her breakfast, as you bade me, and then spoke to her in pedlar's French."

"So she knows it?"

Tandy shrugged. "She seemed to, at first, though she denied that we might have met in any of my old haunts in London. Then she said something that led me to think her a cony-catcher, but when I pressed her on the matter, she became angry—"

"Fearful, I warrant you," Justin interrupted.

"—and bade me leave, and tell you she would not talk to me."

Justin shook his head. "Jesu, what a saucy wench she is!"

Tandy said nothing, remembering how he had found her crying. She had seemed anything but saucy then.

"So she still has not told you where she comes from, or who her master is?"

"No, my lord."

The baron sighed. "By the mass, I had hoped for some other choice than this. I cannot leave her with the sheriff, not knowing who her confederates are, or if they might have power to set her free from any jail or prison. Nor dare I leave her here."

"You cannot mean to take her with us?"

"What choice?" Justin asked. "I dare not turn my back on her."

"Not even from such a great distance?"

"We must needs return, Tandy, and God knows what mischief she could make for us here in the meantime. No, she must come with us. Perchance I can find a use for her, if I can make her more willing. She resists me now.''

"No doubt,'' Tandy murmured.

"Tell me,'' Justin continued, "for I trow you know more of such matters than I. How much gold will buy her affections? I would not insult her by making the first offer too low, but neither would I pay her more than she's worth and so have her think me a fool.''

Tandy shook his head, stunned by Justin's callousness. If nothing else, the baron should be sensitive to the fact that the girl had been virgin until last night.

"Well?'' Justin demanded.

"I am no apple-squire or bawd,'' Tandy said, his voice icy even as anger flared within him, "to be asked for such advice.''

"No apple—'' Justin broke off, a look of amazement on his face, then, shockingly, began to laugh. "In good sooth, Tandy, 'twas not such advice I was asking,'' he said at last, wiping tears from the corner of his eyes. "I mean to buy the allegiance she's given her master, so that she will be my creature and spy for me. I said as much an hour ago. As for what you assumed—why should I pay for what she will give me freely? You heard me remind her last night that she was willing enough at the inn when we first met. Yea, and this morning she called my name while she slept.''

Yea, but was she crying then? Tandy asked himself, but did not speak the question aloud. 'Twas too clear that Justin believed the girl desired him . . . and yet it had been just as clear that Kat felt herself ill-used. Was it possible that she had feigned the tears? No, he decided after a moment: she had been given no warning of his arrival, and her face was already tear-streaked when he entered the bedchamber.

"You frown,'' Justin said, frowning himself. "What's the matter, man? Did you want the wench for yourself?''

"No, my lord,'' Tandy said quickly, startled by the question.

"I hope your friendship and loyalty will not be so easily stolen from me by the sight of a lovely face,'' Justin said, and Tandy became aware that his master was studying him closely.

"Never.''

"Well. We must take her with us then, nuisance though she will of certain prove to be. Pray see to it that she is spared the discomforts of the journey to Southampton, at least.''

Tandy understood at once. "All the discomforts, or some?''

"All.''

He nodded. "I could take her a cup of wine with her dinner. Would that be early enough?''

"Yea, and it will give me time to talk to her yet again. She may yet tell me whom she serves, and then, Fortune willing, we may be spared her companionship. Now, here's a list I have made, of what must be done before we leave . . ."

Tandy forced all thoughts of Kat from his mind as he listened to Lord Harwood, but the thoughts returned as he set about his tasks. The baron had sounded sincere in his wish to be rid of Kat before their voyage, but Tandy could still see the girl's flushed, tear-stained face as clearly as if it were in a picture hung before him; he could still hear her plea for help. For the first time in all the years he had served Justin Lisle, he went about his work feeling himself more servant than friend, no longer wholly a participant in Lord Harwood's plans.

There was a sundial in the garden below the window, and Kat had watched the shadow it cast swing nearly a quarter of the way around its circle when she heard someone unlocking the door of the chamber.

'Twas Lord Harwood. He paid no heed to her at first, merely draping a long garment of pearl-color satin—a cloak?—over the back of a chair and then going to the press, from whence he took a suit of tawny silk, which he draped over the back of another chair. Only then did he look at her.

"Have you had time enough," he asked, "to realize that you must tell me who sent you hither?"

"More than time enough," she replied calmly, "for as I have told you, I sent myself. *I have no master.*"

He sighed. "Have you given more thought to jail, Kat? There would be no such view as this, but there are windows where you may stand to beg alms of the passersby. And you would need to do so very soon, for the paltry few coins in your purse would pay for only a few days' food. Either your master pays you poorly—"

"*I said—*"

"—or you desperately need employment. Which I can provide."

She gave him a skeptical look.

He returned to the satin garment he had set aside upon entering the room, picked it up and held it out at arm's length. 'Twas a gown, not a cloak, she saw now: a most elegant gown, trimmed with silver lace and embroidered with silver thread set with seed pearls.

"D'you like this?" he asked.

She shrugged.

"Would you like to have this?" He sounded impatient. " 'Tis yours."

"I would rather have my own garments returned."

"They are naught but rags compared to this."

"Yea, but I wore them freely."

"There would be more gowns like this, Kat, if you served me."

"No. I will not be your servant . . . or your whore."

"By God's precious blood!" He threw the gown aside as if it were no more than a rag. "What senseless talk is this? Have I asked you to become my mistress?" he demanded, coming closer, pointing an accusing finger at her. "Have I sought you out? Nay, madam, 'tis you who have followed me, even to my chamber at the Jerusalem Tree, and then to my home. 'Twas you who called out my name in your sleep, and who welcomed my kisses."

"Your farewell would be much more welcome," Kat said heatedly. "You need not even show me to the gate."

"No, I need only turn you out, and wait to see what mischief you do me next." He caught her nightgown by its wide collar and dragged her toward him. "I dare not trust you, Kat. Not yet."

She stood less than a foot from him, so close that she had to tilt her head back to meet his gaze. There was fury in that gaze, but also something else, something that might be bafflement. He was still not sure if she was a spy; she had eluded his understanding of her this long. She could not keep that momentary satisfaction from showing on her face.

"You like this, do you?" he asked angrily. "You vexatious witch."

He drew her against him, holding her close as he kissed her, a bruising kiss, nothing like the sweet kisses he had given her at the inn and during her dream last night. She fought him but could not break free, and the kiss seemed to go on forever, until at last she heard someone knock on the door.

He let her go so suddenly that she nearly fell. Her hand pressed to her mouth, she retreated to the window while he went to the door and opened it.

Tandy, again, with more food.

"My lord, I have brought her dinner." He looked questioningly at Lord Harwood, who nodded curtly as he strode past his servant out of the chamber, coming back a few moments later to grab the tawny silk suit. This time he slammed the door behind him as he left.

Tandy looked at Kat. "Would you like to talk to me now?" he asked, his voice so sympathetic that she was tempted, but she forced herself to shake her head.

"Well." He set the tray he had brought in down on a table. "There's stewed chicken, and salad, and a fresh cherry tart. And malmsey. If you would rather have other food and drink, tell me now: I am drawer here but a short while."

"And then turn jailer again?" she asked, forgetting her intention of remaining silent.

"Not if you'll speak to me, girl, and tell me more of yourself."

She shook her head again, and he went away, locking the door behind him.

The dinner was a fine one. *At least I will not starve here,* she thought as she took the glass of malmsey to the window and finished it while sitting on the window seat where any observer outside the walls could see her. *I am more likely to grow fat from lack of exercise.* For a moment she considered walking back and forth in the chamber, as though it were a gallery, but she really felt too sleepy now. She stretched out on the window seat and closed her eyes. Just as she drifted off to sleep, it occurred to her that the wine might have been drugged, but she decided to give that more thought after a nap.

Chapter 16

He remembered trees, and darkness, and men shouting to each other in the distance. Grass-covered ground beneath his cheek. His head throbbing . . .

Then a road, silent in the moonlight except for the occasional stirring of branches by small animals or birds disturbed by his passage. He had to get help: he knew that much. But who needed help, and why, was not clear to him. Still, he had to find help . . . He kept moving, directed by the hedges hemming him in on either side . . .

Then a flickering light, seen as he looked down a narrow lane that intersected the one he was following. He had turned toward it instinctively, a moth to a flame . . .

He sat up, blinking, and stared wildly around at the chamber in which he had just awakened. The room was directly beneath the roof: the slanting ceiling told him that. The floor was covered with rushes. The furniture—the bed on which he was lying, a chest, a table with an earthenware pitcher, a three-legged stool—was plain but serviceable. Where was he?

Frightened for no reason he could clearly understand, he flung himself to the side of the bed and stood up. Dizziness assailed him, and he staggered forward, bumping against the table. The pitcher tipped over, spilling water across the polished oak and the rushes below.

He was clinging to the table, waiting for the dizziness to subside, when the door opened.

He turned his head slowly toward it as a middle-aged man in tawny frieze came in. Behind him, stopping in the doorway, was a plump middle-aged woman, and, half hidden behind her, a girl of thirteen or fourteen. The man gestured for them to leave, but they stayed.

"Up and about already?" the man asked.

"Who—" The chamber reeled and leaped about him—*'tis dancing a lavolta*, he thought dizzily—as he tried to turn toward the man; he clutched at the table's edge. "Who are you?" He assayed a step toward them, and his knees buckled. The man caught him before he hit the floor.

He was hungry, he realized, and there was food nearby.

He opened his eyes. He was back in bed, his head resting on a plump pillow. Seated on a cushioned wooden stool, facing him, was the man he had seen earlier. Beside him on the table was an earthenware bowl, from which wafted steam bearing the tantalizing smell of chicken broth.

" 'Cham Ralph Higham, a yeoman," the man said, as if no time had elapsed since he had been asked who he was. "Now, sir, who are you?"

"I am—" He hesitated. The man had spoken as one from Kent, and he wondered if he should use the same speech. " 'Cham . . ." No name came readily to him. " 'Cham . . ." he repeated, panicking as his own name eluded him. The blackness began to close in again.

He jumped when Ralph touched his shoulder.

"Fear not, lad," Ralph said, his gruff voice surprisingly gentle. "You have but forgotten for a while. It happens sometimes, with a blow to the head like you took. You could not remember last night, either."

"A blow . . . ?"

"You cannot remember even that now?" A slight shake of the head. "Maybe 'tis best forgotten."

His entire skull ached—and it had been throbbing worse before; that memory was still too vivid—but one spot was particularly sore. He touched it gently, discovering a bump, and a cut, but surprisingly little blood.

"My wife washed the cut," Ralph told him. "You were a sight when you came here before dawn this morning, with blood trickled down the side of your head and twigs and leaves all over your clothes. But she insisted on taking care of you, once she got over her fright. Now she's saying she's glad she could not sleep last night and was up sewing, so you saw a light here." He paused. "Can you recall any of what misfortune befell you?"

"I remember shouting . . . men shouting . . ."

Ralph snorted. "More than one, then. Robbers are all cowards. They would not set upon even an unarmed man unless they had companions to help them. But you kept your purse, so you must have defended yourself well, even if one of them got you with a cudgel before they ran off." He fell silent for a few moments. " 'Tis strange," he said, frowning slightly, "that they left you your purse, but perchance they heard someone coming, or else the blow had but stunned you for an instant and they still feared your sword."

Seeming to dismiss the matter from his mind, Ralph handed him the bowl of broth and a spoon, then set a platter of fresh-baked bread on the bed beside him. "Here, now. Eat this, and sleep some more, and you'll be fit and have your memory back when you wake again."

It was late in the afternoon when he woke again. The throbbing in his head was gone, and even the wound, when he touched it, seemed less tender. Despite having eaten all the bread and broth earlier, he felt ravenous again.

He sat up on the edge of the bed, waited a bit to make sure the dizziness would not return, then stood and took a few experimental steps. The floor remained steady beneath his feet. He could leave here now, and go—

Where?

He closed his eyes, biting his lip as he tried to remember more than tattered remnants of last night. Trees, a wood, but where? Men shouting, but who? A lane bordered by hedges, but which direction had he been walking? Where had he hoped it would take him? For all their use to him, the memories might have been torn from another brain, without reference, meaningless.

Sighing, he gave up and opened his eyes.

A doublet lay on top of the chest. His, he supposed, for it was of black silk, matching the hose he wore. It fit him perfectly, too, he realized as he donned it and fastened the buttons. 'Twould be much too small for his burly host, and also rather too fine for a yeoman. 'Twas a gentleman's suit he wore, though both doublet and hose, he noticed, had been torn and mended, skillfully, but with a coarse thread. Mistress Higham's work, no doubt.

The bowl and platter had been taken away, replaced by a pewter basin, beside which lay a rough towel and a sliver of crude, unscented soap. The earthenware pitcher, he saw, was filled with water. He poured some into the basin and was leaning over to wash his face when he noticed the tiny mirror behind the basin, the sort of mirror a woman would wear tied to her girdle. He picked it up and studied his reflection. Mayhap the mirror had been left on the table in the hope that seeing his own face would bring back his memory, but that had been a vain hope. The features might have been a stranger's. He looked well enough, he thought, too worried for much vanity. There were bruises along one cheekbone, and a couple of small cuts on his forehead.

He was still looking in the mirror when the door opened behind him. He turned to see Ralph enter the chamber, carrying a sword belt and a purse.

"I heard you get up," the yeoman said, "but thought 'chud give you time to yourself, in case . . ."

"I cannot remember. Not even reaching your house. Only a little about last night." He had made an effort to keep fear from his voice, but the flat, emotionless tone somehow sounded worse yet.

Ralph's shoulders seemed to sag, but he merely nodded as he crossed the room and handed over the purse and sword.

The purse was full. He was curious about the contents, but instead of opening the purse strings simply fastened the chain to his belt. Had he checked to see what coins the purse held, his host might think he suspected theft, which was not the case. Then he buckled the sword around his waist. For an instant he let his hand rest on the hilt. It felt comfortable, but not familiar: no memories there. He hoped he had not forgotten how to use it.

"There's an inn, and not a bad one, at the village," Ralph said. "Go back down our lane and then turn right. 'Tis less than a mile. Someone there might know you."

"Not, pray God, any of the men I met last night."

He had meant the remark half as a jest, and certainly not as a reproach, yet Ralph looked guilty.

"My wife would have you stay, at least until you remember who you are. She's a kind-hearted woman, and she trusts you." He cleared his throat. "I trust you, too, and could fend for myself if 'chwas wrong about you, but 'cham responsible for others . . ."

He nodded, and the yeoman looked relieved that he understood. 'Twas the daughter. A pretty girl. His host did well to protect her from a stranger, whether he was a gentleman suffering a loss of memory or a rogue pretending to be such. He remembered Ralph's frown as he considered that his uninvited guest had not been robbed by whoever had set upon him.

"I thank you for your kindness," he said, loosening his purse strings, "and would fain—"

"No." Ralph shook his head. " 'Tis but our Christian duty. And you may need all your money before you find your way home again."

If I have a home, he thought, but did not argue. He drew the purse strings shut as he followed the yeoman down a steep flight of stairs and out of the house, which was, oddly, deserted. Ralph must have sent his wife and daughter away when he realized that his guest was up and about.

"I would thank your wife before I go," he said as he stood on the path leading to the lane.

" 'Chill thank her for you. Fare you well."

"Wait!" he called as Ralph turned back toward the house. The yeoman glanced back over his shoulder, a look of suspicion on his face.

"Pray tell me, where am I?" he asked, feeling more helpless now than ever. "Is this Kent?"

Ralph's laughter was good-natured, not mocking, and it quickly stilled, giving way to a look of sympathy. "Nay. 'Cham from there, but this is Hampshire, lad, nigh to Sussex. The innkeeper can give you directions. God speed."

He stood for a few moments on the path after the yeoman had gone back into the house, pointedly shutting the door behind him. There was kindness here, if guarded. There had been security and hospitality when he needed it. He gazed up at the solid, half-timbered two-story house, wishing he could stay for at least a while longer, but that closed door had given him an answer with which he could not argue.

He opened his purse, tilting it so sunlight fell on the silver and gold within. Mostly silver: shillings, a sixpence, some groats and half-groats, a few pennies. But three of the gold coins were pounds, and there were also four angels, two half-angels, a noble and two crowns. It had taken great honesty for the yeoman to return the purse to him, when Ralph could as easily have told him that he had not had a purse with him when he reached their dwelling.

I could leave a pound, he thought, his fingers grazing the edges of one of the large gold coins, but the warning that he might need all his money seemed too apt. Still, he felt this debt must be repaid: he took one of the angels and two shillings and set them down on the path where anyone watching from the house—and he was certain Ralph was— could see them. He looked up at the house again, engraving it in his memory, for he would want to remember it to find it again should he ever be able to repay his debt more generously. Then, turning his back on his temporary sanctuary, he set off for the inn Ralph had mentioned.

The village was small, no more than a dozen cottages huddled together around the inn and an ancient, crumbling church. The inn, too, was small, and seemed shabby to him, though he could not summon any memories of other inns. At least the common room, its walls hung with faded painted cloths depicting scenes from the Old Testament, seemed clean enough. He paused in the doorway to look around. He recognized no one in the room, but there was the consolation that no one seemed to recognize him, either. Until he recalled who he was, anyone who seemed to know him had to be considered a possible enemy.

He sat down at a table by a painted ark that time had left looking insubstantial enough to float on air as well as water. A servingmaid, who seemed uncertain as to how friendly she should be, brought him the food he ordered: bread, a cold joint of mutton served with mint sauce, small beer. All the while he ate, he was aware of the innkeeper watching him. A thin, dour-looking man who succeeded in smiling at certain of his customers, the innkeeper had nothing but scowls for him.

But then, what had he expected? Arriving alone, on foot, dressed in torn finery instead of honest frieze. Obviously neither a common laborer nor a gentleman, what else could he be but a rogue? After paying for his supper—ten pennies, dearer than it should have been—he asked his host about the price of a chamber and was not surprised to be told there were none empty. The girl started to object, but the innkeeper brusquely gestured for her to be silent.

So there was room, but not for him.

For want of another destination, he asked the servingmaid which way to Sussex, and took that route away from the village. 'Twas a mild summer night, and he would not have minded sleeping outdoors and saving the money a chamber would have cost him, had he not feared being set on again—possibly by whomever he had encountered last night. He was glad when the hedges bordering the lane gave way to open fields on either side.

He walked until it was completely dark, feeling well rested after spending most of the day asleep. He might have continued walking all night, had he not seen clouds massing in the southeast. There might be rain before morning.

He left the road at the next farmstead. No lights showed in the windows of the farmhouse, and that suited him; he had no plan to introduce himself to the yeoman and his wife. He wanted only to avail himself of the soft hay in their barn.

Inside there were only a few animals: a horse that whickered once, softly, when he passed its stall, two slumbering cows, a she-goat that bleated and leapt out of his path, a cat that stole away into impenetrable shadows. The air was sweet with the scent of newly mown hay. He looked around, spying a corner where he would be concealed by stacked bales from anyone just coming into the barn. He unbuckled his sword belt, drew his sword, and lay down with the hilt under his hand. The cat came creeping back to lie down beside him. After a little while, lulled by its purring, he fell asleep.

"The ruffian cly you!" a woman said, her voice shrill. "I am no niggling mort!"

"Stow you!" a man retorted. "I'll filch you!"

"You have filched me already, and had all my lour. But I'll couch a hogshead alone this darkmans."

He sat up, his hand closing around the sword hilt. The quarrel he had overheard had seemed dreamlike, the harsh voices and strange words gone now. Then he heard, clearly in the silence, a slapping sound, and the woman cried out in pain.

Stealth would be impossible when his footing was rustling straw. He scrambled to his feet and darted out from his hiding place.

The two standing just inside the door turned toward him. The woman, her hand to her cheek, was bent over slightly, cringing away from her companion. They were mere silhouettes against the starry sky, but he could tell that the woman was short and slender, the man tall and heavy. It was a wonder that his slap had not sent her reeling off her feet.

"Get you gone, sirrah," he said coldly, with as much authority as he could muster. It helped that the man was not wearing a sword. "Let the wench be."

"A gentry cofe couched in strummell?" the man said. His laugh had an ugly edge to it. "Bing a waste, cofe, ere you meet my filchmans." The rogue brandished a truncheon that had been hanging from his belt, concealed by the shadow of his leg.

Wary, he took a step back and drew his dagger. The truncheon was nearly as long as his sword, and if used properly, could parry sword thrusts as well as any blade. And though the cudgel might not deliver the clean, quick death a blade could, it could be just as deadly, in practiced hands.

And his assailant seemed to have the confidence of long practice, swinging the cudgel lightly as he came toward him. Still a few steps away, the rogue reached behind his back and drew a knife.

He dodged just in time, and heard the knife thunk into the wooden wall behind him.

The vagabond closed with him, bringing the cudgel down on his sword blade and forcing its tip to the floor. The supple steel bent but did not break. Growling, the rogue brought the cudgel up to smash him in the face, but before it could touch him his sword had nicked the man's ribs. There was a yowl and a scuttling retreat, but then the vagabond leaned down and rolled a bale of hay toward him. It slammed against his legs, staggering him, and with a victorious shriek the rogue attacked again, the cudgel raised for a final, finishing blow.

The man shrieked again as the sword blade slid between his ribs. An instant later his knees buckled and he toppled headlong onto the straw.

He stared down at his fallen assailant, stunned, scarcely able to believe that he had killed a man. Finally, leaning over, he rolled the vagabond onto his side and pulled his sword free, shuddering at the feeling of warm blood on his hand. Quickly he grabbed some straw and began to wipe his hand and sword clean. For some minutes the woman remained crouching in the doorway, watching him. She had made no sound to indicate either grief or elation at her companion's death, and he wondered if she were afraid of him, too.

"Y'are free to go," he told her.

"Bene," she said. "Am I free to stay?"

He hesitated, then shrugged.

"I thank you," she said. "I have had no cause to thank a ruffler ere now, but he"—she nodded toward the corpse—"deserved to die." She rubbed the side of her face, likely remembering the slap.

So she thought he was a ruffler? He had heard of them, former soldiers or serving men who turned their skill in fighting against honest citizens and other vagabonds alike. He thought of telling her that she was wrong, he was no such thing, but then decided against honesty. He was vulnerable enough, deprived as he was of all personal memory; he would be more so if she knew. And rufflers were feared and respected by other vagabonds.

Nor, he thought unhappily, could he be certain that she was not correct. Perhaps he *was* a ruffler . . . But he did not think so. It had been too much of a shock, seeing someone die at his hands.

She finally moved, walking past him to kneel beside the dead man. He looked on curiously as she searched through the rogue's clothes, first finding a purse. She shook it, then shook her head at the thin jingling made by the few coins inside. "He would spend all lightmans in a bousing ken, while I begged for alms, a demander for glimmer for the first time in my life, telling all who would listen that I had lost everything when my cottage burned down."

"Your cottage burned down?"

She looked up at him, her mouth slightly open in astonishment. "Of course not, cofe."

She reached into her bodice, pulling the neckline down so one breast was bared to the nipple, and drew out a small knife. With this, she slit the lining of the vagabond's doublet, grunting with satisfaction when some tightly folded papers spilled out.

"Gybes, I warrant," she said. The word meant nothing to him. "A niggling mort he knew, a whore he had taken too much lour from, told me he had filched a jarkman to get them." She handed the bundle to him.

It was too dark to read the papers, even by moonlight, but she seemed to think them valuable, so he put them in the pocket of his doublet.

"That pays my debt to you," she said. She had followed him to the door. "You would not have found them without my help." The last was said defiantly, as though she expected him to contradict her.

She turned back toward the dead man. He tried to read her expression, but could see little of her face past the thick tangle of dark hair. Then, aware of his gaze, she tossed her hair back and stared directly at him.

She was an attractive woman, though not truly beautiful; her nose was too short, her mouth too wide. But her skin looked smooth in the moonlight, and her eyes were large and wide-set. Her hair was thick and healthy, if hopelessly tangled, and he was very aware of the high, full breasts thrusting against the thin cloth of her bodice.

"Well, cofe," she said at last, "do we stay here this darkmans?"

He looked toward the farmhouse. There was still no light showing there. Maybe no one was home, but it was more likely that, hearing the shrieks, the farmer and his family had decided that it would be wisest to stay inside, at least until dawn. He glanced at the sky. 'Twould be only an hour or two . . .

"No," he told her, then went back into the barn to retrieve his sword belt. She followed him back through the entrance, and he thought for a moment that she was simply determined to dog his heels, but she had her own objective in mind: the cudgel. He watched her closely as she picked it up.

"D'you want this filchmans?" she asked, holding it out toward him.

He shook his head, swallowing hard as he remembered the heavy club swinging toward him.

"Y'are certain?" She hefted it in her right hand. " 'Tis heavy for me, but I'll keep it. I might need it."

He was about to protest when it occurred to him that her knife would provide her with little protection except in the most desperate fight at close quarters. She would need the club to frighten off other bullies like the vagabond he had killed.

They set off down the road, silent for the first mile or so, and he suspected that she was also listening for sounds of pursuit. Then, when she apparently felt they had put enough distance between themselves and the farmstead, she began to talk.

"Where are you bound, cofe?" she asked.

"London," he said, for want of a better answer.

"Romeville? 'Tis my own town, but a good long walk from Sussex. Why would you go there?"

"Curiosity," he answered honestly.

"Curiosity." She looked heavenward. "Like enough, you'll stand gaping at London Bridge and Paul's. But do not think to see the Rome mort herself. She'll not be there now, cofe, she'll be gone on progress with her court, the good queen and all her gentry coves, and she'll not return till autumn."

He shook his head, thinking she was wrong about the queen—for it must be the queen she meant—being gone on progress already, but was not sure why he felt that way. And in truth, why would it concern him?

Her name was Bess Morsted, and she was a walking mort and a wild dell, she told him, to his confusion. "An autem mort am I. 'Twas in a church in Romeville that my late husband and I were married. I have never been a niggling mort," she asserted firmly, and he recalled her argument with the vagabond. "I begged for him when he filched me," she said, "and I'll foist a purse, or nip clothes from a hedge, but I am no whore."

She had spent most of her life in London, but had recently found it prudent to leave for a time; she did not explain why. For the past few weeks she had been traveling through Hampshire and Sussex, surviving as best she could on the few coins she had brought with her from London, trying always to avoid both the bailiffs and local vagabonds. Then, as she began to make her way back toward her home, she had the misfortune to catch the eye of someone she called an upright man.

He had threatened to set the bluecoats after her unless she agreed to beg for him. He had more than a dozen vagabonds working for him, robbing and pilfering and begging, but he had paid scant attention to them lately, instead concentrating on Bess. He had tried to bed her several times, but each time the threat of the knife she carried had stopped him, and though he hit her a few times when she was not on guard and he thought she had withheld money from him, he seemed wary of making her desperately angry.

"A coward," she said contemptuously.

He remembered the vagabond's attempt to kill him too well to share her opinion of the man. Then, too, he would not want to give Bess reason to use that knife on him, either.

"You know me now, cofe," she said at last. "But I do not know your name."

"No, you do not," he agreed, praying that the amiable tone he tried for cloaked his uneasiness.

She gave him a long, measuring look, all the while not breaking stride. Finally she turned away. Her gaze on the road before them, she said, "Would you have me call you jack, then?"

It had been a saucy question, for she could as easily have used the word *jack* to mean *knave* as to mean the nickname for *John*. He laughed, admiring her boldness.

"Jack will do," he assured her.

She stared at him again, then shook her head. "Well, then, Jack o'Sussex, where shall we couch? 'Tis almost lightmans, and the cackling-cheats will be awake soon, and all the yeomen and laborers hereabouts. D'you see that old cottage there, across that greenmans?"

She pointed across a field in which sheep were lying. He followed her gaze and was disappointed to see a crumbling hovel, most of the thatch of its roof gone.

"There's no roof," he pointed out.

"Aye, and no rain, either."

He shrugged, and she led the way across the field. They discovered the door of the cottage missing, and an ewe with two lambs inside. "Out, you," Bess said, laughing as she swung her cudgel toward them. "I'll not couch with bleating-cheats." The sheep bleated with fright as they ran from the cottage. He stood in the doorway, anxious lest the animals' alarm be noticed, while she moved about the cottage, using a bit of thatch she plucked from the roof to sweep the dirt floor clean, then pulled more straw thatching down and spread it over the floor. Now and then while she worked, she glanced toward him with an oddly shy expression on her face.

She had been carrying a pack strapped to her back. Now she removed it and unfolded the cloth. 'Twas a sheet, he saw, which she draped over the straw. She lay down on one side of the sheet, gazing up at him, then, when he did not move, she patted the cloth beside her.

"You may share my slate, Jack. 'Tis not the best bed, a slate over strummell, but better than strummell alone."

He sat down on the edge of the sheet, mindful of the knife she carried.

"I am not diseased, cofe," she said sharply. "Are you?"

He shook his head.

"Well."

He stared at her. In the dawn light, he could tell that she was young—no older than himself, he guessed, recalling the reflection he had seen in the mirror. Twenty, mayhap. Her skin was free of pockmarks, but it was sunbrowned and lightly freckled: a gentlewoman would kill herself, he thought idly, if she woke up one morning with a complexion like that. Yet it suited Bess, who looked like some healthy country maid. Very healthy. He could scarcely keep his gaze from her breasts, large breasts for a girl so slender.

"What's the matter, cofe?" she asked. "Am I not pretty enough for a ruffler like you? Too brown, am I?"

He shook his head.

Straw rustled as he slid over to her. She threw one arm around his neck and drew his face down to hers.

She seemed in a hurry, unlacing her bodice for him, then pulling her skirts up only a few moments after he had begun fondling her breasts.

Her urgency excited him. He rolled on top of her, fumbling with his hose. Their coupling was quick but satisfactory; she was shuddering beneath him, her legs wrapped around his hips, before he finished.

He rolled off her and lay on his back on the sheet—*slate*, had she called it? another of her strange words—gazing up at a few pink-tinted clouds in a sky that had turned a glorious blue with sunrise. It would be a beautiful morning. He closed his eyes to it, exhausted, and was already half asleep when Bess spoke.

"Jack?"

She had sounded anxious. He opened his eyes and glanced sideways at her. She appeared anxious, too, lying there with her head propped up on her hand, gazing intently at his face.

"Will you take me to Romeville with you? Please you, let me travel with you."

He studied her face, but found no trace there of a cold calculation that would lead her to offer her body to him as part of some bargain. *I am no whore*, she had told him, and he decided now that he believed her. She had wanted him too much; he was sure it had not been pretense. Belike it had been a while since she had lain with a man. Had she not let him know that her husband was dead? 'Twas said that widows were lusty. Certainly she was.

He smiled, a soft smile that was a bit crooked, and touched her cheek gently. "Yea, we'll to London together. Now let me sleep."

But she had other plans.

He woke around noon, when a lamb bounded into the hovel and stumbled over his leg before scrambling away. Bess, sitting up beside him, laughed quietly as she brushed her hair away from her face.

It was warm inside the ruined cottage, warm enough that he was glad they had shed all their clothes earlier. Sunlight had encroached on the part of the hovel shaded by what remained of the roof, where Bess had spread her slate, and his legs were lightly sunburned. He winced as he drew on his hose. Bess shook her head in sympathy and began to dress herself. When they were both dressed, and Bess had again folded the sheet and strapped it to her back, he checked to see that no one was about. Then, her hand in his, they walked down to the road.

"There's a village not more than a mile or two down this road," Bess told him. "There's an inn there, where we could buy dinner if you have any lour. And if not, haply we could use the gybes."

He had forgotten the papers she had given him the night before. He drew them from the pocket of his doublet and unfolded them, looking at one after another. They were licenses to beg.

Bess moved closer to him, peering down at the licenses as she walked.

"Good jarks, those," she said, stabbing a ragged-nailed finger at one seal, then another. "The jarkman knew his trade. Either that, or he nipped the real cheat."

The seals looked official enough to Jack, but if he understood her correctly—and he was afraid to let her know how little he understood of her words, for fear that she would suspect he was not a ruffler—the licenses were counterfeits, and good ones. What, he wondered, was the penalty for being caught with such forgeries? Bess seemed unconcerned—but then, he was certain, she had had ample experience avoiding bluecoats.

"We'll use these only if needs must," he said firmly, folding the licenses and hiding them in his doublet pocket again.

"D'you have lour, then?" Bess asked.

"Aye," he told her. "I have . . . lour."

She nodded, a look of relief on her face that told Jack that, however high an opinion she had of the forgeries, she would not have felt comfortable using them. What had she told him last night? That she had begged for alms when her companion forced her to, but never before. She had confessed as well to being a thief—but no, that had been less a confession than an admission, and one made without any shame. How strange, he thought, that she thought it better to steal than to beg . . . He could not help but smile at her.

She smiled back, then, to his alarm, unfastened the cudgel from her girdle and hefted it in her right hand.

" 'Tis heavier than I like," she said, "so I ask you again—d'you want this filchmans?"

He shook his head, his hand brushing the hilt of his sword.

"Nor do I," she said, and swung her arm, releasing the cudgel to send it flying across the hedge and out of sight. They heard a chicken squawk.

Bess chuckled. "As like as not, I nearly brained the cackling-cheat." She came back to him, slipping her arm around his waist and resting her hand over his on his sword hilt. "You must protect me now, cofe. Unless you would liefer teach me to use your sword, so—"

He interrupted her with a laugh. "I'faith, not you, too—"

His laughter ended abruptly as he realized he did not know what he was starting to say. Bess's remark had almost called up a memory, but it had disappeared before he could catch it, like a fish slipping free of the hook before it could be pulled from the water. He swore in exasperation, and Bess moved away from him.

" 'Twas but a jest, my Jack, sweet Jack," she told him. "By God's body, I would not want to learn fence. 'Tis for coves. What would I do with such skill, turn ruffler?'' Her laughter had an anxious edge. ''Did you teach fence once, Jack? I trow that others have asked you to teach them.''

He shook his head. It made him uncomfortable to try to remember. He held out his arm, and after a moment she returned to his side. To his relief she said nothing more about fencing, instead content to walk beside him in silence for a time, her shoulder and hip sometimes brushing against him.

They were within sight of the village when she spoke again.

''Have I told you yet,'' she asked, and something in her voice made him instantly wary, ''about my kinchin co and kinchin mort?''

CHAPTER 17

Sparrow had been in Southampton a week, waiting for Lord Harwood's ship, the *Lady Margaret*, to sail. As far as he was concerned, the stay had been a week too long.

He disliked Southampton, with its large population of foreigners: Venetians whose colony of merchants had been here for centuries, and Flemings who had arrived in the last few years, setting up factories that were permitted as long as they trained English apprentices and hired an English journeyman for every Flemish worker. The townsmen seemed to welcome the immigrants, especially since Southampton's trade had been drawn away to ports in the West Country. But they were far from welcome to Sparrow, who winced every time he heard a Low Countries accent as he walked through Southampton's streets to the wharves.

The harbor reeked of pitch and rotting fish and seaweed. Sparrow found a place out of the way of the sailors and laborers on the docks and stood there looking out to sea. Innumerable small boats crossed from the wharves to anchored ships and back again. A hulk was preparing to sail, its windlass crew chanting while the anchor was drawn up. He heard the shriek of a boatswain's whistle, then a volley of curses, delivered in half a dozen languages but with an honest English accent.

They had been conveying supplies out to the *Lady Margaret* for days now. Casks of salt pork, beans, flour and beer; livestock cackling or grunting in cages; earthen pots of mutton packed in butter and beef in vinegar. Fresh and dried fruits, spices, vinegars and onions. Ship's biscuit, and rice. And the spare canvas, the timber and pitch and nails needed for repair, had been taken on board and stowed, as had the gear they would need for fishing. Most of the crew were aboard, and this morning the casks of water, left till last so it would stay fresh longer, were being loaded. The ship would sail today.

Justin Lisle was leaving England, and Sparrow found his moods alternating wildly between fury and delight.

He had been stunned when he first learned from Walsingham that Lord Harwood had been given a license to travel beyond seas. The license had been granted only grudgingly by the queen, especially since

Lisle had not come to court himself to obtain it but had sent one of his servants. He had pleaded gout as the reason for his absence and cited an illness that threatened his cousin's life as the cause of his request to be allowed to travel to Spain. Elizabeth had grumbled about *cousins in illness* but had finally agreed, though specifying that the license would be for a period of only five months. *Only.* It made Sparrow's head reel to think what harm Lisle could do, what mischief he could plot, during five months in Spain.

Yet Walsingham himself had seemed less concerned about Lisle than about a note that had been pinned to the lining of his cloak the previous day in London.

The note's presence there had been bad enough, for Walsingham could think of no one who had been close enough to him to leave the note without being observed . . . and he had become quite wary this last six months, after finding three other notes, one somehow slipped into his purse, the others pinned to his hat and to the underside of his ruff. Once this had happened at court; the other times he had been in different neighborhoods in London. He could think of no one whom he had seen on all four occasions. Yet it was indisputable that it was the same person, for the handwriting was the same, an elegant Italian hand, on small pieces of fine paper, and the wavy borders of the notes fit together, much like the copies of an indenture, to form the better part of a sheet of paper. 'Twas as if the author, who did not sign or even initial each note, wished to assure Walsingham of his identity each time, so that by the time the third note appeared, the bit of information it conveyed, about the activities of a certain gentleman in Northumberland, would be assumed to be as correct as the intelligence in the previous two notes. And so it had proven to be. 'Twas fortunate, Walsingham said, that he had acted without hesitation, without waiting for confirmation of the intelligence from another source.

But now Sparrow's master had been given a message he could not accept.

Ware Ridolfi.

Surely that warning was mistaken, Walsingham reasoned. Roberto Ridolfi, a Florentine banker who had settled in England during the reign of Queen Mary, had come under suspicion last autumn, after the plot to wed the Duke of Norfolk to the Queen of Scots was discovered. Walsingham had held Ridolfi under arrest at his house for a month, interrogating him. 'Twas true that Ridolfi had given money supplied from abroad to the Duke of Norfolk and the Bishop of Ross, one of Mary Stuart's agents, but then, as a banker he was close to many at the court and had even at times been employed by the Crown in financial transactions. 'Twas true as well that Ridolfi had been told of the marriage plans, but it seemed that he had known nothing more of the conspiracy, and a search through the papers at his lodgings turned up nothing to implicate him in the plot. The Florentine had been released on a bond of a thousand pounds to ensure his promise to limit himself to his business and cease meddling in affairs of state, and two months later the bond had been returned to him. Since then Walsingham had found himself wondering if the banker might not prove useful to the English government, though he had not yet decided how . . .

And now this.

Walsingham was tempted to burn the note, but instead caution had led him to place it, with the others, in his locked writing cabinet. There it lay on top of the second of the notes, one telling him of a gentleman in Surrey who harbored two massing priests, men who had been young during Queen Mary's reign and were still vigorous and determined to incite the massmongers in Surrey to rebellion. That message, and the one about the situation in Northumberland, and the one about the merchant in London, had been invaluable. It troubled Walsingham greatly that his unknown intelligencer should think it necessary to warn him to beware of Ridolfi. Under the circumstances, Walsingham was pleased that Justin Lisle would be out of the country for a few months, sparing him the necessity of keeping an eye on the baron's activities.

Sparrow could understand that: he felt that way himself at times. There was, as Walsingham had said, always the chance that Lisle might stay in Spain, joining the colony of English exiles there. But unlike Sparrow, Walsingham had no need to prove his usefulness to the Crown. Sparrow had hoped to show that Lord Harwood was indeed a traitor, and discover his fellow conspirators as well, and now that opportunity had slipped away from him. Thinking of that, he ground his teeth together as he began to pace up and down the wharf.

Suddenly he caught sight of a familiar, tawny-haired figure. 'Twas Lord Harwood's manservant, driving a wagon down the dock toward one of the barges that had been taking water casks out to the ship. Sparrow hurried toward him.

The wagon halted just before Sparrow reached it. He could see it carried more water casks, and, slumped between two of the casks, a young boy, sound asleep.

"Holloa, Tandy!" one of the men in the barge called. The tawny-haired servant grinned wearily at them—in truth, he looked as though he had not slept for days—and began lifting casks from the wagon and handing them to the first man in the line of laborers who passed the casks down to the men in the barge.

Sparrow walked along the side of the wagon. The boy lay with his head thrown back, his mouth slightly open, dead to the world. His clothes, from the ancient and ridiculously large cap to the worn boots, were grass-stained as well as grimy, and he reeked of wine. Sparrow pitied the lad, who must have decided that a life at sea, with all the adventure and riches sailors boasted of, was preferable to drudgery ashore. He would soon find out differently. This first, short voyage might not prove to be so bad, but on longer voyages he would learn about the rigors of a sailor's life, the spoiled food and disease. And even this trip would be off to a poor start for the lad, since he had obviously spent his entire last night ashore celebrating in some tavern or ordinary.

Sparrow stood near Tandy as the last few casks, except for those the boy lay between, were lifted from the wagon. Lord Harwood's servant picked up the youth then, none too gently, and started to hand him toward the man at the head of the line, then apparently changed his mind and carried the boy toward the barge himself. As Tandy brushed past him, Sparrow noticed how attractive the boy was, how fair-skinned. That fairness would be gone after his first month as a sailor, and in a year or two, like enough, his teeth would have started to go, too, lost to scurvy.

"Hold!" he told Tandy, and the fair-haired man swung around to look questioningly at him.

Sparrow bit his lip. He had no real authority to demand that the boy be left on shore, and the boy himself might well be furious if he woke to find that the ship had sailed without him. But it angered Sparrow beyond measure that this youth—little more than a child, from the look of those beardless cheeks—had been led to sign on with this crew, to sail on a traitor's ship bound for Spain.

As Tandy handed the lad to one of the men at the edge of the wharf, Sparrow caught another glimpse of the boy's face, one that gave him pause for a moment. The boy reminded him of someone, someone he disliked—but who? He shook his head, dismissing the feeling. This was no time to hesitate, with Tandy already climbing down to the barge.

"Who is this boy, and by what right—" he began, but was interrupted by a voice coming from behind him.

"How now, Master Cadmon? Have you seen enough? I trust all our cargo meets with your approval."

He swung around to face Lord Harwood.

" 'Tis within the terms of your passport, my lord." *And it is well for you that the terms are so vague*, he thought. The license allowed gifts for Lord Harwood's cousin, but Sparrow thought Elizabeth would have had second thoughts about granting the passport at all, had she seen the garments that were those gifts. Sparrow had been amazed when he and his men looked over the clothing late last night, just before it was taken to the ship. The fabrics and the small gems worked into the embroidery might well be worth more than the one hundred pounds in coin that Lord Harwood was being permitted to take out of the country. Yet Sparrow could not object, for the license to travel beyond seas had set no limit on the worth of those gifts.

"Pray remember that, sirrah. Now get you gone. My men have work to do, and you are in their way."

Sparrow heard one of the men standing behind him laugh. Furious, he started away, then turned around, remembering the boy.

The lad was just being lowered into the barge, the man on the dock handing him down to Tandy. As Sparrow watched, the boy's cap slipped. Sparrow caught a glimpse of gleaming fair hair before the cap was pushed back into place. Tandy quickly set the boy down so casks blocked Sparrow's view of him.

Sparrow took a step back toward them, but stopped when he saw the expression on Lord Harwood's face. The baron looked as if he would tolerate no more interference, and Sparrow doubted now that any attempt to intervene on the boy's behalf would be successful. The port authorities might have heeded him if it was his word against that of a servant, but he would be foolish to go up against Lord Harwood with nothing more than an unprovable argument that the boy must have been misled.

His shoulders sagging a little, Sparrow began to retrace his steps toward his inn. It would be time for dinner soon. He prayed that the innkeeper's cook, a Fleming who sang psalms as he worked, would not have indulged his Low Countries taste for carrots and put the filthy vegetable in the stew again.

Tomorrow morning he would leave Southampton. It was a cheering thought . . . as long as he did not reflect that Lisle, too, was leaving the port, free as the sea gulls whose shrill, mocking cries filled the air over the harbor.

CHAPTER 18

Racked by pain and nausea, Kat lay with her head hanging over the edge of the bed, her eyes closed so she would not see the contents of the basin Tandy was holding for her.

"Is your belly empty yet, Kat?" he asked. "You will not be sick any more?"

"Alack, I'll never be anything else," she muttered, trying not to gag again at the sour taste in her mouth.

"Nay, I warrant you'll recover, if y'are strong enough to complain." His smile faded when she raised her head to stare at him. He backed away from the bed and took the basin away to empty it.

She rolled back onto the bed. The sheets were of fine linen and scented with lavender, but the faint perfume was no match for the sour smell of her own sweat and vomit. She was still so weak she was trembling, and her head hurt worse than she would have believed possible.

The bed tilted to one side, then tipped back. Her gorge rose, but after a moment she felt in control again. Seasickness was nothing compared to what she had suffered this past hour or more, since she came to herself again. Anger surged through her, anger great enough that she would have killed Lisle, that whoreson traitor, had she been given the chance.

As for Tandy, she would have let him off with some time in prison: fifty years, mayhap, or sixty. That might make him think twice before he drugged someone's drink next time.

Tandy came back into the cabin, bringing the basin again, a cup and a flagon, and a linen towel that he carried draped over one arm. He set the basin down on the chest at the foot of the bed and poured water into it from the flagon, then dipped the towel in the water and wrung it out before placing it across her forehead. The cool dampness of the towel was more than welcome, but she was too angry to consider thanking him.

"I pray your pardon," he said quietly, "for my poor gibe a few minutes ago. 'Twas a churlish thing to say."

" 'Twas a churlish thing to do, drugging me. What was that you had me drink, when I woke last? Was that more wine?"

"You remember that? Yea, 'twas wine we gave you early this morning, when you started to awaken. But look you, we had no choice."

"You could have left me in England."

"With the sheriff? You would not have wanted that."

She looked away from him.

"Would you like a cup of water now?"

She shook her head, and he started to leave, but before he reached the door she asked abruptly, "What time is it?"

"Four o'clock."

"How long—"

"Four hours." His voice was very gentle. "We weighed anchor at noon."

He went out then, shutting the door behind him. She closed her eyes and began to cry.

She wept without restraint for only a few minutes before forcing herself to stop. Sniffling, she dried her face with the towel. 'Twas useless to cry—she was past rescue now. There was no hope that Nick could reach her, now that they had left whatever port—Southampton, belike—this ship had been waiting at, so lamentations were a waste of time, and moreover would sicken her eventually. She had to think of escape now. Yea, even in Spain there might be opportunity to escape, though her first reaction when Tandy had told her where the ship was bound had been black despair. Even in Spain, she would find some means of escaping from Lord Harwood, and returning safely home. She spoke Spanish well enough—if her tutor were to be believed—that she would not be entirely helpless. *And 'tis best,* she reasoned, attempting a smile, *that Nick will not be with me, for his poor imitation of Spanish would of certain announce us to be English . . .*

She sat up and looked around, seeing the cabin clearly for the first time since she had come to herself.

The cabin was narrow, with this end of it nearly filled by a bed that was little more than half as wide as the great bed in Justin's chamber at Harwood Hall. There were four hangings of fine leather fastened securely to the inward-leaning walls, one hanging on each side of the two portholes. Three chests had been set against the wall to Kat's left. On the chest at the foot of the bed sat not only the pewter cup and flagon that Tandy had brought, and the basin, but also a silver flagon and two matching goblets. Beyond the chest was a small table.

She got up, carefully, and walked—bent over and holding onto the bed for support, like an old woman—to the table. Flimsy as it was, it did not move when she clutched at it as the floor rolled beneath her feet; she was not surprised after that to see that the table's legs were nailed to the floor.

The silver flagon held wine. She grimaced, thinking that she would never willingly drink wine again. Instead she poured herself a cup of water and sipped it, all the while holding onto the table's edge. Through the porthole she could see glassy waves, and could not help thinking of the infinity of waves between herself and her home. She looked away from the porthole quickly, but tears had already sprung to her eyes. She dried them brusquely, set the cup down, and, after moving everything from the lid of the chest, opened it and dug through the contents.

'Twas mostly clothes—Lisle's clothes, she guessed—but near the bottom of the chest she found a sheathed dagger, a very pretty weapon indeed, with its silver hilt curiously worked and the sheath embroidered with silver thread. Perchance Lisle would not miss it for a time. She was determined to keep it, but how to conceal it? She tried placing it inside her shirt, between her breasts, realized the embroidery on the sheath would chafe her skin raw, and slid it down the back of her doublet instead. 'Twas more comfortable—until it slipped to the side, sliding under her arm so that both the hilt and the point of the dagger jabbed at her doublet from inside, and she had to unbutton her doublet to remove it. Exasperated, she set it down on the table and went about searching the other chests.

The first was filled with women's clothing: two kirtles, four petticoats, a gown and a pair of sleeves. All new, all of the finest fabrics and workmanship. Kat sat back on her heels, frowning. Since they were bound for Spain, then these must needs be meant for Lord Harwood's cousin, the woman he was rumored to be in love with. And these rich garments lent weight to that rumor, and to Sparrow's belief that Lisle's love for his cousin had led him to plot against his queen.

The next chest also held women's garments. She searched it cursorily, her frown deepening, then slammed the lid shut. He would not give such presents to another man's wife unless he truly loved her. It shamed Kat to realize that the knowledge hurt her: despite her contempt for him, it had been a small triumph for her to know that he wanted her, to hear that note of jealousy in his voice. That triumph crumbled now, as she was faced with evidence of a love that had endured, despite all obstacles, since the reign of Queen Mary.

She opened the third chest just far enough to see that it, too, contained clothing, and would have slammed it shut again, but hesitated. White velvet and small gold buttons. Could it be . . . ? She lifted the chest's lid further. Yea, it was the nightgown Justin had given her, and, beneath that, the gown he had shown her yesterday. Underneath that were a kirtle, a pair of sleeves, petticoats, a farthingale, two smocks, stockings, and, at the bottom, spools of thread, a paper of needles and pins, and a small cherrywood box bound with brass. She opened the box to discover, cushioned in a lining of velvet, a hairbrush and comb and small mirror, all backed with silver that was ornately worked with the same figures. Kat touched her snarled hair, then removed the box and the needles and thread before closing the chest.

It was but a few minutes' work to sew loops onto the lining of her doublet to hold the dagger's sheath. She slid it into place, then put on her doublet again. The garment was loose enough, she was certain, to conceal the weapon, as long as she remembered to keep her shoulders back. That done, she picked up the comb.

When her hair was finally untangled, she began to brush it, then picked up the mirror. She had to laugh at the grime on her face. They had practically daubed her with mud, taking no chances that anyone who saw her might mistake her for a fair-skinned gentlewoman.

She washed her face—there was no soap, alas—then drank what little water was left in the flagon. Her thirst slaked, she realized for the first time that she was hungry. Tandy had said nothing to her of food. Yet it was suppertime—much past suppertime for her, since she had last eaten yesterday morning. Did they not eat meals at the usual time aboard ship? Or had Tandy perhaps decided that if she were still too sick to drink water, as she had led him to believe before he left her last, she was also much too sick to eat?

She went to the door, expecting it to be locked. It was not. She peered out into another cabin, this one dominated by a table three times the size of the one in the cabin behind her, then crossed that and passed through another doorway onto a deck.

She had been able to hear sailors calling to one another, maybe a dozen men talking at once, before she emerged from the cabin. Now they all fell silent, most of them turning to look at her, though most of those looked away after a few moments. Flushing, she stood where she was for a few minutes, and gradually the talk and activity resumed. She started out onto the deck, taking careful, wide-legged steps. Lisle was nowhere in sight, but when she turned to look at the stern of the ship, she saw Tandy up on the narrow deck above the cabins, standing near the rail, talking to a lad of fourteen or fifteen.

She scrambled up a ladder to join him.

"How now, Kat?" he asked. "D'you feel better?"

"In sooth, I do."

"Seasick?" the young boy asked.

"Aye," Tandy said quickly, and a few seconds later Kat nodded in agreement. So that was to be the story given to most of the crew. As like as not, Tandy and his master wanted it believed, too, that she had been brought aboard drunken, not drugged. This was a weakness for them, Kat sensed, but how could she exploit it?

"I was seasick myself on my first voyage," the boy said, then, unaccountably, blushed.

"Peter," Tandy said, "this is my friend Kat, who also serves his lordship."

Kat raised an eyebrow at that, but Tandy's unwavering gaze warned her against making any protest. And indeed, she thought, there would be no advantage—at least not yet—in telling any of the crew that she was here against her will. Until she learned differently, she had to assume that these men all served Lord Harwood willingly and would have little sympathy for her if they knew she had been caught spying at Harwood Hall.

Peter, she soon learned, had made one previous voyage aboard the *Lady Margaret*. Kat flinched inwardly when she heard that name—she was sure Lisle had named his ship for his cousin. Yet more proof that he loved her.

The boy chattered on, telling her now about his family and their farm near Portsmouth, and it did not surprise Kat to learn that he had a sister who was about Kat's age. *By the Lord, I have found myself a younger brother,* she thought wryly, unable to suppress a smile, and she saw an answering, knowing smile on Tandy's face. Peter noticed the exchange of expressions and fell silent at once, picking up the piece of wood and the knife Kat had seen him holding when she first climbed up onto the deck. He began to carve the wood, his head lowered so she could not see his expression, but his ears, she saw, were very red.

"What's this?" she asked gently. "Is that a dolphin y'are carving?"

He nodded and handed her the carving, still not looking up. She turned the wooden sculpture over and over in her hands. 'Twas nearly finished, with most of the lines of a leaping dolphin already clearly defined. She liked it better, even in its unfinished state, than she had the gilded dolphin on the clock Christopher Danvers had given her.

"I once had—" She broke off, aware that she could not admit to owning that clock. 'Twould lead Tandy and his master to become yet more suspicious of her. "I once saw a clock adorned with the figure of a dolphin," she continued, correcting herself, and went on to tell Peter that his was better work.

By the time she had finished speaking, he was gazing at her again, his face alight with joy at her praise. "I have finished another," he said quickly. "Would you care to see it?" He took a cloth-wrapped object from the pocket of his canvas doublet. "This is for his lordship—please it you, do not let him know you have seen it first. 'Tis the *Lady Margaret*." He unfolded the cloth to reveal an exquisitely carved replica of a merchant ship, the masts smaller than toothpicks.

She held the tiny wooden ship carefully when Peter gave it to her, fearful of snapping one of those tiny masts, then handed it to Tandy. " 'Tis lovely," she told Peter, and thought she saw a fleeting expression of sympathy on Tandy's face. Did he understand, then, how difficult it was for her to admire a replica of the ship taking her to Spain? But that expression had been there only for an instant, before he gave all his attention to Peter's carving, praising it as the best work the boy had ever done. He was returning it to the youth when a movement on the deck below caught his eye.

"There's the firebox now, Peter," he said cheerfully. "The cook must be better."

"Cook was seasick, too," Peter told Kat. " 'Twill be a late supper."

"Late?" She could not keep a note of dismay from her voice as she stared down at the fire just now being prepared for cooking the evening meal.

"Are you hungry, Kat?" Tandy asked, and she again sensed sympathy in the tone of his voice.

"Here." Peter reached into his doublet and brought out a package wrapped in paper, which he gave to Kat. "I could not finish this at breakfast."

She opened up the paper—'twas a ballad sheet, she saw—to find a raisin-filled saffron cake of the type sold in taverns. Only a small piece had been broken off. "I thank you, Peter, but are you certain you—" she began, but the boy interrupted her.

"Nay, I want it not. But I pray you, let me have the ballad again, when you are finished."

She did so, after picking off the crumbs that were large enough to handle and then finally brushing the fine, sandy crumbs that were left off the paper into the ocean. She read a few lines of the ballad before handing it back to him. 'Twas mockery of the pope, and it brought back sharp memories of her first visit to the booksellers at Paul's, a scant few weeks ago—an eternity ago, in experience. "I thank you," she said again.

He looked very pleased with himself as he folded the ballad sheet and put it back in his doublet, then picked up his carving of the dolphin and set to work on it again. Kat marveled at his skill. No woodcarver she or her father had ever hired could match him for such fine work.

"By the Lord, I would fain hire you to carve a new railing for—" she began, then broke off as both Peter and Tandy stared at her in astonishment. She looked away, biting her lip. She had almost mentioned Beechwood.

"By my faith! Would you take my servants away from me?" Justin Lisle said, and she turned quickly to face him, wondering that she had not heard his approach. He was smiling, but the smile did not touch his eyes. "First tell them how you would pay them."

" 'Twas but a wish," she said hastily. "I have never seen such carvings."

"My lord," Peter said shyly, "I had much time to myself while ashore, and thought to carve a small gift for you."

Kat moved a few steps away while the boy presented Lisle with the carving of the *Lady Margaret.* Her heart was still pounding from alarm at her narrow escape. Had she said even a few words more, her captors would have learned that she was a gentlewoman, and then they—or, perhaps, their Spanish confederates—might wish to hold her for ransom. 'Twould make it even more difficult for her to slip away, and, worse, Nick might quickly accede to their demands.

She barely listened to what Lord Harwood said to Peter, but when she glanced back over her shoulder, she saw that the boy seemed even more pleased than he had been by her praise—seemed, in fact, as if he might explode with joy when the baron wrapped the tiny ship in the cloth again and placed it inside his doublet.

A moment later Justin took his leave of them. "Come with me, Kat," he said quietly as he passed her, then, when she hesitated, put his hand on her back to pull her toward the ladder.

She stiffened as she felt his hand press the dagger against her back. It seemed to her that he froze for just an instant and started to take his hand off her back, but then he was insistently drawing her with him toward the ladder. Was it possible he did not realize that she wore a weapon beneath her doublet? She stole a glance at him, but his face was expressionless, giving nothing away.

He preceded her down the ladder and led the way back to his cabin, shutting the door behind her as soon as she had entered.

"Draw," he told her.

She gazed at him blankly.

"Your dagger," he said, in the patient but condescending tone a man would use with a very young child or a simpleton. "My dagger, rather, for I warrant 'tis the one that was in my chest. Draw."

She had thought the dagger cleverly placed, but the buttoned collar of her doublet, while somewhat loose on her because the garment was too big, was still tight enough that she could scarcely squeeze her hand through. Then she found that although she could touch the hilt easily enough with the ends of her fingers, it was almost impossible for her to grasp firmly. She finally caught it between the tips of her fingers and drew it upward, then gasped as she felt the flat of the blade drag against her shirt.

"Enough! Put up!"

She dropped the dagger back into its sheath, almost trembling with relief. Of certain, the point of the dagger, pressed against her by the doublet's collar, would have cut through her shirt and into her flesh, had she drawn it completely from its sheath.

"Take off your doublet," Justin said, and she complied, handing the garment to him before he asked for it. He ripped the sheathed dagger free of the confining loops and tossed it onto the chest.

"You were ill served by whoever taught you that trick," he said scathingly. "You would have either stabbed your own back or cut your own neck before you had the dagger free to use. 'Sdeath, what were you thinking of?"

"My safety," she said in a small voice.

"Your safety? You clotpoll. Had you not bled to death from your own folly—had you by some miracle succeeded in wounding me, or Tandy, or whomever you meant to hurt—my crew would have made short work of you. Mark me, Kat. Your safety on this ship lies in my tolerance of you, and naught but that. Naught but that. Do you understand?"

"Yea, my lord," she replied sullenly.

He yanked the torn loops of thread out of the doublet's lining. "I meant this thread to be used for altering the clothes I have given you, those in the chest where you found it. See that you waste no more." Tossing the doublet back to her, he turned and strode from the cabin.

Sick again, but this time with helpless anger, she lay down on the bed. Sometime later she heard footsteps in the outer cabin, and sat up just as Tandy came into the room with a platter of chicken and biscuits and a cup of ale.

"Pray God, you are not sick again," he said, and she shook her head.

He set the food on the table, then brought in a stool from the other cabin. While she ate, he carried in a trundle bed, which he set between Lord Harwood's bed and the wall.

"Y'are to sleep here," he said, a bit uncertainly, as if expecting her to contradict him. When she said nothing, he shrugged and went out.

It was still too light when she had finished her supper for her to think of going to sleep yet, so she tried on the petticoats and kirtle, all the while standing with her back against the closed door, lest someone seek entry. All the clothes would have to be taken in an inch or two, she discovered, and she set pins where she would alter the garments. At least they were long enough: Lisle's cousin must be tall. By the time she was done, the sun was setting, and she decided to wait till the next day to begin sewing. She refolded the clothes, careful of the pins, and returned them to the chest.

She watched the sunset through the porthole, impressed by the blaze of colors on the water, though for a few minutes unshed tears blurred the display for her as she thought of her desperate situation. She forced those thoughts from her mind by thinking instead of Peter, with his open, friendly manner, and his stories about his sister. There was an ally for her against Lisle, though the boy did not know it as yet. 'Twould serve Lisle right to have his own crew turned against him.

As a velvety twilight settled over the waters, she lay down on the trundle bed, still dressed in shirt and hose. She would have felt too vulnerable sleeping in that sheer smock. She drew the covers up to her chin, turning toward the leather-covered wall, already drowsy even though she had been awake only several hours today. She was half asleep when she remembered what she had read on the ballad sheet wrapping the cake Peter had given her.

Brother Woodenshoe.

She sat up, the last vestiges of sleepiness gone. That ballad had mocked the pope; 'twould be an offense to papists. The boy could not be part of Justin's plotting against the queen, then. Likely there were other good Protestants among the crew as well, men who would be outraged if they knew that their master was conspiring with the Spanish ambassador's secretary. She might find many allies here, given enough time.

She lay down again, feeling more hopeful than she had at any time since first coming to herself that afternoon. Her heart raced as she planned ways to broach the subject of Justin's treason to Peter, after first winning his friendship and trust. She was still wide awake when Lisle returned to the cabin, but she feigned sleep to avoid talking to him, and it was long after he seemed to have fallen asleep, lying perfectly quietly a few feet away from her, that she at last drifted off to sleep, her mind filled with dreams of escape.

CHAPTER 19

Four days.

Kat and Nick Langdon had told her to wait four days before writing to Francis Walsingham, and now, as the fourth full day since their visit to Stamworth came to an end, Jane sat at the writing table in Kat's bedchamber at Beechwood, writing gear all about her but the paper before her as yet unmarked, and prayed that the horses whose hoofbeats she had just heard in the courtyard belonged to her friends. She did not get up to check for herself, having been disappointed too often already. The steward could deal with any visitors himself. She had told him an hour ago that she did not wish to be disturbed.

She toyed with the quill, considered sharpening it yet again, then shook her head. 'Twas her wits that needed sharpening instead. She could think of no way to begin the letter to Walsingham.

She turned around as she heard someone approaching the door. A man's footsteps. 'Twould not be Kat. Her heart leapt at the thought that Nick might open the door, smiling and thanking her for her care for their household while they had been gone. But it was merely the steward, the look of disappointment on his face telling her that his master and mistress had not returned.

"Madam, I pray your pardon for disturbing you, but there is a man here asking to see Master Langdon. He has ridden post from London and is waiting, most impatiently, in the hall."

He has ridden post from London . . . Jane set the quill down slowly. She had been unaware that she was holding her breath; now she released it in a long sigh, and, for the first time in days, smiled in anticipation. "I will speak with him," she said, and rose, turning her back on the writing gear that she hoped she would not need to use now.

He is a man of middle age, Kat had said, describing Sparrow, *spare of build, his hair brown flecked with gray. He has a narrow face and a long, sharp nose. He is of small stature, as drab as his namesake and just as noisy. But you may trust him to fly straight to his master with any message you give him.*

This was the very Sparrow, of a truth, but Jane was determined that he would not fly away at once with the message.

"Good day, Master Sparrow."

Her use of his nickname startled him. "You know who I am, madam?"

"I know who I think you are, but would have you confirm it. Pray tell me who your master is."

He glanced at the steward. She gestured for the man to leave them and, after a less than trusting look at Sparrow, the servant obeyed. Sparrow waited until the steward had quit the hall; then, his voice lowered so it could not be heard more than a few feet away, he answered, "Walsingham."

A sigh of relief escaped her. "I was told to expect you. Master Langdon is not here, nor is his sister. They bade me send a message to Master Walsingham. I have not sent it yet."

"I'll to London with it, by post, as soon as you tell me what it is, madam."

"Then I'll tell you, sir . . . as soon as you tell me what your business with Nick Langdon is."

"He did not tell you? Then why think you that I will?"

"If you do not, I'll send the message in a letter to Walsingham, by one of my servants. Perhaps in a few days I could spare one of the younger boys from his chores."

"You would not entrust matters of state to a child."

"There is nothing in the message I was given to make me believe it concerns the Crown."

"If it concerns Master Walsingham—"

"Like enough," she interrupted, shrugging, "it is a personal matter between them."

"Then why were you told to expect me?"

" 'Tis a mystery, sir, that only you can explain. And I must have that explanation before I give you the message intended for Francis Walsingham."

He glared at her, then turned on his heel and stomped angrily away. She was outwardly calm as she watched him, though inside she was racked by fear that he really meant to leave without telling her about his dealings with Nick. She would give him the message anyway, but it would be humiliating to have to run after him and tell him she had changed her mind. She prayed he would stop—

—and he did, halfway across the great hall from her. For some moments he stood there unmoving, his back to her, then he slowly turned around. He looked more furious than ever, and she was reminded of a caged wild ferret she had once tried to pet when she was a child: the animal had bitten her.

"You must swear," he said, "to repeat none of what I tell you . . ."

Despite her oath, he told her very little. There was a suspected traitor, but he would not name the man. Nick had been sent to spy on him some weeks before. "The first week of May?" she asked, and he nodded curtly. "He was wounded then," she said softly.

"Aye, by a common player he had no business fighting," Sparrow replied: no sympathy there.

"And you are here now to find out what else he might have learned about this traitor?"

Sparrow shook his head. "I spoke too harshly, to him and his sister, when last I was here. I have come to apologize."

Yea, but only at your master's bidding, Jane thought: she could not imagine Sparrow coming to such a decision on his own. Aloud she said, "This traitor. Lives he in Hampshire?"

Sparrow nodded.

"Sweet Jesu. They bade me tell Walsingham that they had gone to visit a friend in Hampshire."

"God's blood! Why?"

She shrugged helplessly.

" 'Twas a fool's errand—and why not, when all else they—" He broke off as he saw the expression on Jane's face. "He's left for Spain. He set sail the day before yesterday."

"They left two days before that," Jane said softly. "Pray God, he was already aboard ship, awaiting favorable winds."

Sparrow was silent for a few moments, appearing to study his dust-coated boots. "Nay," he said finally, his voice muffled. "He rode to Southampton but that morning."

"Then they could not have missed him . . . Will you to Hampshire now?"

"Not alone," he said, and she felt chilled. "I'll to my master, for I will need others to help me. And I must needs know what clothing your friends wore the day they left, and what horses they rode, so we can discover more easily who saw them in Hampshire."

"Nick wore a suit of black silk. Kat wore an old doublet and hose that had belonged to Nick. 'Tis an odd practice of hers to dress thus—"

"Yea, I have seen her in that suit, when I was here the second time." Suddenly he looked surprised, as at some thought that had just occurred to him. Then that expression gave way to one mixing regret and anger. "Wore she as well an ancient cap, so large that it would cover her hair completely?"

"Aye, she had such a cap with her. A most ugly cap," she added, with an anxious laugh. "So you have seen that, too?"

He scarcely seemed to hear her. He was gazing at a spot a few feet to her left, a distracted expression on his face now. "What?" he said after a few moments, then: "Oh. Yea, I have seen the cap. She was wearing it when I met her . . . What about their horses?"

She described them, but there was nothing else she could tell him, so he bade her farewell, idly promising to let her know as soon as he had some news of Nick and Kat. His thoughts seemed far away already, and though she would fain have learned more from him of this traitor in Hampshire, she did not seek to delay him with questions about the man her friends had set off to visit. She was sure he would not answer, for he would suspect that she might travel to Hampshire herself, or send servants—and he was correct: she would. So she merely walked with him to the courtyard and watched as he rode away, the postboy on his horse hard put to keep up. That was certainly not a journey's pace Sparrow was setting back to London, and she was glad of it.

Then, but a quarter of an hour later, she found herself wishing that the spy had set a more moderate pace for London, so there would be some hope of catching him and demanding just when and *where*, in sooth, he had seen Kat's cap. For she had just remembered—fifteen minutes too late, to her great dismay—that Kat had left her cap at Stamworth on the way back from the Jerusalem Tree in early May, and had not picked it up again until she and Nick were on their way to Hampshire. Perchance Kat might have mentioned the cap to Sparrow, that time they met, but the little man could not have seen it, and Jane would gladly have set out after Sparrow herself, poor rider though she was, had there been any chance of reaching him and learning why he had lied to her.

CHAPTER 20

There. The kirtle was finished, the alterations complete at last.

Kat set the needles and thread aside, relieved to be done with them. The last thing that she had expected to find herself doing, after setting out for Harwood Hall, was more needlework, but at least the work had kept her from doing too much worrying, these past several days, during the hours that she was alone in the cabin.

Now, though, with a few hours yet till nightfall, there was work of another sort to do. The time was ripe, she felt, to learn if Peter would help her. She had almost confided in him yesternight, for the boy had seemed so fond of her that she had ventured to tell him that she considered him a true friend, and he had sworn by God that he was her friend and always would be. But there had been too little time left then, with the sun already setting, for her to tell him all. This evening she would have ample time. And now, too, she had clothes to wear that would array her like the gentlewoman she was.

She took off her shirt and hose and washed herself, using a cake of scented soap Tandy had found for her. Then she donned smock and stockings and petticoats and farthingale, and finally the kirtle, to which perforce she first attached the sleeves. 'Twas a perfect fit now, so snug that she had difficulty fastening the hooks along the side of the bodice. For an instant she wished Louise were with her. The thought brought a lump to her throat now, but unlike at other times during the first days of the voyage, she no longer cried.

She fastened a small, neat ruff around her neck, then looked at the gown. 'Twould be magnificent with the kirtle, but she decided against it: 'twas hot out on deck.

As she ventured from the cabin, she felt that she looked very much the gentlewoman, save for her worn leather slippers. Alack, there was no remedy for that: the wardrobe had, oddly, contained no shoes.

She paused shyly for a few moments in the doorway of the outer cabin, then stepped out into the westering sunlight.

The crew had become used to her presence on deck over the last several days, but now the first sailor to glance her way gaped at the sight of her dressed so finely. He said something to a man standing near him, and that man called to another, and within a minute half the sailors were staring at her. With so many eyes on her, she stopped again, only a few steps from the cabin door. She had hoped her new garb would impress Peter, but now she was dismayed to think she might have the crew watching her all the while she tried to talk privily with the boy.

"Marry, you rogues," Justin called from above her, "have you never seen a woman before?"

The taunt was good-natured, but had its effect anyway: the sailors went back to their work. Kat turned around and looked up at Justin, who was standing on the poop deck above the hindcastle, smiling down at her. She felt her heart begin to beat faster. Though she had often seen him smiling or laughing on this voyage, 'twas always with Tandy or the captain or one of the sailors. Whenever he had looked upon her, 'twas with a puzzled expression, or a frown—until now.

"How now, my lord," she said recklessly. "You still stare. Have you never seen a woman before?"

"Not in those garments," he said bluntly, and she blushed.

Laughing, he came swiftly down the ladder to stand before her.

"Turn around," he said, and she did, taking a childlike delight in showing off the kirtle.

"I must compliment your sempster," he said then, "but not, alas, your shoemaker."

"By my faith," she said with mock sadness, gazing down at the battered slippers, "he must have confused my order with another's."

"A plague on such knaves!"

She chuckled, then looked away quickly. 'Twas too easy to forget that Lord Harwood was her enemy, and England's, when he acted like this.

"Kat? Would you walk around the deck with me, that all my sailors may more easily see you? I fear me that some of them may break their necks from craning them about to look at you here."

He was offering her his arm. She hesitated to take it, and after a moment he took her hand and set it on his arm, and they began to stroll across the deck. She lowered her gaze, praying that if her face looked as fiery as it felt, he would not notice. The touch of his hand on hers, and the warmth of his arm beneath the thin stuff of his shirt, called up memories—aye, and memories of dreams, too—that shamed her.

She had lain alone on the narrow trundle each night of the voyage. Justin had not touched her. He would return to the cabin late, after she was likely to be asleep—as she always pretended to be—and go quietly to bed without saying a word to her. 'Twas true that she felt relieved to be left alone, but it was also true—mischievously, shamefully true—that she had spent long hours awake each night, recalling his kisses and caresses. When the sea was quiet, she would listen to the sound of his breathing and wonder if perchance he lay wakeful, too, thinking of her . . .

Now she glanced sideways at him, shyly, from beneath her lashes. He wore a white cambric shirt and black silk hose. His skin, sunburned to bronze, looked dark against the open neck of his shirt, and his hair was streaked with gold. He looked more a privateer, she thought, than a peer of the realm, but she could easily imagine him at court. He would catch the eye of every woman there, including the queen, for he was as handsome as Leicester.

"Nay, more handsome than Leicester," she said, and did not realize she had spoken aloud until Justin stopped and she found herself, with her next step, swinging halfway around to face him.

"What did you say?" he asked in an undertone. "You spoke of the Earl of Leicester. What have you to do with Dudley?"

"I have naught to do with the earl, my lord," she said quickly. "Yet I have seen him riding through London, and thought him a handsome man, though not so handsome as you."

He raised an eyebrow. "Flattery? From you?"

"Nay, my lord, for I had not meant to speak aloud," she said, and felt her cheeks grow warmer still.

"Even more flattering, then," he said, but he did not seem pleased. "And when, pray tell, were you in London?"

She looked down, unsure what to say. Whatever answer she gave must be plausible, must sort with the life he thought she had led. But what, in truth, was *that*?

Then the captain came up and asked to confer with Justin, sparing her the necessity of answering at once. She hurried away, looking for Peter.

She found him at work mending a sail. He seemed abashed to see her in her finery and scrambled to prepare a place for her to sit, bringing a cask over and brushing dust off its top with his doublet sleeve.

She asked him about sail-mending; then, as he became more at ease, she brought the talk around to the subject of his family. A few days ago Peter had told her that she reminded him of his older sister, Mary, but had seemed rather shy after the confession. Now he again mentioned that the way Kat laughed reminded him of his sister, as did the way she treated him seriously even though he was younger than she. The latter was said wistfully, making Kat suspect that few aboard the ship gave the boy the respect he craved. As he spoke of his sister with affection and longing, Kat felt touched, and confident as well. Peter would help her to escape. He need only learn that she was here against her will, and then he would help her. She was sure of it. But 'twould be best if she could also convince him that he must escape with her, that his own safety depended on it.

"Peter, are you not afraid to go to Spain?"

He looked up from his work, an expression of genuine surprise on his face. "Nay. Why should I fear? Lord Harwood has promised our safety, and his cousin and her husband have guaranteed it."

"Spanish promises," Kat said in a slighting tone.

The boy shrugged, forcing needle through canvas again. "They are his lordship's friends, and will let no harm come to him."

"Yea, but will they protect his servants alike?" Peter looked confused now. "Perchance they would fain protect his ship and his crew, but their power is not so great—"

"Don Antonio is a grandee, a close friend of the Spanish king."

"Much less he would care then for the lives of English mariners and common servants. What are we to such as him?"

Peter sighed and put one hand on her arm. "By the Lord, Kat, you must put these fears from your mind. There is naught to fear for us in Spain."

"How so? D'you believe that England has naught to fear from Spain? Would the Spanish king not act to please the Bishop of Rome?" She slid down from the cask to kneel beside Peter, heedless of the damage she was doing to her fine clothes. "Peter, I saw that ballad you had with you, our first day out from Southampton. 'Twas about Brother Woodenshoe." She took a deep breath before asking the question that mattered so much to her. "Y'are no papist, are you?"

Peter shook his head.

"No Protestant is safe in Spain. You risk your life going there."

"But Lord Harwood—"

"Lord Harwood has his cousin to protect him," she said harshly, and Peter shrank back from her a little. She could not blame him: she had been surprised herself by the venom in her tone. "Mark me, Peter," she said, softly now, "you will find no safe harbor in Spain. 'Twould be folly for you to let anyone there see that ballad mocking Brother Woodenshoe."

"But Lord Harwood—"

"Agrees," the baron said pleasantly, and both Kat and Peter jumped. Neither had been aware of his approach.

Kat rose, her face flaming. There was an odd, crooked smile on Justin's face. He had stopped a few feet away from them, his hands on his hips, and despite his smile, she could tell he was angry—as well he might be, if he had heard much of what she said to Peter. Too late, she wished she had returned to the cabin at once.

"I must perforce thank you," he said to her, still speaking in that agreeable voice, "for reminding me of something I should have done days ago."

"Throw me overboard?" she asked with a ragged laugh.

He stared at her, as though stunned by her answer, then, to her surprise, chuckled and said, "Nay, for you remind me of that nearly every time I see you." As his gaze continued to hold hers, his expression become serious again, and abruptly he turned on his heel and strode away.

Peter gave her a fleeting, wary smile, but said nothing. *How now, boy,* she thought, *are you so easily reminded that we have not been friends for long?* But it did indeed seem that Justin had succeeded in driving a wedge between her and this youth whose help she needed.

She gazed down at him thoughtfully, biting the inside of her cheek. What should she say now to bring them once more to a point where she would dare mention escape? She was still casting about for the best ruse, all the while staring at the top of Peter's head while he worked, when the shrilling of the boatswain's whistle cut through all the other sounds of the ship and the sea.

Lord Harwood was again on the poop deck, the boatswain and Tandy and the captain beside him. Peter scrambled to his feet and ran to where the other sailors were gathering on the deck below them. In a few minutes all the ship's crew had assembled. All but one, Kat realized as she tilted her head back to see, high on the mast above her, a ship's boy some five years younger than Peter who had not climbed down from his station but who had stopped watching the horizons to give all his attention to the men on the poop deck.

Reluctant to move closer, yet too curious to stay away, she finally left her perch on the cask to sit on a crate some dozen feet outside the edge of the crowd. She was very conscious of Justin's gaze on her.

"We reach the Spanish coast tomorrow," Justin said, a few moments after she had seated herself, and she swayed a little, stunned to learn they were so near their destination. His gaze had not wavered, and she felt as though he were talking to her alone. Of certain his announcement was no surprise to anyone here but her. Since no one had spoken of their arrival—and since she had been too intent on winning Peter's friendship to mention Spain to him until today—she had assumed that she had a few days left, at least, to make her plans. "By tomorrow evening," Justin continued, "we will be at the port of Bilbao."

He looked away from Kat then, scanning the sailors gathered below him.

"Some of you have sailed with me to Spain before, and know of the dangers. Others have not, but they have been warned. I will warn you once again, for lives and property hang on this.

"Mark me well. There is a saying in Spain: *Con el Rey y con la Inquisicion, chitón! With King and Inquisition, silence!* Remember that. You will not speak to any Spaniard of King Philip, or the Inquisition, or the Catholic faith, or your own Protestant faith."

His last words startled Kat: were *all* his crewmen Protestants, then?

"You will not speak of these matters even among yourselves when you might be overheard by any Spaniard. You will not speak of them even if you are questioned by someone who professes to admire our country and faith. There are agents of the king and the Inquisition everywhere, and you must assume that anyone you meet could be such an agent.

"You will purchase no books in Spain, for the books may be judged heretical, no matter how innocent they may seem to you. You will accept no books or pamphlets as gifts. And if any of you were so addle-pated as to bring a Protestant Bible or other religious book from England . . . or any pamphlet or ballad"—he glanced down toward where Peter had stood when Kat last saw him; she could imagine the boy blushing furiously—"you must needs dispose of them now. Tandy and Captain Sinclair will search the ship this afternoon. Think not that you can conceal books or pamphlets, for both men know the ship and all the hiding places on it better than any of you possibly could, and any man attempting to conceal such materials will be punished."

He paused, his face grim as he looked out across his audience.

"I will not speak to you of the dungeons of the Inquisition, or of the *autos-da-fé*, for of those you have already heard much. But I will remind you that more than zealotry inspires those who would fain accuse us of offenses in Spain, and our accusers' rewards will be more than spiritual. They will receive one quarter of the property of the condemned. One quarter of the value of this ship and its cargo, should they succeed in condemning me, and there are some who would not hesitate to use you to attack me. I would not have any of you be so foolish as to give the Inquisition an excuse for imprisoning and torturing you until you have implicated me in your confessions.

"Anyone you meet in Spain may be your enemy. Remember that, and we may all leave Spain safely."

He turned his back on them then, an action of dismissal, but the crowd was slow to break up as sailors exchanged stories of the Inquisition. Kat remained where she was, chilled now despite the warmth of the air. At last she could see Peter. He looked stunned as he made his way toward her. When he was but a few feet away, he took the ballad sheet from his doublet and tore it into shreds before tossing it over the rail. His face was terribly pale as he turned back toward her.

"Peter—"

"Pray God, his lordship can protect us," the boy whispered. "We have no other hope."

Kat, who had had no other hope than the boy, watched despairingly as he returned to working on the sail. She had wanted to frighten Peter, but only a little, only enough to encourage him to help her escape. But Justin had succeeded in frightening the boy only too well. There was no chance now that Peter would risk leaving the ship in Bilbao. He would see inquisitors and their agents lurking in every shadow . . . as would she.

"Three years in that prison," a man walking past her said, and his companion moaned in sympathy. "He came home lacking all his toes and half his fingers, and lived but a month, and never a night of that month but he woke screaming, great shrieks that would wake all his neighbors."

The boy looked up only for an instant, his face ashen, before resuming his work. Despairing, Kat started back to the hindcastle, wishing she could shut out the frightening snatches of conversation she heard around her, the foreign names of tortures—the *strappado* or *garrucha*, the *tratta di corda*, the *escalera*—which were repeated over and over, as if naming them and the Englishmen who had suffered them was a kind of incantation to keep such dangers away from these sailors, this ship. She was trembling as she stumbled through the outer cabin and into the cabin she shared with Justin, slamming both doors behind her.

She stripped to her smock and lay down on the bed. Crying, she drew her legs up and lay huddled against the pillows, her tear-streaked face pressed against the silk coverlet.

When she opened her eyes next, whimpering a little from a quickly fading dream, it was night, and dark in the cabin except for the light admitted by the portholes. She began to turn over, stretching cramped limbs, then froze as she realized Justin lay beside her.

She could see well enough now to make out the white of his linen shirt and the gleam of light on his leather slippers. He was fully clothed, but his breathing was quiet and even. Asleep, then. But how had he managed to lie down without waking her? And how, in God's name, had she managed to sleep at all, with so many fears assailing her?

Certainly she had not escaped them in her sleep. She could recall little of her dream, other than that there had been an inquisitor in it. And now, fully awake, she could not keep from thinking of the Inquisition again.

The Inquisition was no respecter of women; she had learned that much from Blanche, who had heard the stories from her Flemish friends. Most of the accounts she had read of imprisonment by the Inquisition had been written by men, about men; but women, too, were likely to be arrested, and often only because they had attracted the attention of an inquisitor or his servants. The slightest excuse for arrest would do, and a servant or mechanical could always be found to testify that the woman had not shown proper respect for the Catholic faith. Blanche had been told of women who had spent years in the prisons of the Inquisition, who went to the torture chambers or the *autos-da-fé* heavy with child. That was a threat that none of the sailors, with their talk of the *strappado* and the *escalera*, could ever understand.

She began to cry again then, silently at first, then sobbing, both hands pressed to her face.

"Kat . . ."

She had not been aware of his waking and moving toward her, but suddenly Justin was lying beside her, his arms encircling her and drawing her against him. She pressed her face against his shirt while he stroked her back gently. The welcome warmth of his body was gradually driving away the chill she had felt since hearing his warning to the crew.

His hands stopped caressing her back, and he would have moved away, but she clung to him, lifting one arm to encircle his neck. She raised her head to look at him.

"Sweeting," he murmured, and kissed her.

She slid her fingers through his hair, then down his back as he moved over her. He caressed her breasts, his touch feather-light as he stroked her nipples. She gasped in surprise at the pleasure, and for an instant he paused to look down at her wonderingly, a smile on his lips. He kissed her neck, then her breasts, and she could feel the heat of his mouth through the thin cloth of her smock. His hand slid over her hip, caressing her, pulling her closer. She was trembling with need, but still she flinched and caught her breath when he began to pull the hem of her smock upward.

Had he turned demanding then, she might have refused him, but instead he gazed down at her questioningly, a tender look on his face, and she drew him down against her, and kissed him, and gave up fighting her own desires.

The morning found Kat standing alone at the larboard rail, watching the coast of Spain glide past as they neared the mouth of the River

Nervion, up which they would sail several miles to reach the port of Bilbao. Tandy had told her that much.

Tandy had been the only person she had spoken to all morning. When she awoke, at dawn, hearing Tandy enter the cabin, Justin had already left. She had felt dazed for some time, sitting up in bed, clutching the coverlet against her while Tandy picked up and folded the smock and nightgown lying discarded on the floor. She was not to wear women's garb today, he had explained: 'twould be safer for her in Spain if she went garbed as a boy. He had spoken then about the Nervion and Bilbao, and she realized he was uneasy himself at finding her in Justin's bed. For an instant then she had considered another appeal for sympathy, as she had made to him her first morning at Harwood Hall, but she could not bring herself to do so. Yesternight Justin had taken her virginity, but she had offered it to him, an act that shamed her in the cold dawn light.

She had not sought out Peter's company this morning, and though she had seen him from time to time, he had always been busy about some task or another. She stood alone by the rail. Her face and hands were begrimed. Tandy had saved the twist of dark powder she had been carrying in her purse when she and Nick rode to Harwood Hall. The sailors now called her "lad" or "Ned" when they greeted her or asked her to move aside because she was in their way. It had startled her at first. Justin, she suspected, must have been awake long before she was, to have issued these orders and had them carried out.

She would have given much to have seen his face early this morning, to have some clue as to how he felt about what had happened last night. But she had not seen him yet today.

It seemed dreamlike to her now. She could scarce believe what she had done. For the first time since leaving England, she was glad she was far from her family and friends—Nick especially. I'faith, he would be ashamed of her, as she was ashamed of herself. But he would try to hide his shame, and that would be even worse.

Her face burned again at the thought, and she was glad for the covering of grime that hid her blushing. She blinked rapidly to clear away tears before they could gather and roll down her cheeks. 'Twould not do to let the sailors see her crying, for one might mention it to Justin, and she would not have him know.

She folded her arms across her chest and lowered her head to stare blindly at the waves. She felt hot and cold alternately, and she trembled from time to time, recalling how tenderly he had touched her, lulling her fears until she surrendered easily. The worst of it was that she could not help remembering how much pleasure he had given her.

A plague on her weakness! She clutched the rail suddenly, raising her head to stare fixedly at the coast as she sought to obliterate all thoughts of the ship behind her, the men on it, and Justin Lisle in particular. What a fool she was, to feel this way about him. 'Twas bad enough that she had fallen in love with a traitor, but it was folly beyond measure when that traitor was in love with another woman, and was sailing to meet her on the ship he had named for her . . .

Perhaps half an hour after the *Lady Margaret* had begun her passage up the River Nervion, Kat heard someone approach her. She did not turn. Belike it was Justin Lisle, and she was not sure she could face him again.

"What think you of Spain?" Tandy asked, and she felt her shoulders sag a little as she relaxed.

" 'Tis lovely," she said, glancing over her shoulder at him to make certain Lord Harwood was not there, too. "Yet it disappoints me."

"How so?"

She told him, then, what she had heard of Spain, of the sere plains and jagged mountains that had been described to her and to Nick by the tutor who had taught her Spanish, a middle-aged man who had traveled thoughout Castile in his youth. She did not mention the tutor—she dared not—but even merely repeating what he had told her brought a painful lump to her throat: like everything else about her life until ten days ago, he seemed impossibly distant now. She was stammering as she finished, and averted her face from Tandy's too-curious gaze.

There was too long a silence then, before Tandy spoke, and she feared more questions, but wrongly.

"Yea, Castile is harsh," he said simply, "if you ride far into it. But Lady Margaret's home lies less than a day's journey within its borders. We'll ride tomorrow and the morning of the next day through the Basque provinces."

"So we are not truly in Spain yet?" she asked, and Tandy must have heard the note of hopefulness in her voice, for he looked regretful as he shook his head.

"These are provinces of Spain, Kat, and the Council of Castile and the Inquisition hold sway here as much as in Castile. Think not that you may disregard Justin's warnings."

"I have brought no literature with me that the Inquisition would find heretical."

"Yea, I know that," he responded, and the calmness of his answer triggered the anger she had kept pent up all morning.

" 'Sdeath! You would, of a truth," she said sharply, turning her back on him. For some moments she thought he would not leave her, and she feared that, since her anger was already draining away—'twas not Tandy, after all, who infuriated her—and yet she was unwilling to apologize. Then, to her relief, she heard him walk away.

They cast anchor at Bilbao late in the afternoon. Three other ships the size of the *Lady Margaret* were anchored at the port, and Kat stared at them warily. Would they turn their guns on the English ship?

Kat knew that officials in Bilbao had been advised in advance of the *Lady Margaret*'s arrival by Don Antonio Téllez de Osuna, Margaret's husband. Tandy had told her, too, that Justin would be given a safe-conduct here, signed by the king. But John Hawkins had believed himself safe, too, at San Juan de Ulloa, and he had lost more than a hundred men because he had trusted Spanish promises . . .

A barge was approaching the ship. She leaned over the rail, peering at the men it carried; then, seeing clerical garb, she recoiled, colliding with someone she had been unaware was behind her. Strong hands settled on her arms, steadying her.

Alarmed, she craned her neck to look up at Justin. For the moment she forgot her anger at him: he was merely an English citizen, like herself, and so threatened.

"Is that . . . ?" She waved toward the barge.

He nodded. "Yea, it is likely an inquisitor."

"But Don Antonio—"

"He has no power over the Inquisition. But fear not. There is nothing here to betray us, unless it be our own words. Say nothing within their hearing, and keep out of their way."

Then he was gone, stopping to speak to some of the sailors who appeared as frightened as herself.

As the barge reached the ship, Kat checked her cap to make sure that no strands of hair had escaped, then made her way to a place within sight and hearing of those awaiting the Spaniards. Mayhap she would have been safer completely out of sight, but she had to see and hear what was happening.

The first man to board was a well-dressed *hidalgo* some ten years older than Justin. Justin greeted him, cheerily enough, in Spanish, calling him Don Ferdinand, and accepted from him a document that Kat assumed was the safe-conduct. Don Ferdinand assured the baron that horses had been hired for the journey to Burgos. By then the other passengers of the barge had climbed aboard the *Lady Margaret*, and the don turned toward them—somewhat reluctantly, it seemed to Kat—and introduced them.

There were two friars: the tall man whom Kat had first spotted in the barge, and another cleric so short he seemed a dwarf. Both were dressed in the white hoods and dark robes of the Dominican order. Fray

Tomás, the tall one, was the inquisitor; the dwarfish one, Fray Juan, was his vicar. With them were five rough-looking men, and Kat knew even before hearing the introductions that these were *alguazils*, familiars of the Inquisition. They would guard the inquisitor, and spy for him, and serve him, too, in the prisons of the Inquisition. Blanche had told Kat that these *alguazils*, many of them low-born ruffians who gained status and some immunity from the Inquisition by serving it, were almost as much to be feared as the inquisitors. Seeing them, Kat could well believe it. She began to back away.

"Hold, Kat," Tandy said softly. "You must not seem frightened of them, lest you draw their eyes to yourself."

She stopped.

"See the fellow there to the left of Fray Tomás? The one with the hooked nose?"

Kat nodded.

"He's Basque, by the look of him. They are not like the English, these Basques. They do not look as if people of every nation could be counted among their parents."

Another time she might have been interested in Tandy's attempt to divert her, but now she could think only that representatives of the Inquisition stood less than twenty paces from her.

"D'you know mumchance-at-cards?" Tandy asked.

"What?"

"Primero, then?"

"A game of cards?" she asked in disbelief. "Now?"

"What better way to pass the time?" he asked, taking a deck from his doublet pocket.

Sitting on crates, using a barrel as a table, they played for nearly two hours, while the inquisitor and his servants searched the ship, always in the company of Lord Harwood and the captain. The inquisitor had argued against this—Kat had no trouble understanding his Spanish when he raised his voice—and had also argued that the *alguazils* should be allowed to search individually, but Justin had been adamant. He would accompany them, he said, so they would be sure to find every possible hiding place, every niche where heretical materials might be concealed. He was as determined as they were that such materials not be smuggled into Spain. At last the inquisitor agreed, though Kat was certain that the friar knew as well as she that Justin wished to be with them to make sure that the *alguazils* did not plant any heretical books on his ship for others to discover later.

They began their search below decks, finishing with the cabins in the hindcastle. Justin had managed an appearance of civility at the beginning of the search, but that had given way to a look of irritation by the time they reappeared on deck after going through the crew's quarters. When they at last emerged from the cabins, he looked ready to strangle someone, though his comments to the inquisitor were as polite as ever as he escorted the Spaniards back to the rail overlooking their barge and bade them farewell.

Kat waited until the last of the Spaniards had vanished from sight, then laid her cards down and all but ran to the cabin, Tandy close behind her.

The chests of clothing, so neatly packed by Tandy, had been over-turned, the clothes tossed carelessly across the floor and bed and table. She cried out in dismay at the sight.

"There's nothing amiss here that cannot be set aright in short time," Tandy said, setting his hand on her shoulder for a moment.

" 'Twas needless. Those ruffians—"

"—must needs have vented their spleen somehow, when their search turned up nothing to use against us. Better on these garments than on the crew. Or do you care so much for the Lady Margaret's wardrobe?"

"No. Do you not?"

"Nay," he said, with a rueful smile. "Now if all these were *yours* . . ."

"If his lordship heard you speak thus—"

"He would call me a great calf, and bid me set to work, lest the lady find her wardrobe wrinkled."

"Like her face?" Kat asked, unable to restrain her curiosity.

Tandy had been smoothing and folding a pair of sleeves. Now he paused, glancing at her before saying, "Margaret has changed very little since leaving England." A few moments later, as if aware how much pain his answer had given Kat, to her shame, he added, "But how much she owes to paints and dyes, only she and her maids and the Lord know."

She looked down, her face burning, and busied herself with helping Tandy put the clothes away.

They were soon done, as Tandy had said. As they left the cabin, Kat opened her purse and took out the two half-groats that Tandy had won from her at cards, but he would not accept them.

"By the Lord, girl, anyone playing cards with you would think you more cony than cony-catcher. Not once did you try to cheat."

The odd compliment first startled, then amused her. "In sooth, I wish sometimes that I knew how. Many's the time I have lost more than a groat."

He gave her an odd look, and seemed as if he would say something, but before he could, Justin called to them. He wished to speak to Tandy, alone. Kat he sent back to the cabin.

Peter brought her supper an hour later, and though she would have liked him to stay and talk for a while, he would not linger in his master's cabin. He did tell her that Justin and Tandy had left the ship, and were somewhere in Bilbao checking on the condition of the horses Don Ferdinand had hired for them, making certain they were good enough for the trip. The group that was riding to Burgos would set out early tomorrow morning, and Justin had not wanted to risk being unpleasantly surprised then.

Peter would not be going along. He seemed anxious, and Kat could not blame him, but before she could think of anything to say to him, anything that would reassure him, he bade her good night and left.

She remained sitting at the table while the light waned and darkness claimed the cabin. Finally she went to the porthole and gazed out at Bilbao. She could see very few lighted windows. The streets would be very dark, and who knew what possible dangers they held for two Englishmen—even one with a safe-conduct from the king? Rogues of the kind that haunted every port would not wait to see such documents. What would she and the others on the ship do if Justin failed to return?

We have no other hope, Peter had said.

She prayed that he had been wrong.

But Justin did return, some time after she had lain down to sleep, fully dressed, on the trundle bed. She had lit one candle and left it burning, so when she woke and rolled over to look toward the door, she could see that he was weary, lines she had rarely noticed before framing his mouth.

His eyes met hers, and she lay very still, wondering how he would accept the rejection of him that was evident in the bed she had chosen and the clothing she still wore. Then, after a moment, his gaze slid away and he moved out of her sight, to the other side of his bed. He blew out the candle and sat down on the bed.

Her heart thudding, her eyes wide open on darkness, she waited.

"Sleep well, Kat," he said at last. "The ride to Burgos is a long one."

She heard neither pain nor anger in his voice: he spoke as though they had never been lovers. She closed her eyes then, aware that she was close to tears. 'Twas from relief, she hoped, but she fought the tears anyway. She could not have borne the shame of repeating last night's mistake, but she would be more ashamed—much, much more—if she cried now because Justin, too, thought last night had been a mistake.

An hour after sunrise, Kat, Justin, Tandy, and the four men Justin had chosen to accompany them were rowed from the *Lady Margaret* to the dock. Don Ferdinand was there with several servants who were holding the horses. The English party's spare clothes, and Lady Margaret's wardrobe, had been transferred to leather portmanteaus that were strapped carefully to the backs of the packhorses, save for one horse that was outfitted with panniers. Kat looked at the empty baskets curiously, then turned her attention to her own horse, a placid bay gelding. Except for Justin's mount, a fine Spanish jennet that would have brought a high price in London, the horses were little better than carrier's beasts, fit for an unavoidable journey but nothing else.

The boat from the *Lady Margaret* waited until they were ready to set off before returning to the ship. Kat gazed after it wistfully. She would not feel at all safe again, she thought, until they were back aboard the *Lady Margaret*. Yet she would not willingly return to the ship now and stay there while Justin rode to Burgos. Like Peter, she now believed that her greatest safety was with Lord Harwood.

She turned away from the water in time to see Tandy ride off, leading the pannier-laden horse. Justin seemed in no hurry to follow, but stood talking to Don Ferdinand for several minutes before bidding him farewell and mounting the jennet. Kat and the sailors followed suit, and they rode out of Bilbao. Tandy was waiting for them at the gate of the city, his packhorse's panniers obviously weighed down. "I was cheated," he told Justin cheerfully. "Charged twice what the food was worth. They knew I was from the English ship."

"Truth to tell, you do not look like a Basque," Kat said with a laugh. She had seen many of the long-headed, dark-haired people, like the *alguazil* aboard the *Lady Margaret* last night, while they rode through the streets.

"Y'are right. 'Twas my English face that cost us so much," Tandy agreed.

Justin jerked his head toward a surly-looking guard at the gate. "Pray God," he said curtly, "that your unbridled English tongue does not cost us more dearly."

Tandy fell silent. Kat, too, sobered abruptly. Such levity was unwise with strangers within earshot. Keeping her thoughts to herself—thoughts that would surely see her cast into one of the Inquisition's prison, should they be spoken at the wrong time—she followed Justin up the road leading inland, to Vittoria.

The sun was setting when they reached that town. They had stopped only once, at noon, for half an hour, to eat some of the cheese and freshly baked bread Tandy had bought that morning. They had washed the food down with ale brought in a small cask from the ship: Justin had insisted on that.

Now that rest seemed an eternity ago. Kat's throat was parched.

She was sore from the gelding's bone-jarring gait. When Justin called for them to halt before the inn where they would spend the night, Kat dismounted at once. She hoped this *venta* would be as welcoming as the inns she had stayed at in England, with good food and clean chambers and sheets and obliging servants.

An hour later she had been thoroughly disillusioned. The *ventero* had greeted them with suspicion rather than a warm welcome, and only showing him the safe-conduct had convinced him to let them stay. The rooms were tiny and filthy: Kat set to work at once removing bedbugs and other vermin from the bed in the chamber she and Justin would share, only to have Justin tell her she was wasting her time and they would sleep more comfortably on the floor, wrapped in their cloaks. Their supper would be a very late one, Kat learned to her dismay, since Justin did not trust their host to serve fresh food and instead had Tandy pay the *ventero* a fee to have one of his slovenly servants roast the four chickens he had bought in Bilbao that morning. Kat was tempted to supervise the cooking, but after one look at the soot-blackened, grimy kitchen, she fled back to their chamber.

While she was downstairs, Justin had found a maidservant, a pretty girl no older than fourteen, to remove the infested straw bedding and sweep the room. Now he ignored Kat, instead chatting with the girl in Spanish while she worked, his manner friendly even though he was merely giving her directions. Before the maidservant left, he showered her with warm compliments that brought a blush to her face, and she could scarcely stammer her thanks when Justin gave her a few coins.

Kat, perched on a stool, had been gazing wearily out the room's single tiny window, waiting for a chance to speak to Justin alone. She turned toward him as he closed the door, about to tell him of the dismal state of the kitchen, but he spoke first.

"Jealous, Kat?"

She gaped at him. "Of a *serving wench*?"

"You pretended to be a serving wench once, as I recall," he said teasingly.

He was watching her closely, and she realized of a sudden that he wished to see her show jealousy. He did not know that she spoke Spanish: as like as not, he thought that she believed his talk with the chambermaid had been other than what it was.

"For a truth, I see no reason to be jealous," she said ingenuously, and was rewarded by seeing his condescending smile falter. "If I feel aught of jealousy tonight, 'tis of anyone staying at a good English inn."

"This is not to your taste?" he asked, gesturing at the clean-swept floor.

"I prefer the Jerusalem Tree."

"Yea, so did I." There was an odd tone to his voice, and his gaze was still intent on her. She averted her face to look out the window. "Kat, I would not have wished you to risk this journey—"

A sudden rapping on the door interrupted him.

"Perchance 'tis the maid with the fresh straw for our bedding," Justin muttered, unlatching the door, "but I thought 'twould take her longer than . . ."

His voice trailed off as he opened the door to a Dominican friar.

Her head reeling, Kat clutched at the edge of the stool to steady herself. For an instant she had thought that their visitor was Fray Tomás, for this man looked much like him.

"Lord Harwood?" the friar said, in heavily accented English. "I am Fray Luis. Fray Tomás advised me to expect you in Vittoria this evening."

"I pray you, come in," Justin said, turning to look at Kat just as she almost leapt from the stool. "Will you have a seat, Fray Luis?"

"I regret that I may not stay," the Dominican told him. "I wished only to assure myself—that I may in turn assure Fray Tomás—that you reached Vittoria safely. All six of your servants are still with you?"

Justin nodded.

"The *ventero* told me that a meal is being prepared for you here. So none of your party will be going to a tavern this evening?"

"None of us will go to any *bodegone*."

"That is good," Fray Luis said, allowing a faint smile to touch his lips. "Drink loosens a man's tongue, and it would be unfortunate if there were to be talk of a sort better managed by sober minds. But I forget. You English do not like our Spanish wines."

"Not after those wines are stored in goatskins or pigskins, as the *bodegones* store them. But we have brought some good Spanish muscadel from the ship"—nodding toward a cask Tandy had carried in earlier—"which has never seen the inside of a goatskin."

"Thank God for that," the friar said, and allowed Justin to offer him some of the wine, which Kat poured into the two goblets Tandy had also brought them. Then she retreated to a corner of the chamber, grateful that the friar had shown no interest in her.

"You speak English well, Fray Luis," Justin said after they had sampled the wine and the friar had praised it.

"I have had much practice. I was one of those who accompanied Fray Bartolomé to England, during the tragically brief reign of your Queen Mary."

It was all Kat could do to keep from staring at the Dominican. Fray Bartolomé. That could be none other than Fray Bartolomé de Carranza, the Archbishop of Toledo, whom the English had nicknamed *the Black Friar* for his role in encouraging Mary—Bloody Mary—to persecute heretics. 'Twas only just that the Black Friar had since suffered persecution himself, as his enemies in Spain had drawn the Inquisition's attention to some of the archbishop's writings that could be considered heretical. Carranza was now in prison . . . but this disciple of his was not, and Fray Luis might welcome another chance to try Englishmen as heretics.

Justin's voice gave no clue to his own reaction to hearing Carranza's name mentioned, as the baron calmly asked Fray Luis whether he had enjoyed his stay in England. The friar spoke only of the beauty of the countryside. A most politic exchange, Kat thought cynically, even though she was grateful for it. Peradventure the friar was not seriously interested in trapping Justin into making some statement that could be construed as heresy.

A few minutes later, after Fray Luis had finished his wine and bidden them good night, she said as much to Justin. To her surprise, he laughed.

"I'faith, he would not wish to see us imprisoned here. He knows already that we carry no prohibited literature with us. Fray Tomás would have told him as much. Fray Luis wishes only to see us safely out of his province, so he will be spared the responsibility of arresting and proving a charge of heresy against an Englishman with a safe-conduct from the king. Hence the warning to avoid the *bodegones*, where one of the Inquisition's overzealous spies might lure one of us into reckless talk."

" 'Tis a wonder that a disciple of the Black Friar would be such a—such a politico."

"You have heard of Carranza, then? Well. Look you." He smiled a little, gazing down at her. "The archbishop's success would have taught Fray Luis the value of zeal. But the archbishop's fall, now—that taught him the even greater value of discretion." He chuckled, then abruptly sobered. "Now go find Tandy, and ask him about our supper. Ask him, too, to make sure that none of the men leave the inn tonight. Fray Luis will warn us to be careful, but his discretion does not make him a fool. He dare not hesitate to arrest us if he's given cause."

Kat hurried off, shivering a little.

It seemed that she had been asleep but a few minutes that night when Justin shook her awake. She sat up abruptly, fighting free of his hand. It was still dark outside, without the least hint of dawn, but she could hear horses and men moving about in the courtyard. She ate a hurried breakfast while Justin went to settle their bill and help Tandy supervise the loading of the packhorses. She was ready to leave, her cloakbag packed, her face again well coated with dark powder, by the time he returned to pick up his cloakbag. A few minutes later they were on their way out of Vittoria.

Kat still felt half asleep when they rode through a village just after sunrise. They had to slow their horses to a walk, for villagers thronged the streets, streaming out of the church after mass. They were near the outskirts of the village, the road clear again fifty yards ahead of them, when Kat heard a woman scream.

The sound had come from ahead of them. An old woman wearing a garish yellow tunic over her plain black kirtle was trying to reach the shelter of a hovel, but a group of boys stood between her and the door, taunting her. Other young men closed in on her from the road, making jeering comments as she turned round and round in circles, her hands held out pleadingly, tears streaming down her withered face.

And Justin and Tandy rode right past her.

Kat could scarcely believe that they were not going to stop to help the woman. She spurred her horse to catch up with them, intending to demand that they turn back, then reined in, causing the horse to rear, when she saw one of the youths shove the old woman so hard that she stumbled and fell to her knees with a cry of pain. Kat brought her horse under control an instant before flinging herself from the saddle to run toward the ruffians.

"Villanos! Bellacos! Hijos de putas!" she shouted. *"Dejadla!"*

As she ran she drew her sword, and the boys scattered. The nearest rogue was twenty feet away by the time she reached the woman. As he looked back over his shoulder, Kat gave him the fig. He returned the insulting gesture, but that was the limit of his bravery: he ran on.

She turned her attention to the old woman then.

"Ya pasó . . ." Kat told her gently. *"No dejaré que la hagan daño."*

The woman looked up at her then, an expression of hopelessness on her face . . . a hopelessness Kat could understand now that she finally realized what that yellow sackcloth tunic was, that tunic with a red St. Andrew's cross painted on both front and back.

'Twas a *sanbenito*, the garment of shame and repentance that the Inquisition forced its victims to wear. This woman was free, so she had abjured the heresy she was accused of, but she would have to wear the *sanbenito* for a period of penance—haply all her life—and afterward the tunic would be hung in the cathedral of the diocese, displayed with her name and a description of her offense, so her shame would never be forgotten.

Kat had been reaching out to help the woman to her feet. Now her hands fell and she took a half step back, feeling helpless. She had driven away the woman's tormentors once, but they would return: such harassment was intended as an ingredient in the penance. Her assurance that she would not let those rogues hurt the woman was complete folly. She was racking her brains for something to say to ease the woman's pain when Justin ran up to her and yanked her around, wrenching her arm.

"*Borrico!*" He struck her with the back of his hand, sending her staggering backward to fall onto the dusty grass beside the hovel. He took a step toward her, then paused to retrieve the purse that had fallen from his doublet pocket.

"Have you gone mad?" she whispered as he dragged her to her feet again and pushed her back toward their horses.

"Have you?" he asked in a furious undertone. "Would you bring the Inquisition down upon us, and upon that poor woman again as well?"

She twisted around to stare up at him. His face was drained of color, and he looked bleakly unhappy rather than angry.

He lifted her up onto her horse and sent it down the street with a slap on its rump before she had time to gather the reins. The others were already riding out of the village. Only Tandy had stayed behind; he was holding the reins of Justin's mount. They rode close behind her until she caught up with the others, then cantered on ahead, leaving her to her thoughts, which were far from pleasant.

The outrage she had felt upon first seeing the old woman was still strong within her, but now she also felt a numbing fear that did not leave her as the morning wore on. Twice riders in more of a hurry than the English party caught up with them and passed them; each time Kat tensed as soon as she heard the drumbeat of hooves on the road behind them, and she prayed, as the riders swept past, that they were not messengers sent ahead by someone in the village to tell the servants of the Inquisition in Burgos of a meddling English youth . . .

When they stopped at midday to rest and eat in the shade of an orchard, Kat tethered her horse to a branch well away from the rest of the party. She was too anxious to have any appetite for dinner, and she felt too guilty to want to speak to any of her countrymen, after she had thoughtlessly endangered them.

She turned away when she saw Justin and Tandy come toward her, hoping they would take the hint and leave her alone. But Justin came to stand directly in front of her. For a moment she pretended to study the toes of her boots, then slowly raised her head. His expression was as somber as her own mood.

"I would cry you mercy, Kat, for striking you, were it not that I would do the same again, should you be as foolish again. You heard the warning I gave the crew."

"*Con el Rey y con la Inquisicion, chitón!*" she recited wearily.

"*Habla un castellano excelente.*"

"*Gracias.*"

She had responded to the compliment without thinking, and now she flushed as she realized how much she had given away.

"I see you know more than the handful of insults you used on those knaves in the village. When did you learn to speak Spanish?"

"Well before yesternight," she said, giving him a long gaze that he finally looked away from, his own color heightened by her reminder of his attempt to make her jealous.

"I pray that you will speak more discreetly in Spanish than you have in English—"

"Fear not. I'll be the very soul of discretion in that matter."

"—though you have given me little hope of that," he concluded, and after a final, angry glance at her, strode back to his servants, leaving her with Tandy, who seemed torn between exasperation and sympathy as he regarded her.

His first words, typically, were practical.

"Would you like some food, Kat? You should eat."

"I lack a stomach for dinner."

"I see. And what stole it from you, choler or melancholy?" Then, when she did not answer, he went on, "Stay angry with his lordship as long as you like, yet it will not change the fact that he was right to act as he did."

"I could not have acted differently!"

"Perhaps not," Tandy said dryly. "Y'are very young and headstrong. And I know you meant only to help that woman. But she will suffer more for having been rescued once. Let us hope that she will not have to face the Inquisition again. Maybe the money his lordship left her will assuage her sufferings."

"What?! What money?"

"Did you not see Justin drop his purse?"

She nodded, a bit warily.

" 'Twas empty when he picked it up. I refilled it just now from the coffers. He could have spent but a dozen reals at the inn yesternight, so he must have left the rest for that old woman, spilled into the grass beside her poor cottage. I did not see the coins fall, but I warrant she did, for she crawled to where he had dropped the purse and stayed there for a time before going inside. She was quick about it. I would hazard that not one of the other villagers saw the coins."

"Yea, if there were coins," Kat said sharply, unwilling to accept the possibility that Justin had thought swiftly enough to help that woman, while she had brought her only danger. "Likely the purse was already empty. Mayhap he gave the coins to that maidservant at the inn . . ." Her voice trailed off; she looked down at her feet.

Tandy sighed. "We shall be leaving here soon," he said, and she heard disappointment and perhaps pity in his voice. "We should reach Burgos by suppertime."

She did not watch him as he returned to Justin and the others, but instead untied her horse and let it crop the grass between the trees. Her own hunger had begun to gnaw at her, but her pride, reinforced by anger, would not let her ask for food now. For a few moments she toyed with the idea of riding away, riding north, to France. But she doubted that she could outride the others—especially Justin, on that fine Spanish mare. And she doubted even more that she could reach the border alone. Like enough, she would be stopped and turned over to the authorities. Perchance Fray Luis still had jurisdiction here. She shuddered. Much as she hated being with Justin, she would need his protection for a time.

CHAPTER 21

It was a warm, lazy afternoon; even the bees drifting through the garden sounded sleepy. Supper was still three hours away, and there were no other guests to entertain than the one who would be arriving this evening. With nothing else to do, Margaret Téllez de Osuna, Condesa de Ordaz, strolled through the shadow cast by the high west wall of her formal garden, overseeing two gardeners and a maidservant as they cut blossoms from the rose bushes that gave the Case de las Rosas its name.

"*Aquí, corta éstas.*" She directed the gardeners to several small, perfect buds, then looked at the girl. "*Que las arreglen en una fuente como te he enseñado y que las pongan en la mesa para la cena.*"

"*Sí, señora.*"

Justin would notice the rosebuds at supper. He always did. He always told her that the buds, set like jewels in a bowl of greenery, reminded him of the bowl of flowers she had been arranging that afternoon they had met fifteen years ago, seeing each other for the first time since they were children. During the first few visits he had made to Spain, she had arranged the flowers herself, but not for the last two visits, and not today: she had no wish to prick her fingers on the rose thorns, and moreover he would not know the difference.

"Lady Margaret!"

Margaret looked around to see her personal maid hurrying across the garden toward her. Now what could have excited Edwina? The maid was nearly fifty now, but she was moving as spryly as a young girl, and her face was lit with a rare smile.

" 'Tis Lord Harwood!" Edwina gasped as she halted a few feet away.

"Here already?" He must have ridden hard from Vittoria to reach Burgos so quickly. By the mass, he must be as eager to see her as ever! Such eagerness boded well for her plans.

"Yea, my lady. He and his men are waiting in the hall."

"I'll see him anon. Send servants to make certain he and his party are given refreshments. Then come to my chamber."

Edwina departed in a rustle of silken petticoats, almost flying back down the path. Margaret's own movements, as she gave the gardeners some final orders and made her way back to her chamber, were slower and calmer: 'twould not do to have all the servants see her excitement. But she could not keep her thoughts from racing . . .

She thanked God that Antonio was not here.

Glancing in her looking glass, she decided that her dress—a gown of rose silk faced with ivory sarcenet over a kirtle of primrose satin—would do. They were clothes that Justin had brought her, garments she much preferred to the dark, severe garb favored by Spanish gentlewomen. She dared not wear her English fashions away from her home, nor when she entertained guests who were unaccustomed to her ways, but with Justin she was free to be herself—her English self. And she need never fear that he would call her an *Ana Bolena*.

It still rankled her that her innocent dalliance—an exchange of letters and poetry, nothing more—with one of the *galantederos* of the court had led to such gossip that her husband had sent her away from the court, away from Madrid, to stay in Burgos this past year. She had done nothing that a dozen Spanish gentlewomen she knew had not also done, but they, being Spanish, had been forgiven, while she, being English, was likened to Anne Boleyn. A pox on those gossips for comparing her—once a maid of honor to Queen Mary—to that witch, that goggle-eyed whore, who had seduced King Henry away from Mary's mother, Katherine of Aragon.

It had been a lonely year of exile from the court. She had once come close to summoning her twelve-year-old son from Valladolid, where he was being raised by Antonio's brother Diego in a purely Castilian household free of all taint of England. She had hesitated, though, not sure what she would do if either Rodrigo or his uncle refused to obey her summons, and soon the longing for his company had ebbed. She had found solace in her correspondence, which had become more extensive and more influential than ever. And now, she prayed, Justin would help bring her plans to fruition.

She was looking through her jewelry chest for a pearl necklace and earrings when Edwina burst into the chamber.

"They are being made welcome, my lady."

"Good." Margaret seated herself before the looking glass while the maid combed her hair.

"Think you that I look nearly thirty, Edwina?" she asked.

The maid laughed and shook her head. "I warrant you, you look scarce older than you did when you first met Lord Harwood."

"Beshrew you, old woman!" Margaret said with mock anger. "I was but a babe when I first played with my cousin! Nor was he Lord Harwood then."

"Cry you mercy, madam. I meant—"

"Michaels Court," Margaret interrupted. "Aye."

She had been fourteen then, in the summer of 1555, and dazed by all that had happened to her in the previous year. Because of her family's loyalty to the Catholic cause, she had received the honor of becoming one of Queen Mary's maids of honor, just a month before Mary's wedding to Prince Philip of Spain in July of 1554. Margaret had missed the wedding itself: the English queen, a plain woman who looked older than her thirty-eight years, had left her prettiest maids and ladies-in-waiting behind when she traveled to Winchester to meet and wed her Spanish prince. Margaret had not met the Spaniards until the wedding party arrived in London. Among them—one of the few Spanish nobles who did not quickly flee England in dismay, preferring to serve Philip's father, the Emperor Charles, in Flanders—was Antonio Téllez de Osuna, a slim, fair-skinned, dark-haired man of medium height, then thirty-two years old, with an easy command of English and a winning smile. Don Antonio had been enchanted by Margaret's shyness and loveliness, while she, in turn, had been flattered by his attentions.

At first she had feared that her father would never consent to the match, for turmoil swirled about Prince Philip's entourage. The Spanish noblemen were robbed by English highwaymen and English shopkeepers alike. They were ridiculed in the streets, called Spanish knaves, and told that they should have packed less baggage for they would be going home soon. There was fighting even in the halls of the palace, and three Englishmen and a Spaniard had been hanged.

And then, in late autumn, came the good news that the queen was expecting a child—an heir who would, Antonio argued, ensure the continuation of Spanish influence in England. Margaret's father gave his consent, and she and Antonio were married in February.

The first two months of their marriage were honeymoon for Margaret: she could imagine no better husband than Antonio, no one more kind, more devoted, more skillful in the lovemaking to which he had initiated her. She still wondered how different their marriage might have been, had that blissful season not ended so soon, had she had more time to feel herself the center of her husband's existence.

But he had sent her away, less than half a year after marrying her. And she had gone willingly, no longer enchanted with her marriage.

The problem had begun with the queen. That poor, barren little woman. Margaret could still see her, see those thin, colorless lips moving in silent prayers for the health of her unborn child. Her never-to-be-born child. For there was no child. A false announcement April thirtieth of the birth of a male child, accompanied by the ringing of bells throughout London, had been followed by disillusionment and rumors, even rumors that the queen had died. For two more months Mary remained confined at Hampton Court, resisting the knowledge that she was swollen not with child but rather from dropsy. Hundreds of Englishmen gathered at the gate of the palace, anxious to fight any Spaniard who would come out. A brawl between a handful of Spaniards and Englishmen became a battle, and before it ended, several men were dead and dozens wounded. Antonio judged it best to send his wife to stay with her grandfather in the country, at his estate in Surrey. He had broken the news of his decision to her gently, thinking she would be dismayed, but he had been wrong, for he had been absent too often that spring and summer, cloistered with others in Philip's household. Wounded by his neglect, so that she found herself weary of him and of the fretful court, she welcomed the change of scene and company.

She had arrived at Michaels Court in mid-July. A few days later Justin had come for a visit of several weeks.

Her grandfather, seemingly blind to the fact that his granddaughter and great-nephew were no longer children, had allowed the two of them to spend long hours together unchaperoned. They had become lovers within a few days, for Justin had provided the sympathy and attention Margaret needed after Antonio's neglect. With the Spaniards again as unpopular as ever, she had found it easy to convince Justin that she had been forced into a loveless marriage. In sooth, she had almost succeeded in convincing herself. With no hope now for an heir, Philip was planning to leave for Flanders soon, and his noblemen with him. Margaret's mistake in wedding Don Antonio seemed, during those late summer weeks, a bad dream from which Justin had awakened her.

Then Antonio had come, unknowingly ending the idyll, to take her to his home in Spain.

She had not set foot on English soil since then. Mary had lived only a few more years, years in which Margaret had been unable to travel because of two pregnancies, one of which had ended in a miscarriage. By the time she was well enough that Antonio would consider taking her back to England, Mary was dead, her bastard sister Elizabeth on the throne.

But not, pray God, for much longer.

For years Margaret had been in touch with the English Catholic exiles on the continent, lending what aid she could to many plots, none of which had succeeded. The failure of the rebellion by the Northern earls had been a particularly bitter disappointment. But now that the papal bull had reached England, things would change. That must be why Justin was here. Soon Catholic armies would march on English soil, and she would return—with or without Antonio's permission—to her own country, which would once again belong to the true faith.

Her face was flushed with excitement. She sang a verse of a ballad that had been popular her last spring in London as Edwina fastened the string of pearls about her neck and the pearl drops to her earlobes. Then, with the maid trailing after her, Margaret swept out of her chamber, ready at last to welcome her cousin.

"Well met in Burgos, my lord," she said with a smile. "You and your men are welcome here." The last was not completely true. After scanning the men who had accompanied Justin, she had been hard put not to frown. That wayward rogue Tandy was with him, and the rest of the men looked no more presentable. One, a slightly built lad, was particularly slovenly. But she knew it would offend Justin if she treated his servants with the contempt they deserved.

"Well met indeed, sweet cousin," he said, taking her hand and bending down to kiss it. "You are more lovely than ever."

"Court incense, cousin. And pray do not accuse me of the same if I say that the last two years have also served you well." She kept her voice light, so the listening servants would think her remark mere courtesy, but the compliment she had paid him was sincere.

He was heavier now than when she had fallen in love with him, but the heaviness was muscle, not fat, and she could not help contrasting him with Antonio, who was developing a paunch that sorted oddly with his otherwise slender frame. Antonio's forehead had become creased, too, from too many hours of sharing King Philip's myriad concerns. Looking at Justin, she saw only the faint lines radiating outward from his eyes, lines that instead of dismaying her only reminded her of how often he laughed—and how much she missed his laughter, living here among these too-sober Spaniards! He was still holding her hand, which tingled where his lips had brushed her skin. Reluctantly, she withdrew it from the grip of his hard fingers.

"I would present my companions to you, my lady," Justin said. "You have met William Lofts . . ."

"Tandy," she said, forcing herself to smile as she greeted the tawny-haired servant and the next four men Justin introduced. Her smile faltered as Justin gestured for his youngest servant to approach.

By her faith, the boy was looking at her impudently! Margaret could not fathom that unwavering gaze: there was curiosity in it, and hostility. She was astonished. No man had ever stared at her like that. Bewildered, she turned to Justin, only to receive another shock: he seemed amused by the youth's impudence.

"And this," her cousin said, yanking the cap from the lad's head, "is Katherine. My ward."

Stunned, Margaret stared wordlessly at the shimmering blond hair cascading around the slim shoulders.

"I thought it safer that she travel thus," Justin said, with a slight shrug.

Margaret spared him only a quick, cold glance before returning to her scrutiny of the girl. For it was a girl, beneath the grime. It was impossible to judge whether the girl's complexion was fair, but her features were delicate, and her eyes—still focused on Margaret in that unsettling gaze—were lovely, a dark blue-green fringed with thick lashes.

And she was young, Margaret realized. Of course. Still Justin's ward, the girl had not yet attained her majority and could be no older than fifteen, for all that she looked a year or two older than that.

She turned to Justin. "My lord?" she said coldly, touching his hand for an instant before leading him a dozen steps away from the others. "What means this?" she whispered. "Why have you brought your ward here?"

"She's not my ward."

"But you—"

"She is but a servant, Meg. Just as the others. I have no wards . . . as you should know."

"Then—" She broke off as the meaning of his last words sank into her. Alack, he must think her slow-witted, for it seemed he thought he had been making a jest, telling her the girl was his ward when she should know he had no wards. 'Twas a poor sort of jest, in truth, but he would think her shrewish if she rated him for it.

"Well," she said, somewhat mollified, "since she is a servant, then she may share a chamber with the youngest of my maids . . . if they do not object. Haply they can find her more suitable garb."

"Her own clothes are in two of the cloakbags. And 'twill not do for her to stay with your maids. She will need a chamber of her own, as near mine as possible."

She had not thought he could surprise her further, but he had. She stared at him in disbelief before whispering furiously, "I will *not* entertain your *puta* under my roof!"

"Soft, cousin. She is not my whore. But neither is she a maidservant."

"Would you have me believe she serves as your guard, like the men you brought from the ship?"

He chuckled. "Not without more practice with the sword she sometimes wears."

"*What?!*"

"More softly, Meg. She has talents, useful talents—nay, not those, spare me those dagger looks. Useful knowledge . . . as useful as Tandy's."

"Oh . . ." She looked back at Tandy, remembering what Justin had told her of him. She sighed. "How will I explain her presence here?"

"She is my ward. Please it you, let her keep that guise. Tell no one else, even Edwina, that Kat is but a servant."

"Her wardrobe . . . ?"

" 'Tis meet for a gentlewoman."

"Dress her as you will, coz, but 'twill be wasted effort if she cannot play the gentlewoman. Can she?"

"She's an artful player. Belike that role will suit her, too."

He was on his way back to his companions before she fully realized that he had admitted that the girl had never acted as a gentlewoman.

She swore under her breath, then turned to look speculatively at Kat. She was not Justin's mistress yet, or so he said, and Margaret did not believe that her cousin could lie to her about such matters. But did Kat hope to become his mistress? Very like. And might Justin in time succumb to the girl's prettiness? The answer to that was less certain, the uncertainty troubling. Mayhap, Margaret reflected as she followed him, something could be done about that . . .

"Shoes," Justin said suddenly, turning again to her.

"My lord?" she asked, confused.

"Katherine lacks shoes. They were left on the ship. May she borrow a pair of your slippers?"

"Edwina's might fit her better," Margaret said hastily.

"But my lady, you know my feet are so small!" Edwina protested. The maidservant held her foot out so all could see that it was indeed tiny.

Kat approached her and placed her own foot beside it, then shook her head. "Madam?" she said, looking questioningly at Margaret. "Maybe your slippers—"

"They will fit," Margaret interrupted. "Needs must that they fit." She laughed, somewhat breathlessly. "You must not go barefoot here."

"Marry, I would fear to be mistaken for a friar," Kat said cheerfully.

"Or a peasant," Margaret added, so sharply that Justin and all his party stared at her. Jesu! That girl was already causing her trouble! "Will you excuse me, my lord?" she said to Justin. "I must prepare for supper. My servants will show you and your men to your chambers. Edwina"— glancing coldly at the maidservant who had unthinkingly come so close to humiliating her—"find a suitable chamber for Lord Harwood's ward." And she left as quickly as she could, wishing for once that the English-style kirtle she wore were longer, imagining that all eyes were on her feet.

———

"More paper?" Justin asked, trying to keep from smiling as Kat slid her feet back and forth inside the slippers.

When Kat looked up to take the scrap of paper from him, he saw that she was having the same problem. She looked like a child with a mouthful of comfits. She lowered her head swiftly, her expression hidden as she tore the scrap in two, crumpled the bits of paper and stuffed them into the toes of the slippers. She tried them again, then sighed and held out her hand for more paper.

He choked back a laugh, a sideways glance at the maid assigned to Kat telling him that they were being watched. None of the servants here could be trusted not to repeat whatever they saw or heard, and he did not want Margaret told that her guests had been laughing at the amount of paper needed to stuff the slippers' toes so the shoes would fit Kat's feet. What Kat had said a few minutes ago had been bad enough. He had handed her the slippers, and the paper the maid had provided, and had informed her most seriously—repeating what the maid had told him—that the slippers were ones Margaret had never worn, as they were too large for her.

"By my troth," Kat had said, holding the slippers up and studying the soles, which showed signs of wear, "then her horses must have borrowed them for dancing."

Thank God the maid would know little if any English. Margaret spoke to all her servants except Edwina in Spanish, preferring her conversations in English to be somewhat private. She had told Justin that she could never be certain whether any of her Spanish servants understood English well: there might be spies, for there was the Inquisition to consider, and, well, Antonio . . . He had taken the hint and now never said anything indiscreet within a servant's hearing. Such discretion—like, he thought wryly, all other types of discretion—had apparently not occurred to Kat. He wondered what she had said to the maid before his arrival. What he had overheard was the Spanish girl telling Kat about her family, an innocent conversation at that point. He prayed that she had said nothing about the Inquisition.

Kat seemed satisfied at last with the fit of the slippers, and stood and took a few steps across the room, frowning a little.

"Can you walk in those now?"

"If I could dance wearing pantofles, I can—" She broke off as she glanced up and saw the surprise on his face.

"Where have you danced, Kat, that the dancers wore pantofles?" he asked. He had seen it done only at court.

"Never, my lord. 'Tis but a saying I once heard, and means merely that these are difficult to walk in, as difficult as 'twould be to dance

wearing pantofles. Have you not heard the saying?'' she asked ingenuously.

She's an artful player, he had told Margaret. 'Twas likely Kat was
playing the innocent now, for all the directness of her gaze. But what
did it matter, in truth, if she had once danced wearing pantofles? Her
master, whoever he was, had seen that she was able to ape the manners
of the gentry—yea, even young gentlemen—and 'twas not impossible
that she knew how to dance as well as how to wield a sword or chatter
about St. John's. At the moment he could not complain: 'twould make
matters simpler if she was prepared to play his ward so well that no one
would question it.

He offered her his arm. She took it, as calmly and graciously as if
she were a gentlewoman, and they went downstairs to supper.

"What think you of Spain?'' Margaret asked Kat, her voice coolly polite. The third course of their supper had just been served, and she had
finally realized that she had not spoken to Kat at all after greeting her,
instead asking Justin about the voyage to Spain and the ride from Bilbao. She would have preferred to continue ignoring the girl entirely,
but dared not. 'Twould provoke more gossip from the servants.

" 'Tis a much poorer country than I had thought,'' Kat said, the
tactlessness of her answer not surprising her hostess: Kat was, after all,
but a servant.

"Indeed? I hope you are not disappointed by my hospitality,'' Margaret said, giving Justin a conspiratorial smile. "Are you accustomed to
much grander houses than this? To better repasts than this?'' She waved
her hand to indicate the profusion of dishes on the table. 'Twas a proper
English feast, not the ascetic type of meal that Spaniards seemed to
favor. Most of the time, even when supping alone, Margaret followed
the Spanish custom—it helped her stay slim—but she had arranged an
impressive supper for Justin, with chicken and venison pies, quail and
heron, ham, mutton, cold roast beef, and the fish that Burgos was famous for. The board groaned under enough food to provide a dozen
typical meals for her. And Justin's servant thought Spain poor?

Kat shook her head. "I meant the poverty of the villages and farms
we passed along the way, my lady. England's yeomen and shopkeepers
are more prosperous.''

" 'Tis the fault of the *alcabalas*, the taxes here,'' Justin explained.
"Everything that is sold is taxed at a tenth of its value, each time it
changes hands.''

"Why such ruinous taxes?''

"The armies must be maintained, Kat. And the clergy and highest
ranking noblemen are not taxed.''

" 'Sblood! Is that fair? Why, England would have been ruined, too, had Mary Tudor lived and Philip become King of England!"

"You speak of matters you know nothing of," Margaret said, wishing to interrupt this conversation between Kat and Justin lest any of the servants understand and report it.

Kat gave her a hard look, then, turning to Justin, raised her eyebrows and murmured, *"Con el Rey . . ."*

He nodded, and she fell silent.

Margaret, recognizing the beginning of the saying, suppressed a sigh of relief. At least the girl was wise enough to keep still when reminded that she should do so. Though of a truth, enough had already been said. She prayed that none of the servants was in the employ of one of Antonio's rivals at court, anxious to report that her guests had complained about the king's taxes . . .

"You spoke of Mary Tudor," she said of a sudden, giving Kat a brittle smile. "I was a maid of honor to Queen Mary. 'Twas my first year at court. I was but fourteen then . . ."

She went on talking of the English court while the servants cleared the dishes away and then brought in the dessert: fruit, almond cake and sucket tarts. Kat was silent throughout, which pleased Margaret, who had hoped her stories of the court would put the girl in her place by reminding her of the uncrossable distance between her station in life and that of Margaret and Justin. But then Kat yawned.

"Weary, Kat?" Justin asked. " 'Twas a long ride today. Perchance you should go to bed early."

"Nay, my lord." The girl smiled faintly. "I am not sleepy."

"Haply you found my reminiscing tiresome," Margaret said, trying without success to keep her voice pleasant. "I should not have spoken at such length of Queen Mary's court, when you must feel yourself so remote from it."

"Indeed, I do," Kat agreed amiably. "Remote in time. I was but a child, little more than a babe, at the time you spoke of. But I was not tired by your reminiscing. There is great value in hearing one's elders speak of their youth." She gave Margaret a dazzling smile, then glanced briefly at Justin. "His lordship has told me of his studies at Cambridge."

"Yea, I warrant you have heard a great deal about Cambridge," Justin said, and looked amused.

For once Margaret was speechless. So she was an elder? And past her youth? Had Justin not been present, she would have slapped the girl. At the moment she felt like slapping him, too, for being so heedless of Kat's insolence.

She turned her gaze on him then, and he must have read her distress in her eyes, for he sobered instantly and gave her a look of sympathy before resuming eating, picking lightly at a slice of almond cake. He said not a word to rebuke Kat, but nonetheless the girl again seemed to sense that she had gone too far in her remarks, and she, too, was silent.

"What news from France?" Justin asked abruptly, and for an instant Margaret wondered if he had somehow learned of her plans. Then he added, "How goes the war?"

"They are still fighting," she said with a shrug. "There are rumors that *Madame la Serpente*"—she could not help smiling at King Philip's nickname for the wily Catherine de Medici, Queen Mother of France and his former mother-in-law—"seeks peace with her Protestant rebels. Pray God, she does not find it."

"They are fighting still in the south of France?" Justin asked, looking thoughtful.

"Aye. Monluc and others."

"So there is no chance yet that French troops will ally with Spanish to attack England."

"Nay, there's no hope of that," Margaret said with regret. She had seen that Kat, too, seemed dismayed by Justin's conclusion. Were even servants, then, concerned about their government? What difference could it make to Kat whether the rulers of England belonged to the true faith or were heretics? Unless, of course, the girl hoped to yoke her fortune to Justin's . . .

"Monluc," Kat said softly. "Is he not the soldier known as the Hammer of the Huguenots?"

Justin nodded.

" 'Tis said," Kat went on, "that he would have all heretics who do not repent burned without trial—even the children."

"The quickest way to deal with them," Margaret said. "Examples must be made. One man hanged, he has said, is worth a hundred killed in battle." The girl's stare was unsettling. Margaret laughed awkwardly. "Rebellions are crushed best if crushed quickly."

"Like the rising led by the earls of Northumberland and Westmorland?"

"A tragic example."

"I have also heard," Kat said, "that Monluc spoke publicly of his wish to rape the Protestant Queen of Navarre, that he wished to have Jeanne d'Albret to discover if bedding a queen is like bedding other women. 'Tis said that he has raped—"

"Huguenot slanders," Margaret interrupted. "They cannot prevail against him on the field of battle, so they attack him in whispers behind his back, calling him a *forceur de filles*."

"Yet one Englishman at the French court fought Monluc to defend Jeanne's honor—"

"What care you for a heretic's honor? Y'are not a Protestant, are you?"

"No more Protestant than my lord, I trow," Kat said warily.

"Justin?"

He shrugged. "Kat has lived all her life during the reign of a Protestant queen."

"And that determines her faith?" She looked at Kat. "Would you be Catholic now, if Mary had borne an heir?"

Kat shrugged but said nothing.

Margaret shook her head. " 'Tis a fickle sort of faith, to my mind. I should have guessed it, for your eyes betray you, with that changeable color, that seawater green. Are your feelings so changeable, Kat?"

"I cannot help the color of my eyes, my lady. Would that they were blue, like yours. Blue is for constancy, is it not? And faithfulness?"

Margaret's mouth fell open a bit. Was this impudent child mocking her? Did she know that she and Justin had been lovers?

"I would see more harmony between you," Justin said, and both Kat and Margaret looked at him. "I must leave for Madrid tomorrow, and would leave Kat here."

"You leave for Madrid? Tomorrow?" Margaret asked, stunned. She had expected him to stay at least several days.

"Nay, I will not stay here!" Kat protested. "I will go with you!"

He turned to Kat first. " 'Tis a dangerous journey, and one I would spare you. No, girl, do not argue with me. I have thought about this for days, and you cannot sway me from my decision . . . unless my lady objects"—a glance at Margaret—"and I hope she will not."

"Tomorrow?" Margaret repeated.

"Needs must," he said simply. "Mayhap, by leaving a few days earlier than I had wished, I can spend more time here upon my return from Madrid."

"Why to Madrid?" Kat demanded. "You said nothing—"

" 'Tis nothing that concerns you," Justin said, the tone of his voice discouraging further questions and objections. He looked back at Margaret. "Please you to tell me I may leave her here with you."

Margaret wanted to refuse his request. Justin would be gone at least two weeks, for it took five days or more to ride to Madrid and she doubted he would spend only a day or two there before returning. The thought of having Kat as her guest for that long sickened her. Yet she badly needed Justin to feel himself in her debt now.

"As you wish, my lord. I am honored that you would leave your ward with me." Justin smiled uncertainly; Kat looked openly skeptical. Margaret gave the girl her warmest smile. It had just occurred to her that she would have at least two weeks to deal with Kat without having to be mindful of Justin's interference on his servant's behalf. Two weeks. Much could be accomplished in that time.

"Are you not tired, child?" she asked solicitously. "Perhaps you should go to bed now. I have much to discuss with my cousin, and I would not have you falling asleep at the table."

Kat looked questioningly at Justin, who nodded. She then took her leave with poor grace. Margaret sighed with relief when Kat was gone.

She turned to Justin then. "Let us talk in my antechamber. Edwina would hear your news of England . . ."

Edwina could have listened to the news from England for hours, but she had no more than five minutes to ask Justin questions before Margaret decided that enough had been said to satisfy the curiosity of any servants who might be eavesdropping outside the door.

"Will you play for us, Edwina?" she asked, gesturing toward the pair of virginals in the corner of the antechamber.

Looking disappointed but resigned, Edwina seated herself at the instrument and began to play. As the first strains of melody filled the room, Margaret took Justin by the hand and led him back to her bedchamber, closing and locking the door behind them. The heavy drapes over her windows had already been pulled shut, a barrier to chill night breezes as well as any eavesdroppers in the garden below.

She was smiling as she turned to Justin, her face raised for his kiss. He put his arms around her and held her close to him. She whispered his name over and over between kisses, caressing his neck and shoulders, nearly sobbing with relief that she was in his arms again after so long. With all her heart, she wished that they were very young again, together again back in England, in that first summer of their love—

But they were not. Remembering what she had to say to him—what he must agree to—she drew back a little, catching his face between her hands.

"Sweetheart, we must talk."

"Later," he said, and would have drawn her against him again, but she stood firm, on her face a look of regret that she did not have to feign.

"*Now*, Justin. So we need think of nothing else . . . later."

He released her then. She was surprised and a bit hurt that he let her go so readily, but now was not the time to say so. She went to pour them both cups of wine, and when she turned back toward him, he was sitting on the bed, his back against the pillows.

She handed him a cup and then sat down at the foot of the bed.

"At supper," she began, "you did not ask what I have heard from my friends in Louvain and Douai. Why?"

"Kat," he said simply.

"She is not to be trusted?"

"She is young, and has yet to learn discretion."

"Well." Margaret nodded. "I will remember to say naught to her of my friends among the exiles in the Netherlands."

"What hear you from them?"

"Their last letters expressed hope that, with the papal bull, the Catholic powers would at last unite to invade England."

"Nicholas Sander still believes invasion is the only way to return England to the true faith?"

"Yea, and he has written as much to the Duke of Alva."

"If he argues for invasion as persuasively as he argues for the Church . . ."

"Then he may convince Alva. Let us pray that he will."

Her eyes strayed to the shelf where she kept the books received from Louvain, published by the English Catholic exiles there. There were Sander's *The Supper of our Lord set forth in six Books* and *The Rocke of the Churche wherein the Primacy of St. Peter and his successors the Bishops of Rome is proved out of Gods Worde*. And there were works by Thomas Stapleton, another of her friends, a greater scholar even than Sander— though less determined, she feared, to see the heretic rule of England come to a quick end. She had his English translation of Bede; his *Tres Thomae* with its discussion of St. Thomas the Apostle, Thomas à Becket and Thomas More; his *Fortress of the Faith* and his *Counterblast* against the English Bishop Horne's defense of the oath of supremacy many of Elizabeth's subjects had been forced to take. There were the attacks on the English Church and its defenders—especially Bishop Jewel with his *Apologia Ecclisiae Anglicanae*—by Thomas Harding, who, like Sander, had once been a Fellow of New College, Oxford. There was the catechism written by Laurence Vaux, another exile from Oxford, a Fellow of Corpus Christi. That catechism was one of the matters she had to discuss with Justin, though less important—much less important—than the other. Tucked into those books, and all the others published by other exile scholars who had left Oxford and Cambridge for the universities at Louvain and Douai, were their letters, which she found more heartening than the books themselves. She sent as much money as she could to these men; she admired the war against the English heresy that they waged with words. Yet words were not enough . . .

"What news from Douai, from William Allen?" Justin asked. "Are you still sending him money for his seminary?"

"All that I can," she said. "Yet sometimes I wonder what is gained by this."

"You question his aims now?"

"Nay, I would never do that. England needs the priests he is train-ing. I would only that they be ready sooner. Likely none will be ready to send into England for two years or more. And in the meantime there is confusion among the Catholic clergy left in England. You told me yourself how the judgment of the Council of Trent was not accepted, how some in England still maintain that 'tis lawful to attend the English Church's services if it is done only as an act of obedience to Elizabeth."

"Will not the bull change that?"

"If it is published everywhere. If it is read in full, and understood, and believed. The pope spoke out against attending English services four years ago, and Laurence Vaux wrote a letter to tell all English Catholics that he witnessed the pope's statement, but the letter has not circulated as widely as he wished, nor, alack, has it been believed by all who read it. The priests who will come from Douai will give heart to English Catholics and bolster their faith. Dr. Allen is training them well, better than most priests are trained in England. 'Tis a harsh regime that he has imposed, for he would know who can face hardship. They are taught Hebrew and Greek to aid in their study of the Bible. They are taught to preach, and to argue against the heresies of the English Church."

"They shall be brave new priests, then, and bring England back to the true faith, without need of the pope or Catholic armies."

"Do you mock our zeal? They will be needed in England, but, God willing, those who have imposed the English Church on the people will already be gone, and the priests who will instruct the people anew in the true faith will be able to go openly about God's business, not fearing arrest and torture and execution."

"No, I do not mock you, sweeting," Justin said, his voice quiet and somber. "I laud your efforts."

"Then help me." She went to the bookshelf for the copy of Lau-rence Vaux's catechism, removed the letters he had sent her, and handed the book to Justin.

"What's this? A *Catechisme of Christian Doctrine necessarie for Chil-dren and ignorant people.* Which do you think me, Margaret," he asked, laughing, "a child or ignorant?"

"Neither," she said. "I think you a man who can find a publisher for this in England and see that it is circulated. Copies have already been sent into England, but I would have more distributed there, thou-sands more."

"You are not jesting, in sooth?" He looked at her sharply, then, frowning, glanced down at the book again before setting it aside. " 'Twould be folly for me to try such a thing. What use am I to the

Catholic cause if I am caught with a book that will be denounced as traitorous and popish? Would you have me clapped in the Tower?"

"Nay, of course not, but—"

"Or taken by the Inquisition?"

"For a book defending the true faith?"

"Carranza thought his teachings defended the true faith. Have you proof that this book is permitted in Spain?"

"'Twas brought to me, after the Inquisition examined it."

"Yea, but the wife of a grandee may be permitted materials that would provoke the arrest of an Englishman."

"You will not take it with you?"

"No, I will not."

She glared at him, unable to conceal her anger any longer. "But if you will not do this—not even this—" She caught herself just in time. In his present mood, she could not trust him. But if she could change that mood . . . "Then I must perforce ask someone else."

"Oh?"

Was that a hint of jealousy in his voice already? Good. "There is another Englishman who will do this for me, I trow. I have never dealt with him, but he is trusted by Pierre de Marchant, a French gentleman who is a friend of one of the students at the seminary. Their faith, it seems, is stronger than yours."

"And you would trust an Englishman you have not met to have this catechism published?"

"Aye, and more. Would that I could meet him, for I have heard marvelous things of him, from the letters Monsieur de Marchant has sent me from Paris. This Englishman is oft at court, and belike as conversant as you with other courtiers, even the queen's councillors. I would fain be his friend as well as his ally." And his lover as well? With luck, Justin would think that, and change his mind to keep her from a man he must now see as a rival.

He met her challenging gaze for a few moments longer, then looked away, taking up his wine glass and drinking again before saying, "Who is this Englishman?"

"What need have you of his name?" she asked tauntingly. Marchant had assured her that the man was a most accomplished courtier, and young and handsome as well, but there was always a slight chance that he had lied to her and that his English confederate was old and ugly. She dared not give Justin a name that he would react to with disdain or, worse, laughter.

"None, I warrant," he said at last. "I wish you well in accomplishing this." He got up from the bed and walked to the door.

She could scarcely believe that he was going to walk away. "I would prefer that you help me," she said as he opened the door. "Pray reconsider."

"I will," he said over his shoulder as he walked out into the antechamber, astonishing Edwina, who had not expected him to leave so soon. "Reconsider, that is."

He was about to open the antechamber's door. Margaret darted out of the bedchamber and closed its door behind her, lest any servants passing by outside see that she had been in the inner room. She reached Justin just as he left the antechamber and bade him good night, as pleasantly as ever: appearances had to be maintained. But when she closed the door again and locked it, she drew a deep, shuddering breath and dug her fingernails into her palms.

Edwina looked at her questioningly, then, under her mistress's cold gaze, looked away. Margaret stalked past her into the bedchamber and slammed the door shut. Justin had refused to help her! She could scarce believe it. And he had refused her bed as well! When at last, after so many years of frustration, they had been able to meet while Antonio was away, he had not tried to bed her.

Nay, she reasoned a few minutes later, when the worst of her rage had subsided. He had left because he knew she would refuse to share her bed with him, after his refusal to help. But by now he would be lying alone in a cold bed, and he *would* reconsider his decision. He would be back again in a few hours, knocking quietly on the door of the antechamber . . . and he would be hers.

She called to Edwina to help her undress. She would wear her finest nightgown, and her sheerest smock underneath it. With her heart still pounding, she knew she was too excited to sleep, but she did not mind. She would have hours awake to plan how she would deal with his capitulation.

She knew already that she would be forgiving, once he told her he would help her. She would not demand that he have the catechism published, since he seemed to fear it so greatly. That could always be done by Marchant's friend—though she would tell Justin she would not use his rival, that she would forget about the catechism, that it was of little importance. As indeed it was, compared to the main task she would set Justin, the one which—after this estrangement—he would dare not refuse.

Kat had not expected to be able to fall asleep so soon after returning to her chamber. She was angry at having been dismissed from the table as though she were a child. Worse, she felt herself envious of Margaret. Mock the woman as she would for having large feet, Kat still had to admit that Justin's cousin was very beautiful, with her flawless skin and pale blond hair and blue eyes. She had seemed very much the gentle-woman, in her fine garb and jewels; her face had been artfully painted, and she had worn a perfume of orange blossoms and musk. Lacking paints, perfumes and jewels, Kat had felt plain next to Margaret. In faith, the countess seemed a very paragon . . . save for that temper. Howsomever, might not Justin see his cousin as sweet-natured, after having spent so many days with Kat as an unwilling companion?

Yet for all her anger and jealousy, exhaustion after the journey still overwhelmed her. She was asleep within a few minutes of lying down on the soft bed in her chamber.

She awakened with a start when a hand gently brushed her hair back from her face and neck. She jerked away, crying out wordlessly before she recognized Justin.

He sat on the edge of the bed, a goblet of wine in his hand. His doublet was unbuttoned, his hair mussed.

" 'Tis late," she whispered, then glanced at the clock on the man-tel. Less than two hours had passed since she went to bed. She had fallen asleep with the certainty that he would be spending the night with Margaret; her dreams had been filled with images of him lying entwined with his cousin on the adulteress's bed. Had she been wrong, then? "What do you want?"

He touched her hair again, running his fingers through it. "No welcome for me, Kat?" he asked, and she heard in the slurring of his voice that he was slightly drunk. "By my life, you seemed reluctant to leave me a few hours ago. And I was sorry to see you leave."

His hand moved to her shoulder, tracing the neckline of her smock. She shivered as she lay there staring up at him. Had he spent the last few hours merely drinking with Margaret? Was it possible that the ru-mors that he and Margaret were lovers were untrue? 'Twas clear that Margaret desired Justin: Kat had seen it in her eyes, and certainly the older woman had made herself as alluring as she could. Yet Justin was here now, with her.

His hand had reached the top fastening of her smock, which let go under his expert touch. Aware of the danger she was in—she did not want him, dared not want him—she reached up and caught his hand between both of hers.

"No, sweeting. Let go."

'Twas hopeless. She obeyed him, her hands falling to her sides again as he released the remaining two fastenings of her smock's high neck, then brushed the fabric aside. His fingers moved subtly on her skin, his touch feather-light. Her breath caught in her throat. He leaned down to kiss her—

—and she noticed for the first time a scent of orange blossoms and musk clinging to his doublet.

"Bastard!" she screamed. "You reek of your whore!" She tried to hit him, but in seconds he had her arms pinned to her sides. She glared at him, her vision blurred by tears of rage.

"My whore, Kat? And what are you?"

"I am *not* your whore!" Tears were running down her face now, and she was furious at herself for crying in her anger.

He stared at her for what seemed a long time, then released her, moving away a little. "No, you are not. Cry you mercy. I am drunken and can rule my tongue, it seems, no better than—"

He broke off suddenly, but she finished the statement for him. "No better than I?"

"I'faith, no better than you, wench," he admitted, and laughed raggedly. He shoved his hand through his hair, then stood and walked a few steps away before turning back to her. "Needs must that we talk."

"Very well."

"You showed yourself a most ungracious guest at the table tonight. Now mark me, Kat. You will have to behave better in the future. I am to Madrid in the morning, and until I return there will be no one to intercede with Margaret on your behalf if you push her too far."

"Then take me with you," she said, and had no need to feign the note of pleading in her voice. Holding the neckline of her smock together, she slid out of bed and took two steps toward him.

"Careful, sweeting," he said, and she stopped. "I might almost think you eager for my company."

"My lord, please—"

"No, Kat. And we'll have an end to this argument. And an end to your warfare with the lady Margaret. I'll be leaving one of my men here, so I'll know from him how well you have behaved."

"I am no child, to be told how—"

"You are my ward, Kat, for the duration of our stay in Spain, and will be treated as such."

"Even by you, my lord?" she asked, stung by his condescension. "You were not playing the guardian when you came to my chamber. You sought to share my bed." Her defiant gaze unwavering, Kat waited for his response.

"Yea, I did seek to lie with you," Justin said at last. "And now I can only wonder at that. Good night."

For several minutes after he had left she stood staring at the door, unsure whether to be hurt or relieved. Finally she shook her head, crawled back into bed, and huddled under the covers, chilled now despite the fire. 'Sdeath, she would *not* let him hurt her, she decided just before falling asleep again. She was relieved that he would leave her alone. She was. She would swear to that on all the Bibles in Christendom.

Justin and his party were ready to leave by dawn.

Standing in the courtyard watching them, Kat shivered despite her velvet nightgown; the breeze was a chilly one, the stones of the court cold beneath her bare feet. She had been awakened only a few minutes earlier, by her maid, who had in turn been awakened by the sound of a letter being slid under the door. 'Twas a note from Justin, impersonal advice from a guardian to a ward, primarily an admonition that she show proper respect for the lady Margaret.

Kat's gaze veered from the servants now mounting their horses to the lovely woman standing a dozen paces from them, watching Justin approach her.

Margaret looked as though she needed sleep more than respect this morning. Kat had gotten a close look at her face as she brushed past, and had seen that there were circles under Margaret's eyes that her artful painting could not conceal. Kat had taken some solace from that, thinking that Margaret, having failed to keep Justin with her, might have been too troubled to sleep. That solace had lasted only a few seconds before it occurred to Kat that Lord Harwood might have returned to his cousin's bedchamber after bidding her good night.

Of certain there seemed no quarrel between them now, as Justin took his cousin's hand and then kissed her cheek as he bade her farewell. Kat could not look away, so she saw, as Justin turned back toward his men, a look of triumph cross Margaret's face.

Kat could not bring herself to cross the courtyard to bid them Godspeed. The memory of Justin's last words to her last night was too strong, reinforced as it was by that coldly civil letter he had planned as his last remarks to her before leaving for Madrid. Like enough, he did not want to speak to her now. She was turning back toward the door, about to return to her bedchamber, when she saw that he was riding toward her. She waited for him.

"Good morrow, Kat," he said gently. "Have you read my letter?"

She nodded. "Fear not, my lord. I shall show her the respect she deserves."

He chuckled. "Truly, I would have you show her more respect than that." He sobered then. "Do so for your own sake, girl, for your safety. No matter how much it tries you. Remember, 'tis only for a few weeks."

To her shame, she felt close to tears again, so she merely nodded. He looked questioningly at her, as if he had hoped for something more.

Then Kat heard a rustle of silken petticoats. Margaret was coming toward them.

"I wish you a safe journey, my lord," Kat said huskily. "God speed."

She retreated to the house then, not wishing to see Margaret bid him another tender farewell. Alone in the sanctuary of her chamber, the maid gone about some other duties, she reread his letter, started to throw it onto the embers of the fire, then hesitated. She looked at it again, folded it carefully, and placed it in her cloakbag, unsure why she was saving it.

Her shoulders sagging with weariness, Margaret walked heavily up the stairs to her chambers. With Justin and his men gone, her forced smile had been replaced by the frown she had worn much of the night.

He had not returned to her. She still could scarce believe that. And yet he had kissed her this morning. She had felt sure then that, upon his return from Madrid, he would tell her that he had changed his mind and would help her. And then he had gone to say good-bye to his ward, having left her for last, as if that farewell were the most important to him. Even though Margaret had managed to speak to him after that, and touch his hand for an instant, she again felt uncertain of him. And she could not doubt that the woman pretending to be his ward was part of the problem.

So two messengers would be sent out today. One to Bilbao, there to take ship for France. Perchance Justin would yet agree to help her, after he returned from Madrid, but she would not wait till then, lest Marchant find another patron for his English courtier friend. She would have to sell some of her jewels to make up for the money she must needs send Marchant, but she could see no sure alternative to that sacrifice, not with Justin behaving so ungraciously . . .

And the second messenger would ride north, to a castle in the Pyrenees. Margaret began to smile again at the thought of her plan and its fulfillment. 'Twas the one hope that had sustained her through the endless, sleepless night, and now, recalling how lovely Kat had looked in that rich nightgown and how Justin had spent long moments speaking privately to her, Margaret took a visceral pleasure in the thought of the invitation that she would send to her friend in Navarra today.

CHAPTER 22

On the morning of her sixth day at La Casa de las Rosas, Kat gathered together the books that Margaret had lent her and started toward Margaret's chambers. She had finished them all, though the reading matter was not to her taste. There had been no romances nor books of jests among those Margaret let her see; instead, Kat had been offered religious treatises written by English Catholic exiles at Louvain and Douai. Dry matter indeed, and not likely to convert her, but still she had read the books most carefully. Perchance, if Margaret would discuss the writings with her, she might learn something more about the countess, something of use to Walsingham.

Besides, she had naught else to do. She was not allowed to go riding, or to take long walks. She would fain have whiled away some of the idle hours playing the virginals, but she had misread Margaret's intent when the countess bade her play, the evening after Justin left. Margaret had perchance expected Kat to admit that she could not play. 'Twas clear from Margaret's stormy expression that she had not been pleased by what she heard, and she had soon ordered Kat to stop, complaining that the virginals were out of tune and she would not have them played. Since then Kat had spent much of her time alone in her chamber. She still chatted with the young maidservant when she saw the girl, but she had decided against trying to befriend any of the servants, as she had befriended the boy on the ship. There was no way to tell which of the Spanish servants might be spies for the Inquisition. Like enough, mere Englishness was cause for suspicion here. Margaret herself kept the door of her antechamber locked.

Reaching that door, Kat knocked. The door was opened at once, by Edwina, who looked even more surprised than Kat felt.

"Marry, I thought you were the Lady Margaret," Edwina said.

"So she is not here?" Kat asked, disappointed. "I have brought these books back, and would fain borrow more, if she would lend them to me."

"If you come back in a quarter of an hour, belike she will be here then," Edwina said, starting to close the door.

"May I not wait for her instead?" Kat said quickly, and Edwina hesitated, a doubtful look on her face. The maidservant had been very friendly at first, but had become wary as Margaret made it more and more clear that Kat was not entirely welcome here. Kat had never had much chance to talk to Edwina alone, and it occurred to her now that Edwina would be less likely than any of the other servants here to report to the Inquisition. Mayhap less likely to gossip about her mistress too, Kat thought—but she doubted that. Edwina seemed a born gossip. And even if Edwina would not say much, Kat would at least have a chance to look around Margaret's chambers. "I would fain put these books down."

"Are they heavy?" Edwina said, throwing the door wide and taking two of the books from Kat.

Kat stepped inside quickly, lest Edwina change her mind. She followed Edwina through the antechamber to the bedchamber, where the maid set the books down on a shelf.

"You have read all these?" Edwina asked, turning to take the remaining books from Kat.

"Aye. Have you read them?"

Edwina shook her head. "I can read a little, but not such matter as this. And nothing in Latin."

Kat nodded, remembering Margaret's amazement when she learned that her guest could read Latin. No doubt the countess had hoped then, as when she asked Kat to play the virginals, that the younger woman must needs confess to lacking that ability. Had not the books been theological tomes, and Margaret so zealous in her faith, Kat suspected that she would have been denied reading, too.

She looked around the bedchamber, her gaze lingering on the bed, as she wondered how often Margaret and Justin had shared it. Then she shook her head. There was no time for such thoughts now. She picked up one of the books on the shelf, determined to learn, if nothing more, which other books Margaret read. But as she opened the book, a thin sheaf of papers slid out; she caught it before it could fall to the floor.

"What's this?" she asked, unfolding one of the pieces of paper, seeing at once that it was a letter. The signature stunned her. Jesu, 'twas from the author of the book! "Does the countess keep notes of her own thoughts on each of these books?" she asked innocently. "She must be a scholar indeed." A glance sideways at Edwina sufficed to assure Kat that the maid had believed Kat's praise of Margaret and was pleased with it.

"I warrant you, my mistress is a true scholar, and perchance those may be notes she has written." Edwina leaned closer. "Nay, 'tis a letter—one of many that Lady Margaret has received. 'Tis from the man who wrote that book, I trow. She has many such letters. These scholars write to her oft, for they value her opinions."

Do they, in faith? Kat thought, wondering if Master Walsingham knew of this. Aloud, she said, "They are wiser than John Knox, then, that they do not doubt all women's judgment."

Edwina nodded vigorously. "Indeed they are. See, my lady has Dr. Allen's letters here"—opening another book—"and here"—opening yet another. "And she has letters from Nicholas Sander and Thomas Stapleton and Thomas Harding."

Kat shook her head, honestly amazed. Oh, for an hour alone here, that she might read all that these exiles had written to Margaret!

"You will not believe me?" Edwina asked, having misread Kat's silence. "Here is the latest missive from Lawrence Vaux." And she took a folded sheet of paper from one book and thrust it into Kat's hands. "There. Look. Is that not his very signature?"

"Yea, it is," Kat said softly. "In sooth, I am greatly amazed . . ." She picked up the other letters, glancing through them, wondering how soon Edwina would snatch them back. Oh, for only ten minutes to read! But 'twould not do to have Edwina think she was reading closely. She shook her head again, and forced a laugh. "I warrant you, it is a struggle for me to read the Latin they write in, but 'tis clear as the very ether compared to these scribbling hands . . ."

"Do they write carelessly?" Edwina asked, and Kat nodded, though her own secretary hand was often no more legible. But Edwina had believed her, and now all Kat need do was grimace from time to time and give her head a shake, and the maidservant would haply let her read all . . . if she read swiftly enough.

She skimmed the letters, her hands shaking a little as she read of the exiles' activities, of the seminary William Allen had founded. This was ill news, but she doubted if much of it would truly be news to Walsingham and his agents. But the queen's spy-master would wish to know how much aid Justin's cousin was giving the exiles. Of Justin's own role, however, there was nothing, other than a line in a letter imploring Margaret to seek her cousin's aid in publishing a catechism in England. Kat smiled faintly at that. Would that she could tell Sparrow that all the queen had to fear from Justin was this!

She opened another letter then, and a tightly folded sheet of paper fell to the floor. She stooped to pick it up before Edwina could reach it. Catching a scent of fine perfume, she held the paper near her nose. It *was* scented—unlike any of the other letters. And the paper was of better quality . . . She frowned as she unfolded it, and Edwina moved closer, peering at the letter over her shoulder.

" 'Tis French," the maidservant said.

"Is it?" Kat asked, again pretending ignorance. "Can you read French?"

Edwina shook her head.

"Nor can I," Kat lied, reading as swiftly as possible. Alack, this truly was a scribbling hand, unlike the others, and she could not decipher all . . . but what was this? Whoever wrote the letter assured Margaret that his friend was better situated than her cousin for the work they had planned, and bade her reply soon, and send the amount of money they had agreed upon, lest—

Kat turned the letter over, leaving off reading the text for a moment to glance down at the signature. Pierre de Marchant. The name meant nothing to her. She was about to resume reading when Edwina snatched the letter from her hands. Kat stared at her, amazed. Then she, too, heard the footsteps. She turned toward the door just as Margaret entered the antechamber.

"Edwina, are—" Margaret said, then broke off as she saw Kat. "What are you doing here?"

"She came to return the books, my lady," Edwina said hastily.

"Aye, and stayed to read my letters, I see."

"Nay, I did not—" Kat began, but was interrupted by the maid.

"She has but glanced at them, my lady. I pray your pardon if this has offended you, but I wished her to see the signatures, that she would believe such learned men have written to you."

"In good sooth, madam," Kat said, "I should not have doubted what your maid told me, but I had not known that any English gentlewoman in Spain had such influence, save for Jane Dormer, and . . ." Her voice trailed off as Margaret frowned. Had it been a mistake to mention the other maid of honor to Queen Mary who had married a Spanish nobleman? Was it possible that Margaret was jealous of the Countess of Feria? "I trow that you must have even more influence than she does."

"In some circles, perchance," Margaret admitted grudgingly, but her frown was gone.

"Edwina told me that these scholars at Louvain and Douai ask your opinion of sundry matters. I would fain hear, too, what you think of Thomas Harding's writings. I have read Bishop Jewel's apology for the English Church"—that much was true, thanks to her cousin Blanche— "and I must confess that both men are so learned that I am not certain which to believe."

"You would have me explain their arguments to you?" Margaret asked, a thoughtful look on her face.

"Please it you, if you would."

"I am going into Burgos this morning. Come with me. We will discuss this in the coach."

Kat had hoped to discuss matters other than theology with the countess, but Margaret brushed aside all questions about Thomas Harding and the other exiles at Louvain and Douai. By the time they reached Burgos, Kat was heartily sick of playing the humble student. Her mood was not helped, either, by the stares she received while she followed Margaret through one shop after another. While Margaret had chosen to wear a somber, high-necked kirtle and gown, and her hems brushed the ground, Kat was perforce wearing English fashions, and people gaped at her as if she were a freak displayed in Fleet Street.

Her choler increased when Margaret insisted on showing her the cathedral, where they spent more than an hour. Kat was bored by the priest who guided them around, telling them at great length of the cathedral's history. And she disliked the profusion of spires and the opulent decorations. She much preferred Paul's, or the simplicity of the cathedral at Chichester, with its single spire.

She was in a black humor by the time they returned to the coach and started back to the Casa de las Rosas, and did not think before answering when Margaret asked her opinion of the cathedral.

" 'Tis overwrought," she snapped, and would have added *like all things Spanish, save for the meals*, but seeing Margaret's stunned expression stopped her. "I prefer St. Paul's," she said, more mildly.

"Paul's? 'Tis a true house of prayer, Paul's. It has all the sanctity of Stourbridge Fair, or Paris Garden."

"Nay, 'tis not so bad as that!" Kat protested, but laughed. " 'Tis English, at least. D'you not miss England?"

"Not St. Paul's," Margaret said with a fleeting grin, and for an instant she seemed a young girl again, a mischievous girl. "I miss the Thames. I would fain see London Bridge again, and Richmond, and Hampton Court. Yea, and the countryside. This"—she gestured toward the window, the rolling green hills beyond—"is not so harsh and strange a land as the rest of Castile, but neither is it my home."

She fell silent then.

Kat teetered on the brink of sympathy and then, cursing herself for being a fool, fell over it. "Would that you could return," she said quietly.

"Yea," Margaret agreed, a dreamy expression on her face. "And we shall, when Elizabeth is gone. Pray God, 'twill be soon."

Kat shivered then, more ashamed than ever for feeling so much as an instant's pity for this woman who was an enemy of her queen. She was very quiet during the rest of the ride back to the house, but Margaret seemed not to notice, and favored Kat with a smile from time to time as she reminisced about England.

When they reached the courtyard, they saw several unfamiliar horses and riders. As Margaret descended from the carriage, her steward hurried over to tell her that Don Rafael de Vincente y Marcos had stopped to see her on his way home to Navarra after visiting friends in Burgos; the men were his servants. The don himself was awaiting her in the hall.

"*Se ha de alojar aquí esta noche como huésped. Qué se acomoden sus criados,*" she told him, then turned to Kat, just as the girl stepped down to the ground. "We will have a guest for supper tonight, a nobleman I have met at court. Pray behave as Justin's ward should."

Don Rafael de Vincente y Marcos was a tall, strikingly handsome man in his mid-thirties. His black hair was thick and wavy. Smooth olive skin was stretched taut over the fine bones of his face. His black eyes were wide-set, beneath arching brows; his nose was aquiline; his lips thin but beautifully shaped. He had beautiful teeth, too, and his frequent smiles were dazzling.

During their supper, he smiled most frequently at Kat. And he had insisted that they speak in English, for her sake, though he confessed that her Spanish was excellent.

Margaret, dressed in some of her finest clothes, her hair brushed until it outshone the gold pins holding it in place, could not have been more pleased.

She had first met the don ten years ago, at court. She had been flattered by his attentions, his pretty speeches and gifts. He was a master of the *galanteo en palacio*, the public wooing of the ladies of the court, and yet, even knowing his mastery of such court incense, she had been convinced that only Don Rafael's fear of Antonio had kept him from going beyond the formal game of love they all played to a serious attempt to make her his mistress. Rafael was known to be attracted to blond women; his late wife—who had died but a year earlier, at the age of eighteen—had been blond. Margaret would never know now whether Rafael would have become her lover: she had not been daring enough to invite such attentions until her last few months at court, and then Rafael had not been among the *galantendores* who sought her company. She had seen that he was stalking much younger game.

She smiled at the girl seated across the table, less envious of her youth this evening than at any time during the past several days. She had even seen that Kat was given perfumed soap for her bath, and perfume and paints to use this evening, that she might appear at her best.

"I wish I could show you my home, *El Nido de Aguilas*—the Eagle's Nest," Rafael said to Kat, and went on to tell her of the castle, built four centuries ago on a promontory that could be readily defended, of the magnificent view of the valley below, of the fine hunting in the surrounding forests. "Señora," he said, turning to Margaret, "you must come for a visit, and bring Katherine with you."

"I would gladly, Don Rafael, but must await the return of my cousin. He may wish to return to England quickly, and his ward will go with him. But tell me, sir, how fares your son? He must be thirteen now. Or is he fourteen?"

"Thirteen." He looked back at Kat, the expression of disappointment that had crossed his face when Margaret mentioned Kat returning to England replaced by a melancholy smile. "I regret that I have only one child. My wife died when he was two years old, died after giving birth to a daughter, who lived for only a few days. I have lived alone with my son since then."

Margaret coughed to hide her amusement at his glib dismissal of a long string of mistresses.

"The air is close in here," she said. "I have planned to have our banquet in the north garden. The servants will have taken the sweets out there already." She rose, and an instant later Rafael was at her side, looking regretfully at Kat, who still had not moved, apparently unsure whether she was to accompany them.

"Please it you, join us, Katherine," Margaret told her. "I have ordered that the virginals be carried out to the garden—yea, I had them tuned—and I would have you play for us . . ."

Under a deep blue sky decorated with clouds tinted by the setting sun, the silvery notes of the virginals were the only sounds to be heard for a time. Seated on a bench beside Rafael, Margaret bided her time, an occasional glance assuring her that the don was becoming even more enraptured of the girl.

Kat ended one of the melodies she was playing, looked questioningly toward them, and at Margaret's nod began another. Rafael sighed.

"What think you of Justin's ward?" Margaret asked softly.

"She is as accomplished as she is lovely. A true gentlewoman!"

Margaret shook her head. "You are already in love with her, Don Rafael."

"Doña Margaret, you wound me. You know the love I bear for you, and how I envy your husband—"

"Please, Don Rafael," she said, holding up her hand, "we are old friends, and you must know that I enjoy your company as no other's. But we must talk now, in earnest. There are things you must know. First, that Katherine is no true gentlewoman—"

"Margaret! You wrong her! *Dios*, how can you say . . . !" He gave her a searching look. "Oh, no, señora, do not give in to jealousy. You have no need to be jealous, and it belittles you to belittle her thus."

It stung Margaret that he would think her jealous of the girl. "I speak truly, Don Rafael," she said in a sharp voice, then, more sweetly, continued. "She is no gentlewoman. She is not of gentle birth. Nor is she my cousin's ward."

"Not his ward? But she did come from England with him?" Margaret nodded. "Then what . . . ?" His voice trailed off as he turned his gaze toward Kat again. "Surely not his mistress?"

"By my life, she is," Margaret said, surprised at how easy the lie was.

"She acts very much the lady."

"One of her talents, one of many. And not the most important to Lord Harwood."

She had sounded more bitter than she intended, and he looked at her then, his eyes narrowed.

"You do not approve of her influence over your cousin?" he asked.

For a moment she wondered if he had somehow heard that she and Justin were lovers. Haply there were rumors about it at court—it seemed there were always rumors. She had not considered that what she was doing now might add fuel to those rumors, but it was already too late to help that.

"No, Don Rafael. Nor, in truth, does my cousin. She pleased him at first, and he made the mistake of treating her entirely too well. Now she demands too much."

"To be introduced as his ward, when they travel abroad?"

"Just so. He would be rid of her, but the girl has been using all her wiles to keep him from sending her away. Such women can be very persuasive."

Don Rafael nodded, his gaze again resting on Kat.

" 'Twould be best," Margaret continued, "if she were with a man who could rule her properly."

"And your cousin is not the man?"

"Alas, no."

"But I may be the man?"

"Perchance. I have given this much thought."

"Indeed." He moved closer to her, taking her hand in his. "Tell me of your thoughts . . ."

———

"Look at this." Margaret reached out to touch a hedge clipped in the shape of a crouching lion. "Francisco is such a marvelous gardener, so good with topiary work. Antonio brought him from Seville for me."

The wizened old gardener, who had just finished trimming the hedge of the new shoots that were blurring the outline of the topiary lion, looked up as his name was mentioned. For an instant Kat thought she saw wariness in his expression; then, as he noticed that his mistress was in an unusually good mood, a wide smile revealing missing teeth cracked his wrinkled, dark face.

Kat was pleased to see that even the servants benefited from Margaret's good humor these days—though, she thought wryly, most of them must be baffled by the change. In the days since their visit to Burgos, Margaret had been a most agreeable hostess and a pleasant companion for Kat. The countess still would not talk of her friends at Louvain and Douai, saying that to do so would seem boastful, but in other ways she seemed open and trusting, as though glad to have another Englishwoman for company. Twice they had had breakfast on the balcony of Margaret's bedchamber, and the countess had given Kat some chocolate to drink, and had shown her that 'twas best to wash down the thick chocolate with a swallow of water. They had laughed together when Margaret had shown her the *tarima*, the cushioned dais on which Spanish women were supposed to sit when they received their guests, in the fashion of the Moors who had once ruled Spain. The countess had allowed Kat to play the virginals whenever she wished, and each day they had spent at least an hour or two working in the garden. Margaret had even lent Kat an old calico kirtle so that she would not have to risk damaging her own clothing, though Kat had refused Margaret's offer to have Edwina alter the kirtle for her: 'twas too much work to do on a kirtle that she would return to her hostess in another week or two. Kat sometimes felt a twinge of guilt at the thought that she would be betraying Margaret's trust when she told Walsingham of the aid the countess gave to the exiles.

Margaret herself was dressed simply today in an old kirtle, her jewelry limited to a thin gold chain. Following her down the hill, toward the stone wall that bordered the garden, Kat thought that her hostess looked more like a maidservant in her mistress's castaway clothing than the mistress of the house herself.

They were cutting roses from the vines along the wall when Kat heard a horse whicker, the sound surprisingly close. She looked up, at the woods between the wall and the road. The sound had reminded her that she had not been riding since reaching Burgos. Perhaps Margaret, in her new, benign mood, would agree to let her go riding . . .

"Ka—" Margaret's cry was muffled suddenly.

Kat whirled around. Twenty feet away, Margaret struggled in the grip of a heavily built man whose face was concealed by a mask. He had clapped his hand over her mouth so she could not scream. Another man, also masked, came scrambling over the wall between Kat and Margaret, only to land sprawling among the roses, swearing at the tangle of thorny brambles.

Kat glanced toward the house. The only servant in sight was the old gardener, who must be partly deaf, for he had not heard Margaret cry out. Kat would not call to him—what help could he give against these rogues?

The second intruder was still trying to free himself from the roses. She sprinted past him, toward the man holding Margaret, and seized his sword's hilt as he stared disbelieving at her. As she yanked the weapon free of the sheath, he grabbed for it and then screamed as naked steel slid through his hand. He snatched his hand back, spattering himself and Margaret with drops of blood. She broke free then, but before she could get away he cuffed her, and she fell senseless to the ground.

Kat backed away, holding the sword in the low ward, though her wrist and arm ached already. The weapon was far heavier than the swords she had used for practice. The second attacker was crawling out of the roses, toward her. She lifted the sword with both hands and swung it, clublike, so the flat of the blade struck the side of his head. Nick would have disapproved of the blow—'twas in none of his manuals on the art of fence—but it sufficed: the man crashed sideways into the brambles.

Hearing scrabbling sounds, she began to retreat up the slope toward the house just as two more rogues climbed over the wall. More nimble than their companion, they landed on their feet and came toward her, their swords drawn. The man whose sword hand she had cut approached her too, his dagger drawn.

Aware of a sudden that someone was behind her and closing fast, she spun around—then managed to stay her blow just in time. 'Twas the gardener, his only weapon the pruning knife. As he ran past her, she cried out for him to stop, fearing he would be cut down, but the rogue he threw himself toward merely laughed and struck the knife from the old man's hand with his sword, then, catching the gardener's sleeve, hurled him against the wall, where he crumpled and lay still.

Kat retreated further up the slope, still holding the sword in both hands, as the intruders fanned out around her. 'Twould be useless to scream: no one from the house could reach her in time to help. She continued to back away, frighteningly conscious of the weight of the sword, knowing it was too heavy for her to wield expertly. But if she could put enough distance between herself and her attackers, she might drop the sword and run: these rogues would be at a disadvantage in their heavy riding boots.

"Diego!" one of the men called then, to someone standing behind Kat, to her left.

She turned a quarter of the way around before she realized she had been tricked. She swung back, and the two men who had come within a few paces of her danced back as she took a step toward them. But where was the third rogue? She looked around, and a shadow swept across her face, and then something struck the back of her head, sending her tumbling forward into oblivion.

Margaret lay where she had fallen for several minutes after the last of the men left the garden, then sat up slowly, rubbing her neck. Before they fled, taking Kat with them, one of the men had yanked the simple chain she wore from around her neck, and it had bitten into her soft flesh for an instant before snapping. She hoped it would not leave a mark for long. The chain itself was no loss, a cheap thing Edwina had given her.

She looked down at her clothes and grimaced. They were old clothes, and she did not care that they were torn, but blood from the man's cut hand had seeped through the fabric of her sleeve to her skin. Blood had spattered onto her face, too; she wiped at it, then grimaced at her bloody fingers before rubbing them clean on her half-kirtle.

She started then, hearing a low-pitched, terrible sound.

The gardener was still alive, and groaning in pain. That was fortunate; she would have disliked losing his expert help. She would not have risked him at all, had she not thought a witness would be of use. Thank God she had had the foresight to tell Don Rafael that none of her servants should be killed, unless needs must.

He groaned again, and she grated her teeth at the sound. Slowly she got to her feet, conscious of a multitude of bruises. She flung an unruly strand of hair out of her face. Then, taking a deep breath, she began to scream.

CHAPTER 23

It was a small purse of worn leather, bulging with coins. The drawstrings were of leather, but the purse was hanging from a chain that would discourage any cutpurse.

The chain itself hung from a belt fastened about a jerkin that had been fitted over a tall wooden block on a chair. Cheap, tarnished bells festooned both the jerkin and the belt.

Think of the block as your cony. Jack could hear the advice clearly in his mind. Marry, he had heard it often enough with his ears. *You do not want your cony to feel the purse touched, nor lifted away.*

Jack cupped his left hand around the bottom of the purse—delicately, delicately. One of the bells on the jerkin shuddered but did not ring out his failure.

"Bene, bene," was the whispered comment from behind him, the voice the same that he had imagined a moment before.

Steadying the purse with his left hand, raising it just a bit, he began to work at the drawstrings with his right hand. The chain trembled, but not enough to stir the belt and set its bells to ringing. Looser now. Looser. He could slip his fingers into the purse. He did so, touched the cold edge of a coin, reached further—

And the belt twitched, its bells jangling.

He jerked his hand away, swearing.

The children laughed behind his back.

Before he could turn around, the laughter was stilled by a sharp word from the gray-haired man who had been standing just behind Jack. The little boy and girl looked contrite, but Jack had seen them look thus a dozen times so far this afternoon, and still Bess's kinchin co and kinchin mort had laughed at the next failure.

"Will you try it again, lad?" Ned Daughton asked, a sympathetic look on his face.

"Anon," he said. "I would practice the other again first." In truth, he felt he needed no such practice, but he did need to restore his confidence in himself.

He stepped around the old man, ducking his head to avoid the sloping ceiling. This, the largest of the three chambers beneath the roof of the Turk's Sword, the alehouse that Bess called home, was Ned's bedchamber during the night and a school and shop by day. All about were scraps of leather. Ned had been an apprentice cordwainer at a monastery in Lancashire when Henry VIII dissolved the religious houses after his break with Rome, and the orphan, like most of the other laborers employed by the monks, had found himself without work, with little choice but to become a vagrant and live by his wits. Ned had learned enough of the cordwainer's craft to earn some money still by making cheap shoes for some of his neighbors here in Southwark, but his skill at nipping and foisting had once earned him more. Even now, when his gnarled fingers made it too risky for him to nip purses himself, his skill in teaching the thieves' art was prized highly enough that his students paid well.

All his students, that is, save Jack, whom he treated as a son. Jack had brought Bess home safely, and last night Ned had told Jack that he liked him better than Bess's late husband, Will Morsted, a sometimes honest mariner who had drowned two years before, washed overboard during a storm while crossing the Channel on a merchant ship bound for Antwerp.

Standing before a second purse, this one suspended from a rope by leather thongs, Jack flexed and wiggled his fingers while he thought again how Bess's ill fortune of several weeks ago had become his good luck. She had been forced to leave London to avoid the attentions of an upright man, Tom Waver, who counted the Turk's Sword among the alehouses he considered his territory. Bess had warned Jack against Waver before they reached London, but the warning had been unnecessary. Waver was gone, arrested for killing a watchman; he was hanged at Tyburn the day after Bess's return. Robin Dalling, Waver's lieutenant rogue, was said to be the upright man now, but as yet he had not shown his face at the Turk's Sword. Word had spread quickly that Bess had returned with a ruffler, and that her swordsman had killed an upright man in Sussex. Dalling, Bess had predicted gleefully, was a coward and would be loath to test Jack's swordsmanship. So now Jack found himself acknowledged as the protector of all those vagabonds who congregated at the Turk's Sword. And with most of them, he had their affection, too, for at Bess's urging he had given away the gybes they had taken from the dead upright man.

He should have felt safe here. But his money was running out, and he did not yet know how he would replace it.

Not this way, he prayed as he took the knife and horn sheath from his pocket and slid his thumb into the sheath. There was no honor in being a cutpurse, as any pickpurse or pickpocket could tell you: the more

skillful foists felt nothing but disdain for lowly nips. Jack had not wanted
to settle for less than learning to foist, but Ned had insisted that he
start with the cuttle and horn sheath first, as nipping was easier to learn.
Jack had mastered cutting purses on his second afternoon of lessons,
while he had been trying to pick that purse for more than a week, and
still without success.

He reached toward the purse strings confidently. Ned had sharpened
the cuttle just yesternight, complaining good-humoredly that he used
grindstone and whetstone more often than cuttles themselves these days.
Jack knew that the cuttle's blade would slice through the leather as if
'twere butter. He would have the purse in his hand in an instant—

Then bells rang out, the chiming sounding like mocking laughter
to his ears. For a moment he could scarce believe that he had failed,
and would have thought that the sound came from behind him. But the
rope to which the leather purse strings were tied was still trembling,
and it was perfectly quiet in the room behind him. Too quiet.

He turned to see Ned looking disappointed. That hurt. Yet more
painful was the look of surprise on the children's faces, especially Tom's.
The five-year-old looked amazed that Jack could have failed such a simple test.

"Y'are tired, Jack," the old man told him. "Bess should be back
now. As like as not, she's below in the kitchen, having a cup of ale.
Why not go talk to her for a while?"

Jack took a deep breath, expelled it in a long sigh, then nodded.
He did not speak; he was afraid to say anything, in his current humor. He set down the knife and horn sheath and was turning toward
the door when Bess's three-year-old daughter Amy ran to him and held
her arms up. He picked her up, and she planted a kiss sticky from a
violet comfit on his cheek.

"Kiss mama for me," she whispered.

"There's pleasant work," Jack said, laughing as he set her down.
She clung to his leg for a moment before skipping back to her brother.
"Shall I have anything brought up to you, Father Ned?"

"Nay, there's wine enough left in this bottle," Ned said with a
smile. "I thank you, but you may save your lour."

The remark had been meant as a kind one, but it stung Jack anyway.
He tried to smile, but it felt more like a grimace, and he gave up the
attempt as soon as he had turned away from Ned. Descending the stairs,
he touched his purse and was dismayed anew by how light it felt. He
must have some more lour, and soon.

Jack could hear the talk from the kitchen well before he reached it, but
at this hour he could still hear separate voices, even those not raised in

anger or celebration. The din would come later, when more vagabonds arrived at the alehouse to drink, or to find a place to couch for the night—sometimes in the small barn behind the house—or, if Roger Chickwell were in a good humor, to fence their stolen wares. The last could not always be depended upon, for sometimes Chickwell would remember his oaths to the justices of the peace who had licensed the Turk's Sword, but much of the time Chickwell would buy, and he would give as much as the crown for a pound's worth that the pawn-keepers gave, and sometimes more if he liked the thief.

Bess was in the kitchen, as Ned had predicted, but though she smiled at Jack and waved as soon as she saw him, it was clear that she did not want his company at once, for she presently returned to talking with the woman who sat with her at the smallest of the three tables. Clare Mantry was no older than Bess, and had been her friend since childhood, but the autem mort looked ten years Bess's elder, with sun-browned skin that was already lined, several teeth missing, and a harried expression that never left her face for more than a few seconds during one of her fleeting smiles. Marriage to a hooker had not spared Clare the necessity of spending long hours begging, for her husband was a clumsy drunkard who drank away any lour gained from the stuff he hooked. Jack wondered that Tom Mantry felt no shame.

Yea, and what of you? a sly voice inside his brain asked. 'Twas true that since Bess had realized that the once-abundant money in his purse was vanishing, she had begun spending much of each day away from him, vanishing into the lanes of Southwark to return in the evening with coins or food, or both. It shamed him, and at times it puzzled him to feel that way, for none of the other rogues at the Turk's Sword would have qualms about their women begging or stealing for them, but the feeling was there, not to be denied.

"Jack! Sussex Jack!"

Jack looked around to see who had called to him, and smiled. Simon Norbroke's loud voice would have astonished those people who had taken pity on him today and thrown coins into his clack-dish. Simon was a dommerar. Away from this bousing ken, he folded his tongue under and pretended to be mute, begging silently for alms, all his eloquence in his pitiful gestures and the pathetic way his rags hung on him. Jack had once mentioned to Bess that it seemed the easiest way to beg, but she had told him it could be dangerous, for she had heard of a dommerar who had made the mistake of begging from a surgeon who, discovering how he had been fooled, had cut out the beggar's tongue to end the deception permanently.

"Jack, come meet this rogue. Here's Little George Crispyn, a prigger of prancers, come from Hampshire, and he says he'll turn tinker."

"Well." Jack sat down on the bench across the table from Little George, who was in fact some inches taller than Jack and half again as heavy. "Why would an honest horse stealer turn knavish tinker?"

"Truth to tell," Simon said with a laugh, "he's grown too fat, and must needs go afoot and lead the prancers he prigs, lest they become shoulder-shotten and swayed in the back from his riding them."

"Stow you!" Little George gave the dommerar a shove, but a gentle one. "To the ruffian with you—aye, if even he will have your stinking black soul!" He chuckled. "Y'are an honest dommerar, for your speech is always dishonest. Too fat, am I? A plague on you lean fellows! You find not enough in your clack-dishes at day's end to buy supper, but are too proud to confess as much, and so needs must that there's virtue in starving. 'Sblood, I did well in Hampshire, until last month."

"Last month?" Jack asked, and the horse thief's gaze returned to him.

"Aye, last month. 'Twas to have been a good month for me. I had prigged me two of the finest prancers—and so easily, by the mass! Happened upon them in a wood, where their riders had left them hobbled. One was a great black stallion, black as sea-coal, the other a roan Barbary gelding. Horses fit for the Rome mort herself, they were. I took them to Oxford and sold them there. I rode the roan Barbary, and a swift little horse it was! But the stallion was too wild by half, fit only for breeding. Jesu, I dared not ride it! He had a cloud in his face, to give fair warning, while the roan Barb had a white star on its forehead, to tell all of its sweet temper. I will not sell a horse with a cloud in its face, nay, 'tis too difficult by half. I found some white paint and rid him of that cloud."

Jack had tensed as the prigger of prancers described the horses. Again he felt a memory just out of reach, close as the momentarily forgotten name of an acquaintance not met for too long a time . . .

"So you had good fortune with the horses?" Simon asked, confused.

"Yea, so I thought then, lour enough to live like a king for a time. I found me a chamber at a fine inn, and spent two days drinking and wenching, and then the bluecoats came, aye, with the man who had bought the horses. I told them that I had had the horses from a man who had bought them in London to make the journey to Oxford. 'Twas no fault of mine, said I, if the stallion had a cloud in his face, for the man was wroth that the paint had washed off, and I said I was greatly wroth, too, at having been cheated. But there was more. The horses were stolen, the bluecoats said, and would have me find for them the man who had sold them to me. Aye, and they would stay with me, they would, while I looked for him, and would let me sleep in the jail overnight, to save them coming to my inn each morning to start the search again. But they were lean fellows, weasels like our dommerar here"—jerking a thumb at Simon—"and I shook them off soon enough and took to my heels, never looking back. 'Twas as well, for I learned from a friend that the bluecoats were looking for me all over Oxford, aye, and Berkshire as well." He paused to gulp down some ale, then wiped his mouth with the back of his hand. " 'Tis a pity how a man of my size can be easily spotted. But safer here in London than in the countryside, say I."

Jack pressed his hands flat on the table to still their trembling. Bluecoats. It troubled him that he felt he should remember something about two horses that were of concern to bluecoats. Was he also a prigger of prancers, then? Or was he wanted for worse crimes than that?

"You'll likely be safer here," Simon said then, a bit doubtfully. Most London rogues felt contempt for their country brethren. Jack knew that only Bess's avowal of his courage in rescuing her had spared him the hostility he would have encountered, had he come to the Turk's Sword alone. But the horse thief seemed unconcerned: perchance he was unaware of what he might face here, or, more likely, at his size he had little fear of any man.

Little George was gazing at him curiously. "Y'are the upright man here?"

Jack shook his head.

"This scarecrow Simon told me I must meet you above all others here. Yet if you are not an upright man—"

"He's a ruffler," Simon said quickly. "There is no upright man here."

"Oh." Little George gave Jack a shrewd glance. "What share d'you ask, then?"

"None."

The horse stealer's jaw dropped.

" 'Tis true," Simon confessed, sounding almost ashamed. "He'll have none of our lour."

"The ruffian! Say you so?" Little George stared at Jack with interest and not a little wonder, as if he were some fabulous beast.

Which, Jack thought, he might well seem to many of these rogues. The alehouse's patrons were enjoying their freedom and the opportunity to keep all their lour, but they were used to serving an upright man. It puzzled them that Jack would neither accept tribute nor agree to lead the more daring thieves in armed robberies. And if they had known that Jack spent his afternoon practicing the arts of a foist and a cutpurse, they would have been more than puzzled—they would have been dumb-stricken. He smiled at the thought. Even Simon would be as mute then, here at the Turk's Sword, as he was out in the streets and alleys of London.

Little George would have bought him a cup of ale, but Jack, wanting Bess's company more than ever, declined the offer. After bidding the horse thief welcome to the Turk's Sword, he left Simon and Little George and started back toward Bess's table. He brushed past two heavily painted doxies. The younger one, only twelve years of age, smiled invitingly as she arched her back and pushed her budding breasts against the thin stuff of her bodice. Jack felt pity for her, but no lust. Though the girl had been broken only six months ago by Tom Waver, as like as not she was already diseased.

He sat down beside Bess. As usual, she wore no paint; she needed none. The smile she gave him displayed perfect teeth, a rare sight here in Southwark, and he thought how much more fortunate she had been than Clare Mantry, or Mary Whitston, the young whore. Even though Bess's parents had died, of the sweating sickness so common here in Southwark, when she was just three years old, she had had Ned Daughton and his late wife to take her in. Ned had taught her to steal at an early age, knowing that she would otherwise learn soon enough from other children and he could teach her better than they. She had never been caught, since she always chose her victims carefully: with Ned providing for her, she was never driven by desperation to take foolish chances, and during the years she had been married to Will Morsted she had not stolen at all.

Now, though, Ned could provide less support; he could teach others to nip, but was too old and slow to risk nipping a purse himself. So Bess was forced to spend more time away from the bousing ken, more time stealing. She could do that, or whore. Or watch her family starve.

"I have brought you something," she told him, picking up a bundle wrapped in paper that had been lying on the table. "Open it."

He untied the string and folded the paper back to reveal a length of fine cloth.

"Linen, and good quality," Bess told him, a hint of pride in her voice. "I'll make you a new shirt."

"Thank you," he said softly, fingering the cloth. Had she stolen it, he wondered, or bought it with coins that had been stolen or exchanged for stolen goods? It mattered not one whit: however she had obtained the linen, it still shamed him to take gifts from her. Yet 'twould hurt her if he refused it. He kissed her heartily—once for himself, and again for Amy—then called for ale to be brought to their table.

"Upon my life, I wish I could sew," Clare Mantry said wistfully, touching the fabric with callused fingers.

"I would fain teach you," Bess responded, but her offer was half-hearted. Jack guessed it had been made before, and always refused. It was quicker to steal clothes left to dry on a hedge than to make them. Clare's clothes fit her poorly, but no doubt there had never been money to hire a sempster to sew for her, as Bess had sometimes done.

"Clare!"

The rude bellow from across the room made Bess's friend jump. She smiled wanly as she rose to go join her husband, who had just swaggered in, and would have left the ale Jack had ordered for her, but he insisted she take the tankard with her. It irked but did not really surprise him to see Tom Mantry claim the drink from her when she reached his side.

"Poor woman," Bess murmured.

Jack nodded, but did not speak out against the hooker, remembering how his thoughts against Mantry had only reminded him of his own shame, of the debts he owed Bess.

She let him pay for some of her family's food, but thus far she had refused to let him pay for his share of the lodgings, even when he had money for it. Instead she had insisted that he buy a new doublet and hose, and new shoes, "for when you mingle with the gentry." And she had urged him to give the gybes away, although—as he had realized later—selling them would have brought enough money to care for her entire family for months. "They were yours," she had said calmly when he upbraided her for letting him make such a mistake. "They bought you a welcome here, did they not?" And when he had told her that his welcome at the Turk's Sword was due to her, she had shaken her head. " 'Tis untrue. Yea, and even if it were true, I would not have you welcome here for my sake alone."

So now he was welcome; welcome, and well nigh useless. He had only a few coins left, and in a week or two would be unable to pay for his own food and drink. He was too proud to beg, and unwilling to use arms to persuade a victim to hand over his purse, and too clumsy to be a foist. Were it not that his presence guarded Bess and the other vagabonds at the Turk's Sword from Robin Dalling, Jack would feel no more useful to anyone than Clare Mantry's caterpillar of a husband.

"How now, Jack? Why frown? How went your day?" Seeing his grimace, Bess quickly continued, "I was on Fleet Street today, and saw a monster, a puppy with half another puppy joined to its side. 'Twas dead, long dead by the stink of it, but it cost only a half-penny to see it, and that half-penny was from a friend."

Despite himself, Jack smiled. Bess had many such friends, all of them unwary bystanders.

He forgot his cares for awhile as she chattered on, telling him of her day in London and her visits to Paul's and to Cheapside—which

she, like most others at the Turk's Sword, called Chapmans—and to
Paris Garden. Though she had lived in Southwark all her life, Bess still
had a child's fresh enjoyment of the city. But she was no child when it
came to dealing with the less-than-honest shopkeepers of London. He
had to laugh when she told him of an argument with a haberdasher
over the price of a hat. " 'Twas lined with gummed velvet," she said
with exaggerated indignation, "that would have lasted but one wearing!" And she had refused a joint of beef she had planned to buy from
a butcher after discovering that the joint was old meat washed with
fresh blood to hide the staleness. She had come close, she said, to
thrashing the butcher with the stinking joint.

Yet none of her stories could long banish his awareness that she
had walked through London looking for likely targets, rather than simply to enjoy herself, or to shop. And 'twas his fault that she was forced
to steal again.

Stung by his conscience, he ordered supper for himself and Bess, as
well as trays of food to be taken upstairs for Ned and the children. He
insisted on paying for it all, knowing he had just subtracted another day
or two from the time he had left before his purse was empty. Bess would
have paid for her family's food, but she sensed his choleric humor and
quickly gave up arguing.

The kitchen of the Turk's Sword was more crowded now. The doxies left, their place taken by a bawdy basket, who set her basket of
trifling wares on the table before her, then dug through the bits of lace
and ribbon and papers of needles and pins until she brought out a small
loaf of manchet bread, a wedge of cheese, and a cherry tart. "These
cost me but a few inches of cheap lace," she told Simon, when he asked
about the food. "There's a scullery maid at a house in—nay, you rogue,
I'll not tell you where!" She slapped his hand away when he reached
for the tart.

"Mayhap I'll turn bawdy basket," Bess murmured, and Jack chuckled at the jest. He knew that Bess, as a thief, felt superior to the women
who would carry baskets of trifles from house to house until they found
a maidservant foolish enough to buy their wares with something of
greater value.

Their meal was brought to them, and they ate slowly, interrupted
often by friends who drifted over to their table for a few minutes' conversation.

Young Ned Aubrey was the first to join them. The man was a
counterfeit crank, but no one would know it to see him now, with his
face and hands washed, his hair combed, his clothes worn but carefully
mended and clean. He spent most of each day in a far different guise,
wandering through Southwark dressed in rags, a filthy cloth tied over

his head, pretending to be a victim of the falling sickness so that men might take pity on him. He carried a sliver of white soap that he would slip into his mouth at times, when he would fall to the ground and thrash about, foam dribbling from his lips. Jack had seen him at work once, and had been amazed by his skill in counterfeiting the sickness.

Young Ned had been fortunate that Jack had come to Southwark when he did, for Robin Dalling hated him and would have beaten him and driven him away from the Turk's Sword, depriving him of the one place where he felt safe to leave off his disguise; now he had Jack's protection. From Jack, Young Ned also had a gybe identifying him as a former patient of Bedlam, which he could show to any who questioned his sickness. Like the other vagabonds at the alehouse, he had offered Jack a share of his takings; unlike most of them, he had not been content when Jack refused lour, but had begun the practice of buying a round of drinks for Jack and Bess and himself each evening.

Finished with his ale, he slipped away, knowing others coveted his place at the small table.

Less than a minute later Nicholas Ender shuffled over to their table. Until Jack's arrival he had made his living as a palliard, applying the herbs spearwort or crowfoot, or else arsenic, to his skin to raise blisters before going from house to house to beg. Bess had told Jack that just a few years ago Ender had been perfectly healthy, but the constant self-poisoning had robbed him of his health. She had urged Jack to give him one of the gybes, and so Nicholas was now a freshwater mariner, carrying a paper saying he was a former sailor licensed to beg, after his ship was wrecked, until he reached his home again. Jack thought the man too frail in appearance to ever have been a seaman, but Bess had assured him that she had seen sailors return from long voyages in worse condition.

Like enough, Nicholas earned as much from his begging in a day as did Young Ned, but he was more close-fisted, offering instead of drink some bits of gossip about the city. Jack did not mind; he was already feeling the effects of the ale, and Bess often found the information Nicholas brought them to be of use.

After Nicholas came a tinker, back in the city this last week after months in Surrey; he would steal or beg in London until he could afford his next pack of goods for sale, then take to the country again to earn a slightly more honest living. Jack had talked to him twice before, and then, as now, he had good tales to tell of constables and justices of the peace he had bested. He could make Jack laugh, even if he could not make him believe.

The tinker was good company, but he, too, moved on, and Jack's good humor vanished when he saw who would replace him at the table.

For a moment he thought to send the man away, but could not think of any way to do so without revealing his fear. Then the Abraham man had settled onto the stool and was greeting them, his presence impossible to ignore.

Few Abraham men had ever truly been mad for a time and spent time in Bedlam, but Jack believed it of Hal Oldham. 'Twas not that the man seemed mad now. He could rave, or babble nonsense, when he demanded charity, but his behavior around his friends was quiet and observant, and his face was a mask of perpetual melancholy.

"How d'you fare, Hal?" Bess asked warmly.

Hal's sadness seemed to lift for a moment as he met Bess's smile with a faint one of his own.

"Very well, today," he murmured. "I found this for you." He took a silk-wrapped package from his pocket and slid it across the table to Bess.

She opened it, and exclaimed in delight at the pair of gloves within. The gloves were small, fit perhaps for a child of ten, and heavily embroidered with silk thread and tiny seed pearls.

"Hold them to your smelling-cheat," Hal told her, and she lifted the gloves to her nose and then, with a yet wider smile, held the gloves to Jack's nose. Even in the alehouse kitchen, with its reek of food and drink and smoke and unwashed bodies, Jack could smell the musk and rosewater perfuming the gloves.

"They are too small for you," Hal said with regret, "but I thought you might like them to give to the little kinchin mort when she's older."

Bess stiffened, and Jack knew she had been galled to the quick by hearing her daughter called a kinchin mort. She called Amy that herself sometimes, as a jest, but she had vowed that her children would not be thieves. She had promised as much to Will Morsted, soon after each child was born. She would see Tom as an apprentice someday, she vowed, dressed in blue, his knife at his side. And Amy would stay chaste and marry respectably. The girl would not be a wild dell, Bess would say fiercely; she had not given birth to Amy so that ten or twelve years later she could be broken by some upright man and become his doxie. But she had told none of her vagabond friends of her plans for the children; they would not have understood.

"Faith, y'are a kind-hearted rogue," Bess said at last, standing and leaning across the table to kiss Hal.

The Abraham man looked anxiously at Jack, as though fearful of rebuke. Jack forced himself to smile. 'Twas not jealousy of Hal's friendship with Bess that made him uneasy whenever the Abraham man was around.

Hal had been sent to Bedlam—if the story Jack had heard were true—a few days after waking beside a high road in Surrey. He had lost his purse, if he had ever had one. Worse, he had lost his memory. Clutched in his hand had been a letter to one Henry Oldham from a woman named Margaret, but the man who had awakened by the road had needed someone else to tell him that, for he could neither read nor write. He had made inquiries in the nearest villages, growing more and more frantic when no one could tell him anything of himself or Henry Oldham or Margaret, and had finally been sent to Bedlam for two years. In the fifteen years since then Hal had been in London, stealing when stealing looked easy, and at other times begging, imitating when necessary the madness he had seen in Bedlam. His memory had never returned, and he had ceased to look for his family—if he had any family living still—forming instead a family of friends, the closest being Ned Daughton. Bess he had come to treat as a daughter.

Bess sat down again. Hal picked up the cup of beer he had brought with him and sipped from it, his mournful gaze resting on Jack for a moment before sliding away. Jack felt chilled by the emptiness he imagined behind that gaze. Nay, more than imagined, for was Hal's plight any different from his own—save for those years in Bedlam? And Hal's incarceration could not but make Jack wonder whether he would be taken there by force himself, if his lack of memory became known generally or if—as he sometimes feared—the frustration of his attempts to recall his past drove him mad.

Bedlam. The hospital of St. Mary of Bethlehem, by Bishopsgate. Jack had walked past it and heard screams from within, shrieks that seemed to come from damned souls, though Bess had told him that belike 'twas only one of the inmates being whipped for his correction, haply by some citizen who had paid to see the lunatics. Hal himself said he had never been chained to his bed, as some of the more violent madmen were, but had instead been allowed to wander about the hospital, and had suffered only occasional beatings. Yet he had not been free to leave, and he would cry as he told of the horrors he had seen and his despair at ever being freed from that hell. 'Twas only through the good will of one of his keepers, who spoke often enough with him to recognize that he was not mad for all his lack of memory, that Hal was finally released.

"I have another gift for you, Bess," Hal said, and stood and reached into a pocket at the front of his slops.

" 'Sdeath!" Jack roared. "You would make Bess a gift of what you have in your breeches?"

The Abraham man paused, his hand still in his pocket.

"Stow you, Jack," Bess said lightly. "There are morts aplenty who would want what Hal has in his breeches."

The Abraham man laughed at that, and withdrew from his pocket a fine cup of porcelain on a silver mount.

"How now, Hal! Turned sneak-cup! By the mass, 'tis worse than begging. And y'are carrying your cup in your slops. You'll never lack for a jordan, in sooth!"

Hal reddened at the laughter around him, which ended when Bess said "Stow your whids, Jack!" in a voice that brooked no argument. She held out her hands for the cup, and when Hal had given it to her, held it up for all to see. "Look you, coves. 'Tis a fine cup, and not stolen from any tavern. A pretty gift, Hal."

"Likely stolen from a careless housewife," Jack said. " 'Tis tarnished, I see."

Bess rubbed the elaborately wrought silver mount. " 'Twill be easy enough to polish. I thank you again, Hal."

The Abraham man nodded and backed away, bidding them good night. Someone snickered behind him, and he whirled, then walked swiftly to the door and out.

"Well, Jack," Bess said, her voice so soft only he could hear her. "I had looked for better from you. But then, Will did not like Hal, either."

"Think you I like him not, when I but jest—"

"Think you I am blind?" Her gaze met his coolly. "I'll not turn him off as a friend, Jack. Not for your sake, not for any other man's. Hal was my friend long before I met you, and he'll still be my friend when y'are gone. I would have you treat him as a friend, unless you—" She broke off, staring at him as though seeing him for the first time. "Unless you have good reason to treat him otherwise. Unless you also—"

She fell silent, scant instants after the others in the kitchen had, her gaze on something across the room. " 'Tis Robin Dalling," she murmured.

Jack looked up to see a huge man with two burly companions swagger toward them, shoving the bawdy basket aside when she did not move out of his path fast enough.

Dalling himself was as heavy as his underlings, but while they seemed heavily muscled, the upright man's overly tight doublet betrayed flesh that jiggled softly. Like his predecessor, Robin Dalling owed his rank as an upright man to slyness and treachery rather than brute strength, preferring, if given a chance, to knife his enemies in the back rather than face them. But 'twas said he could fight well enough, if forced, and if he had a weapon other than his bare hands.

He settled his bulk on the stool across from Bess and leaned forward, planting the grease-stained elbows of his doublet on the table. "Good even, dearling," he said with a grin, his gaze lingering on her breasts.

"I have not seen you for many a day. Mayhap you were waiting for an invitation from me?"

Bess flushed but made no reply. It was well enough to defy Robin by avoiding him, but a public rebuke of an upright man might only force retaliation. 'Twas why she had left London earlier.

So Jack replied for her. "I warrant you, she was not."

Robin looked his way, then feigned surprise. "Sussex Jack, is it? 'Twas told to me that you had left London, that you missed the country." One of his companions laughed. " 'Tis a strange thing for a country lad to stay in London. I would not think you would be welcome here."

"Nay, you would not think," Jack said agreeably, in a very quiet voice, and Robin Dalling started up from the stool, only to be stopped by a heavy hand on his shoulder.

His face twisted in rage, the upright man craned his neck to look up at the man who had stopped him, a man larger yet than himself.

John Albers was a ruffler, and while his clothes were tattered after several months of poverty in London, he was still as well-armed as when he had served the Earl of Northumberland. Though Catholic, he had left Northumberland's service rather than rebel against his queen. And behind the ruffler stood Roger Chickwell, the scimitar that had given the alehouse its name still sheathed by his side, but with his hand on the sword's hilt. Even Tom Waver had feared the alehouse keeper enough to avoid harrying the vagabonds who met here, instead counting on their fear of being waylaid outside to convince them to hand over their lour.

Robin Dalling grimaced, but dropped back onto the stool, then shrugged free of Albers's loosened grasp. He faced Bess again, his gaze locked with hers. "You waste your time here, sweeting," he muttered, then took her tankard of ale, drained it, and left as quickly as a pretense of dignity would allow.

" 'Twould seem it was our friend Robin who wasted his time," Albers said with an easy smile as he joined them, taking the stool the upright man had vacated only moments before. "He'll seek you out next time when y'are alone."

"He fears Jack's reputation," Bess asserted.

" 'Twill not protect you forever."

"No," Jack agreed, wondering if the ruffler meant him, or both him and Bess, or Bess alone. He had seen how John looked at her, when she was unaware of his gaze. Peradventure the ruffler could see benefits for himself in an encounter between Robin Dalling and Jack that left the latter dead.

Jack noticed that Albers was looking at him speculatively. Was he

perchance wondering if he could best Jack in a swordfight, and then
become the upright man here? Jack had seen that look several times
since the ruffler first came to the bousing ken a week ago. As recently
as two weeks ago the life of an upright man might not have appealed
to Albers, who for months had sought honest work, subsisting on friends'
charity in London and spending his mornings at Paul's in the hope of
finding employment, before finally drifting, like so much of the human
flotsam of the city, across the river to Southwark. But now the ruffler
seemed embittered by months of cooling his heels by the *Si quis* pillar,
and he had voiced no regret for having taken a purse at sword point
last week, his first theft, and, of certain, not his last.

One of Albers's friends joined them, bringing a pack of cards. They
played for an hour, Jack losing a few shillings, which, happily, Bess won.
Finally Albers and his friend took their cards to another table in search
of better luck.

"Let's walk for a while," Bess suggested then, and she and Jack left
the alehouse, after giving the porcelain cup to Roger Chickwell for safe
keeping.

Outside the breeze was still warm, the Southwark night alive with rau-
cous sounds from taverns and stews. As they wandered along the streets
and alleys, Jack saw a door on which was painted a cross: a plague sign.
He shivered, and Bess noticed and looked curiously in the direction of
his gaze.

" 'Tis but the plague," she said calmly, and he remembered her
telling him that Southwark, with its marshes, was an unhealthy place
to live, but she had learned to deal with the threats to her family's
health. What else could she do? They could not afford to flee London
every time they heard of a victim of the plague or the sweating sickness.
"Fear not. I'll get candles of wax mixed with juniper and rose leaves.
Those are the best preservatives—those, and sprigs of rosemary and rue
left on the windowsills."

"You'll steal the candles?" he asked sharply.

" 'Tis cheapest," she replied, her voice equally sharp. Jack's disapproval of her thievery both puzzled and annoyed her.

They crossed London Bridge, let through the gate by the gatekeeper
and the watch, many of whom knew Bess. Most night walkers they
would treat with suspicion, but Bess they believed to be a widowed
sempster, and some of them would give her clothes to mend, and pay
her well. Tonight one of the younger bellmen told her he had a shirt
he had torn while practicing wrestling at Moorfields, and she chided
him for not having taken off the shirt before practicing, then promised
to get the shirt from him on her way back to Southwark.

Arm in arm, Jack and Bess strolled along Thames Street toward where the steeple of St. Paul's robbed the heavens of a sliver of stars. They passed cup-shotten revelers and other night walkers. After a time, Bess tugged on Jack's arm, and he followed her curiously into a narrower way that sloped upward to the north. Here the upper stories of the houses, leaning out over the street from either side, nearly closed off their view of the sky. In the shadows cast by the buildings, Jack was rarely able to see where he stepped, and they had gone but a short distance when he set his foot down in something soft and stinking.

"God's death! Why are we walking here, Bess?"

"Soft, you noisy cofe. I trow I saw a friend steal down this way."

They walked on a bit further, past shuttered shop windows, and then Bess stopped and gestured toward a pool of shadow a dozen yards up the street. Jack shook his head.

"D'you not see?" she whispered, then, a bit more loudly: " 'Tis rude, Tom Mantry, to hide from your friends."

For a few moments there was only silence and stillness in the shadow-drowned street. Then, with a muffled cough, Tom shuffled bashfully from the shadows to greet them.

He was a corpulent man, looking much older than the thirty years Bess gave him. He moved unsteadily, weaving in and out of the narrow moonlit alley running along one side of the gutter: drunken, though no more so than usual.

Bess shook her head, her tongue clicking in disapproval. "Drunkenness is a vice, Tom, and the most damning one for a hooker. Could you not have contented yourself with gluttony?"

"Stow you, wench!" he grumbled. "Have I not heard enough from Clare this night?" He turned his back on them and set off up the street, staggering a little.

"Likely you have, and that's good, if she's set you to working," Bess said with a little laugh.

"Peace, damn you!" Tom returned in a furious whisper, glancing back over his shoulder. "Will you wake them that I would have sleep?"

Bess and Jack chuckled but then were silent as they followed him.

Three houses further along the street, Tom stopped and looked up at a window on the second floor.

"Aye, that's the one, that's the window," he said in a whisper Jack could barely hear. " 'Twas there this afternoon, a fine lady's cloak."

" 'Twould be finer if 'twere meant for Clare's back, and not for a pawn-keeper who'll give you a few crowns to buy your bouse," Bess murmured.

Tom seemed not to hear her. He took from his pocket an iron hook, the base of which he fitted into a hole drilled through one end of the staff he always carried. Everywhere but at the bousing ken he was careful to keep a hand closed over that end of the staff, for it marked him as a hooker. It was such a habit that he had concealed the hole even from Bess and Jack until now.

When the hook was secured, Tom moved his hands down the staff, lifting it over his head. Drunk he might be, but years of his trade had left him skillful enough that he easily caught the partly open shutter with the hook. An instant later the window stood open. He waited, holding his breath; then, when silence assured him that no one within had heard him, he swung the top of the staff inside the window. Even in the poor light, Jack could see that the hooker's face was gleaming with sweat.

After what seemed a long time, Tom withdrew the staff. Bess gasped when she saw the pale, rich fabric of the cloak. This merchant loved his wife or daughter well, to spend so much lour on her clothing.

" 'Tis lovely, Tom," Bess whispered as the hooker wiped his hands on his frieze jerkin, then took the cloak from the hook and folded it into an easily carried bundle. "Come, let's away, before—"

Tom shook his head stubbornly. "There's more. A cap of velvet, with an ostrich plume." He handed the bundle to Bess, after first making her swear that she would return it to him.

Again he probed the darkness behind the window frame with his hook-crowned staff. His hands shook now from tension and weariness. Bess looked fretfully at Jack, but said nothing. Nor did Jack, fearing to distract the hooker, who was frowning now as he swung the staff a little further to the left.

Suddenly a crashing noise came from within. Tom pulled back on the staff, but it was caught. With an oath, he yanked harder, then stumbled backward as the staff came free. One of his feet slid in a shallow puddle, and he fell onto his rump.

A head topped by a nightcap appeared in the window.

Tom was already scrambling to his feet. Snatching the cloak from Bess, he tucked it under his arm and fled down the street.

Bess tugged on Jack's arm, but for long moments he was frozen, staring up at the furious shopkeeper, who was now bellowing at Tom's retreating figure, unaware of the two who stood in the shadows directly beneath him.

He was in a garden, gazing up at a lighted window in a brick wall, and there were two men there looking down on them, and they must run—

"Run," he said aloud, almost sobbing with fear, and felt Bess's thumbnail dig into the top of his hand then, as the shopkeeper looked down in astonishment at them. Gripping her hand, Jack sprinted after Tom, pulling Bess along with him.

By the time Jack and Bess reached Thames Street, the hooker was already far down the street, running east. They ran after him, sped on their way by the shouts of the shopkeeper pursuing them. They were crossing the high street of Dowgate when Bess cried out in pain, then stumbled to a halt.

"Jesu!" she gasped. "I have turned my ankle."

Jack looked back over his shoulder for an instant. The shopkeeper was not yet in sight. And, in the other direction, far down Thames Street, Tom could scarcely be seen, his running form visible only when the pale stuff of the stolen cloak caught the light from a lantern. He was already past the Steelyard and Church Lane and Allhallows the More, almost to Hay Wharf Lane. Past that lane, just south of the church of Allhallows the Less, was Cold Harbor, with its thieves' sanctuary of tenements where the hooker would be safe. 'Twas likely he would be out of sight before the shopkeeper reached Thames Street.

But they would not, if they stayed here.

Ignoring Bess's whimpers of pain, Jack half dragged, half carried her up the steep slope of Dowgate, past Elbow Lane and the Skinners' hall. He glanced backward every few seconds. They were near the top of the street, opposite the Tallow-chandlers' hall, when he saw a man in a nightshirt and nightcap run into Dowgate, brandishing a long cudgel.

Jack pushed Bess against the wall of a house, his body pressed against hers. "Put your arms around my neck!" he whispered.

"I would liefer wring your neck, your whoreson! What—" She fell silent as she glanced down the street. Jack followed her gaze to see the shopkeeper coming toward them, looking like a poor, clownish ghost in his nightclothes. The cudgel he was now using for a walking stick was nothing to laugh at, though. "A plague on Tom Mantry and his clumsiness!" she said, and slid her arms round Jack's neck, then pulled his head down to hers for a kiss.

"I am glad you bethought this," she murmured between kisses. "I could have run no further."

He chuckled. " 'Tis the only reason y'are glad, of course," he said, cupping his hand over her left breast.

Her laughter was all the answer he got before their lips met again. He slid one hand behind her hips and drew her close against him, making her aware of his arousal, and her response was to press closer yet. It was lunacy: he had stopped only because he knew Bess could not outrun the shopkeeper, and if the man recognized them now, they would be in for a beating—or worse. Yet at this moment, Jack could think of little but how he wanted to tumble her here in the street.

All of a sudden a hand clawed at his shoulder. "You, there," the merchant said, angry but uncertain. "Sirrah, have you seen—"

Bess let go of him, and Jack turned around slowly, slapping the shopkeeper's hand away.

"Sirrah! Who are you, knave, to so address your betters?"

"I—" The shopkeeper swallowed, taking a step back. In the darkness he would be able to see the fashionable cut of Jack's suit, but not the cheapness of the cloth. Jack touched one hand to the hilt of the sword, aware that the finely wrought hilt would catch the light from the nearest torch. "I seek a thief, and two of his companions, one a woman," the man said haltingly. He looked at Bess, his eyes narrowing as he studied her shapely form.

"Then go seek them, sir fool, and leave us be!"

"But sir, she—"

"She's not for you, old man. You must find your own doxie."

The shopkeeper looked back and forth between them for a few moments, his confusion seeming to war with fear of the gentleman Jack appeared to be. At last he backed away, mumbling apologies. After a last doubtful look at Bess, he shook his head and turned around to start back down Dowgate toward the river, peering into shadows as he went.

Bess waited until the shopkeeper was safely out of earshot before kicking Jack smartly in the shins. "Doxie, am I?" She limped past him toward the conduit at the top of Dowgate. Following her to the castellated conduit, he thought he remembered seeing the structure half built, with workmen all about. The image had slipped from his brain an instant later, but for its brief life it had been vivid—though not so vivid as his memory of standing in a garden beneath a lighted window. That image still troubled him, but for no reason that he could determine.

"Is this conduit new?" he asked Bess.

"Aye, it is, cofe," she called over her shoulder. "But a year or two old. Why?"

When he did not answer, she glanced back at him impatiently, then shrugged. She sat down by the conduit spout, removed her slipper and stocking, and soaked her swollen ankle in the cool Thames water.

"Doxie," she muttered when he would have sat down beside her. "I thought never to hear you call me that."

"Would you have had me tell him that y'are a gentlewoman, my lady?" he asked sarcastically.

"Nay, that's no role for me." She was silent for a time, then added, "Though you act the proper gentleman, in sooth."

Jack said nothing. For a few moments there he had not needed to pretend his disdain of the shopkeeper: it had felt real to him. And the memory he had had, of a stately brick house, still teased his mind.

Bess dried her foot with the hem of her petticoat, then donned stocking and slipper again. She rose and took a few gingerly steps away from the conduit.

"Can you walk, sweeting? As far as the water stairs? We can take a wherry—"

"Nay," she interrupted, shaking her head. "Walking is cheaper. Needs must that I go slowly, though . . . and belike we should not go back by Thames Street, if Tom is still sought there."

So they made their slow way along Candlewick Street and East-cheap, with Bess uttering not a word of complaint during the climb up Fish Street Hill. But she paused when they reached the top, and stood for a time gazing at Fish Street's long descent to London Bridge, before she sighed and started down the hill.

They sat down to rest on the drawbridge, looking out over the river to the west. There were still wherries out on the Thames, the boats torchlit now, looking like giant flapdragons on the dark water. Bess leaned wearily against Jack.

"Tell me of yourself, Jack," she said after a time, her sleepy voice audible above the rushing of the waters only because she was so close. "Tell me where you learned to act the gentleman."

" 'Tis not a story I can tell," he said, his answer both truthful and evasive.

She was silent for a long time after that, and he relaxed, certain she was too tired to care that he had evaded her question.

"I know so little of you," she said at last. "But then, you know so little of yourself."

The drowsy note had left her voice, and he was suddenly wide awake too, and wary. "Men know so little of themselves."

" 'Tis true, sir philosopher, but 'tis not what I meant."

"No?"

"Y'are like Hal Oldham, are you not? Much of your life is lost to you. But y'are wiser than Hal. You do not let people know."

"How did you know?"

"You have never spoken of your past. 'Tis not just when I have asked you about it. That I could understand, for such questions mislike some men, and mayhap y'are such a man. But neither have you spoken so much as a byword about the times before we met, and I have known no other man thus sundered from his past . . . save for Hal Oldham. 'Tis why you'll not befriend him, is it not? You fear him, for he reminds you of yourself, and you fear a life like his."

Jack sighed and nodded.

"How far back can you remember?"

"Till the day before I met you." He told her about the yeoman who had helped him and then turned him out.

"And you chose to go with me to London . . . Had you stayed in Sussex, you might have met someone who knew you."

"Perhaps I would have encountered an old friend, had I stayed. But 'tis as likely I would meet with an old foe. And had I not found someone who knew me in a day or two, might I not have met Hal's fate?"

"Bedlam," she said, and shuddered. "Have you no memories at all?"

He hesitated, then told her of the confusion he had felt when the shopkeeper discovered Tom's thievery.

" 'Twas a poor time to start remembering, and for so little a memory." She laughed, and he chuckled too, though in truth the memory still troubled him. It was something of import, he knew: it fit too well with the feeling of guilt he sometimes had, the sense that he had failed someone— a guilt that was entirely separate from what he felt about his inability to help Bess more. Thus far he had tried to dismiss it from his mind, fearing he risked madness if he dwelled on it too much, but the feeling of guilt was very strong again now. *Run!* . . . He shook his head, trying to banish the image of that imposing brick wall, the lighted window.

He told Bess of his memory of seeing the conduit on Dowgate built, too, and she was more interested in that than the other. "You were in London, then," she said. "Haply you have friends here."

"Yea, or enemies."

"Jesu! Y'are as gloomy as a raven," she said, but there was real concern behind the mockery of her words. He managed a smile, to show her he was not so melancholy.

She smiled, too, then held out her hand, and he helped her to her feet.

"Will you keep my secret?"

"Would you stay if I did not? No, of course not. You would not dare stay. So I'll tell no one . . . if you'll promise me one thing . . ."

"Yea?"

"Promise me that, when you remember who you are and where you belong, that you will not leave without telling me good-bye."

" 'Sblood! Bess, why—"

"Promise!"

"I promise," he said, kissing her. "By my life, I swear that I would not leave you without saying good-bye. Indeed, I will never leave you."

"A gallant liar. You should be at court."

"Perchance I was," he said with a laugh.

"Perchance you were," she agreed, very solemnly. Her seriousness troubled him.

"And perchance I have a wife and ten children," he said teasingly, to lighten her mood.

"Nay," she said. "What mort would have you to husband?"

The bellmen they had seen earlier were now at the bridge foot. They took pity on Bess for her twisted ankle and two of them offered to help carry her home, but she laughingly declined their offer. "I would liefer have you defend me from the Spanish," she told them, "than carry me about Southwark."

They then told her and Jack all the news they had of the defenses being prepared throughout the country, especially along the coasts. The Spanish fleet was sailing to Antwerp, supposedly to provide escort to Spain for Anne of Austria, who was to marry King Philip. But who could say whether the fleet might not instead attack England? No one would feel safe until the fleet was back in Spanish ports, and there were none of the watchmen who did not know of men, family or friends, who had been called up by a sheriff to practice with hackbuts so they would be ready to defend English soil. Two of the watchmen knew mariners who sailed on the ten ships that, under Lord Howard, guarded the narrow seas, and the watchman who gave Bess his shirt to mend had heard from a cousin in Kent that his cousin had been set to gathering wood for a beacon fire there, one of many fires that would be lighted to signal an attack by the Spanish fleet.

"Jack Spaniard will never get this far," one of the watchmen assured Bess.

"Marry, if I could believe that—"

"By my faith, Bess," Jack said, "y'are as fearful as—" He broke off. A name had been at the tip of his tongue, but he could not think of it, nor call up the image of a face. He swore, angry at himself, and the watchmen would have upbraided him for being angry with Bess, had she not quickly told them that he was apt to forget names when he had had too much ale, but could not accept his failing with Christian patience.

She and Jack left the bridge for Southwark then, Bess limping more than ever, though all her concern was for Jack. She regretted that he had not been able to remember that name, but there was hope, she told him, in its coming so close. He found scant reassurance in that. Tonight, more than ever, he had been unable to forget about what he had lost and live wholly in the present, and he thought of the emptiness he saw in Hal Oldham's gaze sometimes, and was sickened with fear.

Ned and the children were asleep when Jack and Bess returned home, so they made their way to Bess's chamber as quietly as possible. As Jack closed the door, Bess moved carefully through the inky blackness of the room to the window, which she unshuttered to let in the cool night air. Far in the distance, a bellman cried the hour of midnight. For a few moments Bess stood at the window, moonlight silvering her lovely face. Then she turned toward him, her face only a pale blur again, within its frame of dark hair now frosted by the moon's light.

"You are beautiful," he whispered, drawing her against him.

She was willing, but more passive than usual, letting him undress her but not helping him. He was careful as he at last rolled the stocking down her right leg and over her swollen ankle. The puffy flesh that almost hid her anklebones felt too warm to his touch.

"You need a wet cloth for this," he said, but she caught at his arm when he would have left her.

"Nay, Jack, I need you."

He shed his own clothes and leaned over her. She set her hands on his shoulders, with just enough pressure that when he would have kissed her, he felt himself held away. Instead of the smile he knew so well, she wore a wide-eyed, solemn expression that made her look very young.

"Is something the matter, sweetheart?"

"No," she murmured, and gave him a quirky smile before pulling him down against her firm, lithe body.

For weeks he had been teaching her to take more time in her love-making, drawing out the pleasure, but tonight, after that first, strange passivity, she seemed desperately impatient, urging him to a quick, frenzied coupling. As he lay beside her, gasping for breath, he saw that her face was wet with tears as well as sweat.

"Bess?" he asked wonderingly, touching tears that glimmered on her lashes. "Y'are crying . . ."

She laughed shakily, brushing his hand away. "Mind it not," she said. "I am such a fool." And she would talk no more that night.

Three days later Jack stood in Ned's chamber before the purse suspended by leather thongs. For the fourth time that morning he reached toward the purse. A quick, deft movement brought knife and thumb sheath together, the sharpened blade slicing easily through the purse strings. He turned toward Ned and the children, holding the purse up triumphantly. There had not been a whisper of sound from the bells.

Amy and Tom clapped, and Ned beamed.

"Four times, with nary a slip. You'll do well as a cutpurse."

"I would do better if I were a foist."

"Haply you would," Ned admitted. "Will you try it again now?"

Jack nodded, turning his head a little to look at the next test awaiting him.

It was an old doublet of stained white camlet, bought yesterday for a few shillings from a seller of used clothing, but the shabbiness of the garment did not matter. All that mattered were the pockets and the bells hung about them. Jack moved to where the garment hung from a wooden frame the height of a man's shoulder. Ned had told him that it was a bit easier to be a pickpocket than a pickpurse; he reminded himself of that now, forcing his worries back.

He stood behind the doublet, a bit to one side: Ned had shown him which pocket the purse was in. He took off the horn sheath and slipped it and the cuttle into his own doublet's pocket, then flexed his fingers. Reaching forward, he slid his hand into the white doublet's pocket so carefully that the side of the doublet scarcely moved. So far the bells were silent. His fingers touched the purse, then fastened on the purse strings, and he began to pull it out of the pocket, but before he could even see the purse, the jangling bells were announcing his failure.

"Jesu!" He stalked away from the doublet, his fists clenched, and went to the window. Outside a prosperous-looking fellow—a merchant, like enough—was passing by. There was no purse hanging from his belt, so he must have been carrying it in a pocket. *'Tis safe from me*, Jack thought bitterly.

" 'Twas but the first try," Ned said soothingly as he came to stand beside Jack. "You'll do better on the next."

Jack nodded but said nothing.

Mary Whitston came into sight, staggering a little on the arm of a rogue friend of hers; she was drunk, but laughing, and singing in her high, pretty voice. Watching her, Jack felt some of his anger drain out of him.

He heard the sound of a stool being slid across the floor behind him. The children must be restless. He flexed his fingers. In another minute he would be ready to try again.

"Jack," Tom called.

He turned, and the little boy, who was standing on the three-legged stool he had pushed over to the frame with its white doublet, threw a purse to him.

There had been no bells ringing.

Jack looked down in disbelief at the purse in his hands. 'Twas the one Ned had placed in the doublet's pocket. He swallowed hard, and looked up at Tom. The child's proud smile faltered under his hard stare.

Ned touched his sleeve. " 'Tis easier for a child," he said awkwardly. "The hands are smaller, so they—"

"No!" Jack shrugged free and almost ran from the chamber.

It was early in the afternoon. Bess might not be back for hours, and in any event he was in no mood to talk to her, or to anyone else at the bousing ken. He avoided the kitchen on his way out of the alehouse, brushing past Mary Whitston without a word. "And good day to you, too," the punk shrieked after him, then began to laugh again.

He walked toward Paris Garden.

He heard cries of "A mile, a mile!" and "Good cast!" before he reached the bowling green. He joined the spectators watching a finely-dressed gallant who seemed almost to have learned how to compensate for the lead weight on one side of the bowl he was throwing. It rolled close to the jack, and Jack cried, "Near the mistress!" and the gallant turned to smile at him.

Jack watched for several more minutes, now and then looking over the crowd. Two young gentlemen were betting on the gallant's skill, one wagering that his luck would not last. Jack would have bet against him, for the player's luck, but he could not spare even a penny, should he lose the bet. His purse would soon be empty, and all because he could not foist.

But he could nip a purse.

It was the first time he had thought of it away from the Turk's Sword, and now he remembered that he still had the cuttle and horn thumb-sheath. He would be ashamed if any of his vagabond friends, save Bess and her family, knew he used them, but who was to know? 'Twould be foolish out of all measure, he thought of a sudden, to starve in order to save his pride. He scanned the crowd again, and saw no familiar faces. Hoping that no one here knew him that he did not know, he slipped his hand into his pocket and, unseen, fitted his thumb into the sheath before curling his fingers around the small knife.

There was a stout yeoman in the crowd a dozen feet away from Jack. The rustic was unwary enough of London to wear his purse openly, only leather purse strings holding it to his belt. Pretending to watch the game, Jack moved closer to the yeoman, thanking God for his luck, and praying for more.

It seemed too easily done. Jack moved back through the spectators, the stolen purse hidden in his pocket along with the horn sheath and cuttle, and no one around him cried "Thief!" and no hands seized him to stop him. At the edge of the crowd he glanced toward the sun, shook his head, and walked away, like a man who has just realized that he has idled away too much time. Not until he was well away from the bowling green did he transfer the contents of the yeoman's purse—more than three pounds in all—to his own. He dropped the stolen purse near the bear garden and then made his way home.

Chapter 24

In the lulling heat of late afternoon, on the fourth day after leaving the Casa de las Rosas, Kat and the single captor who remained with her walked their horses up a steeply sloping road.

Kat sweltered beneath the hooded cloak that she had been ordered to wear during most of the journey north and east from Burgos. It was a man's cloak, long and voluminous. Beneath it she wore the doublet and hose that her captors had given her, but the doublet fit too tightly to hide her figure, and the hat they had brought for her had been forgotten on the second morning of the ride north, so they had made her wear the cloak despite the summer heat.

She no longer suffered from the terrible headache that had plagued her for two days following her abduction from the house, but there was still a tender bruise on the back of her head. No further injury had come to her yet. When she had first come to herself, it had been evening, and she had not recognized her surroundings. The hillside on which they had camped offered no view of Burgos or any of the countryside Kat had ridden through on her way to the Casa de las Rosas. Her captors had brought her water to drink and food that she was too sick to eat. They had given her the cloak then, to wrap herself in as she slept, for they dared light no fires to warm them in the chill night. She had lain awake for half of the night, frightened of the men around her. The man who seemed to be their leader had told her she need not fear them, that no harm would come to her. But whenever she had glanced toward the man who took the first watch that night, and then his replacement, she had found them staring hungrily at her, and she wondered who could guard her from her guards.

There were five men in the group. Their leader, who had told her only his Christian name, Pablo, was a reserved man, about forty years old, who dressed simply but well and had the manner of a clerk or a responsible servant. The other four men avoided Pablo's company for the most part, though they took whatever orders he gave them. They were boisterous, strongly built men in their thirties; they wore leather jerkins like those worn by fighting men, and they bragged of their exploits as soldiers years ago, when they had served in the Spanish army in the Netherlands under the command of the Duke of Savoy. They spoke of the famous battle of Saint Quentin in 1557, when the French army had been annihilated and the Spaniards had spent two days sacking the town. It was clear that they were no longer soldiers, but they took offense when Kat called them *salteadores*. They were not highwaymen, they told her. They were *valentónes*, heroes. Kat saw nothing heroic about them, but she held her tongue. If she angered them further, she might discover that their willingness to obey Pablo had its limits. She had been relieved to see the last of them a few hours ago, when Pablo had paid them and sent them on their way.

Now Kat stretched as well as she could and looked around, her field of vision narrowed by the hood. Where was she?

They had crossed the Ebro River days ago, and had been riding through increasingly mountainous country since then. They were in the Pyrenees, but she was uncertain how far east they had traveled. Was this Navarra, or Aragon? They had met no border guards, having avoided roads until a few hours ago. The need for caution had slowed their travel, and Kat guessed that, given a map and a fresh horse, she could have made her way back to Burgos within two or three days. But she had neither of those, and was herself too exhausted to make the attempt. Too exhausted, and too frightened: an Englishwoman traveling alone would be easy prey for either the *salteadores* or the Inquisition.

Like enough, there would be a better chance to escape later, she thought with a sigh.

Pablo, riding close by her side, looked over at her. "It is but a little way further, lady."

"What is?" she asked, but he only smiled and ignored her question, as he had ignored all the other questions she had asked him during the past few days.

Ahead of them, the road began to level out slightly before it disappeared around an escarpment. He urged his horse into a trot, and hers followed suit without bidding. He spurred his horse again, and they rounded the escarpment at a false gallop and suddenly their destination was in view.

The road curved into the mountainside, then out again to another escarpment, and there it ended, beneath the walls of a castle set on the edge of a sheer drop to the valley below. The time-worn stones of the castle glowed in the late afternoon light, and so did the glittering surface of the narrow stream that sluiced down the ravine in the opposite slope to join the small river dividing the valley floor, which was already in shadow.

She had heard this place described too carefully, too lovingly, not to recognize it.

"*El Nido de Aguilas,*" she said, thinking aloud, as Pablo reached her.

"Yes," he said, though her words had not been a question. "Come."

Servants took their horses when they reached the courtyard, and other servants would have led Kat to chambers that had been prepared for her, but she refused to go. Standing in the great hall, she clung to the back of an enormous chair, resisting the anxious maid who tugged at her hand, and demanded to see Don Rafael.

"Later, lady, after you have rested . . ." Pablo said, pleading with her.

"Now!"

Shaking his head, he at last turned away. One quick order sent a manservant scurrying to seek Don Rafael; another convinced the maid to let go of Kat's hand and withdraw unhappily to stand against the wall. Kat rubbed her arm. Her hood had fallen back, and tangled strands of hair, uncombed except with her fingers during the last four days, fell across her face. She pushed the strands back, grimacing. She knew she looked haggard, but she wanted answers to her questions now, and would not wait until whatever time Don Rafael deigned to see her.

She was still standing beside the chair, one hand resting on its back, when Don Rafael reached the great hall. He seemed startled by her appearance.

"Katherine! I am sorry that the journey was so difficult for you," he said in English, "but there are chambers ready where you may take your ease. You may rest now, and later we will talk. I am happy to have you as my guest here."

"Your guest, Don Rafael? Guests are invited—"

"As you were."

"But I did not accept your invitation."

"Nor did you refuse it, madam. You said nothing of my invitation, and I chose to read interest in that silence. It was Margaret who declined my invitation for you both."

"Yea, and she told you it was Lord Harwood's decision. You'll answer to him for this."

"I think not," the don replied, looking amused. "But come, let my maidservant attend you. You are so weary from your journey you are not thinking clearly. We shall talk again after you have rested. Until then." He bowed slightly and turned away.

The rooms Kat was given were in a tower in the castle's outer wall. The lower room was an antechamber, and Kat would have been content to lie on the settle by the fireplace, but the maid insisted that she climb the curving stairway to the bedchamber. There Kat threw off her cloak and then crawled into bed, not bothering to undress further.

She slept until sunset, when she was wakened by the sound of servants carrying in a tub and buckets of hot water for her bath. There was fine rose-scented soap, and after her bath Kat sprinkled herself with rosewater from a crystal and silver casting bottle. The old kirtle that Margaret had given her, which Pablo had brought along in his cloakbag, had been taken away, and the maid told her that Don Rafael wished her to wear instead one of the kirtles in the press, and opened the cupboard to reveal several kirtles and gowns in silks and velvets.

"Did those belong to his wife?" Kat asked the maid, who giggled before shaking her head.

Kat looked over the garments with a critical eye. Nay, these would not have been his wife's clothes, not if she had been the proper Spanish matron Margaret pretended to be. The bodices' necklines were cut rather low, and the partlets the maid showed Kat after she asked about them were little boon to modesty, for they were of delicate lawn and cypress and lace. They would suit a mistress, and Kat was certain that Rafael would have had one—if not many—during the years since his wife's death.

"I will not wear these," Kat told the maid at first, but finally, realizing the only alternative was to don the ill-fitting doublet and hose again, she agreed to try some of the garments to see if they would fit.

Some time later she stood across the room from the maid, who tilted the small looking glass from side to side as Kat tried to judge her appearance. She wore a gown of midnight-blue tabine lined with gold satin over a velvet kirtle, the velvet gingerline figured with white. Her sleeves were of white satin embroidered with crimson and gold thread, her partlet of white cypress. The garments fit her better than those intended for Margaret, and though the maid was dismayed that the hem of the kirtle and gown did not reach the floor, Kat thought them the right length.

She gestured for the maid—Dorotea was her name, she had told Kat—to put the looking glass away. As the girl started to do so, she hesitated, turning toward the stairs as someone opened the doorway to the antechamber. She gave Kat a quick smile. "They have brought your supper."

"I am to eat here?" Kat asked, starting down the stairs.

The small table had been set with silver plate, and another table brought in to hold the platters of food. Don Rafael was in the antechamber, too, splendidly dressed in a doublet of black velvet, the sleeves slashed to show the ash-colored silk lining.

"We are to sup here?" Kat asked.

"Yes, Katherine. I am happy to see you fully restored after your journey."

"We must talk—"

"We must, we must," he agreed with a smile, "but first we will have our supper. I am told you have had nothing to eat since your arrival."

Kat took her seat, and so did the don. The first course was served, and then the servants, including Kat's maid, withdrew. Kat's uneasiness increased as the door closed behind them.

"My lord," she began, but he interrupted her again.

"First we'll sup, Katherine. Then we will talk."

She ate lightly; her appetite had deserted her, and only the knowledge that she needed sustenance convinced her she should eat. When they were ready for the second course, Kat waited expectantly for Don Rafael to call the servants back into the antechamber, for surely they had gone no further than the hall leading to the tower rooms. Instead, to her surprise, Don Rafael served the food himself.

"You will find the venison excellent," he assured her a minute or two later, seeing she had not begun to eat.

"My lord, we must talk."

He sighed. Setting his knife aside, he wiped his fingers and mouth with a richly embroidered linen napkin. "Sweeting, you are very impatient. But then, I am also impatient. So let me hear your petty objections and be done with them."

"Petty! Think you that it was petty to have me taken from Doña Margaret's house? I demand that you take me back at once!"

"Dear Katherine," he said, almost sadly. "That is not possible."

"You fear that she will know it was your men who took me away? I will tell no one of what you have done, my lord, if you will see me returned safely to La Casa de las Rosas." Seeing that his expression had not changed, she added, "Or do you fear that Lady Margaret was badly injured by the rogues in your hire?"

"Doña Margaret was not hurt at all, if those men obeyed their orders. Moreover, señora, though I am touched by your promise of secrecy, should I have you returned to Burgos, it is a promise of no value, for there is no secret. Margaret already knows whose men captured you. The idea, sweet Katherine, was hers."

Kat's head reeled. She set her hands on the table, pressing hard to steady herself. She took a deep breath, then shook her head. "She would not think of such a thing," she said slowly. "Nay, even if she wished me ill—and I warrant she did not—she would not conspire with you as you have said, for she would fear her cousin's wrath. I am his ward, and—"

"No, you are not, Katherine. Margaret told me what you are. And she told me as well that Lord Harwood wished to be rid of you. Knew you not that he had lost patience with you and wanted you no longer? You are lovely, Katherine, but you alienated him. Be thankful that he is not the only man to find you lovely."

She turned her head away, then got up, leaning so heavily on the table that it shuddered under her weight. She crossed the chamber to stand before the fire, her fists clenching and unclenching. Finally, blinking away tears, she slammed one fist down on the back of the settle.

So this was Justin's doing. This was what she had brought on herself by spurning him when he came to her bedchamber, that first night at La Casa de las Rosas. She did not want to believe it, but Don Rafael's next words, though spoken softly, struck at her like hammer blows, beating doubts into hard conviction.

" 'Twas best, we felt, if it seemed that *valentónes* had attacked you and the lady Margaret and then taken you with them. The servants thought you Justin's ward, and Margaret did not wish to be burdened with explaining that she had deceived them, having them treat her cousin's leman as if she were a gentlewoman. They will search the countryside around Burgos, but they will find nothing to lead them here. And by the time Justin has returned from Madrid, all will have concluded that further searching is useless, so he may be saddened by the loss of his ward, but he need not stay in Burgos to continue looking for you."

She cursed herself for trusting in Justin for her safety while in Spain. God's death! If he could betray his queen and his country, how much more easily could he betray her? She bit her lip, thinking of the kind way he had spoken to her before he left for Madrid. A treacherous kindness. And his bidding her to obey Margaret—how useful that had been! 'Twould have been far more difficult for the *valentónes* to reach her, had she stayed sulking in her chamber. Instead she had followed Margaret about like a sheep being led to slaughter . . .

Rafael left the table and came to stand beside her. "This news must trouble you, sweeting. I would comfort you," he said, and would have put an arm around her, but she quickly took a few steps away, then swung around to face him.

"I will not be used thus!" Her voice broke, to her shame, and she had to brush tears away from her eyes.

"Haply this is too soon," he said gently. "I would fain share your bed tonight—"

"No!"

"—but no doubt you would liefer be wooed, as I wooed my other mistresses. Very well. I shall spend more time with you tomorrow. For now, I wish you pleasant dreams." And he bowed and left.

Dorotea came back in then. She had been standing just outside the door, and perchance had heard all that they had said, but her expression gave no hint as to her feelings. 'Twas likely, alas, that she had seen too many other women here, too many mistresses of Rafael's.

But Kat would never be one of them. By her life, she would not! She would find some way to escape. If not the maid, then perchance someone else in the castle might befriend her and help her. And in the meantime, she would let Don Rafael woo her, thinking she would eventually let him lie with her.

And someday, she vowed to herself, someday she would repay Justin for this. She would get back to England, and she would take what she knew of Justin's plottings to Walsingham. And then she would see his traitor's head on a pike on London Bridge.

"More wine, señora?" Rafael asked.

Kat shook her head, not lifting her gaze from the chessboard before her. She resented his intrusion into her concentration on the game. While they played, she could forget for a time that she was a prisoner here. All that existed, outside herself, were the small Italian marble table before her and the ebony and ivory chessboard, with the matching, ornately carved figures, that sat upon it. If she kept her eyes lowered, Don Rafael entered her world only as a smooth, slender hand that moved chessmen in response to her moves.

She treasured this chance to play, this third game of chess, for he rarely allowed her to ignore his presence so completely. For the past three days he had been an attentive and congenial host, spending long hours with her, and while the maid withdrew discreetly to a corner of the antechamber, he never ordered her to leave. Kat knew he was trying to put her at ease with him, and she knew as well that he would never succeed.

He had escorted her around the castle once, proudly showing off the ancient fortress and the improvements he had made in it, but otherwise she was confined to her chambers. A servingman always waited in the hall beside the door to the tower, and while supposedly he was there to convey messages if necessary, Kat knew he was really a guard. Don Rafael apparently had no intention of allowing her free run of the castle, at least not until he was assured of her attachment to him, though since that first evening he had not spoken directly of the relationship he wanted with her.

She never spoke of it, either. For three days they had played an elaborate game in which she acted as though she were Justin's ward, and he treated her as though she were a gentlewoman. It was a game she hated, but it bought her time.

And she needed more time. Dorotea seemed friendlier now, but she was still somewhat frightened of Kat's Englishness, and Kat knew she did not yet dare confide in the girl that she wished to escape. She would be more careful this time than she had been aboard the *Lady Margaret*, when she had decided too early to trust in Peter's affection for her.

At night Kat would lie awake, racking her brains for a way of escaping, if she could not get the maid's help. There was no way directly out of the tower: the windows were mere loopholes. She had toyed with the idea of overpowering the guard somehow, but what could she use for a weapon? The fire-fork? And even if she succeeded in silencing him before he could cry an alarm, how could she hope to steal through the castle unseen, get a horse from the stables in the courtyard, and ride out without being pursued? So far she had thought of no plan with much chance of success, other than getting help from a servant here, someone who knew the surrounding countryside and could guide her safely to France, where she might find shelter with a Huguenot family until she could return to England. And more and more it seemed that that servant must needs be Dorotea, or, perhaps, another servant whom Dorotea could trust.

So Kat had rehearsed, over and over, what she would say to the girl. By now she must have imagined every possible response Dorotea could give to her plea for help, every possible argument that could be used if the girl were reluctant to aid in her escape. Kat suspected at times that she was planning too carefully—would it not be better to respond naturally to whatever Dorotea said, rather than utter sentences that mayhap would seem learned by rote?—but she could not stop: if nothing else, her feverish planning helped keep thoughts of Justin from her mind.

For she had rarely gone as much as a minute without thinking of him—or so it seemed to her. Much of the time, she felt a terrible anger at his betrayal of her, and then her traitorous memory would remind her of the tenderness he had sometimes shown her and, worse, the love she had felt for him, and her fury would be doubled. Alone at night, when she thought the maidservant asleep on the trundle bed, Kat would give vent to her anger in tears, but during the day she tried to hide her feelings, and felt she had succeeded.

"Kat?"

She started, and looked guiltily back toward Don Rafael.

" 'Tis your move," he said.

While she gazed down at the board, he left his chair and came to stand behind her. She sat very still as he set his hands on her shoulders. It was the first time he had touched her, save in greeting her or taking his leave of her, since that first evening. Dorotea glanced at them and then quickly away.

"You are wearing the chain I gave you," he said softly, touching the necklace of ivory and gold beads. "D'you like it?"

"Very well, my lord," she replied, still not moving.

He began to draw the chain back until it was taut against her neck, then, setting one hand beneath her chin, lifted her head so she was gazing straight up at him. He leaned down to kiss her—

And she jerked away, breaking the chain as she flung herself from the chair. Glittering beads rolled everywhere across the floor.

Rafael looked down at the remainder of the chain in his hand, then tossed it aside. His gaze met the maid's for a moment, and he froze then, before turning a resentful gaze on Kat. She swallowed hard. She had shamed him in front of one of his servants, a humiliation that a man as proud as Don Rafael would find hard to accept.

"Out, Dorotea," he said, not looking at the maid, and she hurried to obey him, moving toward the stairs, but he barked, "Not that way, you fool!" and she fled out of the tower.

"I had hoped, señora," Rafael said in a tightly controlled voice, "to have you care for me by now as you care for Lord Harwood."

"As I care for—" Despite her fear, Kat laughed. Then she saw the fury in the Spanish nobleman's eyes, and realized that her laughter had been a mistake. "My lord, pray do not think—"

"Think what, Katherine? I think I have been far too patient with you. Come here."

She shook her head.

"Now!"

She darted toward the door through which the maid had fled, but Rafael caught her before she reached it and began to drag her toward the stairs.

She screamed.

He hesitated, and she kicked at him and screamed again, and he let her go, so suddenly that she fell to the floor. He reached down to help her up, but she flinched back from him, screaming again.

"No, do not—" He held up his hand, wincing. "I beg you, do not scream. Would you have all my servants think I must take you by force?"

"Would you have that be the truth?" she asked, crying now, from fear and anger—aye, and shame that she was reduced to this.

"I would have you as my lover."

She shook her head again. "I will never love you."

"I am certain you will change your mind, in time. And even if you cannot truly love me, I am sure you will at least be grateful for me, for the care I give you, and the protection."

"The protection!" Kat said scornfully.

"Yes, Katherine, for I have protected you. I meant to keep this from you, lest it interfere with my wooing of you. But now I would have you know that rumors of an Englishwoman staying here, rumors spread by my servants, have reached my neighbors. And there is a vicar of the Inquisition staying with one of my neighbors, and he has told this neighbor that he wishes to meet you, to determine if you are any threat to my household, and to give you brief instructions in the true faith if you are not. I have delayed my reply. I would have told this vicar, who should be leaving Navarra soon to return to Castile, that you would not be my guest much longer, and that his questioning of you would only offend Doña Margaret. But now I think I will let him come. Yes, Katherine, I will let him meet you, and then you may decide whether you wish me to continue as your protector."

"And if I do not?"

He shrugged. "Then what happens to you will be no concern of mine. I will leave you now. No doubt you need time to think about this."

Dorotea came back in a few minutes after the don had left. By then Kat had gotten up and straightened her clothes, but she still felt shaken, and she and the maid looked at each other wordlessly. Dorotea looked worried, nearly as worried as Kat felt. Marry, Kat thought, who should comfort whom?

CHAPTER 25

The day was warm, even for Madrid in July, yet a fire burned in the hearth of the largest bedchamber of the house on the Calle Mayor, and the bed was heaped with blankets. Beneath those blankets, the sick man who was Justin's host was shivering. Despite that, Don Antonio Téllez de Osuna, Conde de Ordaz, wanted another glass of orange juice, and he wanted it with ice.

Justin shook his head as he lifted chunks of ice from the covered bowl on the table beside the bed, dropped them into a tall Venetian glass, then filled the glass with orange juice. He had never shared the Madrileños' fondness for adding ice to many of their drinks. A servant was sent daily from Antonio's house to the snowpit where snow from the mountains was stored during the summer months, and Antonio had insisted on having his drink iced, though Justin doubted it was good for his health, especially now.

He handed the chill glass to his host, who thanked him and took a sip, then smiled.

"Do not frown so," Antonio said, in the flawless English he enjoyed speaking. "If my physician demands that I give up iced drinks, then I will. But this is a mere cold, and—" A coughing fit ended his attempt to speak for almost a minute. After it was over, Antonio sagged back against the pillows, but kept a firm grip on the glass, which Justin would have taken from him. "This *is* but a cold," Antonio said again, and Justin prayed that he was right.

The illness had come on suddenly, Antonio waking with a bad cough this morning, but Justin had noticed as soon as he saw his host upon arriving in Madrid that the rigors of serving King Philip were taking their toll of Don Antonio's strength. Antonio was still a handsome man, but his hair was graying and his face was cut with harsh lines. Now, with this illness, Justin could see how his friend would look when old, and it grieved him.

"Perchance you should return to Burgos when you are better, and rest there for a few months," he suggested, but Antonio shook his head.

"The king needs me. I have sent a messenger to tell King Philip of my illness, and I would wager that he returns with some papers for me to look over." He said it calmly, with a trace of a smile, and Justin was reminded once again of the value Antonio placed on *sosiego*.

Sosiego. Margaret sometimes railed against it, that quality of serenity which was prized by the Spanish nobility, a serenity that was no part of her own nature. Yet even she admitted that his serenity served Antonio well in his dealings with the king. Philip was himself the epitome of *sosiego*, but his own habits sorely tested his servants' patience. Margaret sometimes called Philip "The Tortoise," mocking his slowness in coming to any decision, and Antonio himself, though never directly complaining about the king, had told Justin that one of Philip's viceroys, frustrated by the troubles and delays he encountered whenever he sought advice from Philip about situations in that overseas colony, had told one of his officials that if death came from Spain, they would all live forever. "I and time shall arrange matters as we can," the king would say—but that was scant comfort to the councillors whose own work was slowed by Philip's insistence on dealing carefully with even the most trivial matters mentioned in the letters or *consultas* he read, or his penchant for adding further notes to final drafts of letters or orders before he signed them.

Yet Antonio never spoke ill of his king. He had come close to losing his composure only once when discussing Philip, and that had been yesterday, when he and Justin had ridden out to the Casa de Campo. Antonio had wished his guest to see the gardens, especially the topiary work, and also the zoo, with its elephants and rhinoceros. Then, as they were riding past a group of gardeners, Antonio had heard one of them predict that some enemy of his would soon be dealt with as harshly as Don Carlos, the king's late son.

Justin had never seen Antonio so angry. Before they left the Casa de Campo, Antonio had ordered the gardener turned off, never to be hired again for work in one of the royal gardens. Then he had spoken nary a word on their ride back to Madrid. Justin had wondered at his reaction to the gardener's remark.

Don Carlos had died several months after being imprisoned by his father two years ago, and few had seen the imprisonment itself as anything but inevitable. The twenty-two-year-old prince, who had seemed slow-witted since his childhood, had suffered serious head injuries from a fall down a staircase at the university of Alcala when he was seventeen. He was blind for a time, and feverish, and was cured only when his skull was trepanned by the great Flemish physician Andreas Vesalius—though 'twas likely, Margaret had told Justin in all seriousness, that Don Carlos's recovery was owed more to the holiness of a dead Franciscan monk, Diego de Alcala, whose corpse had been exhumed and placed next to Don Carlos in an attempt to drive away the evil sickness in the prince. Neither the trepanning nor the holy remains of the monk had effected a complete cure, however, for after the accident Don Carlos had been subject to mad rages, even attacking some of his father's ministers with a knife. Philip had imprisoned Don Carlos to prevent him from fleeing to the Netherlands, where belike he would have been used as the figurehead of a rebellion by Philip's enemies, much as Philip's grandmother Joanna the Mad had been used by the *comuneros* who had rebelled against her son, Charles V. Philip had personally led the party that put his son under arrest.

But that was common knowledge; it could not have been the possibility that the gardener was referring only to the arrest that had caused Don Antonio to be so wroth with the gardener. Needs must that it was the manner of Don Carlos's death to which Antonio believed the gardener referred.

Not everyone believed that the prince had died as was officially reported, from an illness that ensued after he fasted for three days and then drank great quantities of iced water and devoured an enormous partridge pie. It was widely rumored that Don Carlos had been strangled, on orders from the king. Justin was not sure which story was true, but he was certain that Philip would not have wished his son to go on living for decades as a prisoner, the focus of every rebellion and plot against the throne, as Joanna the Mad had been, as the Queen of Scots was now. And that Philip would condone his son's death under certain circumstances was beyond dispute: had he not said as much at that *auto-da-fé* at Valladolid? Then the question had been one of heresy, but would not the king treat a grave threat to his sovereignty as a kind of heresy?

And if Don Antonio had learned that the king had ordered his own son murdered, then he would have been greatly troubled, but he would not have abandoned Philip. There might well be, Justin reasoned, a great deal of pain hidden behind that mask of *sosiego*. Yet he would never know, for those were questions he dared not ask.

"*Madre de Dios*, you are somber, my friend," Antonio said, recalling Justin from his thoughts. "I regret that I am free to spend a day at home only when I am ill. 'Tis not how I would choose to treat such a beloved guest."

"Pray do not apologize. I am only sorry that you are ill."

"I should be well again in a few days. Will you delay your departure until then?"

"If you wish."

"I would return to my duties at court for a day or two before you leave, so I will have a chance to learn whether Philip has decided to heed the pope's wishes and invade England. That is what you came here to discover, is it not?" he asked with a chuckle that gave way to coughing.

Justin waited until his host had recovered, then said, "I will not deny that the matter interests me, but it is far from the only reason I am here. I had not seen you now, coz, for two years, and I missed your company."

"And Margaret's," Antonio said with a smile.

"And Margaret's," Justin echoed after a slight pause.

"I hope that you will be able to spend some more time with Margaret on your way back to Bilbao. She has missed you greatly, too."

Justin could think of nothing to say. Was it possible Antonio knew that he had once been Margaret's lover? His comments might have been innocent, but still they stirred up feelings of guilt like raked-over coals.

Justin had not lain with Margaret for fifteen years. He could excuse the adultery now: he had been only fifteen, easily swayed by Margaret's beauty, easily taken in by her story of being forced to marry Antonio against her will—a story which, in truth, he thought she had believed then, at least for a time, while she was trying to convince him. But his first meeting with Don Antonio had left him certain that Margaret had married the Spaniard willingly. Moreover, he had seen Antonio as a man worthy of respect and admiration, unlike many in Philip's retinue. He had even found himself wishing at times that his father had been more like this Spanish gentleman. Of one thing he was sure: he would not again help Margaret to cuckold her husband. He was still tempted by her beauty; he still enjoyed holding her and kissing her—but it would go no further. He had been unable to think of any way to let her know of his changed feelings without hurting her, so instead he had come to Spain much less often than she would have wished, and had limited the length of his visits and the time he spent alone with her. Interruptions could always be found; excuses could always be made. He had hoped that over time her love for him would cool, and he believed now that it had: she had seemed more interested in having his help with her plans to return England to the Catholic fold than in having him share her bed.

But if Antonio was suspicious of his relationship with Margaret, there was no way to allay his fears. What could he say? *I no longer love your wife, and I believe she no longer loves me as she once did.* Justin nearly laughed aloud at the thought. Then, aware of Antonio's unwavering gaze, he changed the subject.

"Do you truly expect to hear different news when you return to court? Do you see any chance that Philip will change his mind, and send his fleet against England?"

Antonio shook his head. "There is much less chance of that now than last year."

Justin was suddenly very still. "Last year?" he asked, trying to sound unconcerned, but Antonio laughed.

"That surprises you, I warrant. Yes, the king was eager to help the rebel earls last year. He was wroth with English piracy—with Hawkins, with the English pirates in the Channel. Especially was he angry at Elizabeth, for having acted the pirate in seizing the treasure bound for Antwerp. He would have had the Duke of Alva add his army to that of Northumberland and Westmorland—but the tide of rebellion turned too quickly. Even then, he would have had Alva prepare to invade England, had not the duke argued against such a course. The pope has tried to sway Alva, too, asking him to ally with France against England, but Alva has discouraged such plans, for he has seen enough damage done to trade already and so argues for negotiation rather than war."

"Yea, but does not this papal bull change matters? Will not His Sacred Catholic Royal Majesty"—his voice was edged with sarcasm as he used the title by which Philip was addressed—"heed the pope's wishes? This bull excommunicating Elizabeth—"

"Matters little here," Antonio said, waving a hand negligently. "His Sacred Catholic Royal Majesty"—there was no sarcasm in his voice—"rules here. The pope does not. No papal decree may be published here without the permission of the Council of Castile. When the pope decreed that all who take part in bullfights are excommunicate, our theologians and bishops assured the king that such fights are not sinful. If Philip will not heed Pius's decree on such a matter, why would he aid the pope now, in a military venture that might bleed Spain dry? We cannot afford another war—not now, with the trouble in the Netherlands, with the Morisco rebellion in Granada—"

"But I was told that their commander had surrendered."

"Some still fight on in the mountains, with aid from the Turks and the sultan's servant the king of Algiers. We have lost Tunis to Algiers already this year. Would you have us risk more, that Spanish armies may fight on English soil? We cannot withdraw our armies from Italy, from Granada, from the Netherlands, and we cannot form a new army here in Castile. There are too few able-bodied men left."

"Say you so? I have seen enough able-bodied rogues abroad in the streets here."

"Oh, our *matónes* and *valentónes*? May God deliver us from them. They are rogues indeed, deserters for the most part, and there is trouble enough among our soldiers, especially when their pay is late, without adding more such scoundrels to their ranks."

There was a long silence between them, broken only by the sound of Antonio's coughing. Finally the Spaniard said, "This has disappointed you. It has disappointed Margaret as well. But please it you, let not your disappointment in the king lead you to desperate actions."

"Desperate actions?"

"I would fain hear that you are not plotting with de Spes."

"I am not plotting with de Spes," Justin responded, without hesitation. "By my faith, I am not."

Antonio looked relieved. "I had feared for you. De Spes is a fool. I argued against sending him as ambassador to England, but no one listened to me. De Spes began his clumsy meddling as soon as he left Spain, and Cecil has watched him every second since then, like a wise old hound watching a puppy. Let the puppy disturb him too much, and—" Antonio snapped his fingers. "I would not have you caught in the snares de Spes is setting for himself."

"I would not be. The queen trusts me."

"No doubt, but does Cecil trust you? It is Cecil who governs all. De Spes has told us as much, though he believes Cecil will not long enjoy such power. And Fenelon de la Mothe, the French ambassador, agrees with him. Ware Cecil. If he can dispose of an enemy as powerful as the Duke of Norfolk, then how much more easily may he deal with you?"

"He can do nothing to me without cause, and I tell you again: I have not plotted with Don Guerau."

"Good," Antonio said, nodding. "Then I need not fear for you, unless perchance you have been drawn into this latest folly of Margaret's."

"Folly?"

"Has she not told you of her latest design? She spoke of it when last I saw her, and I had hoped she was speaking in idleness, but your coming here has reminded me that she wished you to help her."

"Oh. The catechism. In sooth, she did show me a catechism, published at Douai, and bade me take it into England and see that it is published there. I told her I could take no such risk."

To Justin's surprise, Antonio began to laugh, then coughed alarmingly for a few minutes. At last, wiping tears from his eyes, he smiled at Justin and said, "What you say relieves me, and I thank God that it was all she asked of you. She spoke to me of some mad plan to have your queen assassinated. Someone else had conceived it and had disclosed it to her, for she told me that they wished to be paid, and how much, and said that she would rather set someone else to such a task, someone like you, who would do it out of friendship and love of the Church." His smile faded. "You are very quiet, my friend. Pray God, my wife did not ask you to murder your queen."

Justin shook his head. He felt stunned. "How could she think that such a design would meet with the approval of the other exiles? Some, to be sure, might be so desperate, but . . ." His voice trailed off. Frowning, he shook his head again.

"I warrant that she has given this plan little thought, and was but repeating something said to her by one of the more disaffected exiles."

"Who told her how much the assassin would demand for his services."

"A sum greater than she could ever raise. 'Twas why she spoke of asking you for help. Otherwise, she must sell all her jewels—and what woman would make such a sacrifice for politics?" He laughed, then continued, more soberly, "As like as not, the person who spoke to her of this plan hoped to trick her into giving him the money. There is no way this design could be carried out without your help, for needs must that the assassin have access to Elizabeth's court, and you are the only English courtier to whom she writes. No doubt she has realized as much herself, and that is why she said nothing of this to you."

"No doubt," Justin agreed.

There was a knock on the door, and then a maidservant announced that the physician had arrived. A moment later Bernardino de Silva entered the bedchamber. Justin looked at him curiously. De Silva was a *converso*, a man who was Jewish by descent but who, like his father, now practiced the Christian faith. De Silva's father and grandfather had been physicians, too: Jewish doctors were renowned for their skill, and Philip's father, Charles V, had employed a *converso* physician. But Philip was not so tolerant—perchance, as Antonio said, because the king's tutor and confessor had been Juan Martinez de Sileceo, who as Archbishop of Toledo had decreed that only those who could prove that they had no Jewish blood in their veins could hold an ecclesiastical office. Justin wondered whether the king knew of Antonio's physician.

De Silva greeted them in Spanish, then switched to English when he was told Justin was from England. "I welcome an opportunity to speak your language," he told Justin. "I studied for a time at the university of Padua and had many friends among the English nation there."

De Silva told Justin he could stay while he examined his patient, but warned that Antonio should rest and not exert himself in conversation. "Though," de Silva added with a wry smile, "I have little hope that will happen as long as he can draw breath and is awake."

"Then I shall take my leave of you until this evening," Justin said. "Mayhap I will go riding until then."

Antonio looked alarmed. "I pray you, do not leave the house today. I would not have you encounter Don Alonso again."

Don Alonso Martinez de Villena was one of the Spaniards Justin had met during Mary's reign, first meeting the nobleman as he swaggered into a tavern. Don Alonso was a proud, arrogant man, but it had been reckless of Justin to call him a popinjay within his hearing. Only the intervention of Philip himself had stopped Don Alonso from forcing his young English rival into a duel. Alonso had been twenty-one then, and already an accomplished swordsman who had killed two men in duels. He had made it clear that he resented Philip's meddling, and Justin had avoided him for the rest of the time he remained in England.

He had not seen Don Alonso again until yesterday, when, returning from the Casa de Campo, they had encountered Don Alonso and three of his servants in the Calle Mayor, not far from Don Antonio's house. Don Alonso had been outraged to discover that Lord Harwood was in Spain, and still more outraged to learn that the Englishman was Antonio's guest. Only a mention of the safe-conduct provided Justin by the king had prevented a fight then and there.

"I do not trust him," Antonio continued. "I would not have you meet him again, as you may if you ride through Madrid."

"Fear not. I plan to ride directly to the gate and then out of the city. I am loath to spend such a beautiful day inside."

"Then take a servant with you."

"I'll have Tandy ride with me," Justin assured him, though he knew that Tandy was already away, off gathering information from his own sources.

"Very well. I shall see you this evening, then." He looked toward the physician, and Justin left the room. As he crossed the threshhold he heard Antonio ask, rather crossly, if de Silva meant to forbid him to drink iced juices. He heard the doctor chuckle, and could not help but smile.

Justin's mood was much grimmer as he rode away from Don Antonio's house. Margaret's words kept repeating themselves in his mind.

But if you will not do this—not even this—then I must perforce ask someone else.

Fool! Why had he not wondered what she meant by *not even this*? He might have learned of her other design then.

I have heard marvelous things of him, she had said, speaking of the English courtier of whom her French friend had told her. For a truth, she had: from what Antonio had said, the payment this would-be assassin demanded was marvelous indeed. And she had been wearing jewels at supper, so she had not sold them all, not by then. But might she have sold them since then?

He would have left at once for Burgos, but could not—not while

Don Antonio was still ailing. Antonio was likely correct: Margaret would be loath to part with her jewels.

He would be glad to leave Madrid. The city had changed greatly in the ten years since Philip had declared it the *unica corte*, the only court, choosing the city over Toledo or Valladolid—which most courtiers would have preferred—because of its dry, healthful climate, which suited Philip, and its central location.

Justin especially disliked the ugly, straggling houses of only one story, the *casas de malicia*. There was no incentive to build taller houses, for the king had ordered that the houses' owners be willing to lodge court officials in the second story of their homes. Justin could not blame the builders of these malice houses, but they had added a meanness to Madrid's appearance that Philip could not remove with all his plans for rebuilding the Alcazar and widening the streets. There seemed to be more poor people in Madrid now, many of whom could be found at noon each day waiting by the monastery of San Luis for the free soup that was given out there. And the streets they thronged were filthy with night soil that was never cleared away, for it was believed that the brisk, dry winds here on this high plateau would purify all such filth.

The climate itself had changed in ten years. Once sheltered by wooded hills and renowned for its even climate, Madrid now suffered harsher weather that the Madrileños themselves had brought on by clearing away many of the forests for wood to build their houses, wood that increased the king's revenues. Now the wind that swept through Madrid's streets carried grit that stung one's eyes and could strip varnish from wood, as Antonio had discovered when a table and two chairs had been left out on a balcony overlooking the Calle Mayor.

A girl strolling across a side street caught his eye. She was fair-haired and tall and slim, and for a moment she reminded him of Kat, and desire seared him. Then, aware of his gaze, she turned to look at him directly, and smiled, and he saw that she was not as lovely as Kat. Still, this girl was fair, and he could have had her: she wore the scarlet cloak of a whore, and as he continued to look at her she gestured toward a house down the street—her *burdel*? For a moment he was tempted, but then he shook his head. Like enough, the *puta* was diseased. She shrugged and walked on.

He rode past the Alcazar, where Philip's double-eagle standard flew, then out the Puerta de Moros. He wanted quiet and solitude, and a ride through the hills between Madrid and the Escorial would might offer heart's-ease. He remembered one especially pretty glade, some fifteen miles from Madrid, where he and Antonio and Margaret had stopped to have dinner after riding out to the Escorial the first time he had seen it, four years ago.

He found the glade eventually, recognizing it by a hollow that Antonio had pronounced an amphitheater. Justin smiled, remembering how the don stood there, entertaining his wife and his guest by declaiming lines he remembered from plays. Then, hearing branches rustling behind him, he started to turn around.

He heard the shot at the same time that the bullet struck his shoulder. He reeled under the impact. His horse reared, and he was thrown from the saddle. The breath was knocked from him, and he lay still on the ground.

He saw the rider then, surrounded by a corona of pale smoke that blew away a moment later. The man wore a leather jerkin like a soldier's, and Justin knew at once that this was one of the scoundrels Antonio had spoken of. As he watched, the man returned his dag to its holster and then rode toward him, a leering smile on his smallpox-scarred face.

Justin kept very still. The rider was too close: he would be trampled before he could get to his feet or draw his sword. His hope now lay in the man's curiosity, or his greed.

The rider dismounted a few steps away. Justin watched his approach through slitted eyes, then, without warning, rolled toward his attacker and kicked the man's feet out from under him. The *matón* fell, but before Justin could get to his feet, the Spaniard had thrown himself at him.

They wrestled, rolling into the hollow. Justin was taller and heavier, and he might have overcome his attacker in a few moments, had his left arm not been weakened. As it was, he was hard put to keep the *matón* from drawing his weapons, and he had no chance to draw his own. Finally the *matón* let go with one hand and tried to gouge out Justin's eyes, but Justin jerked away and rolled, taking the Spaniard with him. The *matón*'s head slammed into a rock, and he grunted, then lay still.

Justin got to his feet and staggered a few paces away, then drew his sword and dagger. His attacker had not stirred. Justin approached the man cautiously, not wanting to have his own trick used against him. He prodded the *matón* with the sword's point, then moved the blade so it touched the Spaniard's throat, then, carefully, made a shallow cut. Blood welled from the wound and trickled down the side of the *matón*'s neck, but still he did not move. He was breathing yet, but raggedly.

Justin searched the man's clothes, hoping to find some clue to his identity, but there were no papers—only an ivory comb, a toothpick, and two purses. One was of greasy leather, creased and worn. The other did not fit with the rogue's garb. It was of straw-colored velvet-on-velvet, embroidered with silver thread. Justin was amazed to find the purse filled mostly with gold ducats. There were a few silver reals, but not a single copper maravedi. The rogue had been paid well.

Justin tucked both purses into his doublet pockets, then relieved the *matón* of his sword belt and pistol, which he tucked under his right arm. He looked around. The *matón*'s horse had run away. Justin's mount was cropping grass some fifty yards down the hill. There were fetters in his cloakbag, he remembered, fetters that could be used to tie up the Spaniard. Justin started down the hill, moving slowly now, for he was light-headed of a sudden. He stopped and looked for the first time at his left shoulder, where the bullet wound was still seeping blood. He tore a strip from his shirt and packed the linen bandage against the wound.

Hearing a noise behind him, he turned to see the *matón* get to his feet and then stumble away. Too weak to pursue on foot, Justin continued on down the hill and caught his horse, managed on the second try to get into the saddle, then rode back up the slope.

The *matón* was no longer in sight, nor could Justin hear him. He was looking around for tracks when he became aware that his shoulder was still bleeding. Swearing, he started back toward Madrid.

A few hours later Justin was sitting on a chair in Don Antonio's bedchamber. Fortified by a large glass of aqua vitae, he had succeeded in making not a sound while Bernardino de Silva removed the bullet from his shoulder and then cleaned and dressed the wound. Still, he could not resist a sigh of relief when the ordeal was over. The physician gave him an understanding smile.

"I thank you," Justin told him.

"I am glad to be of service," Bernardino replied, bowing slightly before resuming his methodical work of returning bandages and medicines and surgical instruments to his bag. "It is always a pleasure to treat a patient who does not fear *quintar*, or believe that he will be defiled if he is so much as touched by a *converso*."

De Silva had spoken mildly. Whatever bitterness he felt was an old wound—though not so old and scarred over that he had forgotten it. *Quintar*. Justin remembered Antonio telling him of that superstition, the foolish belief that Jewish physicians—and hence *converso* physicians as well—killed one out of five of their Christian patients, as a revenge against the Christians. It angered and saddened Justin that Bernardino de Silva was the victim of such superstitions, that this highly educated doctor could be treated with contempt by anyone, no matter how low, who could produce an *ejacutaria* proving he had no Jewish blood.

"*Todos somos de una masa,*" he said softly, and Bernardino paused in his work, then looked up at Justin, an expression of surprise slowly giving way to a smile.

"We are all of one clay. That is true. But that is a statement I have heard, till now, only from *conversos* . . . and from my friend Don Antonio," he added, nodding his head toward the nobleman.

"Would there were more Spaniards like him."

"Aye, but too many are like a patient of mine—also of the nobility—who sent for me at the recommendation of a friend of his, a friend who said nothing to him of my being a *converso*. I treated this nobleman, and cured him of his fever, and he thanked me and paid me most generously. And then a week later he learned that I am a *converso*. He went at once to a priest, who blessed him and then blessed his house to purify it. And he burned the nightgown he had worn when I saw him, and the bedhangings, and the stool I sat on, and would have burned the bed itself and torn up the floor of the bedchamber if his wife had not convinced him to desist, telling him the priest's blessing had sufficed."

Justin shook his head. "You seem little troubled by this."

De Silva laughed. "The man has a Christian doctor now, no more than a mountebank despite his degree. This doctor recommends purges for all ills, and his patient now scarce dares leave his house for an hour at a time."

Justin chuckled, as did Antonio, who said, "I believe I know who this nobleman is, but Bernardino will not confirm my suspicions."

"I am the very spirit of discretion, where my patients are concerned," the physician replied, closing his bag.

"So you will say nothing of Lord Harwood's quarrel with Don Alonso?"

"No. Especially not if you are sure it was he who sent the *matón* after Lord Harwood."

"Does this look familiar?" Antonio asked, holding up the velvet-on-velvet purse Justin had taken from his attacker.

De Silva went over to him and looked at the purse closely. "I could not swear that I have seen this very purse before now . . . but this velvet the color of straw, with the silver—this is the stuff and these are the colors that he wears above all others. Will you send this to the king and tell him of what happened?"

"Nay, this evidence is too slight to convince Philip. But Don Alonso may not know that. I shall send the purse back to him, with a letter advising him to be more careful what he does with his purse."

"A subtle design," de Silva said approvingly. "Let him wonder whether you have told King Philip."

Justin got up from his chair and walked over to him. He took the purse from the physician and hefted it in one hand. "I would not have this returned to Don Alonso when it is so heavy," he said to Antonio.

"No, of course not."

" 'Twould likely do injury to the servant forced to carry such a heavy purse."

"Yea, and his horse, too."

"Hold out your hands," Justin told the doctor, and poured the entire contents of the purse into de Silva's palms. The doctor blinked at the glittering mound of coins.

"This was too much for a *matón* . . . aye, and too much as well for my fee."

"I would have you keep it," Justin said.

"Very well," de Silva said. "I thank you." He poured the coins onto the table, filled his purse, then put the substantial pile of coins that was left over into his bag. "You do not fear that I will come to harm while carrying this much treasure? If I am not set upon by thieves first, and this burden lightened for me, I may suffer a hernia."

"Haply you will," Justin said lightly, "but you may always hire yourself a physician."

De Silva laughed. He picked his bag up and slung the strap over his shoulder. Justin thought he would have bidden them farewell then, but instead, his smile fading, he turned to Antonio.

"Don Antonio. You may have heard that Baron Montigny was once a patient of mine. I know that he is under a sentence of death, but I have been told that the princess Anne will ask that he be released when she reaches Spain. Is there any hope?"

Justin had caught his breath at the first mention of the baron. Montigny, a rebel from the Netherlands, was said to have conspired with Don Carlos. The baron had been arrested nearly three years ago, and after a long trial had finally been found guilty of treason and sentenced to death last spring; he was still being held prisoner in the castle of Simancas, awaiting execution. Justin, too, had heard from Tandy that his sources had learned of Montigny's friends in the Netherlands approaching Philip's bride-to-be and asking for her help, which she had promised. It was unimaginable that Philip would agree to spare a traitor whom he might well blame for the plot that had finally forced him to imprison his son, but neither was it possible that the king would wish to refuse such a request from Anne at the time of their nuptials. Justin had given no thought to the matter at the time he had heard that the Austrian princess planned to intervene, but now it suddenly struck him that Philip must see only one course lying open to him.

Montigny would never leave Simancas. He would die sometime before the princess could reach Philip and make her appeal. And he would be strangled, or killed in some other secret way, and the word given out that he had died a natural death, so that the king could be spared an awkward situation.

Chilled, Justin awaited his friend's response.

Antonio had become quite still when he heard Montigny's name mentioned, but at last he shrugged, the movement jerky and forced, completely unlike his usually fluid gestures. "I have no knowledge of this," he said, but his tone and his expression gave the lie to his words. He was angry, as angry as he had been at the Casa de Campo, but Justin was certain the anger was not directed at the physician. No, Antonio was wroth with himself instead, reminded anew of what manner of king he served, but he was too fair to blame de Silva for reopening an old wound, one that Justin feared would never heal completely as long as his friend served Philip.

De Silva nodded, a look of sorrow on his face. He bade Antonio farewell, then turned again to Justin, giving him further advice on his shoulder wound as they walked together toward the door. There de Silva paused and glanced back at Antonio. "Would that I had some physic for his spirit," he murmured. And then the physician was gone, his cloak swirling behind him as he walked down the hall.

Justin turned slowly back toward the bed. Antonio had been sitting up for the last hour, but now he was lying back against the pillows, his eyes closed.

"Shall I summon any of your servants?" Justin asked.

Antonio shook his head, still not opening his eyes. "I am merely tired, my friend, and would rest again. As should you. I pray that your wound heals quickly. But I must ask you now not to leave my house again until you return to Burgos. Don Alonso will understand the message I have sent him, but he is such a fool that he may not choose to heed it."

Justin agreed, and then left Don Antonio to his thoughts, which he was sure would give the count anything but rest.

Tandy strolled slowly up the Calle Mayor, looking about at the fine shops and houses, some of them five stories tall, though of a truth he had long ago become bored with them. But he was playing a bumpkin, and had dressed for the role, donning old clothing of Spanish cut that he had brought from England. He had rubbed dark grease through his tawny hair, then combed it carelessly. It was unlikely that anyone seeing him now would recognize him as the carefully dressed servant of the English lord who was staying with Don Antonio.

He listened closely to the people around him as he walked. For days he had done little but listen, and when he chanced to overhear an interesting scrap of conversation he had paused and lingered, as inconspicuously as possible, until the talk no longer interested him. Much of his best information had been gathered at the *mentideros*, the lie parlors where everyone traded in news and gossip, but there was always the chance to learn something here, too, outside the shops on the Calle Mayor.

He walked through the Puerta del Sol, spotted a *bodegone de puntapie*, and went over to the stall. He had not stopped to eat breakfast before leaving the house, but he was hungry now. He gave the vendor a few maravedis for two *empanadillas*, and ate the meat pies there. The meat was heavily seasoned with pimento and garlic. He washed his meal down with a draught of wine from a leather jug, then moved on.

On other days he had visited as many *mentideros* as possible, but today he decided he had no time for the lie parlors by the *corrales* where plays were presented. His new friends among the actors who gathered to gossip at the Corral de la Pacheca in the Calle del Principe would be disappointed not to see him. He did spend a few minutes at a *mentidero* where soldiers gathered, staying there only long enough to confirm what Lord Harwood had heard yesterday from Don Antonio. Spain's armies were too wide-flung, in Milan and Flanders and Granada. Philip's call for more troops had brought in a pitiful rabble that the officers were ashamed to lead. No one there said a word about invading England.

Tandy moved on, to the Alcazar.

The Madrileños were proud of their royal palace, though Tandy, who had seen the beauty of Hampton Court and Greenwich, could not understand why. The four towers facing the town did not even match. And while Philip had made some improvements in the building, the changes had only contributed more to its motley appearance, with stone walls abutting walls of brick and mud. But he was not here to admire the palace, for all his gaping.

He strolled through the main gate and into the courtyards. Into the greatest lie parlor in Madrid, into the Paul's Walk of Spain.

Like Paul's, the courtyards of the Alcazar had their vendors, and he bought himself a paper of berries to take the taste of the *empanadillas* from his mouth. As he ate, he wandered through the crowd, watching as couriers and officials were accosted for news, listening to all the gossip. And all the while he made his way, as unobtrusively as possible, toward a corner of one courtyard where he had seen rogues meeting.

They were there again today, the *matónes* and *valentónes*, the killers and heroes. Killers they were of certain, but not heroes. Tandy had paid little attention to them on his previous visits to the Alcazar. They rarely had news of interest to him, and he disliked their bragging of their prowess and—worst of all—of their nobility. All of them claimed to be *hidalgos*, as did so many other Spaniards that Tandy often wondered that anyone was left to work in Spain, for the *hidalguia* would not soil their aristocratic hands with honest labor. Tandy far preferred England's rogues: none of the rogues and thieves he had met in England ever claimed to be a gentleman—at least not when in the company of other vagabonds.

Today, however, Tandy edged closer to the *valentónes* and *matónes*, scanning the faces shadowed by their hats for a particularly scarred face. He saw one man who had been terribly disfigured by smallpox, but his hair was gray, and the *matón* who had attacked Lord Harwood was a young man.

Several of the rogues had just come to Madrid, one group from Valladolid, another from Burgos, and they were as hungry for news as Tandy was, and were listening eagerly to even the stalest gossip. Knowing he would learn nothing here, he began to move away, then, hearing the word *inglesa*, stopped and stood there, munching berries, while the *valentónes* from Burgos bragged of their latest exploit.

They had abducted an Englishwoman, a lovely young girl with fair hair and blue-green eyes. They had taken her from the home of another *inglesa*, also a yellow-haired beauty, but they had not taken her as well. Their orders had been only to capture the younger woman . . . and she was the choicer morsel, by far. She had fought them, using a sword to defend herself, but she had been well worth the trouble. Several in their audience wanted to know if they had enjoyed the English maid, and the *valentónes* from Burgos were offended that the question had even been asked. Were they not men? *Dios*, the wench had enjoyed them!

Tandy, then putting another berry in his mouth, bit down hard on his fingers.

The pain recalled him to his surroundings. He had been almost blind with rage, on the verge of drawing his sword and running them through, but now he was aware again of how many rogues were here, all of them armed. He would have to bide his time. He moved a little ways off, but not so far that he could not see the *valentónes* from Burgos, and waited.

At noon the four rogues left the Alcazar, unaware of Tandy trailing after them. He followed them to a *bodegone* where they spent the afternoon, and thence, at dusk, to a *burdel*. Tandy waited across the street, pretending to sleep sitting up in a doorway. The day had been a hot one, but, as was often the case in Madrid, the summer night was almost cold, and he shivered from time to time as he sat watching the door of the *burdel*. And at last—near midnight, judging by the stars—he had his chance. One of the *valentónes* came out alone. He paused in the doorway and screamed a few insults at someone inside, and a woman's shrieking voice replied in kind. Then the rogue stumbled out into the street and began to stagger back in the direction of the tavern.

Tandy got up and went after him. He had taken only a few steps when he saw a window opened overhead. A man called out *"Agua va!"* and the contents of a jordan were thrown out, splashing the hapless *valentón*, who halted in the middle of the street, swearing as he shook off his cloak.

Tandy stepped carefully around the stinking puddle and approached the *valentón*.

"Amigo," he said quietly, *"deje que le preste mi capa . . ."*

The Spaniard gazed dully at him, seemingly too drunk to react with surprise or happiness or wariness at a stranger's offer to exchange a clean cloak for his befouled one. Tandy removed his cloak, and after a moment the *valentón* followed suit. Smiling graciously, Tandy stepped behind the fellow, then caught both the rogue's arms with his left arm. His right hand held a knife to the *valentón*'s throat.

"Grita una sola vez," he murmured, *"y te aseguro que no has de volver a entrar en un burdel."* And he took the *valentón* to an alley he had noticed earlier.

It took him only a few minutes to learn everything the rogue could tell him, for the *valentón*, once deprived of his sword and dagger, was far from the hero he claimed to be. Indeed, the coward all but sobbed as he protested that he had not raped the English girl.

Tandy shook his head. Would that he could see the man hanged—of certain he deserved to die, but Tandy could not bring himself to kill him in cold blood.

He heard footsteps then, near the alley's opening, and glanced back toward the street.

The *valentón* moved then, lunging at Tandy. There was a tiny knife in his hand, like the cuttle used by nips. He thrust at Tandy's face, belike trying to blind him, but Tandy moved more swiftly yet, jerking his head back so that while the Spaniard's fist struck him, the blade missed. An instant later the *valentón* was dying, Tandy's knife between his ribs.

Tandy stood still for a few moments, breathing raggedly. Then he looked toward the street. No one stood there in the alley's entrance. Nor did he hear any footsteps. And then he did, more rapid steps than before, going away. Likely whoever had come down the street had decided the alley was best avoided.

'Twas a wise decision, and for himself as well, Tandy thought. He pulled his dagger from the Spaniard's chest, wiped it clean on the man's doublet, and then started back toward Don Antonio's house, walking swiftly, but not so swiftly he would call attention to himself.

There were letters as well as his breakfast on the tray the maidservant brought to Don Antonio's chamber. He waited until she left before opening the letter on top, which was from the king. It was of no import, merely a polite few lines expressing concern for his servant's health and repeating the advice he had given Don Antonio in another letter yesterday. Antonio smiled wryly as he glanced at the tray on the table beside his bed. King Philip's advice was already being followed, to his servant's regret; Antonio wished he had not mentioned the advice to his own servants.

He heard someone knock on the half-open door of his chamber, and looked up then to see Justin standing there.

"Come in, my friend! I was just thinking of you."

A look of guilt that Antonio had come to know well flickered across Justin's face, then was gone, carefully hidden behind a smile. Antonio knew the cause of that guilt, and wished it were possible to comfort his friend. Even fifteen years ago, when he first saw Justin and Margaret together and sensed that they had become lovers, his anger at the boy had quickly been subdued by the knowledge that he had been as much to blame as Justin. Margaret had been so young then, so easily hurt, and Antonio had not given her the attention she craved. He had not been able to hate Justin then, and he could not hate him now, even knowing that his wife still loved her cousin. Antonio knew as well that there had been no act of adultery between Justin and Margaret since that summer long ago. The baron had never, until now, visited Spain when Antonio and Margaret were not in the same house, and then Antonio had kept track of their whereabouts, and knew that they had never spent more than a few minutes alone together. On this visit of Justin's, Antonio had been unable to leave Madrid, but he felt he could trust Justin now, and the look on his guest's face whenever Margaret's name was mentioned—and at other times, too, as now—proved him right. Justin still looked guilty, but it was an old guilt, not one inflamed by any recent act. Antonio was aware that none of his Spanish friends would understand his tolerance: his honor had been insulted, and he should avenge himself on both Justin and Margaret. But he loved them both, and there it was.

"I came to say good-bye, Antonio," Justin said, crossing the room to stand beside the bed. "I must leave for Burgos today. One of my men quarreled with a *hidalgo* yesterday, and the *hidalgo* has vowed to seek him out, bringing a small army here, if he must, if my servant will not meet him in a duel.''

''You speak of Tandy, do you not? The maid who brought my breakfast said he looked as though he had been fighting.''

Justin chuckled. ''I'faith, his face is the very advertisement of the event.'' His glance strayed to the table. ''What's this? *Chocolate?*''

Antonio sighed. ''The king has turned physician, and bids me avoid all iced drinks until I am well. Alas, I read his letter to my secretary, and . . .'' He shrugged, then smiled wearily. ''I shall miss you, Justin.''

''Would that I could stay longer.''

''Pray give my love to Margaret.''

There was the guilty expression again, replaced a moment later by a smile. ''Yea, of course.''

''You will be leaving this morning?''

''Aye. My men are already preparing to leave. I came to say goodbye, and to thank you for your hospitality.''

''You know you are always welcome here, Justin. I hope you will remember that, should you find yourself in difficulty in England.''

There was that look of guilt again. Had Margaret perhaps told Justin the same thing? It was very likely.

''I thank you, my friend. I will pray that you recover your health soon.''

''I will.''

''Fare you well.''

''And you, Justin. God speed.''

CHAPTER 26

Garbed in new clothes of satin and taffeta and sarcenet, Jack and Bess strolled along the central aisle of Paul's, smiling and nodding at the gentlefolk they passed.

His thefts in Paris Garden over the past several days had secured enough money to buy the cloth from a mercer in Watling Street. They had taken the cloth to some sempsters Bess knew, who had made the garments for them in just a few days. The sempsters had promised the clothes would be fine enough for the court itself, and Jack had to admit that anyone glancing quickly at them—with himself in his suit of watchet satin trimmed with silver lace, and Bess in her kirtle of azure taffeta under a gown of primrose satin with white sarcenet sleeves—might think the men had succeeded.

It was just before noon, the time when Paul's was most crowded. Jack knew they should choose their cony soon, before people began to leave for dinner, but for a time he was content to wander through the throng, and so, he was certain, was Bess.

He smiled down at her as she tugged at his hand, expecting her to prattle delightedly of her new clothes again. But instead she had her mind on their business: with an unobtrusive nod, she indicated a young gentleman in the aisle a few yards ahead of them. He stood with his hands on his hips, his short Spanish cape pushed back so they could see the purse attached by leather thongs to his girdle.

Their arms linked, Jack and Bess closed on the gallant, their gaze directed toward the ceiling of Paul's as they lauded the craftsmen who had done the work.

Bess's shoulder must have been bruised when she collided with the gentleman, for even Jack was jolted by the sudden tug on his arm. He swung around to look at Bess, stopping with his right hand just a few inches from the startled gallant's side.

"Sweet coz, what happened?" he asked with concern. "Are you hurt?"

The boy had looked angry at first that someone had bumped into him, but his anger had vanished when he saw Bess. "Cry you mercy. I fear I must have been blocking the aisle," he said, reddening. He was younger than he had seemed at first, perhaps no more than seventeen. "Pray forgive me, my lady."

Bess gave him her most charming smile. "Y'are forgiven, sir, though there's naught to forgive. 'Twas my own fault. I was too busy looking about to watch where my own feet took me."

"Nay, do not blame yourself. The fault is mine. I hope you will let me make amends. If you would dine with me—"

"Mayhap another day, sir. We have promised to meet friends for dinner at their house today, and must be on our way."

She bestowed a dazzling, gracious smile on the youth and they started away, continuing down the central aisle a few more yards before reaching the transept and turning toward the north door.

"'Twas a gracious invitation," Bess murmured, "but I warrant he will have trouble paying for his dinner today."

Jack chuckled. The gallant's purse, taken during the first moments of confusion after Bess had bumped into him, lay safely in the capacious pocket of his new doublet. Now they needed only to be safely gone before the youth noticed his purse was missing and raised a hue and cry.

They skirted a group of richly garbed courtiers. The north door was very close now . . .

Then a hand came down on Jack's shoulder.

"Nick!" a voice cried cheerfully from directly behind him. "Nick! By the mass, I thought you were still in the country!"

Jack turned slowly, his hand dropping to the hilt of his sword. "Sir?" he said politely but coldly, his stare daunting as he faced the man who had stopped him, a pleasant-looking gentleman of about Jack's own age, garbed in an expensive suit of murrey velvet.

The gentleman drew back a little. He seemed confused as he studied Jack, then Bess, frowning a bit as he looked her over. The frown deepened as his gaze returned to Jack.

"Master Heyford!" a gentleman called, and the man who had stopped Jack glanced back over his shoulder.

"I'll be with you anon," he said, then turned to Jack again. He shook his head. "I pray your pardon, sir. I mistook you for a friend of mine." He continued staring at Jack for some moments, looking as though he were about to say more, then, abruptly, turned away and went back to his courtier friends.

Bess was gazing after him curiously. Jack caught her arm and pulled her after him, out of Paul's, into the safety of London's streets.

Jack hurried toward Cheapside, Bess half running beside him in an attempt to keep up with his longer strides.

"God's body, Jack! Slow down! There's no alarm, and I would talk to you!"

Jack shook his head slightly and hurried on. He knew what she wanted to talk about. 'Twas bad enough to have it plaguing his thoughts: he would not talk about it as well.

That man had known him.

True, the gentleman had apologized when Jack gave no sign of recognizing him in turn . . . but he seemed disbelieving that he could have been mistaken. He had still looked doubtful as he turned back to his friends, and that, more than fear that the gallant they had robbed would discover his purse missing, had made Jack hurry away before the courtier could engage him in further conversation. The gentleman had seemed surprised—yea, and unpleasantly so—by Jack's clothes. What would he have thought, had he known that Jack carried a stolen purse?

He slowed his pace when they reached Cheapside. Beside him, Bess was gasping for breath.

"Let's return to Paul's," she pleaded. "Let's ask that gentry cofe who he thought you were."

"Now? Would you have us stay at Paul's until our cony descends upon us crying 'Thief!'?"

"But if he did know you—"

"I still knew him not, whether as friend or foe, creditor or debtor. Should I trust him then with the truth? Were you in my place, would you trust him?"

"I know not what I would do."

"And so you would tell me?"

She flushed and looked away.

"I am sorry, Bess. I am not cross with you. Nay, I am not."

"I know," she said quietly.

"Come, let's count this purse. Perchance we can buy gifts for Ned and Tom and Amy."

In the midst of the marketplace, they found a quiet spot between two stalls and checked the contents of the purse, pleased at what they discovered.

"Marry, the cofe could have bought our dinners for a month," Bess said. "I'll have new slippers made for Amy, and hose for Tom and Ned . . ."

"Yea, and new slippers for yourself, too," Jack said as they moved out into the throng again.

"And gloves for you. And maybe a hat to match your fine new suit. And . . ."

He scarcely listened to her prattle, his thoughts returning again to the courtier at Paul's. Nick. The man had called him Nick . . .

Suddenly someone lurched against him. A bony hand clutched at his arm as a thin old man in a buffin jerkin struggled to regain his balance. Jack caught at his scrawny shoulder to help the old man stay on his feet, then froze as he felt a hand in his pocket.

"God's bones!" He clamped his free hand over the old man's wrist just as the ancient was drawing the purse from his pocket, and now the thief was still as well, his head lowered so Jack stared down at his bald pate. Two paces ahead of them, Bess turned around to see what was the matter. The old man had not let go of the purse. Jack dared not release his grip. He did not want to cry "Thief!" to stop the foist: the old man looked as though he would not survive long in jail, even if he survived being caught and belike ruffled by this crowd. Nor did Jack want to call the bluecoats' attention to himself. Yet he could not stand here much longer with this rogue without drawing all eyes to them.

Then Bess moved closer and seized the old man's other arm.

"Bing a waste, foist," she whispered harshly. "My cofe will filch you. He's the ruffian himself in a fight. He'll kick in your crashing cheats."

The old man stared in amazement at her, then at Jack, then at her again. All of a sudden he laughed, a cackling sound, and let go of the purse. His breath reeked of stale beer. Jack released him and stepped away.

"Crashing cheats?" the old man asked. "What crashing cheats?" And he opened his mouth in an ugly grin to show gums that were as toothless as a babe's. He cackled again, then spun away, disappearing in a trice among the stalls.

Jack shook his head. Bess looked at him, her face twisted into an odd expression, then began to laugh.

"I see no merriment in this," Jack said, looking glumly down at his doublet pocket, which had ripped when he caught the old man's hand.

"Oh, Jack, my sweet Jack. Can you not see it? In sooth, he tried to steal your purse because he thought you were a gentleman. He thought you were a gen—"

She fell silent as his eyes met hers. After a moment she swallowed hard. "Aye, and what's to wonder at in that?" she muttered, almost to herself. "So thought the other." She glanced down at herself, then turned away, her shoulders sagging. She had little to say as she set about making her purchases.

Bess's usual good humor was completely restored by the time they returned home, laden down with small gifts: a doll for Amy, a wooden top for Tom, a fine new pewter tankard for Ned, violet comfits and rosewater for Bess, and cloth for new hose. They had stopped, too, at an apothecary's shop in Bucklersbury, where Jack had bought some things for himself.

He did not take them out until they had finished their supper, eating in the kitchen after taking the other gifts upstairs and changing to their old clothes. He drained his cup of ale, and called for another, and then took from his pocket the pipe and tobacco. Bess looked at him dubiously as he filled the pipe and lit it. The exuberant noise around them abated somewhat as people turned to stare at him, and the wench who refilled his cup of ale stayed by their table, watching curiously. No one at the Turk's Sword had ever drunk tobacco, till now.

He put the pipe in his mouth, drew in deeply, choked, and began coughing. Bess waved her hand in front of her face as the smoke drifted toward her.

"I like it not," she announced.

Jack was not sure he liked it either, but he had paid too much for this fashionable novelty to abandon it now. He returned the pipe to his mouth and drew in just a little. Better, though the smoke still seemed to sear his throat. He took a quick swallow of ale, and instead of returning the pipe to his mouth simply held it in his hand, watching the smoke curl up. Peradventure if he drew on the pipe only now and then, its fieriness would be tolerable.

More smoke wafted toward Bess, and she coughed and wiped at her watering eyes. "Jesu! Why would anyone take tobacco?"

" 'Tis said to cure rheums and catarrhs and all such ailments of the lungs and throat."

" 'Tis likely that it smokes them away. But would it not be cheaper to use burning sea-coals as comfits?"

The maidservant laughed and went away.

Jack continued to hold the pipe most of the time, drinking the tobacco only now and then, in tiny sips. Several of their friends came over and Jack proudly showed off the pipe and the small block of tobacco, then let Simon Norbroke, who complained of rheum, draw on the pipe. The dommerar coughed more than Jack had, but he vowed he would try taking tobacco to heal his lungs. He was asking Jack which apothecary he had bought the pipe from—and likely planning, Jack thought wryly, to steal one if possible—when a loud voice cut through their conversation:

"So you have a pipe now, Jack? And I hear that you and the mort were wearing fine new clothes today. Have you come into some money, cofe? Mayhap your father died?"

Robin Dalling swaggered toward them, elbowing people aside. He was trailed by the two rogues who had accompanied him on his last visit to the Turk's Sword. Dalling came up to Jack's table and stood there, his hands on his hips, smirking as he looked from Jack to Bess and back again.

"The lour, cofe. You have had more money of late. Whence came it?"

" 'Tis no business of yours, Dalling."

"Aye, you'll wish it were not. For 'twas told to me by a man I trust that he saw you nip a purse at Paul's today. All these fine men thought you a brave ruffler, and all the while y'are a mere nip."

He looked around; his gaze fell on Michael Webbe, a young nip who had been a student of Ned Daughton's the year before. "Here, lad." Dalling reached out and seized the boy by the collar, to drag him, cringing, to his feet. "You can see by this example, Michael, that you need not be looked down on as a lowly nip. Keep your trade to yourself, cofe, keep your trade to yourself, tell no man of it, and get yourself a sword, and then tell some story of killing an upright man, and say the deed was done so far away that no one can disprove you. You may even find some mort to tell the story for you," Robin added contemptuously, his gaze swinging to Bess for a moment. "You'll still be only a nip, Michael, but none will know. Think what respect you'll have then."

He dumped Michael back onto his stool, then turned to Jack again.

The room was very quiet. There were stunned looks on many faces. Seeds of doubt had been planted about Jack's reputation. They would sprout and grow and ripen within the hour, Jack knew; he would have most if not all of his former friends turned against him unless he could refute the upright man's story.

Then Bess spoke, before he could collect his thoughts.

" 'Tis true he took a purse, Robin, but he's no mere nip."

Jack was glad she had spoken first. He might have denied Dalling's story, but that would not have served. Others in the alehouse might have been at Paul's and seen the theft, or might know someone else who had been a witness. Nips were thicker than clerics at Paul's, and their eyes took in actions their prey were oblivious to. No, there would be no harm in having that story out; he could not be forever looking over his shoulder to be sure no one would observe him when he took a purse.

Dalling glowered at Bess. "You lie in your throat, mort!"

"By God, y'are a brave man, Dalling," Jack said with a laugh, "to insult a woman so. Dare you say as much to me? I say, too, that I am no mere nip. Would you give me the lie as well?"

The upright man's gaze darted about furtively. No doubt he had come here only to shame Jack, and had not meant to take the matter this far. But he could not back down now without branding himself a coward.

"Yea, I would," he growled. "You lie in your throat, nip!"

Jack gave him a cold smile. "Then I challenge you, Robin Dalling, to a *duello*." The upright man began to draw his sword. "Hold. We'll have no fighting in here. I would not have Master Chickwell's kitchen fouled by your blood. Out! Out, you knave! To the alley!"

Outside it was still light, the western sky red with sunset. Jack and Robin Dalling stood in the alley, with everyone who had been in the kitchen around them. Dalling's companions had moved to the edge of the crowd, and one of them started to walk away, but John Albers drew his sword and held it across the man's path.

"Nay, you'll not leave," Albers told him. "I'll not have you call your friends—or haply even the watch—to put a quick end to an honest fight." And the rogue went back to stand beside Dalling's other lackey.

"Jack!" Amy called, and he looked up to see her head in the window, and Tom's, and Ned's. He shook his head angrily, and Ned drew the children back into the room and closed the shutters.

Jack turned his gaze on Robin Dalling then. The upright man had given his staff to one of his men and had drawn his sword and dagger. Dalling's sword was a plain but serviceable weapon of English make; it was neither as handsomely designed nor as strong as the fine Bilbao sword that Jack held, but Jack knew that he could not count on the differences in the swords' quality to settle this match. Skill would decide it, and Jack was still unsure of how skilled he was. Killing a drunken upright man, a man armed only with a cudgel, proved nothing. He knew not whether he was a journeyman or a master swordsman.

But then, neither did Robin Dalling, and from the sweat on his jowly face, it seemed he feared Jack greatly . . .

Perchance driven by his fear, the upright man attacked first, lunging at Jack and striking with such force that when Jack parried, the bilbo's blade curved under the impact.

"Ha!" Dalling cried, then was astonished when the supple blade failed to break. He retreated then, sweating more than ever, already panting.

Jack looked upon him with distaste. This was no fit opponent, this Bartholomew pig of a rogue . . .

"Come on, nip," Dalling taunted. "Come show us if you can fight."

So Jack did, but not recklessly, not driven into a fury by Dalling's jeering, mocking voice as the upright man goaded him. His attack was precise as clockwork, and for all Dalling's bravado, the older man was forced back in a steady retreat down the alley, each of his taunts answered by another hit. Jack's father was a filthy old priest, Dalling said, and Jack cut his sleeve half away from his doublet. Jack's mother was a whore and birthed him into a jordan. A thrust at the face, then, and a wisp of Dalling's beard gone. Ned Daughton was an apple-squire, the upright man said—and then blood trickled from his wrist—and Bess was his whore.

Dalling squealed like a pig as Jack sliced open his doublet, leaving a shallow cut across his ribs. The upright man staggered back, into the wall of a house.

"Run him through!" someone in the crowd called, but Jack merely stood there, studying his enemy through slitted eyes. Kill this fat, cowardly bully? 'Twould be too easy. He felt disgust at the thought. He took a step back, lowering his sword.

Dalling lunged at him then, but Jack caught the upright man's sword with his own and wrenched it away, sending it flying across the alley. Dalling started to go after it, but Jack slapped his belly with his sword and the rogue flinched back, cringing.

"Nay, 'tis mine for my troubles, though it is a poor sort of weapon. Be glad that I'll let you keep your life. 'Tis more wretched yet than that sword, but I trow y'are fond of it. Now get you gone, and trouble me no more."

Dalling edged away, cringing again, but straightened as he got further from Jack. There was even a trace of a swagger restored to his walk as he reached his lackeys and held out his hand for his staff.

The man did not give it to him, instead gazing stolidly at the upright man, insolently unyielding.

Jack heard Simon Norbroke's tittering laugh. So did Dalling, who looked around, snarling, then grabbed the staff from his lieutenant. He lifted it as if he would have struck the man, but his other lackey caught the staff, staying the blow. Dalling gaped at him, then, with a curse, broke his staff free of his lackey's grip and strode away, followed by laughter . . . and, a telling few seconds later, by his men.

When he was some dozen paces away, he swung around and shook his staff at Jack. "Whoreson nip!" he bellowed.

"If he's a whoreson nip," Albers returned, almost cheerfully, "then y'are less than that. Begone, sirrah!"

Dalling swore at him then, but Albers merely laughed as he strolled over to Jack. "He'll not be back," he predicted confidently. "And 'tis unlikely he'll be upright man for much longer."

"You should have finished him, Jack," Bess said, coming up to him and seizing his arm with both her hands in a viselike grip. "You should have killed him."

"By the mass, y'are an Amazon," Albers told her with a laugh.

"Why so bloodthirsty? Let Dalling's own deal with him. They'll likely kill him soon enough. You saw how they were loath to return the staff to him."

"You are too new here. You understand nothing—"

"By God, Bess," Jack said, as patiently as he could. He put his arm around her shoulders. " 'Tis you who fails to understand."

She shrugged free and moved away from him. "Say you so, Jack? 'Sblood, I *know* Robin Dalling. You know him not, or you would not have let him walk away. He'll see you again, Jack, but he'll not play the gentleman with you. Nay, he'll play the jack with you. Pray God, you'll be able to walk away from him. You fool!"

And she ran back into the alehouse.

"Pay her no heed," Ned Daughton said quietly, and Jack whirled around, surprised to find the old man standing there. He glanced up at the window: the shutters were still closed.

"No, they did not watch," Ned assured him. "I told them I would beat them if they did."

"Would you had told Bess the same," Albers said.

"She thinks me a fool," Jack muttered, still stung by her rebuke.

"She fears Robin Dalling more than you. Aye, and she's had reason to fear him. Remember that. And remember, too, that unlike us, she knows no other life than this . . . and perchance that leaves her wiser in understanding the ways of a Robin Dalling."

Jack nodded. Ned was right: his refusal to cut the rogue down must needs be explained to Bess, else it would seem mere folly. "I'll talk to her," he said, and would have gone after her then, but Ned stopped him.

"Nay, let her think it over," he counseled. "Perhaps she'll come to understand on her own. 'Twould be better for her. Besides"—he nodded toward the alehouse, where Roger Chickwell was standing waiting for them, holding the door open—"there are friends who would fain drink carouse to you . . ."

He was not quite cup-shotten by the time he went upstairs, or so he thought. Of certain he was less drunken than most of those left in the kitchen, some of them already under the tables. Yet it seemed to him, as he stumbled across Ned's chamber toward his own, that there was more furniture here now than had been here a few hours before, or, more likely, it had been moved about. He tripped over a stool and nearly fell, then bruised his leg on a table. The bed creaked as Ned turned over. Mayhap the old man, who had come upstairs an hour ago, had been asleep. Jack was sorry to have wakened him.

The noise he made must have wakened Amy, too, for she came out of the chamber she shared with Tom and flung her arms around his legs, almost tripping him again. He leaned down and picked her up and kissed her. Her face was wet with tears.

"Jack, I feared for you," she whispered.

"Hush, now. There's naught to fear." He held her, smoothing her hair back, until she had stopped crying, then carried her back into her room and set her down on the bed, where Tom was also awake and sitting up.

"You showed them, Jack!" the boy said in an excited whisper. "You showed them y'are a proper swordsman!"

"Yea, I did," Jack agreed with a weary sigh. "Now have done with it. We'll talk no more of this."

"But Jack—"

"We'll talk no more of this tonight," he interrupted, relenting just enough that the little boy was satisfied and allowed Jack to tuck him in with his sister. Amy wanted a good-night kiss, and then at last Jack was free to go to the bedchamber he shared with Bess.

He bumped into a stool again on his way there, and was not at all surprised to find her sitting up, watching him. "Faith, we should have moved all the furniture against the walls."

"I trow you moved it all into my path."

"Nay, for we could never have guessed at how crooked a path you would walk."

He took off his clothes and sat down on the edge of the bed. Usually Bess would slide over against him, but tonight she stayed where she was.

"D'you want to talk about Robin Dalling?" he asked.

"No, I have talked quite enough to myself about him. Do you want to talk about that gentleman at Paul's?"

"The cony?" he said, pretending to misunderstand.

"Jack . . ." She shook her head and lay down again, as did he, aware of the distance between them but no more willing than she to be the first to bridge it.

What seemed like an hour passed, and he was still not able to sleep, though he thought Bess was sleeping. At last he got up and went over to the chair where Ned had placed the two swords, Jack's and the upright man's, that he had brought upstairs while Jack was carousing.

He picked up Robin Dalling's sword. It was heavy, but the balance was good: an adequate weapon for a fight, but scarcely that. Certainly it was not for show, with its plain hilt.

Then he drew his own sword from its scabbard. Roger Chickwell had cleaned the blade for him, first with water and then with sheep's tallow, and the fine steel gleamed even in the faint moonlight. 'Twas as beautiful as it was deadly, this sword. Jack sheathed it again, then studied the hilt, which was beautifully wrought, with the handle worked in a spiral pattern and the gilded pommel set with a small ruby.

" 'Tis a gentleman's sword," Bess said softly, sitting up as he turned toward her. "And 'tis yours."

"As like as not, I stole it," he said, but he knew it was a lie: this bilbo suited him too well.

"Nay, it is yours," Bess said again, and he could tell she was crying, though the darkness in that corner of the chamber hid her tears.

He put the sword down then, and went to her, and reassured her without words, for he knew words would only betray him now.

CHAPTER 27

Eight days after receiving Don Rafael's invitation, Fray Francisco de la Vera Cruz arrived at the Eagle's Nest. He was shoeless, and the white robe of his Dominican habit was of the coarsest stuff, but he carried the authority of a vicar of the Inquisition with him, and so he accepted it as his due when Don Rafael's servants deferred to him as though he were a great noble.

The friar greeted his host coolly, conscious for a moment of his own appearance beside that of the don. Fray Francisco was short and slight of build, with the face of a young boy, and not all the riches of Christendom would have made him finer to look upon, more manly and noble of bearing, than his host. But he quickly cast that thought aside, his eyes narrowing suspiciously as he searched the don's face for any sign of Jewish ancestry.

His own blood was pure, thanks be to the Blessed Virgin. He came from a family of poor *hidalgos*, of the lowest rank of the nobility, which was so numerous here in the north of Spain as to seem common. The *poderosos* such as Don Rafael looked down on the *hidalguía*, for many *hidalgos* owned nothing of value besides their ancestry. The disdain of the mighty meant little, though, when the *poderosos* themselves lacked honor because their blood was not pure. *Limpieze de sangre* mattered more than wealth and a great title. Francisco had known that since he was a child. Purity of blood conferred a kind of nobility in itself, and Francisco's family could boast of that nobility as well. Don Rafael likely could not. Almost all the great nobles owed their wealth to rich Jewish or Muslim ancestors; Francisco had read the green books, especially the *Tizón de España*, which proved that was so.

It was not yet time for supper when the friar arrived, so Don Rafael and a servant named Pablo showed him to his bedchamber. The vicar frowned as he surveyed the room.

"Does something displease you, Fray Francisco?" Don Rafael asked obsequiously. "Is there anything you would like to add to your comfort?"

357

Francisco shook his head sharply. The chamber was far too comfortable already.

It had been the same during his stay with Don José. Nothing but
the finest food, the most comfortable bedding, the best wine. Fray Francisco had added flesh to his spindly arms and legs, and he had slept
longer hours than he had in years. All as his superiors in Valladolid had
intended.

Those superiors had told him he was working too hard, demanding
too much of his frail body, and though they had admired his zeal and
the strength of his spirit, they had denied his request to continue as
before. They had taken away his hair shirt, had treated the infected
wounds left by self-flagellation, and then, when he had recovered enough
strength to travel, they had sent him back to his homeland of Navarra
to recover. Not to his parents' home—though he was allowed to visit
them briefly—but to the castle of Don José Murcia de Valtanas, an old
friend of the inquisitor who was Francisco's direct superior. He had been
ordered to stay there for six months, restoring his strength before returning to Valladolid and "more demanding duties"—a hint, Fray Francisco prayed, that he would soon advance from the position of vicar to
that of inquisitor.

And he had rested. He had suffered through more than three months
of rest already—three months of boredom. Don José was a pious man
but an indulgent one, and though he would spend long hours discussing
religious matters with the vicar, Fray Francisco felt his presence there
was of little use to the don, of no use to the Church, and of less than
no use to himself. He felt as though he were being smothered with
pillows. He had honed his religious sense to a fine edge, and it was
useless as long as he stayed with Don José. Worse, that edge was being
blunted. He had been relieved when he learned of an Englishwoman
staying in a castle not far from Don José's home, and he had exulted
when Don Rafael responded to his expressions of curiosity and concern
by inviting him here. There had been a delay while Don José insisted
on first asking permission of Fray Francisco's superiors before allowing
his guest to leave, but this morning the messenger had returned with
that permission, and the vicar had left at once, glad to be sprung from
his cage. He had not expected to find another luxurious cage here.

"A servant will come to escort you to the hall when supper is
served," the don said. "No doubt you will wish to rest until then. You
must be weary after your journey."

Rest was the last thing Fray Francisco wanted, and he was offended
that Don Rafael would treat him as though he were frail, but he forced
himself to smile at his host as he agreed that indeed he was weary. But

he would not sleep, or even lie down, while he waited for supper. He would spend the time in prayer, and that would make the minutes pass more swiftly until he could meet this English heretic.

Rafael could not entirely suppress a sigh of relief after leaving the vicar. After just a few minutes in the bedchamber, the air in the hall seemed freer by contrast, less close, less suffocating. But that, he knew, was an illusion. It was the vicar's presence he found suffocating.

Don Rafael had never had cause to deal personally with any of the powers of the Inquisition before. He had met officials of the Spanish Inquisition's Supreme Council, when at court, but those representatives of *La Suprema* had then seemed to him less like the predators other people had described them as, than sleek, well-fed pets, who posed no real danger to those in the king's favor. He had thought of the Inquisition as a threat only to others, not himself—and he had limited experience even of that aspect of it.

He had witnessed *autos-da-fé* only twice, once in Valladolid and once in Madrid, and then only because other business had brought him to those cities at those times. He had not particularly wished to attend, but he would have drawn the wrong sort of attention by refusing to go, and not only because indulgences were granted to the spectators. At those times the inquisitors had been tiny figures seen from a distance, their threat directed towards victims clearly marked by the hideous *sanbenitos*. He had felt safe enough from them.

He had felt no fear for himself, either, the time in Burgos when a number of *alguazils*, the brutish servants of the Inquisition, had come to a house next to the one where he was staying. It had been in the middle of the night, and he had been on the balcony because the air in his room was hot and still. The *alguazils* had wakened his host's neighbors and soon dragged off a screaming, tearful maidservant. He had felt some pity for the girl after he learned she had been accused of heresy by a man with whom she had refused to lie. Pity, but no real sympathy. He could not imagine *alguazils* coming for him.

Now, though, he had invited the Inquisition into his own home.

He shuddered as he remembered the vicar's face, which might have looked almost angelic, had those boyish features not been sharpened by repeated fasts. And those eyes! Those glittering, feverish eyes . . . unnaturally bright from illness or fanaticism, or perhaps both. Don Rafael had found the vicar's stare unsettling. Fray Francisco reminded him of a hawk sighting its prey.

But if he were disturbed by the vicar, how much more would Kat be? No doubt a single meeting with Fray Francisco would suffice to persuade her that she needed the don's protection. And then, Rafael thought, he would send the vicar away. That moment could come none too soon . . .

"Your English guest will not sup with us?" Fray Francisco asked when he saw that the table was set for two, not three.

Don Rafael shook his head. "She will have already had supper in her chambers. She takes most of her meals there."

"That is wise," the friar said, nodding. "There is less chance then that she will preach heresy to you and others of your household."

"She does not preach heresy," the don said quickly. "Truly, she says nothing of her faith."

The vicar smirked. "Maybe nothing that someone unschooled in the ways of heretics would notice. But what she says may yet work subtly against the true faith. I was told that she speaks Spanish as well as anyone born here, and I was grieved to hear it. Does she speak to many of your servants?"

"Only one, a maid."

"A maid. A young girl?" He smirked again when Rafael nodded. "A young girl who will chatter endlessly, and repeat all that she has been told."

"Dorotea is no idle chatterer. She is wise for her years, and a most devout Catholic."

"Then we must pray that her devotion will be her shield against this heretic. Else I fear for you, and for all your household."

The vicar ate but sparingly of the delicacies set before him, frowning at each as if he disapproved of the Don Rafael's hospitality. The nobleman was offended, but he managed to refrain from asking if anything were amiss. He could not keep silent, however, when he noticed that the vicar always waited to sample each dish until after he had seen Rafael eat some of it. It enraged him to be thus used as the friar's taster, but still he strove for an appearance of serenity.

"Do you fear poison, Fray Francisco?"

"Not here, Don Rafael," the friar said. "Nor did I fear to be poisoned while I stayed with Don José, but the habits of a lifetime"—he shrugged as if he were an old man, not a young one—"cannot be changed so quickly. When I accompany inquisitors, we often must dine with families who know the people we are investigating and who may secretly be their friends. Ergo, there is always the risk of poison. I accept it as another of the burdens that fall on those who defend the true faith. Yet still I cannot help but wish that, like Torquemada, I had a unicorn's horn as a charm against poison."

They spoke very little during the rest of the meal, and then of inconsequential matters—Don José, the fine weather, the vicar's love of Navarra—and Rafael had begun to hope that Fray Francisco had forgotten about Kat, but the friar proved him wrong.

"How came you to have an Englishwoman as your guest?" Fray Francisco asked. Finished with dessert, he was wiping his fingers on a linen napkin.

The question had been asked lightly, almost idly, but Don Rafael was not deceived. That predatory look was back in the vicar's eyes.

"She has been a guest of a friend of mine in Burgos, Doña Margaret Téllez de Osuna, Condesa de Ordaz. Do you know her, or her husband, Don Antonio?" It was a barbed question: there was little chance that this lowly vicar would know them.

"I have heard of Don Antonio," the friar replied.

"He is a friend and adviser of the king," Rafael said. It would not hurt to be certain the friar knew that he—and Kat—had powerful friends. "I met the lady Katherine while visiting Burgos recently, and she expressed an interest in seeing Navarra."

The friar considered that for a moment. "Doña Margaret is English, too, is she not? But of the true faith?"

Don Rafael nodded. "She has many relatives in England still, friends of the Church and of Spain. Katherine is a ward of Doña Margaret's cousin, who is now in Madrid visiting Don Antonio."

The friar was silent again for some moments, his brilliant gaze hooded by lowered eyelids.

Have I said enough? Don Rafael wondered. Would the friar's interest in Katherine be discouraged by mention of Don Antonio?

"I fear," the vicar said at last, "that I must question the wisdom of Doña Margaret's cousin in bringing a heretic to Spain—even a heretic who does not preach," he added with a laugh that made him seem younger yet. Watching, Rafael was chilled by the sight of those bright, avid eyes in that child's face. "What would you do if she began to preach heresy here?"

"I would prefer that such a grievous situation never happen, and thus far I have trusted her discretion. Still, I can see now that it might be best if you spoke with her, and told her of the Holy Inquisition and the fate reserved for those who lead true believers astray. I am certain that she would then be convinced of the need for silence." And submission, he added to himself.

"Your foresight is admirable," the vicar said. Was there a touch of sarcasm in his voice? "When may I meet the lady?"

When a manservant came after supper with the message that Don Rafael's guest wished to meet her, Kat changed from the kirtle she had been wearing, of maiden's-blush satin, to one of velvet, black figured with white. She wore two lace partlets with it, one over the other: the effect was modest if not especially attractive.

Then she waited in the antechamber for the don and his guest.

Within a few minutes she heard footsteps in the hall. The door was opened and she saw Don Rafael. He seemed to be alone. She took a few steps toward the door, then stopped, amazed, when the friar came into view.

Was this some jest? For a moment Kat, gazing from a still-sunlit chamber into the dimness of the hall, thought that Don Rafael had lied to her and, instead of bringing a vicar of the Inquisition, was trying to frighten her with a pretty chorister dressed as if for a mummery in a Dominican's robe. Then the monk stepped through the doorway, and as a shaft of light from the setting sun touched his face, Kat saw that he was no longer a boy, for all his boyish appearance: he was perchance several years older than herself, his face already etched with fine lines. Yet surely he was not in sooth a representative of the Inquisition . . . ?

She looked at Rafael and started to smile, and he shook his head, confusing her even more.

"Doña Katherine," the don said, "I would like you to meet Fray Francisco de la Vera Cruz." He was, for a change, speaking in Spanish. "Fray Francisco, you have the honor of meeting Doña Katherine Lisle, my English guest of whom you were told, the niece and ward of Doña Margaret's cousin."

The young man murmured a greeting, also in Spanish. Kat scarcely listened to it as she stared at Don Rafael, who was explaining that Fray Francisco spoke no English. So she was to be known as Justin's niece now, as well as his ward? Was this meeting all to be pretense? She was sure now that this monk was no vicar—and likely no monk either—for Rafael would have to be a fool to lie to the Inquisition. ‧

"My lady," Rafael continued, "I was telling Fray Francisco of our meeting at La Casa de las Rosas, and of your decision to visit me here for a time." His expression was serious, his gaze intense in a silent demand that she heed him. She nodded slightly, still smiling a bit.

"I have told Katherine," Rafael said to the friar, "that this must be a poor substitute for the meeting she had wished to have with Don Antonio, who had also wished to meet her. Alas, she was ill from the journey when Lord Harwood left for Madrid and could not go with him. I only hope that she is enjoying her stay here."

"Indeed, my lord," Kat agreed, with exaggerated cheerfulness. Fray Francisco stared at her coldly. Was he offended that she was not quaking with fear at his visit? She gave him her warmest smile.

"I thought," Rafael said, a bit loudly, "that perhaps, lady, you would benefit from learning of the true faith from Fray Francisco. He serves the Inquisition as a vicar."

"Does he indeed?" Kat asked, and Rafael looked despairing. *By my life,* she thought, *he did think I would be fooled by this mummery . . .*

"I have heard," said the friar, "that little other than lies about the Holy Office reaches your country, lady. Slanderous lies."

"I would not know, Fray Francisco," she said lightly, "which were slanders and which were truths."

Rafael shook his head again.

The young man's lips pursed in disapproval before he said, "Then it is of the utmost importance that you learn the truth. What have you heard of the Inquisition, my lady?"

"Little, in truth."

"Little of truth, I warrant."

Kat shrugged. "Most of what I read were sailors' accounts, Fray Francisco. I had no way of judging the truth of them, but neither had I any reason to doubt them."

"Sailors' accounts." The little man seemed oddly pleased with her answer. "Of their imprisonment, no doubt? Of the torture they forced the Inquisition to put them to, before they would confess? Yet did they say anything of their shameful attempts to spread heretical doctrine and lead astray followers of the true faith?"

"By the mass," Kat said pleasantly, "you take your role seriously."

Silence claimed the room for the space of several seconds. Smiling mischievously, Kat turned to Rafael, intending to chide him for this mummery, but the don, who was looking at Francisco instead of Kat, spoke first.

"Fray Francisco," the nobleman said, "mayhap you could continue this conversation another time. I wish to show you the rest of the castle tonight . . ." He paused as the vicar turned that cold gaze on him. ". . . so you will know your way about."

"Tomorrow, Don Rafael. I would begin now to demolish the wall of lies that prevents this lady from seeing the truth about the Inquisition. The walls of your castle are, I trust, of sturdier stuff, and will still be here tomorrow."

"Very well," the don said, sighing a little, and he gestured for Kat to return to her chair. He turned the room's only other chair toward Kat's and indicated that the vicar should take it, then seated himself on a padded stool.

Kat sighed, too, but folded her hands in her lap and waited for the masque to continue.

God, how lovely the Englishwoman was!

Francisco had felt stunned since he first caught sight of her. He had seen a woman so lovely only once before—the wife of a rich merchant of Valladolid, investigated by the Inquisition. He had been told there were other women as lovely, but the names he heard were always those of the wives or daughters of the higher nobility, who were hidden like precious gems from the common eye, their beauty concealed by veils when they were seen in public. The merchant's wife had worn no veil when she sat before the inquisitor, and Francisco had found it difficult to concentrate on what was being said. Weeks later, after she had confessed and been given a light punishment, the beauty of her face was almost gone, erased by terror and lack of sleep and hopelessness. Still, she had drawn all men's eyes to her as she was paraded through the streets with the other penitents, stripped to the waist like the rest of them. Her breasts had shown bruises and bite marks then, from the unrestrained attentions of the *alguazils*, and Francisco had been ashamed of himself for watching, but he had been unable to take his eyes off her.

This girl was younger than the merchant's wife, and her beauty was fresher. Francisco found his gaze drawn from the flawless face to the golden hair falling unbound to lie in shimmering waves on her shoulders, then to the shadowed valley between her high breasts, enticingly visible beneath the fine lace filling in the kirtle's neckline. As he stared, her finely shaped hand, with its long slender ringless fingers, came up as though to shield her breasts from his sight.

He looked up then, coloring a little as his eyes met hers, but his shame quickly gave way to anger. How dare she dress so immodestly!

He swallowed hard, his hands gripping the arms of his chair. Forcing his gaze to remain on her face, he assayed a smile and said, as gently as possible, "Tell me of yourself, lady. We should become friends. I would have you understand me and trust me, and believe that what I tell you of the Inquisition is true."

"There is nothing to tell of myself, Fray Francisco. I have lived very quietly in the country until recently. And I have no reason to distrust you."

"All the same, I would have you know more of me, and of the reasons why I serve the Inquisition. Those whose accounts you read attacking the Holy Office must, as you admit, have failed to provide the relevant histories of their own lives, the histories that would let you judge them. You must concede, lady, that the truth of any story is found in the teller and not in the story itself. A saint may speak of marvels beyond the ken of all who hear them, yet he must be believed. A sinner may tell a story which is in no way out of the ordinary, and yet it must be doubted."

"I would never suspect you of dissembling, Fray Francisco," she replied, and there was mockery in her smile.

Was it possible, Francisco wondered, that she felt contempt for him? Mayhap Don Rafael had said something to her of his being from a poor *hidalgo* family.

"You honor me, lady," he said, a bit sharply. "Yet I would first prove myself worthy of that honor. I would ask no man to believe that my blood is free of all Jewish taint unless I could prove it." He glanced toward Don Rafael, but the nobleman showed no reaction to his words. "Similarly, that you may judge for yourself whether I speak truly of the Inquisition, I will tell you how I came to serve it."

"But how will I know, Fray Francisco, whether you are a saint or a sinner?"

His mouth fell open a little. She *was* laughing at him. But as he gaped at her, her expression changed, became repentant.

"Pray forgive me, Fray Francisco. I was merely making a jest, and a poor one. I know that no sinners would be chosen to serve the Inquisition. Why else would the Inquisition's servants be free from investigation?"

Her words were reasonable. Still, the vicar felt himself off balance, sensing mockery but unable to say exactly how she mocked him. For an instant he was tempted to flee the antechamber and leave her to her heretical beliefs and the damnation that would surely be her fate. Then awareness of his power as an official of the Inquisition returned to him, flooding him with confidence, and he even managed a smile to show that he had understood her jest.

"Let me tell you of myself, lady," he said, and then paused for a few moments, folding his hands and looking down at them, praying for guidance to say the words that would inspire belief in her.

"I was born here in Navarra, near Pamplona, the second son of a *hidalgo*. At an early age I decided upon a religious life." He saw no need to abase himself by adding that entering a monastery had been his only chance for education and advancement.

"My abbot's great-uncle had known Torquemada, and from him I heard much of Fray Tomás. I soon resolved to model my life on his. Like Fray Tomás, I scorn wealth"—another glance toward Rafael assured him that the nobleman was not laughing at him—"and practice mortification of the flesh." The woman raised an eyebrow in query. "I sleep on a plank," he explained eagerly, "and often wear a hair shirt under my habit. And—" He broke off, seeing an expression of disgust on her face. How could he have expected this self-indulgent heretic to understand? And yet, for the salvation of her soul, he must make her understand . . .

"While still a novice, still but a boy"—he paused as she smiled, and felt his face burn—"I felt I might be called to serve the Inquisition. But I was not certain of my calling until I attended my first *auto-da-fé*, eleven years ago in Valladolid."

He was quite still for a time, overwhelmed by memories, but then the woman stirred, recalling him to awareness of her presence. He felt almost hopeless as he gazed at her. How could he make her understand?

He rose and began to pace agitatedly about the room. "How can I tell you of that day? The king himself was there, with his son, seated on the balcony opposite the Church of St. Martin. I stood there in that great city where Torquemada had been born, and watched the king swear to support the Inquisition's holy mission. I was close enough to the balcony that I could hear every word Philip spoke. I saw the condemned pass by—they were all Lutherans, guilty of trying to spread their heresy. One was a nobleman of Italy, the son of the Bishop of Placenza. This nobleman, Don Carlos de Seso, was the most dangerous heretic of all. He had served the king's father as *corregidor* of Toro and misused his authority to protect heretics there. That day he was so weakened he could not stand, and two *alguazils* had to hold him up."

"Weakened by torture?" the Englishwoman asked. That look of disgust was on her face again.

"He would not repent! Yes, he was tortured, by those who would have saved his soul, but they inflicted pain then only in an attempt to spare him an eternity of suffering in Hell! But it was of no avail with Don Carlos. He was still gagged when they brought him into the square, so that he would not exhort the crowd to follow his heretical path. But when the gag was taken from his mouth, and he found himself near the king's balcony, he had the presumption to ask Philip why he would allow such punishments in Spain. He asked him, as one gentleman to another—as if a heretic may truly be a gentleman!—how he could let him burn. And Philip replied—and I was honored to hear him—that if his own son, the prince, were as wicked as Don Carlos de Seso, then he would himself bring the wood to burn him." Fray Francisco drew a deep breath. "I prayed then that my faith would always be as strong as the king's was that day."

And then, to his horror, the Englishwoman began to laugh.

Kat laughed so hard she could not talk for a time. At last, wiping tears from her eyes, she turned to Don Rafael.

"By my faith," she said, speaking in English so the vicar would not understand, "your king would have willingly brought wood to burn his own son, would he not? As like as not, he would have wished the Inquisition to deal with Don Carlos for him, to save him the trouble of imprisoning the prince himself."

Rafael had been staring at her; now he looked down.

"Oh, have I spoken too carelessly of the prince? Haply you admired him? I saw you had that book of his in your library, the one time you let me go there." The little book, almost completely covered by a sheet of paper, had been lying on the table. Rafael had seemed unhappy that she had discovered it, and as soon as she opened it, she realized why. Nick had told her that the book had become infamous at the Spanish court, and that none dared admit to being its author, though many believed it had been Don Carlos's work, written when the prince despaired of ever traveling abroad since his father preferred to stay in Spain and continue his ceaseless rounds of his palaces. Of certain, Rafael would not want his enemies to know that he still kept a copy.

"Know you not which book I mean?" she asked tauntingly when he did not respond. " 'Tis the one about Philip's great and noble voyages. The one that reads, 'From Madrid to the Escorial, from the Escorial to the Pardo, from the Pardo to Aranjuez, from Aranjuez to Madrid, from Madrid to the Escorial—' "

"Enough!" Rafael looked up then, and she saw that his face was white with fear. He glanced warily toward Francisco.

Did he really expect her to believe that he was afraid of this young man who pretended to be a monk and a vicar of the Inquisition? Kat laughed again, and said, "There is a saying I have heard, Don Rafael: *Cucullus non facit monachum. A cowl does not make a monk.* 'Sblood, you should not have expected me to believe—"

"*Cucullus non facit monachum!*"

Kat turned toward Francisco, stunned to hear him repeat the Latin words exactly. The look on his face chilled her. He was furious, and she could not believe now that the fury was a pretense.

"What do you mean, lady? You mocked me. You laughed at me. And what were you saying of Don Carlos and the king?"

She looked beseechingly at Rafael, and saw there would be no help from him. He appeared too frightened to think. As she was—almost.

"You misunderstood, Fray Francisco," she said quickly, then paused, racking her brains for some explanation he might find plausible. "I was laughing at Don Carlos—Don Carlos de Seso—laughing that he would think to speak to your king so. I but told Don Rafael that mayhap Don Carlos had some mad dream of infecting the king himself with his heresy, and then that heresy might be spread from Madrid to Aranjuez and then to all the king's palaces and servants. I laughed him to scorn, for being such a fool."

Fray Francisco nodded, but the suspicious expression did not leave his face. "And what you said at the last. *Cucullus—*"

"*A cowl does not make a monk.* 'Tis a common saying. I was telling Don Rafael that although a cowl does not make a monk, faith does—and you have great faith, Fray Francisco." It was a poor answer, she knew, wishing she had been able to think of something else to say. Likely he had clearly heard the mockery in her voice. "Pray continue," she begged. "I would hear more of this *auto-da-fé.*"

Fray Francisco shook his head. "Another time, my lady. I have just now realized that I am very tired from my journey here. I would rest now."

Rafael rose at once. "Let me show you back to your chamber."

He escorted the friar to the door, solicitous as any common servant. Kat followed them and caught at the don's sleeve before he could accompany Fray Francisco out of the antechamber. "I thought this but a jest," she whispered to the don. The vicar was walking away, yet she spoke in English, just in case he could still hear her. "He seems little older than a boy, too young—far too young!"

Don Rafael glanced down at her, and there was still fear in his expression, but there was pity, too.

"Are you fond of sayings, Katherine?" he asked in English, also whispering. "I have another for you. 'Tis said that one suspected by the Inquisition might escape without being burned, but he will of certain be singed. I pray that you will escape so easily." And he shook free of her grasp and hurried to catch up with the vicar.

The guard closed the door, leaving Kat alone with her maid. She turned toward Dorotea, intending to make some jest to lessen her own fear as well as the maid's, but the girl was already slipping from the bench to kneel on the floor. As Kat watched, Dorotea took out her beads and began to pray.

Most of the way back to his chamber, Fray Francisco kept silent. It was only when they were within sight of the bedchamber door that he said, harshly, "She mocked me!"

"It was but a jest . . . though I must confess it a poor one."

"Yet you did not upbraid her for it."

"I did not think it my place. I shall tell Doña Margaret of this misbehavior by her cousin's ward."

"Misbehavior!" He swung round to face the don. "She is a heretic!"

"By happenstance. Not by intent. The true faith has been outlawed in England since she was a small child. She has not been taught the Catholic faith."

"And you think that is all she needs?" the friar asked, looking thoughtful. "Instruction in our faith?"

"I am sure of it."

"Then *if* she respects my faith, *as she said*, I should teach her. I will begin tomorrow."

"But Fray Francisco! I would not have you set yourself such a task, when you are here in Navarra to rest."

"I have no choice, Don Rafael. Would you have her left to her heresy?"

"No, of course not. But—"

"Then I have no choice." He turned and walked into the bedchamber, saying, almost as though to himself, "I had wondered what purpose of God's could be served by my presence here in Navarra. Now I know. Now I know . . ."

CHAPTER 28

Margaret was soaking in her tub, eyes closed, enjoying the warmth and the scented water, when someone knocked on the door of the antechamber. She opened her eyes to see Edwina's questioning glance.

"If it is one of Lord Harwood's men, instruct him to tell his lordship that I am still abed, but that I will come to bid him farewell as soon as possible."

As Edwina scurried off, Margaret lolled back again, frowning as she caught sight of the clock. A quarter past four. A strange hour to be awake—especially since she had been rudely awakened at midnight by news that her cousin's party had returned from Madrid—but Justin had told her he was determined to leave as soon as it was light. He would not leave without bidding her farewell; she had made him promise that. And she had intended to be ready to see him off from the courtyard by this hour. But she had been awake late, finally crying herself to sleep sometime after two, and it had taken Edwina nearly an hour to coax her from her bed.

No matter: Justin would wait. She was resolved to look her best when she bid him God-speed and a safe journey; she would leave him with an image of herself that would have him afire with eagerness to return to her.

And if it chafed him to have to wait, it was no worse treatment than he deserved. She was still vexed with his behavior toward her since his arrival last night, when he talked to her for only a few minutes before retiring. He had pleaded exhaustion as an excuse, and in truth he and his men had looked travel-worn, having ridden from Madrid in four long days. He had told her that the reason for his haste was something he had learned in Madrid, and she could understand the importance of his business. But had he forgotten how much she was the cause of his wanting to see England restored to the true faith? Of certain, he seemed to have forgotten that she had asked for his help when he was last in Burgos. Whereas she had hoped he would return penitent and begging to be allowed to help her, he had said nothing of the matter.

Muttering an oath, she picked up a bar of musk-scented soap and began to wash.

At least Justin's rush to return to England had left him without time to lament Kat's disappearance, or even to question Margaret too closely about it. He had been angry, yes, indeed had asked her if she knew of anyone who might have been responsible. She had told him she knew of no one who would be so villainous, and that none of the inquiries she had set afoot had revealed any clue to Kat's whereabouts. He had seemed disappointed, but did not pursue the matter; it obviously weighed less on his mind than whatever he had learned in Madrid. Apparently the girl had not been his lover, or even a valued servant. No doubt by the time of his next visit to Spain, he would have forgotten that Katherine had ever existed.

She heard low voices from the antechamber, but paid them no heed, not looking up until the door to her bedchamber opened. Edwina peeked around the edge of the door, her face flushed.

"My lady, 'tis Lord Harwood, and he says he cannot wait."

"Woman, I can speak for myself," Justin said, throwing the door wide as he strode into the bedchamber.

Margaret gasped and snatched the towels from the side of the tub, covering herself with them. She glared up at Justin. He was dressed for travel already, in plain black doublet and hose, riding boots, and a leather cape.

"God's death, Margaret! Your maid said you were abed, but 'tis a very strange, damp bed you chose."

"What matters it to you, Justin, unless you share it?" she asked crossly.

"Was that an invitation, lady? 'Twas not spoken like one."

Margaret drew a deep breath, trying to overcome her anger. She had wished Justin to see her this morning splendidly dressed, her face perfectly painted. Now her face had been scrubbed free of paint, and steam from the bath was frizzing her hair. It had been years since he had seen her like this, and she prayed he would not think she looked old, that he would still find her desirable.

"I would invite you to join me, my lord," she said in a honeyed voice, "if I thought you would accept and stay your journey to Bilbao."

Justin shook his head. "My men are awaiting me in the courtyard, ready to leave."

"I'faith, I wonder that you even came to bid me farewell."

He smiled crookedly. "Have I seemed so ungracious, sweeting? I pray your pardon. I did wish to bid you farewell, and to tell you I will be back as soon as I can, and with better gifts than those I brought this time. Some jewelry, perchance."

Margaret could not help smiling. This was the Justin she remembered and loved.

"Would that please you?" he asked, and she nodded. "Well, then. Now I need but find jewels that will suit you but are not too much like any you already own. May I see your jewelry?" He looked at the maid. "Edwina?"

Edwina looked to her mistress for help. Margaret bit her lip. She would not have Justin learn that she had sold much of her jewelry. "I would fain have you choose what you like best, my lord," she said after a moment, "for that would please me most."

He nodded then, and came closer to the tub to take her hand. She felt very anxious as he looked at her. For an instant, when she invited him to share her bath, she had considered standing up, but she had quickly decided against that. He had not seen her naked since she was fifteen, and though she always told herself she had not changed for the worse since then, she feared to put that belief to the test, feared to see disappointment on his face.

Of a sudden, there were tears in her eyes. " 'Tis unfair, Justin, for you to be leaving so soon," she whispered.

"I am sorry, Margaret," he said softly, and kissed her hand, and then left. She threw the wet towels after him.

A few miles past Burgos, Justin led his men off the road, into a small grove where they halted, hidden from view but still able to see if anyone might be following them.

Justin opened his cloakbag and withdrew the papers he needed. His hands were shaking slightly as he unfolded them. He was thinking of Margaret again, recalling the fury he had been forced to hide when he met with her last night and again this morning. Would that he could have avoided her completely! Tandy had suggested yesternight that they avoid the house entirely, stopping but a few hours at an inn in Burgos while word was sent to Margaret that they were perforce traveling in haste and would not trouble her and her household at that late hour but wished only to have Justin's remaining servant pack his belongings and ride to meet his fellows in Burgos. Justin had decided against the plan: 'twould engender suspicion, he had told Tandy. Then, too, he had wished to discover if she had sold her jewels—though he had made his plans already on the assumption that she would sell them soon if she had not already done so.

And he had wanted to see Margaret, wanted to see her face when she told him that Kat was gone.

Now he was not even sure why he had wanted to see her. What

had he hoped to see in her expression? Guilt? Perhaps regret? Instead he had seen only a poor show of sorrow and concern, so shabbily done that it would have disgraced the clumsiest strolling player in England. There had been not the slightest redeeming sign that she truly regretted what she had done. Jesu! How could he have ever loved the woman?

Tandy moved restlessly, waiting, and Justin banished all thoughts of Margaret as he looked at the papers carefully in the dawn light, making certain that he handed Tandy the correct one, the one addressed to Don Ferdinand in Bilbao. It was too dark here in the grove's shadows to examine the seals impressed in the wax, but he had seen earlier that it was Don Antonio's, as Tandy had sworn—though he still did not know the subterfuge Tandy had used to borrow that seal ring during their last hours in Madrid. No matter: it was but one more of Tandy's skills, better accepted without questioning.

What mattered was that Don Ferdinand would accept the seal, and the letter within—copied by Tandy in a hand like that of Don Antonio—explaining that Lord Harwood lay ill in Madrid from a chronic complaint and had asked for his own physician, whom Tandy was to bring with all speed from England. The letter would see Tandy safely out of the port, and Justin handed it to him, along with a letter bearing his own seal, instructing the captain to follow Tandy's orders as if they were Lord Harwood's own. Tandy would give the full reasons for this shift only once they were at sea, safely away from the Spanish coast.

The other letter bearing Don Antonio's seal Justin slipped inside his doublet. Perchance it would afford him some protection, should he be stopped and questioned . . .

"I like this not," Tandy said suddenly. " 'Twould be best if I accompanied you."

"Jesu, man, you are as repetitive as a starling that knows but a few words. Who else could I send in your stead to Bilbao? And which of these"—he jerked a thumb back, indicating the other men—"speaks Spanish well enough to pass himself off as my servant when I am in this guise? Would you have all our plans come to naught?"

"Still—"

"Still disputing?" Justin laughed. "By the Lord, Tandy, I would think you more concerned about my safety than ever . . . did I not also suspect that you wish to see the fair Katherine again, and as soon as possible."

His servant looked down. "Pray God, I will see her again."

"Fear not. You will. And likely she will soon give us reason again to wish her elsewhere. Now come, man, let's be on our way. You must not burn daylight. There is a good doctor you must fetch from England for your master. Get you gone."

For some minutes after they had left, Justin lingered in the grove, watching the road. Then, finally satisfied that they had not been followed by anyone who would report back to Burgos that Lord Harwood had left the party, he turned his horse away from the road and started northeast, toward Navarra.

CHAPTER 29

There was a hand on her shoulder, shaking her awake. Kat groaned and tried to roll away, seeking the oblivion of sleep again. Waking meant only pain . . .

She shrieked as she was yanked to her feet. Opening her eyes, she shook her filthy, tangled hair back from her face. She recognized the alguazil who held her; he was one of three who had taken turns raping her several months ago, after Fray Francisco first brought her to this hellish place in Valladolid, one of las carceles secretas, the secret prison-cells, of the Inquisition. He had raped her several times since then, but not for the last few weeks. There was fresher meat, he had told her coarsely; a twelve-year-old maidservant, a virgin when she was brought to the prison.

Beyond the alguazil she saw the guard who usually brought her meals, but this morning there was no bowl in his hands. There would be no breakfast for her, then. And that meant another audience of torment. They never fed her before torture, not wanting her to vomit.

The alguazil pushed her out of the cell and toward the torture chamber where the audiencia de tormento would take place.

She walked with only a slight limp now, though a week ago she had had to be carried to and from the torture chamber, so badly burned were her feet after an audiencia in which she was forced to sit on the floor while the torturer coated her bare feet with fat and then held a burning brand near them. She had fainted after less than a minute, coming to herself again only when she was back in her cell, being ministered to by the physician who always stood watch over the torturer to ensure that the torments imposed would be moderate. He had used poultices to heal her feet and had given her a drink containing laudanum to lessen the pain, but it had been days before she could walk again, and during that time the alguazils had grumbled at the necessity of carrying her to the torture chamber, where they subjected her twice to the potro.

The potro. She prayed that it would not be the water-torture again. She had suffered more lingering pain after other tortures, from her burnt feet, and from the torn muscles in her shoulders after she had been subjected to the strappado, where she had fainted the first time they had chained her arms behind her back and drawn the chain through a pulley

375

in the ceiling so she was lifted off the ground, then dropped partway and caught. But the potro had seemed the worst to her—and likely the best to her torturers—because she stayed awake throughout, from the moment they bound her, lying down on that ladder where her head was lower than her feet, through the placing of an iron bar in her mouth to hold her jaws open, the plugging of her nostrils, the draping of a long linen cloth across her mouth, and then the first pouring of foul water into her mouth, pushing the cloth into her throat and choking her. She had sobbed, she had gagged and retched and would have vomited if there had been anything in her stomach—but she had not fainted. And each time the drenched cloth had been withdrawn from her mouth to allow her to catch her breath, the inquisitors had been at her side, patiently asking the same questions, patiently insisting on a confession . . .

She shivered.

They reached the torture chamber at last, and Kat saw the two inquisitors, attended by Fray Francisco and a notary, a physician, and two more alguazils, assistants to the torturer who stood waiting, arms folded, in a corner of the room.

Seeing them again frightened her so much that for an instant the chamber reeled about her and she would have fallen if her escort had let go of her. She recovered a few moments later and, lifting her head defiantly, asked if any response to her letters had been received. The older of the two inquisitors shook his head, a look of sympathy on his face. Fray Francisco smiled thinly, and she glared at him. More and more, she was certain that the letters she had written—to Lord Harwood, to Doña Margaret, even to Don Antonio at King Philip's court—had never been sent. As like as not, unless Rafael had informed them—assuming he were still free—they did not even know that she was here. They might suspect that she had been taken prisoner by the Inquisition, but the Holy Office could keep the names of its prisoners and all details of the proceedings against them secret until the auto-da-fé where they would meet their fate. Perchance her letters were even now with the records of her trial and these audiencias de tormentos in el secreto, the archives to which only inquisitors were admitted. But she could not be sure of that, and so she clung to hope.

"Katherine," the older inquisitor said gently, "are you ready to confess now?"

She shook her head. 'Twas of no use to try, for they would never accept her confession.

The charges had been read to her—charges of preaching heresy in towns she had visited, of going into churches to spit on the statues of saints—but the names of her accusers had not been given to her, leaving her unable to confess in detail as the Inquisition required. She must needs give them names—the names of the poor Spaniards whom they had forced, belike with torture, into giving accusations against her. But she could not guess who her accusers were—and dared not guess, in truth, for fear of naming someone whom the Inquisition had not yet snared in its web.

The inquisitor gestured for the alguazils to strip her of her rags prefatory to the torture. At last, as she stood naked before them, she turned her gaze on Fray Francisco, who, as always, seemed flustered by seeing her without clothes and averted his gaze, muttering something about protervos e inpenitentes negativos.

She knew the words: they came easily to his lips whenever he spoke to her, warning her about the death she would face if she remained a stubborn and impenitent denier. He had warned her that she would give the Holy Office no choice, that she would be abandoned to secular authorities for execution by burning. The Holy Office itself could not take her life. Ecclesia abhorret a sanguine. Priests could not shed blood. But a papal bull ensured that blood would be shed anyway, for the secular authorities were required to execute convicted heretics within five days or face charges of heresy themselves.

Resigned to being tortured again—though Fray Francisco had told her that she was not being tortured again, that the torture had merely been suspended, for it could not by law be repeated—she started toward the ladderlike engine where she had been subjected to the potro. Then one of the alguazils caught her arm and stopped her. She looked questioningly at the older inquisitor.

"It has been decided," he told her, "that your confession will be sought by another method."

She shook her head in disbelief while he told her what it was, and screamed and fought the alguazils as they dragged her to a table and strapped her down.

The torturer showed her a shallow but heavy metal bowl, then set it upside down on the hollow curve of her belly, checking to make sure that the bowl's weight held its rim snug against her flesh. An alguazil brought him a wicker cage then, and Kat watched through tears as the torturer took three young rats from the cage, one at a time, lifting the rim of the bowl for an instant to slip the rat beneath it. She shuddered as the rats scrabbled about, their claws scratching her. The older inquisitor approached her again, a hopeful expression on his face, but he retreated again when she glared at him.

And now a brazier was set on the table, and the torturer, using wood-handled tongs, began to lift live coals from the brazier and set them, one by one, on the flat base of the bowl. Kat was aware of the rim of the bowl growing warm, then hot, against her skin, but she paid little heed to it. All her attention was on the increasing tempo of the rats' mad dance inside the bowl, driven by fear of the searing heat above them. In a few more moments her belly would be scratched raw, but she began to exult, hopeful that this torture would fail, that the prediction by the inquisitors had been wrong.

And then she screamed, feeling the first agonizing bite, as a rat tried to gnaw its way through her flesh to escape from the burning metal above it . . .

Kat bolted upright in bed, then sank back against the pillows, whimpering, her hands pressed over her mouth. She did not want to scream aloud, and believed she had not, not this time: though she still seemed to hear her own screams, torn from her throat, echoing within the tower, Dorotea lay sleeping on the trundle bed. Twice before Kat had wakened the maid with her screams, and though Dorotea would try to comfort her, it was a mistake to tell the girl of her bad dreams, for Dorotea would begin to cry and in the end Kat would find herself comforting the maid. Nay, she would let Dorotea sleep . . . though in faith she slept poorly. To judge from her tossing and moaning, Dorotea's dreams were no pleasanter than her own. The maid, too, had listened overlong to Fray Francisco.

It seemed impossible that Fray Francisco had been here only a week.

He had insisted on spending several hours each day in her company, and already she felt she knew him better than many people in Sussex who had been part of her life for years. She knew the awkward gestures of his bony hands, the spastic smile that seemed more a grimace, the way his religious zeal would shake his whole frail body and set his eyes afire. She knew what dreams he had once dreamed, and which he still dreamed. She knew, she felt, entirely too much about him.

And he knew—or so he said—entirely too little about her.

His attempts to draw her out were clumsy, and so far she had been able to evade the point of his questions, but with each day he became more clever. He was not interrogating her; he had no right to do so. Nor had he the right to interrogate her maid, but yesterday he had succeeded in waylaying Dorotea on her way to the kitchen and had held her in private conversation for several minutes. The maid had assured Kat that she had truthfully informed the friar that her English mistress never spoke to her of heretical matters, yet it was clear to Kat that Dorotea had been badly shaken by the meeting with Fray Francisco. Kat felt besieged: she knew it was only a matter of time before a careless comment of her own, or lies wrung from the frightened maid, left her completely vulnerable. Yet she was powerless to end these conversations, to send the vicar away. Only Don Rafael could do that.

She twisted the corner of the blanket into a taut cord between her hands.

Always her thoughts came to this. She could submit to the don, and Fray Francisco would leave. The danger to her would be gone—aye, and the danger to Dorotea as well. The maidservant had never spoken to Kat about Don Rafael, but Kat knew the girl must be aware of why the vicar had been brought here. At times—most often just after Fray Francisco had left the tower—Kat thought she saw a plea in the girl's eyes. That plea had been there, too, after the friar had questioned Dorotea alone. Dorotea might be the most zealous of Catholics, but 'twould reck not if Fray Francisco became convinced that Kat had been preaching heresy to her. Then Dorotea would be forced to choose between a lie that might damn her soul and a truth that would more certainly consign her to imprisonment and torture until the inquisitors had the confession they wanted. Neither way could she save Kat. Yet Kat could save both of them.

She tossed the blanket aside and slid out of bed. The stone floor felt cold beneath her feet as she went to the narrow window and looked out.

Don Rafael, or Fray Francisco and the Inquisition. Yet were those her only choices? Was it not possible that these past days, these hours spent confronting the vicar, had forged a bond between her and Dorotea? A bond so strong that Kat might presume to ask the maid's help in escaping . . .

She had to try. Aye, and soon: Fray Francisco was too unpredictable, his zeal for discovering heretics a keg of gunpowder that might explode at any moment. She would ask Don Rafael to come to the tower alone today, and she would speak to him then and tell him of her willingness to submit, and then the vicar would trouble her no more.

With that decision, her fear of Fray Francisco shrank from a Gargantua to a pygmy. She still feared the Holy Office he represented, but now it began to seem strange to her that she had ever been afraid of the man himself. How could she have been, when he so often seemed uneasy in *her* presence? She had often caught him staring at her as though she were not just an enemy—as she was certain all Protestants were his enemies—but as if he were actually terrified of her. At those times she had had the impression that if she had moved so much as an inch toward him, he would have fled. She could see it now, the bare soles of his callused feet showing beneath the hem of his robe as he raced away—a vicar of the Inquisition, fleeing from her!

She began to laugh, at first chuckling quietly, but her laughter became higher and louder and wilder until she was almost howling and she was leaning helplessly against the wall, tears streaming down her face. Dorotea awoke and came to see what was wrong, but Kat waved her back to her bed, then returned to bed herself, her fit subsiding into hiccups and an occasional giggle. In a few minutes she fell into the most peaceful sleep she had had in weeks.

Awake in his bedchamber, Fray Francisco heard the woman's laughter and shuddered.

He lay on his back on the cold stone floor. Servants had turned down the covers of the bed and set a warming pan between the fine linen sheets, but he would not sleep there. He had extinguished the fire, too. His flesh was betraying him, and he would not strengthen it with creature comforts.

He thought longingly of his hair shirt and leather whip, both left behind in Valladolid at his superior's insistence. How he needed them now! His superior had intended him to regain his physical strength, but with new strength had come the old, shameful lusts.

Since his first night at the Eagle's Nest, his sleep had been racked with dreams of the Englishwoman. She haunted his thoughts during the day, too, and when he was with her he would sometimes sense his body responding to her presence as if he were not a monk, as if he were as ignorant of sin as a pagan. She seemed to be doing nothing that was out of the ordinary, but his gaze would be caught by the gleam of her hair, her sweetly shaped lips, the smooth line of her soft white throat, the shadowed curves of her breasts beneath the veiling cloth—

He moaned, grinding his hands against his eyes as though he could rub away the hated images of her.

Blessed Virgin, he began to pray, *aid me*.

Two nights ago he had awakened from a harrowing dream to find the sheets wet, stained with his seed. Ashamed, and frightened lest the servants discover that he had not yet mastered his body, he had washed the stains from the sheets himself and dried them before the fire, then made the bed again before spending the rest of the night on the floor by the hearth. When the dreams plagued him still last night, he had pushed the rushes away so he slept on bare stone, and had let the fire die down. Still the dreams came. So he had walked that afternoon in the woods outside the Eagle's Nest, had found a long, supple willow shoot, and had hidden it beneath his robe when he returned to the castle. Using the shoot as a switch, he had whipped his back and shoulders until his skin was crisscrossed with welts and the pain had driven all other thoughts from his mind. And though he had slept but little—for now the pain kept him awake—that sleep had been dreamless. He had expected to spend a somewhat peaceful night, plagued less than usual by thoughts of the Englishwoman.

Until he heard her laughter.

He had clapped his hands over his ears, trying to shut out the sound, but now it rang within his skull, its wildness amplified in his memory. Groaning, he staggered to his feet and crossed to the bed. He had hidden the switch beneath the mattress; he withdrew it and ran one hand along its bloodstained length. Then he began to scourge himself again, harder than before, in the hope that he would drive out not only the memory of the Englishwoman's laughter, but also the thought that had come to him a moment after he had heard her. The thought that she knew somehow of his efforts, and was laughing at him.

Don Rafael came to the tower late in the morning, a full two hours after Kat had sent Dorotea to him with a message requesting a private conference. The wait was an anxious one for her. She wore the somber-hued clothes she had worn since Fray Francisco's arrival. As like as not, the don would have preferred to see her garbed in brighter colors, but she could not chance it when the vicar might pay her an unannounced visit at any time. Her hair was carefully dressed, however, and her face delicately painted, with just enough rouge to restore the color that weeks of confinement and sleepless nights had stolen from her.

"Señora." Rafael paused at the top of the stairs. Dorotea waited below in the antechamber, on Kat's orders. Kat would be consenting to become Rafael's leman. He would find her submission more convincing if they were alone in her bedchamber, rather than standing in the antechamber with Dorotea there as duenna.

"You look especially lovely this morning," Rafael told her, and she smiled.

"I thank you, Don Rafael, for your sweet words and for your presence here. Pray God, I have not inconvenienced you by requesting this meeting."

"I had planned to go riding, señora, but my plans will wait until this afternoon."

He had gone out riding nearly every afternoon, she thought with a savage envy. Twice she had even watched him riding in the valley below while the vicar, uncaring that her back was turned and her attention on the freedom of the outside world, had prattled on of the Inquisition.

"I wished to speak with you about the . . . relationship . . . you desired. I realize now that I was stubborn and foolish. You will find me more . . . amenable . . . in the future."

A thin smile touched the don's lips. "And to what may I ascribe this change of heart, Katherine? To myself, or to the vicar?"

She lowered her gaze. "I have come to recognize your good will, my lord, and to appreciate your protection more every day. As for the vicar, I would that you ask him to end his visits to my chambers. His talk, while edifying, has alarmed my maid."

"Your concern for your maid is touching," Rafael said dryly. Not moving any closer, he held out a hand. "Come, sweeting."

She went to him and took his hand, then allowed him to draw her closer and kiss her. His mouth tasted slightly of rosewater, but the kissing comfit he must have eaten before coming to the tower could not entirely hide the garlic on his breath, and she needed all her self-control to stand passively in his embrace.

Suddenly he stepped back and looked at her skeptically. "There's scant appreciation in your kisses, sweetheart."

"My lord, you must give me more time—"

" 'Tis a refrain I have heard from you before. Nay, Kat. No more time." And he scooped her up and carried her to the bed.

He had ripped the partlet from her gown before she could fight free of his embrace again.

"Please you, Rafael, wait a few days, until—"

"Wait!" He glared at her furiously. "I am neither a child nor a simpleton, to be tricked again and again. Why should I wait?"

"I have my monthly course now."

He looked disappointed, and she rejoiced that the gossip she had heard was true, that many men would avoid lying with their wives when the women had their monthly courses. 'Twas untrue that she had her course now, but she judged him unlikely to ask Dorotea about it. She had gambled on the lie gaining her a few days in which to make her escape, and it seemed to have worked as she had hoped.

And then he grabbed her again, dragging her down to the bed and covering her face and neck with kisses.

"Rafael . . ."

"Yes, señora, I will wait." He raised himself on one arm to gaze down at her. He was smiling again, but with genuine pleasure. "I will use the hours to plan our sport."

"And you will send Fray Francisco away?"

"If you will gladly become my love. *Gladly*, sweeting. I will have no pretense of shrinking modesty, nor any pining for Lord Harwood. You do not love him still?"

"After he has cast me away?" She laughed harshly.

"Good." He began to kiss her neck again, then her shoulders and the top of her breasts. "I would have you remember, Kat," he murmured, his lips against her skin, his voice muffled, "that you may look only to me for protection. I will send the vicar away, but I may recall him just as swiftly, should you fail to please me as you have promised. Do you understand?"

"Indeed, my lord."

She felt his teeth graze her breast, and then he bit her, gently at first, then hard enough that she gasped.

"That pleases you?" he asked, raising his head to look at her, and she had the presence of mind to say nothing. "I'll bring you greater pleasures," he promised, then moved away, straightening his clothes as he crossed to the stairs.

"We'll sup together tonight," he said over his shoulder.

"That will please me, Don Rafael," Kat replied, but when the don had descended to the antechamber, she glanced down at her breast and wiped her hand across the red bite mark there. "As much as becoming supper for rats," she muttered, then turned her thoughts to Dorotea.

The girl's sympathies must be won, and quickly. Kat thought it likely that Dorotea would be moved to hear of the sacrifice Kat would make to protect her from Fray Francisco. But would it not touch her more, for a truth, if she saw the vulgar emblems of that sacrifice painted on her mistress's face?

The door below was opened and then closed a few moments later. Rafael was gone; presently Dorotea would be coming upstairs to see to her mistress. Smiling, Kat got up from the bed and went over to the array of paints and perfumes, most of them left by Don Rafael's last leman, which she had spurned till now.

To Don Rafael's vexation, Fray Francisco did not join him for dinner as was his wont. The steward, sent to inquire, returned with the news that the friar—who looked ill—had decided to spend much of the day in prayer but would leave his room to join his host for supper. The don regretfully sent word to Kat that he would not see her until the next day.

It was with relief that Rafael watched Fray Francisco enter the hall at suppertime. The friar looked, if possible, even paler than usual, and there were dark circles from lack of sleep under his eyes, but his walk was steady enough, and he set about eating his supper with his typical grudging appetite. Certainly he seemed well enough to travel . . .

Rafael waited several minutes before mentioning that he had received a letter from Don José. "He pleads with me, as one of his oldest friends, to restore you to his household as soon as possible."

He paused. There was no change of expression on the friar's face to indicate that one of the servants might have told him that the letter had in fact been received four days ago—fortunately, since Rafael would not have enjoyed explaining why he had said nothing of it until now.

"It has of course been a great pleasure for me to have you here as my guest, Fray Francisco, but I would not be so ungracious as to attempt to keep you here after Don José had so kindly made little objection"— he paused again, coughing to hide a laugh—"to your leaving his abode for mine. I have already arranged for your return to Don José tomorrow.

You will be leaving in the morning. I have spoken to Doña Katherine, and—"

He broke off, startled. At the mention of Katherine's name, the friar had jerked as though struck by an invisible whip.

"She is grateful for the instruction you have given her, and will miss your visits, but she understands Don José's prior claim on you as a guest. She wishes me to express her gratitude to you."

The vicar bit his lip. "I should speak to her again," he said, lowering his head. He had spoken so softly that Don Rafael wondered if he were speaking to himself.

"The lady mentioned a headache when I spoke to her this morning. Since she is indisposed, I will convey to her your farewells."

"I thank you, Don Rafael," Francisco replied, still not looking up, "but I feel I must speak to her personally. If she cannot see me today, then tomorrow or the next day . . ."

The don frowned. "But I have arranged for you to leave early tomorrow, that you may reach Don José's castle before the worst heat of the day."

The vicar raised his head then, and his eyes seemed to glitter more than ever as he stared with suspicion at his host. Neither man said anything for some moments. Then Rafael took a deep breath and said in what he hoped was a cheery voice, "However, we shall see if she has recovered by now, and if so, you may say farewell to her yourself this evening."

The vicar's sharp gaze held Rafael's for a long time, then he inclined his head in a slight nod and returned to picking at his supper.

Admiring her handiwork in the mirror, Kat recalled her aunt's warnings against paints and thought, *Anne would be horrified by this.*

Of certain, Dorotea was.

Kat touched her face, which was—except for her vermilion-painted cheeks and mouth and kohl-rimmed eyes—of the same paleness as a whitewashed wall. *Yea, and of the same softness, forsooth.* She would have chuckled, had she dared, but Dorotea was watching her from across the room, a somber expression on her face. She had just offered to help Kat escape, broaching the subject first herself.

It had been so simple. Kat had seated herself before the looking glass and proceeded to daub her face with paint until she looked gaudier than any of the whores she had seen in Southwark. What had Justin called her at the Jerusalem Tree, when he saw her face heavily painted? A Winchester goose? Like enough, he would have to find a worse name for her now, for she looked worse, with her face and neck and bosom covered with a thick layer of white fucus, and gaudy vermilion streaking her cheeks and mouth. The kohl she had used to line her eyes was smeared already by the tears she had shed in sympathy with Dorotea. Now she picked up a brush and a gallipot and began to repair the damage, though she wished more than anything that she could wash her face completely clean of paint. She had planned to do so before supper, had Rafael not told her he would not be coming to the tower to sup with her. This show was for Dorotea, not for the don, who would see too much mockery in it. But the message from him had left her free to wear the heavy paint all day, reminding Dorotea that her mistress had been forced to agree to become Don Rafael's whore in order to save them from the threat of the Inquisition.

And now Dorotea had sworn that she would get Kat safely away from the castle tomorrow night. There was a groom who lusted after her, Dorotea had said. He had offered before to let her take a ride some night on a white jennet for which the don had paid a great deal of money, but he insisted that he must go with her. She had always refused his offer before, but tomorrow morning, she told Kat, she would ask him to have the horses ready that night. She would trick the guard into entering the tower, where, Kat had assured her, they could overcome him and bind him. Dorotea would lead Kat to the stables, and then while Kat hid nearby, she would send the groom back into the castle on some errand or other. And then the two girls would take the horses and ride away. The groom would not dare raise a hue and cry, Dorotea said. He would be too fearful of the punishment he might receive, and instead would wait all night in the vain hope that Dorotea would return both horses safely. By dawn they would be twenty miles from the castle, at the farm of one of Dorotea's cousins, no friend of the don's, a man who was sure to help them.

Kat—who had had much more experience than she liked to recall of plans going awry—thought the plan much less certain of success than Dorotea considered it, but she kept her doubts to herself. Slim hope though it was, it was the only one she had.

She heard the door open downstairs. 'Twould be their supper, which was late. For a moment she thought of having Dorotea go downstairs alone while she washed her face, then decided against that: it would be some jest, to see the servants' faces when they saw her painted thus. She led Dorotea to the stairs and was halfway down before she realized her mistake.

"Katherine?" Don Rafael asked, disbelief in his voice.

It was too late to flee back up the stairs, yet by the Lord! she wished she could. For the vicar, whom she had hoped never to lay eyes on again, stood just behind the don, as still as if he had just seen Medusa.

"My lady," Rafael said after a few moments, "I had told Fray Francisco that you did not feel well, yet he wished to come bid you farewell before he leaves on the morrow. Don José wishes to have him as his guest again." He had spoken too rapidly; now he paused before adding, "I see you are feeling much better now."

"Yes, my lord," Kat replied, her mind eased by his words. For an instant she had thought that Rafael had lied to her, that this would be her undoing.

As she approached them, Fray Francisco seemed to shrink back without moving his feet. He looked away once or twice as she drew close to him, but always looked back in dread and fascination. What was it he wished not to see? she wondered. Her face, with its gaudy paint? Or was it her body, displayed more than was her wont in a tight-fitting kirtle of crimson velvet-on-velvet with a low-cut bodice.

"I am sorry that you must leave us so soon, Fray Francisco, and only wish that we might have had more time to talk. But I understand Don José's desire that you become his guest again."

"I regret that I cannot spend more time with you, lady," Fray Francisco said in a small, strangled voice.

"As do I, Fray Francisco," she responded, hard put not to smile. "I regret it more than I can say. But you will not leave until tomorrow. Will you then spend this evening with me?"

For a moment she feared she had misjudged him in making that suggestion, but then the friar was turning to Rafael, a beseeching look on his face, and Kat knew she was safe. She inwardly breathed a sigh of relief. I'faith, she had been tempted to say more and frighten him even further in revenge for the times he had frightened her, but she knew 'twould be too reckless a course.

"Katherine, you should be resting," the don said quickly. "I would have you regain your health and natural color, not counterfeit health with paint and bright garb."

"As you wish, Don Rafael," Kat said. She turned to the vicar again. "Fray Francisco, I hope your journey tomorrow is a pleasant one, and so, too, your return to Valladolid."

"Thank you, lady. Fare you well." He backed away, as though he were afraid to turn his back to her when she was close. She said nothing more until he was several steps from her, when he finally turned on his heel to hurry away.

"Pray for me," she called, unable to resist that last taunt.

The vicar froze and looked back over his shoulder at her. She had thought his face pale before, but now, as the last vestiges of color drained away, she realized she had frightened him more than ever. She all but clapped her hands with delight, catching herself at the last moment and instead bringing her hands together silently as if in prayer.

Fray Francisco shook himself a little, then said softly, " I will, lady," before vanishing through the doorway. His feet slapped against the stones of the hall in a faster tempo than usual.

"Fool!" Don Rafael whispered harshly. Kat's eyes met his, then she turned away, clapping her hand over her mouth to muffle her laughter. The don grabbed her and shook her. "What was the meaning of this, Katherine? Why did you paint your face like this?"

"I'faith, my lord," she said unsteadily, "I was but showing Dorotea how some English ladies paint their faces. I expected to see no one but the servants who would bring our supper. You promised me that I would not see Fray Francisco again!"

"I had no choice, madam. He would not go without bidding you farewell."

" 'Twas for the best, I trow, for the friar has given us much merriment. I warrant you, no man was ever so startled by woman. Saw you his face?" She glanced toward Dorotea. "Saw you his face?" she asked her, laughing again, and the maid began to laugh with her, and then the don, until they were all holding their sides, while the guard looked on with a bewildered smile.

CHAPTER 30

He had whipped his back until it bled, and that had freed him from the memories of the Englishwoman's painted face and ripe body, freed him long enough to fall asleep before the cold hearth. In his dreams he had been back in the sanctuary of Valladolid, with thoughts of nothing but his service to the Holy Office. When the noise disturbed him he sought at first to ignore it, clinging to his dreams until they tore like rotted cloth, ragged shreds fluttering about him as he sat up and stared at the opening door.

Opening. Yet he had locked it; he remembered locking it—yes, and bolting it, too, as soon as he was safely back in the bedchamber.

What a fool he had been to think there could be safety here!

She slipped into the room almost silently, the whisper of her silk-slippered feet on the floor so faint a sound that, had the fire been lit and crackling, he would not have heard her. She smiled at him as she closed the door behind her, locking it once again. It was a small smile, with her mouth closed, but for a few moments he could not tear his gaze from her lips, painted so red now—

He moaned and threw an arm up to block the sight of her face, with its terrible beauty. "Lady, you must leave at once! You should not be here! If you do not leave, I will be forced to tell Don Rafael—"

His voice choked off as her clothing slid to the floor, revealing her naked body to his sight. Sobbing, he scrambled away on his hands and knees, his face averted from her. She was a witch, for her garments—garments that would have required a maidservant's help for half an hour to don—could not have been discarded so easily. Yea, she was a witch, for he was naked too, and he had been wearing his monk's habit, the coarse cloth rubbing against his raw back, when he fell asleep.

He fled like an animal, crawling across the floor, but she followed him, laughing, until she had him cornered. He turned to strike out at her, but she caught his hand, and he almost fainted from terror.

"Francisco," she murmured, still laughing, and his name was sweet song when she spoke it, and his fear melted away.

She raised him to his feet, as if she were a great lady and he her subject, *but then her hands were touching his rebellious flesh. Knowing hands, whore's hands that set him aflame. Groaning, he stood still for a moment, then swayed toward her, then caught at her and dragged her down with him to the floor, and took her there, on the cold stones.*

Francisco sat up, trembling, sweat pouring off him. He looked around wildly, then threw himself to the floor again, whimpering. She was gone. If ever she had been here. But could any experience so vivid have been merely a dream?

He got to his feet and staggered over to the chest at the foot of the bed, where there was a ewer of water and a basin. Stripping off his habit, he began to wash. As he sponged away the sweat and the traces of his shame, the panic that had flooded his mind gave way to an icy calm. He began to pace around the room, letting the cool air dry his skin.

She had been laughing in his dream, as she had laughed a few hours ago when he fled from the tower. As she had laughed last night, when he had realized that the self-flagellation that had always kept lustful thoughts at bay in the past was no help at all when his thoughts were of her. Somehow she had known that the carnal temptation she offered was defeating his resolve. But how could she have known?

. . . unless she was a witch . . .

Pray for me, she had said, mocking him and the Church he served. But she had mocked him earlier, at their first meeting. *How will I know*, she had asked, *whether you are a saint or a sinner?* He had been suspicious of her question even then, but now it shamed him that he had not recognized it for what it was—a clear warning that she meant to test his faith.

He began shaking again, so violently that anyone watching would have thought him palsied. He went to the bed and took the blanket and wrapped himself in it before sitting down again to think.

She was a witch. He could not doubt it now. Was not the very proof in his dreams of her? Lustful dreams. He knew what his dreams signified. He had read the *Malleus maleficarum*, the book written nearly a century ago by the German inquisitors Henricus Institoris and Jacobus Sprenger. The wise authors of *The Hammer of Witches* had revealed that witchcraft had its origin in a woman's insatiable lust—lust that the Englishwoman had declared without words by her garb and painted face . . . and by the dreams she forced him to dream.

But could he prove that she was a witch? If he were back in Valladolid, with the aid of his *alguazils* and *familiares*, he would have her seized and taken to prison, then stripped and examined for the witch marks that must be on her body. But whom could he trust here? He shook his head. He would have to take her to Valladolid with him, without further proof of her witchery.

And that thought was frightening, nearly as frightening as the witch herself.

His first years in Valladolid he had learned the bitter lesson that the Supreme Council of the Inquisition was reluctant to believe tales of witchcraft, most especially when told by a young monk from Navarra. Most of his superiors were proud Castilians, certain of their superiority to those who lived in the Pyrenees, far from the great cities of Spain. They had discounted his stories of witches as superstition and reminded him that *La Suprema* had put a stop to most witch trials in Navarra half a century earlier, insisting that there be solid proof as well as accusations.

So now how would he be able to convince them that the English-woman was a witch? At the thought of such opposition, he was tempted to abandon his purpose and leave the castle quietly—but then what would become of the don and the members of his household?

He knelt on the bare floor. He would need guidance for this decision. Bowing his head, he began to pray, but only a few minutes had passed before images of the witch once again invaded his mind. He was in despair.

And then he remembered the relic. He hurried to the cloakbag in which he carried his meager belongings.

How could he have forgotten that he had the relic with him? He should have remembered it at once when the witch first began to torment him. No doubt this was part of her sorcery, to make him forget this most precious possession.

It was a small handkerchief, of linen yellowed with age, and much of it was stained reddish-brown with the blood of the martyred inquisitor Pedro Arbués de Epila, Torquemada's delegate in Zaragoza in 1485. Arbués had been struck down in church during matins, fatally wounded by *converso* assassins who had been offered five hundred florins by wealthy *converso* conspirators wishing to stop the Holy Office from discovering the heretics among the New Christians and confiscating their property.

The martyr Arbués was not yet acknowledged a saint, but Francisco knew that the canonization was only a matter of time. Was it not widely known that the church bells had rung of their own accord when the inquisitor died two days after receiving his fatal wounds? And the stones on which his precious blood had fallen had remained wet with blood for two weeks, as many had seen, touching the stones themselves or pressing bits of cloth to the church floor for a relic of the martyr's blood. Francisco had bought this relic from an old pedlar in the market in

Valladolid, and though another monk had warned him that the pedlar was as like as not selling old handkerchiefs stained with pig's blood, Francisco believed otherwise . . .

Now he touched the relic to his lips, breathing a prayer for peace and guidance . . . and at last, with the assistance of the martyr, they were given to him.

Wakened by his steward, Don Rafael had listened to him discourse on household expenses while he broke his fast. Now the steward was gone, and Rafael was dressing to go riding. It would be a lovely morning, and he was anxious to be away from the castle for most of the time until Fray Francisco's departure in a few hours.

He had slept well enough, though sleep had eluded him at first, so troubled had his thoughts been by recollections of the friar's horror when he saw Katherine for the last time. Then at last he had fallen asleep, and his dreams had been sweet ones of lying with Kat, here in his own fine bed—not the bed in that cold chamber in the tower.

His manservant was helping him with his riding boots when someone knocked at the door. The servant went to answer it, and as soon as the door was opened, the vicar burst into the chamber.

"Fray Francisco?" the don said, rising to greet his guest. "I had thought you would still be abed, resting before your journey."

"There are, my lord, more important things than rest. I have been at prayer since midnight."

Don Rafael could readily believe that. The friar looked haggard, his eyes shadowed, but his feverish energy had not left him. Even now he was trembling slightly, as though shaken by a force he could scarcely contain. Rafael had a sense of foreboding as he waited for Francisco to continue.

"I would return to Valladolid immediately, my lord, if you will arrange it. If not, I am certain Don José will."

"Of course I will." He wondered why the vicar had changed his plans, but did not ask: he was not sure he really wanted to know what went on behind those glittering eyes.

"And I will take Doña Katherine with me, to be investigated for witchcraft."

"What?" Don Rafael took a step toward the vicar, who flinched but did not retreat. "What madness is this?"

"Madness, my lord?" Fray Francisco retorted. "Doubt you my judgment as a vicar of the Inquisition?"

The don drew in a deep breath. "Forgive me, Fray Francisco. But you must understand that neither I nor anyone in my household have had cause to suspect the lady Katherine of witchcraft."

"Can you deny, my lord, that you feel desire for her?"

Don Rafael flushed. Had his feelings been that apparent when he first saw Katherine yesternight? Damn the woman for surprising him so, that he would reveal himself to this monk! "That she is a beautiful woman, I will not deny. But she is the ward of a cousin of my friend, and I respect and will protect her."

"It is not she, my lord, who needs protection, but you who need to be protected from the desire she has created in you by means of witchcraft. You are too trusting to defend yourself against her. Even I—" His voice dropped to a whisper. "Even I . . ." His hands clenched spasmodically.

The don understood, and would have recoiled in disgust from this friar's hypocrisy, had he not also feared him. "Is it not possible," he asked cautiously, "that you misjudge her, Fray Francisco? Maybe if you spoke to her guardian, or to Doña Margaret or Don Antonio, you might come to realize that you have viewed her in the wrong light."

"One might almost think, Don Rafael," the friar replied, a menacing note in his voice, "that you do not trust the Holy Office to judge if a woman is truly a witch, and would instead rely on the judgment of nobility with no training in such matters. I can only hope that your dismaying attitude is due to the influence of the witch, and will change after she is removed from your domain."

Don Rafael could not hold the vicar's gaze for long. He looked down at the floor, ashamed of himself for his silence, yet knowing that further defense of Katherine would damn him in the eyes of the vicar. Had he more power at the Court of Castile—were he certain he could gain King Philip's ear on this matter—he might challenge the vicar and refuse to let him take Katherine away. As it was, he could only ask others to intervene, and hope they would be successful.

"Do you wish me to inform Katherine that she will be traveling to Valladolid with you?" he asked in a muffled voice.

"I shall tell her. It would be best, my lord, if you were not exposed to her malign influence again. I will also tell her maid to pack for the journey. You will need time to arrange provisions for our trip, if we are to leave yet today. And we shall need guards, of course."

"Of course," Rafael echoed.

The don sank back down onto his chair after the friar departed. His manservant, who looked as stunned as Rafael felt, offered him a glass of wine, but the don waved it away. He would need a clear head, for the next hour at least. He asked that his writing gear be brought to him.

He addressed the letter to Don Antonio, then paused, trying to force order upon his confused thoughts. This letter must be carefully worded. Katherine's life, and possibly his own, depended upon it.

"Don Rafael." His steward sounded concerned. "A messenger is here."

The don slowly opened his eyes. He was reclining on his bed, pillows propped behind his back, the bed hangings drawn back to let the warm sunlight fall upon him. A goblet sat on the table beside the bed, next to a half-empty flagon of wine. He reached for the glass now and took another sip. He had been drinking rather steadily in the hour since he put the unfinished letter aside.

"What news?" he asked, hoping the briefness of the question would disguise any slurring of his voice. The steward sometimes seemed to disapprove of his drinking.

"I know not. He will not give his message to me. He insists on speaking with you in person, as his message is from a grandee and is meant for you only."

"Which grandee?"

"He would not tell me."

Rafael shook his head, confused.

"Perhaps, Don Rafael, this man wishes you to return to Madrid with him. He has brought an extra horse, saddled and ready to ride."

"Has he brought any other men with him?" the don asked, suddenly wary, wondering if this might be part of some plot by one of his rivals at court.

"No, my lord."

Then the messenger could not expect to force Rafael to go back with him . . . Curiosity fought fear, and won.

"I will see him. Send him in."

Rafael got up, straightened his clothes, and buckled his sword belt around his waist. He splashed water on his face and had just finished drying it when his steward knocked at the door. Rafael called for him to enter.

The messenger preceded Rafael's servant into the chamber. He was a tall man of some thirty years of age, and clearly a gentleman of high rank, judging from his clothes and his bearing, which were those of a courtier. Rafael had never seen him before in his life.

"Don Rafael?"

"You behold him."

"I have come to bring you a letter from Don Antonio Téllez de Osuna."

"So quickly? Do messengers now fly faster than thought?" the don asked with a laugh. He saw the messenger's brows draw together in a puzzled frown, and recollected himself. "Forgive me, sir, but I have just this morning begun a letter to Don Antonio. It would be wonderful if you were here with the answer already."

"I wish that I could oblige you, Don Rafael," the messenger replied, "but I have come about other business. A matter which must be spoken of in private."

"Something more than the letter discusses?" Rafael asked, suspicious again, and held out his hand for the missive, which the messenger gave to him.

Rafael glanced at the seal, ascertaining that it was Don Antonio's, then broke it and read the letter, which consisted of only a few lines advising him to trust the messenger and heed what he said. Folding the letter again, he looked steadily at the messenger, one eyebrow raised. "I see Don Antonio has entrusted his message to you. What is it?"

The messenger looked at Pablo, and after a moment Rafael gestured for the steward to leave them. Surely this man could be trusted not to be an assassin.

When the door had shut, he offered the messenger some wine. The gentleman declined to drink, saying that he had been sent on a matter of some urgency. "I was sent to escort Katherine Lisle back to Burgos. Where is she?"

Rafael had half expected this. Still, "Why do you believe she is here?" he asked with a smile.

"Let us have no games between us, Don Rafael. Doña Margaret has told Don Antonio what befell her guest. She has confessed all, your role in this as well as her own."

Rafael had maintained his smile while the messenger spoke, though it felt more like a grimace now. So Margaret had betrayed him. What had brought her to do so? he wondered. It could not have been remorse—he did not believe Margaret capable of it. No, she must have feared discovery and thought a confession to her husband the safest course. Was it possible that Don Antonio—wishing above all to limit gossip—would content himself with the return of Katherine Lisle? Or would the conde seek revenge at some later date?

"My role in what?" he asked. "Doña Katherine has been a guest here, but that was known to Doña Margaret. I invited Doña Katherine to visit me when I met her at La Casa de las Rosas."

"And did you offer then to send *matónes* to escort her against her will to Navarra? I must tell you, Don Rafael, that Don Antonio will be sorely angered if he learns that any harm came to the lady."

For an instant Rafael was shaken by the threat, but then it struck him that the messenger had referred to the *matónes* Pablo had hired. Margaret had known nothing of that—she had thought he would use his own men. However Antonio had learned of the *matónes*, it could not have been from Margaret.

If, indeed, Antonio did know of this, and this messenger was in truth his servant . . .

Rafael stared at the stranger. His height, his coloring, his noble appearance—all matched what he had heard of another.

"I did not know, Lord Harwood," he said in English, "that you were now Don Antonio's messenger."

The Englishman drew his sword.

Rafael held up one hand. "Put up, sir, put up! You need not fear that I will call my servants. I have no quarrel with you, nor with your purpose here."

"How did you know?"

"The *matónes*. Margaret knew naught of them. How did you know?"

"They bragged of their exploit in the courtyard of the Alcazar in Madrid."

Rafael winced. "I erred in letting Pablo hire such fools. Yet how did you connect me to them? They were never here. They were hired by a servant of mine. *Dios*, did he tell them? I shall—"

"You shall have no need to punish him, Don Rafael. The *matónes* knew nothing of your involvement in this. I learned of this from"—a pause, a bitter smile—"I learned of this at La Casa de las Rosas, upon my return from Madrid."

So Margaret *had* betrayed him . . . though perchance only under duress.

"And now you have come for Katherine."

"I have."

"You may have her . . . if you can take her from a vicar of the Holy Office."

Lord Harwood looked stunned. "You handed her over to the Inquisition?" he asked in disbelief.

"She is still here. The vicar is preparing to leave for Valladolid this morning. He was a guest of mine, you see. I invited him here because the lady had been most uncooperative. Doña Margaret had told me that Kat was your mistress, and I wished to make her mine, but she was stubborn." He sighed. "By God, how wine dishonors men by making them admit what shames them and should be kept secret!"

"Your honor concerns me not," the Englishman said. "To your point, and quickly—or to this one." He pointed his sword at Rafael.

"In brief, I knew that a vicar of the Inquisition was staying with an acquaintance of mine. I invited Fray Francisco here, in the hope that he would so frighten Katherine that she would realize she needed my protection. But my plan miscarried. The vicar began to lust after your mistress, and so thinks her a witch, and now he will take her to Valladolid for trial."

"You fool. Where is she?"

"I shall tell you in a few minutes, but first—"

The sword moved an inch closer to him. "You wager your life now, Don Rafael."

The don could not help but laugh, but was ashamed that his laughter sounded frightened. "I will surely lose it if, rather than fighting you honorably, I merely send you on your way to interfere with an agent of the Inquisition. No, Lord Harwood"—shaking his head—"you must have overcome me and disarmed me. So." He drew his sword, but before the tip had cleared the scabbard, the point of the Englishman's sword was pressed into his doublet. "Lord Harwood," Rafael said in reproof, "I intend only to drop my weapon. So." And he lifted his sword clear of the sheath and dropped it. "And now you must bind me. That chair"— he inclined his head toward the velvet-upholstered chair that was his favorite—"is most comfortable."

Two minutes later, tied more tightly than was comfortable to a plain, hard chair, he told Lord Harwood which passages to take through the castle to the tower where Kat was held.

"And now you must gag me, lest the servants who will find me wonder why I did not cry alarm as soon as you left."

"There are surer ways to silence you."

"But none, I trust, that you would use on a defenseless captive."

"No, by my faith," said the Englishman, with what sounded like real regret. "However, lest your servants believe you have surrendered too easily—" He drew his dagger.

Rafael yelped as Lord Harwood drew the blade lightly across his throat. He could feel the blood trickling down his neck, so slowly that he knew the wound would clot soon. Ashamed of the fear he had shown, he complained mildly, "This will stain my ruff."

"Would you have it all dyed to match?" the baron asked with a laugh, but there was no amusement in his eyes as he gazed at Rafael, and the don had to suppress a shudder. He shook his head, and quietly directed Lord Harwood to the chest where he would find a clean handkerchief that might serve as a gag.

A minute later the Englishman was at the door. He paused to look back and smile at Rafael, who was doing his best not to choke on the foul stocking that Lord Harwood had found in the rushes beside the bed. The baron made a mocking bow, then opened the door and slipped out, closing it noiselessly behind him.

Even while laughing helplessly last night, Kat had wondered if she might have cause to regret mocking the vicar. Now she knew.

Still wearing her nightgown, she sat on the bed and watched Dorotea pack her clothing into a chest. The maid's eyes were red from weeping: she, too, would be required to travel to Valladolid.

Kat's own eyes were dry now, but she had been crying earlier, first when she heard Fray Francisco's charge of witchcraft, when her tears were from outrage that he should dare say such a thing. Neither her tears nor her outrage had moved the friar. I'faith, she had known they would not. But she had hoped, at least, that her tears and Dorotea's would sway the guard, with whom they had pleaded for a time, asking him to let Dorotea leave the tower to speak to the don. The guard had seemed willing to let Dorotea go, but Francisco had forbidden it. There would be no appeals to the don, he had said. The don had made his decision already. Did they not realize that the vicar would not have come to the tower without first advising Don Rafael of his intent to take the women to Valladolid?

Kat and Dorotea had retreated up the stairs then to the bedchamber. Once away from Fray Francisco, Kat's outrage had given way to despair, and she had wept bitterly for a time, scarce able to believe that this was happening. She had stopped crying only when she realized that Dorotea was even more frightened than she was, perforce stemming her tears so she could comfort the other girl.

"My lady," Dorotea said suddenly, "I did not think to ask you which kirtle and gown you would wear today."

Kat laughed a little at the ordinariness of the question. And yet, she thought as she looked down at her nightgown, she must needs dress soon . . . and she should have spoken sooner, for it looked as though Dorotea had packed almost everything but the crimson kirtle Kat had worn yesterday, which still hung over the cupboard door. She was about to ask Dorotea to take another kirtle from the chest when she heard her name shouted by the vicar, who was waiting below in the antechamber.

"Whoreson!" she muttered, infuriated that he thought he could summon her in such a manner. Outrage filled her again. I'faith, he would speak to her politely—else she would not answer.

Then he bellowed again—"Katherine!"—and she swore under her breath and strode to the top of the stairs, where she stopped, glaring down at him in vexation.

"What do you want?"

"Are you not ready to leave yet? You have been up there for an hour." He sounded less sure of himself, and she felt a glimmer of hope. Perchance she could drag out the time before they left. Perchance, during that time, the don would reconsider . . .

"And we will stay here until we are ready!" she told the vicar furiously. "Which will be *much* later if you continue to interrupt us. So get you gone, brother fool! I will send a message to you when we are through packing."

Francisco had taken a step back, as if her outburst had been a physical blow, but now he stood very still for some moments, then slowly shook his head. Kat wondered if he might yet leave the tower, giving them some chance of escape. He reached into his sleeve and pulled out some bit of cloth—a filthy handkerchief, she saw to her disgust—and raised it to his lips, all the while whispering something to himself. Then he replaced the handkerchief in his sleeve and began to climb the stairs.

"I will help you pack," he said, and Kat felt hope desert her.

His face seemed even paler than usual by the time he reached the upper floor, and he was careful not to touch her as he passed her, but his gaze was fierce as he looked around the room, seeing at a glance that Dorotea had finished the packing. He seized the crimson kirtle and threw it at Kat.

"Dress now. We must leave."

"No, not while you are here. Go below, and wait."

He shook his head. "I will not trust you again, witch. You might try to work some magic against me, while you are out of my sight. You might try—"

He fell silent all of a sudden, his head cocked to one side. Downstairs, the door into the tower had been opened. Kat heard a few shuffling sounds, then nothing more.

Was it the guard? Had he fled? Then she was free to try an escape. She began to edge toward the stairway, Dorotea following, but then her path was blocked by the vicar, and she stopped.

"Miguel?" the friar called, glancing over his shoulder toward the stairs, but there was no answer from the guard.

And then they heard footsteps, crossing the antechamber.

"Miguel?"

Still no answer. The vicar crossed himself. "If this is some witchery of yours," he told Kat as whoever was below started up the stairs, "if you have summoned some familiar to help you . . ." He turned his back on her and moved toward the stairs.

Kat stepped over to the hearth and picked up the fire-fork. Her heart was beating very fast. *She* had no familiars to summon, but after hearing Fray Francisco's rantings about witches, she was not entirely certain that he would not have demonic familiars. The fire-fork would be no help against them, but if there was nothing supernatural here and the guard was gone, she was determined to reach that door, even if she had to crack a skull or two to get there. She lifted the fire-fork overhead, ready to defend herself against any mortal enemy.

Then she saw who was coming up the stairs, and her mouth fell open in astonishment.

" 'Sdeath, Kat!" Justin looked around in surprise, then laughed. "I thought to come to your rescue, but it seems you were in little need of my help." Lowering his sword, he came up the last few steps, then turned to face the vicar, who backed away.

"Devil!" Francisco hissed.

"What manner of clergy is this," Justin asked cheerfully, "to be so unmannerly?"

"I know not," Kat said. Aware that she was still holding the fire-fork aloft, she lowered it. She laughed shakily. "I have met none of his sort in England."

"Pray God, you never will," Justin said, looking back over his shoulder at her. "What shall we do with—"

Francisco screamed like a woman and flung himself upon the baron, first pummeling him with his skinny fists, then trying to claw his eyes. Justin staggered and almost fell, then caught his balance and, gripping the monk's bony shoulder, pushed him away. The vicar stumbled backward, toward the stairwell. Seeing the danger, Kat ran to catch him, but he cried out in fear and took another step back, then, arms flailing, fell onto the steps below.

"Jesu," she whispered.

The monk lay at the foot of the stairway, half on the antechamber floor, half on the steps, his neck at an odd, sharp angle to his body. Blood glistened on the edges of several steps above him.

Kat would have run down the stairs to see if somehow Francisco still lived, but Justin held her back. "I'll see to him. Stay here. See to your maid."

A minute later, as Kat was trying to calm Dorotea, Justin came back upstairs with a cloakbag. "You'll find clothes for our journey in here. A paper of dust, too." He went back downstairs then, and Kat opened the cloakbag to find Nick's old clothes—aye, and a dag, too, though Kat left the pistol alone, praying she would not need to use it. Dorotea stopped crying and gazed at Kat in amazement as she donned the doublet and hose and boots, then pinned her hair up and hid it under the cap. Kat ripped open the twist of paper, spilled dust onto her hands, and rubbed it on her face. By then Justin had come back, a grim look on his face.

"Is he dead?" Kat asked, not sure what answer she wanted.

"Sí, está muerto," he replied, and Dorotea began to cry again.

Kat went over to her and shook her a little. "Mark me well, Dorotea," she said in Spanish, "for there is little time. You must leave. Else you will be blamed for a share of this."

"She cannot go with us," Justin said in English.

She looked up at him, angered by his lack of concern for the maid.

"I may yet be able to leave here with you without any outcry, but we could never take her with us without questions being asked. Nor would she be safer with us. They'll seek you and me, not a maid traveling alone. Has she friends who will help her to safety?"

Kat nodded and turned back to the girl. Speaking in Spanish again, she said gently, "Dorotea. The plans we had. You must go alone, and today. Now. Do you understand?"

Dorotea nodded and gave her a fleeting smile before hurrying away.

Kat went to the mirror to check her appearance. Those of Rafael's household who saw her leave would stare when they saw her dressed thus, for they would not expect to see a strange youth here, but she prayed they would not stare so long that they would see through her disguise.

"You may need women's garb," Justin said, rolling the crimson velvet kirtle into a neat bundle. He stuffed it into his cloakbag, and they walked down the stairs into the antechamber.

Justin had moved the vicar's body to the center of the chamber and covered it with Miguel's cloak. The guard lay on his side, bound and gagged, his eyes closed. There was a bruise on his forehead.

They went out into the hall and closed the door behind them. Justin took a key from his doublet pocket. " 'Twas in Miguel's purse," he whispered, locking the door.

He looked down the hall then, as did Kat: it had been days since she had seen it. With the door to the tower locked behind her, the horrors that had occurred there now seemed unreal, mere fragments of a dream from which she had just awakened.

Justin put the key back in his pocket, then, turning to Kat, set his hands on her shoulders.

"Kat."

She gazed up at him, her heart beating even faster than it had when she feared devils had come to Fray Francisco's aid. Was Justin going to kiss her? Did she want him to? She had told herself these past weeks that she hated him, but she knew at this moment how much of a lie that had been.

"Kat," he whispered again. "Your name is Diego, should I need to call you. Should anyone else speak to you, you will not reply. I will explain that you are my squire, and not dumb, but that you are keeping silent for two days as a penance given you by your priest for your insolent prattling. In sooth," he said, with a soft laugh, " 'tis as likely a story as I could tell. Now come with me, and for once in your life, hold your tongue."

He started away then, and had she known of any other means of escape from the castle, she would not have followed. By God, she hated him. How could she have forgotten?

In his bedchamber, Rafael listened to Lord Harwood and Katherine ride away. No servants had yet sought him out. He hoped they would come soon, now that he need not fear encountering the Englishman again. The taste of the stocking was still very bitter in his mouth, though he was no longer gagging on it.

Thank God the slow trickle of blood down his neck had ceased. His fine lace ruff would be ruined, but there were compensations: Kat was safely away, and Lord Harwood, Rafael prayed, had dispatched the vicar.

The don wriggled slightly to ease the pain of his bonds, then, closing his eyes, began to make delightful plans for vengeance on Margaret.

CHAPTER 31

Justin and Kat rode south until they were out of sight of the castle, then left the road, making their way north as quickly as they could. The path Justin chose took them up and down steep, wooded slopes, and along narrow valleys, and they forced their horses to wade some distance up or down each stream they crossed, until Justin was satisfied that their trail would be impossible to follow.

Kat's anger had dissipated within a few minutes of leaving the Eagle's Nest, and as Justin said nothing to her except to warn her of obstacles in her path, she enjoyed the ride for a time. But by late afternoon her hands and face stung from scratches where branches had struck her, and she felt that her very bones were being jolted asunder with each step her horse took. She was grateful when Justin stopped beside a stream that cascaded down a shadow-filled valley.

"This will do for tonight," he said, and she nodded. Sunlight still touched the top of the slope to the east, but it already looked like twilight below, among the trees, and twilight itself would leave the lower slopes nearly as dark as night.

She slipped to the ground and walked stiffly across the sandy bank to the edge of the stream, where she knelt and drank from her cupped hands, then splashed water onto her face. The water was so cold that she shivered.

"Careful, Kat," Justin teased as he knelt beside her, refilling his canteen. "You'll wash the dust from your face."

"By the mass! Is there not enough dirt here to replace it?"

He laughed again, and handed her the canteen, and, still thirsty, she drank from it.

"Are you not curious to know how I came to Navarra?" he asked after he, too, had slaked his thirst.

"I brim with questions," she said dryly, "but you bade me be silent."

He stared at her, then nodded. "Yea, so I did." Then, when she remained silent, he said, "You must thank Tandy when you see him again," and told her of his servant's encounter with the rogues in Madrid. "The *matón* he questioned knew nothing of Don Rafael, but we learned of his visit when we returned to La Casa de las Rosas."

"From your cousin?"

Justin winced. "Nay, Kat. Confessing her sins is something Margaret does only for priests—if for them. 'Twas Roger Frowicke who told us of the don's visit. Margaret's servant had gossiped of his interest in you. 'Twas fortunate that I had left one man behind, else . . ." He looked away, shrugging.

She felt wounded. Could he not say more of his gratitude for what Tandy had learned? Was he not grateful, in sooth? She had been pondering what words to use to thank him, but now she wondered if she might be thanking the wrong man.

"Where is Tandy now?" she asked. "Will we meet him soon?"

Justin looked back at her, his expression stony. "He should meet us at Bayonne in a few weeks," he said flatly.

"Bayonne?"

"We are for France, Kat, to stay with friends of mine near Bayonne . . . unless you would rather return to Castile."

"I never wished to travel to Castile at all, my lord . . . as you may remember."

"Nor," he said after a brief silence, "did I wish to travel to Navarra."

" 'Twas Tandy's wish, then?" she asked, hoping the pain she felt could not be heard in her voice. A plague on Justin!

"No more his than mine, once we learned where you had been taken. But I also learned in Burgos, Kat, that the servants had gossiped about your too-free behavior toward Don Rafael. They said you kept him from conversing with Margaret and that you must have sought to make her jealous."

"By my life, Lord Harwood, you take your role as my guardian too seriously! Is there need for that now?"

"Haply less need than there was this morning."

She lowered her head, ashamed. "Cry you mercy. I have not yet thanked you, yet I rail at you."

" 'Twas no more than I expected," he said, and laughed when she looked up again to glare at him.

"You have said nothing of Don Rafael . . . Saw you him?" *Did you kill him?* she thought, but feared to ask.

"Yea, we spoke. I played the messenger from Madrid, sent by Don Antonio to take you back to Burgos, but Don Rafael guessed the truth."

"Fought you with him?"

"Truth to tell, he disarmed himself, lest I harm him. Yea, and sent me on my way to the tower, too, after I had bound him so that his servants would think he had been overcome. Had he dared, I trow he would have welcomed me and had the path to the tower strewn with fresh rushes and laid with carpets in my honor."

"He did not want me taken to Valladolid and tried as a witch?"

Justin shook his head, then: "You thought he wished to be rid of you?"

"He told me—" She hesitated, then, in a rush of words, "He told me you wished to be rid of me. He told me you had said as much to your cousin."

"Rid of you? Why would I wish to be rid of someone who has brained me with a flagon and then climbed the walls of my house to spy upon me? Why would I wish to be rid of someone who is honest only in deception and trickery?"

His words stung, more than she would have believed possible. She felt tears well in her eyes.

"By God's blood, I must needs have wished to be rid of you, had I given the matter any thought, but I warrant I never said such to—" He broke off, staring at her.

She turned her back to him, ashamed of her tears.

" 'Twas but a jest, girl."

She shook her head. There had been too much truth in his words— truth as he saw it. *Honest only in deception and trickery.* Aye, that was how he would see her. How else?

She felt his hands on her shoulders then, turning her around, and he pulled her against him. For a time they stood there without moving, Kat with her face pressed against the rich stuff of his doublet. Her body was racked with sobs. She cried because of what he said, but from more than that: from the fears that had been bottled up inside her since she was taken from La Casa de las Rosas, from relief that she had escaped that danger, from fear that she would never get safely home again. Justin kept his arms around her, comforting her. He had risked his life to come alone to Navarra to rescue her, and though she might blame him for having brought her to Spain, she knew she had only herself to blame for giving him that opportunity. *Honest only in deception . . .* What would he say, she wondered, if she told him who she was? She dared not tell him why she and Nick had been at the Jerusalem Tree, but if she could invent some tale that he would believe, would it not then be safe to tell him that she was a gentlewoman? Could he do aught then but return her to her home? Belike he would be honorable enough to keep her adventures a secret. For he was honorable in some ways—he had proven that. And she did not *know* of certain that he was a traitor . . .

Then, before she could put her thoughts in order sufficient to speak, he tilted her head back and kissed her, and all thought fled her mind.

He lifted her slightly and carried her off the sandy bank to the expanse of grass that bordered it, then lowered her carefully to the ground. She clung to him as he kissed her face and neck, then unbuttoned her doublet. She could feel the warmth of his hands through the thin stuff of her shirt. He undid the few buttons of the shirt's collar, pushing the cloth aside, then froze.

"Rafael?" he whispered in a pained voice.

In the pleasant madness that had overtaken her, she had forgotten the bite mark on her breast until he spoke. She fought free of his grasp. Rolling away, she dragged her shirt and doublet together. Of a sudden she was ashamed of how easily she would have let Justin take her again. How could she have thought that 'twas honor that had brought him to Navarra? Perhaps he had only wished to reclaim his leman. If all he wanted from her was to lie with her, it mattered not that he could not trust her.

"You have been ill-used," Justin said softly. He touched her shoulder, and she flinched.

"Aye," she said bitterly. "Ill-used. And not by Don Rafael alone."

His hand fell from her shoulder. He sighed.

"I never lay with him," she told him some moments later, though herself not sure why it was important to her that he know that. "I would not."

"So he told me." He was silent for a time, then said, "There's bread and cheese in the pack on my horse. 'Tis poor fare, but the best I can offer."

Pride bade her refuse the food, but lost to hunger. Still, she said no more to him that day, but after the meager supper wrapped herself in a blanket he gave her and, surprisingly quickly, fell asleep.

For most of the next day they rode north and west, their journey a slow one, as Justin still insisted on avoiding roads, even those that were no more than overgrown paths for driving sheep. They said little to each other. Justin had acted conciliatory that morning, when he woke her and offered her food to break her fast, but she had said so little in response that he soon gave up any attempts at conversation. He had looked baffled by her treatment of him, and though she had felt ashamed of it herself, she had not dared to beg his pardon, nor dared she explain. For she was afraid to talk to him. How different he was from Tom Heyford! Tom she had found pleasant company, but never troubling, never disturbing to her thoughts and emotions, which had been as steady as a candle flame in a closed and quiet room. With Justin, it was as if a door had been opened and a breeze had swept across the flame, buffeting it so it leapt about in a mad dance. She loved him, then she loved him not. Words led as swiftly to quarrels as to kisses, and the worst of it was, she seemed unable to judge which way they would lead. I'faith, how could she have ever wished that good Tom Heyford, steady Tom Heyford, would be more like Justin? She could never have thought of marrying him then. She would never have known any peace . . .

So she simply followed Justin, heeding his warnings about a treacherous slope or low branches, and kept her thoughts to herself. Occasionally during the day, as they rode the tortuous path the mountains dictated to them, he would point out a shepherd's hut or a grazing flock, or, half concealed by a thicket, a chamois whose backward-bent horns would suddenly be pointing towards them as the hunter-wary antelope fled. She looked at all he pointed out to her, but without comment. Once a lynx slunk across their path, startling the horses, and Justin turned back to see if she needed help. Torn between thanking him and railing at him for believing her such a poor rider, she could only shake her head as he approached until, with a frown, he wheeled his horse around and began to ride ahead again.

To Kat's surprise, he stopped in midafternoon beside a stream. At first she thought he intended only to rest, but then he began to hobble his horse.

"Why have we stopped so early?" she asked, not dismounting yet. 'Twas but a few hours since they had stopped for dinner.

"We need fresh food for supper."

She could not argue that. She was heartily sick of the dry bread and cheese, and there was little of that left. "But how will you hunt?" she asked. He had finished hobbling the horse and was rummaging through his cloakbag. "With the dag? 'Twould be too loud. Would you have those following us—" She fell silent then as he held up some snares.

"Will you ride on, girl? If you plan to stay, then pray dismount and help me. We will need firewood soon."

He helped her dismount and hobble her horse, but stopped her when she would have left at once to gather wood.

" 'Tis folly to wander about here without a weapon to protect you. D'you know how to use a dag?"

"Nay, but I can use a sword."

"Aye," he replied dryly. "So Tandy told me." But he took off his sword belt and buckled it about her waist. Then, after taking the pistol from his cloakbag, he disappeared into the forest to set the snares.

The stream by which they had stopped seemed but little narrower than one they had crossed a few hours ago, which Justin had told her was the River Irati. Was this some tributary? Kat wondered. Or was it simply the Irati itself, narrowing towards its source? She felt lost, con-

fused by the convolutions of the land. For much of the day their view
had been limited by the soaring oak and beech and fir trees around
them; when they did emerge on a rise, it was to see a carpet of forest
swaddling the slopes they faced. The Forest of Irati. Kat had heard
Rafael speak of it; he came here sometimes to hunt. She knew they
must be near Roncesvalles, and the high road leading across the pass
from Spain to France. Yet Justin preferred to take a northerly path now
rather than ride west to the high road. She hoped he knew enough of
these mountains to find their way safely into France; for herself, she was
not even sure she could reach the high road without losing her way.

She found a few dry fallen branches beneath the poplars and willows
bordering the stream, then wandered a little ways into a stand of oak
to gather more. It was a warm and lovely day. She watched two squirrels
race through interlocking branches overhead, and wished for her bow.
Birds chattered in the trees. She remembered equally beautiful days
when she and Nick and Ned had gone hunting in Sussex, but this day
was bereft of their familiar, beloved voices—Ned's, alas, stilled forever
now.

And what of Nick? She shook her head, trying to dispel the thought
that he, too, might be in danger. Nick was safe and well. Needs must
that he was. Had he not escaped the men Justin sent after him?

She hurried back to the stream. No matter how lovely this forest,
without the sound of other voices, or even the musical baying of hounds
caroling their find to their masters, it was the wilderness that Justin
called it. She was relieved to see that Justin had returned from setting
the snares. His company, troubling as it was, was better than none.

Yea, but what was he doing?

He was down on one knee on the verge of a rocky ledge jutting out
into the stream, staring intently at the relatively calm surface just below
the rock. Past the curving tip of the ledge, water swirled and foamed,
but where Justin was looking the surface was still enough that Kat could
see the bottom through the shallow water. Fat trout drifted lazily through
the sun-dappled water. Oh, for a fishing line, Kat thought wistfully.

The load of firewood she carried was scratching her hands and wrists.
"Where—" she began, and Justin held up his hand to silence her, then
pointed to the nearly flat surface of the rock. Kat set the branches down,
then, a moment later, took off the sword belt and lay that down, too.

Not taking his eyes off the stream, Justin removed his doublet, then
his shirt. There was a wound on his left shoulder, but it was scabbed
over and almost healed—several days old, at least. Kat stared at it.

"How—"

"A rogue with a dag attacked me."

"Why?"

"Haply he wanted to steal my purse. Or"—shrugging—"he might have hated Englishmen."

She did not believe him, but she knew 'twould be useless to ask any more questions.

He lay down at the water's edge then, and lowered his right arm slowly into the water.

He lay there for what seemed a long time. Lulled by the rushing of the water and the warmth of the sun, Kat found herself gazing at Justin's shoulders and back, admiring the muscles. She flushed as she realized the direction of her thoughts, then leaned forward to brush away an ant that was crawling toward the nobleman.

She had just settled back on her heels again when Justin moved, the muscles of his shoulders and arms rippling. The quiet water was roiled and splashed in all directions as Justin twisted toward her, clutching a wriggling trout which he released to send sailing past Kat onto the bank. The fish flopped wildly, and Kat threw herself on it before it could flop back into the stream. Justin tossed her his knife, and she sliced off the trout's head. She was about to start cleaning the fish when she noticed that Justin had again reached into the stream. She moved quietly to the edge of the rock and gazed down into the water.

There were still trout in that quiet little pool below the ledge, but none within two feet of Justin's reach. Nor was he trying to reach them. He lay very still, his arm motionless, and in a few minutes one of the trout drifted closer. Kat expected him to try to seize it, but instead he let it come so close that it almost touched his hand. Only then did he move, bending his fingers a bit and stroking the fish's belly. Kat's mouth sagged open a little. Jesu! He was *tickling* the fish! She and Nick had heard of men in the neighboring villages who fished in this manner, but never had they bothered to learn the method. Angling was simpler by far, and, they thought, more suited to gentry. And yet here this nobleman was content to lie shirtless on bare rock and fish with his own hands . . .

Fascinated, she watched as one entranced while the fish drifted backward into Justin's hand and he caught it by the gills and flung it out of the stream.

"God's bones!" she said in honest amazement, leaving the fish to flop around behind her. "I never thought peers would fish in this way!"

"Kat—" He shook his head then and went back to his task.

He caught one more fish while she was cleaning the first two, then finally got up. The rough pattern of the rock was imprinted on his chest and the inside of his right arm, which looked pale and bloodless beneath the sunburned skin. He began to rub his arm and hand to restore the warmth the cold water had stolen. "There's a flint in my doublet pocket," he told Kat. "I'll check the snares."

She doubted that any animal had been snared yet—likely they would have to wait till morning for a meal of fresh game—but she said nothing. The sight of the succulent fish, the first two already spitted on green twigs, had reminded her of her hunger, not fully satisfied since leaving the castle—and truly not for days before that, since she had eaten poorly after the vicar arrived. If there was any chance that a fat young rabbit had wandered into a snare already, she would fain have it for their supper.

After she had cleaned the last fish, she used flint and knife to set the branches afire. The dry wood burned cleanly, the narrow column of smoke it produced broken up into vanishing eddies by a breeze. No one would be able to spot their fire from any great distance.

Kat sat tailor-fashion between the fire and the water's edge, the breeze at her back as she held the spitted fish—one in one hand, two in the other—over the flames. This close, even with the wind carrying most of the scent away, she could still smell the fish as it cooked. She felt famished. Intent on turning the fish, she heard branches rustle but did not look up. A moment later a pebble dislodged from the bank fell rattling to the ledge on the other side of the fire. Justin was returning in the very nick, she thought. In a minute the fish would be done, and she doubted any would have been left for him if he had stayed away too long.

She looked up then and screamed, a high, thin shriek cut short as her throat closed in panic. The fish fell into the flames.

An enormous bear lumbered down the last few feet of the bank and onto the rocky ledge. Fifteen feet away it halted and rose up on its hind legs. Its reddish eyes blinked as smoke eddied around it; its nostrils dilated as it sniffed the air.

The bear was larger than any Kat had ever seen before, larger even than Ned Grimes. And this one was not tied to a stake, nor was there a bearward or mastiffs or a fence between herself and the beast. Only a paltry few yards of sun-warmed air, through which a dragonfly flickered before its glittering path took it back out over the water.

She felt paralyzed by fright. The bear must have been attracted by the smell of the fish, which now lay sizzling where they had fallen into the fire. Would that she had not dropped them! Maybe she would have been able to distract the bear by throwing the fish to it, but they were out of her reach now. So was Justin's sword, which lay only a few feet from the bear. She dared not try to reach it. Nor could she run away while the bear watched her, for sudden flight would surely draw an attack.

The bear dropped down to stand on all four feet again. Its huge head swung back and forth as it shuffled closer, its long ragged claws scraping the rock. It stopped to sniff the air again.

One of the green twigs she had used to spit the fish lay half out of the fire, that half still not burning. If she could use it to spear the fish and toss it toward the bear . . . She reached toward the twig, then froze as she saw the bear's hackles rise.

"Kat! Do not move!"

Justin was standing at the top of the bank, the dag in his hand. As Kat watched, he took a few steps down the bank.

"Make no sound," Justin warned her—needlessly, for she was too frightened to speak. The bear looked round at him and growled.

Justin mimicked the growl as he stopped, picked up a pebble and flung it at the bear. It flew past the scarred muzzle and bounced once on the edge of the rock before plopping into the stream.

Kat held her breath, her hands clenched so tightly her nails dug into her palms.

The bear turned halfway around. Justin stood motionless on the bank. For a few moments the only sounds were those of the crackling flames and murmuring stream, as the bear swung its head back and forth between Kat and Justin.

Then Justin bent to scoop up a handful of pebbles.

The first whizzed past the bear's head, just missing an ear. The animal's lips pulled back in a snarl, revealing white teeth—fearfully sharp, long teeth. All the bears Kat had seen in England had had their teeth broken short so they would do less damage to the mastiffs. Its head lowered, and Kat held her breath as she recognized a stance she had seen bears take just before attacking a mastiff.

A second pebble struck the bear's scarred muzzle. An instant later another hit the animal's neck.

The bear roared and attacked, moving more swiftly than Kat could believe.

Justin raised the dag and fired. The bear staggered but did not stop, and as Justin tried to throw himself out of its way, the bear reached out with one giant paw and knocked him down. Kat screamed, certain the beast would turn on him and tear him apart, but then the bear stumbled and went down on its side. It lay very still, whitish smoke drifting over its bloodied head.

Kat stood frozen for a moment that seemed endless. Then Justin moaned, and stirred, and she ran to him.

He was pushing himself up into a sitting position, coughing in the foul smoke.

"You knave," she said, nearly crying. "Why did you wait to shoot until the beast was so close?"

"Needs must," he said, grimacing as he looked past her at the bear, "for I have little practice and the pistol less accuracy."

"Then you should have practiced more," she said, brushing at her eyes, which were wet now, and stinging from the smoke.

"Would that I could have practiced, but the bearwards I knew—" He shrugged, then caught his breath sharply.

Kat knelt beside him. The wounds were shallow but ugly; the bear's claws had raked across the right side of Justin's back below the shoulder blade, and strips of flesh hung from the edges of the scratches. They were bleeding freely, and when Justin pressed a hand over them the blood slid over and around his fingers.

"Bring my shirt, Kat," he said gently, and she whirled and ran to where he had left his shirt and doublet beside the stream, shaking her head as if that would clear it. The wounds were not serious—she had seen much worse ones, when her menservants had been involved in fights, and once when one had fallen on a scythe—but if the bleeding did not stop . . .

But it did, as she held the folded shirt pressed tightly against the scratches. Once, as she took the cloth away to see if she had staunched the flow of blood yet, she saw ribs showing whitely where the claws had slashed deepest. He was lucky—nay, they were both lucky—that the bear had not been even a few inches closer, else his ribs would have been crushed.

Returning to the stream, she washed out the blood-soaked shirt, then brought it back to clean the wound. This started the bleeding anew, but in slow trickles that she was able to stop with a bit of pressure. Throughout, Justin sat with his eyes closed, his face seeming colorless beneath the sunburn. She was not surprised when he asked afterward for her to bring the flask of wine. He poured some across the wound, then began to drink. She would have liked some herself, but knew there was too little to share.

She left him then for a few minutes, and when she was out of his sight removed her doublet and shirt, then donned the doublet again over her bare skin. 'Twould perchance chafe her, but she needed the linen shirt for a bandage.

"I had another shirt in the cloakbag," Justin told her when she returned to him, but she paid him no heed as she tied her own shirt around his chest, then took his down to the stream to wash it again.

She was leaning out over the water when she heard pebbles clatter across stone behind her. Terrified, she whirled around so fast she lost her balance and would have fallen into the stream if Justin had not caught her.

"Oh, my lord, thank you—" she began breathlessly, without thinking; then, as she got to her feet, her anger flared. "Why are you not keeping still? You'll start the bleeding anew—"

"Peace, Kat. I must have my doublet, and we must away. The bear will draw scavengers, and I have no wish for their company. Nor would I stay here to discover if anyone still follows us and heard that shot."

She nodded and helped him into the doublet, then picked up the flint and knife. The fire had burned itself down to coals, the fish curled bits of char. She could start another fire elsewhere as well as here.

Justin gave her no argument when she insisted on saddling and bridling their horses by herself. The shadows were very long by the time they were ready to leave. It would be night soon. Kat glanced at the bear, which even in death seemed threatening, then looked around, anxiously biting the inside of her cheek. There might be other bears about.

"Come, Kat."

He turned his horse upstream. Digging her heels into her mount's sides, she followed.

They rode for perhaps a mile, stopping where a rocky overhang sheltered a sandy bank. Justin's face was drawn with pain as he dismounted, but still he would have seen to the horses if Kat had not insisted that he lie down. She opened his doublet to check on the rough dressing; if the wounds had resumed bleeding, they had not yet soaked through the linen.

She left him then to tether the horses for the night. That done, she rummaged through his cloakbag to find the cheese and bread that were left. But when she returned to where he lay beside the stream, he was already asleep. She ate but lightly herself, then returned the remaining food to the cloakbag. So little, so very little.

It was still warm, but the night, here in the mountains, would be cool. Taking their blankets, she went back to Justin and tried to wake him, whispering his name, then shaking his shoulder. He still slept soundly. She unfolded his blanket on the ground beside him and pushed him sideways onto it, then drew the rest of the blanket across him. Then, wrapping the other blanket around herself, she lay down beside him, wriggling until she was so close to him that she could throw some of her blanket over him. Closing her eyes, she prayed that he would recover and they would reach France safely. Some animal ran through the wood nearby, and she groped for the knife strapped to her belt. Clutching the hilt, she lay awake for more than an hour, listening to all the noises of the forest around her, but at last she drifted off to sleep.

She dreamed, and in the dream she was in the secret prison of the Holy Office, and the torturer was holding her hand over a flame.

She came awake with a start, yanking her hand away from the too-hot surface it touched. Her mind fogged with sleep, it was some moments before she realized that her hand had been resting on Justin's throat. She reached out to touch it again. He was burning with fever.

"Justin?" she said quietly, but he did not awaken, even when she spoke louder and shook him. Yet he should have had enough sleep—'twas late in the morning already.

With a small cry of dismay, she pulled the blanket off him and opened his shirt and doublet, then peeled back the bandage from the wounds. The cloth had stuck in a few places, and as it pulled free he began to bleed again. But that slight bleeding was of no concern at all, compared to the angry infection that had taken hold of the wounds.

The flesh around the scratches was inflamed, and the wounds themselves were suppurating. The sight of the pus made Kat feel sick. Her eyes stinging with tears, she replaced the makeshift dressing, not knowing what else she could do.

Digging her nails into her palms, she got slowly to her feet. Her head ached terribly.

She knew that there were poultices that were good for green wounds. Both her aunt and Jane were skillful at making them. But Kat had never tried to prepare one herself—there had been no need. If Anne or Jane were not there, she could always send for a wise old goodwife who lived nearby. She knew she should have taken more time to learn to treat the sick and injured, but other tasks were always more interesting—aye, and more pleasant, she thought, her conscience sorely troubled. She was paying for her idleness now. And so, alack, was Justin . . .

Kat wrung her hands as she gazed down at him. What did one do for a green wound like this? She knew the names of the herbs Anne and Jane had used in poultices: comfrey, and woundwort, and self-heal. But what did they look like? What *exactly* did they look like? Comfrey, she remembered, often grew beside streams, and the plant was covered with rough hairs—but how many other plants might also be so described? And were she to choose the wrong one, she might well poison him. She had forgotten almost everything else her aunt had told her so many years ago, but not the admonition to be absolutely certain that one chose the right herb.

Kat shook her head in mute fury, then dropped to her knees again and began to dab at the wounds with the shirt, wiping away the blood and pus. Then she got the wine flask and poured some wine over the scratches, as she had seen Justin do yesterday, then found the spare shirt he had mentioned and used that as the bandage. She took her shirt down to the stream to wash it.

She was leaning out over the stream when sudden dizziness made her sway and almost fall into the water. She sat down on the bank, still dizzy, her head aching. She wrapped her arms around herself, fearing that she was sick. Who would care for Justin then?

And then she realized what was wrong. She had not yet broken her fast, after eating much too little yesterday. She got shakily to her feet and took the remaining bread and cheese from the cloakbag and devoured it, washing it down with a few sips of wine. She was still hungry when she had finished.

There was a little wine left in the flask. She carried it over to Justin, knelt, and lifted his head. She let the wine trickle into his mouth a drop at a time, watched the muscles of his sunburned throat convulse as he swallowed. Still he did not waken fully.

She felt weak and tired. With the sun directly overhead now, its warmth beating down on her, she was tempted to stretch out on the grassy bank and sleep, but she knew she needed more food. Aye, and Justin would need food when he awoke.

While she had been leaning out over the stream, she had seen fish moving through the shallow water. Could she catch them? There were no rocks jutting out into the stream here, no ledge where she might lie while she dangled her arms in the water. Perchance further upstream she could find another suitable place to fish, but she dared not leave Justin alone. Until he came to himself, he would be helpless against any wild beast that happened across their camp. She would have to fish here.

There was a half-submerged log in the middle of the stream. Like enough, there would be fish near it. 'Twould not be as dry or comfortable a perch as the ledge downstream, but it would do.

She took off her boots and waded out to the log.

An hour later, tired and wet and cold, and possessed of a new, grudging envy of anyone who was skillful at tickling fish, she had her first catch. She lost it when she stumbled and fell on the way back to the shore. But she caught another, and in less time than before, and the second trout, she decided, was fatter than the first. She only wished Justin were awake to admire her catch . . .

She took off her wet clothes and wrapped herself in a blanket, then built a fire only a few feet from where Justin lay. He would need its warmth tonight. While the fish was cooking, she checked his wound. It had stopped suppurating, but she was unsure whether that was a good or a bad sign. He was still feverish. She needed Anne here, she thought,

and her eyes filled with tears that she swiftly brushed away, angry at her
self-pity.

While she was binding the shirt around him again, he moved his
head slightly and muttered something she could not understand.

"Justin?"

"Tell him . . ." he muttered. "Must tell him . . ."

"Tell who?" she asked desperately. "Tell him *what*?"

"Tell him . . . Tell him that the King of Spain will not serve the
pope in this matter."

"In what . . . ?" She did not finish the question. There was no need.
Needs must that he spoke of the papal bull, of the pope's desire to see
Elizabeth deposed. And Philip had decided to do nothing about that?
Upon her soul, there could be no better news!

"Justin, whence had you this intelligence?" she asked, but he made
no response. He was still, and she could only suppose that whatever
tide of dreams had moved him to speak of Philip and the pope had
swept him away again.

She shook him gently and murmured his name over and over, but
he did not wake. Would that he would come to himself! she thought.
If not to speak to her again, then at least to eat . . . But maybe he could
be wakened enough to eat? She took a tiny piece of fish and held it to
his lips, squeezing it a bit so juices trickled into his mouth. His eyelids
flickered for a moment, then were still; he did not waken, nor did he
swallow. She decided against putting the morsel of fish in his mouth to
see if that might waken him; he might choke on it.

Still hungry, she ate the rest of the fish herself, then took her shirt
to the stream, wet it, wrung most of the water from it, and folded it
before placing it across Justin's fevered brow. Then she poured a few
drops of water into his mouth, and this time he swallowed. She breathed
a little prayer of thanks.

She moved away from him then, having remembered what she
should have done ere now, had she been a more conscientious intelligencer.

Glancing frequently over at him, and hoping now that he would
not awaken too soon, she searched his cloakbags and clothing, then his
saddle and saddle blanket. She wished she dared rip open the seams,
but she contented herself with feeling along them instead, pressing the
cloth until her fingertips were sore. She found several well-concealed
pockets, two of them in the saddle, but either they were empty or else
they contained a few coins—insurance against thieves, perchance—and
not the papers she had hoped to find, letters or instructions that might
tell her what business Justin had been about in Spain. She cursed roundly

under her breath as she returned each item to its place, careful to leave no signs of her searching that would betray her later. She felt disappointed beyond measure. And yet she felt guilty, too, for so taking advantage of his injury.

It was midafternoon by then, and the stream was shadowed by the bordering trees. A trout splashed suddenly, startling her and reminding her that she would have to catch more fish.

Her clothes were dry, but if she soaked them now they would not dry again by tonight, and she would need them then, since the small fire would provide little warmth. She would need the blanket then, too. Reluctantly, she unwrapped the blanket from around her and waded out into the stream.

She caught two more fish fairly quickly. The fire had burnt out but she started a new one on the embers of the old, and cooked the fish while shadows deepened.

She ate one of the fish, then wrapped the other in the paper that the cheese had been in. Before nightfall, she wandered up and down the bank gathering more firewood. She checked Justin's wound once again before it was fully dark. The infection seemed less, but she was unwilling to trust her eyes in the poor light. The morning would tell. She wrapped him in the blanket again and lay down beside him to sleep, her back to him, her hand on the hilt of the sword, which she had sheathed again, lest she cut herself while she slept.

She awoke with sunlight in her eyes, and Justin's arm around her.

He was sound asleep—but merely that, she discovered with relief as she touched his cheek and found it warm but not feverishly so. Gently disentangling herself, she made a poor breakfast of cold, dry fish washed down with water. She was taking the refilled flask to Justin, intending to give him a drink, when she stopped of a sudden. Now that his fever was broken, it was better to let him sleep; he needed healthy rest as much as nourishment.

The day warmed rapidly. She was bored, sitting on the stream bank watching him. It seemed he would sleep all day. Finally she shed her clothes and waded out to the log again.

She was climbing back up the bank, pleased at having caught another large trout, when Justin spoke.

"Now I know what you are, i'faith," he said with a smile. "Y'are a naiad."

Kat dropped the fish.

"A clumsy naiad," he added, his smile widening.

Pure astonishment held her still for a moment, and warring impulses held her in check for another. Shamefully aware of her nakedness, she wanted to grab for her blanket, but the fish was tumbling down the bank and might flop back into the stream. After a brief battle, necessity triumphed over modesty: she went after the fish and tossed it well away from the stream before hurrying to her blanket and draping it around herself.

Blushing furiously, she went over to Justin. She feared he would laugh at her, but as she approached, his expression sobered.

"I pray your pardon for my jest. I owe you thanks, and more, for tending my wounds." He tried to sit up, then gasped and lay back again. "You must have knowledge of physic."

She shook her head. "You healed yourself, I trow."

"Be that as it may, 'tis certain I slept late." He squinted up at the sun. " 'Tis almost noon."

"Aye, of the day after the day we came here."

He looked startled.

"You were fevered," she said softly.

"Pray God, I did not rave as I slept, as some men do in a fever."

She had planned to ask him about what he had said, but now she shook her head and told him, "Nary a word."

He looked relieved, which was no relief to her. She could not help wondering what secrets he feared he had spoken aloud. Perchance even what he had said of King Philip and the pope was something he would not have her know. Mayhap that had not been good news to him, as it was to her. If he were in truth her enemy . . .

Marry, she was speculating too much, and likely suspecting too much. If she talked in her sleep, would she want Justin to hear? Had he not already told her that she spoke his name while she slept? She felt her cheeks grow warm again at the memory. And if she were to speak of Walsingham . . .

He was eyeing her curiously.

"I must put my clothes on," she told him, and blushed again as she started away, toward where she had left her garments. Now that he was awake, she could leave the stream bank without fearing for his safety. "I'll be back in a few minutes. And then I will cook this fish I have caught."

" 'Twas caught?" He spoke lightly, mockingly. "I warrant you, it came willingly to your hands."

"A plague on you!" she called over her shoulder, and he chuckled. All was well, she thought; all was well, or soon would be.

CHAPTER 32

Over the next several days, Justin slowly regained his strength as the last traces of infection vanished from the wound and it began to heal cleanly. He slept a great deal; while he slept, Kat watched over him. She would try to leave as soon as he awoke, going upstream to fish or gather berries from a patch of wild strawberries she had found. But she could not avoid being near him while she prepared their meals and while they ate, or in the evening after it grew dark. And during those times, he often insisted on talking to her—as he was doing this evening.

Plague take him, she thought as she added wood to the fire. He was almost as bad as Fray Francisco, with his stories about his life and questions about hers, questions she dared not answer.

"What troubles you, Kat?"

"Nothing troubles me, my lord."

A corner of his mouth twisted cynically. "I have never known a woman to make such a face without cause."

"Then never have you known a woman like me."

He chuckled. "That may be, but I cannot tell. I know too little of you. You tell me nothing of yourself."

"But, my lord, there is nothing—"

"Nothing to tell. God's bones, woman, sometimes it seems you have no more words than a parrot—and less than some I have heard. You spoke more openly the night you came to Harwood Hall."

She paused in her work and looked over at him. "Did I, my lord?" she asked cautiously. Her memory of that night was hazy.

"You spoke of gardens, among other matters."

"Of gardens, my lord?" Kat asked quietly, praying he would not see how anxious she was to know what the *other matters* might have been.

"Yea, sweet parrot, of gardens. You advised me to plant violets, and alleys of thyme and water mint."

Kat smiled.

"And you recommended walnut trees . . . though not secret discourse under them."

She started to laugh, then stopped. Was it possible that she had told Justin of Nick and Sparrow's secret discourse under their walnut tree? Nay, for had she done so, Justin would have treated her far differently.

"I thought it good advice, though odd in its source, coming from a student-turned-maidservant-turned-vagabond," he went on. "Or did you never play at being a student at Cambridge?"

"I thought of it," Kat answered truthfully. She had envied Nick and thought it unfair that he could go to Cambridge and the Inns of Court while she must needs study at home with tutors. Even knowing that noblewomen were also denied the privilege had not left her with any degree of content with her lot. And sometimes she had dreamed of disguising herself as a youth to follow in Nick's footsteps and learn what he had learned. She laughed, a bit ruefully, at the foolishness of her dream. "I feared that I would be discovered."

"By your bedfellow, I warrant. And he would have found it a most pleasant discovery. By the mass, it would have pleased me to have had you share my bed, rather than either of my bedfellows at Cambridge."

"No doubt, my lord, since the one was a drunkard and the other snored."

He laughed. She loved to hear him laugh, and quickly turned toward the fire again so he might not read her feelings on her face.

"Well, there's a start," he said after a few moments. "Now tell me more of yourself, Kat."

"Nay, my lord, I would hear more of you." She struck flint against steel, and carefully nursed the smoldering dry leaves into tiny blazes that licked at the twigs. "Tell me of your visit to Madrid." It was one subject he had said little of during his rambling talks.

There was a silence, for the space of several breaths, before he said, "You would hear more of my stay with Don Antonio?"

"Yea . . . but I would hear more of the city, too. Tell me what you did there, what you saw. What you heard."

She could feel tension between them like a rope stretched taut, almost to the breaking point. Had she asked too much? She regretted asking now.

"I saw a play," he said at last, "at a *corral* in the Calle del Principe."

She was relieved and disappointed at the same time, but relief outweighed disappointment. At least she had not made him more suspicious of her. So she listened without much interest to his description of the play and the *corral* and the spectators, and for the time being pushed the questions she longed to ask to the back of her mind.

The next day she returned from fishing to find Justin standing some distance downstream from the fire, leaning against a tree trunk for support. He had not walked so far unaided since the day he was wounded.

She dropped her catch and ran to his side. " 'Sdeath! Why are you up? You should be resting!"

She tried to put her arm around his waist, to help him back to their camp, but he brushed her arm aside. "I have rested long enough, Kat. We'll leave tomorrow—"

She shook her head. " 'Tis too soon."

"—or the next day at the latest."

"Nay, you cannot—"

"I cannot stay here any longer. Time's a-wasting."

"Is it? I trow time's mending you, and what business matters more than that? You can wait three more days, can you not? Three or four? Till you regain your strength?"

"I could sit a horse now," he insisted. " 'Tis folly for us to dally here."

"But—"

"Jesu, woman! D'you like this life? Would you stay here forever, living on fish and berries? Faith, I'll never willingly eat fish or berries again! And look at me! Look at yourself! Your clothes are filthy rags, your skin is scratched and sunburned—"

"Cry you mercy, my lord, if my appearance displeases you," Kat said coldly. She was shaking with anger. She was heartily sick of her ragged boys' garb, and she had scarce dared to let herself think of the damage being done to her skin. Yet she had thought of the sacrifices she was making as little more than inconveniences, compared to the risk Justin had taken in rescuing her from the Eagle's Nest and the wound he had suffered protecting her from the bear. And now it seemed that the way she looked offended him . . .

She whirled and strode away, back up the slope toward their camp.

"Hold, Kat!" he called after her. "You misunderstood—"

"Would that I had," she muttered, and continued on her way. She doubted he could walk fast enough to catch up with her, but still she wished he would try: 'twould teach him a badly needed lesson if he fell on his face.

Reaching their gear, she began to rummage through the cloakbag, looking for the comb she had tossed in there before leaving the castle. She could not find it. Finally she picked up the cloakbag and took it with her as she made her way back upstream.

She washed her clothes first, then bathed and swam for more than an hour in the small pool a few dozen yards upstream of the spot where she usually fished. When she finally left the water, she found that her doublet and hose, which she had stretched out to dry on the sun-baked rocks, were still damp. Why had she not thought to bring a blanket with her? What would she wear if she needed to clothe herself hurriedly?

Then she remembered the crimson velvet kirtle in the cloakbag.

She pulled it out and unrolled it, then draped it over a blackberry bush near the stream. She could wrap the kirtle about herself like a toga, should she need to cover herself before her own clothes dried. Indeed, the half-kirtle alone would do.

With the kirtle out of the cloakbag, it was easy to find the comb she had packed. She began to comb through her sadly tangled hair.

When her hair was nearly dry, she checked the doublet and hose again. Still damp. She looked around at the kirtle, which she had been so reluctant to bring with them.

By her life, it was of lovely stuff, the two-pile velvet gleaming jewel-bright in the sun, more gorgeous here than it had ever seemed in the dimness of her tower rooms. She ran her hands over the cloth, marveling at the softness. The kirtle seemed out of place here, draped across the blackberry bush, a bright emblem of civilization in the wilderness. Her doublet and hose were more suited to this life, but not only were they still wet, they were also poor rags, as Justin had said. Why should she not wear the kirtle for a while?

She pulled it on over her head, careful of the pins fastening the bodice to the waistband of the half-kirtle.

She had trouble with the bodice fastenings—would that Louise or some other maid were there to help her—but finally they were all secured. For a few moments she stood motionless, staring down at herself. Then, lifting the skirts that in the absence of a farthingale hung to the ground, she spun around in a little dance, laughing.

She felt giddy when she stopped, borne up by a reckless gaiety that brought back memories of her first real outing in London, when Nick had taken her to Southwark and Paul's. At the thought of her brother, her smile faltered, but only for a moment. He was safe and well; he had to be.

She lifted the trailing half-kirtle a few inches again, then made her way to the strawberry patch. For the past few days she had gathered the berries in mere handfuls, or pocketfuls, but now she picked enough of the ripe strawberries for a feast, holding her skirt out to form a cloth bowl to hold them. The fruit, which had seemed almost jewellike to her before, looked dull next to the gleaming velvet. Returning to where she had left her clothes, she nudged her doublet with a bare toe. The heavy cloth was still damp. She sighed, then, careful not to spill any berries, she turned and walked down toward their campsite.

———————

Justin had made it back to the campsite without crawling, but he had had to stop twice, leaning against trees for support, and he was in a foul humor by the time he reached his blanket and collapsed onto it. Even more vexing than his weakness was Kat's stormy departure. Why should she have been hurt by what he said? In sooth, he had spoken to her honestly and bluntly, but was that not his right? God's bones! Did the little vagabond, who had played at being a student and then a maidservant, and then trespassed on his own land, expect him to treat her as a lady?

But you did, an unsympathetic inner voice reminded him. *At La Casa de las Rosas, you did.*

He regretted it now, though it had seemed the only solution at the time. No doubt she had been confused by his changeable attitude toward her. God knew he felt confused, with her acting the lady one moment and a very tomboy the next. Though truly he was glad for that tomboy side of her nature, and that she was not of gentle blood. The gentlewomen he knew would all have complained bitterly about riding through this wilderness, let alone staying here while his wound healed.

He finally realized she must not intend to return soon to clean the two fish she had caught. He set about cleaning them himself, using the tip of his fine Bilbao sword rather than the knife, which she had kept with her. Then he built a fire and cooked the fish and ate one of them, setting the other aside on some leaves for her.

More time passed, the trees' shadows continuing to wheel around in Nature's sundial. He began to fret.

Despite what he had said to her earlier that day, he had not felt overfearful for her safety before. Though her trips upstream to fish and forage for berries took her out of eyesight, he was certain he would be able to hear her if she screamed for help.

. . . if she had a chance to scream.

With an oath, he got to his feet and turned around, determined to find her. Then he froze, his heart thudding heavily. A little sigh, half wonder, half relief, escaped him as he watched her approach.

She was a vision of crimson and gold. A silent, almost dreamlike vision, since her bare feet made no sound on the grassy bank. She held her skirt bunched together at one side, as if to carry something—berries? he wondered, bemused—and she had picked up the other side of the skirt, too, since the kirtle, unobstructed by a farthingale over Kat's slim hips, was so long that its hem brushed the ground otherwise.

He remained standing where he was as she drew closer. Her skin, which he had so rudely described as sunburnt, was a lambent gold a shade darker than her hair, which tumbled in a silken cascade over her shoulders. Her own coloring was as luxuriant as that of the dress she wore, and it seemed to him that the most careful painting was indeed a poor substitute for this natural beauty . . . though in truth he could think of no other woman who might, after days in the wilderness, seem so gilded and polished by the sunlight and water.

She stopped perhaps a dozen feet from him and made a low curtsey, careful still of the strawberries he could now see cradled in folds of velvet. "My lord." Her voice was warm and held a hint of laughter, but seemed for the moment free of the sharp edge of mockery he heard too often from her.

For a few moments he stared, entranced, then recollected himself and made a leg as gracefully as he could. "My lady." To address her so seemed only proper now.

"I hope you are pleased with your stay at the Court of Irati."

"Well pleased, lady, now that I am again in your company."

She blushed and turned away to put the strawberries on her blanket. Glancing up shyly at Justin, she said, "I would that these were strawberry wine, my lord. 'Tis simple fare—"

"I am content," he said, and when she looked doubtfully at him, added, "Only a churl would complain of such fare." He went to her and held out his hand. After a moment's hesitation, she let him help her up.

"Content to stay?" she asked. She tried to withdraw her hands from his, but he tightened his grip. "Content to stay until you are well?"

"Perhaps. Will you dance with me, madam?"

"Dance?"

"Can you not hear the musicians playing?"

"You mishear, my lord. 'Twas a lark."

He shook his head. " 'Tis a coranto being played, of this melody." He whistled a few bars. "Can you not hear it?"

She closed her eyes, then, to his surprise, pursed her lips and whistled the next few bars. He laughed in delight.

"Will you dance now?" As she still seemed reluctant, another thought struck him and he asked, "Can you dance?"

"My lord! I hope that you jest, and do not insult me in earnest. A coranto, you said?"

Truth to tell, she could dance, and amazingly well, he thought, for a vagabond. Who had taught her? he wondered jealously, then put the thought from his mind, losing himself for a time in the pleasure of her grace and her laughter. First he would whistle or hum a tune, then she would take it a few bars further, then he would continue. He could not have been happier if they were at court, with the queen's own musicians playing for them.

He had forgotten his injuries and his weakness, but too soon he grew breathless and weary and had to stop. She had been laughing, but she looked concerned when she saw he could no longer dance. She put an arm around his waist to steady him, but when she would have helped him back to his blanket, he drew her against him and kissed her.

Her lips tasted sweetly of strawberries. He clung to her, feeling light-headed, aware of the warmth of her skin beneath the velvet. She did not draw away from him, not even when he began to unfasten her kirtle. Not even when the garment slipped away to lie in a pool of shimmering crimson at her feet.

Somehow he found the strength to lift her and carry her a few steps to her blanket and lay her down.

He set her down on the strawberries. She laughed, then shivered as he licked the crushed fruit from her back. Her eyes were very wide, as though in fear, but she seemed unafraid as he continued to kiss and caress her, and he would have sworn she wanted him as much as he wanted her. They coupled, then rested, then coupled again. Afterward he lay with his head on her breast, watching a hawk circle lazily above them.

"I love you," he said, startling himself.

She said nothing for a few moments, then, her voice drowsy, murmured, "What? What did you say?"

He could not repeat what he had said. It seemed madness now. "Nothing," he whispered, and her response was silence. When he sat up to look down at her a few minutes later, he thought she was sleeping, but then she opened her eyes and smiled at him.

He began to kiss her again, her face, her neck, her shoulders, and she tensed as the trail of his kisses neared the last faint traces of the bite Rafael had given her. He kissed the bite then, and she relaxed, but the guilt he had felt when he noticed the bite again did not leave him, and he moved away from her to look her in the face.

"Pray forgive me, sweeting. I was wrong to leave you with Margaret."

"You did not know what would happen."

"I knew her well enough that I should have suspected . . . Forgive me. Would that I had not gone to Madrid."

Something in her expression changed then. He was not sure what, but it seemed that the look she gave him was guarded.

"Some good may have come of that journey," she said at last, and he felt suspicion well up inside him as she looked away. "You saw your friend Don Antonio. And, if you learned aught in Madrid that would seem good news to me, I would welcome hearing it."

"Good news?" he asked in a tightly controlled voice, and her gaze swerved to him, then away, before she shrugged.

"Know you not what I mean? There was talk in England, before we left, that Spain might serve the pope and invade England to restore the Catholic faith. Perchance you heard something in Madrid that would tell you whether 'tis so."

Oh, she was clever, Justin thought savagely. She said nothing to indicate whether or not she hoped that Spain would invade England, but almost any answer he gave would betray his own feelings on the matter.

"Why would such news concern you, Kat?"

"Why, my lord?" She still did not look directly at him, and her refusal to meet his gaze only fueled his anger. "Such news must needs concern me," she went on, "as it would any other honest English-woman."

He laughed. "You, Kat? You—honest?" And, taking his clothes, he left her and walked as far into the trees as his strength would take him. When he returned to the stream at last, it was sunset, and she was already wrapped in her blanket, seeming to sleep. Likely it was pretense, but he let her be, and was glad to be left alone.

They rode away from their camp the next morning. Justin had insisted that they leave, and Kat could tell from his stony expression that he would brook no arguments. Nor would she have given him any. Why should she care whether he sickened after a day's travel? And she was glad to be away from the stream, with its reminders of how Justin had loved her and then scorned her in the space of an hour.

They camped that night in an open field in Basse-Navarre, miles across the Spanish border. They did without a fire, supping on cold mutton pasties Justin had bought in the first village they reached after riding down out of the mountains into the foothills. None of the villagers had seemed overcurious about them, or surprised by their shabby appearance: years of war had left them with little capacity for surprise. The old man who had sold them the pasties had greeted them in the Basque tongue, saying "*Egunon,*" but had switched to broken English after he realized what country they came from. He had flooded them with gossip and rumor, and while he had seemed disappointed that they had little to say, the generous payment for the food had left his wrinkled, sunburnt face wreathed in smiles. Kat had felt like smiling, too, but kept her happiness to herself, as Justin hid whatever he felt at the news.

The fighting was over in France, a truce called between the king's forces and those of the Huguenot leader Coligny while peace was negotiated. Some travelers who had passed through the region had told the old man that a treaty had already been signed, but others had said the negotiations still went on. There had been more recent fighting here in Basse-Navarre, with the town of Rabastens besieged and finally taken by Monluc's army no more than a few weeks ago, but the Hammer of the Huguenots had been wounded badly, and a pedlar had told the old man that Monluc was dead. Kat thought that Jeanne d'Albret, Navarre's queen, must be rejoicing at that news. She would gladly have drunk a toast to the Huguenots who had so bravely defended their faith, had she dared. As it was, she kept her thoughts to herself and went to sleep early.

Justin woke her before dawn, and at sunrise they were again on the road to Bayonne. Kat's thoughts kept straying ahead to their destination. Justin had told her that his friends were Huguenots, like many of the gentry here in Gascony. As such, they might well see a Protestant Englishwoman as an ally to be befriended. In truth, were it simply a matter of needing their help to return to England, she thought she might well be able to count on their aid. But Justin's presence complicated matters. She doubted Justin would let her return to England without him, and she doubted, too, that his friends would believe her if she told them honestly that he had abducted her. No, she would simply have to bide her time and wait until Justin returned to England to effect her escape . . . unless some other opportunity presented itself.

Monteronne lay some dozen miles to the southeast of Bayonne. They came within sight of it early in the afternoon, stopping on a knoll as Justin pointed out their destination.

Kat gazed wistfully at the chateau overlooking the village some half mile away on the valley floor. Its stone walls were in good repair, its fields and gardens well tended. Pigeons fluttered about on the roof of the dovecote, and smoke curled up into the sky from two of the chateau's chimneys. Throughout the day they had seen neglected fields and wanderers with bandaged wounds, but Monteronne showed no sign that the civil war had ever been. It promised peace and comfort and safety, and Kat, who had ridden for two days in near-silence and desperate hope, felt herself shamefully close to tears. She looked away from Justin, praying he would not notice.

"Gabrielle de Charron sees to her home most carefully," Justin said. "Aye, and to her guests as well. Even if Jacques has not yet returned from the war, she will make us welcome."

"Both of us?" Kat asked, remembering her reception at La Casa de las Rosas.

"I shall introduce you as my wife," Justin said, and laughed shortly as Kat craned her neck around to stare at him in astonishment. " 'Twill save us from making more awkward explanations. And from your performance before Margaret, I trow you can conduct yourself in the manner I would expect of my lady wife. Look not so frightened, sweet. We will have separate chambers, so that I may rest undisturbed until I have recovered my strength.''

Kat felt her face grow warm. Confused, she looked down at her hands, folded neatly over the reins.

"Such bridal modesty becomes you, Kat," he said, and as her head snapped up and she glared at him, he added hastily, "as does silence. A shy demeanor will serve you well . . . By the way, the Charrons speak English well, but their servants do not. Dare I hope that you speak French as well as Spanish?"

"A little," she said coldly. "I will manage."

His mouth twisted in a cynical grin. "Yea, of course you'll manage. What need had I even to ask if you spoke French? By my life, I wonder that you wanted to go to Cambridge. What could they have taught you there?"

"Very little, i'faith, judging by some of the graduates." She paused, smiling a little. "Saving your lordship, of course."

He sighed. "Mark me, *wife*. You will neither do nor say anything here to shame me . . . or you'll have ample cause to regret it. Do you understand?"

Kat nodded stiffly, her lips pressed tightly together to keep back the angry retort on the tip of her tongue.

"Now listen well," Justin said, and, setting heels to his horse, began to ride slowly toward Monteronne. "I'll tell you the story I have invented for how we met and came to wed. Gabrielle would never believe the truth . . ."

"So I fear," Kat muttered, but attended to his words.

CHAPTER 33

Tandy had always thought of St. Paul's as England's second heart, and in some ways more vital than her first, the court. The news that flowed through the court was filtered through courtiers and officials, while at Paul's one might hear everything worth mentioning in England, if one listened closely enough to this babbling current that mixed yeoman with courtier, merchant with thief, cleric with heretic, soldier with traitor, masters—in all walks of life—with prentices. Tandy had been in London two days now, and during those two days he had spent every hour that could be spared from his master's business here at Paul's, listening, listening.

He was dressed well today, but not too well: few would notice him, but those who did would see a neatly barbered man in a plain suit of willow-color silk grosgrain. Ever since leaving the *Lady Margaret* four days ago, landing at night on the coast of Kent, Tandy had been careful not to attract undue attention to himself. To act openly, but inconspicuously—that was best; that had always been Lisle's own policy and counsel. Tandy only hoped that 'twas working as well for his lord in Navarra as it was for himself here in London.

He shook his head slightly. It did no good to wrap himself in worries like this; it only blinded and deafened him to the scene about him. And he needed to learn all he could, for Lord Harwood . . . and for himself.

The nagging suspicion that he had seen Kat before her appearance at Harwood Hall—and not just at the Jerusalem Tree Inn—had become stronger as the *Lady Margaret* sailed back to English waters, stronger still as Tandy rode from the coast to London, strongest yet here at Paul's. He had hoped that spending more time at St. Paul's would bring that memory back to him, but he could not dally here much longer. In a few days the *Lady Margaret* would leave the waters off Kent's coast and sail for Bayonne, with or without him, and he knew that tomorrow morning, at the latest, he would have to give over chasing this will-o'-the-wisp and ride for Kent, if he were to be there in time to signal the captain of the ship to pick him up again. He had alternate plans, in case he were delayed, but they were cumbersome and Lisle would be displeased by the delay.

The ceaselessly moving crowd that had thronged the Mediterranean, the main aisle of Paul's, was beginning to thin: it was nearly suppertime. There would be little new gossip to be gleaned from the talk by staying longer, and his innkeeper served a fine supper. Gathering his cloak about him, his hand resting on his purse to discourage thieves, he began to make his way toward the door.

It was then that Tandy saw him.

A fair-haired young man, no more than twenty or one-and-twenty, with fine regular features and sea-green eyes. Eyes the same color as Kat's. The youth was alone now, but Tandy remembered having seen him here once before, late in May, when he had been here looking for an old friend, a verser, who could often be found in Paul's looking for a cony to invite to a tavern, where he could be easily fleeced in a game of mumchance-at-cards. Tandy had just located his friend when he saw the young gentleman, who reminded him greatly of the youth he and Lord Harwood had encountered at the Jerusalem Tree. The lad had turned his back to Tandy then, and taken a step to one side, all the while talking to another young gallant, and Tandy had found himself gazing at a lovely young gentlewoman, whom he would have been content to stare at all day, had not the verser tugged on his elbow and directed his attention to another old friend who had just come up to them. When Tandy next looked back, the gentlewoman was gone, and within a few minutes he had forgotten about her.

Until now. Now, he would wager his life that it was Kat he had seen then.

The fair-haired gentleman was now turning away and walking toward the door. Tandy could not let him get away.

"Ho, there! Sir! You in the gray cloak!" He pushed his way past the people still standing in the aisle, getting jostled and cursed in return. "Sir! Please you, stop!"

The fair-haired man whirled around, freezing for an instant, a wary look on his face as he scanned the crowd. Then his gaze locked on Tandy, and the wariness gave place to open fear. The man bolted for the door.

Tandy ran after him, but his path was blocked by a stout cleric who seized his arm. "What am I, sirrah? Am I a pin to be bowled off my feet? Would you make of this holy church a bowling green for rogues like yourself?"

Tandy apologized, but the cleric still hung onto his sleeve, berating him, until at last Tandy broke free, tearing his cuff, and ran for the door.

There he paused. The fair-haired man had disappeared from sight, and Tandy knew 'twould be futile to search through the booksellers' stalls. Given such a lead, only a fool would be unable to lose his pursuer, and that look of wariness had assured Tandy that the gentleman he sought was no fool. Perhaps no gentleman, either. He had been dressed as one, but then, so had the verser, and any number of other rogues in Paul's. Conies were easily caught by men who looked like gentlemen.

He sighed heavily, leaning back against the door.

" 'Twas not him," someone said from behind him.

Tandy turned to see a man several years younger than himself, and somewhat taller, with curly, light brown hair and a pleasant face.

"Pray your pardon?"

" 'Twas not Nick Langdon, if that's who you thought it was. I have seen that man here before, and he favors Nick most wondrously, but he's not Nick."

"The last time I saw him here," Tandy said cautiously, "he was with a woman a few years younger than himself. Hair as fair as his, and a face that would make Helen of Troy weep for envy. She wore a peach-color kirtle, which suited her well."

"Very well," the man agreed. He wore a look of wistful sadness. "Nick's sister, Kat—Katherine. He told you naught of her?"

Tandy shook his head.

"Well, think not that you were slighted more than others. He had never told me of her loveliness, either, but spoke only of a tomboy who plagued him unmercifully when he was home. They have gone home again, to Beechwood in Sussex. Would they had stayed in London longer."

"You miss their company?"

"You have seen her, man."

"Are not visitors welcome at Beechwood?"

The man smiled ruefully. "Some, perchance, but I'll not press so hard again. Howsomever, should she return to London again . . :" He shrugged, and smiling more warmly this time, bade Tandy farewell and walked away.

Tandy began to stroll toward his inn. The fair-haired man did not reappear, but he was no longer of concern to Tandy. Nick Langdon and his sister Kat were. Tandy was unsure where in Sussex Beechwood lay, but he would find out, and he knew—he *knew*—he would be made welcome there.

Jack was in Thames Street before he stopped running. There had been no sign of pursuit since leaving the courtyard of Paul's, and logic told him the tawny-haired man in willow-green would have given up the chase there, amidst the jumble of booksellers' stalls. But the sense of danger that had seized him when he turned and saw who had called to him still held him, shaken, in its grip.

Tawny hair, and a scar under the left eye . . . Where had he seen the man before? He could not remember, and the failure to remember this time seemed so much worse than all the rest that he could have beaten his head against a wall in frustration. The uneasiness he had felt weeks ago when that gentleman addressed him familiarly as "Nick" was naught compared to the fear growing in him now. There was danger, great danger, and he walked through it blindfolded.

Jane sat at the table in the parlor at Beechwood, turning a letter over and over in her hands, wondering what to do with it. Nick's steward sat across the table from her, an anxious look in his eyes.

The letter was from Anne Norland, Nick and Kat's aunt. Jane had met her several times, and liked her, but she could not bring herself to open the letter. Mayhap it contained some news that Anne would not want anyone other than Kat or Nick to learn. As like as not, it contained some question to which Anne would expect a reply . . . one that Jane could not give. She had toyed for a minute with the idea of having the steward write a reply, explaining the unfamiliar handwriting by saying that Kat had injured her hand and was unable to write, but such an explanation, Jane had to admit, would bring Anne down to Sussex posthaste to nurse Kat back to health. She had thought, too, of sending Anne a letter herself, without even opening Anne's letter, merely acknowledging that her letter had arrived and explaining that she was helping the steward manage Beechwood while Nick and Kat were away. That much had the advantage of being the truth. But then she could not think of any reason why her two friends should be away from their home so long that would not arouse Anne's curiosity and risk bringing her here. And that Jane did not want. She could put off their servants' questions with some story that Kat and Nick were visiting friends in Hampshire, but that would never work with their aunt. It had not even worked for long with their steward, who had seen worried looks on her face so often that he had eavesdropped on her conversation with Sparrow, hearing just enough that he convinced her later to tell him all she knew. Sparrow's choler would overwhelm him if he knew of this, Jane thought wryly, but it had been a relief for her to be able to confide in someone here, to have someone to share her fears.

So far, however, the steward had been of little help in coming up with a story to tell Anne. And then his eyes lit up.

"I know," he said excitedly. "You may tell her that Master Nick and Mistress Kat are visiting friends and that you have sent her letter on to them. She may wonder that you do not name the friends, but she will wait for their reply. Should she write again, saying that she had not heard from them, you may tell her that haply the carrier lost it.''

Jane thought about it a few moments, then nodded.'' 'Twill gain us a week or two, at least. And perhaps by then—'' She fell silent, her throat closing painfully.

"I'll get my writing gear," the steward said, and got up from the table.

Just then someone rapped on the door.

'' 'Tis unlocked," Jane called, and a maidservant came in.

"There's a pedlar here, madam, at the gatehouse. A handsome fellow," she added thoughtlessly, and blushed. "Would you have him sent away, or let him stay to sell his wares?"

"He may stay," Jane said. "I'll join you in a few minutes."

The maid all but skipped out of the room.

Jane looked back at the steward, who looked as relieved as she felt to be spared—for a few hours, anyway—the trouble of composing a letter to Anne Norland. Smiling like a schoolboy released from his studies early, the steward took himself off to attend to his other duties.

Jane set Anne's letter aside and made her way down to the gatehouse.

Already smallwares had been spread across the table there: lace, silk cords, ribbons of silk and velvet, and shining buttons of all sizes. A few lengths of bright cloth had been draped over a chest. Nearly a dozen maidservants were in the room, poring over the items and waiting for Jane's arrival, for it was her prerogative to choose first from the wares for sale. Jane paused in the doorway, watching with amusement as the pedlar held a crimson silk ribbon against one maid's raven-black hair. '' 'Tis the color for you, sweeting," he murmured, then, aware he was being watched, turned to look directly at Jane.

The rogue showed not a trace of shame at having been caught openly wooing the maids. His smile only became warmer as he approached her and made a leg, a trifle clumsily. "Lady, I could gladly gaze upon you forever, but needs must that you leave. My livelihood depends on the money I make, and your beauty outshines these humble wares."

One of the maids giggled, then clapped her hand to her mouth to smother the sound. Jane felt her face grow warm, but she was not angry at the girl; she felt an urge to giggle herself. Who would have expected such court incense from a pedlar?

"Then you must starve, sirrah, for I shall not leave."

"Then, though I may starve, my eyes will feast . . . Yet dare I hope that you will buy some trifle?"

She shook her head, but walked past him to the table.

He hovered at her shoulder, a tall, slender man dressed in a fine suit of willow green. He must do well to afford such a suit for himself, she thought. There were many women—and not just innocent maids or lonely widows—who would be happy to buy his wares along with the court holy water he spouted. He was a handsome man, and a small, crescent-shaped scar beneath his left eye did not so much mar the handsomeness as render it more acceptable because flawed.

She took her time looking over the wares for sale, more because she did not wish to offend him by a perfunctory survey than because she really wanted anything. She could not complain about the smallwares; they seemed to be of good quality. At last she turned away from the table to study the cloth, which was neither shoddy material nor stuff that could not be bettered at any nearby mercer's.

She gestured for the maids to return to the table, then turned to the pedlar. "These are fine wares, sirrah, but I have all that I need at the moment."

"Madam," he said, very softly, "if you would see more special, private wares . . ."

She stared up at him, her cheeks flaming, but there was nothing in his expression to indicate that he had meant anything improper. Too discomfited to speak, she lowered her head, unable even to face him for the moment.

"Fine cloth, madam," he murmured, and there was kindness in his voice, "fine cloth brought from London . . ."

He knelt beside an unopened pack on the floor. Regaining her composure, Jane watched with bemused curiosity as he opened the pack to reveal some very fine cloth indeed. She ran her hands over a rich black velvet-on-velvet; the price he quoted her was high, but she decided to buy a few yards for a kirtle. She had a length of white silk that would go nicely with it, and silver lace . . .

Below the velvet was an ash-color silk grosgrain, and she decided she could use a few yards of that, too, for a doublet. Underneath the grosgrain was a length of plum varicolored velvet, finer stuff than the other, but Jane knew 'twould be dear and did not even ask the price. Idly wondering what other treasures might yet be hidden in the pack, she lifted the plum velvet, then caught her breath when she saw what lay beneath.

It was cloth-of-gold, in seawater green the exact color of Nick's eyes, and Kat's. It seemed to catch every bit of light in the room, shimmering as she lifted it free of the pack. All thoughts of economy fled her mind. The cloth was not for her: its brilliance would merely draw attention to her own drab coloring. But either Kat or Nick would look splendid in this . . .

"How much?" she asked the pedlar.

He looked regretful. "Madam, the cloth-of-gold is not for sale."

"Someone else has paid you to bring it from London?" If so, she would offer him more than he had been paid—if he would take it.

"Nay, madam, the cloth is mine to sell if I wish."

"So." She tilted her head to one side. "Think you that I cannot afford it? I know I am garbed plainly, but pray do not judge my purse by my dress. Tell me your price, and I—"

"Lady, I would give you the cloth if you were the woman I wish to see wear it, but you are not." He wet his lips fretfully. "Cry you mercy. You are fair, but I once saw a gentlewoman in Winchester, with golden hair and eyes as green as the sea." One of the maids gasped; the pedlar glanced at her for an instant, then went on, "I could not learn her name, nor have I seen her again, but I think of her always. When I saw this cloth, I bought it, though the price was dear, for I could see that it would become her more than any other, and, if God wills, I shall see her again someday, and make her a gift of it."

"To woo her?" asked a sharp-tongued maid, and there was a ripple of laughter among the maidservants that quickly died as Jane glanced over her shoulder at them.

She turned back to the pedlar. "And so you wear the willow for her?" she asked quietly, thinking how, in her heart, she wore the willow for Nick.

She looked again at the cloth-of-gold in her hands, and thought of Nick's eyes. Perchance the gentlewoman the pedlar had seen had been Kat; perchance not. But she wanted the cloth, and there was a way she might persuade the pedlar to sell it to her . . .

She began to walk toward the door, taking the roll of cloth with her. "Come with me," she told the pedlar. "There's a portrait I would show you, of the mistress of this house. 'Tis possible you would have seen her in Winchester."

He stared at the portrait of Kat for a long time without speaking, his face expressionless.

Jane's gaze shifted constantly from the pedlar's face to the picture and back again as she wondered why he showed neither recognition nor disappointment. Frowning, she looked at the picture again.

Kat was garbed in black; she had still been in mourning for her father, dead less than two months when the picture was made. She had not wanted to pose for it, and had done so only because Nick had told her that their father would have wished it, since he had arranged for it just before he fell fatally ill. The picture-maker, who was from Antwerp, had succeeded in capturing Kat's sadness, betrayed in her eyes and the curve of her mouth, as well as her loveliness. She had been thinner then, not regaining her appetite until several months after her father's death, and her face had seemed paler, and with the contrast of the black dress, she had looked very delicate.

The pedlar sighed heavily, looking away from the picture at last.

" 'Tis not the lady you seek?" Jane asked fearfully. She still held the seawater-green cloth-of-gold, loath to give it back to him.

He shook his head. " 'Tis somewhat like her, as if she had a sister as melancholy as she is sanguine. The gentlewoman I saw looked as if she laughed often."

"You must understand that this picture was made but a few months after her father's death last year, and she mourned his loss greatly."

He looked back at the picture then, and she wondered at the expression of shame on his face. This man had more compassion than she would expect from a pedlar.

"Would that I could show you a picture that would more truly portray her nature," Jane said. "Alack, the other portraits of her are less true than—nay, wait. There is another . . ."

Walking a short distance down the gallery, she stopped in front of a table and began to open the drawer on the left side. Pray God, the locket was still here, she thought. It had been a gift to Kat from Nick. One day late last winter, Nick had sent a letter to London, to an Italian artist who lived in Blackfriars. The Italian had arrived a few days later, and soon completed a faithful likeness of Kat. Nick had a locket made for the limning, which he gave to his sister to give someday to the man she loved. Belike she would always keep it, she had told him mockingly. She had shown Jane where she kept it—*in the gallery where it belongs*, she had said with a laugh—and added that maybe she would hang it on the wall someday, with a handkerchief for a curtain. Now Jane prayed that Kat had not been so foolish as to give it to Christopher Danvers.

She sighed with relief when she saw it, near the back of the drawer. She walked quickly back to the pedlar and opened the locket and held it in front of his face.

"Is this the gentlewoman you saw in Winchester?"

He stared at the portrait, then shook his head, and her heart sank until he told her, " 'Tis the most faithful picture I have ever seen. In sooth, this is the very woman—unless the picture-maker painted another and missed her likeness completely."

She let him hold the locket for a time, and he gazed at the picture of Kat as if it were a text he would commit to memory.

He looked regretful as he at last closed the locket and gave it back to her. As she was returning the locket to the table drawer, he said, "You may have the cloth, of course."

"I shall pay you a fair price for it."

"Nay. 'Tis a gift, the only proper one a common man such as myself may give to a gentlewoman. I would accept no payment. Unless—Unless I might see her again, to present the cloth myself."

"Would that I could take you to her, but she is not here now. She has gone to Hampshire, to visit relatives"—how much easier it was to lie to a pedlar than to Kat's aunt!—"but should be back soon. I wish to surprise her with a gown made from this cloth."

"Then if I came back this way next month, mayhap I could see her? Perhaps even in the gown you will make?"

"Yea, if she's—" Jane caught herself, and managed a quick, brittle smile. The pedlar's innocent question had dredged up all her fears about Kat and Nick at once. "Of certain, you can see her then," she said forcefully. "But you must let me pay you for the cloth, so it will also be my gift to her."

After some argument, he accepted a few pounds from her. 'Twas much less than the cloth was worth, Jane knew, but he would not take more, and she would not let him take less. Any less, she had told him, would leave her feeling ashamed.

They went back to the gatehouse then, where a few more maidservants, who had been busy in the stillroom earlier, were eager to make some purchases. Then the pedlar loaded his packs onto his horses and rode away, leaving Jane with six yards of cloth-of-gold and several of the other stuff, giggling maidservants to shoo out of the gatehouse and back to their chores, and the bittersweet task of sewing garments quickly, in the hope that Kat and Nick would return before the pedlar did.

There were walls, but he knew how to scale walls; watchdogs, but he could handle them; locks, and with those, too, he was familiar.

At two hours past midnight he walked silently along the gallery, lit now only by moonlight that fell in neat squares on the floor. He reached the curtain-shrouded portrait he had examined first and paused to lift the curtain aside and look at it, though in the dim light the woman's face was little more than a pale blur. He sighed, then moved on to the table and opened the drawer. Taking out the locket, he went to stand by a window and checked the limning to make sure he had what he sought. He slipped it into his pocket then, and took from his purse a few coins, which he left on the table.

Then he left, as silently as he had come.

Jane picked up the coins, one by one, counting them, though she had known before she saw them how much money was here: three pounds— the four angels and three nobles she had given the pedlar. She folded her hand around the coins, tightening her grip until their edges cut into her fingers.

She was afraid to open the drawer of the table. Would that she could believe he came here only to return her money . . .

She had run here from her bedchamber, dressed only in her smock, though a maid had now draped her nightgown over her shoulders. She stood barefoot on the rush-covered floor of the gallery, aware that the two maidservants who had told her about the coins were whispering about her. Perchance they thought she had gone mad. They had discovered the coins and acted as obedient, honest servants, one staying to watch over the money, the other coming to her chamber, where she had just awakened, to tell her about it. What were they to think when she ran to the gallery as if she had been told that the house was afire?

She finally summoned enough courage to open the drawer, pulling it further and further out until she could see the very back. Other trifles, which she had noticed yesterday, were there: a gold toothpick of Nick's, a thimble, a broken chain that Kat meant to have sent to a goldsmith's for repair. The locket was not.

She slammed the drawer shut, then hurled the coins as far as she could down the gallery. They fell onto the rush matting without making a sound. Just as silent, Jane thought, as his feet would have been . . .

The maids had stopped whispering, but now both stared at her as if they thought she belonged in Bedlam.

"Our pedlar is an honest thief," she told them flatly. "He has paid for the locket he stole, the locket with your mistress's picture."

And she went back to her room to dress, so she could ride to the sheriff's house and tell him about the pedlar.

Near the end of the second week of August, the court, which since the nineteenth of July had been at Chenies enjoying the hospitality of the Earl of Bedford, dislodged, like some monstrous snake disturbed from its nest, and crawled away in a two-mile-long train of coaches and wagons toward its next destination on the progress. Sparrow had ridden beside the train for a few hours, looking for acquaintances in the queen's household who might have news of interest to him. Those few he had found had related nothing but worthless gossip. Now the sun was high and the day hot, and he cursed the fate that had forced him to ride between London and Bedfordshire during these dog days of summer.

He had come to Chenies to meet with Walsingham, but had found his master so busy with preparations for his mission to France, where he would serve as the queen's envoy to the peace negotiations, that he had little time for his servant. Little time, and less sufferance.

Since last spring, Walsingham had received two more of those unsigned letters on ragged-edged paper. The first, in June, had warned him of a plot to poison the queen. Sparrow and one of his agents had stopped the would-be poisoner, but had failed, alas, to keep the evidence from being destroyed. Walsingham had rated them for that, and Sparrow still smarted from the scolding. The second letter had been slipped unseen into Walsingham's cloakbag a few days ago, when he was in London. That had advised him to fear another plot from France rather than Spain, and had said moreover that Spain would not attack England. 'Twas impossible, as yet, to prove the truth of the latest letter, but it had reminded Walsingham of his agents' earlier failure, and he had berated Sparrow again, saying that he was better served by those who were not in his pay than by those who were.

Angered by the memory, Sparrow yanked unawares on the reins. His horse danced sideways, nearly colliding with the mount of a dust-coated popinjay of a courtier, who swore roundly at him for his care-lessness and called him a clotpoll and a bumpkin. A furious retort was on the tip of Sparrow's tongue, but he swallowed his ire and apologized before riding away, toward the rear of the train. A noisy quarrel might lead to his being ordered away, and he wished to see the queen one more time before returning to London.

He passed a few dozen more slowly-moving wagons, then reached a stretch of empty road. The queen's party, all of it—outriders, guards, equerries, her councillors and maids of honor—had come to a complete stop. Her Majesty's golden coach had halted at the edge of the road, by a meadow dotted with wildflowers. Elizabeth herself stood some ten paces from the coach, watching a group of countrypeople who were dancing some poor country dance for her entertainment. *There be bump-kins*, Sparrow thought, wishing that choleric popinjay were here, that he might instruct him . . .

He dismounted and left his horse with a page standing beside one of the coaches, then moved closer to the queen. Elizabeth wore white today: a kirtle of white taffeta that shimmered in the sunlight, and a gown of white cypress so light that in the breeze it drifted about her like a shining mist. Next to the rustics—whose clothing, though color-ful, was of cheap cloth—she seemed like a goddess. Yet there was no condescension in her manner as she smiled and clapped her bejeweled hands, and she laughed aloud in delight at a pair of children who awk-wardly mimicked their elders' dancing.

Her delight was not shared by the courtiers around her, Sparrow noticed. The scraps of conversation he overheard were all the usual complaints about the progress and its discomforts: 'twas clear from what these ladies and gallants said that the necessity of spending days on the road, only to arrive at a destination where they would likely be forced to live in crowded, uncomfortable quarters, was the worst fate they could imagine—save that of being away from the court. They could scarce bear the thought of six more weeks of this progress, before the queen returned to Windsor.

To Sparrow's alarm, the queen's guards seemed bored and wearied, too. When the dance ended, they remained standing where they were while the queen approached the countrypeople, who now knelt on the grass, their heads bowed. Sparrow glared at them, but the few who glanced in his direction seemed to look right through him. The agent turned his gaze back to Elizabeth, who had bidden her subjects rise. The two children offered her a cap woven of flowers and vines, and she placed it on her head, laughing, and thanked them graciously, then turned to walk back to her coach.

Behind her back, one of the countrymen slid his hand up his sleeve, then started after her.

Sparrow hurtled across the five yards separating him from the rustic and threw the man to the ground, but before he could overpower the assassin and deprive him of whatever weapon he had hidden up his sleeve, three pairs of hands seized him and yanked him to his feet.

"Hold, gentlemen!" Elizabeth said sharply. "I know this sparrow-hawk. He's a creature of Walsingham's. Let him go."

The guards released Sparrow, who glowered at them as he straightened his clothes. Two other guards held the countryman.

"How now, little hawk?" the queen said. "This was a curious sort of dance, to follow the other."

"Indeed, madam, but I thought 'twould be more to your liking than murder." He looked briefly at the frightened, sobbing rustic, then back at the queen. "Your guards were careless, I fear, in letting this rogue so close to you, for I warrant you he meant you harm. Look in his sleeve! I saw him reach into it, as he followed after you."

The man shook his head wildly, but his sobbing made his protests unintelligible. The queen stared at him, her normally pale skin even whiter than usual, so that the paint on her cheeks and lips seemed in contrast dark as blood. "Search him," she told her guards.

The bumpkin writhed in their grasp, and sobbed more loudly. Sparrow looked on with satisfaction. In a few moments his vigilance would be recognized. Everyone would know that he had saved the queen while her own guards stood idly by, and he savored the triumph already, a triumph whose sweetness overwhelmed the bitter memories of his talk with Walsingham yesternight. He watched eagerly as the guards subdued the man and then rolled up his sleeve.

There was laughter, then silence, as the queen came forward to take what had been hidden by the sleeve. She spoke in a low voice to the terrified rustic, whose blubbering gave way to quieter sniffling and watery smiles. Then she turned toward Sparrow, her hands concealed by a bunch of drooping wildflowers tied with a red ribbon, and the agent wished the ground would open and swallow him.

"Well, my sparrowhawk," she said at last, and her voice was unsteady, as though she were trying not to laugh, "I must thank you for saving me from this posy . . ."

CHAPTER 34

They could hear women laughing in one of the rooms below, the sound coming through the bedchamber's open window.

Kat recognized one especially loud laugh. 'Twas one of the maid-servants who worked in the kitchen. Then the maid said something, so quickly that Kat missed all but the last word, a name that was nearly shrieked as the maid began laughing again.

Margot.

That was enough to tell Kat what they were laughing about, and she chuckled herself, and so did Marie, the maidservant who was comb-ing Kat's hair.

It was her tenth morning at Monteronne, and for the moment, Kat felt at peace. So, it seemed, did everyone else here.

Peace was all she had heard spoken of: the peace agreement signed at St. Germain-en-Laye two weeks ago on the eighth of August, bringing an end to the civil war that had racked France for almost two years; the peace that these people expected to return to their own lives now that the fighting had ended. Kat was not entirely sure that this Huguenot household was not being too hopeful, for the hostilities just ended had been the third civil war in France in ten years. But the accord signed at St. Germain had guaranteed the Huguenots freedom of worship in certain towns and in the dependencies of high Protestant nobles, and that had been accomplished despite the opposition of the papal nuncio and those who, for one reason or another, represented Spanish interests. The government was weary of fighting, and Catherine de Medici was in no mood to listen to the powerful Guise family or others who supported the Catholic interests and those of Spain and wanted the war to con-tinue until the Huguenots were defeated.

And Margot—Marguerite—de Valois, Catherine's daughter, the subject of so much gossip and cause of so much laughter here at Mon-teronne these past weeks, was one of the reasons.

The seventeen-year-old princess was a pawn in the royal game of alliance by marriage. Her father, Henri II, who had died when she was a child, had intended for her to wed Henri de Bourbon, son of the

441

Queen of Navarre, but that plan had been discarded after Jeanne d'Albret publicly admitted to being a Calvinist on Christmas Day of 1560. Since then Margot's mother had sought a Catholic husband for the princess, dangling her unsuccessfully as bait before Don Carlos of Spain, then Rudolph of Hungary, the emperor's son, and then King Sebastian of Portugal. But now that Catherine de Medici wished to have peace with the Huguenots, it was rumored that she was again negotiating with Jeanne d'Albret for a marriage between Henri de Bourbon and Margot. Unfortunately for Catherine, Margot had plans of her own. The princess was widely known to be hot-blooded: it was said that Catherine forced her daughter to drink potions of sorrel to cool her blood, and there were even rumors that two of the princess's brothers were among her conquests. Perhaps, Kat thought, the Medici woman would have preferred incest to the lover Margot had taken this past spring.

Margot had fallen in love with Henri, Duc de Guise, said to be one of the handsomest men at court. When the king, Charles IX, Marguerite's brother, learned of the relationship, he had gone to his mother's apartments in the middle of the night, clad only in his nightshirt, and after consulting with her there, they had summoned Margot. Her brother had beaten her senseless; some said that her mother had helped him. It was rumored that the king was so incensed against Henri de Guise that he ordered his half brother, the Bastard of Angouleme, to shoot the duke during a hunting party, but the duke was warned in time. Knowing his life was still in jeopardy, the duke had quickly arranged to marry the Princesse de Porcien, a widow much older than himself. His uncle, Charles de Guise, Cardinal of Lorraine—whom Catherine suspected of plotting to marry his nephew to her daughter—had prudently withdrawn to his Abbey of St. Denis. The leadership of the Catholic cause in France was in disarray.

And here, in the south of France, the Huguenots had had another reason to rejoice, for, as Kat and Justin had learned when they reached Monteronne, the rumors they had heard in Basse-Navarre had indeed been true: Monluc was badly wounded, having been shot in the face with an arquebus. Kat's maid had told her that Gabrielle de Charron had drunk a toast to the unknown defender of Rabastens who had shot the Hammer of the Huguenots. Sad news had come the next day when they learned that Rabastens had been taken and all its people killed by Monluc's avenging soldiers, but Gabrielle still believed that Monluc would never again lead either armies or intrigues against the Huguenots.

Marie finished arranging Kat's hair, then went to get the gallipots of paints the baroness had given Kat. Although Kat had diligently washed her face with a lotion that Gabrielle promised would help her sunburned skin return to its original fairness very quickly, her face looked more sallow than fair after two weeks of avoiding the sun, and she was glad to have the paints . . . though in sooth she was not sure for whom she was painting her face. 'Twas not for Justin, of certain.

He had spoken truly when he said they would have separate bedchambers. At first the decision had seemed the only practical one, for the ride to Monteronne had weakened him, and the fever had returned. Two physicians summoned by Jacques de Charron had attended him for the next several days, and no one had questioned Kat's sleeping in another chamber. But Justin had been well for a week now, and still no one had asked Kat why she did not share her husband's bed. Maybe Justin had given some explanation to his host and hostess, but Kat did not try to find out. Belike Seigneur de Monteronne and his wife assumed there had been some quarrel between the two, for they must have noticed that Kat and Justin treated each other civilly but without much affection when they met at table, and never sought each other's company. Yet the Charrons acted as though they saw nothing amiss.

As far as Kat knew, Justin had told them only that Kat was a gentlewoman from Hampshire, that they had been married a few months, that they had been visiting his cousin in Burgos and had found it necessary to leave hastily. He had not explained the reason for their flight—sans servants and belongings—nor why he and Kat had ridden across the Pyrenees, rather than leaving from Bilbao on his ship, which had arrived in Bayonne a few days ago. Kat was amazed that Jacques and Gabrielle had accepted everything without question. She could not have done so.

She had just finished painting her face when she heard a frantic scratching on the lower half of the door. Marie went to open the door, and Gabrielle's pet spaniel bounded into the chamber in search of the scraps Kat had saved from her breakfast.

"A plague on you," Kat told the dog fondly, scratching his neck while he gobbled up the bits of meat and bread. "Aye, and a plague on me for ever starting to feed you."

Then she picked the spaniel up and went looking for Gabrielle. With luck, she would find the baroness alone for once. Kat meant to ask Gabrielle how she and her husband had come to know and befriend Justin . . .

Conscientious as Gabrielle de Charron was about her duties as mistress of Monteronne, she yet maintained a vast correspondence and spent many an hour at the desk in her antechamber. It was there that Kat found her, a letter in her hand and a worried expression on her face, though the frown was replaced with a smile an instant after she looked up and saw Kat.

"Good morning, my child," Gabrielle said, coming to take the spaniel from Kat. "So you have found this little vagabond again. Thank you for returning him." She took a step back, surveying Kat from head to toe. "You look very lovely today. That color becomes you."

"I thank you, madame," Kat replied, made awkward by the compliment. The carnation taffeta would have become her hostess, too, which is why it had been purchased by Jacques de Charron.

As on every other occasion Kat had seen her, Gabrielle was wearing clothes of plain dark-gray cloth. Despite her husband's wishes, despite his frequent gifts to her of fine velvets and silks in the colors that most flattered her, she had not worn bright colors for more than ten years, since her brother was put to death as one of the Huguenot conspirators captured near the royal chateau of Amboise. Monteronne contained chest after chest of gorgeous stuff, fine wools as well as silks and velvets, and it was from those rich stuffs that Kat's new garments had been made, by sempsters Gabrielle had hired.

"I have received this morning a letter from Geneva," Gabrielle said, sitting down again, the spaniel on her lap. "Would you like to hear it?"

"Yea, I would, madame," Kat said, praying she did not sound as reluctant as she felt. Much of Gabrielle's correspondence was with Huguenot exiles in Geneva; they sent her advice and pamphlets and news of the community Calvin had founded before his death six years ago. Kat had at first been as curious to read Gabrielle's letters as she had been to read Margaret's, but that curiosity had quickly waned. There was little news in the letters from Geneva that Walsingham was unlikely to have already from his own sources, and Kat found what she learned of the Calvinist community not to her taste.

"This letter is from Monsieur Bohier," Gabrielle said, "he of the unreadable handwriting." She gave Kat a sly smile. "He sometimes praises Geneva too highly, does he not?"

"Sometimes, madame," Kat confessed, realizing that Gabrielle had not believed her excuse for not reading all of Monsieur Bohier's old letters.

"Mayhap his letters make you wish that the laws of Geneva were not so strict. You would have the city permit plays, and dancing, and cards, would you not?"

"Perhaps," Kat said, very cautiously, "if Monsieur Bohier did not take such pleasure in recounting the punishments of those who have transgressed . . . Truth to tell, there are few people of my country who would live as those in Geneva do. 'Sdeath, not even—" She broke off, seeing Gabrielle smile, and blushed. *Not even Blanche*, she had been about to say, thinking that her cousin would in time find Geneva, with its outlawing of plays and dancing and other innocent pastimes, a dull place indeed. And as for herself, Kat thought wryly, that oath alone would have earned her some punishment, had she uttered it in Geneva.

"Not even your queen?" Gabrielle asked.

Kat laughed and shook her head, thinking of the woman she had seen at Hampton Court.

"It may be," Gabrielle said softly, "that her faith is less strong than John Calvin's was."

"Nay," Kat said, shaking her head again. " 'Tis unlike his, however. There are those who counsel her who would have England more like Geneva, but she has said she will not make windows into men's souls. It is her belief that there is but one Christ Jesus and one faith, and the rest is a dispute about trifles."

"Oh?" Gabrielle looked offended.

Kat frowned. She had somehow diminished Elizabeth in Gabrielle's eyes. How could she explain? "Perchance," she said slowly, "it is more a matter of policy than of faith. The queen, as a prince, must needs think of her subjects, and since her father's reign those subjects have been Catholic and Protestant and Catholic and Protestant again. She must be politic to rule them."

"Politic in her beliefs?" the Frenchwoman asked skeptically.

"Politic in her decisions concerning her subjects' beliefs. By my life, she sometimes has little choice. My father told me that soon after Elizabeth was crowned, the canons of Oxford sought her advice on the burial of the bones of the woman who had been married to Peter Martyr, the Protestant canon of Christ Church during the reign of Elizabeth's brother Edward. Mistress Martyr died during the last year of Edward's reign and was buried in the cathedral, but when the king died and his sister Mary became queen, Mistress Martyr's remains were taken from the cathedral and thrown into a dungheap in the garden. The canons wished to return the bones to her tomb."

"I see little reason to ask the queen's advice on such a matter."

"Like enough, there would have been none, had they not found two sets of bones in the dungheap. One, of course, was that of Mistress Martyr; the other they knew must be that of St. Frideswide, Oxford's patron saint, whose bones had been taken from the cathedral and thrown there some years earlier."

A smile was tugging at the corners of Gabrielle's mouth. "Might that have been during your queen's brother's reign?"

"It was. And now no one could tell which was Mistress Martyr and which was St. Frideswide."

"I see . . . What was Elizabeth's advice about the bones?"

" 'Mix them,' she said. So the remains were buried together."

Gabrielle laughed for a long time, a low, musical sound that delighted Kat. "I should not laugh," she said at last, her voice shaky. "There is more tragedy than comedy in this, and, I fear, half the tragedy is what this comedy has done to your queen's faith. I pray that she will have fewer such trials, and years of peace in which she may turn her thoughts to God. Alas"—and she picked up the letter—"Monsieur Bohier writes that this will not be so." She began to read. " 'Le Tigre'—" She glanced at Kat. "That is the Cardinal of Lorraine, Charles de Guise. He is known as the Tiger, for his fierceness and cruelty."

Kat nodded; she had heard the nickname before.

" 'Le Tigre,' " Gabrielle said, reading again, " 'will not stay caged at St. Denis for long, but will seek his own freedom to hunt and slaughter where he will. His own freedom, and that of his niece, the Queen of Scots. For if his ambitions have been thwarted in France, then they must, like a pent-up flood, seek outlet elsewhere. I have been warned of this by men whose judgment I trust, and I would have you warn those friends of yours in England of whom you have told me.' "

Gabrielle put the letter down and turned to face Kat. "I count you as one of those friends now, as much a friend to us as your husband is. I will tell Justin of this letter, but I felt I must also tell you."

Because it seems Justin rarely speaks to me? Kat wondered, but kept silent as Gabrielle continued:

"Think you that your queen is safe because her cousin the Queen of Scots is still held captive?"

"I—" Kat paused, then shrugged. "I know little of such matters, madame, but the queen is well served by her advisers."

"Yet some of them would see Mary Stuart freed."

Kat hesitated a few moments, then nodded. She could not dispute that.

"Never!" the Frenchwoman said vehemently. "Never free her! Never forget that Guise blood flows through her veins. I fear that your Queen Elizabeth may be swayed by men who have been deceived by Mary's youth and beauty into believing her the victim she pretends to be. I was deceived by her myself, once. I met her at court, soon after her wedding to the dauphin. I saw—I thought I saw—a child, a woman little more than a child, who was pretty and delicate despite her great size. Then I could understand those who said she surpassed other women as much in spirit and beauty as in height. Yet at Amboise—"

Gabrielle turned away then to stare out the window, and Kat knew she must be thinking of Amboise. Amboise, where, ten years ago, the Guises had triumphed over their enemies, executing dozens of Huguenots before the eyes of the French court.

The Guises had ruled France in all but name then, for Mary Stuart's husband, François II, had been but sixteen years old when his father, Henri II, died—sixteen, and more than willing to sign a royal decree that left his wife's uncles, the Cardinal of Lorraine and François, Duc de Guise, in control of all matters of state while the king, no more interested in ruling than prepared to do so, went hunting with his friends. Under the Guises, heretics were hunted more savagely than during Henri II's reign, and those who aided them were also treated as heretics; and the Cardinal of Lorraine, faced with the enormous debt run up by François II's father, cut royal expenditures by throwing officials and soldiers out of work. Within several months, discontent with the Guises was so widespread that a Huguenot gentleman, Jean de Barry, Sieur de La Renaudie, was able to set in motion a plot to enter forcefully into the king's presence and demand reforms, including the arrest of the cardinal and his brother the Duc de Guise.

La Renaudie, alas, had been a fool, disregarding warnings from Calvin and other Protestant leaders, and plotting so openly that the Guises were aware of his efforts almost from the beginning. The conspirators assembled at Nantes, then marched up the Loire toward the royal chateau of Blois, where the king had been residing. But before they reached Blois, the cardinal told the king of La Renaudie's plot, persuading him that the true intention of the conspirators was to capture the king and hold him for ransom. The court removed to the more easily defended chateau of Amboise, twenty miles away. This threw La Renaudie's plans into confusion, and his supporters, wandering in bands through the forests along the Loire and wearing white scarves around their necks to identify themselves, were easily captured and taken to Amboise. Jean de Barry himself was shot and killed in the forest of Chateaurenault. The cardinal, anxious to implicate Louis, Prince of Condé—who, like his brother Antoine de Bourbon, was a prince of the blood and rival of the Guises—in the plot, tortured many of the Huguenot conspirators before putting them to death, but was unable to extract a confession that would condemn Condé. The executions had continued for days, offered as entertainment for the ladies and gentlemen of the court, who had watched as Huguenots were beheaded, or hanged, or beaten senseless—or spitted, two or more together, on iron rods before being thrown into the Loire to drown. Gabrielle's brother Martin, Justin had told Kat, had suffered that last fate. It was said that Martin, like many of the other Huguenots, had gone to his death singing French psalms in defiance of the cardinal.

"At Amboise," Gabrielle said again, so quietly her voice was little more than a whisper, "while the court watched the executions, the young king—so I have been told—cried often while his subjects died, and only permitted it because the cardinal had convinced him that the

Huguenots were his enemies. But his wife, the young queen, Mary Stuart, shed no tears. I have heard that the king and the queen mother
and even the Duc d'Aumale, one of the cardinal's brothers, went to the
cardinal to beg for clemency for some of the Huguenot leaders, but Mary
Stuart was not with them. You must never forget, Katherine, that the
Queen of Scots is of the same blood as *Le Tigre*."

Kat was silent, struck less by what Gabrielle had said than by what
she had not said: the baroness had not mentioned that her brother had
been among those slaughtered at Amboise. Before arriving at Monteronne, Justin had told her that Gabrielle was stronger than her husband,
stronger in her faith and stronger willed. Jacques de Charron, he had
said, would have been content to live the simple life of a country gentleman, unconcerned with matters of religion. The seigneur had gone
to the wars as much to keep peace at home and to keep his wife from
donning armor as from personal conviction. Kat had disbelieved Justin
then, had indeed been amused when she first met Gabrielle de Charron
at the thought of this diminutive woman—more than a foot shorter than
the queen whose "great size" she had mentioned—going to battle for
her faith. She could believe him now.

Then the Frenchwoman turned away from the window, and Kat
thought she saw the brightness of unshed tears in the baroness's eyes
before her back was turned again as she faced the desk. She spoke to
Kat without looking at her.

"You must excuse me, child, but the messenger who brought me
this letter awaits a reply. One of the servants told me that your husband
was talking to mine in the library. That was an hour ago, but haply you
may still find them there. *Au revoir*."

Kat knew she was being dismissed, and accepted it: this was no time
to ask Gabrielle about Justin. She took her leave gracefully, then, shutting the antechamber door behind her so Gabrielle could be alone with
her memories and her grief, went to find Justin and their host.

Justin and the Seigneur de Monteronne were still in the library, she
realized, hearing their voices as she came in sight of the room's open
door. She stopped suddenly, pretending to busy herself with rearranging
a vase of freshly cut roses on an Italian marble table. Likely they had
not heard her approach; her footsteps, cushioned by the rushes on the
floor, would have made little sound. She could linger here for a while
and listen. 'Twas the best opportunity she had had for eavesdropping
since coming to Monteronne.

"Paris?" Jacques demanded. "Why must you go to Paris?"

"Because I must," Justin replied, sounding both amused and weary.
"And what better time than now, when there is peace?"

"The peace was made with King Charles and his mother, not the people of Paris. They have ever hated our cause, and prefer war to peace with those of the Religion. Why, last month, when they still hoped the peace accord would not be signed, the clergy and people of Paris offered their own money to continue the war for at least several more months."

"Then I must needs remember," Lisle said dryly, "not to ride into the city wearing the white cape of a Huguenot."

"Better you not ride into Paris at all," Jacques said, ignoring Justin's sarcasm. "No business can be important enough to take you there."

"Alas, this is, but pray do not ask me to tell you what it is, for I cannot."

What business was Justin about now, Kat wondered, that he would not even disclose to his friend? She was not surprised that he had said nothing of his plans to her, but why would he conceal them from Jacques?

And then she remembered what he had said in the Forest of Irati. *The King of Spain will not serve the pope in this matter*, he had said while fevered, talking unawares. She had taken it then as good news, and had wanted to believe it meant the same to Justin—though his refusal to tell her more of what he had learned in Madrid had rekindled her suspicions of him. Now he had added more fuel to that fire. If he had gone to Spain seeking help for English papists—perchance some promise to invade England—and had been rebuffed there, would he not then look to the other great Catholic power? And, as he had just said, what better time than now, when there was peace, and King Charles's soldiers were free to fight elsewhere than on French soil?

"Then I shall not question your reasons for traveling to Paris," Jacques said heavily, "but I will give you two more reasons why your plans to go there leave me filled with foreboding. I do not trust this peace. I pretend to rejoice in it—nay, I do rejoice in it, while it lasts, but I fear it cannot last. The pope will not permit it. I have been told, by one who has never lied to me in the past, that last year, when he wrote to congratulate Catherine de Medici on the victory of Jarnac, Pope Pius urged Catherine de Medici to exterminate all Huguenots in France. I believe that. It is well known that the soldiers he sent to aid King Charles after the victory, when he expected to defeat the Huguenots completely, were given orders to take no prisoners, but to put all Huguenots they captured to death. He will never accept the peace of St. Germain, this pope. He was Grand Inquisitor before he was pope; he is still more an inquisitor than a prince of the Catholic Church."

"But the peace agreement has been signed, despite his wishes."

"Only time will tell how long the king can abide by the agreement.

It will not be an easy peace, and I fear that when it is broken, it will be broken first in Paris."

"Because the clerks and merchants of Paris offered their own money for the war?"

"That, and more."

"The second of the two reasons you mentioned?"

"I hesitate to tell you of it, for I know you scoff at foretellers of the future."

"By God's blood! Jacques, you have not become a follower of Nostradamus or some other astrologer?"

"Never! I have nothing but contempt for those at court who made a prophet of that imposter before his death, and who still read his verses more carefully than they read the Bible. No, I would not consult an astrologer. But there is an old woman of the village, Madeleine Goujon, who has a certain reputation as a seeress— No, my friend, do not laugh. More often than not her visions come true. She predicted this wound of mine—"

"Jacques. Jacques." Justin's tone was gentle but disparaging, as if he were giving a reproof to a child. Kat grated her teeth. She knew that tone of voice too well. "Predicting wounds from war is like foreseeing rain from storm clouds. No doubt she has predicted a wound for your son as well, and yet you know from his last letter that he is well."

"No wound for him, she said, though she foresaw danger will follow him home." Jacques sounded troubled.

"Indeed?" Justin laughed. "I pray that she is wrong, but then if she is right there is all the more reason for me to leave for Paris."

"Do not make light of this, Justin. Paris she saw awash in blood, the cobblestones running with blood. She saw Huguenots dying, men and women and children; she saw babes run through with swords and then tossed into the Seine."

"There has been a war, Jacques, and thoughts of death would be much on her mind. Let not the fears of an old woman trouble you so."

"She has rarely been wrong in her predictions."

"It is my experience that with seers and astrologers alike the close predictions are remembered, the mistaken ones forgotten. It is this benevolence of memory that makes prophets of them, nothing more."

"For your sake, and your wife's, I hope you are right."

"My wife . . . I would prefer, Jacques, that she not be told of this plan of mine to go to Paris," Justin said, and Kat clenched her hands into fists. "It would cause needless trouble. I will not tell her until we have left Bayonne."

"As you wish," Jacques said doubtfully. "Yet if you believe she would not wish to have you go to Paris—"

"It is more that I fear she would not accompany me willingly."

"Ah. Then perhaps you could leave her here with us?"

Kat shut her eyes tight, praying that Justin would agree. 'Twould be simple, once he was gone, to convince the Charrons to send her back to England.

"No. I would not wish to trouble you."

"But—"

"She gave me little choice but to bring her with me on this journey, and though I regret that she has found travel less to her liking than she had once believed it would be, I cannot leave her with my friends while I complete my business in France. I would not wish to have no choice but to sail back to Bayonne after I have left Paris."

"We could arrange passage back to England for her, so she would arrive home near the time that you returned."

"No. I am sorry if I seem ungrateful for your offer, but I must have her with me. It is no longer honeymoon with us, but she is still my wife, and I would miss her company. And I would fain have her see Paris."

"Very well. You said you will be leaving soon. How soon?"

"In a week or two. I would not have my servants stay too long in Bayonne, lest, with too much idle time, they begin to keep company with the wrong sort of men."

"Smugglers? Ah, but even if your men do not know Bayonne, they will be safe enough if they frequent only the most reputable inns and taverns, and avoid those known to be dishonest."

"Such as Le Dauphin Sautant?"

"The very worst of a bad lot. The lowest sink of Bayonne, for all its fair appearance to the innocent eye. I trust you have warned your men against it."

"I have, though one would perforce go see the sign, once he had heard of it and been told it was like yet not like a leaping dolphin he had carved. Now let us talk of more pleasant matters. Would you sell me the horse you let me ride this morning?"

Kat had dug her nails into her palms until pain flared. Now she relaxed her hands and stared down at the red marks the nails had left. *I would miss her company*, Justin had said. 'Sblood! The Devil himself could not outlie him. She rubbed her palms until the marks disappeared, listening idly while the Seigneur de Monteronne and Justin talked of the fine horse Jacques had bought a few days ago. It seemed to her that Justin was not truly interested in buying the steed, but had mentioned it only to change the subject from his plans to go to Paris. As like as not, he would say no more of them, so there was no reason for her to eavesdrop any longer. She took a deep breath to calm herself, then approached the door of the library, her steps deliberately heavy so they would hear her.

"Katherine! My lovely child! Come in!"

The Seigneur de Monteronne was a florid-faced, stocky man of medium height. Until two weeks ago his arm had been in a sling while he recovered from a sword wound that had fractured the bone, and he still moved that arm stiffly. The injury—received during the battle of Arnay-le-Duc in June—along with the resumption of peace talks, had led to his commander's decision to send him home to recuperate.

She smiled now as the baron took her hand and escorted her to a window seat, then sat down beside her. Justin, who had stood when she entered the room, now seated himself again in a high-backed chair he had pulled up to the window, which overlooked gardens and a sparkling, trout-filled stream beyond. The dense woods that covered most of the foothills around Monteronne formed a shadowy wall beyond the stream, with only the tops of the trees catching the sunlight to show a brilliant green.

"Your dress, madame, the color—it is my favorite!" Jacques told her. "I am reminded—" He broke off, shrugging. "I am reminded that I am becoming an old man who lives too much in the past."

"You are far from old, monsieur. But please you, do not let me interrupt your conversation. Did I hear you speaking of riding when I came in?"

"*Oui*, Katherine. Your husband is well enough to ride now without tiring himself. Perhaps even well enough to hunt?" he said, looking toward Justin.

"In sooth, I believe I am."

"Then I will have my huntsman locate a stag to be our quarry." He turned again to Kat. "Would you like that, madame? Would you like to learn how we hunt in France?"

"*Oui*, monsieur." She got up and went to a bookshelf across the room, returning to his side with a book bound in gold-embroidered brown velvet. "Madame Gabrielle lent me this book."

"*La venerie*," the seigneur said, taking the book from her. "Gabrielle gave this to me several years ago, soon after it was first published. Have you read it?" he asked, and when Kat nodded: "Good. But we must have a hunting costume made for you! Will you have it sewn of green cloth? Monsieur du Fouilloux"—he tapped the book with a finger—"does not believe it necessary to wear the traditional green while hunting the stag, but on this one point I will dispute with him."

"Green will suit me. And thank you, monsieur. You and your lady wife are most generous."

The seigneur took a watch from his doublet pocket. "I am late for

an appointment with my steward now. These household accounts . . ."
He sighed and rolled his eyes, to Kat's amusement. She had heard from
Marie that despite his complaints about his duties at Monteronne, the
baron preferred life here to either battlefield or court. While he had
been away, letters had arrived every few days, needlessly reminding his
well-trained servants to tend the dovecote, shear the sheep, weed the
wheat and barley—in short, to do all the things that they would have
known should be done, even if they had not had Gabrielle de Charron
to oversee them. He had been delighted to be back at Monteronne in
time to oversee the harvesting of the wheat, which he had insisted on
doing in spite of his doctors' recommendations that he rest. How very
much like her father, Kat thought fondly, smiling up at him as he said,
"You must excuse me. I will see you at dinner." He left then, after
kissing Kat's hand.

For some moments after Jacques had gone, Kat remained in the
window seat, staring at Justin. Had Jacques left so hastily in order to
force them to talk to each other? *It is no longer honeymoon with us.* How
foolish of Justin to make such a statement to his host! Now that the
matter was out in the open, the seigneur—unless she misjudged him
completely—would think it his duty as Justin's friend and hers to help
effect a reconciliation. She sighed at the thought, then rose and started
toward the door, but as she passed Justin, he reached out and seized her
by the wrist.

"One moment, lady," he said softly.

She looked down. His eyes were a cold, hard gray in this light.
"Yes, my lord?"

"It is my hope that your reading taught you enough of the hunt
that you do not disgrace yourself, or me. 'Twoud be awkward for you if
it became too clear that the only venery you are familiar with is practiced in a bed rather than a wood."

Kat wrenched her arm free. "Indeed, my lord? You would do better
to address such remarks to a mirror, seeing that they befit you better
than myself. And who would know better than you," she demanded,
"how innocent I once was of bedchamber venery?"

"Kat—"

"You need not fear I will disgrace you," she said, and stalked out.

The next afternoon, Kat kept to the sanctuary of her bedchamber, having pleaded weariness as an excuse not to go riding with Justin and
Jacques earlier. She had guessed that Jacques would find some pretext
for leaving them alone again. She had heard Jacques's voice half an
hour ago, so they must have returned from riding, but still she stayed
in her room. Gabrielle had joined her husband in this campaign to

reconcile Kat and Justin, too, insisting yesterday that both agree on her
plans for Kat's new riding costume—for she knew that Justin would want
his wife to look as lovely as possible, she explained, and Kat would want
to please him . . . Kat groaned at the memory.

Would that she dared confide in the Charrons, telling them honestly who she was—aye, and telling them, too, what Justin was. She was
moved by their generosity and kindness, and she feared what Justin's
base plottings might do to them someday.

She had racked her brains, but had been unable to think of any
explanation for Justin going to Paris, other than to find support there
for the Catholic cause in England. The peace of St. Germain was no
guarantor of peace with England—on the contrary, it left the French
king free to consider wars on soil other than his own. And if the pope
lamented the accord with the Huguenots, what better way to appease
him than with some plot aimed at his enemy Elizabeth?

And with England secured once again for the Catholic faith, her
treasury closed to the Huguenots whom Queen Elizabeth had aided,
what hope would there be for the Protestant cause in France, once the
peace accord was broken?

Her heart ached for the Charrons, especially Gabrielle. Unlike herself, they had not been foolish enough to find themselves drawn to
Justin despite the suspicion—warranted, if not yet proven—that he was
a traitor. They believed Justin to be an honest gentleman, a true friend.
How deeply they would be wounded when they learned what he truly
was . . .

Gradually she became aware of sounds from downstairs, voices raised
in excitement. She left her bedchamber and hurried toward the stairs,
her own worries driven away for the moment by curiosity. It sounded
as though everyone in the household were trying to talk at once. What
could have caused such a hubbub? she wondered. Then, as she reached
the top of the stairs, she heard someone call the name "Michel" and
she understood.

The Charrons' son had returned home.

He was in the hall, the center of a milling crowd. Gabrielle was
clinging to his arm, while Jacques stood beside them, a broad grin on
his face. Kat had thought her knowledge of French excellent, but she
could not keep up with the rapid flow of questions and answers she
heard as she slowly descended the stairs and walked toward the Charrons. The servants moved aside to let her through, but she stopped when
she was still several feet away, suddenly shy, not certain she should
interrupt this reunion.

Then Gabrielle spotted her and drew her forward.

"Michel, this is Katherine Lisle."

Michel swept his elegant cap off his head and bowed low over her hand as he greeted her. He was a slender youth not much taller than Kat, and only a few years older; he reminded her of Nick's friends, and she smiled at him warmly. His own smile was dazzling. He had a heart-shaped face and dimples and dark hair; with his slight build, he resembled his mother much more than Jacques.

"Mademoiselle Lisle?" he said, a puzzled look on his face.

"Madame, not mademoiselle," Justin said, and Kat started: she had not heard him come up behind her. Now he set his hand on her shoulder. "You have had the honor of meeting my wife."

"Justin!" Michel cried, seizing the Englishman's hands in his own. "I am happy beyond measure to see you here. How many years has it been since we last met? Five? Six?" He looked at Kat again. "Your husband is a master of fence. I was but sixteen when he was last in France, a pompous age—"

"You were a very peacock," Justin agreed, and Kat thought she saw Michel's smile falter for a moment; then he laughed.

"*Oui.* I cannot deny it. I thought I knew everything there was to know of fighting with a rapier, but Justin cut my pride down to nothing—"

"Did he, i'faith?" Kat murmured, and Michel stared at her in surprise.

"But then he built my son's pride up again," Jacques said quickly. "He taught him lessons in swordsmanship that his Italian master of fence had neglected."

Michel nodded. "*Par ma foi,* I was so much better a swordsman that I would have been even more of a peacock, had your husband not already taught me the folly of such vanity." He looked rueful.

"And now I warrant you could best me in a duel," Justin said. "Certainly you have had practice enough in the war just past. You must tell me of the battles."

Michel smiled again, and Kat was unhappily reminded of the sailors who had responded in like manner to Lord Harwood's comments, flattered by any attention he paid them. Likely he would answer any question Justin asked, tell him anything—even those bits of information that would be of value to the Huguenots' enemies.

Michel must have noticed her frown, for he gazed at her wonderingly. He looked as though he were about to say something to her, and then Kat felt Justin's hand tighten on her shoulder an instant before he said, "Jacques has told me you were at St. Germain. Will you tell me about it?"

And a torrent of words was unleashed.

———

Michel was still talking eagerly at supper, anxious to tell them every-thing—or so it seemed to Kat—about his adventures in Coligny's service these last few years. Sometimes, to her dismay, he would begin to say too much of the Huguenot forces' weaknesses and strengths, and at those times Kat, fearful of Justin hearing too many secrets, would ask him again about the Admiral.

Michel could not praise Coligny too highly. To Kat it seemed that the young soldier all but worshiped the Admiral, whose followers still called him by the title given him by King Henri II, who had made him Admiral of France before his capture at the battle of St. Quentin and the imprisonment that had led him to Calvin's writings and his con-version to the Protestant faith. Michel was insistent that Kat realize that Coligny could in no way have been responsible for the assassination of François, Duc de Guise, in 1563, as the Guises claimed—saying he had hired the assassin—and continued to claim even after the king's council found Coligny innocent. Kat, amused by Michel's defense of his hero, was laughing as she assured him again and again that she could never have believed the Huguenot leader guilty of such a crime. In truth she did believe Michel, for she remembered what Blanche Gardiner had told her in London of Coligny's sense of honor, his religious zeal, his austerity and bluntness. But it amused her even more when Michel began to imply that only supernatural forces—God's intervention on behalf of his lieutenant on Earth—had saved Coligny from the attempts on his life: the hiring by the Cardinal of Lorraine of fifty Italians who were paid one thousand crowns each to poison the Admiral and the Prince of Condé; and the more open attempt by Catherine de Medici and her son, King Charles, who less than a year ago had had Coligny condemned to death by the Parliament of Paris and had executed a straw effigy of the Admiral, then offered a reward of ten thousand écus for his capture alive or two thousand écus for his assassination.

Michel had news of the court, too, for he had been in Paris before leaving for Monteronne—an admission that made his father grimace and Justin smile. He had seen old friends, many of them Catholic, and he seemed so glad to have been able to enjoy their company once more that Kat wondered if, for all his zeal and his devotion to the Admiral, the war just past had not been little more than a game to Michel—a tournament, a mock battle to be fought honorably but then forgotten, as if the differences that inspired the war vanished once the treaty was signed. She saw a troubled look on Gabrielle's face that became more intense when Michel spoke of a young woman he had seen in Paris.

"Isobel de Maisse?" Gabrielle asked sharply. "The daughter of the Seigneur de La Ferriere?" Michel nodded. "Is she not one of the Flying Squadron?"

The Flying Squadron. *L'Escadron Volant.* Now Kat understood that sharp tone: she had heard of the Flying Squadron from Nick and his friends.

L'Escadron Volant was the name given to the band of aristocratic young women who were Catherine de Medici's most subtle and dangerous agents—intelligencers, seducers, corrupters. They included the queen mother's maids of honor, but *honor,* Kat thought, was not a word that suited them. They were Catherine de Medici's most effective weapons, much more efficient than Italian poisoners or paid assassins. Jeanne d'Albret, the Queen of Navarre, might now be celebrating the concessions made to the Huguenots by the Treaty of St. Germain, but Kat doubted she would ever forget that her husband, Antoine de Bourbon, an apostate who had abandoned the Huguenot cause, had, after being wounded in the siege of the Protestant stronghold of Rouen, died in the arms of Isabelle de Rouet, *la belle* Rouet, the member of the Flying Squadron whom Catherine had assigned to watch him and make certain he did not switch his allegiance again.

"Perhaps she is," Michel admitted, "but you need not fear that the Medici woman will use her against me. I am not important enough to interest her," he concluded, sounding so wistful that Kat had to suppress a smile.

"That is a great comfort to me," Gabrielle said dryly, and the talk turned to other matters—inevitably, the matter of hunting.

Michel seemed pleased with the plans for a hunt, especially when he learned that Kat would join them.

"Do you enjoy hawking as well, madame?"

"Even more, in truth."

"Then we must go hawking while you are here."

"Thank you, monsieur, but the hawks are molting now." She was unable to keep a slight tone of regret from her voice. Jacques had shown her the mews, of which he was proud; he was also—and justly—proud of his fine collection of hawks and falcons. The birds were fat and torpid now, during molting, but Kat's experienced eye had recognized their quality. She had especially admired a magnificent female Greenland falcon, more than two feet in length, which must have cost Jacques a prince's ransom.

"Then you must stay until the molting season is over." He looked from Kat to Justin. "Will you stay that long?"

"I cannot say," Justin told him.

"But surely you would not wish to disappoint your wife?" Michel said.

Justin put his hand over Kat's. "My wife has not yet been disappointed by me. Have you, sweeting?"

"Never," Kat replied in a low voice, but she had hesitated before answering, and she kept her gaze directed downward. Justin's hand tightened around hers as he waited for her to say more, but she kept silent, not raising her eyes again until the conversation had resumed, with Jacques telling Gabrielle about the price Justin had offered for his horse that morning. As Kat looked up, her eyes met Michel's; his held puzzlement and sympathy. He offered her a shy smile, leagues apart from the dazzling, court-polished smile she had seen when they met, and much more moving.

Kat was not surprised when, the next day, Michel offered to show her around the manor, and she accepted at once. Perchance it would be easier to confide her suspicions about Justin to Michel than to his parents. And even if she could not confide unreservedly in him, he could be a valuable ally.

In early afternoon they were in the mews. They made a tour of the several molting chambers, and Michel took two pairs of hawking gloves and handled each of the fat, sluggish birds, allowing her to handle the best-behaved of the lot, including the Greenland falcon she admired so much. Kat would have gladly spent the rest of the day here, in these clean, warm, dry rooms. Monteronne's falconer was as conscientious as his mistress, and Michel was unstinting in his praise, pointing out the tiny braziers that were ready to be used to drive away chill and damp when necessary; the clean dry sand, nearly two inches deep, covering the floor; the baths whose water was changed several times a day; the fat geese and quail that formed the rich diet for the molting hawks.

Michel led her back to the small room containing the hawks' furnishings—the hoods and varvels and jesses, the bells and lures and gloves. "I have thought sometimes," he said, "that were I not heir to this, were I forced to choose some other station in life, then I would as lief be the falconer as anything else."

"I have felt the same way at times," Kat said, as she watched him put the hawking gloves away, "when I was younger . . ." She smiled a bit wistfully at the memory. How often she and Nick had envied the falconer and head groom and kennel master! To spend all day with the hawks and horses and dogs they loved, untroubled by tutors who found more joy in Latin grammar, had then seemed a better, more carefree, life. No need to trouble yourself, if you were a falconer or groom, with thoughts of war or policy or creeds . . .

She shook her head slightly, as if to throw off the melancholy that threatened to settle over her, and reached out to touch a gorgeous hood of black leather with gold braces. The hood was trimmed with gold lace and crowned with a small tuft of white feathers.

"For the Greenland falcon?" she asked, though already sure, from the hood's size and magnificence, that it could be for no other.

"*Oui*," Michel replied. "I hope that you will be here long enough that you may fly her."

"I think not," Kat murmured. The falcon was in the last stage of molting, having just lost the beam feathers, the longest feathers in the wings. It could fly now, and had been fluttering from side to side of the molting room when they entered, but it would fly much better when those feathers had grown in. And by the time that had happened, and the falcon's weight was reduced to the point where there was no risk that, when flown, it would be disinterested in food and would rake away or take up a perch in a tree, she would no longer be here. "My lord has not said for certain, but I believe we will be leaving soon. Perhaps in a week."

"A week!" His open astonishment assured Kat that Michel was not privy to Justin's plans. "Could you not convince him to stay longer, madame?"

"I fear that my wishes count for little with him," she said softly.

Michel looked as though he wanted to ask her about that, but he said nothing. Mayhap, she thought, he still hesitated to say anything against a man who was an old and trusted friend of his family. But there was a solemn, contemplative look on his face as they left the room to walk back to the chateau. Michel was silent, and so was Kat, again brooding over the fears that had plagued her since learning of Justin's plans to go to Paris. She was so lost in thought that she failed to notice Justin approaching them.

"Faith, you both look melancholy! Michel, I hope that my wife has not been begging you to show her your hawks."

"It was I, sir, who offered to show her the mews," Michel said hotly, before Kat could respond.

Justin raised an eyebrow. "Indeed?"

"I wished to see more of the manor," Kat said quickly.

"You could have seen all of it yesterday, sweeting, had you gone riding with me," he said, taking her hand as they climbed the steps to the house.

"There you are!" Gabrielle said as they entered the hall. "The sempsters are almost finished, Kat, and would have you try on your hunting costume now."

Kat was glad of the chance to escape, but ten minutes later, through with fitting the green velvet coat and safeguard, she returned to the hall, looking for Michel. Worry seized her when a servant said that Michel had gone back outside and was talking with Lord Harwood. She feared Justin's ill humor would lead him to warn Michel away from her

. . . and Michel would no more accept such a warning than Nick would, under similar circumstances.

They were not in sight, but she saw that the door to the mews was open. As she stepped inside the door, she heard their voices, and sighed with relief. Justin was merely asking Michel about the Greenland falcon; she would not have to intervene to prevent a quarrel. She was about to start back to the house when Justin spoke again, a different tone to his voice than before.

"You said nothing yesternight of any talk at court about war with England. Of certain, some of the Guisards must wish for it."

"They are out of favor for the moment."

"Yea, but only for the moment . . . and if Mary Queen of Scots were to be crowned Queen of England, with the help of her brother-in-law the King of France as well as her uncle and cousin, then they might need never fear to fall into disfavor again."

"Mayhap."

"And are there not others besides the Guisards who might urge the king to send his armies against England? Monsieur de Salvandy, for one? His daughter, for another? Yea, so I thought . . . And what of Monsieur de Marchant?"

"Marchant?" Michel asked, and Kat held her breath. Marchant. 'Twas the same name as that signed to one of the letters Justin's cousin had received, the letter recommending someone other than Justin for the work they had planned . . .

"Would he not wish to fight battles on English soil?"

Michel exploded with laughter. "Pierre de Marchant?" he said at last, his voice shaky. "A soldier? Never. Never."

"So he feels no ill will toward Elizabeth? He would not rather see Mary Stuart on England's throne?"

"He hates Elizabeth . . . or so I am told . . . but that was gossip . . . They say—"

"Madame, may I help you?" the falconer said, and Kat jumped. She had not heard him approach from outside.

Michel had stopped talking. He must have heard the falconer.

"Is my husband here?" she asked, a bit loudly. "I was told that he and Michel had come out here."

"Aye, sweeting, we are here," Justin called, and in a few moments he and Michel emerged from the interior rooms.

"I thought that perchance we might ride around the manor this afternoon," she told him. She had no wish to spend more time in his company, but could think of no other reason she could give for having been looking for him.

"As you like." Justin said, and she realized that he had no particular desire for her company now, either. Had he sought her out earlier only to keep her away from Michel?

"Shall I come with you?" Michel asked, and Kat quickly told him she would like that. She ignored Justin's angry glance and started back toward the house, the two men beside her. She would need to change to her old doublet and hose, she explained, but she would meet them in the courtyard in a few minutes . . .

They were in the hall dividing the ground floor of the manor house when they heard a commotion from the courtyard: hooves clattering on stone, dogs barking, servants calling out. Gabrielle heard the noise, too, and ran into the hall. She hurried with them to the doorway opening onto the courtyard, where they stopped at the top of the steps.

Several riders were there, two of them leading packhorses. All but two of the riders were men—servants, to judge by their clothes, which were dusty and sweat-stained. They looked haggard and travel-weary, as did one of the women, who also seemed to be a servant. By contrast, the other woman seemed exquisitely composed and was garbed as elegantly, in a costume of azure silk, as if she had just set out on a ride.

As Kat watched, the woman straightened her cloak, then at last raised her head to reveal, beneath a pretty velvet hat sporting white ostrich plumes, a pale oval face with large dark eyes and delicate features, a face so perfect, so serene, seemingly so untouched by any mortal feelings, that it would have served even the least-inspired picture-maker as a model for an angel.

"Isobel!" Michel whispered, then plunged down the steps, calling out, "Mademoiselle de Maisse! Mademoiselle!"

Kat heard Gabrielle's sharp intake of breath, but it was Justin she turned to look at first, for, incredibly, he was laughing, very quietly.

"Voilà!" he said, in a soft, chillingly light voice. "L'Escadron Volant est arrivé!"

CHAPTER 35

Gabrielle had planned an especially fine supper, for Michel had arrived so late the previous afternoon that there had been no time to prepare any of his favorite foods. Now, alas, Mademoiselle de Maisse joined them to feast on salad, *ragout* of venison, roast partridges basted with sweet butter and herbs, asparagus, pheasant *fricassée*, artichokes, *pâté de foie gras*, roast pheasant with chestnut stuffing, and tarts made with the last of the season's late-ripening strawberries. The men were so distracted by Isobel's beauty that none of them thought to compliment the baroness on the meal. Ironically, it was Isobel who paid her hostess one compliment after another, saying she had never had a better supper, even at court. The compliments seemed to torture Gabrielle, who perforce had to thank her unwelcome guest.

Unwelcome but, shame to say, not uninvited.

Michel had told Isobel in Paris that she would like Monteronne, and invited her to come visit him if she were ever near Bayonne. Kat doubted he had believed she would ever accept the invitation. Never, she felt, would he have dreamed that Isobel would leave Paris two days after he did, traveling by coach on the King's Highway to Orléans before buying horses to ride for the remainder of the journey. She had traveled swiftly: had Michel stayed another day with the friends he had stopped to visit in Bordeaux, she would have reached Monteronne before he did. And *that*, Kat thought, would have been some scene to witness: what would Gabrielle de Charron have done if one of *L'Escadron Volant* had alighted in her courtyard and Michel had not been here to confess that he had invited her? Bid her fly away again? Very like. Even after observing Michel's delight at Isobel's arrival, the baroness had considered sending the girl away, and only Jacques's plea for caution and tolerance had stopped her. With the ink scarcely dry on the Treaty of St. Germain, he had argued, was it wise to insult one of the queen mother's maids of honor? *Infinitely wiser than to welcome her into our home*, Gabrielle had replied, but she had nevertheless gone to greet Mademoiselle de Maisse and assure her that she was welcome at Monteronne.

"We planned a hunt for tomorrow," Michel told Isobel. He spoke in English, for Isobel had insisted on using that tongue once she learned that the Charrons' other guests were English. "But I fear your journey may have left you too weary to consider such sport for a few days." He looked at his father. "Could we postpone the hunt?"

"Of course," Jacques said at once, and Kat shook her head a little in disbelief. Jacques already had his huntsmen searching the oak forests near Monteronne for spoor of large stags. Gabrielle looked at her husband with disappointment, then sighed and went back to eating.

"*Merci*," Isobel said, then, after a glance at Justin, continued in English, slowly, "Thank you, but I am certain a good night's sleep will refresh me, so I may join your hunt tomorrow."

She smiled prettily while Jacques and Michel praised her spirit, then turned to Justin. "Will you be joining us, monsieur?"

"*Oui*, mademoiselle, my wife and I will."

Isobel glanced fleetingly at Kat, then returned her attention to Justin. "Good. I wonder, monsieur . . . does the English hunt differ from the French?"

"Do you make a study of venery, mademoiselle?" Kat asked suddenly.

Justin seemed to wince, and the Charrons were very still—Michel looking as though he had just discovered a bone in the bit of meat he was chewing—but Isobel appeared unaware of the *double entendement*. In the face of her lack of suspicion, Kat felt somewhat ashamed.

"*Oui*, madam," Isobel said. "Do not English ladies study *la venerie?*"

Kat was nonplussed. By the mass, had Isobel actually understood her gibe?

"In sooth, on that subject, most are ignorant indeed compared to some ladies of France," Justin said.

Isobel looked blank for several seconds, then, apparently deciding to accept Justin's words as a compliment, she bestowed a gracious smile on Justin.

"Of course," he went on, "there is more to English gentlewomen's lives than venery."

Isobel's smile faltered. "Is that not true for everyone?"

What sort of game was this? Kat wondered. She had thought Justin's remark about ignorance an insult aimed at her, but now it almost seemed that he was launching a subtle attack on Mademoiselle de Maisse. Michel seemed to think so, too, judging from the look of outrage on his face.

"*Par Dieu*, there is much more to life than hunting," Michel said, staring challengingly at Justin, "and we have had enough talk of venery. Let us speak instead of fencing. *Mon ami*, you once proved yourself more than my equal, but that, as you yourself confessed, was years ago. Would you try your skill against mine again, tonight?"

Jacques had hired musicians from the village to play for them after supper, but now he bade them wait, and the hall was cleared and the floor swept clean of rushes to provide surer footing for the fencers. Michel went upstairs and came back with a pair of blunt foils, which Justin inspected and pronounced satisfactory.

Without further ceremony, the match began.

Kat was amazed by the speed with which Justin and Michel thrust and parried. She had never seen Nick fence with any of his friends. Years ago she had watched him fence with their father, but that had been with heavy longswords and bucklers, not light, quick rapiers. She had thought that she had learned to strike quickly during her practices with Nick, but now she realized that he must needs have held back, slowing his movements to suit with hers, for their practices had been but limping pavanes to this coranto. Before her thick brain could recognize a blow or thrust and think how it should be parried, the parry had been accomplished and another blow struck.

They were well matched, Justin and Michel, she thought, for as they moved back and forth the length of the hall, neither seemed to gain an advantage over the other. Their duel was an elegant dance that would have been deadly if their swords had not been dull-edged and button-tipped. Yet Michel might have an advantage, for while Justin looked grim, the younger man smiled, elated at now finding himself the equal of the man who had beaten him years ago. As the two came closer to the end of the hall where Kat was standing with Mademoiselle de Maisse and Jacques and Gabrielle, Michel glanced toward them, his smile widening—

—and then vanishing, as the button on Justin's foil pressed against his shirt over his heart.

"Time enough to seek applause," Justin said, loudly enough for all to hear, "when you have won."

"Another match?"

"If you wish."

And now Kat saw that both swordsmen could move even faster, for Michel attacked with lightning speed, and Justin fell back beneath a rain of blows, seeming to fear the younger man, until without warning Michel's foil was caught by Justin's and wrenched free of his grasp. Michel seemed stunned to find himself of a sudden weaponless. He stared mutely at the Englishman.

"Another lesson," Justin said, laughing breathlessly, "on care triumphant over carelessness. Stay on guard. Ware security."

"Were you hired as my tutor?" Michel asked.

"D'you still need one?"

Michel did not reply. He took the foils back to his room, and it was ten minutes or more before he returned. The musicians were playing by then, but no one felt like dancing, and half an hour later Jacques paid the musicians and sent them away, and they all went to bed early.

Kat was nearly asleep before it struck her that Justin's lesson for Michel—*Ware security*—was little different from what Nick had told her Francis Walsingham had said. How ironic, she thought, and then, a moment later, decided that perhaps it was not ironic after all . . . for who would be more of a danger to Walsingham and the prince he guarded than a man of his own mind?

"And this bitch, too, is of Souillard's lineage," Jacques de Charron said, patting the head of a white hound, and Kat dutifully praised the dog. Her host was proud that two of his fine pack of hounds were descended from King Louis XII's favorite hunting dog. She trailed after Jacques as he made his way across the clearing, watching the kennel master and his assistants tend the dogs, petting and calming the hounds and treating the bloodhounds' noses with vinegar so their sense of smell would be keener.

The hunt would begin soon: the head huntsman had found a trail he liked, with fresh large tracks revealing a hollowed-out hoof. It would be a good-sized stag—larger, perhaps, than any Kat had ever hunted at Beechwood. Yet her excitement about the hunt had been dissipated by seeing Justin and Isobel in close conversation on the other side of the clearing, and she had made her way towards them, taking advantage of Jacques's eagerness to show off his fine pack of hunting dogs, tawny and white alike.

Now the huntsman came up to Jacques, carrying fresh dung that had been found along the trail and brought back for his inspection. Kat excused herself and moved away, closer to Justin and Isobel, who stood some twenty feet away, gazing out into the forest as they talked.

She could hear only snatches of their conversation over the noise of the people and dogs behind her, but what she heard was enough to tell her that Justin was asking Isobel much the same question that he had asked Michel: which nobles at the court would urge the king to war against England? Kat edged closer, desperate to hear the reply.

"I would not know, my lord," Isobel said. "Who would reveal their thoughts on such matters to me?"

Likely anyone the queen mother set you after, Kat thought, torn between frustration at the demoiselle's evasive answer and amusement at the realization that Justin must be feeling similar frustration.

"I warrant you, few men would withhold anything from you," Justin responded, taking her hand in his.

Kat felt stabbed by jealousy of a sudden. 'Twas foolish, she knew. Justin merely sought to learn more of the French court from Isobel. Aye, and was it not better for her that he was now asking questions of Isobel instead? Still, she felt stricken.

She turned around, hearing someone approach, and her feelings must have shown on her face, for Michel glanced over her shoulder for a moment, then looked at her with pity. "Your husband has become a rogue and a knave," he said quietly, then, raising his voice, told Justin and Isobel that the hunt was about to begin.

Kat loved to hunt, to ride at breakneck speed through a forest, the baying of the hounds a joyous music to her ears—finest still when the dogs had, like these, been chosen as carefully for their voices as for their speed and strength and skill. Her fears and worries fell away, and for a time she felt as carefree as when she was a child, hunting in the beech woods near her home in the company of her father and Nick and Edward Neale. The sun was high, sending shafts of light down between the branches, piercing the forest's shadow even where the trees grew thickest, so the green-clad riders ahead of her were now limned by the sun, now shaded and almost invisible against the dark green leaves about them. Both Justin and Isobel were well ahead of her, sometimes out of sight, and Kat put all thought of them from her mind as her gray palfrey followed Michel's dappled gelding in pursuit of the stag.

Their quarry was nearly as clever as a hare, running through streams and once through a flock of sheep to confuse the dogs, but those stratagems caused only brief delays before the chase began again. There was a longer, anxious wait when the huntsman had to call the dogs back; the stag they had been pursuing since dinner had followed the trail of another stag, a smaller one, abandoning the other deer's path at the edge of a brook, and only the huntsman's keen eyes had let them catch their mistake before they wasted all their energy on a lesser quarry. As it was, they had to retrace their path a few hundred yards, then wait while the bloodhounds sniffed up and down the banks of the brook. Kat was near enough to Justin to overhear his conversation with Mademoiselle de Maisse, but all they spoke of—all anyone spoke of, while they waited—was the hunt.

Then the cry was taken up again, and the pack was off, the riders close behind them.

Soon they were closing in on the stag; Kat caught glimpses of it far ahead, between the trees. It was a splendid animal, with at least a dozen tines to its antlers. Spotting a low branch ahead, Kat ducked to one side, and just then her horse stumbled. Caught off balance, she was thrown from the sidesaddle.

Her fall was broken by a bush, which saved her from serious injury, but the twigs scratched her face. She was still trembling with shock, swearing at the branches that snapped off in her gloved hands as she tried to pull herself up, when Michel rode up, swung down from his mount and ran over to assist her.

"Are you hurt?"

"Only in pride," she said, but was grateful as he pulled her free of the brambles and helped her to her feet. She leaned against him for a few moments, then, aware that a servant had followed Michel and was watching them, she straightened and took a step away from him.

"The mare," she said. "I must see to it."

She went over to where the palfrey waited, twenty feet away, its reins caught on a branch. The mare did not seem to be lame, so she could ride it back to Monteronne, but she was not certain she could gallop it again. Michel sent the servant away, telling him to rejoin the hunt; they would rest here for a time.

He offered her a drink from a flagon of wine. The sounds of the hunt were distant now; they would never catch up, even if Kat's horse were sound. She was beginning to feel sorry for herself—and sorry, too, that her fall had made Michel drop out of the hunt—when they heard the huntsman's horn sounding death for the stag. The hunt was over.

It was warm beneath the trees, the branches keeping the light breeze from them. Kat unbuttoned her coat, then removed it; a few moments later she took off her safeguard, too. Beneath the velvet outer garb, she had worn a silk kirtle with cypress sleeves that she would have to be careful not to snag, but she was too glad to feel cool at last to worry overmuch that her clothes were unsuited for this place. Michel took off his green taffeta doublet and draped it over an exposed tree root to make a rude chair for her, and she sat down. She patted the space beside her, and a moment later he sat down, too, and they drank some more of the wine.

Had they started dismembering the stag yet? she wondered. She felt no need to be there. The aftermath of a hunt always saddened her, as the stag was cut apart, its organs given to the dogs. She would never give up hunting: it was good sport, and she liked venison for her table. But she respected her quarry—especially a cunning stag like this one— enough to mourn its death a little.

She proposed a toast to the stag, and they drank. Michel proposed another, and they drank again. He began to invent a sonnet in the stag's honor, a sonnet so outrageously bad that she laughed until she felt weak. She was leaning against his shoulder, shaking with laughter, when she heard riders approach and looked up to see Justin, leading a bay that she remembered one of the servants had been riding. Behind him was Isobel.

He stared at Kat and Michel for some moments without saying a word, then: "Cry you mercy, lady, if I have interrupted your dalliance. I was told your horse might be lame, and thought that the reason why you were not with us, but now"—he glanced at the safeguard and coat Kat had removed—"I see that I was wrong." He looped the bay's reins around a branch, then wheeled his horse and rode off. A few moments later, Isobel followed him.

Kat got up and smoothed her half-kirtle. "A plague on him," she muttered. Michel helped her to don her overgarments again, and then they rode back to Monteronne, Kat mounted on the bay, Michel leading the gray mare.

Isobel de Maisse stretched languorously as she stood before the fire, its warmth drying the last traces of water that she had missed with the towel. A sweet scent mingling herbs and perfumed soap hung in the air; the water in the tub was still steaming, since her maid had brought more buckets of hot water to add to it while Isobel indulged in a long bath.

Isobel wondered if Lady Harwood had also spent the time before supper soaking in a hot bath. No doubt she was bruised from her fall. Lord Harwood had seemed more annoyed than concerned when told of his wife's fall, and Isobel was sure that her own skills as a horsewoman had appeared better yet by comparison with the Englishwoman's clumsiness. The queen mother, who loved to ride and hunt, insisted that the ladies of *L'Escadron Volant* be excellent horsewomen, and Isobel was glad of that now.

The queen mother. Isobel grimaced as she thought of Catherine de Medici. That coarse old woman, daughter of Lorenzo de Medici, the Duke of Urbino, heir of an Italian family that had accumulated sufficient wealth and power as merchants and bankers to become rulers of Florence. The old nobility held her in disdain: *the banker's daughter*, Mary Stuart had called her, or *the Florentine*, overlooking the fact that Catherine's mother, Madeleine de la Tour d'Auvergne, was descended from the noble houses of Auvergne and Aquitaine on her father's side and the royal house of Bourbon on her mother's side. Perhaps Catherine would have been derided less if she had been a beauty, but she was stolid and plain, with bulging eyes, greasy skin, and thick lips. Only her hands were beautiful. But she made up for her natural deficiencies with charm and cunning.

For years people had underestimated Catherine de Medici. She had been humiliated in her marriage to King Henri II by Henri's celebrated affair with Diane de Poitiers; then, when Henri died, she had seen her influence with her son, François II, undermined by the Guise family. But she had been wise enough to take the reins of government into her hands when François had died, having herself appointed *gouvernante* during the minority of her son, Charles IX. And though she had sometimes come close to losing control of France since then, she had persevered. Isobel despised the Florentine as a woman, but the queen mother was her means to power, and so she would use her . . . though it meant letting herself be used for a time.

Isobel had first heard stories of *L'Escadron Volant* when she was only a child, but even then she had listened carefully. The second daughter of a seigneur who also had four sons, she knew that her hopes for an advantageous marriage rested more on her beauty than her dowry, and that she could use that beauty to its greatest advantage at court, where she could hope to find her own husband, rather than have her father choose one for her—likely a neighbor to whom the court would be anathema and who would force her to live in the country and manage his house. She decided then to become one of *L'Escadron Volant*, and paid heed to what was said of those renowned demoiselles' methods, their successes . . . and their failures. That of Isabella de Limeuil, for example.

Mademoiselle de Limeuil had once been so highly regarded by the queen mother that Catherine had sent her after no less a quarry than the Bourbon Prince Louis de Condé. It could have been as splendid a chance for the demoiselle to distinguish herself as that given *la belle* Rouet, Mademoiselle de la Limaudiere, who had seduced Condé's brother Antoine, King of Navarre. But Mademoiselle de Limeuil had foolishly fallen in love with Condé, and had either neglected to ferret out secrets from the prince or else failed to pass them on to the queen mother. Nor had the demoiselle persuaded Condé to change religions. Worse yet, she had carelessly become pregnant by her lover, only to have Condé deny the child was his. Catherine de Medici was intolerant of failure, and Mademoiselle de Limeuil had been sent away from court, to the convent of Aubonne, then later forced to marry an Italian—a merchant turned banker!—Scipion Sardini, a gentleman of the queen mother's suite who was said to be no more happy with the marriage than his wife was. Isobel de Maisse was determined not to suffer such an ignominious fate; she would never make such a huge mistake.

Nor would she want to make a lesser mistake. Catherine de Medici was likely to become violent if disappointed. Isobel had heard other maids tell of beatings, and seen the bruises that bore silent witness to the queen mother's temper. For if Catherine would spare not even her own daughter, how much less likely that she would be lenient with a maid of honor?

But now Isobel wondered if it might not be worth the risk of a beating—for bruises would heal in time—if she had a chance of returning to court with unanticipated and valuable information. Information such as the reason for an English nobleman's presence in France soon after he had been in Madrid . . .

She was still pondering what to do while she painted her face and then dressed with her maid's help in a kirtle of blue cloth-of-silver and a gown of white branched velvet figured with blue and crimson. It was while she was looking over the meager selection of jewelry she had brought with her that she reached her decision.

She had been asked by the queen mother to discover which of the Charron men, the seigneur or his son, was more vulnerable, and to seduce him. Both Jacques and Michel de Charron were trusted by Coligny, and might have knowledge of the Admiral's plans, which were still of interest to the queen mother despite the peace accord.

But what the Charrons knew, Isobel reasoned, would as like as not be known by a hundred other Huguenot nobles. She wanted more than a pat on the head for confirming what Catherine de Medici had already been told by other spies. She wanted to be able to give the Florentine news she could get from no other source, and she wanted recognition of her ability to identify the best quarry. Most of all, she did *not* want to waste her time seducing Michel de Charron, only to be scolded or beaten later should the queen mother, learning that Lord Harwood had been here, decide that Isobel had ignored an opportunity to discover some Spanish or English plot.

So it would be Justin Lisle, and not Michel de Charron or his father. And since she could not guess how much time she had, she took from the jewelry case the silver pomander the Florentine had given her.

"Marguerite," she told her maid, "bring me a glass of wine. Not the claret in that flagon—I would have Rhenish wine, if the Charrons have any."

Then, with her maid out of the bedchamber, Isobel locked the door and went to open the lid of a small mahogany chest, one of several she had brought with her. This one contained her perfumes, but she ignored them as she set her fingertip on one of the strips of fine wood inlaid in a decorative pattern on the inside of the lid. She pushed it a fraction of an inch to the right, opening a gap into which she moved a very narrow piece of wood, scarce wider than a toothpick, that without close study seemed to be part of a wider strip. Now there was room to slide another piece of wood across—and she heard a faint click. She lowered the lid, and the marquetry fell away on delicate hinges to reveal several velvet-lined niches into which stoppered glass vials had been wedged. Isobel selected one of the vials, opened it, and sniffed the fine white powder to make sure of the contents.

Then she twisted the top of her pomander, and a segment folded out into her hand. Like the other segments, this one contained a perfume, but unlike the others, here the perfume was only a thin layer next to the exterior. The center of the segment was hollow. She poured the powder into it, then pushed the segment back into place. Closing her hand over the pomander, she pressed the knob on its top. She opened her hand and looked down at a sprinkling of powder on her palm, then brushed it back into the vial, which she returned to the hidden compartment, replacing the marquetry and pushing each piece of wood back into place.

Now she was ready.

Sparrow, Kat decided, had sorely misjudged Lord Harwood. 'Twas of little use to have men like her brother spy on him. Nay, what Sparrow should have done was to find someone like Isobel de Maisse. In a trice, Justin Lisle would have been eating out of her hand, as tame as any lap dog.

As he was now.

Kat watched angrily over the top of her cards as Justin kissed the demoiselle's sugar-smeared fingers. Isobel had been feeding him sweetmeats ever since they had all come out to the garden for the banquet after supper. Kat had hoped that the fresh air would clear his head, for he seemed cup-shotten, but it had not worked. While she and the Charrons played cards, he sat with Isobel on a stone bench beside the banquet house, acting as if the others were not there, no more than twenty feet away.

'Twas fortunate, Kat thought, that she did not have a sword nearby, for she could have murdered him . . . Her eyes met Michel's for an instant, and she saw that he, too, was furious with Justin . . . though whether because Justin was neglecting her, or because Justin had stolen Isobel's attention from him—or, more like, a mix of the two—Kat could not say. Michel started to get up, but Kat put her hand on his arm, staying him. She remembered last night's mock duel too well; she would not have them fight.

It was Jacques's turn, but he seemed to have forgotten that. He looked vaguely ashamed as he glanced from Justin to Kat, and he opened his mouth to speak, but she forestalled any words of sympathy he might have offered, recalling him to the game as she gave him a brittle smile.

Not long after that, Justin and Isobel went back to the house.

Kat watched them go from the corner of her eye, scarce believing that Justin would do something so thoughtless—nay, so lunatic, rather, given his pretense of being married to her. Did he think that she—if she must needs pretend to be his wife—could overlook this dalliance completely? She prayed they would come back outside in a few moments, but they did not. Sighing, she put her cards down, excused herself, and went after him.

She was in the great hall when she saw them at the top of the stairs. Isobel was leaning against the wall, her gown pushed down her arms, and Justin was kissing her breasts.

"My lord husband!" Kat's cry seemed to echo off every wall. Justin raised his head and peered down at her. *He is cup-shotten*, she thought, and suddenly feared that he might drunkenly announce that she was not truly his wife. "My lord husband," she repeated, more softly, her gaze pleading with him to think before responding.

He straightened then, and Isobel would have fled, but he held her beside him, his arm around her neck, his hand resting between her breasts. "My lady wife."

Kat sighed with relief. Gathering her skirts, she ascended the stairway. "Get you gone, mademoiselle," she told Isobel, but Justin continued to hold on to the Frenchwoman.

"What right have you, madam—" he demanded, but she interrupted him.

"My right as your wife."

Isobel broke free then, and, clutching the front of her gown across her chest, ran down the hall to her bedchamber and slammed the door shut behind her.

Justin had watched her go; now he turned back to Kat. "Well, *wife*," he said. "Mayhap that was your right, i'faith. But what of *my* rights as your husband?"

Then, before she could flee, he caught her and slung her over his shoulder and carried her to his bedchamber.

"Whoreson!" she said when he had set her down.

He laughed. " 'Twas you who bade me remember that here you are my wife."

" 'Twas your invention, my lord, not mine. In truth, I would have as lief played the lowest servant as your wife. I am here through no choice of mine."

"No? Then whose choice was it, Kat? For I warrant you gave me none. You have plagued me since I met you. Would that I could send you away and forget you, but you have made that impossible. You troublesome wench! So you would rather play the lowest servant than my wife? By God's blood, I swear that even that would be a role too high for you, my lady vagabond. Had I not taken pity on you, you would be a jailbird now, maybe in some prison in London. And how would that suit you, my lady of Marshalsea, my lady of Bridewell?''

That was too much. She slapped him.

For some moments it seemed as though he had been turned to stone. Nor could she move, so amazed was she by what she had done.

Then he slapped her in turn, and she reeled back and fell to the floor. She sat there for a few seconds, stunned, then touched the side of her face gingerly.

"Jesu," he muttered, reaching toward her. "Kat, I—"

She gasped and flinched away, then scrambled to her feet and darted past him, out the door and down the hall to her own bedchamber, where she locked the door behind her.

It was perhaps five minutes before he came to pound on her door. Marie, who had been holding a water-soaked towel against the side of Kat's face, looked at her for direction, but Kat shook her head. At last the noise stopped, for a few moments, and then they could hear him pounding on another door. Isobel's, Kat realized. That noise soon stopped, and then she felt like crying, though she was not certain she could have said why.

Gabrielle de Charron could not sleep. She was grieving for both Justin, her friend, whom she hated to see falling under the spell cast by Isobel de Maisse, and for his young wife. Her maid had told her that servants in the kitchen had heard voices raised in argument after Katherine had returned to the chateau. Gabrielle wished now that she had asked Jacques to speak to Lord Harwood. Drunk as Justin had been, he still might have allowed an old friend like Jacques to separate him from Mademoiselle de Maisse. And it would have spared Katherine the need to confront him.

She sighed and closed her eyes, then, hearing a soft sound in the antechamber, opened them again.

Someone knocking at the door? At this hour?

She slid from the bed quietly, careful not to wake Jacques, whose light snoring continued without interruption.

In the antechamber she paused by her desk, wondering if she had imagined the sound. Then she heard it again, and went to the door and opened it.

A woman stood outside in the hall, clad in a nightgown, a veil over her face.

"Kat?"

"I pray you, let me come in."

By the time Gabrielle had lit the candle on her desk and turned back to Kat, the girl had removed her veil. Gabrielle moaned in sympathy when she saw the dark bruise around Kat's left eye.

"Your husband?"

The girl nodded. " 'Twas Isobel's doing, for she was the cause of our quarrel." She told Gabrielle what had happened, then said vehemently, "Needs must that she leave Monteronne."

Gabrielle sat down, gesturing for Kat to do the same. She was silent for perhaps a minute, then: "*Chère* Katherine. Would that I could send the demoiselle away, but what reason could I give if the queen mother asked why I offered such an insult to one of her maids of honor? What transgressions could I name?"

Kat looked astonished, then pointed to her bruised face.

"Was it Isobel's hand that caused that mark? *Non?* Then what transgression?"

"She would seduce my husband."

"Or he would seduce her. Who could prove which was the seducer?"

"She drugged his food and drink."

"Can you prove it?" Gabrielle asked, more hopeful than she had been since Isobel's arrival.

"I saw her toy with her pomander while she fed him sweetmeats, and earlier while she spoke to him at supper. Then her hand would oft reach across his cup. I trow there was some drug in the pomander, which she added to his food and wine."

Gabrielle nodded slowly. She, too, had noticed Isobel toying with the elaborate pomander, which the demoiselle had worn in masculine fashion on a chain around her neck, but she had thought nothing of it then.

"But can you prove it?" she asked again. "Would Mademoiselle de Maisse let us see her pomander and examine it? And even then, what might we find? She would be foolish to leave any drug there. If she has brought some potion or philter with her—and if any is left—it will be well hidden by now. Would you have us rip her belongings, even her clothes, to shreds, till we find what you seek?"

Kat looked away, blinking back tears.

"I am sorry, Katherine," Gabrielle said gently. "I dare not accuse her, nor send her away. Would that I could think of some reason why the demoiselle might choose to leave on her own . . ."

Kat was very still. "That's it," she said at last, and chuckled. "*Au revoir*, Isobel . . ."

Isobel de Maisse had fallen asleep quickly, her mind at ease, soon after Justin had given up hammering on her door. She had known it was best to avoid him tonight, while he was in a fury. Tomorrow, if he complained about her refusing to open her door to him, she would tell him that she had been frightened, reminding him of the rage his wife had kindled in him. As for the English baroness and her anger at Isobel—that mattered for little. Isobel had dealt with jealous wives before, and they were rarely matches for their husbands.

Content that she had done a good day's work, she drifted off to sleep, only to be awakened when a sword blade was placed across her chest, just below her neck.

She gasped at the shock of the cold metal against her skin and would have sat up, had she not felt the edge of the blade begin to cut into her flesh. Astonished, she stared up at the masked figure who stood beside the bed, holding the sword and at the same time pointing a dagger at her maid.

"Soft, mademoiselle. Do not scream. I am a friend."

The voice was distorted, the words slightly difficult to understand: the mask must be one of those held against the face by a string attached to a marble kept in the mouth. The intruder spoke hesitantly, and with a strange accent—what was it? She studied him in the poor light cast by a single flickering taper on the other side of the bed. His doublet and hose were black, of good cloth, but somewhat the worse for wear. His riding boots were coated with dust. He wore an ugly, shapeless cap. She might have thought him some ruffian, were it not for the richness of the sword he carried, a dress sword with the guard and hilt gilded and elaborately worked in some shape she could not discern from this angle. A courtier's sword.

"Who are you? What do you want?"

"I have come to tell you that she who sent you here would have you elsewhere. I regret that you traveled so swiftly, mademoiselle, for I hoped to overtake you before you reached this place. You may forget *le beau* Charron. There is more worthy game to be hunted, but you must leave Monteronne to catch it."

"Leave now? But—" She bit back the words. She would not tell this stranger, this emissary of the queen mother, about Justin Lisle. He would scoff at her suspicions about the Englishman, and bid her obey the queen mother's orders anyway—and what choice would she have? And then he, too, would know of Lord Harwood's presence here, and he would give that news to Catherine de Medici first, depriving Isobel of what might be a *coup d'éclat*. No, she would save what she had learned of the English baron for other ears than his.

"What worthier game?" she asked, not really expecting an answer.

"A quarry that is now in La Rochelle."

"A Huguenot?"

"They roost there, do they not?"

Jeanne d'Albret had her headquarters in La Rochelle. Might this worthier quarry be one of the Protestant queen's household?

"Do I know him?"

"He has seen you, mademoiselle, and in his letters approved what he saw."

Whoever the unnamed Huguenot was, then, he was important enough to Catherine de Medici for her to go to the trouble of intercepting his letters. It seemed more and more likely that he was someone close to Jeanne d'Albret. Someone close enough to know some of her secrets. Someone trusted enough to influence her . . . or to poison her, subtly, if the woman he loved directed him to do so. He could be a dagger aimed at the Queen of Navarre's heart, and Fortune had chosen Isobel to hold that dagger.

"Let me sit up," she said, and the queen mother's emissary lifted the sword, held it raised for a moment, then sheathed it, and the dagger. Isobel could see the design of the hilt now, a curiously wrought M. She stared at the emissary, idly rubbing her neck, which had been lightly scratched. "Who are you? Do I know you?"

He laughed. "I am but a messenger, mademoiselle. My identity is of no moment. But I will tell you that I have seen you, and that perhaps you noticed me. I wore"—he paused, then laughed again, as if amused by the memory—"a suit of purled satin, the color *giuggiolino*."

Giuggiolino! He had used the Italian word for the color, not the French, *zinzolin*. Was he Italian, then? *Par Dieu*, that was it! The slight hesitations in his speech, the trace of an Italian accent—so like the queen mother, who had never learned to speak French properly. And the M on his sword hilt—for Medici?

But where had she seen him before? She racked her brains but could not recall seeing a slender courtier—an Italian—in a suit of purled satin, the color that of horseflesh.

She shook her head. The puzzle could be solved another time. The Florentine might freely tell her, when she returned to court.

"How soon must I leave? And do I travel to Paris first or at once to La Rochelle?"

"You must leave this morning, mademoiselle, as soon as it is light, and you will go neither to Paris nor La Rochelle, but to Bayonne. Tell no one here where you are going."

"No. No, I will not." Michel de Charron might follow her, and he would be nothing but a hindrance now. "But why Bayonne?"

"I await another command from our mistress, that may come tomorrow or a month from now. Until then, you must wait, but in a place where you will be free to receive visitors. You will hire lodgings at Le Dauphin Sautant . . .''

He left a scant minute later, after advising her to keep her stay in Bayonne as discreet as possible, waiting in her chambers at the inn until he brought her the anticipated message from Catherine de Medici. She should be ready to leave Bayonne on an hour's notice.

She watched him descend a flimsy ladder that he must have stolen somewhere. Then, picking up the ladder and carrying it under one arm, he ran away, across the garden, until he was lost to sight.

A suit of *zinzolin* purled satin . . .

She sighed. There was no more time to waste in such idle musing. Turning her back to the window, she set her maidservant to packing for their ride to Bayonne.

Kat rubbed her arm where the ladder had bruised it. She could still taste the marble and string she had held in her mouth, but the wine Gabrielle had given her was helping to take that taste away.

The candle on Gabrielle's desk had burned low. In the bedchamber, Jacques was snoring peacefully. He had not wakened even when Gabrielle returned to put away her mask and the sword that they had had made for their son but not yet given to him.

Her head had begun to throb again where Justin had hit her. She touched the bruise lightly and winced.

"I could give you syrup of poppy," Gabrielle offered.

"Nay, but thank you. I would be awake early, and with my head clear." She laughed softly. "I will enjoy watching the demoiselle leave."

His head ached, worse—much worse—than it had ever ached before, and there was a vile taste in his mouth.

He tried to sit up, but that made the pain so much worse that he lay down again to think . . . or to try to. His head seemed damaged inside and out.

'Sdeath, what had he been drinking last night? He remembered a few cups of claret at supper. What had he had to drink afterward? He recalled that they had been in the garden for the banquet, and he had been with Isobel de Maisse.

. . . and now he remembered that Kat had been furious with him. Jesu. How imperious she had looked, standing there at the bottom of the stairway.

While he was at the top? With Isobel?

He groaned as he remembered pushing her gown off her shoulders and pulling her bodice down to kiss her breasts. What a drunken fool

he had been! He had meant only to divert Isobel from Michel de Charron, and perhaps learn why she had been sent to Monteronne. Instead,
he had nearly succumbed to her himself.

He remembered bringing Kat here to his bedchamber, carrying her.
She had still been angry with him. But he could recall nothing after
that. He would have hoped they had settled their quarrel in bed, were
it not for the fact that he was still fully dressed.

Likely she was still angry with him. He rubbed his face. Likely Isobel
was angry, too. 'Twas enough to make him want to stay in his bedchamber. He did not relish the thought of meeting the two of them at
dinner. Perchance he should try to make amends to Kat, at least, before
then. He glanced at the clock. 'Twas nearly ten. He had less than an
hour.

He pushed himself up, ignoring the pain in his head as best he
could, and walked unsteadily to the door and opened it.

The door of the bedchamber Mademoiselle de Maisse occupied stood
open. From within came the sounds of someone sweeping the floor.
Curious, he approached the doorway and looked in. A smell like that
of a perfumer's shop assailed him.

A maid was sweeping up damp rushes and shards of glass. She told
Justin that one of Mademoiselle de Maisse's servants had dropped a
chest containing her perfumes. The latch had broken and several of the
bottles inside, which had been broken by the fall, had spilled out onto
the floor. The chest had been badly damaged, and Madame de Charron
had offered one of her own to replace it, but the demoiselle had declined
to accept the gift, saying that the chest could be cleaned and repaired.
Isobel had, however, been so angry with her clumsy servant that she
had beaten him with her shoe.

Justin, suppressing a smile, asked the maid to which bedchamber
the demoiselle had moved. 'Twas certain she would not have stayed
here.

The answer astonished him. Mademoiselle de Maisse had left, giving no reason for her departure. Neither had she answered the seigneur's
son when he asked where she was going. Michel had seemed troubled
that his guest was leaving, but his mother, the maid confided, had not
looked troubled at all.

Justin could well believe that.

He left the bedchamber and its reek of perfume and walked down
the hall to Kat's bedchamber.

At first he thought that her maid would not admit him. Marie had
opened the door just enough to peer out at him, then closed and bolted
it again while she spoke to Kat in hushed tones. Justin waited quietly,
pretending a patience he did not feel. Mayhap, he thought, he should

have bathed and dressed in fresh clothes before coming here, but he decided he looked more penitent this way. It was not sackcloth and ashes, but his rumpled clothes would testify that he had come to her as soon as he had awakened, humbly to beg her forgiveness of his drunken folly. But he was beginning to feel that not even the most humble petitioner should be made to wait so long when the door was opened again at last.

He walked past Marie into the chamber. Kat was standing in front of the window, but she was not looking out. Instead, her gaze was on a picture over the hearth, a picture of one of Jacques's ancestors.

"Well, my lord?" she said coolly. "You wished to speak to me?" Her chin was raised haughtily. "Haply about Mademoiselle de Maisse?"

Truly, she made it difficult to apologize. His patience had already worn thin during the wait outside her door, and now he found himself vexed. He had hoped to begin by confessing his drunkenness; the less said of Isobel, the better.

"She has left Monteronne," he said.

"Yea, I know. I saw her leave."

Prudence counseled him to drop the subject, but he could not: Kat had sounded too smug just now, and he asked suspiciously, "Did you bid her—"

"By the mass!" She clenched her fists in a fury, but still did not turn to look at him directly. "Did I bid her leave? You dare ask that, my lord? Think you that I would usurp my hosts' rights here and send away their son's guest, one of the queen mother's maids? Upon my life, I warrant"—she paused, sighed, then turned to face him—"I warrant you must think me as unseemly in behavior as yourself."

He stared in disbelief at the terrible bruise on her face. The livid flesh around her left eye was so swollen her eye was half shut. Even cupshotten, would he have struck her? But the answer was in her pitiless gaze, from which he had to look away, sickened.

"Kat," he whispered. "I'faith, I am sorry—"

"Get you gone, my lord," she said, her voice breaking, and when he looked at her, he saw she was crying. He reached toward her, thinking to comfort her, but she took a panicky step back, her fear so palpable that he stopped, so ashamed at that moment that he felt it monstrous that he should still be living.

"Go!" she begged, and this time he left.

He walked blindly along the hall and down the stairs. He was near the door leading out to the courtyard when Gabrielle de Charron called to him.

"Isobel has left."

He stopped, nodding, but did not look around or reply.

"She has told no one where she is going . . . unless you know."

He turned toward her then, thinking he had heard the same smug tone in her voice that he had thought he heard in Kat's. "Did you . . ."

Gabrielle shook her head. "No, *mon ami*. I did not see her last night, after you returned to the chateau with her." He winced; she seemed not to notice. "And it was the noise her servants made that woke me this morning. I did not ask her to leave. Nor," she added with a tight smile, "did I ask her to stay."

" 'Twould be discourteous to plead with a guest so impatient to leave."

"*Oui*," she agreed. "It would have been discourteous." Her manner became serious again. "My husband must go to Bidache on some business. Will you go with him? You will be away only a few days."

Justin hesitated. He glanced back toward the stairway.

"Her bruises will fade," Gabrielle said softly, and his face burned with shame. "Her anger as well. But she will need time, Justin, and it would be best if you were away. Bring her back some gift. I am sure she will forgive you."

He looked questioningly at her.

"*Oui*, I only guess. But *I* would forgive you. Once."

CHAPTER 36

The dog days of summer were two weeks past, but London still sweltered in late August, and there were new cases of plague every day. Yet neither the heat nor fear of contagion had kept the crowds away from Bartholomew Fair in Smithfield. On this, the last day of the fair, Jack and Bess had brought Tom and Amy with them, and Ned as well.

"Puppets!" Amy shrieked, pointing toward a puppet show with one hand and tugging at the hem of Jack's jerkin with the other, leaving grease and crumbs of gingerbread on the cloth. "Puppets?" she repeated, this time pleadingly.

Jack was reaching for his purse, ready to come up with the pence they would need for the show, when Bess swooped down on her daughter.

"Not now, sweetheart," she said, rubbing an already soiled handkerchief across the little girl's face; both Amy and Tom were greasy from eating the roast pig for which Bartholomew Fair was renowned. Then, before the child could start to cry: "Mayhap we'll go later. You saw a puppet show scarce more than an hour ago." Taking Amy by the hand, she resolutely led her away from the booth and its brightly colored puppets.

Jack looked around for Tom. In the few moments that his attention had been distracted by Amy, her brother had made his way into the throng. He swore as he started to push his way through the crowd, the largest he had seen since they hanged John Felton, the papist who had posted the bull excommunicating the queen on the door of the Bishop of London's palace, on a gallows erected in Paul's Yard in front of that very palace. He had thought that press was terrible, but this was worse. Haply he would never find Tom again. He rued Bess's decision to bring the children, for all that he understood it. They had started begging her to take them to Bartholomew Fair a month ago, and had been so eager that they had even accepted the daily doses of wine mixed with ginger and sage and bramble that she had given them to help keep them safe from plague—though they, like Bess and Jack, had refused Ned's concoction of powdered dried ivy-berries in vinegar, which the old man

481

claimed was a more potent medicine. The fair had been all that the children had talked about for a week, and Bess had set aside nearly a pound for them to spend there. It would kill her if they lost Tom here, and Jack was not sure he could live with himself, either, if the boy disappeared.

And then he caught a glimpse, past a merchant's fat legs, of Tom's bright orange-tawny tunic. He shoved two yeoman aside and ran after the boy, catching him, he saw, just in time. Tom was stalking a richly dressed gallant who was regaling the *buonaroba* on his arm and seemed heedless of the fact that others might be interested in the purse tied with silk cords to his girdle.

Tom yowled in protest as Jack yanked him around, but despite his struggles was picked up and carried back toward his mother and sister.

"The ruffian cly you!" Tom whispered furiously. "I would have had that purse. I would have given it to mama!"

"Yea? And what chair would you have climbed on to reach into it, you giant, you?"

"I need no chair to nip—" The boy cut the sentence short, but Jack had understood it too well.

"Where's your cuttle?" he asked, and when Tom would not answer, he stopped walking and, pinioning the child against his chest with one arm, used his free hand to search the pockets of Tom's tunic. He had found what he sought in a few seconds: a small cuttle, just the right size for a child's hand, and a tiny horn sheath that would fit the boy's thumb. He pocketed them himself, after just a quick glance. The sheath had been cunningly made. Bess, he knew, would want to know which of their friends at the Turk's Sword had been foolish enough to give her son these dangerous toys, but when he asked Tom from whom he had had them, he was dumb-stricken by the answer.

Robin Dalling.

Jack had not known that the upright man had been anywhere near the Turk's Sword in the last few weeks, but Tom had seen him in the alley one day, and had been so pleased by the upright man's gift that he had agreed not to tell his mother about it. Jack was vexed to think that Dalling would ever come near him again, but he had heard stories that the man was determined to reassert his control of the bousing ken and the rogues and thieves who stalled there. Two men Jack knew had told him at different times that they had seen Dalling at Moorfields, wrestling any man who would accept his challenge, and besting many of them. And another friend had heard a rumor that the upright man was practicing with a sword, too, having found himself an Italian fencing master who had sought shelter at Whitefriars one night after using too much of his skill on one of the worthies of the Chandlers' guild.

Jack had kept all the gossip from Bess, and asked those who gave him the news to do so, too. 'Twould serve no purpose to have her fretting. Moreover, he thought Dalling too much of a coward ever to challenge him again. Still, the upright man had risked coming to the alley by the Turk's Sword . . . even though his mission had been the low one of giving a child toys that, if used, could put him in the stocks or jail.

Perhaps, Jack thought, Bess should not be told of this. She might go after Dalling herself.

"A favor for a favor," he said to Tom, and the boy was amenable to the trade of promises of silence, though Jack had to promise Tom a piece of gilt gingerbread, which he bought him before taking him back to Bess, who was waiting impatiently for them, Amy by her side.

"Marry, a runagate co," Bess said, eyeing her son with mock disapproval. "Should we keep him, or let someone else take him home?"

"No!" Tom yelled, and Jack handed him over to her for a scolding that would surely keep the boy safely near them—for another hour, at least.

They walked on, through the jumble of booths and stalls erected for the fair at the priory of St. Bartholomew. They stopped to listen to the verses of a ballad-maker, who offered to write for them a ballad mocking their enemies, but Bess shook her head and told him, laughing, "Faith, I have none—or none that I need fear," and Tom caught Jack's eye before turning away, his hand pressed to his mouth. They moved on, to watch a juggler whose tricks were worth a penny, in Bess's opinion, and while they watched him they ate Catherine pears purchased from a costermonger who had set his baskets down nearby.

Ned remembered then that Little George Crispyn was still at the fair, having been tried yesterday in the Court of Pie-Powder and set on the pillory till the end of the fair, so they all went to see him. They found him talking to a merchant set on the pillory beside him, a cloth merchant who had been accused of not giving good measure. Little George was glad to see them, and seemed cheery enough, though he complained that his back ached from standing stooped over, for the pillory had not been made for a man of his height. Jack thought Little George should be happy, since the former prigger of prancers could have come to a far worse fate. The clotpoll, thinking to imitate other cony-catchers he knew of, had sold a piece of folded paper with needles glued inside it to a woman who sold bottle-ale at a booth at the fair. He had learned that she was wroth with a man who had promised—alas, without witnesses—to marry her, and then married another. Little George had told her to mark the man's name on the outside of the paper and then give it to him as if 'twere a letter; when her former lover opened the letter, George had promised her, the needles, which had been magicked, would break free of the paper and fly at the man as if shot from a gun and wound him most grievously. The woman had changed her mind about using the magic—more likely, Jack believed, because she feared punishment than because her conscience had troubled her—and had demanded her lour back from Little George. Then, when he would not give it to her, she had gone to the Court of Pie-Powder, complaining that he had sold her needles that broke too easily. Little George had not argued too much in his own defense, as like as not fearing that to do so might prompt her to admit that she had bought magicked needles and denounce him as a cunning man. The charge of sorcery would have brought him a year in jail at least, and might have cost him his life if the court had decided that the needles were meant to kill and not merely wound. So now he was content with the lesser charge and sentence, though he confided in a whisper to Jack that he feared, every time he saw a bluecoat, that it might be one of those who had searched for him in Oxford and Berkshire.

As they walked away from the pillory, Tom asked why the fair's court was called the Court of Pie-Powder. Bess shrugged and looked to Ned, who confessed he did not know, either. Tom looked up at Jack then.

" 'Tis from the French words *pied-poudreux*, from the Latin *pede pulverosus*, for dusty-footed."

"Dusty-footed?" the boy asked, glancing down at his feet, which were indeed dusty.

"Dustyfoot," Bess told him, "is another word for pedlar. 'Tis the court that tries pedlars who come to fairs."

"But Little George is not a pedlar," Tom said, a bit loudly. "He's a prigger—" His next words were muffled as Bess clapped her hand over his mouth and smiled at the people around them.

"By the mass," Ned said, his gaze thoughtful as it rested on Jack, "we have a scholar with us."

"Aye, he's that and more," Bess said sharply. "Amy, would you see that puppet show?" she asked, pointing to a stall.

Mary Whitston, the younger of the two punks who spent much of their time at the Turk's Sword, was among the audience for the show, and she gave them a strained smile before looking back toward the garishly clad wooden figures on stage. There were hundreds of whores at the fair; with so many rivals, no doubt she would think half an hour spent at a puppet show little loss. And haply the entertainment would ease the look of worry on her face, which no amount of paint could conceal. Last week Mary had learned sad news of Hal Verrick, a blacksmith who lived in Islington, a man whom Mary had loved so well she had charged him only half the usual price. He had pox now, and though

Mary as yet showed no signs of the French disease, she was frightened, as were those customers of hers who knew of Hal's sickness. Deprived of half her usual income, she was willing to venture out to the fair, scary though it was for her to be so far from home and the sanctuary of the Turk's Sword.

"God, she looks fretful," Bess muttered. "She'll get no customers this way. Poor chit." Bess had once disliked the girl, whom she suspected of being too interested in Jack, but since the news about Hal Verrick she had taken pity on her, even giving her a small looking glass for her thirteenth birthday two days ago.

"I should give her some money," Jack whispered.

"Not for her wares, you will not, or you'll lie no more with me."

"Nay, not for her wares. For the doctor."

"Then she'll take your lour, and thank you for being a fool, and spend the coin on ale to help her forget her fears. Nay, Jack, save it for when she needs it, if she needs it. If she's poxed."

But would that not be too late, in truth? Jack wondered. He might help Mary pay a doctor, and then, like Hal Verrick, she could half starve herself, and sit in a bath of hot water mixed with cinnabar in the kind of tub used for pickling meat, and breathe the foul steam, and sweat, and pray that the treatment would work. But the prayer might be all that could save her, Jack thought, for though doctors would swear that the powdering tub and the tub-fast would cure the pox, Jack could not recall hearing of anyone who had been cured. Nor could anyone else he knew. Perchance the girl would be better off spending the money on ale . . .

His gaze was caught then by a heavily painted woman who stood beside a girl of fourteen or fifteen clad in a plain russet kirtle. They, too, were watching the puppet show, but the older woman talked all the while, and it seemed to Jack that her every other word was *London*, while the girl replied in the broad accent of the West Country. Another young whore was a-making, he thought. Mary Whitston would have been another such a year ago, fresh off some carrier's wagon that had just reached Smithfield, come to London to find her fortune, and easy prey for the first bawd who found her—and there would always be a bawd or two waiting for the carriers arriving in London, waiting to see what new maids had come with them, for these unwary country girls were easy pickings. Jack was tempted to introduce the newcomer to Mary Whitston and let the punk tell her what life in London could be like, but the bawd would then set the bluecoats upon him, rather than be cheated of her newest punk, and belike the girl would not believe him anyway.

The show ended, and they moved on, to a booth selling the roast pig they wanted for their supper. They washed down the slices of pork with bottle-ale. Ned was tired, and complained of his weary feet, and then began to grumble about how the fair had changed for the worse since its origins as a cloth fair, the greatest in England.

"Peace!" Bess cried at last, laughing, but with that telltale line between her brows that betrayed her annoyance. "Your grandfather may have seen it so, but not you. No one else I know speaks of such a fair held here. It changed long before your time."

Ned shook his head in annoyance, but held his tongue as he looked about with open dislike at the noisy crowd. Then his glance fell on the children, and he looked concerned, and a bit rueful.

He looked up and caught Jack watching him. "They should be in the country, not here," he said softly, and Jack, thinking of the bawd and her cony that he had seen a few minutes before, nodded agreement.

Bess glanced at them both, her expression one of disgust. " 'Sblood! They wanted to be here. Would you deny them a day at the fair?"

"There are fairs in the country," Ned told her. "Finer fairs than this. When I was a lad, I used to go to Stourbridge Fair, by Cambridge. 'Twill start in a few weeks. Half the pedlars here—"

"Dustyfoots," Tom corrected.

"Aye, dusty of foot they are. Half of them, I warrant, will soon be on their way to Stourbridge Fair, and I envy them, for there's room for a proper fair on that common, and 'tis no more than a mile from Cambridge, so you have all the students as well as the townsfolk."

"And not kings and queens, too?" Bess asked.

"Mock me if you will. You have not been there. I have. And 'tis better than Bartholomew Fair, for at Stourbridge it is never so hot."

"I mind not the heat," Bess said. "It makes the ale taste better."

"You would not need to swelter to enjoy the ale at Stourbridge Fair. I warrant you, the brewers there are better than them that brewed this," he asserted, raising his bottle.

"Mayhap this, too, will be improved by memory," Bess said. "Will it not, Jack?"

He barely heard her. He was listening to another voice, sitting at another table . . .

"And you would swear that the ale you drank at Stourbridge fair was the best you had tasted all year . . ."

He laughed, and agreed with the tall, strongly built gentleman seated to his left, a man with russet hair and gray eyes. Across the table was a slightly built youth who smiled at their laughter but did not laugh himself.

"Jack!" A woman's voice, somewhat shrill. "Jack, what—" He ignored her.

The youth wore a ridiculously large hat, which covered his hair com-

pletely. His face was filthy, but if you looked past the dust you could see delicate, pretty features.

"Jack!" A bony hand shook his shoulder.

"No!" He batted the hand away, then, hearing Ned gasp with pain, knew once again where he was. The remembered scene had slipped away. For a few moments his sense of loss was so bitter that he felt near tears; then, seeing Ned cradling his hand, an astonished look on his face, Jack drew a deep, shuddering breath. "Cry you mercy, Father Ned," he said quietly. "I forgot myself for a moment."

"Or remembered," Bess murmured.

Jack saw a look of understanding sweep over Ned's face at his grand-daughter's words. So she had told him that Jack had lost his memory. But he could not find it in his heart to feel betrayed, and not just because he was not surprised that she still felt more loyal to the old man than to himself. His thoughts were on the two faces he had seen.

The gentleman, with his russet hair and beard and rich garb—his face affected Jack in the same way as the sight of the tawny-haired gentleman at Paul's. Those two were connected in some way . . . some troubling way.

But the youth troubled him more. He felt concern—aye, and guilt, too—as he called up that face in his mind's eye once more. But why? Who was the lad?

He pictured the russet and the tawny heads together, and suddenly an almost sickening fear thrilled through him. He shook his head, then wiped a hand across his forehead; he was sweating profusely.

"Are you sick, Jack?" Bess asked, concerned.

He swallowed hard and shook his head. The children were watching him solemnly, as was Ned. He wished he could get away from them, so he could ponder in solitude the things he had remembered. 'Twould be useless, though, for already the images were fading from his memory. By the time he reached some quiet place, he would have little left to med-itate on but the words of the descriptions he had pinned on them: *the russet-haired gentleman; the pretty but filthy youth.*

"Nay, I am not sick," he told Bess, but his voice was shaking, and when she suggested they go home, he did not argue.

The sun set while they made their slow way home. They passed several plague houses, each marked by crosses and the words *Lord have mercy on us.* Watchmen stood guard to make sure that no one left the houses or opened the doors and windows. It would be hellish in those places, Jack thought, even for those not yet sick, as they suffered the heat without the slightest breeze to cool them and waited to see if they, too, would break out in the buboes that announced the pestilence.

Back in their rooms at the Turk's Sword, Bess put the children to bed at once, absently feeling their foreheads as she did every day now, checking for fever. She wiped grease from the pomanders they had carried, withered oranges stuck with cloves, before putting them away. Ned sat down on a joint stool and began to rub his feet. Jack went after water so the old man could soak his feet, and by the time he got back, the children were already asleep.

He followed Bess into their chamber.

The small room was stifling hot. Jack opened the single window further, careful not to disturb the rue that Bess had placed on the windowsill to ward off plague. There was a light breeze, but he could feel it only when he leaned out the window; not a bit of the cooler air entered the bedchamber. He sighed heavily. 'Twould be an uncomfortable night.

"Do you wish you were back in Sussex?" Bess asked softly from behind him.

"Why do you ask that?" As he turned to look at her, she shifted uneasily from one foot to the other.

" 'Twould be cooler there, with less danger of plague . . ." Her voice trailed off. She looked down at the floor.

" 'Twould be lonely as well." Jack went over to her and took her hands in his. "Look at me," he said urgently, and when she did: "Know this, Bess, that I had no life before I met you. There's nothing in Sussex for me."

Hope flared in her eyes for a moment, then died away. "But you remembered something today."

" 'Twas but a will-o'-the-wisp, and one that pleased me not," he said honestly. "I have remembered nothing that I would fain return to."

"I am glad," she said, then bit her lip. " 'Tis wrong, perhaps, to wish you to stay as empty of memory as Harry Oldham, but I am glad."

She wanted to make love then, though they had not for the past two nights because of the sweltering heat. And he might have put her off now, had he not sensed that she would read more into his reluctance than his desperate weariness. But then her ardor inflamed him, and their coupling was more fierce than tender, though afterward, lying atop her, his ragged breathing becoming more steady, he saw the tenderness return to her face.

Then, without warning, she laughed. "Sirrah," she said reprovingly, "you are dripping sweat on me, and I on you. Get off."

He laughed and rolled away. He felt cooler at once, and oddly guilty at his sense of relief. He reached out and took her hand. "I love you, Bess."

"I love you, too, Jack," she murmured drowsily, her fingers tightening around his. A few minutes later her hand went slack, and from that, and her quiet, steady breathing, he guessed she was asleep. He envied her that peace for a few minutes more, until he joined her in sleep.

There was a man at the window, looking downward, his features disguised by darkness as he stood silhouetted against the candlelight in the room behind him, but his tawny hair seemed gilded as the light glinted off it.

Nick stared upward, his breath caught in his throat, as a second man, russet-haired, joined the first. Lord Harwood!

For an instant everything seemed unreal, a dream from which he must soon wake. He had never imagined they might be discovered. Then the reality of the scene slapped against all of his senses at once. He was aware of the coolness of the night breeze that bore the garden's fragrance, of pain from flesh bruised by his fall, and, most of all, of the weight of the girl sprawled on top of him.

"Get off!" he whispered, pushing her away, half helping her to her feet after he got to his. And then she just stood there, tilting her head back to gape up at the window.

"Get them, Tandy!" Lord Harwood commanded, and the tawny-haired man was gone from the window.

"Run, Kat!" he cried, and seized her arm.

"Run, Kat! Run, Kat!"

He was sitting up in bed. The candle had guttered out, and he looked wildly around in the darkness. A hand touched his arm, and he cried out in alarm before Bess's quiet voice calmed him somewhat.

"Peace, Jack. Peace, my love. There's no harm here." She tried to pull him back down beside her on the coarse, sweat-dampened sheets, but he resisted her, and after a few moments her hands fell away. "Have a drink, Jack, and put your mind at ease. 'Twas only a nightmare." She paused, and when she spoke again, she sounded worried. "Though I would never have guessed you were frightened of cats."

"Nor am I." He got up and poured himself a glass of wine. 'Twas cheap stuff: he had never really liked it, but until now had not known why.

"But you were shouting about a cat," Bess said. "I heard you." There was a pleading note to her voice, as though she were begging him to agree and lay her fears to rest.

He shook his head, unwilling to look around at her. His clothes lay draped across a chest. He dressed quickly, turning toward the bed only to take his sword belt from the bedpost. Bess was sitting up, and as his gaze swept across her she drew the sheet up over her breasts in unusual modesty, as though of a sudden she knew him for the stranger he now felt himself to be.

"Not a cat," he said heavily, as he buckled on the sword belt. "Kat. Katherine."

"Your wife?" she asked in a small voice.

"My sister. I have no wife." He hoped it would be some reassurance. He could give her no more. He had to be alone now; he needed to think. He went out without saying another word, and though he was careful to move quietly so as not to wake the children, old Ned raised himself on one elbow to look at him curiously. He tried to give the old man an easy smile, but it froze into a grimace. He sighed with relief as he closed and locked the door behind him.

Sunrise found him north of the city, in Moorfields. A few servants and housewives were already there with linen they had washed, spreading it out to dry in the sun. 'Twould dry quickly. It promised to be another hot day.

His head ached as though he had had too much to drink last night, but he no longer felt as though he wore two identities like two suits of the same size, neither fitting when worn together. He had weathered a storm of feelings: revulsion at some of the things he had done these past two months, hatred of himself for not being there to help Kat—pray God, she was safe!—and terror at the thought of losing Bess. He was still far from comfortable—he felt now as if a tailor had taken both suits, cut them into strips, and worked them together into garments of double thickness, as odd and garish as a fool's motley. But he could wear this new suit, for a time. He had no choice.

He got up and brushed the dew from his hose. He had stayed away long enough. Now he had to speak to Bess. 'Twould be painful, and his mind shied away from thoughts of it to memories of last night, when he had loved her, simply and honestly. But he could not hold to those memories. Nothing was simple now, and last night might as well have been a century ago.

He started back toward Southwark, keeping a wary eye on the people around him. One thing had not changed since yesterday: he wanted no encounters now with people he had known before leaving Harwood Hall. He would not be able to explain his appearance, and he doubted he could still give as convincing a performance of not recognizing a friend as he had given to poor Tom Heyford at St. Paul's that afternoon.

Bess was waiting for him in the kitchen. The bruised-looking flesh beneath her eyes betrayed her weariness. He doubted she had slept much after he had left.

"You came back." She sounded wary, and looked wary too, and he realized she was still not certain of his return. How long, he wondered, would she have continued to wait for him despite her doubts? He was touched, painfully so.

"Needs must that we talk."

She nodded. "Yea, but not here." She took his hand and led him out of the Turk's Sword and down the alley toward Paris Garden. There were few people about.

"How much have you remembered? Everything?"

"Aye." He stopped, set his hands on her shoulders and turned her to face him. "Bess, I must leave. My sister was in danger when I last saw her. I must see if she is safe now, and if not, help her . . . if I still can."

"If . . . ?" Her eyes widened with understanding. "Oh, Jack . . ." She reached out to touch his face, then froze.

He caught her hand before she could yank it back. "D'you fear to touch me now?"

"I know not who you are!" she wailed. "Not even your name!"

A drunkard staggering past with a whore with whom he must have spent the night turned to stare at them, then snickered, but he quickly looked away as Nick glared at him.

"My name is Nick," he told her in a low voice. "Nicholas Lang—"

"Nay, tell me not! I would not know your full name!"

He gaped at her, wondering if worry and lack of sleep had robbed her of her wits.

"Y'are a gentleman, are you not? Y'are of gentle birth?"

Reluctantly, he nodded.

"Then you will not be returning, even after you have seen to your sister. And Jack—Nick—I do hope you find her safe, and I will pray that you will be safe and well and happy. But you must not come back. We can no longer have aught to do with each other. And I would not know who you are or where you make your home, lest I be tempted to follow you."

She spoke sense, but it was a cruel sense. "Bess, I cannot go away and just forget you."

"You must."

"I cannot leave you here. You would not be safe, nor would your children, nor Ned. There is the plague to fear, and Robin Dalling, and if you were ever caught stealing, by a bluecoat who was not your friend . . ."

"As like as not, I would end as so many of my friends have. Yet they were my friends, and that's the rub. How could I go with you, Nick?" she asked remorselessly. "Would I fit into your life? You cannot marry me—for a truth, you might be ashamed to admit you know me.

Nay, do not shake your head. You will feel otherwise after you are back with your family and friends. Yea, and someday you must marry. Think you I will be your light-of-love, waiting for you to sneak away from your wife's bed?''

He shook his head again. There were no good answers to her questions. He had already racked his brains for hours, having suspected that she would refuse to go with him. "If work could be found for you, honest work—"

"I still would not live in your home, Nick, nor anywhere near it. Please you, do not ask me to do that. I could not stand to see you, knowing I have no part of your life."

"You are too proud, Bess."

"Aye, so Robin Dalling told me, too," she said bitterly, and Nick jerked his head back as though she had slapped him. "Pray your pardon. I should not speak to you so. But I cannot accept your offer, kind though it is. Yet if . . .''

"Yea? If what?"

"If you would do me a favor . . .''

"Bess, I owe you my life."

"Nay, you saved mine."

He placed a finger across her lips, silencing her. "You kept me alive, Bess, when I was helpless. I needed more than skill with a sword to survive, and you tutored me. Without you, I might have ended in Bedlam, like Harry Oldham. I owe you everything."

"Then will you take my children with you?" Seeing his stunned expression, she hurried on: "Oh, I know they have some bad habits already, and Tom will have his hands chopped off someday if he does not learn to keep them off other people's purses. But they are young enough to mend their ways. They could be trained as servants, or apprenticed."

"You would give them up? Bess, you love them."

"Aye, love them enough to want them away from here. Think you I would see Tom in prison? Or Amy broken by an upright man, as Mary Whitston was, whoring and poxed before she's thirteen? I cannot protect them forever, Nick."

"But will it not hurt you, Bess, to see your children only now and then?"

"I will not see them at all! I told you, I would not know who you are or where you go. I trust you to care for them. They must not return to look for me, either. Not ever. Only God knows what—" She broke off, looking away, blinking furiously.

Only God knows what they would find. Yea. Perchance she would be dead, or in prison, or, like Mary Whitston, dying of pox . . .

"But what will Ned say?"

"He will say," she said firmly, "that he understands. I would have him go with you, to spend his last years safely and in more comfort, but—"

"He would not leave you."

"No," she agreed. "So. Tell me. When will you be leaving?"

His first thought that morning had been to hire post horses for his journey and travel fast, but he could not do that if he took the children. And a carrier, though safe for them, would be too slow for him. He wanted to be home soon.

"I must buy a horse—two horses. Can Tom ride?"

"He sat a pony once, while a pedlar led it."

Nick frowned. He would have to take Tom up behind him, and hold Amy in front of him. Still, he would need two horses, since the one they rode would weary quickly, and they would have packs besides.

"I'll to Smithfield, then."

"Have you enough lour for two horses?"

"Perhaps not, but I can nip a purse if—"

"No! No, I will not have you steal, Nick, not to help me. I have saved some lour against a rainy day. Ned keeps it for me. Come back with me, and I'll give you the lour, and you can be off to Smithfield at once, with no need to cut a purse."

He saw it would be useless to argue. He could repay her, too, sending a servant back here with some money as soon as he reached Beechwood. So he started back toward the Turk's Sword with her.

"I would not have everyone know that you are leaving, and the children with you," she told him. "So we'll meet in Lambeth Marsh, and I'll tell my friends, when they ask, that Ned and I took the children to stay with a goodwife he knows in Islington, to keep them safe from the plague."

"And if anyone asks about me?"

"I'll tell them I threw you out. Look you, you will want to take a pack with you when you leave for Smithfield. Can you grumble and play the churl?"

"I'll attempt."

"And I'll throw a bottle at you. 'Twill aid your playing. Mind that you must duck," she said, and laughed then, but her eyes were too bright, and she brushed at them as she looked away, pretending great interest in a sleeping beggar.

Lambeth Marsh, west of Paris Garden, was a melancholy place, with its streams and pools and willows, a place for disappointed lovers to sigh and weep. Yea, and a place for traitors to meet and plot, Nick thought as he sat waiting for Bess. 'Twas here that Lisle had met with Muñoz, unaware that one of Sparrow's intelligencers was spying upon them. 'Twas here that it had all been set in motion. And was Lisle still free, or was he even now in the Tower, awaiting trial? Nick could not recall any of his friends at the bousing ken gossiping about Lord Harwood, but he was not certain that they would have heard about an arrest, or talked about it after. Truth to tell, he could not even be sure that he would have paid heed to the gossip, if there had been any, for the name would have meant naught to him. 'Twas a discouraging thought.

Fortunately, he had little more than an hour to wait before Bess came into sight, carrying a large cloakbag—a new one, likely stolen—and leading Tom by the hand. Ned was with her, carrying another cloakbag and Amy. Both children looked as if they had been crying. Nick was glad he had missed the scene at the Turk's Sword.

Ned set Amy down but kept hold of her hand. He looked tired and very, very old in the bright afternoon sunlight. "We are grateful that y'are doing this for us, Jack—pray your pardon, sir, I meant—"

"Nick. And do not stand upon courtesy with me, Ned. 'Tis I who must needs thank you, for all you have done for me. Would that I could stay with you longer, but I cannot."

"So Bess said. I hope you find your sister well, sir—Nick."

"Nay, do not sir me, Father Ned. I have not been dubbed a knight, nor have I any other titles."

With Ned's help, he secured the cloakbags to the saddle of the smaller horse. Tom watched curiously, reaching out now and then to touch the horse's flank. Nick doubted that the boy could ride well enough to sit a horse alone, but certainly he seemed willing to be taught. Amy, on the other hand, hung back, seemingly frightened of the beasts.

"Amy, come here," he called.

Bess had to urge her forward, but at last she came to him. He picked her up and carried her over to the horse they would ride. Both animals were very gentle—and old, too, alas, but he could afford none better. The horse-corser had even set his own three-year-old son on the jades to show that they were tolerant of children. So Nick did not hesitate to hold Amy beside the horse's neck and tell her to stroke its mane. Her timidity quickly gave way to delight, and soon she was patting its velvety muzzle. By the time he had mounted the horse and let Bess hand Amy up to him, she seemed eager for the trip.

Nick himself was less eager. There was a forlorn expression on Bess's face, and he wished he could stay another night. But it was not possible, not while he did not know what had happened to Kat. Nor was he certain that a prolonged leave-taking would not be more painful yet.

Assured now that Amy would ride with him, he handed her down to Bess, then dismounted. Bess was kneeling on the ground, her arms around both children, and they were all crying. Nick's own eyes stung with tears as he looked on. Ned came over to hug him and bid him God-speed, then withdrew a tactful distance so Nick could take his leave of Bess in some privacy.

She saw he was waiting, and stood up, but the children clung to her hands. It wrung his heart to think of separating them.

"Bess, you must come with me."

She shook her head.

"But who will protect you when I am gone?" he asked, and regretted a moment later that he had mentioned his worry in front of the children. But then an instant after that, hearing Tom's wail, he was glad, for the children might be able to convince her when he could not.

"John Albers will protect me." She tousled her son's hair. "Stop crying like a babe, cofe. You know John Albers."

"The ruffler."

"Aye. He's a good man, and good with a sword," she told Tom, and he looked less frightened.

"And no one has seen him for these last three days," Nick reminded her.

"He'll be back," she said firmly, and Nick had to believe her. Albers had never stopped looking at Bess as if he wanted her, and he would return when he heard Jack had left her . . . if not before then. And she knew it, as well as he did.

"Nay, he'll not be back," a rough voice said, and Robin Dalling pushed through a thicket and swaggered toward them. One of the ruffians who had been with him at the Turk's Sword trailed him, his own swagger less confident. "I left him lying in a ditch by Aldgate, a foot of good steel in his back. 'Twas my best dagger, too, but the dog had howled so loud that I feared the watch would be there in a trice." He stopped some dozen paces from them and looked from Bess to Nick to Ned, and then back at Bess. " 'Slid! Y'are all teary already, and I have not yet killed this cofe of yours."

"Nor have you yet bumped your head on the moon," Bess said coldly, "and that will happen before the other." She pushed the children toward Ned, who held them close. "And stow your whids, Dalling. You call Albers a dog, but you were not fit to lick his shoe."

"I'll learn you to cut more benely, mort, when I am done with this cofe," Dalling replied, almost pleasantly. Then he looked at Nick, and his eyes narrowed. "Well, Jack. Well, Jack. You bested me once, with your pretty rapier and your subtle Italian tricks, but no more. I have turned schoolboy, I have."

" 'Tis no news to me."

"Is it not?" the upright man asked, his eyes widening again. " 'Sblood! Is that why you would leave Southwark now? Would you run away from me—aye, and Bess as well? Would you turn tail against them that took you in, you coward, you ingrate dog?"

"Have a care, Dalling," Ned warned. "He's no ruffler, but a gentleman, in sooth."

Dalling laughed. "Nay, he's a Jack gentleman, planning to be a Jack-out-of-doors. But you need not sleep under any hedge tonight, my Jack, for I'll see you to a bed of dust that you'll never leave again." And he drew his sword and dagger.

Nick drew as well, told Bess to stand back, and then waited for Dalling's next move. This was poor ground for a fight, too spongy by half, with the grass and weeds just tall enough to hide fallen branches that could trip a man. He scanned the ground as well as he might, never taking his eyes from the upright man for more than an instant.

"By my faith! You dare not even look at me in the eye!" Dalling exclaimed, and attacked.

In those first few seconds Nick had to confess to himself that this bravo had learned, and learned well, and across his mind strayed the idle thought that he would fain know the fencing master's name, so he could look him up himself. But then he slipped on the muddy grass and almost fell, and came within inches of having his throat cut. Thereafter he thought only of his weapons and Dalling's, and the intricate dance they performed in the air. The upright man could deal stronger blows from the high ward than Nick could; he found that out after he parried the blow and nearly dropped his own dagger, his wrist was so numb. But then he noticed that Dalling had forgotten—if he ever had known— to parry with the first or second parts of his dagger's blade. He stepped back and struck a blow that he knew Dalling would have to reach to parry, and the Spanish steel of his sword blade came down near the point of Dalling's dagger and snapped it off.

"Would that I could thank Albers for keeping your good dagger," Nick gasped, "but I'll not believe that he screamed when you stabbed him, for he was a brave man, and y'are a coward and would have run away no matter what."

"Whoreson rogue!"

Dalling sprang at him again, wild with rage, but Nick parried his sword's thrust and then delivered a home thrust, a *stoccata* to Dalling's heart, which the upright man tried to parry and missed with his short-ened dagger. He yanked his sword free, and Dalling toppled onto his face in the mire.

"You were not schooled well enough," Nick murmured. He sheathed his dagger, then dragged his sword across the grass to wipe off Dalling's blood and sheathed that, too. He felt sickened at what he had done, for all that he knew it had had to be done. Aye, and he had avenged Albers. Still, the thought did not cheer him. For all his playing at weapons, he had never killed a man ere now, save for that ruffian who had threatened Bess that first night he met her, and that fight—in the darkness, moments after waking, his mind numbed by sleep as well as the blow that his memory loss had been—had seemed dreamlike, far from real. This was much too real, this killing, in broad daylight, of a man he had first met weeks ago . . . a man who was no true match for him in a duel. He prayed he would never need to kill like this again.

"Jack!" Bess screamed.

He whirled around to see Dalling's companion draw a knife. God's death, how could he have forgotten! He began to draw, but knew he would be too late.

And then the man cried out, his dagger spinning free. He clutched his shoulder, from which the hilt of a small knife protruded. Bess's knife.

Nick ran toward him with sword and dagger drawn, but the man fled, clods of dirt and clumps of grass flying from the heels of his boots. Nick chased him only a few yards, then stopped, breathing hard, and watched until the rogue was gone from sight. Then he turned and walked wearily back to Bess, who had retrieved the rogue's knife and was clean-ing the mud from it with the hem of her gown.

"I thank you."

"And I thank you. I need fear Robin Dalling no longer."

"Aye, but what of him?" Nick asked, inclining his head in the direction the ruffian had vanished. "You have another enemy there, Bess."

"Perchance."

"Nay, not perchance. Of certain. You dare not go back now. Albers will not be there to protect you."

"Can I not protect myself?"

"Against a dagger in the back? No more than Albers could."

"He's right, Bess," Ned put in. "We cannot return to Southwark."

"Come with me," Nick said.

"No!" Her eyes flashed anger. Amy whimpered, more frightened by their argument than she had been by the swordfight. Looking guilty, Bess picked up the little girl, hugging her tightly.

"Come with me," he said again, more gently. "I'll not plead for you to stay, if you would leave my home. But I will not leave you here now."

"But your sister—"

"Has done without my care these past two months. And she would be the last to bid me leave you alone to deal with an enemy . . . as I willy-nilly left her."

She was silent for a time, then: "I must go back to the bousing ken for my stuff."

"Nay, Bess," Ned told her. "Jack cannot wait here. What if that rogue comes back with his friends?"

"But I am afraid!" she said at last, and Nick began to laugh, and Amy pleaded with her mother not to be afraid, until Bess, too, had to laugh, even through tears.

Finally she sobered, and turned to her grandfather. "What say you?"

" 'Tis your decision, girl."

She bit her lip, then sighed heavily and turned toward Nick, her shoulders slumping. "We'll go with you, then. But I'll not stay."

"We'll see," he said, smiling, and went to refasten the cloakbags so Ned and Tom could ride the smaller horse. A few minutes later, with Amy on the saddle before him, Bess sitting behind him with her arms around his waist, and her grandfather and son following, Nick rode out of the marsh, south toward Sussex.

CHAPTER 37

Three full days passed after Isobel's departure before Kat left her bed-chamber again. Most of the swelling around her eye had subsided by that first evening, but for the next two days the bruise was still too dark to be hidden by paint, and Kat did not wish the entire household to know that Justin had struck her. Marie, she believed, would keep it a secret . . . if only because Gabrielle had ordered her to. Jacques had been told that there had been a quarrel—Gabrielle had used that to convince him to take Justin with him to Bidache. Michel and the Char-rons' servants thought that Kat was staying in her room because she was suffering from a megrim, and Marie sent everyone but Gabrielle away from her door with whispers about *migraine*.

Gabrielle had seemed all sympathy to Kat at first, urging her to let Justin believe himself entirely to blame for their quarrel. They might suspect that his food or wine had been drugged, she told Kat, but they had no proof . . . and then, too, Justin had been dallying with Isobel: there was much he should rue about his behavior.

However, there were limits to Gabrielle's sympathy, as Kat discovered when she asked her help in leaving Monteronne before Justin could return from Bidache. She had told Gabrielle that she wished to return to England, to her home, but the baroness would not hear of Kat going back to her family before trying once more to make her marriage work, and at last Kat had given up: Gabrielle would not help her get away. But Michel might.

The paint she had applied to the bruise covered it so well that even she had scarcely been able to see it in the looking glass. Still, she felt anxious as she made her way down to the parlor, where, as she had hoped, she found Michel having breakfast.

"Kat! *Bonjour!* You must be over your *migraine*. I am glad you are well again."

"Thank you, Michel."

"Will you have breakfast?"

"Thank you, but I have broken my fast already. I was looking for your mother," she added. 'Twas a lie; she knew Gabrielle had left the chateau.

"You will not find her here. She has gone to the village. There is a feud there, between two families, and in the past they have asked my father to be the arbiter. But today, with him gone . . ." He shrugged.

"Oh."

"The day is too fair to spend inside. Will you go riding with me?"

" 'Twould please me greatly."

"Then I will have the grooms ready our horses while you change clothes. I will meet you in the courtyard. I have a surprise for you," he added, but only chuckled when she asked him what the surprise was, and would not say more.

She changed to her doublet and hose and boots, then ran down the stairs and out into the courtyard—

Where she stopped, dismayed.

Michel, already mounted, was carrying the Greenland falcon on one gloved hand. It looked sleek and ready to hunt, and her heart had sunk when she saw it.

"*Voilà*, madam," Michel called cheerfully as he rode up to her. "Your hawk—Katherine, is aught amiss?"

"Amiss? Nay. Nay. But I must confess that I am astonished that . . . I am astonished."

"I asked the falconer to begin preparing her the day we visited the mews."

Any damage that would be done had already been done, Kat thought unhappily as she studied the falcon. All traces of the fat it had carried while molting were gone. She could do no more than pray that the falcon's molt had not been ruined when the falconer restricted its food to leave it hungry enough to hunt game rather than rake off. She could guess what Jacques's reaction would be if the last of the bird's new feathers came down weak and thin. It amazed her that Michel had risked incurring his father's wrath merely to please her. Aye, and it gave her hope, too, that Michel would help her get away from Monteronne.

Michel had brought a glove for her, of thick leather to protect her hands from the falcon's talons, and splendidly embroidered with seed pearls. She put it on and took the Greenland falcon from him, and they rode out of the courtyard and down the slope away from the chateau, to a glade beside the stream where Michel believed they would find plentiful game. There they stopped. Michel looked at Kat expectantly, a smile on his face.

Now, the test. She was of a sudden fearful that the falcon might still be unready to hunt.

She bent her arm, bringing the falcon closer to her, then leaned forward and with her teeth and right hand freed the bird of its hood. Its dark brown eyes blinked in the sunlight as it looked around, and it shifted slightly on her wrist. She looked questioningly at Michel. At his nod, she cast the falcon into the sky.

Any fears she had had that it might rake away vanished as the falcon drifted in circles high above them. While Kat, rapt with joy, watched the falcon, Michel rode through the thickets bordering the stream to flush out game. The falcon soon took two partridges and then a fat rabbit, which completely filled Michel's game bag.

"I should have brought another game bag," Michel said. "Shall we go back?"

Kat had not seen a chance to mention her quarrel with Justin yet, for though she doubted Michel would have forgotten Justin's behavior a few days ago, he seemed uninterested in talking about it—perchance unwilling to remind her of it. But she could delay no longer.

" 'Tis warm out here," she said, wiping her hand across her face. She saw the paint smeared on her fingers as she turned back toward Michel.

" 'Twould be cooler—*Mon dieu.* Your *face.*"

She looked down, as though ashamed that he had seen the bruise.

"I knew you had quarreled," Michel said, "for all the servants talked of it. But this . . . Does my mother know? Yea, of course she would. And yet she permits him to stay—ah. Is that why Justin has gone to Bidache with my father?"

Kat nodded.

"I was to have accompanied him. He is staying with a man whose son is one of my best friends. But then I was told—nay, ordered—to stay here . . ." He shook his head angrily. "And when your husband returns? Does my mother expect you to forgive him?"

Kat shrugged. "What choice is there?"

"You must leave him!"

"How? I have no money for passage to England."

"I have money aplenty," he assured her. "Shall we leave tonight? After everyone is asleep? Will that give you enough time to prepare?"

"Yea, 'twill be enough time. Indeed, I am ready to leave now."

"But I am not, Katherine. I can have all in readiness by midnight. I will have these horses. The groom will believe me if I tell him I wish to go riding with a demoiselle from the village, for I have—" He broke off, his face reddening, and Kat was reminded of how young he was. "I will wait for you in the wood near the chateau, by a great oak, a tree twice the size of those around it. Come. I will show you where it is, and the path to it from the chateau."

When Kat and Michel got back to Monteronne, they found Jacques had returned from Bidache and was waiting for them in the courtyard, his face dark with anger. The falconer stood beside him, anxiously twisting his hat into a thick felt rope.

"Michel!" Jacques called when he saw them.

"Go on into the chateau," Michel murmured to Kat as grooms ran to take their horses.

"Nay, let me talk to him. Mayhap I can explain—"

"Explain what?" Michel asked lightly. "*Foi de gentilhomme*, I have done no wrong. This"—he took the game bag from the saddle—"is the proof. Let him argue with it." He slung the bag over his shoulder, then, still carrying the falcon, strode across the courtyard toward his father.

Kat could hear Jacques berating his son as she walked up the steps to the chateau, and though she winced inwardly as she listened, she was not entirely unhappy about their argument. 'Twould only make Michel likelier to help her, in further defiance of his father.

She entered the hall, but before she could reach the stairway, Justin called to her, stopping her.

"My lady."

She turned around slowly. He was standing by a window, from which vantage he must have been watching the scene in the courtyard.

"Do you wish to rebuke me for my sins, my lord? No doubt you are certain I am to blame for this." She gestured toward Jacques and Michel.

Justin looked amused. "No, lady . . . unless you are to blame." His smile faded, and she wondered what her own expression had revealed. "Did you bid him ask the falconer to end the molt early?"

"By my faith, I did not . . . though I must needs confess that I did tell him we might be leaving soon, for Par—" She fell silent, but not nearly soon enough.

"For Paris? And how did you know that?"

She could lie, but if he sensed the lie, he would be more suspicious than ever. The truth was better. It scarce mattered now, when she would be gone in another twelve hours.

"I heard you talking to Jacques," she said, "when you were in the library. You told him you would leave for Paris in a week or two."

"You were eavesdropping?"

"Not by intent, my lord," she said. "Gabrielle had bidden me go to the library, saying I would find you there. I was in the hall when I heard you two talking. Are you satisfied?"

"Indeed," he said, and laughed suddenly, to her surprise. "I feared you had been climbing walls again."

And then he walked away, leaving her to wonder if perchance he did suspect that she had somehow tricked Isobel. A plague on him.

Michel did not join them at dinner, and she feared that their plans were for naught, but then he was with them at supper, and though he and his father had less to say to each other than usual, it was almost as if the morning's quarrel had never occurred.

Justin she saw at both meals, for he sat next to her, as attentive to her now as he had been to Isobel de Maisse a few days before. Michel looked on warily, likely wondering if she might change her mind about leaving Lord Harwood, and she sought to reassure him with smiles. Yet she found herself smiling at Justin more and more, and laughing at his jests, and even blushing once, when he said that the musicians who played for them were better than those they had heard at the Court of Irati.

"The songbirds, you mean?" Gabrielle asked, puzzled.

"Yea, the songbirds," Justin replied, his hand resting lightly on Kat's for an instant. Desire thrilled through her veins, and she cursed her treacherous heart for reminding her of those sweet hours now.

It was with relief that she escaped to her bedchamber after supper. Marie was not there, for Kat had told her earlier that she would be free to spend the night with her family in the village, and the maid had been only too happy to fly away. Belike she had already left the chateau.

Michel would be leaving Monteronne soon, too, Kat thought, to wait in the woods a mile or more from the chateau until well after dark, when he would return with all stealth to wait for her under the great oak. She envied him. He had at least something to do to fill the hours.

At ten minutes of midnight, Kat stole quietly from her chamber and down the hall, a cloakbag in one hand.

The hours had passed very slowly. At half past ten Kat had packed the cloakbag with spare clothes and a comb and two small gallipots of paints: enough, she hoped, to last her until she reached England. Then she had finally extinguished the candle and waited restlessly in the dark, so none would know she was awake, only now and then getting up to check the clock, which she had moved to a table where moonlight fell upon it. The chateau grew more and more still around her, all but the library, whose lighted windows overlooked a part of the garden she could see. But finally even the card game Justin and Jacques had been playing there had ended, and that room, too, was dark and silent. It was twenty minutes after eleven then. Kat waited another half hour, to give Justin and the seigneur time to reach their chambers and retire, before she picked up the cloakbag and opened her door onto the darkened hall.

She moved as quietly as possible along the rush-strewn hall and down the stairs. Her heart was thudding so loudly she feared someone would hear it, or the breath that seemed to rasp in her throat. The cloakbag seemed heavy already, dragging at her arm. She had to bring it—Michel had convinced her of that—but it slowed her, and threatened to betray her if she swung it carelessly against some doorjamb or chair, and worse, it would make mock of any story she might tell for being up and about at this hour of the night. She would have left it in the great hall, had she not been afraid that Michel would insist on coming back after it—if some servant had not already tripped over it and raised a hue and cry.

Somehow she escaped from the chateau without being seen, and ran awkwardly toward the woods, the cloakbag pulling her to one side.

It was not hard to find the path Michel had pointed out to her, for the oak leaning out from the woods could be spotted from a distance even in poorer light than the moon gave tonight. Yet once Kat had reached the entrance to the wood, she paused. In the darkness, their branches stirred by a breeze, the trees seemed alive, and every winter's tale she had once heard of ghosts and fairies and hobgoblins returned to her now, much more frightening than when she heard them beside a warm fire, in the company of her family and friends. 'Twas folly, she knew, to think on such things: was she in any more danger here than in the Forest of Irati, when she had not thought of sprites and fairies at all?

But Justin had been with her then. Now she was alone, and she could not know in certain that Michel was waiting beneath that great oak. Haply he had been delayed. Haply someone had waylaid him. Someone, or something. She shivered, watching the branches sway against the sky. An owl hooted—an ill omen, i'faith—and she shivered again.

Yet she dared not go back. She set the cloakbag down and unbuttoned her doublet, then turned it inside out and put it on again. 'Twas an old wives' fable that to wear a coat inside out was a charm, but some said that ghosts and fairies were no more than that, too. Like to like.

Picking up the cloakbag again, she ventured into the wood.

She had only a few hundred feet to walk, but that was space enough to wonder a thousand times if Michel would be there, and what she would do if he were not. Then she came within sight of the tremendous oak, and saw him waiting below the canopy of its branches with their horses tethered beside him, and she gave a cry of relief and ran toward him.

"Kat!" he cried. "I feared you might have been discovered and followed."

"She was," came the response from behind her, and she stumbled to a halt, dropping the cloakbag as she whirled to see Justin walking toward them, carrying a sword, though he wore no sword belt.

"I could not sleep," Justin told her. "I wished to talk to you. But when I left my room—softly, so as not to wake anyone—I saw you stealing away. With a cloakbag, forsooth. So I followed."

"Par Dieu," Michel said, "she was fortunate indeed to escape that talk you intended, since you came with a sword."

Justin shook his head. " 'Twas a flagon of wine that I first carried, but this seemed more meet. I feared she might come to harm in this folly."

"What folly? She leaves, that she may come to no greater harm than you have done her."

Justin looked from Michel to Kat and back again.

"So this is no dalliance, but a rescue? Or 'twould be if there were need of one. I trow you have been misled."

"Then 'twas by my own eyes, for I saw the bruise left by your hand."

Justin sighed, and closed his eyes for a moment, and in that moment Michel drew his sword.

"No!" Kat stepped between them.

"No, by my life," Justin agreed. "I would not fight you. But neither would I let you leave with her."

Michel took a few steps to the side, and Justin turned slightly, following him with his gaze but moving no more than needs must. His would be the cooler head in this fight, Kat knew. And so he would win, and kill or maim Michel in that victory, for these were no blunt foils they carried.

"Enough!" She moved closer to Justin, blinking back tears as she faced Michel. "I would not have your blood on my hands. I will go back."

"Katherine—" Michel sounded anguished.

"I have no choice." She picked up her cloakbag and started back to the chateau. Justin caught up with her and took the cloakbag, and as they walked back together, he looked over his shoulder from time to time at Michel, who followed them at a distance.

They found Gabrielle waiting for them, just outside the courtyard. Mercifully, she was alone. Or maybe not so mercifully, Kat thought, as they paused beside her and watched her watch her son approach. Gabrielle had said not a word to them, but her sorrowful gaze had taken in everything: Justin's sword, the cloakbag, the two horses . . .

When Michel was close enough to hear Gabrielle without her needing to raise her voice, she said, "One may see many things that should not be seen, if awake and watchful too late, but never . . ." She shook her head. "You said you were going to the village. Go, now. You are late."

"I will not leave her with—"

"You will not! You will not give your father even a day of peace. But I will *not* have this, Michel. I will not have you give him no choice but to send you away, never to return again. And I am afraid he would do that, should he learn of this dishonorable behav—"

"Dishonorable? Was there honor in Justin striking his wife? Was there honor in you refusing to help her?"

"Michel, no!" Kat said. " 'Twas wrong of me—" She fell silent as Gabrielle held up her hand.

"Perhaps not," the Frenchwoman said to her son. "But I see in that no reason why you should ape our foolishness."

"Am I a fool to want to protect her from her husband? You knew he struck her—"

"*Oui.*"

"—and yet you did nothing."

"He is sorry! And he will not hit her again. Will you?" she asked Justin, and he shook his head.

"And you would believe him?" Michel asked furiously. "Why? He hit her once. He—"

"He may have been drunk."

"Do you believe he will never drink wine again?"

"And there may have been some drug in the wine."

Justin started, and looked at Kat. She could not meet his gaze.

"I cry you mercy, *mon ami*," Gabrielle said to Justin, "for not telling you of our suspicions, Katherine's and mine, but we had no proof. Nor would that excuse what you did."

"But if his behavior is not excused—" Michel began, and his mother interrupted him.

"It is at least explained. Would you think about that, my son? Would you *think*? But not here. Go. Go now, before we are all seen together, for this tells too much of a tale without any words needing to be said."

Michel hesitated a few moments, then left. Gabrielle watched him ride away, then, shaking her head, took both Justin and Kat by the arm and walked between them into the courtyard.

"We should leave now," Justin said as they approached the steps up to the chateau's door. "My wife is half through with her packing already. We could be gone before Jacques wakes."

" 'Twould be best," Gabrielle said simply, and Kat kept her thoughts to herself.

Half an hour later Kat was in her bedchamber, adding a few things to the last of the three cloakbags Gabrielle had given her—for the baroness had insisted that Kat take all her new clothes with her—when Gabrielle came in.

Kat looked at her warily. 'Twas the first time she had been alone with Gabrielle since returning to the chateau, and she would understand if the baroness had harsh words to say to her. But Gabrielle said nothing for a time, only stood there looking at her sorrowfully, until Kat's vision blurred with unshed tears.

"Madame, I am so sorry . . ."

"So am I, Katherine. I blame myself, for not comprehending how much you wanted to leave Justin. I love Justin. Had I borne a daughter as well as a son, and were Justin not already married, I might have wished her to marry him. That may have made me deaf to your pleas. If you do not wish to leave with him tonight, then tell me so, and I will see that you are not taken from Monteronne against your will."

The Devil himself could not have tempted Kat more. But before she could accept Gabrielle's offer of help, she was overcome by guilt. She had already caused conflict between Michel and Justin, and brought enough trouble to this family.

"I thank you, madame," she said softly, "but I have decided that I should go with my husband."

"Then," Gabrielle said with a sigh, "I will merely give you this." She handed Kat a heavy purse full of gold écus, and refused to take it back. "Put it in your cloakbag, and do not let Justin know that you have it. Perchance someday, should you change your mind again and wish to leave him, you will need that money. I trow you had none of your own?"

Kat shook her head.

"That is always a mischief, for a wife to have no money of her own."

"Aye," Kat said, thinking how she might have left Monteronne while Justin was recuperating, had she had enough money to buy passage on a ship. "Aye, it can be." And she thanked Gabrielle, and added the purse to her cloakbag, and then Gabrielle helped her carry the cloakbags downstairs, to where Justin was waiting.

With the point of a knife, Isobel de Maisse pried at the tiny rectangle of wood that so frustrated her, but as before, it stubbornly refused to budge.

She sat back, wiping sweat from her face. Her hands were shaking from her efforts, and the knife's handle had left a red imprint on her palm.

For the last few days, whenever her maidservant was away from their room at Le Dauphin Sautant, she had tried to open the intricate lock inside the lid of her perfume chest. She had made the attempt at least a dozen times now, but always in vain: the mechanism must have been damaged when that lout of a servant dropped the chest.

She flexed her hand, trying to ease its soreness so she could try again before the maid returned. She had sent the woman away to buy them some tolerable bread, better than what they could get here at the inn.

Par Dieu, how she hated this place! And where was the Florentine's emissary, the Italian gentleman, he of the ready laugh and the sword decorated with the Medici initial? Where was he? She would have believed that she had come to the wrong inn, but this was the one to which every person they had asked had directed them, and there had been no mistaking the sign, with its outline of a leaping dolphin, and inside the dolphin the painted figure of a young man wearing rich garb and a crown, also leaping. She had even wondered if there might be two inns of the same name, but her servants had made inquiries, and that was not the case.

So where was Catherine de Medici's messenger?

Isobel reminded herself again that he had said she might have to wait a month for her instructions. But how could she bear to spend so much as another week here? The inn had seemed fair enough when she first looked upon it, but the first night here had taught her that those who stayed here were coarse and dangerous. Most were men, and those who were not thieves or smugglers seemed no better than thieves. And the women—what few she had seen—had to be whores. She would have left the next day, had she been able to think of a way to leave the emissary word of where she had gone, but she trusted her host no more than she trusted his guests. She was trapped here until the Italian gentleman came for her. She would as lief have been in the dungeons of the Conciergerie in Paris. Though perhaps not: she might find herself there, were she to leave here before learning from the emissary where his mistress wanted her to go next. Of certain, she would be beaten. Yet she was beginning to wonder, seriously wonder, if a beating might not be preferable to spending much more time here.

Suddenly there were voices outside her door. Two men had stopped there and were talking about a ship that had weighed anchor late this morning, leaving so hurriedly that all the idle men along the quay had been hired to help load the ship with victuals and casks of fresh water.

She listened idly. One of the men was wroth at the ship's captain, whom he had spoken to a few times during the weeks the ship was here. The captain had refused to consider smuggling for any amount of money—he would not even come to Le Dauphin Sautant to talk business, the man complained. Isobel had to laugh, though quietly: she could understand that captain's reluctance. Would that the Italian gentleman had been so wise, but no doubt he had judged the inn only by its appearance from the street. Else he would not have bidden her come here.

At last the men went away. She turned once more to the chest, wiggled her fingers a few times, and set to work again.

CHAPTER 38

The sleeves and stomacher were finished.

Jane laid them out on the satin coverlet of Kat's bed and stood back to admire her handiwork, shimmering green and gold in the afternoon sunlight. She had lined the sleeves with gold tissue and trimmed them with gold lace and glass beads. For the stomacher, she had worked the cloth-of-gold with gold thread, embroidering three large roses on it, then veiled it with the finest black cypress she could find. These would be fine gifts for Kat, and had used no more than a few yards of the cloth-of-gold; the rest she had taken to a tailor who was fashioning of it a doublet for Nick.

If he ever returned to wear it . . .

She had seen Sparrow four more times since their first meeting, but each time he had stopped by Beechwood for only a few minutes to see if Nick and Kat had returned. He had had no more news for her than she for him. It seemed impossible to her that Kat and Nick had vanished so completely that not even Walsingham's agents could find them. Someone must know where they were . . . if the two were still alive.

She shook her head, banishing that thought quickly, then hurried from the chamber. She needed to find something else to do now, so she would have no time for brooding such fears. Would that she could have trusted herself to make that gift for Nick. 'Twould have kept her busy. Alas, she had never sewn men's clothes, and would liefer start elsewhere than with such fine stuff as cloth-of-gold.

She made her way downstairs. Perchance she could help with some of the work in the kitchen or stillroom. But as she turned toward the kitchen, a groom burst into the hall.

"Madam," he gasped, " 'tis Master Nick, coming down the lane from the north!"

Jane gaped at him, almost unable to believe what she had heard.

" 'Tis Nick!" the man said. "I saw him myself!"

With a little cry, she ran past him out into the courtyard.

Her thin-soled slippers were not meant for wear outside the house.

Before she had left the gate twenty paces behind, she had bruised her foot on a stone. She slowed to a limping walk but continued on.

Nick was riding up the lane toward her, surrounded by half a dozen of his servants. With him were two strangers—nay, four strangers, she realized, noticing that there were two children riding with the old man. Children who looked much like the black-haired woman who rode behind Nick.

Nick reined his horse in when he saw her. He and the woman dismounted, but she stayed by the horse while he approached Jane.

"Thanks be to God that you are back!" She did not even try to hold back her tears as he hugged her.

"Yea, I thank God that I am home again. 'Tis good to see you, Jane. Where's my sweet sister?"

The question chilled her. She drew back, her eyes wide and unhappy as they met his, and he groaned.

"Oh, no. Oh Lord, no . . ."

He ordered chambers prepared for the people he had brought with him. They seemed ill at ease in the house, especially under the speculative gaze of the servants, most of whom were better dressed than these strangers, but Nick did his best to make them feel welcome. He talked with the old man and the woman as though they were his equals, and jested with the children, until the chambers were ready. Jane had questions aplenty for him, as well as news, but she waited, unwilling to interrupt. Not until his companions had gone upstairs did he turn to her.

"Shall we sit down in the parlor?" he suggested. "I am famished, and we have much to discuss."

He dined on salad, cold roast chicken, Catherine pear pie and muscatel while Jane told him what had happened at Beechwood since he and Kat left. Her voice shook at times as she spoke, no matter how hard she tried to keep it steady. So far Nick had told her only that he had stumbled and fallen in the wood near Harwood Hall, losing his memory and not regaining it until two days ago, but that revelation had been shattering. He knew no more than Sparrow of Kat's whereabouts . . . unless Sparrow knew more than he had admitted.

" 'Tis all I have to tell you," she said at last.

He reached across the table and took her hand. "Good Jane. 'Twas kind of you to wait for us at Beechwood like this."

"What else—" Her voice broke; she looked away. He tightened the grip on her hand. She wished she could feel his arms around her again.

"Fret not," he said. "We'll find her yet. Lisle would not have dared harm her."

"Pray God, you are right." He gave her hand a final squeeze before releasing it. She felt the loss of contact keenly. To keep from showing her disappointment, she said, "Now you must tell me of what happened to you since leaving Harwood Hall."

He was silent a long time before replying, sunk in thought, and she could not help but think that he seemed much different than the young man she remembered. The changes the last two months had made in him were much greater than the cut of his hair and beard, or the poorly fashioned clothes he wore. He seemed much older now than when he left for Harwood Hall. He had acted carefree and boisterous as he tried to keep the children amused earlier, but while the old Nick had worn that carefree manner like a second skin, the man now seated across from her seemed more like a grave shadow of that young gallant. She would have been grieved by the change, had she not also sensed new strength in him, a tempered strength, forged by God only knew what trials.

"There's little enough to tell," he said at last. "I have told you already that I fell and struck my head. When I woke I found myself in a yeoman's house, with no memory of who I was or how I had come there. As soon as I could, I set out for London. On the way, I met Bess, and she and her grandfather allowed me to stay with them in London."

There was more to it than that, Jane knew. Much more. "Bess is a lovely woman," she said softly.

Nick glanced at her, then away, but said nothing. Jane sighed inwardly. She knew that he and Bess had been lovers: 'twas plain to see when either one of them looked at the other.

" 'Twas generous of them to take you in," she went on.

He nodded. "I mean to repay them by finding them a home away from London. There is plague there now."

Jane nodded, as though his answer had satisfied her, though it had not. How had his friends lived, that they would be so willing to leave their home and work behind? She could scarce believe that people making an honest living, no matter how poor, would abandon their trade on the spur of the moment—and from what Nick had said earlier, they had all left London the evening before last, on the same day that he had regained his memory. Some folk might have jumped at the chance of a different life offered by a gentleman in their debt, but Jane did not think that was true of Bess and her grandfather. They had appeared more uneasy than happy with their new surroundings. The little girl had seemed awed; only the little boy—Tom? Was that his name?—had looked around with an avid eye.

Someone entered the room behind them. Jane turned to see Agnes Fuller, one of the maids.

"Yea, Agnes?"

"Madam, cry you mercy. I would not disturb you, but I have lost my purse. The strings were old and worn thin, and haply broke at last." She touched her belt, from which hung two strands of ancient silk cord. "I was in here earlier this morning, and thought it might have fallen from my belt. I have already searched the chambers upstairs, and the gallery and the great hall. Have you seen it? 'Tis a small purse, of maiden-hair brown velvet."

"Nay, Agnes. Would that I could help you, but I have not seen it."

"Then I must have left it elsewhere," the girl said, with a small, wavering smile. " 'Tis of little matter, I suppose. There were only a few coins in it . . ."

But all you had, Jane thought.

Nick shifted in his chair, and Jane glanced at him, her attention caught at once by the guilty look on his face.

Just then they heard light but quick footsteps from the great hall. A few moments later Bess tripped into the room. She was somewhat out of breath, but with her cheeks flushed and her thick dark hair in disarray about her face, she looked even prettier than she had earlier, when she had been pale and wary. Jane felt a pang of jealousy, and chided herself for it.

"I have found your purse," Bess blurted out, not bothering to apologize for intruding. " 'Twas on the floor by the hearth. The strings were badly frayed, so I cut them off for you. 'Twill still serve to tie to your girdle, I warrant."

"Aye, and more securely this time. I thank you." Agnes ran her hand over the cords, which were not more than two inches long now. "I would reward you—"

"No," Bess said, with a quick shake of her head. " 'Twas naught. And would you not do the same for me?"

"With all my heart," Agnes said. Then, after thanking Bess again, Agnes excused herself, explaining that she should be about her tasks.

Bess remained in the parlor. With the maid's departure, the wary expression Jane had seen earlier had returned to her face. She moved slowly toward Nick, one hand digging into a pocket of her half-kirtle and emerging with a tiny figure of carved ivory that usually stood on a table in the gallery.

"Tom picked this up," she said, looking ashamed, "and by the time I saw he had it, he could not recall where it belonged. Or so he said. If you'll tell me where it belongs, I'll put it back."

"I'll return it," Nick said, taking it from her.

She flushed. "I have spoken to him, and it will not happen again."

"I know." He reached out and took her hand, and again Jane was stabbed by envy. "Do not worry yourself, Bess."

She gave him a fleeting smile. "Y'are kind, Jack. I thank you. Now, I must get back, before—" She caught herself, and glanced at Jane, then sighed and smiled again. "Before there's more mischief. Children, you know."

"Aye," Jane agreed, the corners of her mouth curving upward a bit.

She waited until Bess had left before looking at Nick again. "Well, *Jack*," she said with a wry smile. "You may be thankful that Agnes is a goose, and of an unsuspecting nature to boot. Will you tell all of it now?"

He started to protest, then looked down at the figure in his hands and had to laugh. At last he began to talk again, and the tale was much longer than the one he had told before.

He still did not confess that he and Bess had been lovers, and Jane suspected he knew 'twas not necessary. She only hoped that the jealousy she felt was not so obvious to him.

After she had sworn not to tell anyone else, he admitted that Bess and her father had made their living in less than honest ways, but he was more than willing to defend them, and most of their friends at the Turk's Sword as well. He seemed more than a little surprised—aye, and greatly relieved, too—that Jane did not condemn their thievery and dishonest begging. But she could not: she had offered charity to vagabonds before, when they came to Stamworth, and had heard enough stories to convince her that for every thief or rogue who had become one out of laziness or malice, there was at least one other who had had no other choice but starving. Ned she sympathized with, and she pitied Bess, and the children especially.

"You will let the children stay here?" she asked, thinking she would take them to Stamworth if Nick would not have them here. She would have to keep an eye upon Tom, though.

"Yea, verily. But Bess will not stay."

Jane nodded, gladdened by his reply, and at the same time guilt-ridden that she felt glad.

"And Ned will insist on going with her, though God knows he's too old to be traveling."

"If you could find them a place to stay near here . . . and honest work . . ."

"I have bethought me of that. Truly, I have racked my brains. 'Twould mean Bess could keep her children, and safely. But I can think of no place for them in the village, nor would Bess stay so near." He looked away then, frowning.

No, Jane thought, the woman would not wish to be too near Nick. She understood Bess's feelings, for often enough she had thought 'twould be best to move away herself. But Stamworth was her home, and Kat her best friend, and she had always been able to contrive some hope that someday Nick might love her. Poor Bess had no such hope. She had lost him irrecoverably when he returned to his life as a gentleman, and she knew it, and Jane pitied her more than ever.

She drew idle patterns on the tablecloth with her index finger, looking at her hand but not really seeing it, as she wondered what might be done.

Suddenly she looked up at Nick. "Mistress Adams! At the Golden Griffin!"

"Southampton . . . ? 'Twould be far enough to suit Bess. But do you think she would take them in?"

"She has been in your debt, Nick, since you and Kat took her in that time when you found her on the high road by your lane, too sick to travel further. She swears she would have never made it back to Southampton at all, except in a coffin, if you had not brought her here and sent for doctors and had her stay with you for those two weeks. She tells me you have given her no chance to repay you."

"She's repaid us already with a week's lodging, and offered us more."

"Aye, but she holds that as naught against the debt she owes you. I warrant you, she would be glad to help you in this. You have told me she would talk of how close her late husband had come to a vagabond's life, after King Henry dissolved the monasteries. And she loves children." He still looked uncertain. "At the least ways, write to her."

He nodded slowly. "Very well. I could see that Tom was apprenticed to a good tradesman in Southampton, if he does not wish to stay at the inn. Amy would be happy there, and Ned . . ." His voice trailed off, and she knew he was thinking of Bess again.

"Ask Bess first. I trow she will approve the plan."

He nodded again, but said nothing more, and after a time she began to feel herself an intruder. So she excused herself then and went away, leaving him alone to wrestle with his thoughts. 'Twas not, she feared, a match he could win.

Nick sent a messenger to Southampton that night. The man was back by the next afternoon, bringing word that Mistress Adams would welcome meeting Nick's friends, whenever they could come. Plans were made to set out for Southampton early the next morning.

In the meantime Jane saw little of Bess and her family. Nick had spent the day showing them around the house and grounds, and though Jane would not have minded accompanying them, she felt it would be best to leave Nick these hours alone with the people who had been his family for the last two months. She would have gone home, but Nick had asked her to stay at Beechwood for another few days, in case Kat returned while he was away on his trip to Southampton.

She saw him that evening for a little while, encountering him by accident when she went to Kat's room, thinking to put away the sleeves and stomacher she had made for her. Nick was there, sitting on the bed, looking at one of the sleeves. He looked up when she came in.

"Well met, Jane. Needs must that I thank you in my sister's behalf. When you told me that you had fashioned these gifts for Kat, I had not expected them to be so fine. Nay, I mean—"

"You mean well," Jane said, laughing. "But I trow I would starve if I had to make my living as a sempster."

"I doubt that." He handed the sleeve to her, and she folded it and its mate and put them away, with the stomacher, in a chest. "Kat will truly like your gifts."

He spoke as though confident that she would return. He had spoken that way each time he mentioned her, Jane thought. Would that she felt the same . . . but she could play at confidence. "I hope she will," she said lightly. "You have willy-nilly paid a dear price for them."

"The locket?"

She nodded. She had told him yesterday of the thieving pedlar, and of the sheriff's fruitless search for him.

" 'Twas foolish of me to show him the picture."

"Nay, it was not. Had I seen the cloth, likely I would have done the same. No stuff could suit Kat better. And you had no way of knowing that he was a thief and not merely a common pedlar."

"In truth, he was not a common pedlar. Had I left him alone with the maidservants, he would have flattered them out of their every penny."

"Aye, and mayhap their clothes as well," Nick said, and she blushed.

"He was a handsome man," she confessed. "Tall—a hand taller than you—and with tawny hair, and a neat beard, and pale blue eyes."

"In good sooth, a perfectly beautiful pedlar. I trow I am lucky that this house was not bartered for one of his smiles."

"Beshrew you, Nick. Said I that he was perfect? Nay, he was not, for he had a small scar, of the shape of a crescent"—her fingertips traced a pattern below her left eye—"high on his left cheek. An old scar, not— Is aught amiss?" she asked uncertainly, seeing Nick's expression change abruptly.

"Tandy . . ." he whispered.

"What?"

"Lord Harwood's manservant, whom we met at the Jerusalem Tree. He has such a scar, and fits such a description."

"Lord Harwood's servant?"

"Yea, and a trusted one, for 'twas Tandy who was with Lisle when he met with the Spaniard. Jesu! If Kat did not escape, then might not Tandy have been left in England as her jailer? If Sparrow or his agents could find Tandy . . . I must talk to him. I'll send a messenger presently. He will have an hour of light yet in which to ride. I would liefer have waited till my return from Southampton, but now I shall not."

"And if he gets here before you return from Southampton?"

"What chance of that?"

Just past four in the afternoon of the day after Nick's messenger reached him, having ridden hard from Sussex, Walter Cadmon, nicknamed Sparrow, who had ridden hard from London, came within sight of Beechwood and slowed his post horse to a trot.

'Twas far from cheap to ride post, and he had paid for the horses and postboys out of his own purse, with no assurance that his master would repay him. *Come post-haste*, Nick Langdon had written. *Would that I knew why*, Sparrow thought angrily. If it proved that Master Langdon had misled him and that by making this journey in such haste he had been shoeing the goose, then he would—Nay, he knew not what he would do to Nick Langdon, but the popinjay would rue that letter . . .

And no matter what news the boy had, Sparrow thought, he would answer now for his silence these past two months. As like as not, nothing he would say would be trustworthy. 'Twas what followed of choosing intelligencers because they had been at the Inns of Court. There were far too many papists there, and no doubt they encouraged all manner of contrivers.

Yea, there was little hope that Nick Langdon could ever be trusted. The boy had made mischief enough already. 'Twould take news of great import to redeem him now, in Sparrow's eyes.

And if there was no news of import, Walsingham, too, would be sure to complain about it.

Two days after his humiliating mistake near Chenies, Sparrow had received a letter from Walsingham that he wondered had not arrived in cinders, for the message was so hot. Walsingham had felt himself shamed by his agent's mistake, even though the queen had graciously allowed that a knife could have been concealed as well as a posy, and her guards had in truth been lax in not seeing the possible danger. Still, Walsingham's enemies at court now mocked him for his agent's error. Sparrow's master had reminded him again of his other failures, including his failure to find proof of Lord Harwood's treason. The last had especially rankled

Sparrow, for it was unfair: 'twas Walsingham himself who was to blame for that, having shackled him with Nick Langdon as an agent.

If Langdon had some intelligence of use, then all would be well and good. If not, Sparrow resolved, he would rid himself of the Italianate gallant, and give Master Walsingham a piece of his mind, too, on the subject of these Inns of Court men.

Faith, there was solace in that thought. Sparrow was almost in a good humor as he rode through the gate of Beechwood and dismounted in the courtyard. And then he was told by the groom who had come running to hold his lathered horse that Master Nick had gone to Southampton, and might be back today, or might not.

That evening the great hall of Beechwood rang with the music of a pair of virginals, its loudness most often overpowering the noise of the argument in the adjacent parlor. Jane, foreseeing trouble, had asked that Kat's virginals be brought downstairs and set on a table in the hall. After supper, she had sent all the servants but Louise up to the gallery, where the steward, who had a good strong voice, was reading to them from the *Book of Martyrs*. Soon after, Nick had returned from Southampton, already in a surly mood even before he heard that Sparrow was here, in the parlor, and wroth at having to wait for him. The moment the door of the parlor had banged shut behind Nick, Jane had told Louise to begin playing, as loudly as she could. That had been nearly an hour ago, and though the quarrel still raged on, the servants had likely heard little of it and—pray God!—nothing of the secrets of state that Nick and Sparrow should have been whispering rather than shouting.

Suddenly the parlor door was flung open and Sparrow stalked out. He bestowed a venomous glance on Jane before giving her his back, and she sighed with relief as he vanished around the screen and ran heavily down the outside stairs.

Then she looked around at the parlor door again. Nick still had not come out. She approached the door warily. He sat with his head resting on the table, his forehead on his crossed arms.

"Jane?" He did not look up. "Pray have the steward bring me a bottle of aqua vitae . . ."

So she went upstairs and told the steward what his master wanted, then betook herself to her bedchamber. Nick, she was sure, would not want to talk to her again that night.

She was wrong. He knocked on the door of her bedchamber half an hour later.

"Marry, will you speak to me?" he asked, not coming in at once. "Though I trow to do so will make you suspect to Master Sparrow, for I have been at Gray's Inn, that nest of papists and contrivers."

"Then you are forsaken indeed," she said, as gravely as she could, and gestured for him to enter the room.

He had taken but a few steps inside when he stopped, glanced back at her, then walked the rest of the way to the open clothes press in which she had hung his doublet, which the tailor had finished that morning.

"You had more of that cloth-of-gold! By the mass, this will suit Kat well!"

" 'Twill suit you better, I warrant," she said, and smiled when he looked around in surprise. "Please you, try it on. The tailor used one of your old doublets for the pattern, one that Harry told me fit you best. Try it on, for I would learn if he did good work."

"I'll be all night merely buttoning it," Nick told her, running his hand down the two dozen gold buttons on the front of the doublet. Another dozen buttons closed the cuffs.

"Then let me help."

Save for the few seconds, two days ago, when he had embraced her upon his return, she had never stood so close to him before. Her hands shook a little as she helped him with the buttons, and she stepped back quickly when she was done.

"Well?" she asked.

He went to stand before the looking glass, and turned from side to side, admiring himself.

"By God's blood, I'll to the court tonight. The Rome mort herself must see this."

"Who?"

"The queen. She's called the Rome mort in pedlar's French."

"Oh. I hope you will not take that canting tongue back to court with you."

"What, would you have me at court without a tongue? Then I would be the finest dommerar in the land."

"Beshrew you, Nick! Y'are cup-shotten."

"Perhaps," he admitted. "But I have reason to be . . . as you may have heard."

"I heard as little as I might, though I am near deaf from Louise's pounding on the virginals."

"I thank you for having thought of that. Master Sparrow and I were much too wroth with each other to think to speak softly, lest some eavesdropper overhear us."

"Eavesdropper? My own servants at Stamworth could have heard you. Nay, you were not so loud. Louise's playing sufficed to keep your talk private. What said Master Sparrow to your news of Tandy?"

"Naught to our purpose. He saw Tandy at Southampton, but could not swear that he sailed with Lord Harwood. Like enough, he did not, for Sparrow says Lisle has not yet returned to England."

"So he told me. But will he search now for Tandy, in the hope of finding your sister in his care?"

Nick hesitated, then shook his head. "He has searched enough already," he said quietly.

"And will search no more."

"Nay."

"For Sparrow believes she is not in England," Jane said. "He is sure she sailed for Spain with Lord Harwood."

Nick looked startled. "You knew? Yet you said naught to me of this?"

"I suspected, and would not have added to your fears. Sparrow would tell me only that he was searching for both of you, but on his first visit here, when I told him how Kat was garbed, he spoke of that outlandish hat of hers, and told me he had seen her wear it here. And I knew that could not have been, for she had left that hat at Stamworth when you . returned from the Jerusalem Tree. I wondered if he had perchance seen her in Southampton, but not known her . . . but I thought 'twas also possible that you had told him that she had worn the cap at the Jerusalem Tree, and that was how he knew of it."

"You did not ask him?"

"I'faith, he would not stay for questions on his next visits to Beechwood, but stopped only to ask if I had news of you." She hesitated. "Yea, and I feared to ask, for I prayed that my suspicions were wrong. I will not sleep easily tonight, knowing of certain that she is in Spain."

"Nay, she is in France now, if she is with Lisle. His ship was seen at Bayonne by a friend of one of Walsingham's intelligencers."

"In France?"

"There is peace there now. She is safer there than in Spain."

"Aye, if she is in France. If she is still with Lord Harwood."

"I pray that she is. Better with him than alone in Spain." He laughed, a brief, ugly laugh. " 'Sdeath! What have I come to, that I must needs pray that my sister is with a suspected traitor!"

"Kat went with you of her own accord. Indeed, if I know her, she gave you little choice. You must not hold yourself accountable."

"Yea, verily, for I dare not. It seems I am incapable of being accountable."

"Did Sparrow say so?" she asked, wishing she had not let the little intelligencer get away yet. She would have liked to have had some words with him.

"Yea, and I had no sound argument against him. God knows I failed, both as Kat's protector and as Walsingham's spy."

"What failure? Was it your fault that you were discovered? Was it your fault that Kat fell?"

"I bade her climb."

"Nay, you told me that you asked her if she could climb the wall. Do not tell me now that you forced her to do so, or bade her climb beyond the point where she could do so safely. I will not believe you. I say again, 'twas not your fault she fell. Nor did you fail as Walsingham's intelligencer, and if Sparrow said so, 'twas to hide his own failure, for he should have listened to what you told him in May of what you learned at the Jerusalem Tree."

She shook her head angrily. "Nick, sweet Nick. Nick, you fool. Would you be the Atlas of England, and do every man's work? And then torture yourself when you cannot bear a burden no mortal man could bear? You say you cannot be accountable. I deny your major. Had you been able to bring Kat safely away—aye, had you been able to keep her away entire—you would have. Look you, you have brought Bess safely from London. I know of few gentleman who would have done so, and many—more's the pity—who, coming to themselves as you did, would have left at once, with nary a backward glance. Yet you brought her here, and took her to Southampton, and found a new home and a new life for her. You would see her safe and happy."

"Would I? Would I?" He laughed bitterly again, and she stared at him in bewilderment.

"Does she not like the Golden Griffin?"

"Yes, she likes it. And Mistress Adams likes her, of a truth. Aye, and so does an ostler who works there. He likes her too well by half. When I left the inn this afternoon, they were standing together under that gilt sign, and I swear he would fain have had his arm around her."

"I see . . . Is he an honest man, this ostler?"

Nick sighed. "He is. He was a sailor once, but he swears he'll no more to sea. Bess told me that he reminds her of her late husband. Mistress Adams hopes to make a match of it."

"And y'are against it?"

"I know not what I am. I am a fool," he said, and turned away.

Jane's heart ached for him. She had expected to hear someday that Bess had found a new love. 'Twas what she would do, if she were Bess. But not so soon! Not half so soon . . . And yet she could not blame

Bess for the pain that she was causing Nick to suffer now. Mayhap the woman had decided that a clean break with Nick would be kindest at long running . . .

"Do you wish her well?"

"Yea, of certain."

"Then you are not a fool."

He still would not turn to face her. He was crying, soundlessly, the tears leaving bright tracks down his cheeks. She put her hands on either side of his face and, standing on tiptoe, she kissed him, gently, on the mouth.

"Jane, you are too good to me," he whispered.

"I love you."

"Nay . . ." He looked disbelieving.

"I have loved you for years, I swear it. Upon my life, I love you."

Suddenly his arms were around her, pulling her against him. She buried her face in the rich silk of his doublet, then jerked back, realizing that she was crying, too.

"I thank God you are here, lady," he said, and kissed her, less gently than she had kissed him. "Will you stay with me?"

"I would not be sent away," she said, and took his hand, and led him to the bed.

CHAPTER 39

" 'Tis the first of September today. My dad should be leaving for Stour-bridge Fair soon," Peter said, a bit wistfully.

"Did you ever go there with him?" Kat asked.

"Once," he said, and looked as if he would say more, but went back to his carving instead.

I'faith, he misses his home, Kat thought. All Peter had talked of since she returned to the *Lady Margaret* had been his experiences in Bilbao and Bayonne, and the most outrageous sailors' tales he had heard there. He would tell her any of those she wanted to hear—but nothing, alas, of what he thought his lord was about, or even where Tandy, who to her surprise was not aboard, had gone. She had believed Peter entirely given over to the sailor's life, but now it seemed that a vein of melancholy ran beneath his surface happiness. *He might yet make a yeoman.* 'Twas a pleasant thought.

She was sitting with her back to the starboard rail, on a cask upon which Peter had placed a length of canvas to protect the fine stuff of her kirtle. If she looked over her shoulder, she could see the French coast. For two days now, the *Lady Margaret* had sailed slowly up the coastline toward La Rochelle. For all his haste in leaving Monteronne, Justin appeared to be in no hurry to reach Paris.

Of a sudden, the ship's boy high overhead on the mast called out:

"A sail, ho! A ship!" He was silent for a few moments, then cried: "I make it to be *L'Orfraie*. Aye, 'tis *L'Orfraie*! *L'Orfraie*!"

Peter's head whipped around, and he stared past Kat toward the bow. "There!" He pointed toward the horizon ahead of them. The ship was tiny in the distance, little more than a dark speck against the bright water, but Kat knew the ship's boy who had identified it had a glass made in Italy that Justin had given him.

"*L'Orfraie*," she whispered, as the cry was taken up by the men on deck. Mingled fear and excitement coursed through her veins. *L'Orfraie*, the *Osprey*, was a Huguenot pirate ship, and while she felt she could count its Protestant captain as an ally, how would he feel about those aboard the *Lady Margaret*? If many in England knew the ship was named for the wife of a Spanish nobleman, and suspected its owner of Catholic sympathies, then it was likely such rumors had reached the Huguenot port of La Rochelle and the privateers there. Would this privateer stop the *Lady Margaret*? And if it did, was there any chance that she might be able to convince its captain that she was an ally and should be returned safely to England?

"Fear not, lady," Peter said, taking her hand and squeezing it. "Jean d'Arnaud, the captain of yon ship, is a friend of his lordship."

"A friend?" she asked in a small voice, all hope that this encounter would mean her freedom dashed. She wished she could doubt him, but Justin, who walked past them now toward the bow, the captain beside him, looked very pleased to see the pirate ship.

"How much do you know of Monsieur d'Arnaud, lady?" Peter asked.

Haltingly, for her attention was on the men clustering at the bow and the ship bearing swiftly toward them, she told him what few facts she had gleaned from conversations in London and pamphlets she had read there. She had heard that Jean d'Arnaud was of noble birth, the son of a wealthy seigneur in Burgundy. The seigneur's wife, Jean's mother, had converted to the Calvinist faith, to the fury of her husband, who remained true to the old religion. She had succeeded in converting Jean and his younger sister, but not the older son. Unable to tolerate Jean's beliefs, the seigneur had disinherited him, and the young man had become a privateer, one of many sea captains who, with their English counterparts and the Sea Beggars from the Netherlands, preyed on Catholic ships. His piracy was as legitimate as it could be, Kat knew, for he was one of those Huguenot captains to whom Jeanne d'Albret had issued letters of marque.

"Heard you anything of his sister's fate?"

Kat nodded grimly. Françoise d'Arnaud had followed her brother to La Rochelle, and there met and married Charles Rondier, a young Huguenot of gentle birth. The couple had sailed to Florida, to the Huguenot colony of La Caroline, and both had been killed in the massacre when the fort was attacked by Spanish soldiers. Jean d'Arnaud had good reason besides religion to hate Spain and its allies. 'Twas a wonder that he, like the Charrons, did not suspect Justin . . .

Peter bent down and picked up his jerkin, put his knife and the carving he was working on away in a pocket, then slung the jerkin over his shoulder. "Shall we go watch from the bow?"

As *L'Orfraie* neared them, she saw that the ship was longer than the *Lady Margaret* but no wider, and carried even more sail. The ponderous merchant ships that plied between Spain's ports and the Netherlands would be easy prey for this aptly named sea hawk. She felt a childlike excitement as she watched the pirate ship, and wished Nick could be here: he had spoken more than a few times of *L'Orfraie*. Then her mouth twisted as she reflected that the only way Nick could be here would be as Justin's captive, like herself—'twas far better that he was safe in England, for all that he must be worrying about her now.

Soon *L'Orfraie* was close enough for her to be able to see its crew, and her gaze was drawn to a tall, lean, broad-shouldered man standing on the poopdeck, now and then lifting a glass to his eye to study them. Even at this distance, she could tell from his stance that he was in command. Then another man came to stand beside him, and she forgot the pirate for the moment as an excited murmur ran through the *Lady Margaret*'s crew at the sight of that familiar tawny head.

Tandy! She knew it was absurd to feel so pleased by Tandy's return. He had befriended her, true, yet he was Justin's lieutenant, and she had no doubt that if Justin ordered him to drug her again, he would obey. Still, her lips parted in a wide smile as she saw Tandy raise his arm to acknowledge the sailors calling to him. Not until Justin appeared all of a sudden before her, his gaze cold and suspicious, did she remember that she was truly without real friends here.

She would have retreated to the cabin then, but Justin took her arm and held her by his side while Jean d'Arnaud and Tandy were rowed over from *L'Orfraie*.

Arnaud came aboard first, and Kat saw that her initial impression of him had not been wrong. He was almost as tall as Justin, and perchance a bit thinner, but she could see the play of strong muscles beneath the thin black silk of his hose and shirt.

"Justin, *mon ami*! It has been too long since our last meeting!" He clasped Justin's hand, then laughed and hugged him briefly, but as he drew back again his gaze moved curiously to Kat, and his expression changed.

He looks, she thought with some bewilderment, *like a man who has just seen an old acquaintance and is struck by the changes the years have made.* But she was sure she had never met the Frenchman before. Of certain, she would have remembered him.

Arnaud was a handsome man, black-haired, with an aquiline nose and high, sharp cheekbones and brilliant eyes that would, she thought, tempt people to call him a hawk. His eyes, framed by thick, dark lashes, were a light gray, their paleness startling against skin that was even more sunburned than Justin's. *As dark as a Moor*—or so a popinjay like Christopher Danvers would say—but Kat found the sharp-featured dark face attractive, especially when Monsieur d'Arnaud smiled, his white teeth gleaming in contrast to his dark skin.

"There was business that kept me in England," Justin said, drawing the Frenchman's attention away from Kat.

"So this man of yours has told me," Arnaud said, nodding toward Tandy, who was just then climbing onto the deck.

"I thank you for returning him to me," Justin said, turning away for a moment to greet his servant, leaving Kat again the object of the Frenchman's brilliant gray eyes. She smiled uneasily at him before she, too, turned to greet Tandy.

"Mistress Katherine," Tandy said quietly, and bowed over her hand.

Kat was bewildered by the unexpected formality. Justin frowned at his servant. If Monsieur d'Arnaud saw anything odd about Tandy's deference toward her, his features did not betray it.

" 'Tis good to see you again," she murmured.

"And I am glad to find you well and safe," Tandy replied, looking sharply at Justin as he spoke. The nobleman's frown deepened, an ominous line appearing between his brows.

"Mademoiselle, pray forgive me for not introducing myself at once," Arnaud said. "I am—"

"Jean d'Arnaud," Kat said with a mischievous smile. "I have heard much of you, monsieur."

"I hope it has not been too slanderous," he replied. "But I am at a disadvantage, for I do not even know your surname, so I cannot tell whether I have heard of you ere this, Mistress . . . ?"

"Kat," Justin said firmly.

"Kat?"

"Just Kat."

"*Vraiment?* Only the one name?"

"She is the only one of her kind," Justin said impatiently, "like Medusa, and needs but one name to identify her."

"And does she, like Medusa, turn men who look upon her to stone?" The privateer smiled at Kat. " 'Twould be a trifle to pay for looking upon such beauty."

She reddened. "I did not know, monsieur, that they bottled court holy water in France."

"Holy water?" he asked, looking puzzled, but before she could reply, Justin set a hand on his shoulder.

"Come, my friend. We have much to talk about. Let's go to my cabin."

They started off, Tandy with them, but before they had taken more than a few steps Justin turned back to Kat.

"Mistress Katherine," he said lightly.

"Yea, my lord," she replied, wary of the mockery in his tone.

"Be a good wench and bring us another cask of wine, will you, sweeting? And ask cook for some food."

She stared at him in disbelief.

"Well, Mistress Katherine?"

"Aye, my lord," she whispered angrily, and Justin smiled and started walking toward the hindcastle again, only to find Tandy standing in his path, his expression openly resentful. Tandy grudgingly stepped aside, and the baron stalked past him without a word, Arnaud following and glancing back at Kat for an instant, one eyebrow raised in an unspoken question.

Tandy stood there for a while, his gaze fixed on Kat and melancholy now, and Kat would have asked him what was the matter, but then Justin called him, and he went.

When she entered the cabin fifteen minutes later, two sailors carrying a cask of wine and a tray of food following in her wake, she found Justin lounging on the bed. Tandy was seated on a joint stool. Arnaud, who had been walking restlessly about, stopped and smiled warmly at her.

"Ah! Mademoiselle! I have just heard that you spent some weeks with my friends the Charrons. I trust all is well with them?"

"Indeed, monsieur," Kat said, stepping aside as the sailors moved forward to set the wine and food down on the table. "Jacques de Charron was wounded during fighting in June, but has regained his health, and now that his son Michel has returned home, he and Madame de Charron have their heart's ease."

"*Bien.* But I had heard that a demoiselle of Queen Catherine's retinue was planning a sojourn at Monteronne. Did she not arrive?"

"You are very well-informed, monsieur," Kat murmured, raising an eyebrow. "Isobel de Maisse was at Monteronne, but she stayed only a few days."

"She was not welcomed by the Charrons?"

"*Au contraire.* The Charrons were most genial in their attempts to entertain her . . . as was his lordship."

The Frenchman grinned at Justin. "I must ask you about that, *mon ami*, but later, and not in the demoiselle's company." He approached Kat and took her hand. "Will you join us, mademoiselle? We were discussing the future of this newest peace. It is said that Coligny—"

"I am afraid Kat would not be interested," Justin said, interrupting. "Would you, sweeting?"

'Twould be useless to argue that she wished to stay. "You are right, my lord," she said regretfully, withdrawing her hand from Arnaud's. "I will wait outside—"

"On deck," Justin said softly, and she glared at him.

"—on deck, until you are finished with this business." Plague take him! Aye, and herself, too, for having witlessly told him that she had been eavesdropping at Monteronne . . .

She walked out, through the outer cabin where she had hoped to wait, and onto the deck that was barred with long shadows now in the late afternoon sunlight.

An hour later the air in the cabin was thick with smoke. The food was gone, and most of the wine. Jean sat on a chest beneath the porthole, a pipe in his mouth. Justin had sworn under his breath when the Frenchman had produced the small pipe and tobacco pouch from his purse. Jean had learned to drink tobacco from John Hawkins, whom he had known for years, and Justin wished he had not. He had finally complained after half an hour, but by then the cabin was filled with the noxious fumes, and although Jean had seated himself beneath the porthole, saying the smoke would then blow out of the cabin, Justin could have sworn the opposite was true. His eyes were watering, and his mouth tasted of dirty ashes.

Tandy looked as uncomfortable as his master felt, but he had said nothing about the privateer drinking tobacco. Nor much of anything else, Justin realized, unable to think of anything of significance his servant had said after reporting on the matter on which he had been sent to England.

They had been discussing the mischief that might have been done to the Huguenot cause by the wild statements of an English Catholic who had left England recently to study at Louvain. The man had told his friends—and word of it had reached the French court—that the fleet Queen Elizabeth had prepared to defend England against any risk of a Spanish attack, which was officially at sea to provide an additional escort through the Channel for King Philip's bride-to-be and her escort of Spanish ships, intended, on its return, to attack Calais and claim it again for England. Jean had been told that Henry Norris, Elizabeth's ambassador in France, had learned of the rumors being spread and had written to Cecil of them, so 'twas certain that the queen would soon send word to the French king denying any such plans. But neither her denial nor the failure to attack Calais would completely eliminate French suspicions, especially of the Huguenots, for the student had said that Huguenot intelligencers were working for the English in this.

'Twas wicked gossip, and Justin had to wonder whether the student was doing so much mischief by himself or whether the Cardinal of Lorraine might not have had a hand in spreading the rumor. Jean had the same suspicions, but the privateer had so far been unable to discover any proof that Le Tigre was involved in the gossip-mongering. He had asked, tactfully, if Justin had heard anything else about the gossip in Louvain. Margaret's name had not been mentioned, but Justin had still felt defensive, and had merely shaken his head in response. Neither of them had said anything in the minute or two since then. Justin had been considering whether to bring up the subject of the Duke of Anjou, the proposed marriage between Queen Elizabeth and Henri, the duke, the younger brother of Charles IX. The match—which Justin would swear would never happen—was of endless interest to Huguenots, who saw in such a marriage an alliance between the Protestant monarchy of England and the Catholic monarchy of France that would preserve this fragile peace between French Huguenot and French Catholic.

Now, though, he spoke to his servant instead.

"Tandy, you have had naught to say about your reasons for staying in England past the expected time."

"I thought we would talk of it later, my lord."

His eyes met Justin's for only an instant before moving away, but in that quick glance there had been an element of challenge that—save for that odd confrontation on deck earlier—Justin had not seen in years, not since those first weeks after Tandy's return to Harwood Hall from the exile Justin's father had imposed upon him. Theirs had been an uneasy friendship then, Justin often sensing that Tandy did not quite trust him, and that Tandy's behavior—more that of an equal than a servant—was meant to dare Justin to send him away again, if he would. But why on earth was the man behaving this way now?

"I would liefer discuss it now," Justin said sharply. If Tandy had by chance run across one of his enemies in England, and been turned against him by anything he had heard, Justin wanted it out in the open now.

" 'Tis a subject best discussed later," Tandy insisted, glancing at Jean.

The Frenchman noticed, and laughed. "I'll wait on deck, *mon ami*, and so give you at least a short reprieve from this healthful smoke you detest so much."

"There's no need for you to leave, Jean," Justin said. "You know I keep no secrets from you."

"This concerns a trespasser, my lord, at Harwood Hall," Tandy said, and Justin regretted his last words to Jean.

"A trespasser?" Jean asked, curious now. "A spy, perhaps?"

Tandy shook his head. "A slovenly youth in ill-fitting clothes, who crossed the wall with a companion."

"Did you have this young trespasser disciplined?" Jean asked, but his voice betrayed less interest than before.

"Too straitly, I fear," Tandy replied.

That challenging look was back again, and Justin felt a surge of annoyance that this new problem involved Kat. She seemed to cause trouble for him everywhere he turned. And now, with Tandy's surly behavior toward him and the odd subservience the man had shown to her, it appeared to Justin that his servant had become infatuated with the girl, mayhap to the point where he had sulked in England for a few days before returning to Justin's service. Or, worse, he might have been making inquiries about the girl—a waste of time, certainly, for vagabonds like Kat belonged to a community that shifted like sand at the sea's edge.

He stared in exasperation at Tandy, hardly aware that he had begun to drum his fingers on the tray lying beside him on the bed. Jean studied him for a few moments, then shrugged and started to leave the cabin, but paused when Tandy spoke to him.

"Monsieur, now that you have seen Mistress Katherine, needs must that I ask. Is it not the very likeness of her?"

"Aye, it is. *Foi de gentilhomme*, it is," Jean said, then left, closing the door behind him.

Justin waited a few moments, then: "By his faith as a gentleman, is *what* a good likeness?"

"Would you not rather swear by your faith as a gentleman?"

" 'Sdeath, if you try me more, I will perforce cease to act like one. I would have less talk of faith, and more of the matter at hand."

"Oh. The matter at hand," Tandy said, and Justin could have struck him for his insolence, but with an effort he kept his anger under control as Tandy reached into his doublet and brought out something that he held for a few moments in his cupped hand. "By my faith, the matter in my hand," he said, then tossed it to his master, who caught it neatly from the air.

It was a locket.

"Please it you to open it," Tandy said, and Justin did, and caught his breath at the portrait. 'Twas the very likeness of Kat, as Tandy had said.

"This is why you stayed in England? To hire a picture-maker to paint this?" He was furious to think Tandy had delayed him for so petty a reason, but at the same time he marveled that such a great likeness could be painted from the directions Tandy must have given the picture-maker.

"That is what I told Jean. I told him, too, that you had requested it, so remember that if he speaks of it again. But nay, I did not hire a picture-maker. I found that locket and picture ready-made, in a manor house in Sussex."

Silence held the room as Justin stared first at Tandy, then at the picture again. At last he closed the locket.

"Well, my lord?"

"What, pray tell, were you doing in Sussex?"

"Does not the picture itself explain that?"

"Marry, it prattles like a gossip and bellows like the town crier. Nay, of certain it does not explain it. It explains nothing. Now answer my question."

He listened to Tandy's incredible story without interruption, and though his own thoughts were stormy, he tried to keep all expression from his face.

"You wasted your time," he said when Tandy was done. "Aye, and mine as well. Had you not stayed in England on this wild goose chase, we might have left Bayonne before—" He broke off, shaking his head.

"How can you say I wasted my time? Look at that picture! 'Tis her!"

"There is some likeness—"

"Some? 'Tis her very likeness!"

"Even if it were, that does not prove that whoever sat for this picture looked like Kat. Your picture-maker is no more honest than your courtier. They paint with court holy water. Haply the woman this is supposed to be is older and less fair, with a squint in one eye."

"And what of the rest I told you, that I remember now having seen her in London, at Paul's?"

"From a distance. And have you never mistakenly greeted someone you thought an acquaintance, only to discover him a stranger? It is possible that this woman may favor Kat."

"By God's blood! Even the name is the same!"

Justin laughed. "And that is proof? Think you that Katherine is a rare name now? I tell you, Tandy, that if you stood at Paul's Cross and summoned all Katherines in a loud enough voice, you would have half the women in London come running. Nay, you must have better evidence than this."

Tandy gazed at him for a long time, disbelieving. "You cannot accept this, can you? You will not believe. Nay, you dare not, after what this girl has suffered since you took her prisoner. 'Tis easiest for you to dismiss her as a common vagabond, a wretched young woman whose life might have been worse yet if you had not captured her and kept her with you against her will. Belike you think that when you someday wish to let her go, a few coins will be reparation enough. She'll thank you for them, and you'll feel content. But you cannot salve your conscience so easily if she's a gentlewoman. What possible amends could you make—"

"You go too far, sirrah!" Justin took a step toward him, his face livid with anger. " 'Tis obvious the wench has bewitched you, too, or you would have thought more on this matter, and said less. God's light! What sort of gentlewoman would have gone disguised as a boy to the

Jerusalem Tree? What sort of gentlewoman would have trespassed at Harwood Hall?"

"Her sort. For upon my life, she is what I say she is."

"Then why, in God's name, did she not tell us who she was, if indeed she is of gentle birth?"

Tandy shook his head slowly. "I do not know, but we could ask—"

"No! The wench is trouble enough already, without you letting her think that we suspect her to be a gentlewoman. You may have done much damage already, greeting her so foolishly, as though she were some great lady of the court! I'll hear no more of it, and you'll say naught to her, nor treat her differently than you have before!" He crossed to the door, then swung around to face his servant. "And Tandy . . ."

"Yes, my lord?"

"Bear in mind the example of Mademoiselle de Maisse. Not all spies are common folk. Even if Kat were a gentlewoman—and I warrant you, she is not—that would mean nothing to me."

Tandy's gaze was cold and unwavering. "You could better convince me of that, my lord, if you believed it yourself."

Justin swore and stalked angrily out of the cabin, eager to leave its smoky air and unwelcome ideas behind him.

Kat had been surprised to see Jean d'Arnaud leave the cabin alone.

She had been talking to Peter again, sitting by the starboard rail and staring at *L'Orfraie* while the boy recounted stories of the pirate ship. He was telling of the capture of one Spanish ship and a particularly craven nobleman who had left his ailing, terrified wife hostage while he returned to Spain, when Kat noticed Arnaud coming out onto the deck.

Silhouetted against the westering sun, he seemed incredibly dark. What would they call him at the English court? she wondered. For if Robert Dudley had been nicknamed the Gypsy, and Walsingham was dubbed the Moor, then what would they say of this man, who made the earl and Master Walsingham seem delicately fair by comparison?

She shook her head at the fanciful notion, and that movement seemed to catch his eye, for he paused, looking at her. Smoke curled up from the pipe in his hand, a black scrawl on the bright sky.

She sat gazing at him for a while, summoning her courage. Finally, telling Peter "I must talk to him," she left the boy to approach the privateer.

"Monsieur d'Arnaud. I did not expect to see you again so soon. Have you finished with your business with Lord Harwood, then?"

"For the moment."

"I have been admiring your ship," she said, nodding toward *L'Orfraie*. "Do you plan to continue your voyage south now?"

"I have no definite plans, mademoiselle."

"Is there any chance, then, that you might soon be sailing in English waters?"

He shrugged. "Are you interested in returning to England, mademoiselle? I had heard you were bound for Paris."

" 'Twas not my plan."

"Nor your desire?"

"No, monsieur."

"Jean."

"Jean."

"And your reason for wishing to return to England?"

"I wish to see my family and my home again, monsieur. I have been away longer than intended," she said, relieved at being able to speak the truth, if only for a few moments. "And I fear Paris."

"Why? Justin would protect you."

"But I no longer want him as my protector, monsieur."

"Does he know this?"

"I trow he does."

"And he knows you wish to return to England?"

"Aye."

"Then I shall ask him if he would have me take you there," he said with a smile that made her think he was jesting with her.

"Monsieur d'Arnaud—Jean," she said, with as much patience as she could muster. "I would return to England whether he agrees or not. I ask this of you not as a favor for him. I will pay for my passage."

The Frenchman sighed. "Mademoiselle—"

"Kat."

"Kat. There are many risks I will take, but interfering in lovers' quarrels is not one of them."

"Justin and I are not lovers."

"No? Do you not share that cabin? I saw a woman's clothes there, lying across a chest."

"Yea, and mayhap you also saw the trundle bed on which I sleep. We are not lovers."

"But have you been?" he asked, and she flushed and looked down at her feet. "So I thought."

"That is over," she whispered. "And I would leave him now, and not be taken willy-nilly to Paris. Will you help me?"

"Kat . . ." He set a hand on her shoulder.

She raised her head and saw a look of sympathy on his face. "Please you, take me to England," she pleaded. "I will pay you well. I have money."

"Mine?" Justin asked pleasantly from behind her.

She whirled around. "No, not yours."

"No? I hope 'twas not stolen at Monteronne."

"*Par Dieu*, Justin," Arnaud said, "that was not called for."

"Nay? You met her scarce two hours ago, and you would tell me how to deal with her?"

"Perchance someone should."

"Truth to tell, half the world already has."

The Frenchman smiled crookedly. "I doubt that, *mon ami*. But perhaps so much advice should be heeded, and then she might not want to leave you."

"I care not if—"

"Nay, you do."

"Jesu." Justin glowered at his friend, then abruptly laughed. "It seems that everyone I know professes to know my mind better than I do. Come, let me see you to your boat."

Knowing there was no hope now that Arnaud would take her with him, Kat bade the Frenchman good-bye and walked back to the hindcastle. She was in no mood for anyone's company, not even Peter's.

She left the doors open as she walked about the cabin, holding fans that Gabrielle had given her in both hands and waving them about to try to clear the air of all traces of tobacco smoke. The cabin grew darker as the sun set, but she did not bother to light a candle. Through the porthole she saw the boat taking Arnaud back to *L'Orfraie*; soon after he reached her, the pirate ship weighed anchor.

An hour later she was sitting on the chest beneath the larboard porthole, the fans beside her, when she heard Justin walk through the outer cabin. She knew the sound of his walk, she thought wearily, as well as she had known her father's, or her brother's. Alas, to be so familiar with someone who was her enemy.

He paused in the doorway. "No lights, Kat?"

She made no answer. He stepped into the cabin, closing and locking the door, then went to light the lantern by the bed.

In its glow, she could see that he looked very tired.

"Have you had supper?"

"Nay, but I want none."

"I pray your pardon for what I said about your stealing the money. In good sooth, I did not believe it stolen, though by my life! I would liefer have believed that than have learned that Gabrielle gave it to you. She did, did she not? 'Twas her, and not Michel?"

Kat nodded.

"And she gave it to you, to use when you wished to leave me?"

There had been enough pain in his voice that Kat hesitated before nodding again.

He sighed and looked away, out the starboard porthole. At France— though the coast, Kat knew, would be only a dark ridge between the paler darkness of the sea and the sky. At France, where he had friends who had sided with her against him. She felt sympathy well up in her, but forced it back down again.

"It seems," he said at last, speaking very slowly, "as if all my friends who know you feel I have mistreated you."

"Not your cousin."

He laughed, the sound humorless. "Nay, not Margaret . . . but then, I was speaking of friends. No, Margaret has no sympathy for anyone but herself." He was silent again for a time, then: "Have I mistreated you, Kat?" When she did not reply, he laughed again. "In faith, what need that I ask? I need but think what would have happened, had I arrived in Navarra even a day later . . ."

"That was not your doing."

"Would you have me blame my cousin? By the mass, who left you with her? And then at Monteronne I struck you."

" 'Twas the drug."

"If there was a drug."

"If not, then like enough, 'twas the wine."

"I must confess to the wine," he said wryly. "But I have been cup-shotten before, yet never hit a woman. It shames me that I hit you."

"My lord," she said very softly, "I hit you first."

He turned around then, a stunned look on his face.

"But not so hard," she added, wishing suddenly that she had not made the confession. Would he be furious that she had not admitted as much to his friends?

He began to laugh, genuine laughter this time, laughter that went on until he was leaning helplessly against the wall. When he could speak again, he said, "I would take solace from learning you struck first, but I fear you had reason enough, in my fondling of the demoiselle."

" 'Twas not that. Nay, I was wroth with you for that, but 'twas not uppermost in my mind when I hit you."

"What was, then?" he asked, smiling.

"You called me your lady of Bridewell, and Mistress Vagabond."

"And that hurt you more than the other?" he asked, his smile fading.

"Yea," she said, then, realizing how foolish that must seem, said, "Nay. Nay, I know not." She bit her lip, uncomfortable with the seriousness of his gaze.

"You would not be called a vagabond?"

" 'Tis not a name I would choose, my lord."

"But you have given me no other . . . save Kat."

"I am like Medusa," she said bitterly, "the only one of my kind."

"I am mocked by my own words. Would that I could call them back. Would that I could change many things."

"What things?"

"How I met you."

There was a painful lump in her throat, and she could no longer meet his gaze. 'Twas her wish, too, that she might have met him in another way, and for other reasons. Would that he were not suspected of treason . . .

"Or if I could not change it," he said, coming to her and drawing her into his arms, "I would fain lose all memory of it, at least for a time . . ."

She began to cry then, but he kissed the tears away, and by the time he lifted her and carried her to the bed, she had forgotten her sorrow, for a time.

CHAPTER 40

It was, finally, silent in the room, save for the sound of Margaret's weeping.

Antonio looked upon his wife with pity. A few hours ago she had been a graceful picture of beauty and nobility as she greeted him and Don Rodrigo Molina de Encinas. With a scant hour's warning that her husband was returning from Madrid, and bringing with him a representative of the Council of Castile who would be their guest for a few days, she had managed to transform herself into the epitome of a Spanish gentlewoman. With her hair tucked smoothly under a lace cap, her sweetly curved figure hidden by a severe, high-necked gown of black silk, and her face so subtly painted that Antonio would have thought she had gone without paints completely—had he not known that she could use a subtle hand when necessary—her appearance had given the lie to any of the court gossip Don Rodrigo would likely have heard about her. If she had felt at all uneasy about her husband arriving unexpectedly with a high official of the court, her behavior gave no sign of it as she played the hostess in the *estrado de cumplimiento*, directing servants to provide refreshments while she sat on cushions on the *tarima*. Under other circumstances, Antonio would have been amused by her performance, especially since Margaret had not kept secret from him her contempt for the old custom, adapted from the Moors, that required women to sit on the cushioned dais while men took chairs. But she had assumed her place on the *tarima* with a good grace, giving no hint that she felt either demeaned or discomforted by the position.

All grace had fled her now. Crying had left her face looking ravaged and old, the paint washed by tears into tiny lines Antonio had never noticed before. More paint could be seen, splotches of black and pink, on the soggy handkerchief she held crumpled in one white-knuckled fist. She sat with her head lowered and shoulders slumped. The defiance she had shown for awhile, after first realizing that Don Rodrigo was here to question her, had been whittled away by the official's sharp questions.

"Doña Margaret," Don Rodrigo said gently, and Margaret flinched before raising her head warily to look at him. "I am sorry that these questions have distressed you so. Please be assured that I meant you no harm, and that I will inform the Council of Castile that you have been very open and cooperative." He turned to Antonio. "Don Antonio, I wish to apologize to you, too, and thank you for permitting this investigation."

A knot of fear in his chest that Antonio had been unaware of was suddenly released. For days he had been telling himself that Margaret was innocent of this relationship with Justin—if not of the other—and refusing to consider the possibility that an interrogation might disclose damning facts. He had not realized how worried he had been until just now.

"I am glad that we could help you, Don Rodrigo."

"As am I," Margaret said quickly. Her eyes, so dull a few moments ago, were now alight with hope, but she still looked wary, and her hands fretfully twisted the stained square of linen and lace.

Don Rodrigo smiled briefly, not looking at either of them as he shuffled through the stack of papers on the table beside him, writing down a few words here and there.

Antonio already knew most of what was in those papers. Don Rodrigo had shown them to him last week, just before they left Madrid.

The documents began with a transcription of a letter from Don Francisco Muñoz de Herrera in England. Philip's ambassador's secretary had been disturbed by something he feared he could not dismiss as mere coincidence. In his last meeting with Lord Harwood before the Englishman left for Spain, he had mentioned to Lisle the name of a young English gentleman of strong Catholic sympathies who was becoming impatient with the slow turn of events and had implied to Muñoz that he might take matters into his own hands. Three weeks later the gentleman had been questioned by two of Walsingham's agents after he had stopped overnight at an inn on his way to join the court. The agents had expressed an unusual interest in a fine pair of gloves, crafted by an Italian who had lately joined the gentleman's household, and intended as a gift for the queen. Unfortunately, the gloves had accidentally been dropped into the fire as the gentleman was handing them over to Walsingham's men, so they could not be subjected to the examination which would have brought an end to the false and malicious rumors of a new plot to poison the English queen. The Italian glovemaker had been taken to London for questioning, and the gentleman was home again, brooding his sorrows, denied the court for a time.

Was it possible, Muñoz had wondered, that Lord Harwood had let slip the gentleman's name to the wrong person?

There had been more to the letter, pages more. Don Francisco had poured out all his suspicions in his tiny, meticulous secretary hand on a dozen pages of gauze-thin paper, which had made its way to Spain carefully sewn into the lining of a cloak. Never once daring to directly accuse Lord Harwood of treachery, ever mindful that Lisle was a close friend and relative of Antonio, Muñoz had nevertheless woven a fine net of improbable coincidences to fling over the Englishman. Nearly every failed intrigue of Don Francisco's mission could be linked to Lord Harwood in some way.

It would have been a convincing, damning document, had not Philip been so cautious—or had it not been widely known that Muñoz was overwilling to ascribe his own failures to others. But Philip was, and it was, and since Antonio was more respected by the king than was Don Francisco, nothing had been done with the letter. Philip kept it in his ever-patient grasp, and waited.

Then Don Rafael de Vincente y Marcos had arrived in the capital from Navarra, with news of the murder of Fray Francisco de la Vera Cruz, and with the letter bearing Don Antonio's seal that Justin had carried.

Only desperation could have brought Don Rafael to Madrid with such charges against the wife of a grandee and her cousin. But with the Inquisition demanding an explanation of the murder of their vicar, Don Rafael's desperation was understandable. Antonio could almost pity the man. Almost.

Don Rodrigo, finished with his papers, gathered them neatly into his hands and rose. He turned toward the door, then paused, looking back at Antonio.

Antonio held up his hand, silently asking a moment's leave of his guest, then went to Margaret, who still sat huddled on the dais. She looked up at him fearfully as he pushed a stray wisp of hair back from her face.

"Antonio . . . ?"

"I'll send Edwina to you." He knew she would want to see to her appearance before leaving the *estrado*.

She caught at his hand, holding it to her face for a moment. "Antonio, I am sorry . . ."

He looked into her eyes, wondering how deep her apology went, and if she might be asking his forgiveness for more than just this humiliation of discovering that Justin Lisle was not the friend of Spain he had once appeared to be.

"So am I, my love." He gently extricated his hand from hers and turned to walk with Don Rodrigo from the room.

Antonio showed Don Rodrigo to the bedchamber. The council's representative had indicated he planned to rest before supper, but wished to speak to Antonio first.

The chamber was cool, much cooler than the *estrado* had been, with its windows and doors closed to discourage eavesdroppers. Here the doors to the shaded balcony had been thrown open, and a breeze heavy with the scent of roses stirred the silk curtains.

Antonio waited patiently as Don Rodrigo put his documents away. He felt aches in every joint and muscle. After days of riding, two hours of sitting perfectly quietly in an uncomfortable chair was not the rest he would have liked, and he planned to retire to his own bedchamber after hearing what his guest had to say.

At last Rodrigo turned to face him. For a moment there was a look of concern on his face, then he smiled warmly. "My friend, do not look so troubled. I fully believe your wife's explanations, and will so inform the council."

"And Don Rafael . . . ?"

"He will have much to answer for. But that is, perhaps, a matter best left to the Inquisition," he said with complacence, and Antonio felt chilled. "We have, as you know, accepted your explanation that your seal was stolen for a time, and that the letter was a forgery. Whatever happened at the Eagle's Nest—and no doubt many people will have to be put to the question before all the truth is known—we are certain of your innocence, and of your wife's as well."

That certainty, Antonio knew, would save them from prison . . . but not from the gossip that would soon be heard in every palace and *mentidero*. It might be best if he and Margaret left Spain for a time. Philip had once spoken of appointing him to be a viceroy, but had changed his mind, saying he needed Antonio's sound advice here. With this scandal, that high office would be denied him, Antonio was sure. But another post in one of Spain's colonies might still be within his reach . . .

He smiled at the thought, then became aware of Don Rodrigo's shrewd gaze.

"I am happy to have this unpleasant business behind us. Could you be persuaded to stay with us for a while, rather than returning to Madrid at once?"

"I would be happy to stay, Don Antonio, were it not necessary that I be back in the capital to await replies to the messages we have sent."

"Messages?"

"To France. We received word that Lord Harwood's ship was in Bayonne, and that it had been there for some time."

That was bad news indeed. Antonio had been wounded by learning of Justin's betrayal of their friendship and of the Spanish cause in England, but not so deeply that he still did not wish his friend safely back in his own country.

"So you sent a messenger there?"

Rodrigo nodded. "We have a spy there, who can play the *matón* if need be. And another messenger is on his way to Paris, to the French court. Should Lord Harwood escape us in Bayonne, he may still stay in France, and we shall see if Madame la Serpente can be persuaded to capture him and return him to us, so he may be dealt with properly."

"By the Council of Castile?"

Don Rodrigo shook his head. "By the Supreme Council of the Inquisition. He has murdered a priest, if Don Rafael is to be believed, and he has murdered him to stop him from bringing a heretic to trial."

That, Antonio knew, would be an *auto-da-fé* that the king would attend, to see the burning of an English nobleman who had betrayed Spain as well as killed a priest. He would be expected to attend, too, were he still in Spain. The thought sickened him. So, too, did the realization that Justin would likely find no refuge in England after all, for there would be spies willing to play the *matón* there as well as in Bayonne . . .

He took his leave of his guest a few minutes later and went to his own bedchamber. His clothing had already been unpacked. Wine and fruit had been left on a table, and both the window and the door to the balcony were open to admit the cooling breeze.

His head aching, Antonio lay down, fully clothed, on the bed. For a long while he was perfectly still, save for the occasional quivering of his tightly closed eyelids and the jumping of a muscle in his jaw. At last he got up and closed the window and balcony door. Hot and airless as the room might seem without the breeze, he felt he had to shut out the mingled scents of flowers and dust, which reminded him far too much of church incense, and funeral wreaths.

CHAPTER 41

'Sdeath! Kat thought. *Will Justin ever finish his breakfast?*

It was their fourth morning in Paris. On the other mornings, Justin had rushed through the meal, as though eager to be away from the inn. Today he was dawdling, and that and his melancholy expression worried Kat. Perhaps there would be no ride through the city this morning? 'Twas a miserable thought. Their rooms in L'Oison Noir on the Rue St. Honoré were comfortable, and the innkeeper, Denis Cotart, was a pleasant host and kept a good table . . . but outside, all of Paris was waiting to be seen. She had been forced to stay here, with Tandy to watch her, throughout their first full day in the city, and only her body's demand for rest after the bruising four-day ride from Le Havre had made the confinement tolerable. Justin had been away all that first day, but for the last two days his business had separated him from them only during the afternoon and early evening. The past two mornings they had gone riding through the city, and Kat had been able for those few hours to forget her own cares as she took in the sights and sounds of Paris.

She shifted restlessly in her chair by the window. Tandy, noticing the movement, looked up from the second cup of wine he had decided to savor while waiting for Justin, but the nobleman appeared indifferent to Kat's agitation. She gave him a dark look before lowering her gaze to study her fingernails.

They were clean, scrupulously clean, in contrast to her dirt-smudged face. It was a small act of defiance, a protest against Justin's insistence that she stay disguised as a boy until they returned to the *Lady Margaret.* She could see no reason for it, especially when she had to stay in their chambers at the inn most of each day. She rubbed her cheek, grimacing at the rough texture the dust had given her skin.

She looked up again as Tandy cleared his throat and addressed Justin.

"My lord, have you decided yet whither we shall ride today? If we wait much longer, Kat will wear out either her chair or the seat of her hose with her squirming."

542

If Tandy were trying to lighten Justin's mood—and Kat suspected it was more that than an attempt to shame her—he failed. The gaze Justin turned on him was so harsh as to be unsettling, and when he glanced at Kat she felt chilled suddenly, and at the same time concerned.

In truth, he looked not only grim, but also years older now than he had looked during the last several days of their voyage up the French coast to Le Havre, after their encounter with Jean d'Arnaud. He had seemed carefree then, rarely without a smile.

That had changed the afternoon they reached Le Havre.

Justin had taken Kat's doublet and hose and boots from the chest where they had been stored and told her that she must needs wear them for the journey to Paris. *Would that you could travel in the guise of my lady wife,* he had said, *but 'twill not do in Paris, when you lack a maidservant.*

Must I go? she had asked. *I would prefer to stay here, on the ship.*

His expression had changed then. He had been gazing at her lovingly, but 'twas clear that her request startled him. For an instant he looked betrayed—aye, and grief-stricken—and then the stony mask he had worn for most of the last week was in place.

You will go, he had told her. *Nill you, will you, you will go.* And so had ended her plans to take the money Gabrielle had given her and buy passage on a ship to England. He had even made sure, before they left the ship, that she had no more money with her than the few coins she had had in her purse since he captured her at Harwood Hall.

His anger had had an echo in hers, for all that she had been moved by seeing how her request to stay in Le Havre had astonished him. Had he thought that she could stay with him forever? Those last few days on the ship had been sweet beyond measure, as for a time they were lovers with no concerns other than each other. She had found herself wishing that the voyage could last an eternity, for she had known that when they reached port, their loving perforce must end. She had banished that sorrowful thought from her mind until they cast anchor at Le Havre. But it seemed that Justin had given little thought, if any, to her leaving him, and for the last week he had again treated her with suspicion, as his prisoner and his enemy.

"Is there some part of Paris you would see today?" he asked her now, but she hesitated to answer. She had a destination for today's ride in mind, but was not certain it would be wise to mention it.

Two mornings ago, on their first ride through Paris, they had kept to the Right Bank of the Seine. Yesterday they had ridden across the Pont-au-Change to the Ile de la Cité. She had seen enough of the Cité, for there was little to see on the island except the Cathedral of Notre Dame and the Palais. For a time she had been agreeably distracted by the bustling courtyard of the Palais, once the palace of the French kings, now the site of Parlement, the Cour des Monnaies, the Chambre des Comptes and the Cour des Aides. It reminded her somewhat of St. Paul's, with its throngs of court officials and clerks and priests from the royal chapel in the center of the courtyard mixing with those who came to buy from the booksellers and other vendors, as well as fashionable Parisians who were there to be seen as they promenaded in the *grande salle*. She had no wish to see it again, though. Nor did she want to return to Notre Dame, with its great stained-glass windows that left the interior in perpetual gloomy twilight.

The Left Bank, with its universities, would be well worth a visit. But they had not nearly finished seeing the Right Bank.

She would have been unaware of the limits of their ride, had not Tandy drawn a rough map of Paris for her. On that ride two days ago, Justin had led them first all around the Louvre, then up the Rue d'Autriche and across the drawbridge and through the gate into the palace's courtyard, with its beggars and petitioners and gaping rustics, to show Kat the difference between the ancient walls on the north and east and the fine new Italianate walls to the south and west. Then they had ridden back along the Rue St. Honoré, past their inn, to the vast marketplace of Les Halles. They had finished their morning's tour with a visit to the Cimetière des Saints-Innocents. Tandy had visited it once before, and felt Kat should see the cemetery and its surrounding cloister, especially the frescoes of the Danse Macabre that had been painted a century and a half ago in one of the charnel houses, the *charnier des lingeres*. Kat felt more sickened than fascinated by the frescoes, and by the rest of the Cemetery of the Innocents as well, with its shops and vendors' stalls along the arcade, which was all a great charnel house, with the bones that had been exhumed from the graveyard when new graves were dug stored beneath the roof in open-sided chambers so they were impossible to ignore. Yet the Parisians who came to the cemetery to shop or just stroll about did seem to ignore the heaped bones overhead, and the smell of cadavers as well. Saints-Innocents was almost as busy as the Palais. Kat, who had no taste for this grisly juxtaposition of the living and the dead, had made no protest when Justin suggested they return to the inn, though she had suspected, correctly, that she would not be leaving their chambers again that day. She felt she had seen more than enough.

Not until that afternoon, when Tandy sketched the map for her, did she realize how much of the Right Bank she had missed seeing.

Eastward from the Cemetery of the Innocents, past the Place de la Grève and the Hôtel de Ville, was the most fashionable part of Paris. Here had settled the nobility and wealthy clergymen and judges. Kat felt a simple curiosity about the imposing *hôtels* Tandy told her had been built there, but she also wondered that Justin expressed no interest in visiting the area, especially after Tandy let slip the fact that during his last trip to Paris with Justin, the nobleman had been curious to see what new building had been done in the Marais, as the area was known.

Was that where he went to attend to his business? And did he choose not to take her there lest he encounter someone he would not have her learn that he knew?

She dared not ask him directly if they could tour the Marais, so she asked instead to visit the Bastille. If Tandy's map—aye, and her memory of it—could be relied on, needs must that they ride through the Marais to reach the Bastille.

"The Bastille?" Justin sounded disbelieving. "Why would you wish to see that?"

A plague on his questions. Unprepared, she could answer with naught but a shrug.

"The Quartier Latin would be more to your taste, I trow."

Argument would only rouse his suspicions, so she went quietly to get her cloak. Perchance tomorrow, if they were still in Paris, she could broach the subject again. He would not be able to offer the Latin Quarter as an alternative then.

They crossed the Pont-au-Change to the Ile de la Cité. There Justin, who seemed to have cheered somewhat since leaving the inn, asked Kat if she wished to visit the courtyard of the Palais again, and haply make a purchase or two. She declined, and could not help wondering if the offer had been meant to somehow recompense her for being denied the visit to the Bastille. If by some chance he felt guilty about refusing her request, she had no intention of letting him ease his conscience so quickly. With any luck he would agree tomorrow.

So they left the Cité, crossing to the Left Bank on the Pont St. Michel. The bridge was lined by houses, and this morning its narrow way was jammed by a cart that had collapsed, spilling pottery across the width of the bridge. The potter was scurrying back and forth, trying to salvage what had not been broken by the accident before it was smashed under foot or hoof or cart wheel. Until they could pass the broken-down cart, they had no choice but to ride at a halting walk.

While they waited, Kat felt the skin at the back of her neck prickle. She was sure someone was staring at her, and she looked around wildly, though the crowd pressing around them seemed interested only in getting off the narrow bridge as soon as possible. All but one: a lean fellow in ragged finery who lounged in a doorway, smirking as he surveyed the crowd. Some thief, no doubt, selecting his prey. It could have been his gaze she had sensed, though she doubted it, since the sensation persisted and he was no longer gazing her way. She looked around again, but could see no one staring fixedly at her. 'Twas but her imagination, she decided.

She sighed heavily, and Tandy turned to face her, and gave her a crooked smile.

"I, too, would liefer be on London Bridge," he murmured.

She was about to tell him that he had not divined her thoughts, when of a sudden, as if conjured by his words, images of London rose up in her mind. Tears stung her eyes. For a truth, she missed England. Paris was new to her, but she would fain trade its novelty to be home again. She had heard that Parisians said that Paris was not a city but a world, but they could have their world. 'Twas a poor one, next to London. The narrow Seine could not compare to the Thames, with its gleaming expanse dotted with great ships and wherries and noblemen's barges. Nor could Notre Dame equal Paul's, or the Louvre, with its mismatched walls, equal the grace of Hampton Court. Nor, as Tandy had reminded her, were any of the four bridges spanning the Seine, the Pont-au-Change, the Pont St. Michel, the Petit Pont, and, most of all—for it was least of all, with its houses built of brickbat instead of stone—the Pont Notre Dame, the equal of London Bridge. Her longing to be back in London was a palpable thing, and she looked away, not wanting Tandy to see her cry.

Soon she had put such thoughts from her mind, as they meandered through the Quartier Latin on the Rive Gauche. The young men around her would not let her stay melancholy for long. The students who thronged the narrow, winding streets were a noisy lot, and much of their talk was in écorche-Latin, a vulgar, fantastical mix of French and Latin that often left her bemused and frowning in concentration until she laughed aloud as the meaning of a phrase or word struck her. Many of the students were poor, ill-clad and terribly thin, but even these possessed an exuberance that reminded her of Nick and his friends from Cambridge and the Inns of Court.

Justin, too, seemed to relax as the morning progressed. He began to jest with some of the students who spoke to them, and when they stopped later at a street corner where a liripipiumed scholar had nailed up a thesis that he was eager to defend, Justin managed to stay in a good humor despite the scholar's insulting comments about the English and their universities.

Then it was close to midday, and Tandy suggested that before returning to the inn they stop for dinner at the Pomme de Pin, on the Ile de la Cité.

"The Pomme de Pin?" Kat asked. "François Villon's Pomme de Pin?"

"Yea, 'tis the tavern he wrote of," Tandy replied. "You have heard of Villon?"

Of certain, she had heard of Villon, that student, thief, and vagabond. Nick had brought her a book of his poetry, which they had kept hidden from their father, fearing he might not approve of all of it.

To Kat's delight, Justin agreed to stop at the tavern. They started back toward the Cité, but by a roundabout way, for Kat wished to see the Place Maubert.

As they approached the Place, they saw fewer and fewer scholars, more and more artisans and merchants. "This is bourgeois Paris," Tandy told her as the street suddenly opened up before them. Kat nodded but did not speak. Her eyes were riveted on the immensity of the Place, which Gabrielle de Charron had told her of. Heretics had been burned here, but there was no sign of stakes or ashes, and Kat found it difficult to reconcile the busy Place with the lurid tales she had heard. Why, some of what she saw was almost comical, like that fat flower vendor, now approaching them at a lumbering run, pushing her wheelbarrow full of flowers before her . . .

Kat called a warning, but it was too late.

Justin's mount was skittish, and now, as the wheelbarrow rattled toward it across the cobblestones, the horse reared. The woman let go of her wheelbarrow and it skidded on for a few feet more. The horse struck the wheelbarrow's edge with one hoof and tipped it over, sending flowers cascading to the ground, to be trampled a moment later. The vendor wailed in dismay.

"By God's blood!" Justin's voice was sharp, but still held a hint of laughter. "Are we to be the targets of every idle Parisian?"

"Anglais," the woman said, and sniffed loudly. She looked at the ruined flowers, and her lower lip began to tremble.

Justin started to dismount, but a gesture from Tandy stayed him.

" 'Tis but pretense, my lord," Tandy murmured. "Like enough, if your horse had not upset the wheelbarrow she would have done so herself, in the hope that you would buy all her flowers. I have seen such cony-catchers in London. I would not be her cony."

"Then perforce I must be," Justin said, and got down. "I would not have her complaining that an anglais trampled her wares. Such complaints would be ill-timed, with Walsingham here now."

Walsingham? Kat pricked up her ears, but Justin said no more of the man, and she dared not ask him why Walsingham was here. 'Twould appear too curious. As like as not, the sort of vagabond he thought she was—if he thought her anything so innocent—would not even know who Walsingham was.

He paid for the flowers, so generously that the vendor set to work picking up those that were not ruined and gathering them into a huge posy, which she tied expertly with a length of string before presenting to Justin, who accepted it awkwardly.

" 'Tis a nosegay fit for Gargantua himself!" Tandy said, laughing.

Justin frowned and looked down at the flowers—roses and poppies and marigolds in bright profusion—that completely covered his forearms. Then he walked the few steps to where Kat was waiting and held up the giant posy for her to take.

'Twas in her mind to jest as Tandy had, but something in Justin's eyes stopped that jest and made her catch her breath. She reached for the flowers, and her fingers touched his, and she froze, her gaze locked with his. There was grief in his eyes, but love, too.

Then the flower seller sniffed again, yet more loudly than before. "*Bougre*," she said spitefully, turning away to right her wheelbarrow. "*Un bougre anglais. Le diable m'emporte.*"

Justin looked around at her, dumb-stricken by the insult.

Tandy looked as though he had a mouthful of cherrystones. Then he could not contain his laughter any longer, and the very walls of the houses in the Place Maubert seemed to ring with it. Kat, too, could not help but giggle, for all that she knew that she was to blame for the vendor thinking Justin was a bugger. But then, he was not entirely blameless, for 'twas he who had insisted that she go disguised as a boy. The thought made her laugh the more.

Justin's face was dark with anger as he mounted his horse again and rode back toward the Seine at a smart trot. He took the Petit Pont and the Pont Notre Dame across the river, not slowing at all between the bridges as he crossed the Ile de la Cité. Kat and Tandy had no chance to remind him that they had planned to stop at the Pomme de Pin. But 'twas of no matter that they could not ask: Kat doubted they would have liked the answer.

A page was waiting for Justin at L'Oison Noir, holding his horse directly beneath the sign with its picture of a black gosling.

"Monsieur Lisle?" he asked. "Seigneur de Harwood?" Justin nodded. "My mistress, Mademoiselle de Salvandy," the boy continued, in slow and careful English, "would fain have your company for dinner today, if it please you."

" 'Twould please me greatly," Justin said, and bade the boy wait while he went inside to change clothes.

Kat and Tandy waited in the courtyard until the ostlers came to take their horses. While Tandy was talking to one ostler, Kat stared at the page without really seeing him, her thoughts in a turmoil. Mademoiselle de Salvandy? Was that not one of the names Justin had mentioned to Michel when he asked him which French nobles would favor war with England?

"Mademoiselle de Salvandy," she murmured, not aware that she had spoken aloud until Tandy looked over at her, a sympathetic look on his face. Like enough, she thought sourly as she turned away and went into the inn, he thought she was jealous of the demoiselle. But she was not—in truth, she was not.

She met Justin on the stairs. He was wearing his best suit and also some light perfume she had not known he had with him, and she felt the jealousy she had denied surge up again.

"May we not go with you?" she asked, though she knew 'twas hopeless.

He laughed and shook his head. "I shall be back by tonight," he said as he moved past her.

"Say you so?"

He looked back up at her, startled, then laughed again, and went out.

She was still in a choleric humor when Tandy came upstairs a few minutes later, but she agreed to play cards to while away the idle hours. She lost more often than she won, losing every time when the game was one of skill rather than chance, for she could not keep her mind on the cards. It frustrated her beyond measure to know that Justin was even now meeting with an enemy of Queen Elizabeth's and she could do nothing about it. Finally she threw her cards down on the table, making Tandy jump.

He leaned over and peered at the cards. "You'll never win with that hand," he said, and shook his head.

"I have lost already," she told him, and he seemed to understand that she was not speaking merely of the cards, for he looked concerned, and was reaching for her clenched fist when someone knocked on the door.

This time she jumped, then sat very still, thinking—nay, praying—that Justin had returned early. But it was only their host, Monsieur Cotart, with a flagon of wine and a head full of gossip.

He had just received a letter from his son, who had moved to Rouen and bought an inn there.

"And a fine inn," he assured them. "Robert stole two of my best cooks when he left, and my prettiest maidservant, the rogue!" He radiated fatherly pride. "Thank God he did not set up here in Paris! I would have lost half my customers. But in Rouen his wife can be near her family, and he has the best inn there. Why, your queen's envoy, Master Francis Walsingham, stopped there on his way to court!"

"Walsingham?" Kat asked, praying that she sounded somewhat less interested than she felt. "Is he England's ambassador to France?"

"No, your ambassador is still Henry Norris. I met him once. A fine gentleman, for all that he is English. And so is Monsieur Walsingham, for all that he dresses all in black, as if in mourning. Or so my son tells me in his letter. No, Monsieur Walsingham is a special envoy. I have heard rumors that your queen wished him to help with the writing of the peace agreement at St. Germain—as if we French needed such help! *Par Dieu*, even our heretics are capable of negotiating for themselves! But she did not send him quickly enough for that, so now he is here to offer the king and his mother felicitations on the new peace. You had not heard of this? He has been here for weeks."

"My lord may have spoken of it," she said, shrugging slightly. "I may not have been attending."

Monsieur Cotart shook his head disapprovingly, then changed the subject.

Kat listened with half an ear while he droned on and on. Walsingham was not mentioned again, and with Tandy here she dared not ask the questions that burned in her mind: *How long will the envoy stay? And where may I find him?*

By the time Justin returned that evening, so late the streets were nearly dark, Kat had reluctantly admitted to herself that her first rash plans of escape and flight to Walsingham were all but hopeless. She had almost no money at all, so she could not buy clothes fit for a gentlewoman to wear to the court, and she would not be taken seriously if she went there garbed as she was. Nor, for that matter, could she be sure that she would be believed by French officials even if she were richly garbed. How could she prove who she was? If she could somehow reach Walsingham and talk to him, she could identify herself in a way by recounting the details of his conversation with Nick. But how many officials would come between her and that meeting, officials whose main purpose in life was to keep petitioners waiting in antechambers? And what if Walsingham left for England again before she could speak with him?

She did not relish the thought of being alone, friendless and almost penniless, at the French court. Michel had spoken too eloquently of the feral nature of some of the courtiers, and if Isobel de Maisse were any example . . . Marry, if she should meet Isobel there . . .

She shivered.

"Are you cold?" Justin asked.

He was lying on the bed, his doublet folded neatly beside him, his shirt unbuttoned. He had not brought a nightgown in his portmanteau, needing the space for the elegant suits he wore about his business here. Kat had brought a nightgown, though, an old nightgown of Tandy's that was much too large for her but at least, in its plainness, suited her disguise as a manservant. She wore it now as she sat tailor-fashion on the trundle bed, pretending to read by the fitful light of a single candle.

"A little," she admitted. It was cool in the room, with a breeze blowing through the unshuttered windows.

"Close the windows, if you wish," Justin offered.

She shook her head, disappointment bringing a painful lump to her throat, then chided herself for her reaction. What had she expected, for Justin to ask her to come lie beside him, as he had one evening on the *Lady Margaret* when she complained about being chilled? Those times, those feelings, were gone.

And yet she longed to touch him, if only to smooth his brow. He looked weary, his eyes darkly shadowed as he lay back against the linen-cased pillows, waiting for the wine he had been drinking to dull his senses enough for him to sleep, and seeing him like this, the jealousy she had felt earlier was overwhelmed by concern. His visit with Mademoiselle de Salvandy could not have been entirely pleasant, for he seemed cheerless tonight. Whatever the business was that had brought him to Paris, it must not be going well. She took some small comfort in that, hoping that his intrigues would fail, leaving Justin little choice but to return to England and perhaps quit this contriving forever. But even that, she realized, would not render him above suspicion in Walsingham's eyes. And Kat herself would owe an accounting of sorts to Walsingham, and her account—both what she had heard at Harwood Hall and what she had since come to suspect—might well help condemn Justin to a traitor's death.

He rescued me from the Inquisition.

Aye, there was that debt she owed him, but the debt was hers, not her queen's and country's. So could she, as payment of that debt, refrain from telling Walsingham all she knew?

It was a cruel choice, and she wished again there were some way she would not have to make it, but she had been able to think of none.

The words of the book swam before her eyes. She shut it and lay down, facing away from Justin, and drew the coverlet up to her neck. A long time later, after he had finished the wine and extinguished the candle, she fell into a dream-wracked sleep.

Men ran through the cobblestone streets of Paris, clutching dags and muskets and swords and knives and pikes, assailing each other in the pale dawn light. Some few were soldiers, but many were plain citizens in their nightclothes, their feet bare, and this was no invasion by troops, for fighting occurred between the nightclad as much as between the soldiers and those disturbed from their rest.

There were women, too, and children out in the streets. A wild-eyed man in bloodstained shirt and hose swung a halberd to strike down a sobbing lad no more than eight years old, then seized the boy's younger sister as she tried to dart past and flung her against the side of a house. Her head cracked against the stone, and she slid to the ground, leaving a bloody smear on the wall. Crowing with satisfaction, her murderer raised that halberd and started away down the street, strolling amid the carnage as though on a holiday promenade.

Suddenly a woman sprang from the doorway behind him. She hesitated in her flight, giving out a low wail of despair as she saw the bodies of the boy and girl. The man heard her and whirled around. Bellowing "Huguenote!" he raced after her as she fled. She slipped in a pool of blood and fell, and before she could regain her feet the blade of the halberd was swinging down . . .

Kat started awake with her hand pressed to her mouth, stifling a scream. She had fought free of the coverlet, and though she was bathed in sweat she felt cold, cold. Gasping, she sat up and glanced fearfully toward the windows. It was still dark outside, and the street was silent: it had been that dream again, nothing more. Would that she had never heard Jacques telling Justin of the visions of that old woman in Monteronne, for now Kat was dreaming of such scenes.

Justin stirred and murmured something inaudible. She looked to where he lay, the covers cast aside. He murmured again, flinging an arm out, but did not wake. Was he, too, troubled by bad dreams?

Certainly he would soon be troubled by the chill in the room. Her gaze went to his coverlet and blanket, but she feared he might wake if she tried to draw them over him again, and she did not want him to wake to find her so near. She would be hurt if he acted as if he suspected her of some treachery, peradventure some wish to harm him while he slept. Yet she would feel wounded even if he did understand that she only wished to protect him from the chill. She would be hurt, terribly hurt, if he did not try to draw her down beside him, even though there would be only false comfort in his embrace.

Instead she went to one window and closed the shutters. She moved to the other, then paused, her gaze again on Justin. Her eyes had adjusted to the poor light in the room, and she could see the fine muscling of his athletic body. In sleep, no matter how troubled his dreams, he was innocent of all contrivings and intrigues, and she could not look at him without remembering the texture, the scent, the taste of his skin, the welcome heaviness of his body on hers. She could not look at him without longing.

She drew in a deep, shuddering breath, then began to close the shutters, but one of her hands slipped and the shutter banged against the window frame.

There came a rustling sound behind her, as Justin moved again. "Kat?"

She kept her face to the shuttered window, fearing to turn and see him watching her, perchance reaching toward her. "It was cold," she said at last. "Pray your pardon for waking you. Go back to sleep."

For a few moments it was perfectly still in the room, then he settled back on the bed again. She waited awhile longer, then, keeping her gaze from him, made her way back to the trundle bed and curled up there, miserably certain that he had, indeed, simply gone back to sleep.

Chapter 42

Kat woke to the sound of breakfast being served in the next room: the clinking of dishes being set on the table, Tandy talking to two maidservants. Hurriedly she grabbed for her nightcap and tucked her hair into it, careful to make certain every strand was hidden, then hastened to rub dust on her face, checking the results in a small looking glass.

Justin waited impatiently by the door while she washed and dried her hands. He was fully dressed already, and from his garb—a suit of popinjay-blue satin, the doublet sleeves slashed to show straw-colored silk—it was apparent there would be no ride through Paris for the three of them this morning. He would be about his business instead, and early. She could not help wondering if some of his business was with the demoiselle with whom he had had dinner yesterday.

He looked her over critically, no doubt making sure her disguise was complete, then opened the door and led her into the antechamber. The maidservants were just leaving. Tandy, in tawny hose, an unfastened shirt, and light leather slippers, stood at the table pouring wine for Justin and then ale for Kat.

She murmured her thanks as she took the earthenware cup from him. Justin did not bother to sit down. He took a slice of bread from a platter and stood munching it. Tandy hesitated a few moments, then, after asking his lord's leave, took a seat and began helping himself to breakfast.

It was suddenly too much for Kat—the frustration of the night before, Justin's cool indifference to her as he went about his business, Tandy's easy acceptance of the prospect of a day shut in these rooms. She glared at Tandy, then turned to face Justin. Insolently she looked him up and down, trying to keep her expression as cold as his had been when he had surveyed her a few minutes before.

Anger grew in her as she saw a smile touch the corners of his mouth.

"Does my suit meet with your approval, Kat?"

" 'Tis overmuch finery for a visit to the Bastille, my lord. Was it not your plan to ride there today, now that I have seen the Left Bank?"

"The Bastille has stood for two centuries, Kat. 'Twill wait another day, or longer, if need be."

And your contriving will not? she thought, but said nothing as she gave him her back and walked over to the window. Already the Rue St. Honoré was busy. The day promised to be a fair one again, and all she would see of it was what was visible from the small windows in these chambers. Nor would there be any chance of escape. She was reminded of the long days in the north tower of El Nido de Aguilas, when she was held captive by Don Rafael. Her hand shook as she tightened her grip on the cup's handle.

"Would you like me to bring you some gift?" he asked, infuriating her more. "Something to help you while away the hours?"

"I have books enough," she said curtly. Justin had bought several books when they visited the Palais.

"Then perchance a lute would please you more? I passed a shop yesterday that sells them. D'you play? If you do not, then haply Tandy could play, and you could sing."

"Like a caged skylark?" she asked bitterly, and vowed to herself that once she was home again, she would set her caged songbird free.

Justin sighed, and tried to take her arm, but she jerked away, spilling ale onto his doublet and hose.

"God's death!" He brushed some drops of ale from the satin, but most had soaked in, and the smell of ale clung to him.

"I am sorry, my lord."

"Say you so?" he retorted, and she could not quite suppress a smile. In truth, she was not entirely displeased to have caused him this small trouble, when he had caused her so much.

He went back into their bedchamber to change, and came back out ten minutes later in a suit of black silk slashed with silver tissue. By that time, Kat had begun to feel ashamed of the petty satisfaction she had taken from the accident.

"My lord, I am truly sorry. I'll see if I can clean the ale from your suit."

"Nay, Tandy will see to that. Will you not?"

His servant nodded.

"Then *au revoir*. I'll be back tonight," he said, and went out.

Kat looked over at Tandy, who was just finishing his breakfast. It had been a hearty one, and he seemed content.

"Well," he said, when he noticed her watching him. "What will you this morn? Mumchance-at-cards, or primero, or noddy, or post and pair, or trump?"

Stated thus, she had to laugh at their dilemma, though her laughter was bittersweet.

"Noddy, I trow," she told him. "Yea, I'll play noddy, for all that I am noddy to play it with you, when you always win. But let me change first. I would not wear this nightgown all day."

She went into the other room and changed quickly from the nightgown to her doublet and hose and boots. Then her gaze fell on the popinjay-blue suit, which Justin had hung on the bedposts. The doublet was nearest her, and she ran her hand over the rich cloth, smiling ruefully. Likely the stuff would stain. 'Twould be a pity. She doubted Tandy could clean it properly—if the rogue would think to clean it at all today, before his master returned to remind him. Perhaps if she rinsed the stains now, and dried the cloth with a towel, that would serve . . .

She picked the doublet up and carried it over to the basin. As she would have done if she had been at home, she checked the single outer pocket, then ran her hands over the cloth to make certain there was nothing in any secret pocket that might be damaged by the water. Discovering a hard lump the size of a large coin, she turned the doublet inside out, found a pocket opening beside a seam, reached in, and drew out a gold locket on a chain.

Kat turned the locket over and over in her hands, and the chain, which had been wrapped neatly around it, fell free. The locket looked oddly familiar. But where had she seen one like it before?

Then, her curiosity getting the better of her, she opened the locket, and her mouth fell open as she stared at a picture of herself and knew what she held.

Whence came this? And how long had Justin had it? Her mind was of a sudden roiled with new fears and doubts, but one thing was certain: he had lied when he pretended he did not know who she was. He had lied, and she could never trust him again, not even in the smallest matter.

She closed the locket, but kept it in her fist.

Justin knew who she was. Aye, and knew who Nick was, too, for he must have had this locket from her brother. Mayhap she had talked in her sleep, betraying herself, if only by speaking of Beechwood or some friend who could have identified her—to Tandy? Was that where he had been, in England? But that mattered little. What mattered was that Justin knew . . .

But then why had he said nothing to her? Why had he not asked her how a gentlewoman came to spy on him? And why had he not said anything about returning her to her home? By the mass, once he knew she was a gentlewoman, he should have seen some profit in setting her free, if only by demanding some ransom from Nick . . . unless he believed he could never set her free.

The thought frightened her. And she was angry as well as frightened when it struck her that he might demand a ransom from Nick when he had no intention of letting her go. She knew her brother: he would pay. Even if it meant selling Beechwood, he would pay.

She had to escape. Her fears of being alone and penniless in a strange land seemed mere trifles now. But how could she get away?

"Kat?" Tandy called. Wood scraped across wood as he pushed his chair back from the table. She heard him approach the door.

Jesu, she was still holding the locket. She stuffed it back into the doublet pocket. Half the chain hung out, but there was no time to remedy that, only time enough to fold the doublet so the lining was hidden, and the chain with it.

"I thought to clean this," she called to Tandy, not looking around, fearful that she might look guilty. She would not have him know that she had discovered the locket. "But I am not sure that I can."

"Leave it. I'll see to it later."

She nodded, still not facing him.

"Is aught amiss?" he asked.

She put her hand to her face, then squeezed her eyes shut as hard as she could, and kept them squeezed shut for a few seconds. 'Twas a trick a player had taught her last year. When she took her hand away and turned to face Tandy at last, she was blinking and her eyes were teary.

"By my faith, Kat, what's wrong?"

" 'Tis nothing," she said, then sniffed. "I would fain go out, for it is a fair day, too fair to spend here playing cards like prisoners in a cell. But we must needs stay here."

"You would go out," he said, and though there was suspicion in his voice, there was very little of it—much less, she would warrant, than Justin would have shown.

"Aye."

"To the Bastille?"

She shrugged. "I would like to go there, of certain, but I would be anywhere but here, in these rooms. I would see the Palais again, or Les Halles . . ."

"You would buy something?"

"Or just look at the wares. 'Sblood, Tandy, are you not weary of these rooms?"

He laughed. "Yes, I am."

"Then pray let us go."

"Yea, let's go."

He gestured for her to precede him out of their chambers. She would have no chance now to tuck the locket chain into the pocket so Justin would not know she had found it. But that was of no concern now, for if luck favored her, she would never see him again.

Would that I had learned more players' tricks from that player, Kat thought a few hours later. Though she had perforce played a role every waking minute since being captured at Harwood Hall in June, she had never needed more skill than she would in the next few minutes. And Tandy, she knew, was a cunning audience. Had he not seen through the flower seller's pretense yesterday? She would have to hope that his fondness for her would blind him for a time—that, and his weariness.

They had been to almost every stall and shop at the Palais, and Tandy's arms were full of her purchases, all those she could not hold herself. She had bought cheesecakes and comfits, a small bottle of brandy, two yards of lace, a length of plush for a hat and feathers to trim it, a fan, a toy lute with strings that produced a tiny unmusical sound when plucked, and two leather-bound books—one by Rabelais, the other the *Heptaemeron* by Marguerite of Navarre, François I's brilliant sister. Tandy had talked her out of buying the parrot.

He was sore of foot already, for he still wore the slippers he had worn at the inn, and she had suggested that they walk, rather than ride, to the Palais. Once there she had wanted to see more of it than she had seen two days ago, so they had walked through the *grand salle*, with its marble floor and gilt ceiling and statues of French kings, where Mary Queen of Scots had married the dauphin of France. They had visited the Saint-Chapelle to see the two fine new altars and the rood screen Henri II had added to the chapel, and then Kat wanted to see the seven chambers of the Court of Parlement again, especially the Chamber of Paris, with its carving of a lion, the beast lying down with its tail between its legs, as a reminder to all who entered the chamber that no one, no matter how great, was above the court. They had also gone to the Chamber of Comptes, to admire the portraits at the entry of Temperance, Prudence, Justice, and Fortitude. Tandy had begun to complain that the soles of his slippers would be worn through even before they started their tour of the vendors' shops and stalls.

Pray God, he was weary enough now that he would heed her next suggestion.

"Let's go to the Pomme de Pin for dinner."

"There's a pleasant thought. I would gladly set these down," he said, glancing down at the heaped purchases in his arms.

"Which way is it?" she asked, and then, "God's life! I meant to buy just a few more things . . ."

Tandy groaned.

"Nay, they are not heavy. In sooth, they are not."

"Are they winged?" he asked suspiciously.

"No, nor are they clawed," she replied. He had not even let her stop to look at a cage of ferrets that were for sale. "There are two books I would buy, and a gallipot of perfume. Have you money enough for them, and dinner as well?"

"I trow I do. How much are the books?"

"Truth to tell, I cannot remember. But I do remember that the perfume was but a few deniers. D'you remember the *parfumeur*'s stall? Would you buy the perfume for me while I get the books? We could leave for the Pomme de Pin the sooner."

"Could I not buy the books for you instead?"

There was no hint of suspicion in his voice now. He sounded merely weary, and she was reminded of how he had waited impatiently while she bought the women's things among her purchases, always pretending that she was a young man looking for gifts for his sweetheart.

"Nay, you cannot, for I cannot recall the titles—though I warrant you, I shall find them quick enough, for I know where they were on the shelves. But perchance I should go to the *parfumeur*'s stall, too. She might have some other perfume that I would like as well . . ."

Tandy groaned again. "We'll be all day in this market. No, I'll get the perfume. Here, take my purse." He unfastened it from his belt and handed it to her. "Give me a sou. A few denier may not be enough."

"Indeed, it will," she said. Now that the purse was in her hands—of a truth, luck was with her, for she had not dared hope for this!—she was reluctant to part with a denier more than needs must.

"A sou," he said again, shifting the packages in his arms and holding out his hand. She gave him the coin.

" 'Tis a perfume compounded of orange-flower water and musk, and 'tis in a white-glazed gallipot, not one of the green-glazed pots. Be sure to get that one, and no other, for she sells others that are somewhat like it but not half so pleasing . . . unless haply there were some I did not try yet," she finished doubtfully.

"A white pot, the perfume of orange flowers and musk. I'll remember," Tandy said, and took himself off hastily. She almost laughed to see how he fled before she could change her mind.

She fastened the purse to her belt—'twould not do to have it stolen—and, after handing her purchases to a startled rustic, slipped away through the crowd.

The woman at the perfume stall could not find the perfume he wanted. She was adamant that the perfume Kat spoke of was in a green-glazed pot; the white-glazed pots, most of them, contained perfumes made with rosewater. Perhaps one or two of the white pots contained a perfume of orange flowers, from a batch she had made last week, but she could not be sure. Tandy, she said, could try them for himself.

He would have gone then to find Kat, but he realized he was not even certain which booksellers' stalls, in which part of the courtyard, she had returned to. So he stood there, as patiently as he could, while the *parfumeur* opened each white gallipot in turn and let him sniff the contents. A few minutes later his head was reeling from the scent of roses and musk. None of the white pots, as she had averred, contained perfume of orange blossom.

Perhaps she had sold that gallipot since the young man had been here? he asked hopefully. Like enough, Kat would accept that explanation, and not insist on returning here herself.

But no, the *parfumeur* had sold none of her wares since his young friend had stopped at her stall.

Sorely disappointed, Tandy went back to the place where he had left Kat, and sat down on his heels, his back against a wall, to wait for her.

Ten minutes later, he began to worry. A few minutes after that, he started around the courtyard, stopping at each bookseller's. Within half an hour, he had nary a doubt of it: he had been tricked.

This was the last place in Paris Kat wanted to be. 'Twas also, she prayed, the last place where Justin and Tandy would look for her.

Three mass graves had been closed since her visit here three days ago, but two more had been dug, two mouths yawning in that flesh-eating soil, that earth that, it was said, could *manger son cadavre en neuf jours*. The bones uncovered when those graves were dug had already been removed, joining those heaped in the open-sided penthouses above the cloister surrounding the churchyard.

It was late in the afternoon. Kat's head ached, and she felt sick to her stomach and dizzy. She bitterly regretted not having eaten breakfast, but she could not eat now, surrounded by the sight and stench of death and decay. She had bought some rose comfits and put one into her mouth an hour ago, but then had quickly spat it out again as her stomach threatened to rebel. There were vendors of foods of all sorts, from pastries to fruit, along the arcades, but she would have to wait until leaving the cemetery to eat and drink.

And leaving this place would have to wait until nightfall.

She dreaded having to stay while shadows collected and vendors and buyers left the cloisters, but Tandy would be looking for her now, maybe running up and down the streets—or riding up and down, if he had returned to L'Oison Noir for a horse. She would have a better chance of slipping unseen through the streets after darkness fell. She would cross the Seine then, and find a room at some inn on the Left Bank. By then, she was sure, Tandy would have given up his search for the night. She certainly need not fear that tomorrow he would go from inn to inn on the Left Bank, with its multitude of university students, asking if anyone had seen a raggedly dressed youth. The innkeepers would laugh him to scorn. Mayhap he would not search for her at all after today. No doubt Justin would be glad to have her gone . . .

She shook her head, dismissing the thought and the pain it caused her.

Tomorrow . . . Tomorrow she would buy women's clothes, and don them, and then go to another inn. And from there she would send a letter to Francis Walsingham. She would say nothing more than that she hoped to see him before he left Paris—she dared say no more—but she would sign it with her own name. He must have suspected by now that Justin had taken her prisoner. If her letter reached him—would that she could be certain of that!—he would wish to learn how she came to be in France.

How many écus, she wondered, would it take to persuade a court official to hand her letter to Master Walsingham? And how many more to persuade the messenger to hand both letter and bribe to the official, instead of keeping the money for himself? She might have to bribe the innkeeper to learn who the most trustworthy messenger was. She wished she could go to the court herself, but it was impossible: she lacked money enough for the inns and the bribes and also for clothes fine enough that she would be accepted at court as an acquaintance of Queen Elizabeth's envoy.

She strolled round and round the cloister, stopping now and then to look at the wares for sale. Vendors were watching her with more suspicion each time she passed, no doubt weighing the possibility that she was a thief. She could not fault them for their wariness, since she had seen more than a few shabby ruffians during the hours she had spent here, and twice she had seen merchants cry *"Larron! Larron!"* and run after fleet-footed thieves . . . thieves who might well return in a few hours. Tandy had told her that during the night many of the vagabonds of Paris took refuge in the churchyard of the Innocents, for here, as in the liberties of London, they need not fear arrest. She hoped she would be well away before the most dangerous vagabonds arrived.

Sweat trickled down her neck and the sides of her face as she left the shaded portion of the arcade and walked through the sunlight. Her hands twitched: she sorely wanted to wipe her face and neck, but she dared not. Already some of the dust she had applied to her face might have washed away, and she did not want to rub her face any cleaner.

Later she would find dirt to apply to her skin again, but not now, not here. She shuddered at the thought of taking some of the soil from the graveyard and rubbing it into her skin. She did not want to think of what soil that was said to eat cadavers in nine days would do to her face, if she must needs leave it there for several hours.

Suddenly the skin at the back of her neck prickled. Someone was watching her . . .

She stopped and then turned slowly around to look about her in apparent boredom.

Two vendors were watching her, but she was accustomed to their scrutiny and certain it had not been their gaze that she felt. She scanned the crowded arcade, seeking, without finding, two tall men—one with tawny hair, one with russet—before looking out across the graveyard.

Besides the grave diggers, the only moving figure was that of a scholar, his liripipium flapping as he staggered drunkenly past the edge of the nearest open grave, shaking his fist as he ranted at the dead in slurred but exquisitely proper Latin. Death himself, motionless, incarnate in stone, a skeleton draped in ragged cerements, held the center of the churchyard. Death, too, raised his fist here, but in that frozen gesture was a power that made the scholar's anger seem mortally feeble.

She shivered. Tearing her gaze away from the statue, she scanned the arcade again.

She recognized no one among the throng, saw no one other than cautious merchants and their customers, none of whom seemed interested at the moment in the ill-clad, dirty-faced youth. She shook her head slowly, unhappy with the mischievous imagination that had now twice led her to believe she was being watched.

Keeping her gaze directly ahead, she continued on her way around the cemetery. The sensation of being watched persisted, but she would not allow herself to stop and look back again: such obvious uneasiness would only draw unwanted attention. But she slowed when she again reached a shaded portion of the arcade, intending to linger here until she had stopped sweating. She smiled as a child crawled across the pavement a few yards ahead of her, pursuing a rolling ball.

Then the ball rolled to a stop, and she saw it was a skull, no larger than the child's head.

She gasped and stepped back, and shrieked as a hand fell on her shoulder and strong fingers dug into her flesh.

She was yanked around, and would have fallen if another hand had not caught her, steadying her. She gaped up at a grimly smiling, terribly familiar face.

"Well met in Paris," Christopher Danvers said.

CHAPTER 43

Tandy's steps lagged as he approached his room at L'Oison Noir. The sun would be setting soon, and he was very weary. He had been back once before, but had left again as soon as he had ascertained that neither the girl nor his lord had been back to the inn.

The door to the antechamber that was his room was ajar now, and there were no sounds from within to indicate servants at work: Justin must have returned. Steeling himself, Tandy swung the door wide open.

Justin sat at the table, leafing through one of the books Tandy had left there a few hours earlier. His expression was coldly thoughtful as he looked up at his servant.

"Where is she?" he asked, very softly.

"I know not," Tandy said, and gave a terse account of the events in the courtyard of the Palais. " 'Twas foolish of me," he admitted. "I did not think—"

"Nay, you did not. You were a very sheep's head. Aye, and her cony as well, for all that you would not be caught by that cony-catching flower seller."

Tandy's face burned with shame and anger, but he could say nothing in his own defense.

"You have looked for her?"

"Everywhere. Every tavern, every inn, every street and alley. But 'tis well nigh hopeless. How many such youths are there in Paris, garbed in an old suit?"

"There is that hat she wears to cover her hair."

"Yea, and have you noticed how many students affect all manner of hats, from turbans to copintanks, of all stuffs and colors? Her hat is but one more novelty among many, and thus invisible, in sooth."

Justin nodded slowly. "But there is her face, and that is not one among many, I warrant you. I trow that some who see her must notice the fairness beneath the dirt on her skin."

"Mayhap y'are right," Tandy said, shrugging, "but how to describe her face so precisely that the words make a very picture of it?"

Justin stared at him in disbelief. "You did not take the locket with you? I left it in my doublet when I changed this morning, but did not remember it until an hour later."

Tandy shook his head.

Justin got up and went into the other chamber. Tandy followed, watching as the baron picked up the doublet from where it lay beside the basin of water.

"By the mass! You did not wash this with the locket in it?"

"Nay, 'twas Kat who meant to wash it, but—"

"Kat?" Justin opened the doublet, and Tandy saw the chain hanging from a slit in the lining. "Jesu. She found it. I left the chain wrapped around the locket." He took the chain and pulled the locket out, then opened it. " 'Tis unharmed. Likely she found it before she began to wash the doublet."

"Yea, for I called to her, and found her standing there, and the doublet was still dry. But not her eyes, in faith. She was crying, but would not have me see. And when I saw, she told me that she was sad to be kept inside here on such a fair day."

Justin sighed.

"I warrant you, 'twas why she ran away."

"Was it?" Justin asked. "Was it? Then was it fear of discovering it someday that led her to attempt to escape when we were at Monteronne? Marry, you fool, you cannot blame her finding this for your losing her."

"Then why was she crying?"

"I know not!" Justin almost shouted. "She's a woman. She weeps. And we burn daylight in this idle chatter."

"There's scant daylight left."

"Then all the more reason," Justin said, tucking the locket into a pocket of the doublet he was wearing, "to make haste. We'll start at the Palais, and show the picture to all who might have seen her."

"Show a picture that you said could not be of her?"

It was a barbed question, and for an instant Justin looked murderously angry, but then he sighed again, loudly, and smiled wryly, and nodded. " 'Tis our good luck, is it not, that it so greatly favors her? Now," he said, as he walked past Tandy and out the door, "pray tell me where you have searched already . . ."

CHAPTER 44

"And then we went to the Louvre," Kat told Christopher, "and were there in the courtyard, and a rustic and his wife saw us and thought us Parisians, and Nick perforce would take advantage of their witlessness and spend an hour telling them where they must go in the town, and what they must do, and I trow that half the directions he gave them were wrong, though I know not whether 'twas of intent . . ."

Her voice trailed off. Christopher, who was trying to catch the attention of a drawer—but with scant luck, for the tavern was busy—seemed not to be listening. She thanked God for that. She had racked her brains for tales to tell Christopher of what she and Nick had been doing in Paris, and her imagination was nearly exhausted.

Perhaps he was as weary of her stories as she was of telling them. Pray God, it was so. Then he might soon take himself off to return to the company of the friends with whom he was staying, and she could go on about her business, which he had so unfortunately interrupted.

In those first moments after meeting him at the Cemetery of the Innocents, she had hoped that he might be as eager to leave her company as he had been when she met him at Paul's in June. But that hope had been lost when he invited her to join him for supper. Too surprised to think clearly, she could think of no reason to refuse his invitation. At least the twenty minute reprieve, during which they walked from the cemetery to this tavern on the Left Bank, had given her time to come up with a story explaining why she was here in Paris, a story that she prayed he might accept.

So far, he seemed to accept it. And why not? He knew of the adventures she and Nick had had as children, when she would go about disguised as a boy. This new adventure she invented as her explanation could be seen as but one more, and if their greater age made it seem greater folly, then that mattered little. What cared she if Christopher thought her a fool? What mattered was that he believed that she and Nick had decided of a sudden that now was the time to visit Paris, with a peace treaty signed and not yet broken. She had told him that they had been here only a few days.

He had said little of his own reasons for being in Paris, other than that he had been invited here by two friends and that he, too, had thought 'twould be best to visit Paris now. "And I wished to avoid the court's progress," he had told Kat. "I have gone twice before, and 'twas enough of packing and unpacking and sleeping in tents or sharing rooms in some ancient manor house."

"I'faith, another reason why I would not like the court," she had told him waggishly, "and one that you never gave me before."

Then she wished she had held her tongue, for the look on his face told her it had been unwise to remind him of anything they had said to each other during the days when he was wooing her. She had quickly gone back to her fanciful stories of what she and Nick had done in Paris, and he was soon in humor again.

But when would he leave? She was weary, and wanted to look for a respectable inn and hire lodgings for the night. 'Twas still light outside, the sun having set less than an hour ago, but she was no longer afraid of being found by Tandy or Justin if she walked through the streets before nightfall. She had made it this far, in Christopher's company, without being seen . . . though in truth she had felt uneasy, and had glanced around from time to time, wondering if they would be espied. Wondering, too, if she could count on Christopher for help if she was seen by Justin or Tandy.

The popinjay she had remembered Christopher Danvers as being would have been of little help, but he had changed in these past months, and now seemed a tougher, shrewder man. He had exchanged his court finery for a black leather jerkin over a doublet and hose of plain tawny silk. His debts might have forced that change on him, but his expression, too, had changed, and she did not think penury alone could account for that. He had often played the fashionably jaded courtier for her, but the elegantly disdainful curl of the lip—an expression she had always suspected he had practiced before a looking glass—had been replaced by a set, cynical twist to his mouth.

"A penny for your thoughts."

"Nay, they are worth a shilling, at least," she said, and laughed. "I was merely thinking that y'are a changed man, Christopher."

"Through no choice of mine," he replied, so bitterly that she flinched.

"Y'are still angry with me?"

He sighed then, and took her hand. "Yea, somewhat, I must confess, and yet more sorrowful than angry. And I would not have had you marry me when you love me not, for all that I loved you. Would that you had loved me, though. Would that you had married me."

"Soft," Kat whispered, and pulled her hand free of his. "What will anyone seeing us think, with me garbed thus?" And he laughed at that.

I would not have had you marry me when you love me not, for all that I loved you. Truly, he sounded honest, more honest than she had ever heard him. Was it possible that she had misjudged him? She was suddenly ashamed that she had suspected him of drugging the wine he had given her for breakfast that day. No doubt she had wounded him with that letter she left for him. She hoped that the wound had healed somewhat. Like enough, it had: *I loved you,* he had said, not *I love you.*

How different her life would have been if she had loved him! Of certain, she would not be here now. Perchance she would never have met Justin, for she doubted that she would have gone to the Jerusalem Tree as she did, without first getting the counsel of the man she intended to marry, whose honor would be tied to her own. To have never met Justin . . . Would that not have been a blessing?

But she could not convince herself of that. For all the trouble he had brought her, her heart was still his. She prayed that would change someday, but 'twould take a better man than Christopher Danvers to help her forget Justin Lisle.

She had yet one more thing to say to Justin, but she would say it in a letter, which she had resolved to send to him tomorrow. Sometime then, before she changed to women's garb, she would find a messenger to convey a warning to him. Needs must that she do so, for she dared not lie to Walsingham. She had not yet determined the precise words to write, but 'twould be short, for if she said too much and the letter fell into the wrong hands, she might herself be found guilty of aiding a traitor. *Flee,* she would tell him, *but not to your home. You are suspect there.* She hoped he would heed her. 'Twould mean he would be saved from a traitor's death, as long as he stayed on the Continent instead of returning to England. Mayhap he would continue to plot with other papists here, but she felt there could be little danger from one more contriver added to so many . . .

"Kat?" Christopher asked. "I pray your pardon if what I said troubled you."

She shook her head. " 'Twas not that. I was merely remembering that I was to meet Nick for supper, and I am late. I must go now."

"I'll walk with you back to your inn. The streets of Paris are no place for a gentlewoman to walk alone."

"Even if she is not garbed as a gentlewoman?"

"Even then."

"I thank you, but 'twill not—"

"Yes, it will. I would go with you, Kat, and see you safely back to your brother. At what inn do you lodge?"

She could think of no inns other than L'Oison Noir and La Plume Vermeille, an inn she had seen just north of Les Halles. She feared to name it—their path there would take her too near L'Oison Noir—but she had no choice, so she told him they were staying there. Then, seeing Christopher's look of surprise, she wondered if haply she had named an inn as infamous as Le Dauphin Sautant in Bayonne. But there was no help for it now. And no matter how dangerous the inn, she would be there only a few minutes, for she would take her leave of Christopher outside—Nick would be her excuse; she would say she feared that her brother would be wroth with Christopher because she was late—and go inside only until she thought Christopher was well away.

They left the tavern and walked north through the twilit streets. They had gone only a short distance when Christopher said that he must needs stop at the house where he was staying, on the Place Maubert, lest his friends delay their own supper for him.

"Of a truth," Kat told him, "you need not continue so far with me. I do not fear to walk back alone."

"I will not hear of it," Christopher said, and took her hand, and at the next corner turned and led her west, toward the Place Maubert.

The Place was nearly deserted at this hour. Kat saw one vendor, a woman with a wheelbarrow, who she thought looked much like the flower seller they had encountered yesterday, but the woman was standing in deep shadow, and she could not be certain.

Christopher took her to a finely built four-story house, and would not agree to her waiting outside, so she followed him through the door and entryway and upstairs. The rooms were clean and well-furnished but not especially elegant, and he must have guessed at her thoughts, for he told her that the house was not owned by his friends, who were gentlemen, but by a merchant whom they knew, who had lent it to them while he and his family were away for some months in Orléans. They had borrowed it for him to stay in, and stayed here themselves at times, though they also had lodgings in the Marais.

Kat raised her eyebrows a little, wondering that gentlemen would choose to live amidst merchants when they had finer lodgings. She also wondered why Christopher would have accepted lodgings here. She would have thought him too proud. But as they said, beggars should be no choosers.

They walked through two more rooms overlooking the courtyard, which was all paved over, save for a small garden in one corner, with a single tree and a flower plot. In the second room a servingman greeted them. He seemed surprised by Kat's appearance, and even more by Christopher's holding her hand, but then he shrugged and averted his eyes and told Christopher that the *messieurs* were in the gallery.

Christopher escorted her through the doorway to their right, into a room that ran the length of the courtyard. 'Twas a small gallery compared to the one at Beechwood, but it had fair, large windows and a long padded bench on which two gentlemen were sitting, facing each other as they talked quietly. They looked up at Christopher and Kat a few moments after the door was opened, and Kat stopped on the threshold, struck by the contrast between them. They both appeared to be about the same age as Christopher, but there the similarity ended.

One of the gentlemen wore a suit of plain brown satin that would have seemed drab but for the sheen of the rich cloth. He had a long, thin face, sunburned skin and black hair that wanted careful barbering.

The other gentleman was clad in doublet and breeches of an intricately patterned three-pile velvet of crimson, black and gold. His stockings were of white silk embroidered with gold thread, and fastened with garters of gold lace. Gold tissue lined his black silk cloak. But it was his face, more than his rich garb, that held Kat's gaze.

His face, framed by gold curls—that she would swear had been put there by a *fer à frisotter*, as the French called their curling irons—seemed to have been painted. The whiteness of his skin exceeded Nature's own artistry, and Kat was sure that if it was not due to some fucus, then surely he washed his face with some preparation that bleached his skin. And the redness of his cheeks and lips looked like paint, too. She had heard that sometimes men who had been ill painted their faces to counterfeit health, and Nick had told her that some courtiers were known to paint their faces to make them more fair—but always with a light hand, so no one might notice the artifice. This man seemed not to care if anyone might think he was painted like—she almost laughed at the thought—like a Winchester goose.

"Christopher!" the painted gentleman called, laughing. "You astonish me! They will now call you *L'Échangeur*, as they called the late King of Basse-Navarre *L'Échangeur* when he left his wife and her heresies for the sweet arms of *la belle* Rouet. Yet it is not your faith you are changing, nor have you changed for the sake of a woman. I applaud you," he went on, in his perfect English, and he clapped his hands—hands that were as white and delicately beautiful as Elizabeth Tudor's, Kat noticed—lightly, mockingly. "But"—and he smiled mischievously—"could you not have done better than this ragamuffin?"

Kat saw that Christopher's face had reddened, but whether 'twas from anger or from shame, she could not say.

"This is no ragamuffin, monsieur," he said coldly, "nor any *boy*."

And he yanked Kat's hat from her head, causing her to cry out as her hair was pulled before the pins tore loose. The two Frenchmen stared at her wordlessly. "This *gentlewoman* is of Lord Harwood's party."

Now it was Kat's turn to stare at him. "How did—Were you on the Pont St. Michel?"

"Yesterday? Yea, I was there."

"Christopher," the man in brown satin said, "we were told of no woman with Lord Harwood, but rather of two menservants."

"Of which she appeared to be one. I have seen her in this guise before. Her home is near mine, in Sussex. I have known her for years."

"But," the satin-garbed gentleman went on, in English as perfect as the other's, "you said nothing about—"

"I knew nothing about it," Christopher said, interrupting. "By my faith, I did not even know that she knew him."

"I have not known him for long," Kat said, though she felt a bit confused by their concern about Justin.

"Long enough," the velvet-clad gentleman said, and laughed again. "Long enough, Madame Lisle. Now, madame. Pray tell me. Why is your husband turning the Marais upside down looking for me?"

Her mouth fell open. She was astonished by both the revelation about Justin and the assumption that she was married to him. "He is looking for you?" she said at last. She was unsure whether 'twould be wisest to deny being married to Justin.

"You did not know?"

She shook her head. "He tells me nothing of what he is about."

" 'Tis a pity, madame." The painted face looked thoughtful.

"Christopher," Kat whispered, "how is it you learned that I was with Justin?"

" 'Tis known that he was at a chateau near Bayonne with his wife," he replied in an undertone. "I knew not who that might be, though, until I saw you with him. 'Twas very quick, Kat. Marry in all haste, repent—"

"At leisure. Yea, but I have repented in haste as well."

"Indeed?"

"Justin tells me naught of his business," she said, still whispering, but putting as much bitterness as she could into her voice. "I am dragged from place to place, and given no reason for gadding abroad."

"I would not think you one to complain of gadding abroad," Christopher responded. "In good sooth, had I not known otherwise, I would have believed what you told me about coming to Paris with your brother."

She looked away, biting her lip.

"Why did you lie to me?"

She sighed. "I feared that you might return me to Justin if you knew that I had left him. I knew not if you were friends. I know very little of his life."

"You have left him?"

"Yea. I would fain return to England and seek my brother's help in ending this marriage."

"And then be free to marry again?"

She nodded. "Pray help me, Christopher," she pleaded, turning to him, but before he could reply, the gentleman in brown satin approached them. His friend still lounged on the bench, but he watched them with interest.

"Madame."

"Monsieur . . . ?"

"Guy de Saint-Amant," he told her, bowing. "My *confrère* is Monsieur Pierre de Marchant."

The velvet-clad gentleman got up to bow and then sat down again. Kat stared at him. *Pierre de Marchant.* The man who had written to Justin's cousin Margaret. She remembered Michel de Charron's laughter when Justin had asked him about Marchant . . .

"Madame Lisle," Saint-Amant said, "I would know if you sympathize with your husband on the matters that concern us."

"Would that I knew what you mean, monsieur."

"I mean," Saint-Amant said, a hint of impatience in his voice, "that I would know if you also oppose the heretic Church of England."

Kat gestured helplessly. She could not lie and say she was a papist. Christopher knew better. "Monsieur, I know not how to answer."

"Was my question too difficult for you?" he asked sharply.

"Nay . . . but I have given little thought to such things."

"You have—" Saint-Amant began indignantly, but Christopher interrupted him.

"I warrant you, she is telling the truth. Katherine was a country gentlewoman, with no ties to the court. Nor was her father part of any faction."

"Was he Catholic, or not?"

"He was not," Christopher said calmly, "no more than Lord Harwood is, to all outward appearances. Were he alive, and a Frenchman, he would be a *politique.*"

"A *politique*!" Saint-Amant spat. "*Par Dieu*! This is just what we need—another *politique*! I wonder that Lord Harwood married her!"

That brought a burst of laughter from Marchant. "Guy! *Foi de gentilhomme*! Think you that he married her for her religion? No one—*Non*. Perchance you would . . ."

Saint-Amant ignored him. He took Kat's hand and stared directly into her eyes.

"Are you a *politique*, madame?"

"Guy, to what purpose is this inquisition?" Christopher said, a bit impatiently. "As I have told you, she has lived quietly in the country, where these conflicts scarce touch her. She saw London for the first time just this summer."

"Oh?" Saint-Amant's gaze had not wavered, and now his grip on Kat's hand tightened. "And just what, madame, did you think of what you saw there?"

"Monsieur," Kat asked in genuine confusion, "of which sights do you speak?"

"Come, madame," he said, and led her a few yards down the gallery, stopping beside a table on which sat a crumbling stone bust of what seemed to be a child.

"This is what was left of the statue of a cherub," he said in a harsh tone, "after heretics destroyed the Church of St. Bartholomew. Or perhaps it was St. Martin's. It scarce matters which, so many were destroyed. You could not have visited London without seeing their ruins. And you could not have seen them"—his hand tightened painfully around hers—"without thinking of all that had been destroyed with them. Could you?"

For a truth, Kat had given scant thought to the shattered churches, many of which were already overgrown, blending with the city's older ruins. But that answer would not serve her with Saint-Amant—or, for that matter, with most other French papists, many of whom had been eager to buy any relics of the old English Catholic churches that reached France. Nick had told her that some men had prospered from that market, even smashing unbroken statues on purpose to sell the separate pieces for as much as the entire statue would otherwise have brought.

"I think, monsieur," she said slowly, hoping to distract him, "that you were fortunate Paris was spared such destruction."

"Paris, spared?" Saint-Amant was nearly shouting. "You think Paris has been spared? It has been nearly half a century since heretics smashed a statue of the Virgin near the Porte Saint-Antoine, and there have been countless more desecrations since then. And not only of churches. 'Twas the Huguenots who were to blame for the explosion that damaged the Bastille seven years ago."

There had been no proof of that, so far as Kat was aware, and she knew that the people of Paris had very nearly retaliated by massacring the Protestants. At other times Protestants had been executed in revenge. But she said nothing in their defense, for the moment too afraid to speak. Saint-Amant's eyes were glittering now as Fray Francisco's had when he spoke of the Inquisition.

"The entire city could have fallen to the Huguenots," Saint-Amant said, his voice softer now, subdued, almost mournful. "I was here then, three years ago, when Huguenot forces blockaded the city. We had peasants seeking refuge within the city walls, bringing their cattle with them, and carts of grain, so that the Huguenots would not have them. There were Huguenots encamped in Argenteuil, madame, and in Charenton, and St. Denis. They came into the very faubourgs of Paris, destroying what they would. They even burned windmills!" He laughed, a choked, horrible sound.

"And the churches . . ." He drew a deep, shuddering breath. "What they did to the churches outside Paris . . . Two years ago I met a Huguenot noble wearing a fine linen shirt he bragged had been made from an altar cloth stolen during the blockade. Had my comrades not restrained me, I would have killed the man. And they took not just cloth and vestments, but all the gold and silver they could carry—the chalices, the crosses. Sacred things, to be melted down for their treasury. As if they needed the wealth, with their pirates making the Channel unsafe for honest merchants. You could ask Monsieur Richier, whose house we occupy, if he feels he has been spared! He has lost thousands of sous to the pirates. Yet even so, he will tell you he was fortunate to have been in Paris and not outside the city walls, for there, had he fallen into Huguenot hands, he would have been forced to loan them money if he had any, and to work for them if he had none."

He paused for a few moments, breathing raggedly, as if he had been running.

"You were at Monteronne. You met Gabrielle de Charron. You must have been told of the execution of the Huguenots at Amboise."

Kat nodded.

"I know that *la formidable* Gabrielle, whose pen has caused so much mischief, had a brother among the traitors who were executed, so I was sure that you would have been told of it, by her servants if not by Gabrielle herself . . . But were you also told," he asked, very quietly, "of the battle of Orthez, a year ago last month? 'Twas a Huguenot victory, madame . . . and they celebrated it by slaughtering the three thousand Catholics who had surrendered to them after being assured that they would not be killed. I lost several cousins at Orthez, the youngest of them a boy of twelve."

There were tears in his eyes. Suddenly he let go of her hand and turned away, to face the stone cherub's head. After a moment he reached out and touched one of its stone curls, and Kat wondered if he were seeing another face, that of a twelve-year-old boy. She felt close to tears herself.

"Monsieur," she murmured, "these are atrocities of war, not the fault of either faith. With the war ended—"

He laughed abruptly. "*Par ma foi*, Christopher was right. You do not understand. You cannot understand. Madame, do you think the Huguenots will be content with the terms of this peace? No, they will not. Our faith is an abomination to them, and soon they will begin to do what they have done before. They will hold their *prêches* outside the doors of our churches—if they do not drive the Catholics out so they may hold their own services inside. They will mock our processions, and steal chrism so they may grease their boots with it. They will not let us be. Think you that if they ever have the upper hand, they will accept our faith in their midst?"

She was still, not willing to shake her head again and so confess he was right, not able to nod and deny his argument. She had been wrong to think that he was like Fray Francisco, who had driven himself into a frenzy of hate for an enemy who could not touch him while he was safe within the bastion of the Inquisition. Guy de Saint-Amant had suffered personally from the war between the religion he believed in and the faith that opposed it. His cause was Gabrielle's, but reversed, like an image in a looking glass.

"The war has not ended, madame. It has only been papered over for a time. The accord is on one level. Beneath it, we still fight. What else can we do?"

Then he took his leave of her, with an oddly formal courtesy, as if he were bidding her *adieu* after some masque at court, when they had talked only of pleasantries.

"Guy, Guy, Guy," Marchant said, after the door had closed behind his friend. Kat turned to see him shaking his head. "He is too serious, madame, to be a good host, so that role perforce falls to me." He rose then, with a sinuous grace she envied, and came over to them. "Have you had supper?"

"Yea, we have," Christopher told him.

"Then would you play at cards? Or billiards?"

"Monsieur," Kat said, "I cannot stay."

"No, madame," Marchant said, gently yet so insistently that Kat could hear the threat behind his words. "You can stay. You will. You must. We have much to talk about. Do you play billiards? The table is upstairs . . ."

"Verily, you know nothing of your husband's business?" Marchant asked. It was his turn to play, but he stood resting his *billard*—like Kat's, of fine wood that had been polished to a brilliant sheen; unlike hers, banded with gold—on his shoulder as if it were a soldier's musket.

"Nothing, alas."

"But you were in Spain with him."

"Yea, but he left me at Burgos, with his cousin, while he went on to Madrid to visit her husband. I would liefer have seen Madrid."

"You did not like the lady Margaret?" he asked slyly, and she knew he knew of the rumors of Justin's love for his cousin.

"Upon my life, I like the ship well," she said, and he laughed, and lowered the *billard* to the billiard table, and proceeded to win another game, his third.

"I wonder," he said then, "that you have not asked him to rename that ship."

"Likely I will someday . . . if I stay with him that long."

"Kat wishes to leave her husband," Christopher explained. "She would divorce him."

"*Vraiment?*"

"*Oui*, monsieur," Kat replied. "I married too hastily."

"I see . . . Yet even if I had not been told this," Marchant said, "I would not wonder that you did not welcome the chance to spend so much time with your husband's cousin. From what I have heard of her, she would not want you as a guest, either."

"You have heard much of Doña Margaret?" she asked.

"*Chère* Katherine . . ." He smiled indulgently. "I have not only heard much of her, but also much from her. We exchange letters often. The last letter I had from her was sent in late July."

"Did she mention me?" Kat asked, hoping she did not sound as fearful as she felt.

Marchant laughed again, and leaned his weight on his *billard*. "*La grande* Margaret, mention a rival? Especially one who has stolen her cousin's heart?" He shook his head, and Kat felt relief sweep through her: these Frenchmen did not know that she had been pretending to be either Justin's servant or his ward while in Spain. The change in roles between Spain and France might be explained, but not easily.

"No," Marchant went on, "she wrote to me of this business we are about, and bade me set our plans in motion. 'Twas then that I sent for Christopher. Now all is nearly ready, and of a sudden your husband is in Paris, searching for me, asking my whereabouts of my friends in the Marais."

"And you choose to avoid him?"

"Perchance I am too cautious, but . . ." He shrugged. "Margaret said nothing of him to me in her letter. Nor—or so it seems—was he told precisely how to find me. So I can only speculate on his reasons for being here. Has Margaret sent him because she has changed her mind about our plans? 'Tis unlikely, for he would have known better how to reach me. Has Lord Harwood decided that she should have changed her mind?''

"If he even knows of your plans."

"*Chère* Kat—may I call you Kat, as Christopher does? *Merci. Chère* Kat, why else would he seek me? No, he has been told of her plans, and haply disapproved . . . but even that, I confess, is not likely. No, there is a much likelier possibility."

"Which is?"

"That he has heard of our plans, and Christopher's part in them, and that he wishes to take Christopher's place."

"We are of one mind in that opinion," Christopher said. "But he shall not take my place."

"No, he will not," Marchant agreed. "*La gloire* will be yours."

What glory? Kat wondered, but was loath to ask so directly, lest she seem overcurious and make him more suspicious of her. Instead, she went back to another matter that puzzled her.

"You say that Margaret sent you money. You seem in little need of it." She gestured around the room with her *billard*.

"*Foi de gentilhomme*, I did not need the money. I have enough for my own wants. But Fortune has been less kind to Christopher. And the Italian we must pay for his creation . . . *Par Dieu!*" He shook his head. "He asks a king's ransom."

" 'Tis fitting, is it not?" Christopher asked. "A king's ransom . . . for a queen's death."

Kat dropped her *billard*. She gaped at Christopher, scarce able to believe what she had just heard. "Elizabeth?"

"Of certain, Elizabeth," Marchant told her. He glanced at the clock on the mantel. "I am late to meet my friends at the Louvre. Christopher, will you see our guest and new *consoeur* to her bedchamber? I trow the room over the stables would be best . . ."

She wanted to flee at once, but knew there was little if any chance that she could escape from the house with Christopher beside her, watching her. Then, too, he was armed, and she was not. Would he let her go rather than risk killing her? 'Twould be foolish to wager that he would do so. For all his talk of love, she knew he valued her much less than his life, which might be forfeit if she could reach Walsingham with news of this plot. Her safest course would be to hide her feelings as well as she could while she bided her time, waiting for an opportunity to escape.

So she went with him quietly, even taking his hand as they descended the steep stairs, and not letting go when they reached the bottom. She said nothing to him, not trusting her voice yet. In truth, she felt dumb-stricken. She feared that if she opened her mouth at all now, what would come out would not be measured words but instead a wordless scream, a scream born of fear and anger at their plans to kill Elizabeth—aye, and born of anguish, too, because they assumed that Justin, if he knew of their plans, would want nothing more than to play the assassin himself. Would they were wrong about that, she thought— yet why should she doubt them, when Marchant knew so much of Justin and his cousin? She would never have believed that it could hurt so badly, after all these months of suspecting Justin of treason, to have her suspicions confirmed—and alack! by such rogues as these . . .

They walked through the gallery and another chamber after that, stopping before a door that Christopher unlocked with a key Marchant had given him.

The room was small and meanly furnished, with a single tiny window. Kat grimaced as she looked around at what was obviously a servant's bedchamber.

"If this is how you treat your friends, Christopher, then I pity your enemies!"

"You pity Queen Elizabeth?" He was smiling, but his gaze was direct and unwavering.

"Is she truly your enemy?"

"She is no friend of mine. Nor is she one of your husband's, for all her innocence of his contrivings. He is not enough a creature of hers, like those new men she has raised to power—Cecil, Walsingham—or like Leicester and Hatton, who are besotted with her. There will be no preferment for him at her court, any more than there has been for me. 'Sblood! To think of the time I wasted dancing attendance on her, in the hope that she might someday grant me a monopoly! But I cannot dance as well as Hatton, nor have I known her as long as Dudley. I may hope for nothing from her . . . nothing but more chances to squander my youth fawning over a woman who looks right through me half the time when I stand before her, more chances to squander my estate—if my father leaves it to me—on gifts for her and finery to wear at her court. I matter not one whit to her. Why should she matter more to me?

"And what of you, Kat? Gave you any thought, when you married Lisle, to what the queen might say? Though he is no creature of hers, yet she would decide when the court gallants may marry, and whom they may marry. Have you seen the queen since you married?"

Kat shook her head. "She knows naught of this. We married in secret."

"Then may God help you when Elizabeth finds out. But you would find little favor in her eyes even if you had not married. Y'are too fair. Have you ever met her?''

"Once, at Hampton Court, in June."

"And did she not seem envious of you?"

"Mayhap there was some envy there . . ."

"Some! I warrant she had words with any man who paid you too much heed, as soon as you were out of earshot."

"Even before, in faith," Kat admitted, and could not help smiling at the memory of how quickly the queen had scattered the band of admirers Tom had dubbed *shadow men*.

"There, then. You'll be happier with Mary Stuart as England's queen."

His words recalled her mercilessly to the matter at hand. "Will I? Little I have heard of Mary Stuart is good."

"Then little was the truth. You have heard slanders. She has been unjustly accused. The proof of her innocence will come when she is released. The people of England will accept her as their queen."

"Will they?"

"They must. What other heir does Elizabeth have than her cousin Mary?"

"But if 'tis believed she has gained the throne through some murderous plot—"

"There will be no proof. We have been promised a most cunning and subtle poison by an Italian, a Florentine, which will not do its work until hours after it has been swallowed, and then 'twill seem that the queen has been stricken by a fever. I will be well away from the court when she sickens. No rumors or scandals will mar my return to London after Mary Stuart is crowned Queen of England. Very few people will know what I have done, but Mary will be among them, and I trust she will reward me generously."

"And do you trust this Italian, too?"

" 'Twas he who provided the poison that killed Coligny's brother François d'Andelot last year, when 'twas said he died of a fever. The same sickness nearly killed the Admiral himself, for they drank of the same cup. Yea, I trust this Italian. This plot cannot fail."

"Aye, but will its success be your downfall?" she asked desperately.

"What do you mean?" he asked, his eyes narrowing as he looked at her.

'Twould be folly to appeal to his conscience, she realized. All his thoughts were of his advancement. Aye, that was it . . .

"No doubt Mary Stuart would reward you, for I have heard gossip that she means to reward the man who killed her half brother, the Earl of Moray. But what if your French *confrères* turn against you, once the deed is done and Elizabeth is dead? Monsieur de Saint-Amant is already sickened by war. 'Twas clear from what he said. What if he changes his mind about this plot? 'Twould be dangerous for you even if he did so afterward, and made your role in this known to others. But if he changed his mind before you could reach Elizabeth, and you were discovered with the poison on you . . . Christoper, I would not see your head stuck on a pike above London Bridge.''

"There's no danger of that. I trow that Saint-Amant dwells too much on the cruel face of this conflict, but if he wavers, Marchant will steel his resolve.''

"Marchant?'' Kat asked, laughing. "That painted jackanapes?''

"Pierre de Marchant has killed at least a dozen men in duels that Saint-Amant knows of, and he will not swear that he knows of all. And Marchant has all the reasons Saint-Amant has for this contriving, and one more: love.''

"Love?''

"For Henri, Duc d'Anjou, the king's brother, the heir, whom their mother the Florentine would have wed to Elizabeth. Anjou has said he will never wed Elizabeth. He says she is an old creature with a sore leg.''

"An old creature!'' Kat laughed again, then sobered. At thirty-seven—for her birthday had been just last week—Elizabeth might seem old to a youth of seventeen, which was Anjou's age. Old, at least, when proposed as a bride . . . "I warrant you, she has no sore leg, for when I saw her at Hampton Court, she danced most nimbly.''

"Marry, you would do well to say nothing to Marchant of that. He goes into a frenzy whenever anyone so much as hints that the duke may yet bow to his mother's will and marry Elizabeth. Pierre would kill Elizabeth with his own hands, if he could get to her, to keep her from wedding his lover.''

Kat was dumb-stricken for a few moments. "His lover, you say? I thought that when you said he loved the duke—''

"That he loved him as his liege lord? No. Marchant believes that Henri will be king someday, for his brother Charles is sickly. And he would fain be the king's *mignon*.''

Kat shook her head, but could not banish from her mind the image of Marchant's painted face.

"Anjou . . . He . . .'' She hesitated. *"Le duc est un bougre?''* The thought was too unsettling for plain English.

"He loves women as well.''

"I had heard that he and his sister . . .''

" 'Tis true.''

She shook her head again, amazed that anyone could have contemplated the marriage of such a man to Queen Elizabeth.

"Seek you to dissuade me from this course, Kat?" Christopher said suddenly, reminding her that he and his friends contemplated not the queen's marriage but her death. "Why do you plant these doubts in my mind? Would you have your husband act in my stead? I warrant you, that is why he is here. He would like to see England returned to the Catholic fold, but so would many others, and he has done naught for that cause—unless you count the encouragement he has given his cousin in her plotting. And now that it is at last time to act, and success is sure to be ours, he would step in and be the agent of this victory. But I will not let him."

"Nor would I wish him to replace you in this," Kat said vehemently. Even knowing that Justin was a traitor in spirit, she would not have him become one—aye, and a murderer as well—in deed. "I mean that with all my heart, Christopher. I swear it."

He looked doubtful.

"I swear it," she said again, and the doubt seemed to lift from his face, to be replaced by puzzlement.

"Then would you dissuade me so that Elizabeth may live? 'Twould be to no purpose, Kat. She is dead already, to all intents and purposes, for so many would have her dead that 'tis certain she will not live to be forty. Needs must that she die soon by someone's hand. Why not mine?"

How easily he dismissed the guards and the tasters—aye, and the intelligencers—surrounding Elizabeth, protecting her from harm. And yet, she thought fearfully, did he not know the forces ranged against the queen better than she did? If a poisoner could get to Coligny and his brother, then—despite all the confidence in Walsingham that Nick said the queen had expressed—there could be no security for Elizabeth either.

"I fear for you, Christopher," she said.

"Sweet Kat." He put his arms around her, holding her close. She was loath to have him touch her, but dared not draw away, even when he kissed her, but when he sought to unfasten her doublet, she broke free of his embrace.

"Nay, Christopher. I am yet a married woman, and would be an honest one."

"You would be faithful to a man you'll soon divorce?"

"Even to him, lest my conscience trouble me sorely. Would you have me otherwise? If I cuckolded him now, would you trust me not to cuckold you later?'

"Then you will marry me? I warrant you, Kat, I can make you love me, if you will give me time."

"Yea, I'll marry you. I swear it," she said, then added, so she would not be completely forsworn, "on my honor as a married woman."

" 'Sdeath! To be both denied and promised your sweet love upon the same honor! You try me, Kat! But I will wait. We'll talk more of this at breakfast."

Kat nodded. "I am very tired, in truth."

"Then I wish you pleasant dreams," he said, and Kat wondered what sort of monster he was, to talk of regicide and then of pleasant dreams. "Good night, sweetheart." And he took her hand and kissed it, then went out, closing the door behind him. A few seconds later she heard the key turn in the lock.

"Christopher!" She tried to open the door, then hit it with her fist. "What's this, sirrah? Why d'you lock me in?"

"Sweet Kat," he called to her, laughing, "I would protect you. I fear you may wish to go out and come to harm in the streets."

"You would protect me? Then why is there no bolt *inside* this door? What if I would protect myself?"

"From Marchant?" he asked, and laughed again. "There's more danger there for me than for you, sweeting. And as for Saint-Amant, he's a very monk in his habits. Nay, Kat, you may rest undisturbed. Sweet dreams."

She heard him walk off then. Going to the window, she watched him pass by each of the gallery's windows. Belike he went upstairs, for she could not see him after that.

The window latch was rusted shut. 'Twould not open no matter how fiercely she tugged at it. Not that there was any hope of escaping through the window anyway, for it was too small, but perchance, had she been able to open it, she could have called quietly to someone for help . . . though that, she supposed, was a slim hope indeed. The only people likely to enter this courtyard were the servants of the household.

She quit trying to open the window only when her fingers were bruised and blistering. Then she went to lie down on the bed. 'Twas far from comfortable, for beneath the worn featherbed, which was scarce a finger thick, the mattress was lumpy, stuffed with straw. She thought idly that it would be much better if the mattress were stuffed with feathers, and Christopher and his *confrères* stuffed with straw. They would be mere men of straw then, and she would not need to fear this plot of theirs. She could sleep easily then. As it was, she feared it would be hours before she slept, and she was right.

In a bedchamber at the Louvre, Isobel de Maisse stretched languidly and smiled up at Don Rodrigo Soria de Helicia, a secretary of Francés de Alava, Spain's ambassador to France.

"Isobel, I have missed you," Rodrigo murmured, kissing the bruises on her shoulders, bruises left there by the beating Catherine de Medici had given her yesterday.

The bruises were bad enough, but the blows to Isobel's pride had been worse. She had been tricked! Someone had been clever enough to trick her into leaving Monteronne and abandoning the mission the Florentine had sent her on. If only she knew who had tricked her . . . She could not even be certain that the stranger claiming to be an emissary from the queen mother was a servant or a friend of the Charrons, for it was possible that one of her rivals here at court had plotted to discredit her.

Unfortunately for her, the Medici woman was less interested in the fact that someone had dared to trick one of her maids of honor—and less interested, too, in the news that an English baron who had just come from Spain was visiting Monteronne—than she was in berating Isobel for letting herself be fooled by the masquerade. She had raged at Isobel for almost half an hour, punctuating her argument with blows from time to time. She could not believe that Isobel could be tricked so easily, Catherine said. Isobel could have told the queen mother that some of the fault was her own, for having no special watchword to identify her emissaries: Catherine had more than once summoned Isobel by sending messengers unknown to her, messengers who could have proven no more trustworthy than the one who had sent her to Bayonne. But it was wisest not to point out Catherine's own failings to her.

Instead, Isobel, once she was no longer too sore to leave her chambers, had sought comfort in the arms of Don Rodrigo, who loved her so much that he had asked her to marry him. She had so far declined, in part because she would spare herself the certain shame of having the Spanish king refuse to give his consent to the match, but also because she had no wish to live the life of a Spanish lady. Better to be immured in a convent, like poor Mademoiselle de Limeuil. At least she had been set free . . .

Yet although Isobel would never wish to marry Don Rodrigo, she found solace in his company. It was pleasant to listen to him denounce the queen mother for beating her, for all that she knew he would never dare say such things in public.

"Where have you been these past weeks?" he asked now. "No one knew."

"I went to Bayonne," she told him, unwilling to have him know she had been staying with the Charrons. She had told him nothing of Catherine's reasons for beating her, other than that she had displeased the queen mother, and she would not be queried more closely now. "I have friends there, whom I had not been able to visit these past two years, while there was fighting. I wanted to see them again."

"Before the war resumes?"

"*If* the war resumes," she replied, not wanting to discuss with him what she thought the chances were of this peace lasting. At times she suspected him of not being so much in love with her that he would forgo all opportunities to learn state secrets from her, so that he might pass them along to de Alava.

"Bayonne . . ." He looked thoughtful. "Did you hear anything about an Englishman there, a nobleman, by the name of Justin Lisle?"

"Lisle?" She drew her brows together, frowning. "The name is unfamiliar. He was in Bayonne?"

"So we have heard from Madrid. The Council of Castile wants him returned to Spain, for he has killed a priest, a priest of the Inquisition. They sent one messenger to Bayonne, and another to Paris, in case he is somewhere else in France."

There was nothing surprising about learning that Spain had at least one intelligencer in Bayonne—Isobel had always assumed as much—but Catherine de Medici would be pleased to learn that a messenger had been sent to that intelligencer recently. Perhaps, if the identity of Spain's agent was not known, it could be learned by checking to see if the messenger's activities had been noticed. She was glad that she had decided to spend the night with Rodrigo.

"Has your ambassador spoken of this to the queen mother or the king yet?" she asked.

"No," he said, and she was even more glad, and gladder still that de Alava was sometimes too cautious in his diplomacy.

Many at court knew that Lord Harwood was in Paris and searching for Monsieur de Marchant. *Dieu*, there had been enough ribald jests made about his inquiries into Marchant's whereabouts! But de Alava, it seemed, had not heard, nor had Don Rodrigo. Few at the French court would entrust the Spaniards with more information than they requested. And it might be days, Isobel supposed, before de Alava decided how best to broach the subject of Lord Harwood to the queen mother. Certainly a blunt demand from him that the English baron be captured and deported to Spain would not be welcome now, with the pro-Spanish faction at the court in disgrace, and with the special ambassador from England still here. Walsingham had been received courteously by King Charles and his mother, to the great vexation of Spain's ambassador, who had told Rodrigo that the English envoy had been haughty and uncourtly in his first meeting with the rulers of France.

"Maybe he should say nothing until Monsieur Walsingham is gone," she suggested. With luck, Rodrigo would think she was helping him more than herself by counseling postponement.

"I know you are right . . . and yet Don Francés frets at any delay. The council wants him to do all he can to see that Lord Harwood is returned to Spain."

"Because this Englishman—Lord Harwood—killed a priest?"

"Because of that, and for other reasons."

"But you do not know those other reasons."

"Isobel! You imply that Don Francés does not trust me! In fact, he read the entire letter to me. Lord Harwood not only killed a priest while he was in Spain, but earlier, while he was in England, he betrayed Spain's friends there. He was believed to be himself a friend of Spain, but he has proved to be a most treacherous friend . . ."

He went on to tell her all that was in the letter. Isobel listened avidly, while pretending no greater interest than was necessary to keep him talking, and then when he would tell her no more of Lord Harwood, she changed the subject to the latest court gossip about the Duke of Guise's new marriage. Yet all the while she chattered of other matters, her thoughts were on what Rodrigo had told her. Pierre de Marchant would be very interested in this news . . .

She looked past Rodrigo, to the clock on the table by the bed. It was a few minutes past three. Soon she would be able to take her leave of him. She always left early, so she would be back in her own rooms before dawn. Perhaps he would not be suspicious if she left by four this morning. And at that hour, there was still some chance that Marchant would be here at the Louvre. He would not welcome any intrusion, but he would surely forgive her, once he heard what she had learned.

CHAPTER 45

At dawn, Tandy followed his lord along the Rue St. Honoré toward the
Cemetery of the Innocents.

They walked through a heavy, silver-gray mist that shrouded everything more than a few paces away with a tricksy, constantly shifting
veil. Tandy had to shake his head now and then to reassure himself
that he was not still sleeping, for his own thoughts were as hazy and
unreliable as the forms around him.

He had had but a few hours' sleep. It had been well past midnight
when he and Justin stumbled back to L'Oison Noir. Since early evening
they had been combing the Latin Quarter, for Kat's obvious liking for
the Left Bank had made it seem the most likely place to find her. They
had questioned street vendors and shopkeepers, tavern hosts, clerics,
beggars, lawyers, and students. Justin had mentioned once that Kat might
have sought shelter with someone she already knew in Paris, and Tandy
had agreed 'twas possible, but neither of them had spoken of that possibility again. Both knew that in such a case their search would almost
certainly be hopeless.

That there was scant hope at best, was a thought Tandy constantly
pushed aside.

He had lost count of the taverns they had visited, often following
student guides from one poorly marked door to another through streets
cloaked in darkness. It seemed that they had been to dozens, but he
doubted they could have checked each tavern on the Left Bank even if
they had searched all night. And Justin had seemed determined to do
just that, even though his voice had been worn down to a hoarse whisper by his incessant questioning of everyone they met. Then a rogue
they had met in an alley had made a clumsy grab for Justin's purse while
the nobleman was carefully describing Kat. Tandy had seen the thief's
move and blocked it, but the ruffian had gotten away and the incident
had convinced Justin to end their search for the night: he had no wish
to advertise Kat's description to half of the city's rogues, lest they seek
her themselves to capture her and hold her for ransom. There would be

fewer rogues about by day, and they would be easier to recognize in sunlight than in torchlight.

They had made their way back to L'Oison Noir, where Tandy had lain awake for more than an hour, his tired brain fashioning such perils for Kat that he thought he would never sleep. When at last he drifted off, he could still hear Justin moving about restlessly in the other chamber.

He still did not know whether Justin had slept at all. When he had awakened, scarcely a quarter of an hour ago, it had been to see the nobleman making his way quietly toward the door to the hall. It had suddenly occurred to Justin that Kat might have run to the churchyard of the Innocents, hoping her obvious dislike of visiting the place a few days ago would ensure that no one would look for her there.

The idea had seemed half mad to Tandy, and Justin had admitted that it might be, but he was determined to turn every straw. He had told Tandy that he could stay at the inn rather than accompanying him on what might be a wild goose chase, but Tandy would not hear of being left behind, and after dressing hurriedly he had followed Justin out into the dark, dismal morning.

Now he was suffering for his decision. His feet had been sadly abused by his trekking about Paris in thin-soled slippers yesterday, and this morning it seemed that each stone on the street picked out a different sore spot. He was glad to stop when Justin paused outside the entrance to the churchyard . . . until he saw what was leaving it.

The skin at the back of his neck crawled as he watched the night-time denizens of the cemetery leave its shelter for the streets of Paris.

A stooped old woman in motley rags shuffled toward Tandy without seeming to notice him until she was just a few feet away. Then she whipped a few stalks of some dried weed from beneath her tattered cloak and shook them in Tandy's face, cackling with glee as he swore and stepped back. She danced away, her swollen, rag-bound feet rising and falling in a heavy, clumsy jig, still cackling as she vanished into the mist. Mad as a March hare . . .

There was no hint of madness about the next vagabond to pass Tandy. The man looked haughty as any noble as he stalked past, his hand resting on his sword pommel. He turned a challenging, one-eyed gaze on the Englishman. A patch of black velvet covered his right eye, concealing the ruin attested to by the puckered, livid scar cutting his brow and cheek above and below the cloth. His doublet and breeches were of good silk, but worn and mended. If not once a gentleman, then a former soldier, Tandy guessed. Peradventure fallen on hard times through an unsanctioned duel that had also cost him his eye. Howbeit, the man had not lost his pride.

The same could not be said for the pack of beggars and thieves that followed him at a safe distance. Most were filthy, reeking ruffians, who looked as though they might have spent the night rolling in the foul earth of the graveyard. Pocked and scarred and maimed, their teeth rotted or missing, these outcasts evoked more horror and pity from Tandy than did the heaps of bones in the charnel houses. A few of them edged toward Tandy, their hands outstretched for alms, and he wished he could have helped them. But if he opened his purse for these few, their companions would also want alms, and he and Justin had not enough coins with them to satisfy all the beggars that might still be sheltering here. He shook his head warningly and reached for his sword instead of his purse, and they retreated readily enough.

Finally the last beggar had gone past. Still Justin hesitated, seeming reluctant to enter the cemetery. "I hope—I pray—that she did not spend the night here, but perchance someone saw her here yesterday."

Who? Tandy wondered as he followed Justin into the churchyard. The vagabonds were gone—and he doubted he could have gotten any honest answers from that lot. He doubted, too, that any vendors would have arrived yet. But mayhap they would meet some servant of the church, or maybe a grave digger . . .

The arcade was perfectly still as they walked down it, columns emerging from the mist ahead of them as their identical counterparts vanished behind. He glanced over at the shifting blur toward the center of the graveyard, where a breeze was making an effort to shred the mist. Suddenly a bony, upraised fist appeared. Tandy swung around to face it, his hand moving to his sword.

" 'Tis Death," Justin murmured.

It took Tandy a few moments to realize Justin was merely naming the statue, and not their fate. In those moments the breeze had snatched more of the shrouding mist away, revealing the bare stone ribs. Tandy let out his breath in an exasperated sigh.

They had gone barely another ten yards when Tandy tripped and stumbled, nearly colliding with Justin. Swearing violently, he looked back to see what had tripped him. The string of oaths caught in his throat when he saw the slipper-clad foot.

The foot protruded from a scholar's gown, which was stained dark red across the breast.

He stepped closer to the body, then nudged its foot with the toe of his boot.

The man groaned.

Tandy jumped back, and Justin laughed. Stepping around Tandy, he leaned down to pick up something the mist had concealed from Tandy's eyes: an empty flagon.

"No wound here, Tandy. He was felled by drink. Or so 'twould seem." He knelt by the scholar to look more closely at the stain, plucking the now-dry cloth away from the man's chest. "Nay, no wound. 'Tis fortunate for him that none of those rogues stumbled across him last night."

They continued along the arcade, turned a corner and proceeded down another straight, covered walk. They had gone but a few paces when they heard hammering, somewhere ahead of them in the mist.

The sounds led them to a stall where a vendor was setting up early and making repairs. The lower of two wide shelves was crowded with small, roughly carved wooden statues—some meant to be saints, others animals or mythical beasts—that jumped in unison, scattered nails rolling among them, with each blow of the vendor's hammer.

Tandy thought their approach too silent to be noticed over the noise of his work, but the vendor turned to face them when they were still several paces away. A burly, cheery-faced man, he stood watching them with such a careless air that Tandy thought the man must needs be a fool, to seem unconcerned about who might approach him while he was alone in this place. Then Tandy noticed that the vendor was still holding the hammer, and that changed his mind: even a swordsman would do well to think again before threatening this fellow.

"*Bonjour,*" the man said cautiously, his gaze flicking from Justin to Tandy and back.

"*Bonjour,*" Justin replied, continuing to approach. He halted as the vendor tightened his grip on the hammer and shifted his weight slightly. His movements slow and easy, Justin took out the locket, opening it as he held it out toward the Frenchman. "*Nous cherchons deux personnes. Il se peut qu'ils soient passés par ici hier. Ma nièce*"—he placed the locket in the vendor's outstretched hand—"*et son frère, mon neveu, qui se ressemblent . . .*"

My niece, and her brother, my nephew, who resemble each other . . . It was the familiar speech, too familiar to keep Tandy wide awake, and he scarce listened to what was said until a sudden exclamation woke him from his drowsing.

The vendor was asking Justin to again describe his nephew's clothing. As Justin described the garments Kat had been wearing yesterday, the vendor began to nod excitedly. Yes, he had seen the youth yesterday afternoon. The boy had seemed to be idling away an hour or two while he waited for his English friend.

"*Son ami anglais?*" Justin asked.

The vendor described the Englishman. He was sure that the man had been well-known to the boy, and they had both spoken that bar-

barous language as well as any Englishmen the vendor had ever heard. Was the nephew then not French?

Justin explained that his late brother-in-law had been English, but his sister had returned to France and was raising her children here.

The vendor nodded his approval. He regretted he did not know more of English so he could tell more of their conversation, but he had recognized a few words. *"Ils ont parlé du supper, monsieur,"* he said, and added that they had mentioned the Left Bank, then explained solemnly that that meant the Rive Gauche.

"Ont-ils parlé d'un certain cabaret ou auberge?"

The vendor shook his head. *"Non, monsieur, ils ne l'ont pas mentionné, je le regrette."*

Tandy sighed heavily. Without the name of a tavern or inn, they had the entire Left Bank to comb again.

Justin appeared less disappointed. He thanked the man courteously, smiling as he handed him several écus, then led the way toward the street again, walking so fast that Tandy did not catch up with him until they were out of the churchyard.

"You may as well return to the inn, Tandy. You have had little sleep, and you searched longer than I did yesterday. Y'are footsore enough without retracing yesterday's steps."

Tandy shook his head slowly. "No, my lord. I'll not be sent away. 'Tis more likely that we'll find her, now that we have a description of her companion."

He had meant to cheer Justin, but instead of smiling the nobleman grimaced. "Her English friend?" he said savagely.

Tandy's mouth opened, then closed again. In faith, he must have been half asleep while he was listening to the vendor. Else he would have given more heed to what had been said about Kat's meeting with an Englishman she seemed to know well. He felt disillusioned as he wondered if Kat had been meeting with a confederate, a friend of hers who was no friend of theirs.

Justin looked more angry than disillusioned. As like as not, he was wondering if *l'ami anglais* was Kat's lover as well.

Then Tandy shook his head. 'Twas foolish to heed such doubts, when he knew for a certainty that Kat had not planned her flight from the inn. She had made up her mind to leave during those few minutes alone, when she had found the locket. Whoever the English friend was, he could not have been someone she had planned to meet.

He would have said as much to Justin, but the baron was already half a dozen steps away, hurrying toward the Left Bank.

The last tavern they had visited the night before had been on the Rue St. Jacques, and Justin had decided to start there today. They crossed the Seine on the Pont Notre Dame. On the way across the Ile de la Cité, Justin questioned a tinker and a carpenter, two students, and a finely dressed little page who was scurrying about some early errand and had scant patience with their queries. On the Petit Pont a gentleman who at first seemed offended by their hailing him later decided, after seeing Kat's portrait, that he wished to accompany them to find *la belle demoiselle*, and they wasted several minutes persuading him that his assistance was not needed. By the time the man finally desisted and continued across the bridge to the Ile de la Cité, Justin's face was flushed with anger, and Tandy was again hard put to keep up with his master as he strode swiftly from the bridge to the Left Bank and down the Rue St. Jacques.

A maidservant was desultorily sweeping the paving in front of the door of a house across the street from the priory of St. Julien le Pauvre, now and then stopping to peer southward down the mist-cloaked street. She started when she heard their swift approach, whirling about with an anxious look on her face that vanished when she saw that they were young, and dressed as gentlemen.

"*Bonjour, messieurs,*" she greeted them, smiling at Justin, then, when he seemed impervious to her charms, bestowing an even warmer look on Tandy. She continued to glance at him coyly from beneath her lashes while she listened to Justin and looked at the picture of Kat. No, she had not seen either his niece or his nephew.

Her wanton manner vanished as Justin described Kat's English companion. She had seen the man, *un beau monsieur*, several times during the past few weeks, here and there in the *quartier*. But since she had seen him on a different street each time, she could give them no clue as to where he might be lodging. And she had not seen him at all for two days now.

Tandy felt torn between gratitude and annoyance. Again they had learned something, but 'twas again too little!

Justin thanked the girl most graciously, however, and was reaching for his purse to get a coin for her when she turned away from them to gaze down the street. Tandy, following her gaze, could see nothing but mist, but he could hear the sounds of feet and wheels on the cobblestones. Then he saw a wheelbarrow full of flowers, and behind it, a shadowy figure.

"*Attendez, messieurs!*" the girl cried. "*Voici quelqu'un qui peut vous en dire davantage.*"

Justin groaned as the plump figure of the flower vendor they had seen two days ago on the Place Maubert emerged from the mist.

"Marie!" the maidservant called, gesturing excitedly. *"Dépêche-toi!"*

The woman took one or two quicker steps, then, catching sight of Tandy and Justin, slowed down again. Her expression hardened as she approached them and settled her wheelbarrow next to the wall. Rubbing her palms where the handles had left deep red marks, she came the final few steps toward the door.

"Le pain?" she asked the maidservant, ignoring the two Englishmen.

The girl looked puzzled, but turned away to pick up a cloth-wrapped bundle lying in a corner of the doorway. The vendor drew the cloth back to sniff the loaf of bread. *"Bien."* She gestured at the wheelbarrow. *"Pavots ou roses? Ou soucis?"*

"Roses. Mais, Marie—"

The vendor held up a hand to silence her while she returned to the wheelbarrow and gathered a nosegay of roses, which she gave to the girl.

"Marie, ces messieurs—"

"Tu perds ton temps chez eux, ma petite."

The maid looked even more puzzled. 'Twas clear that she could not understand why her friend thought speaking to the gentlemen was a waste of time.

The vendor glanced contemptuously at the Englishmen, then back at the maidservant. *"Ce sont . . . du moins celui-ci et—"*

"Nous cherchons ma nièce et mon neveu," Justin interrupted.

And not just his niece and nephew, the maid explained, but also the handsome English fellow they had seen before. Had Marie seen him recently?

The vendor looked back and forth between the girl and the men again, plainly reluctant to help, just as plainly reluctant to refuse to answer the girl.

"Oui," she said finally. *"Hier après-midi, à la Place Maubert. Avec ton mignon,"* she added, gazing coldly at Justin. She told them of the house she had seen the two enter.

"Merci," Justin said, placing coins in both women's hands.

As the Englishmen ran to the nearby Rue Galarde and east along it toward the Place Maubert, Marie shouted after the bugger, telling him that he should have bought more flowers for his *mignon,* and then perhaps the boy would not seek another. She heard him swear in response, but he did not stop or threaten to come back, and she chuckled.

The maid asked Marie if she had not seen the girl, too.

"The girl?"

His niece, the maid explained patiently. The one who looked so much like the boy, with the same coloring, the same height—She broke off then, staring down at a locket in her hand. It was the Englishman's, she told Marie; he had forgotten to take it back.

"Here," she said. "Look." Opening the locket, she held the picture in front of Marie's face. "They said her brother looks like her. By God, he must be a beautiful young gentleman."

Marie frowned, remembering the boy she had seen two days earlier, how beautiful he would have been if his face had not been so dirty. And his hands had been delicate, too, slim and elegant, seeming barely strong enough to hold a horse's reins, let alone the weapons that a youth of that age would have spent years learning to use . . .

"My God!" Marie closed her eyes for a moment, then opened them to gaze again at the picture of the girl she had seen two days ago but not recognized as a gentlewoman. She took the locket from the maid's hand. "I will return this to the gentleman," she said. And she would apologize as well, for the mistake she had made and the insult she had offered him. By her faith, if the girl had come to harm . . . !

She ran after the Englishmen, calling over her shoulder for the maid to watch her wheelbarrow.

For some moments after the vendor had vanished down the Rue Galarde, the maid stood gazing after her, her mouth slightly open in surprise. Then, after looking around to make certain no one was watching, she seized the handles of the wheelbarrow and began to trundle it as fast as possible toward the Place Maubert.

CHAPTER 46

"This is not very like our last breakfast together, is it, Kat?" Christopher Danvers asked.

Kat shook her head. "Truly, it is not." She looked around the tiny chamber. 'Twas out of all cry that it looked nothing like her bedchamber at Beechwood, whose comfort she would appreciate much more when she returned to it—if ever she returned. And their breakfast, too, was a mean one, of bread and butter and ale . . . though Kat had chosen to drink only water, fearing that the ale might conceal some drug.

"At least I am not sick," she said, smiling at Christopher. "I have never drunk wine at breakfast since that day, nor never will again."

"Not even watered wine?"

"Not even that."

"Then I will see to it that you have only the finest ale for our breakfasts—or the purest water, if you would have that instead."

"Y'are kind."

"I would fain always be kind to you."

'Sdeath! She would sicken yet from this court holy water. But needs must that she give him no cause to suspect her, for she would have him give her freedom to roam the house at will today. She would never be able to escape if she were kept in this room.

"What will your brother say if you divorce Justin?" Christopher asked.

"I'faith, Nick would not have me anywhere near the man," she said honestly.

Christopher raised an eyebrow. "You married against Nick's wishes?"

Lord, why had she not thought of that before she spoke? 'Twould be odd indeed for her to give no consideration to Nick's opinion of any man she planned to marry.

"I was besotted, and heeded no one."

"You were too innocent, Kat."

"Yea, but no longer," she said, and saw his expression change, and realized those words had been more foolish than the others.

He had been standing by the door while he finished his ale. Now he came over to the bed and sat down beside her and took her hand.

"Would that I could have been your first husband," he murmured, and leaned toward her to kiss her, but she averted her face.

Her movement had been instinctive, and he seemed to sense that, for his face darkened with anger. "What's this, sweetheart? Do I please you less than Lord Harwood?"

She jumped up and took a few steps away. His sword belt was lying on the table beside the bed. He had taken it off when he sat down for a few minutes to eat, for she had teased him about coming armed to breakfast. She was as close to the sword now as he, but it was sheathed, and she knew that even if she could reach it before he did, she would have no time to draw it.

"You please me too much, Christopher, and I would not be dishonored while I am still Justin's wife."

"Marry, who's to know?" he asked, getting up and coming toward her. "Would it behoove me to tell anyone that my wife had once been less than honest? Nay, 'twould not. You may trust me, sweetheart, and with trust, you may love me . . ."

"*Christopher!*"

He started, hearing his name shouted from the other side of the house. Kat almost slumped to the floor, so great was her relief.

"Is that Marchant?" she asked. "Or Saint-Amant?"

"It matters not which it is. Am I their lackey, to be summoned in such a manner?" He reached for Kat, then stopped as his name was bellowed again. Whoever was shouting was closer now, likely in the gallery. "By God's blood! I'll not accept this!"

He went to the door and flung it open and started out, but got only halfway across the room before Saint-Amant and Marchant entered from the gallery. A woman Kat had never expected to see again was with them. Kat had followed Christopher as far as the door of the bedchamber, but the instant she saw the woman she darted back inside, to the bedside table. She drew the sword and dagger and dropped the sword belt behind the bed, then turned toward the door, the sword held behind her. The dagger was hidden behind her, too, lying near at hand on the edge of the table.

She had scarce turned around when Christopher came back into the room, the others following him. She watched him carefully, fearing he would realize what she had done, but he seemed to have forgotten his sword belt entirely as Marchant berated him in French, calling him witless. Kat could not argue with the judgment, but she wondered at its cause.

Assured that Christopher was no immediate threat, she turned her gaze to the Frenchwoman, who was staring at her in disbelief and growing anger.

"You!" the woman said.

"*Bonjour*, Mademoiselle de Maisse," Kat said civilly.

The demoiselle noticed Kat's old cap on the bedpost, seized it, and threw it onto the floor. "It was *you!*" She lunged toward Kat, but was held back by Marchant.

"No, mademoiselle. I know not what quarrel this is between you, but we need Madame Lisle. Remember that."

Isobel struggled to regain control of herself, but at last was able to manage a smile. "Very well. I shall repay Madame Lisle later."

"For what?" Christopher demanded.

"For great tricking," Saint-Amant told him.

"Even more than you know," Isobel said furiously, then, when Marchant turned a curious gaze on her, added, "but some of it is a private matter."

Marchant shrugged. "Such will wait. For now, what concerns us are matters of state and religion."

Christopher looked confused. "What has Kat to do with this?"

"Tell him," Marchant said to Isobel.

"Last night I heard news of Lord Harwood from a servant of the Spanish ambassador. Much of it concerned a Spaniard named Muñoz, a secretary of Guerau de Spes, Spain's ambassador to England. Muñoz was contriving with Lord Harwood to bring an end to Elizabeth's reign."

Though that was of certain no news to Kat, she still felt as though she had been struck, to have Justin's treason thus confirmed.

"Alas, Lord Harwood betrayed him. All those with whom they contrived, or whom he spoke of to Lisle, were betrayed to intelligencers, servants of Walsingham's."

Kat's head whirled, and she nearly dropped the sword. And then a fierce joy thrilled through her veins. Justin was no traitor to England! She had never been so happy to be proven wrong.

"This cannot be," Christopher said, shaking his head. "He loves his cousin the condesa, and she—"

"Be that as it may," the demoiselle interrupted, "Lord Harwood is no friend of the Catholic cause. He proved it beyond argument when he was in Spain, for he killed a priest, a vicar of the Inquisition."

"Nay, 'twas an accident!" Kat cried, and they all stared at her. " 'Twas an accident," she said more softly. "He lost his balance and fell downstairs."

Christopher sighed. "You were with Lisle then."

"*Par Dieu*, she has been with him in every step of this," Isobel said harshly.

Christopher shook his head sadly as he looked at Kat. "Then what, pray tell, shall we do with her?"

"Bait a hook," Marchant said with a laugh. "A hook with which to catch Lord Harwood. Perhaps he would come if I summoned him—"

"How could he stay away?" Isobel asked, smiling.

"—but 'tis certain he will come if his wife sends for him."

"And then what will you do with him?" Kat asked.

"Why, return him to Spain, *chère* Kat," Marchant said in a kindly tone. "What else? I would have the good will of Spain as well as France."

"'Twould do much to prefer you in England," Christopher said, "once Mary is queen."

"England." Marchant waved his hands slightingly. "Why would I want to live among barbarians?"

"We are not—" Christopher began, but Marchant interrupted him.

"Enough!" He looked back at Kat. "And we will send Madame Lisle with him. The Holy Office might want to put her to the question, too."

"Christopher?" Kat gazed at him pleadingly.

He shook his head.

"And you said you would fain always be kind to me," she said, and laughed, and brought the sword out from behind her back.

"Nay, do not draw," she told Marchant. Saint-Amant was still in his nightgown, and no threat, being unarmed. "Over there." She gestured with the sword for them to move to the far side of the room. When they had done so, she began to edge toward the door, not taking her eyes from them.

"Your own sword, Christopher?" Saint-Amant asked. "You fool!"

The Englishman cuffed him, only to be cuffed himself, in the face, by Marchant, one of whose rings left a bleeding cut beside Christopher's mouth.

"The key," she told Christopher. He looked stunned, and for an instant she wondered if she would have to repeat the command, but then he threw the key toward her. It fell to the floor at her feet.

She stooped quickly and grabbed the key with her left hand, catching it between thumb and dagger. As she straightened she saw Marchant bend over and draw a knife from the top of his boot. She ducked to one side as he threw it, and the knife stuck in the wall behind her. She pulled it free, never taking her eyes from Marchant, and shook her head in warning when his hand moved toward his sword's hilt.

"No, monsieur. I trow I can throw a knife better than you. You would do well to stick to billiards."

And she stepped back through the doorway and slammed the door shut, then inserted the key in the lock and turned it a second before the doorknob was rattled furiously. Someone pounded on the thick wood of the door. She prayed that it was Christopher—'twould only be just.

She withdrew the key and backed away, gasping, so light-headed that she stumbled a little as she turned around, still holding the sword point raised slightly, still in the low ward that she felt safest using. No one was in sight. She tucked the key into her doublet and sprinted from the room, just as a chorus of voices came from behind her, calling for help.

She was running so fast by the time she reached the end of the gallery that she skidded on the rushes as she turned toward the entry and nearly slid into the manservant, who retreated from her sword with a cry of fear. She hesitated only a moment, then sped on, to the stairs and down into the narrow entryway, where she came to a shuddering halt at the sight of a young page who stepped back when he saw her, drawing a lavishly trimmed but serviceable walking sword.

'Twould be quickest to order him aside, but he might refuse to obey, and she feared—much more than she feared for her own safety—that she would injure him. She would not have a child's blood on her hands. So she told him breathlessly that the demoiselle had been hurt, had fallen down the stairs, and that she had been sent to summon a physician.

He looked uncertain, and Kat wished she could have thought of a better story, one that would have explained why she, a woman wearing men's clothing and carrying a sword and two daggers, had been sent for the doctor. Perchance she was armed because the gentleman doubted the doctor would wish to come at this early hour? 'Twas lunacy, and she felt laughter welling up in her, and knew that would be impossible to explain.

"*Dépêchez-vous!*" She gestured toward the stairs—with her sword hand, alas, realizing an instant too late that if the page attacked her now, she would have to defend herself while in the broad ward.

But he still hesitated. She was wondering if she would indeed have to run him through when she heard Isobel calling for help, her voice barely audible. Kat thanked God for the thickness of the bedchamber's door and the rusted latch on the window.

The page reacted then, brushing past Kat to run up the stairs.

She fled down the passageway and out into a shrouding mist. She paused for a moment as she desperately tried to remember where the house was located on the Place, then ran west, toward streets that were invisible to her now, streets that would lead her to the Petit Pont.

She drew stares from the people she passed, but none of those amazed by the sight of a strangely-garbed woman carrying drawn weapons seemed

to think it prudent to try and stop her. Reaching the far side of the
Place, she saw a street opening off it, a wide street that must needs be
the Rue Galarde. She raced down it, then paused at the first intersection, but that street looked unfamiliar. She ran on.

She could hear someone running after her now. Glancing back, she
could not see him, so belike he could not see her, but he needed sight
less than she did, for he could merely follow the sound of her flight.

She paused again, though panic bade her run on without stopping,
and peered at the buildings at another intersection. Was this the right
way?

And then she heard someone running toward her from the west.

Nay, it could not be. Her enemies could not have traveled so swiftly
to have gotten around her. Yet she held her ground, standing in the
low ward, and would have aimed a *stoccata* at the man running toward
her if he had not called her name.

"Kat!" Justin halted and drew his own sword.

Alack, he did not trust her. But why should he? And she dared not
lower her own sword, for the man who pursued her was very close now.

She moved sideways toward Justin in an awkward dance, looking
from him to the mists behind her, then back again as Tandy came
running up to stand beside his master.

"Justin, we must flee," she said quickly. "They know what you
are—Marchant knows what you are. They know y'are no friend of the
papists. Muñoz has discovered all, and they would have you sent back
to Spain."

"Marchant? You were with Marchant? But your English friend—"

"Danvers? How did you know of him? I knew not that he was in
Paris until I met him yesterday. He was once my suitor. But Danvers is
Marchant's creature. They contrive to poison the queen. Pray believe
me! We must flee this place, and escape back to England!"

He shook his head, a look of disbelief on his face.

"You must believe me! I serve Walsingham in this, for he sent my
brother to spy on you, and I learned of his mission and went with him!"

"Walsingham? Why—"

"*Why* can be explained later. Now we must flee, lest—"

And then it was too late. Marchant came into sight, stopping only
a few paces from them. His hair had fallen across his face. Now he
brushed it back with his dagger hand.

"Lord Harwood?" He spoke as politely as if he had been at court.

Justin nodded. "Monsieur de Marchant?"

"You have found me at last," Marchant said, "and I did not even
need to use this Amazon who is your wife as bait." He laughed. "Now,
my lord, if you will return to my house with me . . ."

"I think not."

"*Vraiment?* But you must!"

"Will you compel me?" Justin asked. "With your one sword against our two?"

"Three," Kat corrected, turning to face Marchant, and holding herself ready in the low ward.

Marchant smiled at her and shook his head. "Two, *chère* Kat. Two, against five."

And Christopher came running out of the mist to stop beside him, followed a moment later by Saint-Amant, who had buckled his sword belt over his nightgown. They were followed by the page and the manservant Kat had nearly knocked down as she fled the house on the Place Maubert.

"Now, messieurs, madame," Marchant said. "Put up your weapons, and unbuckle your sword belts and set them down. I would not hurt you, but nor would I be hurt."

"Alas, I have no such scruples," Justin said, and attacked him. An instant later Tandy made a thrust at Christopher Danvers, which Christopher parried.

Kat saw in those first moments that Marchant was a skilled swordsman, much better even than Michel de Charron. He was confident, too, for when Saint-Amant would have joined the fight against Justin, Marchant ordered him away. He smiled widely, baring his teeth.

What was it Christopher had said? That Marchant had killed a dozen men in duels?

"Jesu!" She moved toward him, only to have her way blocked by the page. The child looked terrified but held his ground.

She could not—she *would* not—run him through . . . but peradventure she could disarm him. She thrust at him, more slowly than she could have, and he parried with his pretty sword, so tardily that she almost ran him through despite her intentions. For a second they were both as still as statues, the boy looking almost amazed that he had succeeded in parrying her thrust. And then she slid her sword's blade along his and twisted it, sending the gilded weapon flying through the air.

"I thank you, Nick," she breathed as the child ran off into the mist.

She turned toward Justin, and found herself facing Saint-Amant.

"You'll find me a more equal opponent, lady," he said, and struck at her with a *punta dritta* that she parried just in time with her dagger, but awkwardly, so that her wrist seemed torn.

She backed away, more frightened than she had ever been before. Justin and Marchant were still engaged, and Tandy was fighting both Christopher Danvers and the manservant, who hung back like a cowardly dog and made only an occasional thrust at him. As she glanced at them, the servant's blade drew blood from Tandy's dagger hand.

"Put up!" Saint-Amant said. "I would not kill a woman."

"Nor would I let you," Justin said, leaping back from Marchant and whirling round to strike at Saint-Amant, who parried skillfully.

Kat thrust at him then, for Marchant had closed with Justin again, but Saint-Amant beat her sword away easily and laughed at her, then delivered a *stoccata* that snagged Justin's sleeve. She attacked him again, and was beaten off just as effortlessly. Justin, she saw, was beginning to tire, and Marchant had recognized that, too, for there was a look of elation on his face.

Then something flew past her and struck Marchant in the face, and he staggered backward.

It was a brickbat, she saw when it had fallen to the cobblestones. And it glistened with blood.

"*Mon visage!*" Marchant dropped his dagger and raised his left hand to his face, then jerked it away, staring in horror at the blood on it. Saint-Amant seemed frozen as he gaped at the ruin of his friend's face, the bone showing through where flesh had been razed from the cheek.

"Monsieur!" Kat called, and struck as he looked back at her, running her blade through his right arm, just above the elbow. He dropped his sword and struck at her with his dagger, but she parried and beat it from his hand. Clutching his arm, he retreated.

Marchant was at last gazing at Justin again, such hate in his eyes that Kat wondered if he thought that somehow Justin had thrown that brickbat. Then he lunged toward Justin, but the baron stepped aside, parrying Marchant's thrust, and delivered a *punta riversa* that pierced Marchant's shoulder near the collarbone. Blood poured from the wound down the rich velvet of his doublet, a crimson smear on the crimson and gold and black pattern. Marchant backed away, but Justin followed him, and in a few more thrusts had beaten the sword from his hand.

Marchant turned and ran. A few moments later Saint-Amant hastened after him.

That left Christopher and the manservant, alone against three swords. The manservant took quick note of the odds and fled. Christopher fought on against Tandy for a few more moments, then he, too, ran away, disappearing into the mist after his *confrères*.

Kat went over to Tandy, whose left hand was cut, but he shook his head when she would have looked at the wound.

"Let's away," he said, and they ran.

They had gone no more than a dozen paces when someone caught at the back of Kat's doublet, dragging her to a halt. She screamed and broke free and whirled, then stopped just in time before delivering a blow that would have cut the flower vendor down.

The old woman held out something to her. 'Twas the locket. Kat accepted it, but was too surprised to thank her. Then she saw what the woman held in her other hand.

"*Vous?*" Kat asked, and the old woman glanced at the brickbat and cackled. "*Merci. Merci beaucoup.*"

"*Oui, merci,*" Justin said, and took Kat's arm and dragged her after him along the street.

"*Pardonnez-moi, monsieur,*" the woman called after him, then began to laugh, a sound that was soon lost in the distance.

They ran most of the way back to L'Oison Noir, stopping only to catch their breath. As soon as they reached the inn, Justin called for Monsieur Cotart and had him set his ostlers to work readying their horses. They would leave at once, he told the innkeeper. They had been set upon by a gang of Catholics who blamed the English for the peace accord and its favorable terms for the Huguenots.

Monsieur Cotart barked commands to his ostlers, then, wringing his hands, followed them up to their rooms and apologized profusely for the barbaric behavior of his fellow Parisians. He was eager that Justin know he would always welcome Englishmen at his inn. And Englishwomen, too, he added, staring at Kat, as he had stared at her often since first seeing her with her hair uncovered. He sent maidservants to fetch a bandage for Tandy's hand and a turban for Kat to wear, then descended to the kitchen himself to pack a portmanteau with food and wine for their journey. They would be welcome to stay at his son's inn when they reached Rouen, he told them. He had already written to Robert of his fine English friends.

As they rode off, he stood beneath the sign of the black gosling and waved to them, a worried look on his face.

Kat could not help wondering how much Justin had paid Monsieur Cotart. It must surely have been a great amount, but then, she mused, his help had been worth every denier.

It had taken them four days to reach Paris from Le Havre. They made it back in three.

Marchant seemed to be asleep at last.

Christopher Danvers closed the book from which he had been reading aloud and set it aside. He rubbed his eyes. He was weary of reading, but listening to someone read was the only thing that soothed and distracted Marchant, except for the syrup of poppy that put him to sleep, and the physician had warned him against taking too much of that. So Christopher had been set to reading to him, as if he were no more than a manservant. He had complained just once, and Saint-Amant had told him that if he would not do as they bade him, then he could leave. Alas, that was no choice at all. He had too little money to maintain lodgings of his own in Paris, far too little to return to England, unless he would become a beggar at his father's door in the hope of being received as the prodigal in the Bible—and there was, in sooth, no hope of that.

So he read. For three days now, he had spent much of his time reading, whenever Marchant was awake, even if 'twere late at night. The only times Marchant was awake and not demanding Christopher's company were when the physician came to change the dressing on his face, and then for a short time after that, when the sound of sobbing could sometimes be heard coming from his bedchamber. The physician could give Marchant little hope that his face would not be monstrously scarred, for the wound had become infected and was healing badly. Several other renowned physicians had been brought to the house, but none of them could offer any better treatment than Marchant's own doctor, who had studied at Padua.

Christopher stood and stretched. This idleness chafed him. By now he should have been on his way back to England, the poison with him, but Marchant would not even discuss sending him. 'Twas folly to delay, with Lord Harwood and his wife on their way back to England with news of their plot. The poison had been delivered by the Italian only a few hours after the fight in the Rue Galarde, and had Christopher been able to leave at once, he might have been able to reach the English court before Lord Harwood could, and peradventure find some way to add the poison to Elizabeth's food or drink. There might still be time— or so he had told Saint-Amant. But perforce he must wait here while Marchant cried over his wound. Christopher had reminded Saint-Amant that the siege of Rabastens had not stopped when Monluc was shot in the face, and that had been a much worse wound, shattering the bone. He had thought Saint-Amant might be recalled to the importance of this war they were waging against the heretics. Instead, Saint-Amant had struck him, leaving Christopher stunned and wondering if perhaps he had misjudged the reason for the man's alliance with Marchant. Was it possible that Saint-Amant loved Marchant as much as Marchant loved the Duke of Anjou?

Le duc. That was all Marchant spoke of, it seemed. Would Anjou still love him? He had sent word to the Louvre that he had been wounded by a ruffian and could not come to the court for a time, and

Anjou had sent a reply graciously accepting his excuse. There had been no encouragement for Marchant in that, and yet the Frenchman seemed relieved that the duke would at least not see him before the wound was healed. Christopher thought that a mistake. Had Anjou come here, mayhap he could have been persuaded to send soldiers after Lord Harwood and his party and prevent them from leaving France. But that, too, was a decision that should have been made at once, and when Saint-Amant spoke of inviting Anjou to the house during those first hours after the fight, Marchant had seemed almost lunatic in his insistence that he would not let the duke see him. He wanted Anjou's love, not his pity. So another opportunity had been lost.

And now Christopher perforce wasted his time reading to a disfigured *mignon*, while Lisle sped back to England with news of this plot, and the poison that had cost them so dearly began its quick deterioration. 'Twould be useless in another month, the Italian had told them, but he would not consider returning their money, for he had fulfilled his share of the bargain. Nor, as he pointed out, could they prove to him that the poison was never used. He had kept all the money that Margaret had sent them, and now Saint-Amant and Marchant were more close-fisted than ever. Christopher had had no gift of real value from them since they had given him the ruby ring months ago, and that had been sold in July, to pay for the lodgings he needed in London while he waited for word from them.

Suddenly Marchant moved, holding his hands up and opening his eyes, and the movement was so graceful that Christopher realized he had not been asleep at all. The Frenchman turned his hands from side to side, and the huge stones in his rings caught the light and threw jewel-bright spots of color against the walls.

"They are beautiful hands, are they not?" he asked.

"Yes, they are," Christopher said truthfully. "More beautiful even than Queen Elizabeth's hands, and she takes great pride in their beauty. Yet yours are indeed more beautiful."

"Of certain," Marchant said, a bit sharply, "for she is old, and I am young. I have no fear that my hands are not more beautiful than hers, as the duke would see if he ever were forced to meet her. In truth, I think that my hands may even be more beautiful than his."

He would do well to keep that opinion to himself, Christopher thought, remembering what he had heard of Anjou's pride in the beauty of his hands. A strange sort of pride, for a youth who also enjoyed acclaim as the hero of the Catholic victory at Jarnac.

"I am sure they are," he told Marchant, "though I have never seen the duke."

Marchant nodded. With the bandaged side of his face turned away from Christopher, his features looked beautiful still, reminding the Englishman of the carving of a cherub Saint-Amant kept in the gallery.

"D'you think," Marchant asked, very seriously, "that he loves me more for my hands than my face?"

For the first time in days, Christopher pitied Marchant more than he resented him.

"I cannot say for certain," he said slowly, "for I do not know the duke, but it is possible, monsieur. 'Tis possible."

And Marchant smiled, and admired his hands for a while longer, and then went to sleep.

CHAPTER 47

As the *Lady Margaret* cast anchor at Southampton, Kat stood at the starboard rail, looking out at the town from a vantage she had never had before. Justin stood beside her, his arm around her waist.

She was reluctant to leave the ship, for all that she knew they must make haste. Justin would ride post to the court—wherever it might be now, if the summer progress had not ended—and she would ride post back to Beechwood, and once there send a messenger off to Sparrow, to tell him that they had misjudged Lord Harwood.

In truth, she was eager to see Nick again, for all that she did not want to be separated from Justin for even a few days. And she agreed with Justin that what they had to do could be done quickest if they went their separate ways. He dared not take the time to accompany her to Beechwood, though he had vowed to come there as soon as he could. He would have some words with Nick then, he had said.

She chuckled to herself at the memory of his anger, and he glanced at her and smiled, and offered her ten pounds for her thoughts, but she would not tell him. 'Twould simply start the argument again. No matter how often she told him that it had been her decision to go to Harwood Hall with Nick, that she had given him no choice, Justin still insisted that Nick should have found some way to keep her at home. He would not let her take all the blame for her misadventure, and though she knew he was wrong, she could not help but love him for his stubborn defense of her. Her only worry was that Nick would be just as insistent in blaming Justin. Needs must that they would argue when they first met, but she prayed that at least they would not come to blows, for she was sure they would become friends . . . if they did not kill each other first.

She leaned against him, and he tightened his grip on her waist. The sailors were readying the small boat that would take them ashore. Soon they would have to part, for a time.

They had had little chance to talk during their flight to Le Havre, for they had ridden until exhaustion stopped them, then slept, then ridden on again. But once on the ship they had had all their time for each other, and both of them had been moved from laughter to tears to laughter again to discover the depth of their misunderstandings of each other. In the end there had been more laughter than tears, and so all was well . . . or would be, once the queen was warned of this plot, and Justin's reputation cleared of all suspicion. Kat felt as if a great weight had been lifted from her spirit. She thanked God that she had met Christopher in Paris and learned of his contriving—else she might now be back in an English harbor, but mourning the loss of a lover she thought to be a traitor, with Justin perforce staying behind in France, unable to return to England until he could think of some way to prove his innocence of crimes that had not even been named to him. How strange, to owe this happiness to Christopher . . . Now, if only Nick would learn to like Justin, her happiness would be complete.

Pray God, he would, for she hoped to marry Justin.

He had asked her already to marry him, but 'twas clear to her that his reason for asking was to save her honor—what was left of it. She would not have him on those terms and had told him so, bidding him wait until they knew each other better. They were still too much strangers to one another, she had said, for they had acted toward each other as if players in some masque until these last few days. She wanted to know him as well as she had known any other suitor. He should wait and ask her in a month or two, if he still wished to marry her, and if she still loved him, she would say yes. She would not marry him otherwise.

Not even to save me from your brother, should he threaten to run me through for dishonoring you? he had asked.

Nay, not even for that, she had said, but she had promised to strew flowers and branches of bay and rosemary on his grave, if Nick did run him through, and he had thanked her most soberly.

"My lord?" Tandy called. The boat was ready.

Tandy got out first when they reached the wharf, and reached down to help Kat up the last steps of the ladder.

"I'faith, this is easier when y'are awake," he told her, and she laughed. Now that she knew Justin was innocent, she felt carefree and could look back with amusement on much of what had happened to her. It had especially delighted her to learn that she had been taken out to the ship while Sparrow was here—yea, under his very nose! She would chide him for that, when next she saw him.

She felt exultant. 'Twas early yet: by tonight she would be home. By tomorrow or the next day, Justin would have reached the court, to warn Elizabeth of the plot against her. Before another week was out, they would be reunited, with no further bars to their happiness.

She began telling Tandy of her plans for Sparrow and what she would say to him—and what she would say about him to Walsingham, when he returned from France—as they walked from the wharf to the dusty street. "I have a crow to pluck with him," she said cheerfully, "if one can pluck a crow with a sparrow."

Then, of a sudden, the man himself appeared, as if he were the Devil and were summoned by being named. He walked out from behind a shed and stood before them, blocking their path.

"Lord Harwood, I—"

"Master Sparrow!" Kat cried, startled but happy to have him so soon delivered into her hands for the verbal lashing she intended to give him. "D'you know me now, sirrah? You did not recognize me when you saw me here in June."

Sparrow glanced at her, then shook his head before again facing Lisle. "Lord Harwood, I am here at Francis Walsingham's behest, to see that you are conducted to London, to the Tower, for questioning."

As he spoke, soldiers armed with guns and swords came out from hiding to surround them.

"Your sword belts," Sparrow said, and Justin and Tandy began to unbuckle theirs.

Kat looked around in disbelief. "Nay, you fools!" she cried, and grabbed Sparrow's arm. "He is not what you suspect him to be! I will swear to that!"

Sparrow shook her off. "Y'are in love with him," he said spitefully. "I saw you standing by his side at the rail. Alack, Mistress Langdon, I had thought even you were wiser than that."

She would have struck him then, but he caught her wrist and stayed the blow.

At that moment, Tandy swung his sword belt into the faces of the soldiers nearest him. They staggered backward, one falling, and he leapt over the man and raced away.

"Shoot him!" Sparrow cried, and the two soldiers with dags turned and fired at Tandy, who stumbled and fell to one knee, then got up and ran on, a bright blossom of crimson spreading across his shoulder.

Kat looked around at Justin, who stood within a circle of sword points, surrounded by half a dozen soldiers. His face was very pale as he stared after Tandy.

"Go after him, you clotpolls!" Sparrow said, and the two men who had shot at Tandy ran after him.

Sparrow looked back at his captive then. "My lord, you will go with these soldiers, and I pray you will go quietly."

"Nay!" Kat cried. "He's innocent! Y'are a fool to suspect him of treason!"

" 'Tis not for a witless girl to decide," Sparrow told her. "Haply you should go with him, but I have been asked to take you back to your home. Would that you had had the sense to stay there, madam, and attend to your needlework."

She cuffed him then, and he raised his hand to hit her in turn, but protests from the soldiers made him change his mind. He let his arm fall to his side, his hand knotting into a fist.

"I have proof of my innocence," Justin said then. His voice was very steady, very cold, and he looked upon Sparrow with contempt.

"Yea, there were letters—" Kat began, but Sparrow interrupted her.

"I'll have no talk of secrets of state here. If there is proof, 'twill wait to be discovered until you are in the Tower and we have talked at length. Master Walsingham will want to see you, once he returns from France."

"No less would I see him," Justin said, but before he could say more, Sparrow gestured for the soldiers to take him away. Only two soldiers remained behind. Kat glanced from one to the other, and knew 'twould be useless to flee: garbed as she was in women's clothes and pantofles, she would never be able to outrun them.

Sparrow had watched Lisle escorted away. Now he turned to Kat and would have taken her arm, but she shook free of his grasp. "You whoreson fool! I tell you, he is no traitor! There are letters he has sent, letters to Master Walsingham!"

Sparrow stared at her for a few seconds, then shook his head. "Nay, 'tis not true. I'll not believe it."

"Yes, you will, for he'll prove it!"

"Never!" he said, and would not listen to anything else she said.

Because she refused to leave Southampton with him, saying he was a varlet and a knave and she would not trust him, Sparrow took Kat to the Golden Griffin, the only destination she would accept. There he hired a room for her, setting the soldiers to guard her door while he rode to Beechwood to tell Nick she was back.

She could not leave her chamber, but Mistress Adams came to visit her, and then, after supper, she heard a light rapping on the outside of her door—very low on the outside. She opened the door to see a little girl, no more than three years old.

"Y'are Jack's sister, are you not?" the girl asked.

She shook her head. "Nay, I have no brother of that name."

"I'll send her off, madam," the soldier said.

"You look much like Jack," the child insisted.

"Do I indeed?" She stooped to look the girl in the eye. "And just who is this Jack?"

"Amy, you fatbrain!" another child's voice piped, and Kat glanced down the hall to see a boy about two years older than the girl. Her brother, likely, for they favored each other. "Will you never remember? His name is Nick, Master Nick, now."

"Nick? You know Nick?" she asked wonderingly. "That's my brother's name. You know him?"

The girl nodded several times. "He bought me gingerbread at the Bartholomew Fair."

"Did he?"

"He bought some for me, too," the boy said. "He bought more for me than for you."

"Nay, he did not!"

"Did so! He likes me better than you!"

"Nay, he does not!" the little girl insisted, tears in her eyes. " 'Twas only to keep you from nipping that purse! You told me!"

Kat shook her head, amazed. The guard looked amused.

"Tom, you runagate co!" a woman called from below. "Amy! Why are you up there, and what's this quarrel?"

A woman came running up the stairs. 'Twas a maidservant Kat had seen earlier, when she arrived at the Golden Griffin. She was raven-haired and young and pretty, though her skin was sunburned. It was obvious at first glance that the children were hers. Was she the reason Nick knew these children? Kat wondered. In sooth, the woman was *very* pretty, but nothing like the *buonarobas* she had heard Nick describe. And the children had spoken of the Bartholomew Fair. That was in London! Why would he have taken these children there?

"Good even, Mistress Katherine," the woman said. "I am sorry that my children troubled you."

"Marry, they did not," Kat assured her, "though I wondered at first who your daughter—Amy?—meant when she spoke of Jack."

" 'Twas his first name," Amy explained patiently. "He was Nick later."

"No, he was Nick earlier," Tom said.

"Was not!"

"The ruffian cly you both!" the woman said. "Stow your whids." And they were silent.

The woman shook her head. "They knew him first as Jack," she said quietly.

"Did they?"

" 'Tis a long story . . . and belike one Jack—Nick—would liefer tell you himself."

Kat would as soon have heard the tale from her, for she was weary of this waiting and would fain be diverted, but 'twas clear that the woman was reluctant to tell the story herself. She apologized again for troubling Kat, took her children by the hand and turned back toward the stairs, hesitating as she heard someone start up them, treading heavily.

'Twas Nick, still wearing his riding boots. He saw Bess and the children first, and paused, smiling, but a bit tensely, until Amy ran over to him and hugged his legs. Then his smile became soft and fond as he ruffled her hair. The smile faded as he glanced up at the girl's mother.

All was not well between them, Kat realized. What mischief had Nick been up to? 'Twas clear that changing his name—to Jack, forsooth!—had not changed his habits.

And then he noticed Kat watching him. He gently pried Amy's arms loose, and he came toward her slowly, a look of wonder on his face.

"Kat . . . Sweet sister . . . I feared I might never see you again."

And then he was hugging her, and she was laughing and crying at the same time. The black-haired woman shooed her children downstairs, glancing back once before she followed them, and Kat saw a look of mingled sorrow and happiness in her eyes. But before she could wonder much about it, Nick was asking her a dozen questions at once, questions she was loath to answer within the guard's hearing. So they went into her chamber, where they could talk in private, and closed the door behind them.

By God's most precious blood! How sweet it was, Sparrow thought, to see Lord Harwood in the Tower of London at last!

The baron had not yet sent for furnishings of his own—Lisle expected to be out of the Tower very soon, the warden had told Sparrow—and the chamber was so meanly furnished that Lord Harwood had to sit on a joined stool, like a poor yeoman. He did not seem humbled yet, but this confinement would humble him in time, Sparrow was sure. And he would have much time here, despite his assurance of the contrary to the warden.

He had been here since yesterday, and Sparrow, who had reached London last night, could have seen him then, but he had thought 'twould be better to wait. Lord Harwood could only benefit by extra hours to muse upon his cheerless surroundings and to look out upon Tower Green and contemplate the certain fate of the traitors who had been executed there. Death they could not escape. Their only choice had been between Heaven and Hell, and Sparrow prayed that Justin Lisle would choose Heaven—not because he cared one whit for the man's soul, but because to choose Heaven, Lisle must needs repent and confess.

Sparrow wanted that confession soon, before Walsingham returned from Paris, and his master would be back any day now, to attend to some business in England before returning to France to replace Henry Norris as England's ambassador there.

Unfortunately, Lord Harwood was still far from repentance, as his first haughty words to Sparrow proved.

"Well, sirrah. So you have come at last. Would that you were as impatient to learn the truth of my innocence as you were to accuse me falsely."

"What is false or true has yet to be seen," Sparrow told him flatly. "What proof do you offer of innocence?"

And Lisle told him of the letters that had been delivered so stealthily to Walsingham, the letters that had prompted him to chide Sparrow and say he was better served by his unknown intelligencers.

Sparrow might have been dumb-stricken by the news, had Kat Langdon not already said enough to warn him that those unsigned letters might be what Lisle would claim as proof. It had been a troubling thought for a few hours. Then he had remembered that Walsingham had received one letter while Lord Harwood was on his way from Harwood Hall to Southampton, so he could not have delivered it himself. 'Twas unlikely he would have sent a servant with it. His most trusted manservant, the one who had escaped—successfully, alas—at Southampton a few days ago, had also been at the wharf, and 'twas clear these last few days that he also had been in Spain and France with his lord, for all that Nick Langdon told stories of seeing a man who looked like him, and of a pedlar who Mistress Spencer claimed looked like him. Was it likely, in any event, that Lisle would have trusted such secrets to another? Nay, it was not. So how else could he have learned of the letters? Sparrow had wondered, and had finally realized that the author of the letters must have been a friend or acquaintance of Lisle's. Somehow Lord Harwood had learned that this unknown intelligencer was sending word of various plots—whether all were of Lisle's contriving or not, Sparrow could not say—to Walsingham, and had done away with the man, for there had been no more letters for six weeks now. Which made Lisle a murderer as well as a traitor.

So he admitted that he had heard of the letters, and he appeared to give an ear to Lisle's description of them—and indeed he knew the very gist of the messages, though he could not recite them word for word, more proof of his guilt—but all the while he listened to the man's voice more than his words, listened for hints of weaknesses that could be exploited. And when Lisle had finished talking, Sparrow, too, was silent for a time, as if considering his statements seriously.

"Will you write the text of one of these letters for us," he asked then, "that Master Walsingham may compare the hand to that in the letters he received?"

"They are not in my hand," Lord Harwood admitted, sighing a little.

"Oh?" Sparrow asked, hard put to conceal his feeling of triumph. "Then whose hand are they in? Who wrote them for you?"

"One of my servants. Tandy. William Lofts."

"Is that not the rogue who ran away at Southampton?"

"He's no rogue!"

"But was that not the man you speak of?"

"Yes."

"I see," Sparrow said, and though he felt like crowing, he forced himself to nod with exaggerated thoughtfulness instead. "And so you cannot produce this servant, to prove that he wrote those letters."

"Nor can you prove that he did not!"

"But need I do so? 'Tis you, my lord, who have been often in Spain. 'Tis you who went to France, for business that you have not explained other than to warn of some plot to poison the queen—"

"Nor will I explain my business to you, sirrah!"

"—when your license to travel beyond the seas mentioned only Spain. 'Tis you who skulked about London to secret meetings. If there was no evil intent in all these doings, then 'tis you who must prove that . . . and you have no proof, no proof that we may look at and touch. No proof at all."

"But I have," the nobleman said, to Sparrow's astonishment and dismay, and told him where he could find it.

Never in all his life, Sparrow knew, would he sleep in a bedchamber as magnificent as Justin Lisle's chamber at Harwood Hall.

He had been inside many houses owned by gentry before, but rarely further than their halls, and he had never seen a bedchamber as fine as this one, with its great bed of oak inlaid with ivory and hung with silk embroidered with silver thread and crystal, its chairs upholstered in velvet or gilded Cordovan leather, its Italian tables with marquetry of ivory and marble and topaz, its silver basin and ewer, its huge press filled with more suits than Sparrow would own in a lifetime. Envy gnawed at him so sharply that he felt sick almost to death. And now he hated Lisle as well as envied him. To live like this, with such wealth and standing, and still to be a traitor! Sparrow was still sure of Lisle's guilt. But by God's death! *why* was he a traitor?

Sparrow could understand little men betraying their prince, if they were greedy and they were offered money enough. He could understand men of ambition becoming traitors, if that ambition were thwarted. He could even understand zealots betraying their own country for the cause that maddened them. But Lord Harwood was none of these things . . . and yet he was a traitor. Was it possible that he loved his cousin Margaret so much? Sparrow knew for a fact that Lisle and Margaret had been lovers; there had been endless gossip about them, and as for the truth of the gossip, he had heard it attested to—aye, and sworn to—by two servants of Margaret's grandfather's household who had watched the young lovers during that summer fifteen years ago. It seemed strange beyond measure to Sparrow that any man would risk losing so much for the love of a woman . . . but had not King Henry torn England asunder, that he might have Anne Boleyn? 'Twas madness, a lamentable madness . . . but a common one, afflicting high and low alike. Alas, it could wreak much greater harm when it afflicted those of high station, such as Lisle.

How much harm Lord Harwood had done, only time would tell. The Earl of Lennox had heard weeks ago that the Duke of Alva might send several thousand soldiers to Scotland to aid the followers of Mary Stuart, and while the invasion had not yet occurred, Sparrow could not help wondering whether Lord Harwood had had a hand in its contriving. Nor would it be known for weeks whether the Spanish fleet conducting Princess Anne of Austria to Spain would later be used against England, and Lord Harwood might well be involved in that. The timing of his visit to Spain was much too suspicious . . .

He stood at the fireplace, warming himself. He had requested that the fire be built, for he was weary after the swift ride from London, and the bedchamber, unused for months and shut off from the rest of the house, with the heavy satin drapes pulled against the sun's warmth, was chilly this fall afternoon. Finally he rubbed his hands together and set to work.

He had locked the door against busybodies, despite the complaints of Lord Harwood's steward, who had finally been driven away from the chamber by one of the soldiers Sparrow had guarding the house. Now he took his time searching the room, looking for anything that might incriminate the baron. The locked writing cabinet he left for last. Whatever he might find there, he was sure 'twould not be the papers Lord Harwood described. Sparrow was certain that he had been sent off on a wild goose chase, to gain Lord Harwood another few days' respite, time in which Walsingham might return and be won over.

That possibility worried Sparrow. He remembered the warning that the secret intelligencer had given Walsingham months ago: *Ware Ridolfi*. But Walsingham would not. During the time that he had held Ridolfi under house arrest to question him about his role in the plot to marry the Duke of Norfolk to the Queen of Scots, Walsingham had so enjoyed the Italian's company that he put all his suspicions aside. To Sparrow, that was plain folly. And now he feared that Lord Harwood might be able to work the same magic that Ridolfi had—even if Lisle could not prove that he was innocent of treason—were he not able to prove the opposite.

Sparrow searched for more than an hour, but could find nothing that suggested treason. Grumbling to himself, he went at last to the writing cabinet and unlocked it with the key he had taken from behind a figure carved on the mantel, where Lord Harwood had told him he would find it.

He rummaged first through the letters, but they were of a nature such as any nobleman might receive—though the queen would perhaps be interested to hear some of the comments Lord Harwood's friends had made about her. Then, and only then, did he open the small drawer in the upper left corner of the cabinet, fully expecting to find it empty.

Alack, it was not. And the papers were as Lord Harwood had described them, as Sparrow had heard Walsingham describe them—torn just so, in quarters. Sparrow had no doubt that when he took them to London and gave them to Walsingham, they would fit like the pieces of an indenture with the letters Walsingham had already received. And Lord Harwood would walk free.

His head whirling, his hands shaking, Sparrow took the papers out of the drawer. He was scarce able to believe in their existence even when he held them. Feeling chilled again, he walked over to the fire.

Even these, he knew, were not final proof of the baron's innocence. For if the baron or one of his servants had discovered that an associate of theirs was informing Walsingham of their activities, and had forced from that associate—perchance through torture—the words of the letters, was it not possible that the existence and location of these papers had also been revealed? 'Twould have been simple work to find them and bring them here, as insurance against charges of treason.

But would Walsingham agree with his reasoning? Or would all the months of work he had done be tossed aside as so much rubbish— aye, and like enough, himself with it? And Justin Lisle trusted in his stead . . .

Blind with anger, he ripped the papers in two, then stared down, aghast at what he had done.

How could he explain this? Even if he insisted that the sheets of paper, when found, had been torn in eighths and not in quarters as Lisle had said, Walsingham might suspect that his intelligencer had thought to destroy the papers and had then changed his mind. 'Twould be the end of any trust between them.

Sparrow hesitated, biting his lip, then tossed the papers into the fire, where they flared like burning leaves before settling onto the logs and being utterly consumed.

He would stay until the fire had burned down, he decided, and stir the coals and ashes with the fire-fork, before he left. Just to be sure. He pulled one of Lord Harwood's fine chairs over in front of the fireplace and sat down to wait.

There were walls and watchdogs and locks to deal with, but with all of them Tandy was familiar. Too familiar, of a truth, for the strangeness of stealing into his own home made him clumsier than was his wont, and slower. Or haply that was not it, and 'twas his weakness that slowed him. The physician he had seen in Southampton, who now no longer owed him a debt that had been incurred years ago in London, had cleaned the wound and bandaged his shoulder, but could no more replace the blood Tandy had lost than he could cure the plague. He had told Tandy that only time would mend his weakness. Time that Tandy feared he did not have, though he had perforce stayed a few days in Southampton, after discovering he was too weak to mount the horse he had hired, let alone ride it here.

Now he could already feel his strength ebbing, and he was glad that the guards who had been set about the house were lackwits and half asleep to boot, for he would prefer to leave at a walk rather than a run, after he had what he had come to get. He would have liked to stop to see his brother, too, and learn what news he could, but dared not, for fear of being discovered.

The bedchamber door was locked, but he unlocked it with a bit of twisted wire that he had oft found useful, and let himself in. The curtains were drawn, shutting out the moonlight, and he made his way to the fireplace by memory and touch, stumbling just once, over a chair that was not where he remembered it.

He sniffed then, at the scent of ashes. There had been a fire lit here recently. He wondered that his brother would permit that, then put the thought from his mind as he ran his hands over the marble carvings on one side of the mantel. Finding the carving of a lion's head, he reached into the crevice behind it for the key.

'Twas not there.

He leaned against the mantel, dizzy with fright for an instant. Maybe some maidservant had come in to dust the room and had knocked the key unawares from its hiding place.

Yea, but had she moved that chair as well? And lit a fire? Would a servant have been permitted to do that, in his lordship's bedchamber?

He shook his head. These conjectures were useless—nay, worse than that, for they wasted precious time. He stood up straight, holding onto the mantel for a moment until he felt steady on his feet, then crossed the room to the writing cabinet. 'Twas but one more lock, after all, though he was loath to ruin it with his wire.

But the key was there, already in the lock.

His breath rasped in his throat as he turned it and reached for the drawer in the upper left corner. 'Twas empty. He could have wept, but there was no time. He had to get to London, and back south again to Beechwood, before his strength gave out entirely.

He closed the writing cabinet again, leaving the key where he had found it, then made his way out of the house. He was near the wall when he almost walked into a guard, fast asleep under a hedge until Tandy's noisy step woke him. He had to wrestle the man, but luck was with him in that the guard was too surprised and frightened to think to call for help before Tandy could deliver a blow to his chin that knocked him out.

Tandy got to his feet, rubbing his knuckles, then scrabbled over the wall and ran to his horse. His wound was bleeding again; he could feel the slow trickle down his back. But there were no doctors who owed him a favor between here and London. Nor would he have stopped to see one, had there been.

When Sparrow returned to the Tower, he found Francis Walsingham there, talking to Lisle. Sparrow was vexed to hear from the guards that Walsingham had been there for hours already. He hurried in and found his master looking weary, and harried as well.

" 'Tis a very strange tale that Lord Harwood has told me," Walsingham said to Sparrow after greeting him.

"Very strange indeed. He sends me after papers that do not exist."

"You did not find them?" Lisle asked sharply.

"There was nothing there, nothing to match the description you gave . . . though I searched most thoroughly."

"I warrant you did," the baron said coldly.

"But I could not find what was not there."

"Peradventure," Walsingham suggested, "the papers were taken by some servant, who thought them discarded because they were torn, and wished to use them himself."

Sparrow stared at his master. 'Slid! Walsingham was already seeking excuses to believe Lord Harwood. "Took them from a locked cabinet?" he asked bluntly—more bluntly than Walsingham liked, he could tell, and he regretted speaking so hastily.

But before Walsingham could reprove him, Lisle spoke again. "Needs must that I agree. I trust my servants more than that."

"And not even the least trustworthy servant," Sparrow added, "could steal what was not there."

"Faith, Master Cadmon," Walsingham said irritably, "he knew of the letters, and described them to me. Did he not describe them to you?"

"Aye, but not word for word . . . save for the one of only two words."

"Ware Ridolfi," Lisle murmured, and Walsingham flushed. "As for the others, I plead a less than perfect memory of them."

"Yea, and a hand that matches them no better than your memory does."

"I have told you, they were written by my servant, who—"

"Who has vanished, and is most conveniently not here either to prove your story or give you the lie."

"But how else," Walsingham asked, "could he have known of the letters, had he not arranged that they be written and given to me? I have told but a few men, and I have trusted them not to tell others."

"Haply he learned of them from their author," Sparrow said, and told Walsingham of his suspicions—all but his suspicion that Lord Harwood could have had the papers from the unknown intelligencer, for there was no need to admit to that. To his great annoyance, Lord Harwood laughed, but there was solace in Walsingham's thoughtful look.

Walsingham crossed to the window and looked out, silent for a long time. "There is much to doubt in this, Master Sparrow," he said finally. "But also much to doubt, my lord, in your claim that you could produce the sheets of paper that would prove your story."

"I thought I could," Lisle said simply.

"But they were not there, and you have confessed that no servant would have taken them."

"Perchance some thief took them instead," Lord Harwood said, gazing at Sparrow, who stared back boldly.

Walsingham, his back still to them, asked, "A thief?"

"Truly, there was a thief, my lord," Sparrow said lightly. "Or mayhap he was a trespasser. He was discovered in the garden by one of my men, but not captured, alas. I learned of it just last night."

"So," Walsingham said, turning toward them then, "someone was in the house, other than you and your men and Lord Harwood's servants."

The baron glanced down, smiling. Likely he hoped 'twas his servant Tandy, Sparrow thought. Likely he hoped 'twas Tandy who had the bits of paper now . . .

"Aye," Sparrow said, "someone was there. Two nights ago, several hours after I left. He could not have taken the papers . . . if there were any.''

"Jesu!'' Lisle struck the wall with his fist. "I tell you there were papers in that cabinet, to match those you have seen already.''

"Then where are they, my lord?'' Sparrow asked.

"I know not where *those* are now,'' Lisle said sharply, "but perhaps you may find some like them, pieces of sheets of paper torn with them.''

"Where?'' Sparrow asked, feeling sick. How was it there were two sets of paper?

"Nay, I'll not tell you.''

"My lord, if this is some jest . . .'' Walsingham said, looking more weary than ever.

"Would you bid your Sparrow fly to fetch these papers?''

"At once.''

"Then I'll not tell you . . . unless another is sent in his stead. I trust my servants, sir. I do not trust yours.''

"You slander me!'' Sparrow said.

"Say you so?'' Lisle asked mildly. "Even if that were true—and I swear it is not—'twould be less injury than you have done me. I say you found those papers and destroyed them.''

"And I say you lie in your throat!'' Sparrow retorted, drawing his sword.

"Put up, sir!'' Walsingham commanded. "Would you draw on an unarmed man? Let's hear no challenges in this place. 'Tis an affront to the queen.'' Then, when Sparrow had sheathed his sword again, Walsingham turned to Lord Harwood and said, "My lord, 'tis a most serious charge you make. Why would Master Cadmon destroy evidence?''

"Truth to tell, I know not . . . but I know the evidence was there for him to find, and yet he did not bring it back.''

"Would it satisfy you if I went with him to search for these other papers?''

"By the mass, if you do not trust me—'' Sparrow began, but fell silent when Walsingham held up his hand.

"I would not have this disputed,'' he told Sparrow, then, to Lisle: "Would you trust me?''

"Yea, I would.''

"Then where may we find these papers?''

"Tandy had lodgings at a tenement by Aldgate, above a cordwainer's shop,'' Lisle said, and gave them precise directions. "I cannot swear that you'll find such papers there—''

"Of certain, you cannot,'' Sparrow interrupted, but was silenced again by a glance from Walsingham.

"—but he took extra pieces of paper to London with him once, for he feared the message he had to write could not be explained on one piece of paper.''

"Yet no message I received took more than one sheet . . . so the other pieces of paper might still be there," Walsingham said, and Sparrow was rankled by the hopefulness in his voice.

Lisle shrugged. "They may, or they may not, for he may have ruined a piece or two. I warrant he had at least one left when he was here in London last month, to give you that last letter, for he came here directly from Kent. Had there been no paper, he would of necessity have gone first to Harwood Hall. But whether that note was the last of the pieces of paper, I cannot say."

"Let us hope it was not," Walsingham said, and Sparrow bristled and thought, *Let us hope it was,* but said nothing more as he followed his master out of the chamber.

They returned to the Tower a few hours later, having turned Tandy's lodgings by Aldgate upside down.

Lord Harwood leapt up from his stool when the door opened, his countenance one of hopefulness, but that changed when he saw their faces.

"You did not find those papers," he said. It was not a question.

Walsingham shook his head. "There were no papers at all."

"Had Tandy been there?"

"Aye, long ago," Sparrow told him.

"We thought to ask the cordwainer," Walsingham explained. "He said he has not seen Tandy for many a week." He rubbed his face. "I pray you, my lord, think of something else that may prove your story, for I would not have us hold you suspect, on account of a warning that you may have given us yourself."

But Lisle merely shook his head, and after a time they went away.

CHAPTER 48

The apples in Beechwood's orchard were ripe now, and tomorrow the servants would begin to harvest them, but this afternoon Kat and Nick and Jane could still walk here in peace and quiet. Nick picked three apples from a tree, and gave one to his sister and another to Jane, and they walked on along the sandy path, eating the sweet fruit. 'Twas a fine crop this year, Kat thought, wishing she could take more pleasure in it.

" 'Tis sad news from Sparrow," Jane said after a while.

"Yea," Kat agreed bitterly. "He's turned from sparrow to raven, and would foretell Justin's death."

"Nay, the news is not that grim," Nick objected, but without force.

Indeed, the news from London had been grim. And how like Sparrow, to make Kat think at first that there was hope! Justin had never told her that the notes he had had Tandy take to Walsingham had been written on sheets of paper that were torn like indentures, so each might bear witness that subsequent messages came from the same source. Sparrow had been told that unused sheets of paper, torn like the others, could be found at Hatwood Hall.

At that point in Nick's reading of the letter, Kat had crowed with happiness and seized his arm and told him that it must have been a hard letter for Sparrow to write. Nick had smiled and agreed and read on, but then his smile had vanished and for a few moments he had read silently, and Kat had looked on in trepidation, already fearing what he would tell her, what she would then read for herself when he handed the letter to her.

She was certain that Sparrow had found the papers, for needs must that they had been there. I'faith, would Justin lie about a matter of such consequence? So Sparrow had destroyed or hidden them. Nick had confessed he thought that was possible, for he, too, had no great love of the man . . . but was it likely? Then she had rated him as a doubter who would never believe that Justin was what she knew him to be—a loyal subject of the queen, and an intelligencer by whom Walsingham had been helped unawares. And then she had cried, and Nick had comforted her as best he could, but of what use were words now? Justin was in the Tower, and he might never come out again, except to walk out to a scaffolding on Tower Green and lay his head down on the headsman's block.

Nick had chided her gently for being so fearful, reminding her that as yet no formal charges of treason had been made against Justin. Even an hour earlier his argument might have allayed her fears, but now, having read Sparrow's letter, there was cold comfort in what Nick said. For if Sparrow would not balk at destroying evidence, then what chance that he would balk at counterfeiting evidence, should such forgeries suit his purposes? Kat had not felt so despairing since Justin was first taken to the Tower.

"Will you write another letter to Cecil," Jane asked Kat, "and tell him of your suspicions?"

"And accuse one of Walsingham's own intelligencers of great malice and treachery?" Nick asked.

"Upon my life, I will," Kat said, ignoring her brother. He had expressed doubts when she wrote the first letter she had sent to the queen's secretary of state, too, and had told her that she was burning daylight writing it, for Justin would need more of a defense than she could give him. Perchance he was right: Cecil had sent her a letter in reply, but had told her only that he had taken what she said under consideration. He had bidden her not to come to court, too, if her only reason was to seek an audience with the queen about this business, for Elizabeth had many matters of state to concern her now, and Lord Harwood was among the least of them. That had left Kat wondering if she perhaps had hurt Lisle's cause, as Nick had warned she might. But she had been able to see no other course but to write the letter, and so she had spent her first day back at Beechwood working on it, and then had sent it off, all twenty close-written pages of it, with a servant whom she had told to ride post-haste to the court. What Cecil and Walsingham would do with it now, she did not know. Mayhap they would, as Nick had suggested, use only that portion of her letter describing how she had been taken from England against her will, submitting that as evidence and omitting the rest. And yet, she reasoned, if it were their purpose to charge him with that as well as treason, then they would not even need her letter, for Nick would perforce have to testify to the truth of that charge—as would she, if she would not perjure herself. At least they had her written defense of him against Sparrow's suspicions, and if it sorted with his own testimony—pray God, it would!—'twould aid him somewhat.

Unless they suspected her of having been corrupted by him and now being in league with him. Nick fretted over that, despite Kat's and

Jane's efforts to reassure him. *As they say, the crow thinks its own bird fairest*, Nick had told them. *If Kat would defend a traitor, then maybe 'tis because she is a traitor as well.*

By my troth, I am as much a traitor as he is! she had cried, but he had warned her to keep that claim to herself.

While she had been musing over these things, Nick had asked Jane about her readiness for Michaelmas. Now she listened idly as they talked of the feast they had planned, with both households together at Beechwood, and enough geese, fattened and ready for roasting, to feed an army, and as many cakes and apple pies and puddings as the cooks could prepare. Every other year, Kat had reveled in the feast day of the archangel Michael—aye, and in the preparations for it, too—but this year she had left all planning to Jane and her brother. 'Twas odd of Nick to accept this work being thrust upon him . . . but then, he had changed much in these last few months.

She smiled at them now. Nick had taken Jane's hand a minute ago, and had not let go of it yet. As like as not, he was too rapt in thought to feel awkward at the moment. Most other times, he seemed as unsure around Jane as he had seemed with Bess, the maidservant at the Golden Griffin. Kat would have seen at once that he loved Jane, even if he had not told her so. But alack, he had not quite stopped loving Bess, and Jane knew it, though she had said nothing of it to Nick. She understood that more time was needed, and though she had never spoken too openly of the matter, she had told Kat once that she would have thought less of Nick, had his feelings toward Bess changed the moment he regained his memory and knew himself to be of gentle birth. Kat had to agree that only time's passage would avail, but she still fretted at its slowness. Would that she could help them with this tangle . . .

Would that they could help her with hers. Would that anyone could help. For how could she go on with her life, if Justin's ended in a traitor's death?

The thought sank her in melancholy, from which she was pulled by the sound of laughter.

"What's the matter?" she asked, smiling.

"Jane was just telling me of Gossip Merton," Nick said.

"The old woman who sells you wildflowers to strew with your rushes each summer?"

"The same," Jane said, and chuckled. "She is about her gossiping again, saying the queen's on progress only to have the bastard Leicester begot on her away from London."

"That old slander?" Kat made a wry face.

Jane nodded. "I was not laughing at that. Such gossip is most malicious, and I have told my servants that they'll be fined a penny if I hear they are repeating it. But 'twas what Nick said . . ." She giggled.

"What was it, good brother?" Kat asked, looking at him warily.

"I said merely that if such gossip is to be believed, then the queen must bear children on schedule, conceiving them on All Saints' Day and dropping them at Lammas-tide."

"Fie, Nick! Fie, you rogue! 'Tis lèse-majesté to speak thus of the queen."

"No more so for me than for Mistress Merton."

"Yea, but 'tis unlikely Elizabeth will ever hear of her gossip, or care one whit what such a gossip says, while if you prattle on thus at court someday, your head will roll for it."

Your head will roll for it.

She had been jesting, but her own words recalled to her Justin's plight, and she looked away from them quickly, pretending to choose among the apples on the nearest tree for another to eat. She would not have them see the tears in her eyes.

Jane was in a somber mood as she rode back to Stamworth. This news of Lord Harwood was ill news indeed, and Kat's fear had been writ plain on her face, even when she was smiling. Jane wished she could see Master Sparrow again. She would fain roast him like a Michaelmas goose, until he chirped the truth about the papers he had been sent to fetch.

When she reached home, she found the house abustle, but not with preparations for the feast two days hence, the packing of flour and sugar into sacks and geese into crates to convey to Beechwood. Instead, there was a hurly-burly over the discovery of a wounded man on the road an hour earlier, lying on his back, his face badly sunburned, his horse cropping the grass beside him.

"Wounded?" she asked her steward.

"Aye, 'tis a gun wound, but not a new one, for it was bandaged and even scabbed over but has broken open again. The back of his shirt was all blood."

She ran up the stairs to the bedchamber where they had put him.

'Twas the man she had hoped it would be, but she could ask him no questions. The maidservant watching over him said that he had not come to himself since they found him.

Should she send for Kat? Jane wondered, then decided against it. 'Twould be cruel, if it proved that he had no news that would cheer her. Kat had already had her hopes raised and then dashed once today, and once was enough.

But perchance he brought something better than news?

She had her servants bring her his cloakbag and wallet, but what she sought was not there, nor was it in his purse. Marry, now she knew how Kat had felt earlier, she thought as she settled down again on the side of the bed and gazed at the familiar face, with its crescent-shaped scar.

And then she remembered something Kat had said to her of the habits of spies. She looked thoughtfully at his clothes, which had been draped over the foot of the bed after he was stripped and then clothed in a nightshirt. All his clothes were there, save his bloodied shirt, which she knew would not have contained what she sought, anyway.

She turned his doublet inside out, and found, along the inside hem, at the bottom of the left front side of the garment, some crude stitching that in no way matched the rest. She tore it out, using her fingernails in her haste, and dug inside the lining, and pulled out four pieces of paper, quarters of one sheet, whose torn edges, she knew, would be close matches for the torn edges of some letters in Master Walsingham's possession. Proof of Lisle's innocence.

But yet not quite enough, not enough to be indisputable. There was one thing more that she needed, and then she would ride at once to Beechwood.

She went to sit on the bed again, and the room gradually darkened, and she lit candles, and still she waited. At last, when it was so late that she could scarce keep herself awake, Tandy's eyes opened.

For a few seconds his gaze flitted about the room, as if taking note of all obstacles and exits, and then it settled on her, and rested there.

"Well, pedlar," she said cheerily, "there are smallwares I would buy from you." She held up the rough-edged rectangles of paper. "But I would have you write something on them first. Pray God, you can remember the text . . ."

She left for Beechwood a quarter of an hour later, after giving two of the pieces of paper, one with writing on it and one without, to her steward for safe keeping.

She woke Kat, and held the papers up before her, and her friend understood in a trice.

"Tandy?"

Jane nodded.

"Is he well?"

"Not yet, but he will be."

"God be thanked for that," Kat said, and threw her nightgown over her shoulders and ran to Nick's bedchamber, Jane close behind her.

Kat pushed the bedhangings aside and climbed onto the mattress and shook her brother awake.

"Up, you slugabed, up! We have much to do!"

Nick sat up, groaning, and looked around groggily. "Jesu, what hour is it?"

" 'Tis nearly three of the clock. Up, you rogue! We are for Windsor, to the court, to see the queen!"

And in his confusion he looked to Jane, and she smiled at him, and nodded, and held up the bits of paper as if they were a trophy.

CHAPTER 49

On the morning after Michaelmas, Kat went to Windsor Castle for the second time. She was alone, though Nick had been with her yesterday. He had not been invited to this interview, so instead had left their chambers at the Garter Inn, where they had been forced to lodge because there was not room in the castle for all the court, to go with a friend to hunt the deer for which Windsor Forest was famous. Kat was glad not to have him along with her. There would be more opportune times for his next meeting with Justin.

She walked up Castle Hill into the Lower Ward, then past the ancient stone tower built by Henry II. In the Upper Ward she was met by a gentleman usher who led her to the stone terrace below the queen's apartments on the north side of the ward. There Elizabeth was walking rapidly back and forth for her morning exercise, two white-clad maids of honor struggling to keep pace with her.

To Kat's great relief—she had worn pantofles to the castle, and was not sure she could walk so fast in them—the queen stopped when she saw her and waited for the girl to reach her and make her greetings before starting to walk again, but more slowly. The queen was silent, except for asking Kat her opinion of the view, which she answered honestly was a magnificent one. Looking down the escarpment over which the castle had been built, Kat saw the Thames, a wide silvery ribbon in the morning light. Looking out across the Thames, she could see as far north as the green hills of Buckinghamshire.

Elizabeth approved her approval. " 'Tis why I wished this terrace built, that I might walk here and enjoy this view in greater safety. This"—she gestured at the terrace before them—"was but wooden planks and railings in my sister's reign."

Kat complimented her on the terrace, and again the queen seemed pleased. *She can never be overfilled with compliments,* Nick had told her. *She is a very abyss in that respect.* Kat prayed that they would soon get to the business for which she had been summoned, and not talk idly much longer, for her mind was still troubled and she doubted she could wring much court holy water from it.

"What was it like," Elizabeth asked suddenly, "to go about freely, garbed as a boy? Nay, tell me not, for likely 'twould make me more jealous of such freedom." She stopped and looked out over the Thames, and Kat wondered what it must be like, to never go anywhere without at least a small army of attendants.

"I could have done so once," Elizabeth said after a brief silence, wistfulness in her voice. " 'Twas six years ago, almost to this very day. We were at St. James's Palace. 'Twas when Robin was created Earl of Leicester. Sir James Melville was there, Mary's ambassador from Scotland. He told me that I could meet my cousin if I would leave the court secretly, garbed as a page, and have my women tell all who asked that I was sick and keeping to my chambers . . ." She started walking again, silent for a few seconds, then murmured, "Would that I had gone. How different matters might be now, had I met Mary before—" She broke off.

Kat said nothing. 'Twas a subject she feared to discuss—a quicksand, as Nick so truly called it.

And then they turned and started back, and Justin was standing there. The gentleman usher had brought him, but he withdrew now, as did the maids of honor, at a word from their mistress.

Justin knelt as they approached, and the queen greeted him warmly and raised him up again.

"I thank you, madam, for sending your own barge for me," he said, and Kat understood how he could look rested after traveling so quickly from London. He had not ridden post-haste. Rather, he had been sped here in comfort by twenty-one watermen, and had had ample time to rest and refresh himself in one of the two cabins.

"Would you not agree that it was no less than I should do," the queen asked, "now that I have learned that I have long accepted your protection unawares?"

"Nay, madam, you owe me nothing, for all my payment is in being an Englishman and able to serve you."

"Court incense, my lord! God's death! I have enough of that and suchlike twittle-twattle from other men. I would have honesty from you."

" 'Tis what I have given, madam."

"Say you so? But Christopher Danvers has not yet been seen in any English port, by any of my thousand spies."

"I can tell you only what he planned. Whether 'tis attempted in good earnest, only time will tell."

"Hmmph! But I cannot employ Time as my intelligencer, for he has only hindsight, and needs must that I have foreknowledge of the plots against me."

"I have endeavored to give you that."

"I believe you, my lord. And I am truly sorry that this mistake was made. I would not, for all the world, have anyone else suffer wrong imprisonment in the Tower, as I suffered it. Pray believe me."

"I do, Your Majesty. Your speedy redress of this wrong is witness for you."

"I thank you for your confidence, Lord Harwood," Elizabeth said dryly, and Kat realized that Justin had erred in implying that more than the queen's word might be needed to prove her remorse. But any fear she had that the queen might be truly angry vanished when Elizabeth smiled.

"I could rate you, you know," she said mischievously, "for setting so many of my men to scurrying after you like fools chasing a will-o'-the-wisp."

" 'Twas not my intent."

"I trow it was not . . . and yet, my lord," she added, becoming more serious, "you cannot blame us if you are seen as a wolf and not a shepherd, and hunted down, when you skulk about in shadows and will not show your true face until you are forced to do so."

"I blame no one, Your Majesty."

"I thank you for that," she said, and smiled again. "There is a title Cecil thinks 'twould be fit to bestow upon you, but we must give it more consideration before deciding. We would have you stay close to the court till then."

"I shall, madam."

Was that it? Kat wondered. Were they to be dismissed now, the interview over? Then why, in God's name, had she been summoned?

She looked questioningly at Justin, and their eyes met for a long moment. They had scarce glanced at each other till now, not wishing to offend the queen.

"There is one thing more, my lord," Elizabeth said then, and Kat became aware that she was watching them, a look of amusement on her face. "You will marry Mistress Langdon, and in all haste. I have been told that she is not with child—"

Kat stared at her. How had she learned that?

"—but you have dishonored her, and so you will marry her."

Alas, to be commanded to wed! She glanced at Justin, and saw a look of dismay and anger on his face. 'Twas clear he did not want this. Like enough, during the idle hours in the Tower, he had had enough time to think over his proposal of marriage and realize it had been foolish. But now he would marry her because the queen commanded it, and resent her all the days of his life.

"Your Majesty," she said softly, afraid to speak but more afraid not to, "you have said naught of what you may owe me, for the service I have done you."

Elizabeth's eyes widened in astonishment. Looking past her, Kat could see Justin shaking his head in warning.

"In faith, you are right, Mistress Langdon," Elizabeth said after a brief silence, and her voice was taut and cold. "You may claim some reward, if it is within reason."

And then remove yourself from my court, Kat added for her, reading the unspoken words from her face.

"I trow it is, madam. I wish to be allowed the freedom to marry whom I choose."

Elizabeth laughed shortly. " 'Tis a great reward you ask. Even princes are not often granted that freedom, in sooth." She was silent for a time, then abruptly nodded. "Aye, you may have it. I give you leave to wed whom you please." She turned her back on Kat, dismissing her with the movement. "Lord Harwood, you must perforce look elsewhere for a wife. But we will speak more of that later. For now, I would hear more of this plot to poison me . . ."

The gentleman usher came up to lead Kat away. She followed him blindly, scarce noticing the people about her, the courtiers and the gorgeously clad yeomen. He left her in the Upper Ward, and she walked down through the Lower Ward and then down to the high street and the Garter Inn, all her thoughts overwhelmed by what had happened.

Packing to leave took but a few minutes, and then she sat down to wait for Nick. She prayed it would not be a long wait, but feared it would. Haply he would even want to stay several more days at court and see his friends, but she would away this afternoon. If she stayed in Windsor as late as this evening, she might see Justin, for as like as not, he would have to find lodgings in the village. 'Twould hurt too greatly to see him, knowing that he was safe now, but that she had lost him forever. She was ashamed that she could not take comfort from simply having the suspicions of him disproven. There had never been any guarantee that they would marry, and she would never have wanted him if he did not love her.

The minutes piled slowly together into hours, and at long last it was midday. She was near the end of a long debate with herself, about whether to have dinner in her chamber or go downstairs to the common room, when the door crashed open in the next room, Nick's room. Likely he was drunk, she thought. She hoped he was not too drunk to ride.

But it was Justin, not Nick, who stood in the doorway. Seeing her, he took two steps into the room and then flung the door shut again. The doorknob had gouged the wall where it had struck.

Not taking his eyes off her, he shook his head slowly. "Kat, you lackbrain . . . I had thought you could not be more foolish than you were when you came to Harwood Hall, but I know better now. Nay, I fear that I have not yet plumbed the depths of your foolishness."

"Then y'are lucky, are you not," she asked coldly, "that you need not marry me?"

"You fool! I wanted to marry you!"

"Nay, you did not. I saw your face."

"And I saw yours. You looked stricken, in truth."

"So did you. I thought you had changed your mind and no longer wished to marry me."

"Why would I change my mind?—No, do not answer that," he added, smiling, and she could not help but smile in turn. "I warrant there would be too many reasons, if I but thought of them."

"Then mayhap you should not marry me."

"What, and die without ever marrying? For I would never have another. 'Twould be a cruel fate."

"No more than mine, my lord, for I, too, would die unwed, and I have been told that maids who die will lead apes in Hell."

He looked thoughtful, then shook his head. "The Devil would never have you."

"There's solace in that," she said, laughing, and then her laughter choked off. "Oh, Justin, what have I done! I have offended her, and now we will never marry!"

"Why not?"

"But you heard her grant my request."

"Yea, for the freedom to marry whom you will. Will you have me, Kat? Would you be my wife?"

"Yea, with all my heart." And she ran to him and embraced him, and then he carried her to the bed.

They were still there that evening when Nick returned and walked without knocking through the door that they had forgotten to lock.

"Jesu!" He stared open-mouthed at them, and though Kat and Justin had been merely lying in each other's arms, the covers drawn over them, Kat could not help but blush and pull the covers up to her neck.

"Jesu!" Nick said again. "You dare tumble my sister here, and—and in my bed!" He drew his sword. Welladay, he was drunken, Kat saw.

"Nay, not again," Justin said, and sighed.

"Hush," Kat told him, and sat up, clutching the covers against her.

"Nick, good brother, hear me out. Justin and I are to wed. The queen commanded it."

She glanced sideways at Justin, and saw him fighting a smile.

"Is this true?"

"Upon my life, she did command it," Justin assured him.

"I'll tell you more of this," Kat said, "but now get you gone, and wait for us downstairs. We'll be down when we have dressed."

He lingered in the doorway. "The queen would have you marry?"

She could not say him yea, not without lying directly, and she would not do that. What they had told him so far had been only half a lie, and he would forgive them that . . . or so she prayed. "Truly, it was what she commanded," she said, careful not to add that the command had been revoked.

"Pray put up," Justin said. "I would not fight my brother."

"Why not? I have fought him often enough," Kat murmured, and he laughed.

Nick shook his head. "My *brother*." He sheathed his sword. "I'll await you downstairs. I must hear everything the queen said."

"Nick!" Kat called after him as he left, closing the door behind him. "Say nothing of this to anyone else yet!" But he did not reply, and she could not be sure that he had heard her. Alack, what if he said aught of this to his friends? He was as much a gossip as Mistress Merton, and Kat would not have Elizabeth hear it bandied about that she had supposedly forced them to wed.

She would have to dress hurriedly and reach him soon, lest he tell all his courtier friends the half of the truth that she had told him.

But when she would have climbed out of the bed, Justin caught her and drew her down beside him again, and after struggling for a few moments, she gave up. Let Nick gossip, and let Elizabeth hear of it and become angrier with her still. Let all Hell break loose, for that matter. Tomorrow she would fret about it, if needs must, but not today. For now, she cared not at all what might happen—not one whit. She was with Justin and nothing could disturb her.

And then she thought of something that did.

"Alack, the door is still unlocked!" she said.

And she went to lock it.

ABOUT THE AUTHOR

A fan of historical novels since her childhood, Cynthia Morgan wanted to create as authentic a picture of Elizabethan England as possible in *Court of Shadows*. During the several years she worked on the novel, she read hundreds of books about the period as well as scholars' facsimiles of Elizabethan writings about fencing and the London underworld. She also read Elizabethan plays, especially Shakespeare's, almost every day.

Morgan, who lives in the Midwest, has free-lanced as a rock journalist and has written science fiction stories that have been published in *Omni* and *Isaac Asimov's Science Fiction Magazine*, among others. For two years she was a moderator of a conference on Soviet technology, society, and international affairs on BIX (BYTE Information Exchange), *BYTE* magazine's international computer conferencing system. She is currently working on a novel set in seventeenth-century Germany.